Intro

The core of my chronology is that most citizens are honest. Citizens deserve the benefit of the doubt. Citizen's deserve human rights in their own country. I personally believe smoking pot does not constitute criminality; morally or constitutionally. I believe there is absolutely nothing wrong with citizen smoking cannabis.

I am not going to pretend cannabis is wrong for the government's sake, because the government is dead wrong in all of it's cannabis warfare program on it's citizen's. The enormous pro-marijuana movement's position is that these cannabis using citizens are in no way second class citizens.

There is a better way for our government to spend our tax dollars instead of morally micro-managing our personal lives. There is a better way to have our police force operating. There is a better way for the government to treat its citizens. When the government dictates the beliefs in which you should believe, social habits you should be comfortable with, and the morality you should behold, things which all contribute to robbing the value of a person's individuality, It's time to change the standing of the guard.

I predict real crime will go down through "Legalization of Cannabis." The legal coding of citizens that constitute criminality by crook cannabis users is the root of the problem in our criminal system. This book is not meant to discredit the good and honest police officers of the law who are misguided legally and obligated to impose by force a prohibition through unjust and outmoded laws. Cops who are crooks should be exposed and incarcerated much more severely for not only the crime but for breaching their trust with the citizens.

Government officials should also be treated more severely when caught in "Circles of Corruption." All the bad elements of corruption in the government and the police force should not only be reduced, but also eliminated. Cocaine, heroin, power, money and greed are the real corruption's. This stagnated stalemate in the drug war has to end. The government sponsored drug war is a losing game for all concerned.

Our government needs to accept and promote more individual freedom issue's. Our government needs to identify and act on real crimes forasmuch as incarceration of it's counter culture cannabis citizens. No tax paying citizen deserves to be investigated, interrogated and degraded by our government for smoking a joint. No hard working citizen deserves to be beat over the head or killed by our police force for smoking a joint of marijuana nor suspected of smoking one. No free citizen should have their lives threatened and home invaded by a overzealous militarized trained police force. No free citizen's earned possessions should be confiscated and forfeited to the court or should they go to jail for smoking a joint of marijuana, especially in the privacy of their own home.

We need real citizens and politicians with the intestinal fortitude to fight to regain freedom of personal choice. The mis-information propagated on our citizens concerning marijuana by our government must stop.

The present laws on the books about marijuana, directly contradict the constitution, which I also believe is contributing to "The Criminal Crumbling of the Constitution." This is not the way our forefathers meant it to be. This is not the way many citizens of our country or the world community see it. Our government is often in contrast with many of our citizens who believe marijuana is a friendly socializing or medical product. The medical benefits of marijuana have been proven effective day in and day out for thousands of years. Medical marijuana initiatives are being passed by two-thirds majority in every state where it has reached the ballot box and shows that change is near at hand.

For some smoking marijuana is a spiritual thing and the government should understand those needs. Marijuana is a natural plant that has never hurt anyone. The marijuana plant is not a synthetic or processed hard drug. In the last ten thousand years there has not been one documented death by any government attributed to marijuana use.

There should be nothing wrong with a citizen cultivating industrial hemp in our country. The hemp industry was wronged by our government, and by the self interested industrialists when they banned hemp in the United States in 1937. The chemical lobbyists from hemp's competing industries and their special interest groups literally pulled the wool over America's face.

Regardless of our past history the fact remains that the vast amount of viable hemp products and their need in today's world markets cannot be ignored. Industrialized hemp in the United States must be restored immediately for agricultural, industrial, ecological, and social reasons. Agricultural planting of over thirty million acres of industrialized hemp for paper in the United States yearly is better than cutting down ten million acres of timberland every year. The yearly harvest of timberland takes twenty to fifty years to replenish for a paper fiber harvest. Industrialized hemp would be the number one or two, agricultural money crop in America in two to three years if given the chance.

These unrealistic marijuana and industrialized hemp laws in a modern free society do not justly serve all the hard working tax paying citizens as they are now established.

This book is dedicated to the free spirits of America. Hopefully, this book will show that the little man can be heard in a big way. It is time to stop the senseless violence perpetrated on our cannabis citizens. The reader's of the novel "2002" and the present bigoted politicians have an education coming! I want to settle this argument once and for all in America. I am going to enjoy this!

Chapter 1... In the midst of today's society there seems to be a mad attempt to create crimes where there are none. In the meantime real crimes are being ignored and treated more passively. We all live and walk in this land together. There should to be continuity in regards to how we see our fellow humans. Citizens have a right to trust their government. The government has an obligation to be trustworthy to a nation that was conceived in a belief in liberty and justice for all.

In the twilight of a hot dusty Texas evening, the blue Houston skyline seems to be hanging over Hidalgo Park. The park is located in the middle of the crowded metropolis. A large and lively crowd congregated around the parks baseball field. Two rival fast pitch softball teams are competing for the "Steer Horn Trophy" given out to the winner of county's bar league championships!

The Amarillo Saloon team challenged, the Cactus Club team, for the leagues best bar team. The coveted Texas steers horns prize mounted on redwood, is a handsome trophy to hang over the victorious teams bar. The winning tavern's team is rendered the honor to hang the steer horns up in their tavern until the following year. They would also have major bragging rights in Houston's softball league circuit. The Captain of the losing team must also agree to shave his head and party with the winning club.

The umpire yells "Batter Up!" with the Cactus Club leading six to four in the top of the sixth inning. Their is a base runner on first and second in scoring position with a full count of three and two. Clint Cole the pitcher reels off a fast softball pitch in an underhanded motion to slugger "Jamming Jake" Feira.

The umpire screams. "Strike!"

Jake was the home run champion last year for the Amarillo Saloon. On the Amarillo Saloon's team was "Gangly Girt" a Lt. on the drug squad playing first. Ramone Ramirez another member of the drug squad is the pitcher. Officer Logan Lamarz is playing second base. Officer Luke Little is playing shortstop. Officer Denton Dukes plays third base. Jake plays center field. Officer Tim Harmon are the right fielder. Officer Larry Hangum was the left fielder. Those two cops were known, while patrolling the neighborhoods in the squad car as "Harm em" and "Hang em." The bat boys are Norman Dirkskin the police chiefs son, and Frank Forrester JR the commissioners boy.

Playing first base on the Cactus Club team is Chico Sanchez who is dressed in his sparkeling red, white, and blue hemp uniform. Chico is also a rising star in the Houston Astro's minor league organization. Wherever there is a baseball mitt and a bat you can find Chico.

Playing second base is Aaron Adams an air brush artist. Aaron works for "Ink Slingers" in South Houston. Aaron's business is unique because he uses strictly toxic free hemp based paints and cannabis canvas and hemp made T-shirts.

The Cactus Club's shortstop is Chris Capshaw, a college student computer major, who is quite a computer hack. Chris often plays computer games involving participants from all over the world.

On third base is Manny Manning, a DJ at one of the local pop stations in Houston. Manny is also a musician, and plays sax in nightclubs throughout Texas.

The left fielder is Rudy Ridge. Rudy guest hosts as a DJ on a three-hour show called the "Routing Rudy Roadhouse" along with Manny who is also the main DJ for the radio station once a week. The rest of the week he drives truck, with his wife Maria across country.

Playing center field is Mike Moran. Mike is attending law school right now, he intends to become a lawyer. Playing right field is Miles Innis, he works for a Houston Newspaper. Miles is newly hired fresh out of college, and he is ready to journalistically expose the world with the zeal of a thirteenth century crusader.

The catcher Igor Irons is a construction worker who also does cement and asphalt work. He runs all the heavy equipment, like caterpillars, asphalt paving machines, rollers, and generally controls the whole asphalt conditioning crew. Igor's company build roads and highways.

The softball players girlfriends and their friends are in the bleachers hoping their respective teams will win the softball championship.

Stanley "Stash" Hopkins and Thai Thait are sitting at the park bench in the playing field background. Near the edge of the park by the waterfront, Stanley was rolling a joint on a piece of newspaper.

Suddenly a 1967 Corvette, equipped with a 427 engine and a four speed transmission went screaming down the hot surface of the roadway, burning the rubber from his rear wheels most of the way.

The wind from the car caused vortices which raised the newspaper right out of Stanley's hands. The prepared marijuana cleaned and already to be rolled into a joint sat in the middle. Raising into the air three to four feet upwards, it began to drop down, Stash caught the newspaper without losing a morsel of weed.

Stash and Thai look at each other in amazement; laughed. " Did you see that?" Stash surprisingly says to Thai "That's unbelievable!"

Thai answers. "Yea!" while Stash continued to roll a fat joint out of the good green bud that was now back in his hand after the newspapers magic carpet ride.

Everybody enjoyed themselves with rising curiosity for the outcome of the late spring tavern softball league game. Cactus's Clubs team members enjoyed using marijuana as a recreational high, which is "Illegal." They prefer marijuana use over alcohol and tobacco, which everyone knows is "Legal." All

4

the Cactus's Clubs team firmly believed, marijuana is less harmful than legal recreational substances readily available at any party store and should be made just as legal. Team members of the Cactus Club's team lead respectable lives with regards to their responsibilities of everyday life. Unbeknownst to them at this time, they will soon be propelled into a movement for social change, because of their beliefs.

"Jamming Jake" stood at the plate, waiting for another softball pitch from Clint to approach. Runners on first and second Jamming Jake poised sternly at the plate, unloads on the first pitch. Crushing the softball over the four hundred foot fence of centerfield far above the center fielder's head. As he rounded the bases, Jake arrogantly flips the bird to the Cactus Club team on the sidelines.

The lead changed from six to four in the sixth inning in favor of the Cactus Club, to seven to six now in favor of the Amarillo Saloon. Jake's arrogant flip of the bird draws immediate boos and hisses from the Cactus Club's team mates and their fans on the sidelines.

After rounding the plate, Jake trots to the Amarillo Saloon teams bench. The high fives and cheers are in abundance surrounding Jamming Jake, who hit for the cycle."

The Amarillo Saloon's first base man, Ramone, who is also on the Narcotics Squad of the Houston Metropolitan Police Force, comes to the plate.

Clint and Ramone give each other a cold stare. Clint knows he has to get this guy out, to get out of the inning. The first pitch to Ramone brushes him back off the plate. The second pitch was crushed on the line drive to Chris who is positioned at short stop. Chris jumped straight up into the air and caught the ball to end the inning, and drew immediate cheers from the Cactus Club sidelines. "Way to go Chris," Clint echo's in affirmation.

The Cactus Club comes up to bat in the sixth inning. Igor Irons the muscle pumped construction worker is at bat. The first pitch is blasted over the fence in deep left Center field tying the ball game seven to seven.

No two more opposite teams in terms of entrenched points view could be found in an athletic match up. All of the of the new uniforms for the Cactus Club are made from hemp, and they just got their color schemed version of hemp baseball caps. The Amarillo Saloon failed to score in the top of the seventh inning. The Cactus Club team loved sporting their Cannabis views and their red, white, and blue hemp softball uniforms in front of the Metro drug squad.

Miles while standing on the grass part of sidelines says to Clint. "I love beating them in softball. They're all like the "Bad Attitude Bears."

Clint responded back to Miles. "Cactus Club winning again this year would really send the drug squad to the Amarillo Saloon Pronto."

Chico squatted in the "On Deck Circle" near the sidelines, with Chris in the batter's box by the plate. Chris hits Ramone's under handed pitch over the third baseman Denton Duke's head for a single to left.

Igor earnestly says to Clint and Miles. "They'll leave the Amberillo Saloon stone cold drunk from drinking Jack Daniels after losing another championship game to us.

Clint questioned. "I'll bet they don't have any rogue cops waiting for them?"

Igor clipped. "I'll bet they crisscross the center of the road all on the way home from their saloon."

Rudy hurriedly walked up and said. "Them steer horns looked great on the Cactus club's wall for the last two years. Let's make it three."

Clint agreed while nodding his head and said. "Ya, we got to beat these guys." to Igor.

"We will" Igor said confidently. With the score now tied in the seventh inning, seven to seven this was becoming an exciting hard fought softball game.

Chico with a full count and hitting left handed was now standing in at the plate waiting for the pitch to arrive. Chico swinging for downtown crushes Ramone's pitch over the right field fence to break the deadlock in the bottom of the seventh inning to win the championship.

The fans on sidelines for the Cactus Club were ecstatic! Champaign bottles were now cracked. Open bottles sprayed the bubbly water on the winning players. Blue-grey smoke clouds were rising in the wind from the eruption of firecrackers and sky rockets that were fired off from behind the bleachers by the celebrating fans of the Cactus Club.

This was the third year in a row these two teams met as a rivals in the championship playoff. This was the ultimate match for the league championship and one place where the cannabis crowd dominated.

Clint's wife Chantel and Igor's wife Illylia, were cheering, and everyone was hugging everyone. "You were right" says Clint to Igor's statement "We won."

All the players stood in the middle of the baseball diamond. High fives, congratulations, and general enthusiasm was hand in hand everywhere. As the bleachers emptied onto the field from the Cactus Club's baselines, Igor's kid Vladimir or Vladdie as he is known was elected equipment manager and picked up all the players equipment. Vladdie was busy trying to collect all the bats, gloves, and balls amidst the crowd running around the field. Rudy's kid Marty the team's batboy began to gather the baseball equipment as well. Vladdie smiled appreciatively.

The Texas steer horns championship prize for the year, were now raised into the air. Igor carried the steer horns about the field among the other triumphant players and friends. Stash, Thai and their friend Bernard immediately ran across to the field joining in the celebration and victoriously they began jumping around.

Chantel's Uncle Mel who had a wild, and not always savory or honest past, was on the field celebrating as well. Mel had been in prison for a quarter of his life, and was now up in years. He mellowed quite a bit in his golden years. Mel even slowed down on his drinking. Never the less he was enjoying the event, and the winning celebration on the field.

All of the winning players, friends, family and fans from the Cactus Club's team were making there way to the club, while one of Ramones friends from the loosing team, threw eggs at the passing victorious cars.

The Cactus Club's team kept their composure and proceeded to drive on without incident. Chris, a none drinker and an occasional toker, road his on the road off the road motor bike on one wheel most of the way to the Cactus club. Mel's pick up followed as close as he could. All the other vehicles followed blowing their horns all the way! The multi colored lighting was shining on the Cactus Club Sanguro Cactus shaped sign. The sign is in the caricature of a Mexican who is wearing a large Sombrero hat. The front of the Cactus Club has a large cactus garden encircled by a hemp marine rope. The assorted and colorful cactus garden protruded all the way to the road surrounding the momentous sign.

Upon pulling into the parking lot of the Cactus Club parking lot, the cars pulled straight under the red, white or blue illuminated car port. The designated color under the car port determined which side of the club you park on.

At the Cactus club the celebrating team and patrons continued to party into the night. Friends and other patrons began to flow outside the doors of the establishment while some of the team tried to lunged to get in.

Once in the large open club, you immediately noticed the soft colors of the south western art decor and live plants with multicolored Indian pottery surrounding the interior perimeter of the club.

The bar owner Roger bought the first round of drinks as promised. He was happy and proud when the team he sponsored had won the first championship, then won a second time, and now had won a big three years in a row. Buffalo Steaks were served to the whole team and their entire families. Everyone laughed as they watched Igor shave Ramone's head clean.

Clint laughing said to Igor who is vigorously shaving Ramone's head. "Shave him well."

Igor running the buzzer over Ramone's head responded. "I won't have a problem with these sheep shears."

Miles was taking a picture for the newspaper said. "I like that clean look Ramone has," while snapping a few more embarrassing photo's.

Igor claimed. "Look he's got the tattoo of a police badge on his head, underneath all this hair."

Everyone really broke into a roar at that point. Ramone's face was beat red, but he grinned and bared it."

The crowd at the Cactus Club joyfully stood around watching. Everyone was smiling, laughing, and toasting the Cactus Club's victory. Even Ramone sheepishly raised his glass in the air for the toast. The winning team let him clean up and served him a buffalo steak as well. Ramone didn't stick around long after the embarrassment.

Roger's wife Doris waited on tables, while everyone else was getting festive. The cannabis paintings shaking on the wall were air brushed by Aaron. The load noise was coming from music played by Manny, who is singing to the beat of Rhythm and Blues. Everyone gathered around the bar in celebration. The

Texas Steer Horns were already in place on their perch above the bar mantel. Manny is singing one of his favorite original blues tunes called "Rolling in the Rapids of Love" to the crowd.

Radiant Rudy's costuming and marvelous Maria's dance style were matchless in contests, that were sponsored at various dance clubs. Tonight they were practicing a newly choreographed spicy dance routine, which; they both had been working on. Other competing couples usually had no chance against them. A large crowd had gathered in jubilation and admiration for Rudy and Maria's exciting dance style. Their execution of dance is as precise as any champion figure skater.

Rudy and Maria, and their kids also skate in local competitions at the Houston Skate land. Skate land had six skating rinks in one building. Rudy, Maria, and their kids have always been an active skate family. Seeing the sensational sure footed skating of Rudy and Maria proved firsthand, that they possessed terrific talent.

Clint and Chantel jabbed with Igor and his wife about the play they made in the third inning, throwing Ramone out at home plate. "Team work." Chico yelled out from the back of the club.

Everyone else yelled. "Team work!"

Miles the newspaper reporter's friend "Jazzo" assisted by video taping the league's soft ball games high lights for a commemorative video of the "Steer Horn's Championship.

The event was also going to be featured in the next days paper. Miles joined in the conversation to get some game comments.

"Congratulations!" Miles relayed the rest of the winning baseball team as he walked over. "Team work!" Loudly was the response from victor's. Miles continued to take notes from the players.

All four pool tables were full of patrons. Perry had been controlling one table on a consistent basis all night. He met every challenger and then gave them a sound thrashing.

Shorty sitting at the end of the bar yelled out. "Game time!"

Perry feeling his alcohol yelled out in an arrogant way. "Next rack boy!"

Shorty was spitting tobacco juice into a spittoon on the clubs floor, while taking side bets on the pool games.

Rudy and Maria were leaving Houston the next day. They were driving a commercial semi truck and trailer, through twelve states and three provinces of Canada in thirteen days. They were now talking about their trip with Chantel, while Clint was still talking to Igor about the team winning the game.

Maria told Chantel they intended to go to a tourist area in Las Vegas, where UFOs supposably landed. Chantel then told Maria about a trip Clint and she were planning to take to Clint's sister's Betty's house in Colorado for Thanksgiving. They were also intending to fly or drive up for an another ski trip vacation to Arapaho basin ski lodge.

Rudy was now in a discussion with Clint and Igor. They were listening to Rudy explain about the "Cannabis Café" he had seen on a news program, and they were intending to visit that Cannabis Cafe in Vancouver, BC Canada.

Clint asked. "What did you say Rudy?"

Rudy responded. "Yea Clint were going to the Cannabis Cafe in Vancouver. Their is a place called the "Cannabis Café.""

Clint answered in disbelief. "You can casually stroll into in Downtown Vancouver and vaporize marijuana or smoke marijuana?"

Rudy's enthused "You can smoke marijuana, or vaporize it." They all laughed.

Igor inquired. "What's that?"

Rudy conveyed. "It's a technique of marijuana use that the some of the patrons at the Cannabis Café use."

Clint's consulted. "Vaporizing?"

Rudy enounced. "Yes They heat the bud up with a control heat which heats the pot up enough just to release the THC. Theirs no burnt ashes. Theirs no need for a match or a butane lighter."

Clint professed. "That sound's different."

Rudy's expounded. "It's different. I hear it's a much safer and cleaner method of use. I'll let you know how it is."

Igor told Rudy "Heck you don't have to go that far to smoke a joint. I have a joint of marijuana rolled up in my pocket." They all laughed.

"But I want to go somewhere marijuana smokers are not persecuted or prosecuted. Somewhere the government is more tolerant of people's personal rights." explained Rudy!

They all liked that idea. Clint regretted. "This cat and mouse game with the government and marijuana users is old."

Maria informed. "Canadian politicians and police have relaxed the laws for marijuana use."

Clint responded. "So I've heard and I'm glad you guys are going to check it out. Who in hell would ever believe that marijuana use like the cannabis cafe's is legal or at least tolerated that close to our boarders."

Igor alluded. "For legal use?"

Rudy responded. "I don't know about that! They have a "Cannabis Café" up there and Maria and I are going to definitely check it out. It's going to make the whole trip interesting." The night was getting late and people were starting to leave the Cactus Club.

"It's about time!" Rudy said to his wife Maria.

Maria answered. "I agree!" Maria was tired because of her long day of working in the green house. Maria worked at Clint's farm.

Igor ranted. "That's great! Bring me back a "Cannabis Café' souvenir".

Rudy cracked. "No problem."

Clint countered. "Me too."

Rudy howled. "OK" As everyone drove off out of the parking lot in different directions home.

Mel was still drinking at the other end of the bar, and playing darts with Chris. After beating Chris three straight games in a row, Mel stopped and looked out the window with the rest of the patrons. They were all watching the four police cars that had gathered across the street from the club. The cops were chasing patrons down as they left the Cactus Club.

Roger confessed to some of his patrons, that were commenting about the police cars. "I don't like the police stalking my patrons as soon as they drive away from the Club. How do they expect me to stay in business. That along with a new ordinance proposal for no smoking in taverns will finish me here."

Old Mel would commented. "Why do you think they call them pigs!" The crowd would react by oinking, "Oink!" "Oink!" "Oink!" "Oink!"

After winning a few more games of darts Mel decided to leave. Mel started singing a country tune he had learned in prison called "How Pigs Stink!" Another patron began to sing while adding a verse to Mel's tune. "Bad laws, Bad cops equal no respect for piggy wiggy's." The bars patrons as they watched what was happening out side across the street started signing along with Old Mel's tune.

Mel had had enough partying for the night and wanted to go home to get ready for the next day's work.

Mel had a nice pick up truck on which he had done a lot of work. He painted the truck in multi colors resembling very much like a tie-dye shirt.

Clint always said to inquisitive admirers of the truck "Don't ask me how he did it, but he did!" Mel supported himself with a small business of a body shop, and had learned his auto body trade in prison.

Mel did all the work himself to the truck, and was leaving the bar parking lot with his prized customized bright multi colored tie dye looking pick up truck, with the bull horns on the front of the hood, and beautiful chrome rims flashing!

Officer Larry Wetters, who is a new patrolman trying to make a name for himself at the Police Dept, is sitting in his Squad Car in the parking lot across the road from the Cactus Club.

After watching Mel drive his truck out of the parking lot, Officer Larry Wetters decided to follow Mel. Officer Wetters undoubtably would have no problem finding a reason to pull Mel over. Larry was going to get Mel on anything DUI if possible.

Mel had been drinking, but wasn't stone cold drunk, never the less Larry decided to pull over behind Mel's customized pick up truck. Mel had driven his truck only six blocks when he got a flat tire, and was already in the process of changing the tire on the custom truck.

As Mel changed the tire, Larry proceeded up to Mel's truck. Mel said. "How you doing."

Officer Wetters demanded. "Drivers License and Registration." Mel complies with the officer.

Larry realized Mel is a friend of the Cactus Clubs baseball team who had just won the game. Many of Larry's friends were on the Amarillo Saloons team.

Officer Wetters decided to promptly arrest Mel. Officer Larry said. "Turn around Mel."

Mel pleaded. "For what?"

Officer Wetters deemed. "You've been drinking! I'm going you cuff you! Turn around now!"

Mel burst out to the cop. "No! I'm not going to jail!"

Larry decreed "Mel your going to jail!" Larry steadfastly says. "I've already got Norton's tow truck on the way."

Mel glared at Larry. "For what!"

Officer Wetters sarcastically stated. "Your drunk!"

Mel responds "You didn't even give me a breath test." Officer Wetters says. "I don't have to give a mountain maggot like you a breath test."

Mel being a red neck from the moonshine hills of Kentucky and schooled in prison not to take any shit from anyone, especially after being insulted in such a way. Mel grabbed the Officer Wetters up and proceeded to kick his ass.

By then the tow truck driver Norton Nowens was there, he also promptly got his ass beat and kicked after trying to interfere with Mel and the overzealous cop.

Mel proceeded to fix his tire on the shoulder of the road. When Mel was finished, he promptly drove off on his way home, leaving the two injured men to fend for themselves.

The truck driver was roughed up, but not as bad as the cop Larry. Norton the tow truck driver loaded Larry into the tow truck and took him to the hospital.

Dirkskin the police chief sent Girt over to pick up Mel at his home immediately after he found out about Larry.

Mel surrendered peacefully to Girt and Tim Harmons his partner on patrol. Officer's Girt, Tim and Dirkskin all went to the callboose to make sure old Mel was incarcerated.

Mel end up getting three years in prison for this un-called for overzealous police incident, and went back to his old institutionalized habits in prison. Mel would throw as many horseshoes as possible, Mel stayed sharp as a razor while biding his time playing horseshoes. Uncle Mel was a good guy at heart. He stood his ground even if it meant going to jail.

Since losing the tavern championship to the Cactus Club soft ball team, the Amarillo Saloon team has been heavily drinking liquor at the Amarillo Saloon. The Amarillo Saloon is the local cops favorite hang out. After parking in front of the square brick building, Officer Denton left his drug dogs locked in his truck's cage before he walks in the Amarillo Saloon to see a couple of his friends before starting his shift on the expressway.

Once on the inside of the Amarillo Saloon the decor was dimly lit and made of brick sectioning off the surroundings. You might have to look in fifteen separate different areas before you could locate your party. There is a card room where they played five card stud for green backs too. In the pool room is also a place where the alcoholic cops were gambling for green backs. The dart room was the only place they were playing for the hell of it. In the sports lounge they were betting on everything that came up on the sportscasters odds screen. The dining area was partitioned off in many private areas where many cops held secretive meetings, while dinning at the expense of the tax payers open ended drug forfeiture expenditure account.

Ramone arrived at the saloon and began playing cards with the rest of the drug squad bald head and all. Everyone in the saloon had been talking about Ramone getting his head shaved before he arrived. Everyone had laughed heartily when freshly shaved bald Ramone did arrive. Ramone was now drunk as the rest of the bunch. It was after hours at the saloon, but everyone was served drinks until dawn.

During the coarse of five card stud Ramone scowled. "I want to start busting those guys for anything we can! That whole crowd at that Cactus Club is to uppity!"

Luke raising the ante of the game pledged. "I'll help you anyway I can."

Guzzling whisky high balls Pete called his hand and raged. "Let's burn them pot heads!"

Jake while drinking a shot of red eye urged. "There're all pot heads lets burn em they'd look good in county orange. I'll help! Larry and Pete will help!"

Police officer Greg Greathead overheard the drunken police card players, and didn't like to hear his police colleges targeting some of his pot using friends who were on the Cactus Club's team. Some worked at Clint's green house. Greg grew up with most of them and he knew they were not a criminal element. Deep down Officer Greg would never bust any of his friends for smoking a little pot.

Greg had heard enough cop collusion when he all of a sudden fumed. "Ramone does losing a soft ball game mean that much to you?" in a sarcastic way!

Ramone filled with hard liquor and embarrassed in front of his friends explosively jumps up suddenly in front of all the police officers. Ramone enraged shoves Greg's head on through the dinner counter's partition. Greg tumbles over the partition holding on to Ramone's head locked now in his fore arm. The two police officers started going at it extremely hot and heavy, before all the other drunks could respond. All the officers finally began to separate Ramone and Greg, who were still cursing and scrambling to get at each other.

Police Chief Dirkskin and Capt. Renard hearing all the commotion came running from the adjoining card room, when Chief Dirkskin said. "What the hell's going in here?"

Ramone fighting to get free bellyached. "Greg started it by sticking up for those pot heads." Capt. Renard while Logan and Jake hold Greg at bay snapped. "You'd better go home for the night Greg! Luke drive Greg home now!"

Luke responded. "OK Capt." after Logan and Jake release Greg Luke and Greg turn to leave together

Chief Dirkskin advised. "I think it's time for everyone to go home. Party's over for the night." as everyone started to leave. Girt suddenly bursts through the heavy door and blurts out. "Chief, Larry got beat up by one of those guys from the Cactus Club."

Dirkskin grilled. "Who got his ass whipped?"

Girt came back. "Larry did by old Mel! We've got him in jail right now, and Larry and the tow truck driver are at the hospital getting patched up."

Ramone enthused. "One rat down! And a nest to go! I want Clint!"

Jake now throwing at the dart board with Clint's picture on it boasted. "Bulls eye!" but the dart lands slightly off center of Clint's head.

Logan decreed. "That's sounds good to me, I need some over time." as all the drunk cops laughed.

Capt. Renard asked. "Chief, can we continue the party everyone has calmed down now?"

The chief responded. "OK, boys but settle down. I'm leaving for the night. I'll see you all tomorrow. Good Luck on that rats nest!"

Chapter 2.... Rudy and his wife Maria were now on their way to glitzy Las Vegas with a semi-load of pool tables, where their commercial cargo is to be delivered. On their way through the scenic south western part of the United States Maria took photos of the scenery on the way.

Once they dropped off the load of pool tables off at a downtown Las Vegas convention center, they decided to go straight to the UFO area. The UFO area had been advertised as a Nevada tourist attraction. Someone claimed a UFO landed there. On their arrival in the area with their new Kenworth Semi, Rudy noticed a cop near by. Rudy had already parked the semi-trailer at a truck stop. The cop was sitting in his squad car looked directly at Rudy and Maria's Semi. The crusty cop seemingly stared at the couple's semi with intense interest. The patrolman got out of his squad car and started to walk toward the Semi.

Once at the semi the patrolman asked them. "What are you doing in this area?"

Rudy responded. "My wife Maria and I just dropped off a load of pool tables in Las Vegas. Were here to see the Nevada UFO sights."

The cop asked Rudy his name and Rudy complied. The curious officer noticed Maria's good looks immediately.

This cop has done this type of interrogation many times before trying to drum up an arrest, so he can freely arrange groping on helpless women. Sometimes the cop would let teenage girls out of their traffic tickets for sex. He was what some would call a predator cop.

"Rudy!" The officer said. "I want to search your truck, and I'm going to cuff you while I do the search."

Rudy surprisingly said. "You do! What for?"

The patrolman quickly responded. "Oh, contraband, illegal immigrants, drugs, whatever."

Rudy questionably said. "What for?"

"Because I've got probable cause." The patrolman says and quickly cuffs Rudy to the front bumper. He orders Maria to take the suitcases and travel logs out of the semi truck.

The patrolman Kermit "Tear'em up" Tarrington quickly found while going though the suitcases a small bag of marijuana containing possibly five or six joints.

Kermit eyed Maria with lust. "Step back here to the back of the truck." Out of Rudy's sight with the semi now running because Kermit reached in and turned the ignition on. The noise of the engine was to disguise Maria's anticipated screams and moans.

Kermit then quickly cuffed Maria's hands, behind her back having the cuffs loop the airlines to Maria's rear. "Get on your knees bitch and give me head and I'll pretend I never seen this marijuana. If you don't give me a blow job I'll charge you both with felonies and sell this semi in the next public sale. My buddies are looking for a good semi anyway." While this sex fiend cop laughed.

Now with Maria facing Kermit, the patrolman now freely searched her person, feeling every part of Maria's firm body slowly, as she squirmed to get free, Maria screamed for Rudy, who was cuffed in front of the Semi, to help her.

"Rudy!" she screamed "He's raping me!" With Kermit's continuing forceful sexual advances he said, "Shut up bitch!" to Maria, and grabbed her throat, until she regressed because of the pain.

The nervous patrolman quit the assault, because of her screaming. He noticed a man across the street standing in front of his van.

The man in the van across the street had been illegally broadcasting from a homemade radio station from his van. The rogue radio station master named Rip alerted people on the highway that an officer of the law was groping a helpless woman. Rip told the people on the highway to come and help the women in duress or call some real police.

The Nevada patrolman had by now called his usual tow truck company to tow the Semi-truck. The patrolman always got his kick back from the tow company later.

Rudy on the other side of the truck was asking, Maria if she was OK. Maria sobbed. "I want to get out of Nevada."

Rudy avowed. "I'll call an attorney as soon we get to jail." Rudy knew the patrolman was taking them there anyway.

Charges for the small amount of marijuana were drawn up as felony interstate transport of drugs. Bail was set at ninety-three thousand dollars. It would take twenty percent of that amount to get the Semi-truck and Rudy alone out of jail.

Rudy called a team of high dollar lawyers out of Las Vegas to represent him in court. Rudy drained his credit cards to get himself bailed out of jail. The bail bondsman named Harold immediately took Rudy to the Semi from the jail. Kermit was inside the Semi truck when Rudy and Harold's arrived at the police compound to pick up Rudy's semi.

Harold observed and raided to Rudy. "Look that cop is trying to plant something in your semi!"

Rudy scrutinized to Harold. "Looks like we caught that culprit before he could pull a fast one I hope. Kermit didn't think I'd be out of jail this fast."

Harold portrayed. "He's dumb as well as dirty isn't he?"

Rudy proclaimed. "I'm glad your here as a witness to this guys kangaroo court antics."

Kermit surprised looks up and sees Rudy and Harold standing behind him and quickly jumps back out of then semi truck. Kermit was anxiously shoving an unknown package into the military style pocket of his uniform. Kermit red faced and now facing Rudy angrily persisted. "Get out of here and don't ever let me see you around here again."

Harold the bail bondsman now standing there next to Rudy remarked. "Move it out of here while you still can."

Rudy responded. "That won't be a problem." Rudy jumped in the semi and rolled hard out down the highway out of that cop's jurisdiction.

When the judge saw those high dollar lawyers walk in from Las Vegas for Maria's court hearing he took a start. Rudy's attorneys were well known in the Las Vegas area. They were the best criminal defense's attorneys available Jack and Jim Jarret. They were quite effective in their handling of all their law procedures. They dogged the criminal justice system to the bone. Relentless in their pursuit to make, the judicial system work fairly for all., judges and police with scams did not escape these two legal scholars.

The Judge Lloyd Deems quickly knew the scam of drug forfeiture was not going to work. Deems quickly lowered Maria's charge of felonious marijuana possession down too a misdemeanor. Maria was released immediately from jail.

Rudy and Maria were now back on the road in their Semi-truck on the way to their next load, some nursery supplies of southwestern decor to be delivered in San Francisco and some in Vancouver, BC. There was also a complete line of assorted cactuses from Nevada nurseries which were also to be delivered in Vancouver, B C They were scheduled to report back to their Houston, Texas Trucking terminal in eighteen days.

Jack Jarret called from his law office to talk with Rudy on his cellular phone, while Rudy and Maria were heading quickly for the California State line. Rudy answering the mobile call says. "Hello"

Jack asked. "Hello Rudy, How you guys doing?"

Rudy responds. "Were doing."

Jack divulged. "Rudy, I've heard about that radio broadcast hacker from the T V news this afternoon."

Rudy questioned. "You have?"

Jack answered. "Yes, I'll try to locate the man so he could be a possible witness to the cops attempted rape." Jack's law team brother Jim was on the three way conference call also of Maria.

Jim posed. "Our administrative assistant Susan will locate the news reporter, who did the commentary about that rogue broadcast hacker."

Jack pressed to Rudy. "I know this is a crooked cop. I've heard about him before."

Rudy acknowledged. "This broadcasting radio hacker is a hero for reporting this crime by that criminal."

Jack resolved. "Don't worry we'll find this guy."

Rudy affirmed. "Maria and I want that cop fired and put in jail. What he tried to do to my wife was more than enough to set me off cop or no cop."

Rudy's lawyers from Las Vegas assured him they would press for a civil rights violation action before they all left the one room courthouse in the middle of the Nevada desert. Rudy tried not to let this incident bother him so he could complete this trucking trip. Rudy decided he would, take care of the whole matter upon his arrival back in Houston. Rudy had never been in this type of position before, and never thought cops could be this cruel and corrupt.

Rudy and Maria couldn't wait to get to the California State line. They wanted the sorry state of Nevada's injustice behind them. Rudy and Maria stopped at the first rest area in California to celebrate being out of Nevada, and added a complete round of sex in the sleeper of the semi for a few hours of gratifying relaxation before hitting the road again.

On their way up north along the coast of California to San Francisco, Rudy conveyed to Maria. "I want to pull over at a truck stop in San Francisco."

Maria answered. "That's fine let's stay over a night in the City by the Bay."

Rudy proclaimed. "Really!"

Arriving in San Francisco, Maria walked over to the news stand to get a daily newspaper. She immediately shows Rudy an article from it and reads off the head line which states. "Medical Marijuana Laws have been passed by a large majority of the voters. Cannabis clubs are handing out marijuana at different clubs throughout the city. The article further says that the San Francisco Police Chief is reported as saying. "This is not Amsterdam and we will enforce the Federal marijuana law."

In a related article the assistant police chief who just came back from Amsterdam where he spent a week exploring Dutch policies of legalization of marijuana, hash, and prostitution said. "In my Dutch policy observation, I've come to the realization that their is a much better way to ensure public safety. The Dutch government and their police note that there is no mayhem in the streets, because of their liberal marijuana laws, their respect of individual freedom and their coffee shop policy's. I'm impressed with the Dutch government citizen friendly approach."

Rudy consoled. "This approach concerning marijuana has left Dutch officials with more time to bust real criminals and major dealers of hard drugs such as heroin and cocaine. When marijuana, and hash was officially tolerated over thirty years ago citizens immediately had alternatives to prescription drugs, unregulated illegal hard drugs, alcohol, tobacco, and household inhalants. The Dutch can prove hard drug use went down, because of their liberal marijuana policies."

Maria read. "When regulated prostitution was legalized in the red light district of Amsterdam, reports and convictions of criminal rapes went down dramatically. The would be rapists now had a place to buy sexual relief with no criminal penalties. Sexually transmitted diseases like AIDS are in check and receding because of the Dutch prostitution health regulations for safe sex. The prostitutes themselves became much safer and healthier because of the new prostitution policies. The Dutch police could now concentrate more on harden criminals and white collar crime."

Rudy and Maria were both heavily interested in reading the series of articles while they were sitting in the cab of the semi. Rudy reading his copy of the newspaper told Maria, "Dutch officials reported to the San Francisco assistant police chief that. "Marijuana is officially tolerated in Holland. Your American marijuana laws have double standards. If your connected or rich you can buy your way out of a marijuana bust. If your poor, or a economically strapped working man, and unconnected your branded and convicted a criminal. It's the American government's way to monetarily enslave a class of people." Maria said. "Those Dutch official's are all right with me."

Rudy excited. "Me to!"

Maria read another headlining article and said. "Twenty-one staffers and politicians of the White House were found after an investigation to have used drugs of all sorts. Zero tolerance on one hand for citizens and flagrant drug abuse on the other hand for governmental officials. Do as I say, not as I do, or I'll get you is the American governmental attitude."

Rudy insisted "Look here the Dutch official said in the newspaper. "You don't buy any marijuana or hash off the streets. You just go into any of Holland's different coffee shops sit down and relax and enjoy yourselves.

Rudy himself was smoking a joint at the time and said. "It's about time marijuana users get some respect and treated fairly for their individual beliefs." Maria and Rudy were going to leave the next morning for Seattle after a good night sleep.

The next day the semi was heading north up the highway. Their northern route through Seattle was smooth sailing. They kept the semi rolling on a fast pace straining relentlessly to get to Vancouver, BC. They want to freely smoke in a place that respects freedom with tolerance.

The city of Vancouver known as "Hollywood North" in Canada's south western most part of the country. Rudy and Maria were due to arrive in the late morning just before lunch. A logging protest song in defiance of the logging industries forest hungry demands was playing from the semi's radio "As the Next Redwood Drops." while the chorus of the song sang. "No Need to Flatten our Forests."

Rudy rattled. "That's a catchy tune!"

Maria agreeably said. "I like the melody."

As they approached Vancouver, British Columbia, The snow-capped mountains to the right on the east of them provided a breath taking view. "Awesome" Maria constantly distinguished to Rudy.

On the left stretch out like pristine blue carpet was the Pacific Ocean, white capped waves were flowing endlessly on the beaches, as they headed north. Rudy and Maria went directly to the truck terminal unloading area to deliver some of their nursery supplies. Rudy and Maria then parked their semi-truck in the terminal bay.

The terminal employees loaded the next cargo listed on the Bill of Lading in the semi-trailer ready to be delivered to the next destination. The rental car they acquired, near the wharf in Vancouver for their lay over was Maria's favorite color a light Maroon.

They started out for the Cannabis Café, with the tree line displacing an awesome silhouette on the peaks above them to the east. The well known Cannabis Café was to be the highlight of their journey's quest.

They arrived in the heart of the Vancouver downtown district near Robson square, and parked their vehicle in front of a chili dog vendors. Maria crossed the street to buy a fancy souvenir Vancouver scarf.

Rudy told his wife "You look beautiful in that scarf"

Maria snuggled up. "Thanks" They then walked down west Hastings to the Cannabis Café.

The "Cannabis Café" offered an extensive experience in marijuana and hemp educational encounters and was the personally targeted destination of their trip. It was advertised as "North America's First Marijuana and Hemp Cafe."

Entering the cafe they walked past the tall hemp stalks display. Maria says. I like how the cafe decor is in marijuana art."

Rudy responded. "That's sharp." There was a big sign which said. "Legalize It." Pro-marijuana Reggae music a new hit song "We Won with Weed" is playing in the back ground from a tourists boom box. The aroma of marijuana was evident all through the Cannabis Cafe. Maria had made special reservations for them, before they left Houston.

Maria looked at brochures with all forms of hemp food recipes such as hemp seed oils, flour, yogurt, milk, hemp-tofu, and many other items of hemp seed nutrition. Some were even being served all around Rudy and Maria. The menu says hemp seeds do not contain any THC, so people weren't going to get stoned from that part of the hemp cafe experience. All the hemp and vegetarian food was fresh and delicious as advertised.

The Cannabis Café is also smoke and alcohol free. They promoted healthy life styles with a complete line of juice and vegetarian servings. As Rudy and Maria sat in their booth and looked at the menus of assorted hemp food, they couldn't help noticing the entire interiors contained an intricate hemp decor. The menus advertised that assorted hemp food was delicious and nutritional as well. They took awhile to decide on what delicacy of hemp seed food to try.

The managers worked closely with their employees and patrons. They suggested hemp to-fu for Maria to try, while Rudy was over at the desert bar trying different hemp food samples of cookies made from hemp flour, butter and cheese, there were other baked treats all made from hemp. Rudy finally decided on pasta with hemp pesto, and a salad with hemp oil. They both topped off their hemp dinners with ice cream made from hemp as well.

Rudy passed a dish of hemp ice cream to Maria. "I wish I could get this hemp ice cream back home."

Maria gushed. "I like the taste of this natural flavored hemp ice cream."

Rudy *d. "I can't believe all the different flavors of their hemp ice cream, and all the hemp food is high on vitamin content."

The manager informed Rudy that. "The Cannabis Café opened to challenge the marijuana prohibition and we are enjoying an astounding success. This is a friendly, peaceful, pleasurable, and productive atmosphere.

Rudy mused. "I like how your government is respecting the peoples constitutional rights."

"We are more tolerant in BC." A customer named Victor interrupted. "Our crime rate is less then yours because of it."

Maria said defiantly. "I wish our country would recognize us as good and decent people instead of trashing us citizen's just for marijuana possession or use."

On the coffee table was a Cannabis Canada magazine which explained about the cannabis culture. It included every conceivable topic on industrial, recreational, cultural, social, medicinal, spiritual, and historical Cannabis points. It explored the social and legal effects of criminalizing cannabis. Featured in this months magazine was an article on grading seed strains from the "Cannabis Cup Competition" in Amsterdam. There were also articles on U S marijuana medical advances, Commercial Hemp symposiums, and Canada's drug policies were reviewed. The magazine also recommended the Hemp BC Legal assistance Center on Hastings St. which backed all forums for Cannabis's constitutional challenges.

Another magazine on the table was "Cannabis Culture" which advertised "Marijuana and Hemp around the World." The publisher Marc Emery covers the topic and the cannabis industry in depth. He is also the former owner of Cannabis Cafe. Sister Icee's has since taken over the duties of the Cannabis Cafe."

After Rudy and Maria were done at the eatery, and had looked at some of the marijuana magazines articles, they went on and tried one of the Cannabis Cafe's customer's compact portable vaporizer.

Victor explained. "Marijuana is ingested with a vaporizer pipe device, which heats the marijuana enough to activate the THC of the buds and release it's THC. It is the safest way to inhale marijuana in the vaporizer method."

Rudy enthusiastically said. "Every method has it's madness."

At the Cannabis Cafe there were literally thousands of different types of pipes, bongs, marijuana memorabilia, and paraphernalia on display. A wide variety of marijuana seeds from catalog's were also on display for sale as well.

Maria and Rudy had never heard of a vaporizer type pipe, let alone try it. The patron told Rudy to go over to table, that he already had it set up for They rushed to the booth was the first to try the vaporizer. "Wow! That's really smooth. You hardly know you got a hit of anything let alone THC"

Maria recapped. "Really!"

Rudy exclaimed to Maria. "Really it's not bad."

Victor smiled along with wife Vivian who was watching Rudy and Maria vaporize the THC from the green buds. Everyone was smiling now.

Maria agreed. "That bud is sure tasty."

Rudy confessed. "Isn't it though" agreeing with Maria.

Victor commented to Rudy. "Smooth Ahhyy"

Rudy responded. "Superbly smooth bud."

Maria had to try the vaporizer again and so did Rudy over and over. The vaporizer would heat the bud of marijuana up enough to emit the THC, but no fire or combustion.

Victor explained. "This vaporizer technique has ten times less tar, than that realized from the conventional smoking of marijuana method. No flaming buds means smoking."

Vivian acknowledged. "The Cannabis Café challenged the Canadian cannabis prohibition. Prominent Canadian politicians called for the Attorney general to stop the marijuana war and quit arresting marijuana users. They claim decriminalization does not increase use, which all studies have indicated."

Victor goes on. "The Vancouver police said they would not make arrests for simple possession of marijuana unless other more serious laws were violated. Criminal penalties to control marijuana use have failed."

In the next booth over, a Vancouver couple were enjoying themselves, the lady setting there turned around suddenly, and introduced herself to Maria as Margie. Margie in turn introduced her boyfriend Terry, to Rudy and Maria.

Rudy told them. "Were from the Houston area."

Terry immediately asked them. "How are the Houston Astro's doing?"

Rudy answered. "OK but I'm still waiting for them to get to the World Series."

Rudy had just finished telling them about the softball championship they just won and exclaimed. "I can't believe I'm in a downtown metropolis while smoking marijuana."

Terry popped off. "You're not smoking Rudy, your vaporizer Tokin, which is smokeless by definition!"

Rudy looked directly at Terry asked. "Don't the Vancouver police bother you?"

Terry contended. "No, The Vancouver Police usually do not press charges for any drug use, unless other aggravating events occur. If you maintain a responsible manner theirs no problems. In Canada Vancouver is the most liberal part of our country for excepting different people's cultures and lifestyles. "

Terry explained. "The government set a reasonable marijuana policy, so young Canadians are not tormented and prosecuted. We in Canada don't want criminal charges sticking on the record of young Canadians, and further holding them back from employment and passport restrictions. The government realizes there are too many people smoking pot and they can't stop people smoking marijuana any way. People are not criminals just because they smoke marijuana."

Rudy and Maria both said. "Wow" and the same time in amazement. Every one laughed.

Terry, Margie, Rudy, and Maria all left together and as they passed the "Little Grow Shop" on main street they stopped. Rudy had seen some of the stores hemp wares for sale in the front window. Lighting, grow room hardware, plant additives, and everything else from books and video's on how to grow marijuana to mushroom products.

They all walked into the Hemp Mercantile store." Maria walked up to the Cannabis cosmetics counter and looked at and tested the samples of hemp balm, moisturizers, oils, and saves. On the shelf behind the counter were hemp shampoo's, soaps, wash clothes and bandages, all made from hemp commercially grown in Canada. Assorted hemp woven products were covering one wall much like tapestries.

The hemp furniture display consisted of lamps, futons sofas, tables, chairs and even hammocks were all made from hemp grown in Canada. Hemp office stationary was off too right side with books, cloth and paper towels, note pads, envelopes, card board and assorted commercial hemp packaging samples, They were being being sold and used in the world economy. Newspapers and magazines that were sold there were from the ink to the paper were made from hemp.

All of the environmentally friendly hemp paper was of the finest quality fibers available with a shelf life of over two thousand years. The back of the store was set up with a hemp apparel section consisting of hemp jackets, jeans, pants, dresses shirts, jumpers, lingerie, vests, coats, sweaters, shorts, hats gloves, socks, belts, shoe's sneakers, and Oxford's. Products like hemp briefcases, wallets, and even checkbooks, and money were just a few of the accessories on sale were all made from hemp fibers as advertised.

Advertised and on display for industrial use were hemp bedspreads which could be used in hotels, such as canvas bags and sheets, Environmentally safe hemp fuels, inks, industrial oils, natural pesticides, parachutes, twine, rope, fish nets, were also displayed and the list went on, and on, and on. Even hemp wicked lamps with clean burning hemp oil stood on display throughout the store.

Household items like hemp curtains, aprons, yarn, pillows, bed linens, table clothes, assorted fabrics, hemp samples and the hemp list went on. Building materials like hemp particleboard, insulation, paneling, plywood, caulking, flooring, all made from hemp sat around the display floor. The realities and possibilities were endless again for everything made from hemp. Custom hemp orders were taken every day for large amounts of assorted hemp products.

Rudy asked Terry. "What's the Canadian government's view?"

Terry complied with an update of current cannabis events. "Concerning cannabis in Canada were growing by leaps and bounds. Were growing and were smoking more freely."

Rudy was surprised to hear Terry talking so freely and open about the marijuana industry. Rudy honestly felt like someone was always looking over his shoulder which is a common feeling in America.

Terry went on to tell Rudy and Maria about the mayors present position. "Total incarceration is impossible and putting people in jail at such alarming and damaging rates is unrealistic."

Rudy asked. "And your government is trying to do something fair about it?"

Terry disclosed "Canada realized the systematic criminalization of it's citizens for cannabis use was real problem."

Maria asked. "How far along has the pro-marijuana movement progressed in Canada?"

Terry continued to tell the attentive Rudy and Maria that "The recent Canadian legislation's in regard to marijuana prohibition was turned over. The Canadian government felt that all this chasing marijuana users around was hampering the judicial system. Serious crime had to take priority over marijuana cases. Marijuana they realized wasn't important enough to put colossal numbers of man power hours and resources to fight a fruitless and endless marijuana fight against its citizens."

Terry went on to tell Rudy and Maria. "The money we are now saving on fighting the marijuana drug war is now going to fighting serious crime."

Terry lectured. "Look at the U. S. You have a higher incarceration rate with your drug sentencing guide lines that are much stiffer and drugs have not slowed down one bit have they?"

Rudy confided. "I agree! Buying drugs is like buying a six pack of beer as far as availability. Everywhere I have ever been people have smoked marijuana socially."

Terry attested. "The same is true for me. I find it socially expectable almost everywhere. It definitely isn't a hard drug no matter how much marijuana you smoke."

Rudy knew that what Terry was saying was right and he knew things had to change back home. Maria and Rudy just lived through an American injustice nightmare happening on their way though Las Vegas outskirts during a tourist expedition.

When the United States Police and the Judicial System of the government are Cohorts in a conspiracy to steal a citizen's money, and civil liberties, it's a sad day for all Americans.

Rudy and Maria were caught in the quagmire. Is this really life in America, they thought. Terry and Marge both said at the same time after hearing Rudy and Maria explain what happened.

"That's terrible!" Margie said. Rudy and Maria nodded their head in agreement.

Terry emphasized. "The Canadian Media and political leaders are advocating decriminalizing soft drugs. Police chiefs as well as legislatures were advocating the decriminalization as well. The Ottawa Chief of police went on to say in an article, "Soft drugs do not fall into the sphere of criminal enforcement. Drug use alternatives should be developed further suggesting containment though health and welfare regulators. Human and social costs of the marijuana drug war are enormous. Involving the trauma of the officers as well as the citizens." The chief said in the article."

"I like that!" Rudy chortled to Terry "It's neat to see the police administrators taking a new look at the governing factors by implementing tolerance with the users of Marijuana. There are still a few overzealous cops in Vancouver seeking promotions by busting marijuana smokers."

Margie professed. "One veteran police officer openly said to the media that, "The police and government officials exploit the marijuana war to keep their financial budgets for their branch of government or police dept healthy."

Victor explained. "The benefits from promotions and overtime is big money for the cops and the courts. That's why they use these SWAT teams every day for maximum media exposure. The cops that bust the most marijuana users get the biggest promotions and the most pay. Nobody is willing to pay these marijuana officers so they pay themselves by busting marijuana users to increase enforcement budgets."

Margie depicted. "One constable quoted in today's paper said. "The drug war is senseless, it's very counterproductive."

Terry recapped. "Another police chief for the Halifax police is more interested in dealers of crack cocaine, than hunting down people who use marijuana."

Rudy implored. "Now I'll go for that. If they can get the crack out of the community that would be a major social accomplishment."

Terry said the police chief further admits. "Marijuana is a very low priority for the Police dept. Pot smokers gathered at Halifax Common to protest Canada's drug laws and smoked marijuana. Citizens were smoking pot right in front of the police."

Rudy asked. "Was there any arrests?"

Terry reasoned. "There were no arrests, during the marijuana protests. How do you like that Rudy?"

Rudy let out a loud yell. "Yea!" in full agreement.

Terry expounded. "There are many police officers in Canada who refuse to arrest people for possession of small amounts of marijuana anymore."

Margie disclosed. "Another Canadian legislature came out of the closet as well, stating he smoked pot and inhaled. "Like most every one else from my generation, I tried it" he proclaimed."

Terry continued. "Look at all the billions we have spent in the marijuana drug war. All it does is make the organized crime groups rich, because of the black market underground for the drugs. The financial drain on police, courts, and prison systems has to be reduced to be effective".

Rudy stated. "Your making more progress here in Canada then we are in the United States. I can see that right now."

Terry informed. "The World Health Organization consisting of nineteen countries, concluded that cocaine has little long lasting effects. They advocated decriminalization to end the drug war altogether."

Rudy cross-examined. "You can't legalizes cocaine."

Terry avouched. "I'm just telling you. All What the World Health Organization said. They're taking it a step further than legalizing Marijuana."

Rudy confessed. "Cocaine 's to heavy for me, even if it was legal and sold as a shot of liquor. I still wouldn't do any. It's too mind altering and controlling."

Terry agreed. "There just looking at the existing methods of illegal drug control. They don't agree with how the drug issue is being handled presently. Monitoring all our citizen's twenty-four hours per day so they don't ingest or inhale marijuana is a futile battle that can't be won anyway. It is less harmful to let the citizens choose their own personal destiny."

Terry divulged. "A hemp activist and cannabis store owner proclaimed, the police and government at a twenty five percent tax rate is losing a quarter of a million per year, because of the under ground market in Vancouver, Canada alone."

Margie concurred. "Other senators were high on legislation for marijuana." The Toronto Star reported that, New Brunswick Liberal Senator Rose-Marie Losier-Cool stated recently. " I'm in favor of decriminalizing marijuana. Numerous other Senators were named in the article as well for supporting full decriminalization of marijuana. The Toronto Star newspaper itself has given favorable coverage for medical marijuana."

Rudy asked. "How is your government treating the issue of medical marijuana?"

Margie explained. "One judge allowed a medical marijuana defense for a Canadian patient who was arrested for growing a few marijuana plants. The medical marijuana therapy to alleviate pain from epilepsy was allowed. The judge said. "It was unconstitutional for the police to deprive the man of marijuana medicine approved by his physician. The Canadian Charter of Rights and Freedoms states citizens have the right to life, liberty and security." The judge said. "Health is fundamental to the life and security of each person." The judge further noted that the federal Justice minister is also under increasing pressure to decriminalize marijuana altogether."

Terry remarked. "One judge recently was asked to throw out a marijuana conviction because criminal codes, and marijuana prohibition conflict with the Charter of Rights and Freedoms. Decriminalization or criminalization of marijuana now has to be worked out. Health officials are exploring taxing methods in Canada once legalization occurred. Part of the cannabis tax would be delegated for health costs."

Rudy and Maria were glad there were some politicians trying to put sanity into the government. The trip to Vancouver was very hemp informative, far beyond what they had anticipated. Rudy and Marie liked what they seen.

Rudy openly stated. "Things are different to the north across the border in Canada. I see you got "Medicinal Marijuana Clubs established here in Canada?"

Terry admitted. "That's true! Commercial Cannabis Compassion Center's have opened up here and there nationwide. Some lawmakers have argued that banning marijuana violates the "Canadian Charter Rights" for citizens."

Marge induced. "It won't be long and Canada will legalize pot. Everyone knows it."

Marge told Maria and Rudy they were going to go for a horse carriage ride in Stanley Park. Marge asked if they wanted to come along. Rudy said "Were ready when you are not thinking twice." As they left the Cannabis Café stoned and being all stoners they could all socially relate. Being stoned on marijuana is by far not as intoxicating by alcohol. They could recreationally enjoy the day with out falling stone cold drunk on hard whisky. Marijuana use is just a safe and enjoyable feeling even intellectually tranquil.

Downtown Vancouver is quite unique with it's fashionable shops and seaside markets. The downtown metropolis is with in walking distance of beautiful Rainforested Stanley Park, which virtually surrounds the city. You could spend an entire week, walking around the Parks sea wall trail, they call it Lotus land.

The respective couples now boarded separate carriages and began touring the park with increasing amazement. The setting was quite romantic for couples entering into the scrumptious colorful, Foliage Park. As the carriages rolled down the park fairway, Terry said. "Cultivate your mind" as he passed a joint to Rudy.

Terry and Rudy passed joints to each other from carriage to carriage as the moved along. Both couples were cuddling in their perspective   carriages between passing the joints. The buggy driver was hitting the marijuana joints as well. Police drove by as they hit the marijuana joints, and the police waved back at them as they waved at them too!

Rudy raved. "That's a knockout! That don't happen back home in the land of the free. You know the United States." They all laughed. The carriages stopped while they looked at the Brockton Point lighthouse.

Rudy divulged. "What a nice feeling to be free and not be discriminated against."

Terry relished. "Cats ass ain't it, Rudy?"

Rudy confessed. "You know that's right!"

The horse carriages were now going by the huge Vancouver Aquarium in the midst of Stanley Park. Rudy and Maria were scuba divers with an interest for sea life. They wanted to stop, but knew they had a schedule to contend with. They decided to stay with the horse carriages rolling down the cobble stone path on this sunny afternoon.

Stanley Park was breath taking in itself. Close to a thousand acres of evergreen forests, near the heart of the metropolitan city, was such a natural setting with majestic cedars, firs and hemlock's embracing all around. The horse carriages clattered down the forested lane by a lost lagoon. This was a sanctuary for birds of all types. The Swans gracefully propelled themselves across the lagoons surface, and the Canadian geese swam nearby a varied assortment of ducks all swimming in their natural habitat. Rudy and Maria smoked their last joint with Margie and Terry.

This is quite a change from Houston's asphalt jungle. "Ahh" Terry spoke to Rudy "Did you hear last year about that Snow boarders gold medals."

Rudy avowed. "Oh Yea, The Olympic committee gave the gold medal back to him because marijuana wasn't a performance enhancing drug. Also in some circles of the real free world marijuana is legal."

Terry explained. "The International Olympic Committee agreed on that issue they in essence said it was all right for athletes to test positive for that type of drug, and could still compete and retain your gold medal."

Margie conveyed. "The Canadian Officials said It's only a little bit of pot, let him have his medal."

Rudy induced. "Yea, the guy won the Gold. Ah! And allot of other countries marijuana is legal and in some countries has always been legal."

Terry added. "Like India. And like Spain, Netherlands, Germany, Australia, ECT."

Rudy asked. "You know Terry! Didn't the cops bust a couple of them Olympic snow boarders right after the Olympics."

Terry professed. "Yea your marijuana drug laws in the United States charged these two Olympic athletes with felony charges for possessing two grams of marijuana."

Rudy griped. "That's insane!" Maria nodded in agreement!

Terry affirmatively nodded. "That's your guaranteed freedom in the police state of the United States of America."

Rudy said. "Yea the cop smelled a little marijuana, called in the marijuana drug dogs and found a lousy two grams."

Maria said. "Two grams! That's insanely ridiculous?"

Rudy explained. "Ya! Now these good young men are charged with a felony, just like a bank robbers, murders, and rapists."

Terry protested. "These young men were travelling to another snow boarding event to compete. Let them live their young lives without hassle. Let these young people make there own personal decisions in life. You can only guide young people so long in making life's decisions. You have to respect their choice and let them go. Most people end up just fine when you leave them alone concerning marijuana use."

Rudy agreed. "Really you're not a criminal just because you safely choose express your individuality."

Margie agreed. "That's right Rudy!"

Rudy protested. "We got to fight the injustice in our country."

Terry agreed. "Yea that's some kind of poor excuse you call freedom in your country."

Rudy informed. "I'm on the snow boarders side. They're not felon's in my eyes."

Terry railed. "Mine either!"

Rudy quipped. "I wouldn't mind partying with them guys."

Terry agreed. "Me either they sound like good people to me."

Maria summarized. "Those skiers are not any kind of felons or people that need to be caged."

Terry noted. "Margie, tell them about the hemp emporium raid."

Margie asked. "Rudy did you know your government sent Navy Criminal Investigative Service officers under cover to buy marijuana from the Cannabis Cafe and Hemp BC?"

Rudy answered. "No I haven't heard."

Margie explained. "The American military cops couldn't buy the marijuana at Hemp BC or the Cannabis Cafe so they went elsewhere in Vancouver to buy marijuana. The United States foreign cops then came back to the Cannabis Cafe and smoked their pot. The United States military officers then assisted the Vancouver police in their search warrant which led to the arrest of the owners and patrons of the establishment."

Rudy remarked. "I see big brother is trying to run the drug policy here in Vancouver. That seems to me like solid evidence that the United States is trying to enforce their marijuana war policy here in Canada."

Terry mustered. "Your government has no business on our sovereign soil gathering evidence to bust Canadian cannabis citizens at internationally recognized hemp emporiums. The previous owner Marc Emery and Sister Icee has had to put up with Vancouver police raids in their fight to end the marijuana prohibition in Canada. Sister Icee doesn't need help from the American military sticking their nose in the internal affairs of our prohibition."

Rudy persisted. "Marijuana legalization is coming fast as more and more citizens across America and the world are letting their positions known. That is why the politicians don't want to put the marijuana issue to a vote because they know the pro-marijuana voters will out number the prohibitionists. The people are fed up with the governments insane war against good citizens."

Terry pleaded. "I wish the United States would keep their citizen unfriendly marijuana drug war attitude out of our country. Canadian's are making progress with the hemp and marijuana issues. Were handling the legalization of marijuana in a very sensible way by respecting all our citizen's view's."

Rudy reassured. "I agree with you Terry. I don't like what our government has come too. Are we supposed to live the way our government and police want us to live or are we free to choose our own lifestyle? And I've heard WWII Vets from our country say the same thing, that there are to many laws, which are now a hindrance to a free society."

Terry moralized. Sister Icee said. "Marijuana is a plant. You can't prosecute people for smoking flowers. It shouldn't be regulated any more than parsley or broccoli. There's no harm in it, it's the weed of wisdom."

Rudy quietly told his wife Maria. "I like Terry's down to earth humanitarian philosophies."

Maria confided. "I agree!"

Terry continued. "Merchants around this country are fighting to sell marijuana plants in their stores just like other plants. These merchants are protesting for their civil rights. They want seed sales for marijuana like other countries with similar laws. They want to sell drug paraphernalia like bongs and pipes just like they do in other communities. They want to be able to trade, barter, grow or sell small amounts of marijuana with out interference, or being labeled less than human or criminal. The merchants are requesting Parliament and the courts of justice to re-examine the laws of marijuana and it's use. Banning hemp stores in the communities eliminating municipalities from hemp merchandising is unfair. Legalizing, regulating, taxing, is a much more sane and reasonable conclusion for medical and recreational use. Let's get rid of the under ground trade in marijuana which thrives on unimpeded. Let's get the marijuana trade above board. Let the marijuana trade thrive freely. We live in a democratic society. Truth is always a healthy change. We should deal with marijuana issue fairly for all citizens. Use of marijuana is so widespread and accepted in more social circles than not to be ignored any longer."

Rudy listening to Terry intently suddenly yelled out. "Tell it brother, tell it!"

Terry told Rudy that. "Pro-activists are fighting the marijuana issue on religious grounds as well. They say the Charter of Rights here in Canada guarantees religious freedom protection. Smoking joints at certain church sessions has been practiced for years and around the world for centuries. They see marijuana use as a sacred plant with healing powers that are beneficial in sacraments. Interpretation should be left to the church about which religious sacraments they should practice. It should be the church congregation has the right to choose" summing up his thoughts.

Rudy spoke out. "I agree Terry, I sure don't understand how these marijuana laws got so far out of hand."

Terry said. "It's people's lives they should freely choose their own path in life. In the bible there are many references to herbs, hashish, holy men, and religious sacraments." The pastor of that church says biblical passages from the book of psalms from Christian Bible's over a hundred years old cite use of marijuana in many sacraments Prophets used hashish in religious practices. "They were the leaves that healed nations," the Bibles scriptures had many different references to cannabis. Someone has edited out some of the cannabis scriptures from the newer Bible's.

Rudy asked. "I wonder what else has been altered?"

Terry continued their religious conversation stating. "Moses used cannabis oils in religious acts. Nobody said it was drugs than. They say marijuana use enhances our perception of reality. Gives them a peaceful feeling to meditate their thought's."

Rudy professed. "That sure is food for thought." After ending their keen cannabis conversation they were all leaving the park. They had to depart from their newfound friends.

After the couples exchanged addresses Margie lit a Thai joint she had stashed.

Rudy chuckled. "That bud tastes great!"

Terry agreed. "Yes! It's the best around these parts. We get it from the Chinese community. They bring the Thai grass in from the Far East."

Terry and Margie decided to visit Rudy and Maria next year after Maria had invited them.

Terry stated to Rudy "I'd like to go to a Houston Astro's game."

Rudy responded "No Problemo Sen`or."

Maria conveyed to Rudy as they were departing. "They are really nice and hospital people."

Rudy confessed. "I agree I hope they come visit us in Houston."

As a last gesture Terry yelled out. "If your not faint hearted or afraid of heights, go visit the Capilano Canyon Suspension bridge."

After the welcoming and that send off by their new Canadian friends Rudy and Maria did visit the Capilano Canyon Suspension Bridge. The view was the best one of the city from the towering mountain they were on. The mountain sky train lift was in view, as well as the magnificent back drop sky line. You could see the rolling waves and the beaches in the scenic background. The Lion's Gate bridge spanned across the harbor, much like San Francisco's Golden Gate Bridge, and it was a profound view as well.

After viewing the suspension bridge, Rudy and Maria decided to head back to the heart of the city. Rudy and Maria wanted to go to the Gastown district in downtown. It was getting late and they wanted a nice dinner, before they retired to our hotel for evening.

Once in the Gastown district, they walked by the Gassy Jack statue at Water and Carrall streets intersection. Vancouver was virtually built around this landmark hotel saloon from the old days. As Rudy ate his steak medium rare, Rudy couldn't help telling Maria how he had some respect for the governors and police dept of Vancouver. Rudy wished that back in America, they could have their freedoms back, without any senseless repercussions. Maria said she wanted to see the day of freedom of individual choice with out persecution as well.

When Rudy and Maria left the restaurant, they walked by another street attraction. It was the Gastown Steam Clock, one of the most photographed items in downtown Vancouver for the tourists, who congregated to pose in front of it. It was dazzling. Photos taken by the tourists seemed endless. Every few seconds the gravity falling ball would fall, from the steam driven clock blowing all of whistles as it went. Once every hour it would discharge a large steam whistle, from the crowds reaction this city street contraption was one hell of an attraction.

The following morning Rudy and Maria left Vancouver, they were about twenty miles north of downtown Vancouver. They both thought the pleasant tolerant attitude concerning pot had given Vancouver a good reputation on humanitarian grounds alone. The city councilors had given credence to Amsterdam as well as respecting peoples rights. Peoples rights were more important than any outside interference from an alien party, including the government and police. This was the most tolerant metropolis in North America. Their feelings were optimistic as they left the community, they were both comfortable with what they had experienced.

As they drove by the Tilford Gardens. You could see different floral arrangements from the distance. Rudy had to pull the semi truck and trailer over and unloaded what was left of the cactuses that were loaded in Nevada. Rudy and Maria decided to tour this magnificent Botanical garden. Maria would have none to do with driving here and unloading the cargo with out stopping for a quick tour of all the flowering gardens.

The gardens consisted of green shrubs, trees and colorful ornate flowers was located among colorful flowers where there fountains with different water and rock creations. This was an internationally renowned botanical garden. Weddings were performed there after advanced bookings. The beauty of their floral gazebos and the ornate elegance of the white gardens while walking past the end less grace of the Japanese garden was immensely intriguing. Back drops for photos were in endless an array of colors in many varieties Japanese tourists seemed to flock to this part. They were big on taking photos. Rudy and Maria were witnessed, and were told as well, that some of the special events occurred daily at the Historic Park and Tilford gardens.

Rudy and Maria believed as they left, that Vancouver was a paradise to live in and for the tourists and the tourist industry. On the way east in their semi loaded with hemp industrial machinery, they had just picked up on the outskirts of Vancouver Maria was excited! They leisurely traveled over the rejuvenating snow-capped Canadian Rockie's. The inspirational forefront of emerald lakes surrounded by pristine alpine meadows is unparalleled beauty for any outdoor enthusiast. She was pointing out all the mountain goats, They especially noticed the large rams with their big horns. The wild flower foliage was radiant, in early July. Rudy and Maria were planning to arrive in Alberta, Canada in the early morning hours.

They went straight to the drop off area, which; was a large hemp-farming complex, that served all the farmers in the area with their hemp industrial equipment needs. Half the load on the semi was unloaded as scheduled from the bill of laden, and the truck was re-filled with new hemp combine heads.

A dock worker named Skip was driving the high low and unloading the semi.

Rudy walked around the front of the semi and asked. "What's all the commotion down the road."

Skip explained. "It's a Stampede!"

Rudy asked surprisingly. "Stampede!"

Skip said. "Yea, the Calgary Stampede, Every summer it's the main town rouser."

Rudy asked. "Do a lot of people attend?"

Skip went on to explain to Rudy and Maria that the most popular event in Alberta was the Stampede. "The festival lasted ten days billing itself as the "Greatest Outdoor Show on Earth!"

Maria inquired. "Do they have a rodeo?"

Skip responded. "Yes but it's more than a simple rodeo, with bull riding and all the other competitions. They set up big mid ways with an Indian village and they have big tribal following's of different arts and crafts, and live stock and fireworks. Alberta's first inhabitants were Indians. The Indians are in full display at the Stampede."

Skip offered while still unloading the hemp machinery with a Hilo. "I'll run you both down there for a quick tour."

Rudy revealed. "To bad we didn't have time or we'd go."

31

Maria hesitantly agreed nodding her head in a yes manner, before she abruptly changed her mind and said to Rudy. "Please Rudy let's go! Skip will take us for a quick tour."

Rudy looked at Maria and Skip and said. "Let's go!" Rudy figured the Calgary Stampede would be an exciting event and one not to miss if given the chance.

Skip explained. "We can be there in no time flat."

Rudy boasted. "This is one heck of a cow town." Skip laughed "It's one hell of an event all together," as they arrived and were walking up the fairway. Eugene a friend of Skip's was walking slowly while looking at the hand made Indian crafts. Skip walked up and tipped Eugene's hat from behind. The hat fell just over the fore head and stopped on the bridge of Eugene's nose. Eugene turned and lifted his hat up at the same time busted out laughing when he realized it is Skip clowning around.

Eugene suddenly said to Skip. "Good going on your cannabis court case. I'm glad to see you didn't back down."

Rudy asked. "What court case?" Skip pulls a paper out of his back pocket and hands the newspaper to Rudy.

Skip answered back. "This one."

Rudy pronounced. "You got busted here for one once of marijuana, pleaded guilty and refused to pay a one hundred dollar fine so the judge gave you five days in jail."

Skip explained. "That's right. I told the Judge I'm not a bit remorseful. I'll smoke pot as I please, no matter what. I told the judge I'd rather go to jail, than to give them any money in fines."

Eugene hammered. "You made the press releases every where."

Skip snapped. "Then it was worth it! If we can bring attention to the injustice."

Rudy blared. "I want to shake your hand Skip for being one of the people standing up in the pro-marijuana and hemp movement."

Skip steadfast stated. "Oh Ya, their is no wavering here." as Skip now pulled out a joint, which Eugene quickly lit and passed around the horn."

Rudy now smiling said again. "Like I said! But on a lighter subject, I haven't seen this many cows since I drove a load though Nebraska." as they all laughed together.

Maria asked. "The stampede grounds isn't far from the Saddle Dome is it Skip?"

Skip responded to Maria. "No, the Saddle Dome isn't that far away. Wow! I've never seen the Calgary Stampede grounds so filled with patrons this event gets bigger every year."

Rudy canvassed. "There are people of all classes and walks of life here."

Skip browsed. "That's for sure."

Rudy thanked Skip for all his help for a third time after reminding Skip they both had a schedule to keep. After Skip dropped them off, Maria and Rudy then jumped in their semi and headed out with a fresh load traveling east.

As they passed the Calgary Tower in the downtown area, Rudy told Maria. "I would like to come back up to Canada for a vacation just to see the great sights!"

Maria agreed. "The people of Canada seemed so down to earth and friendly. I'd love to come back here with the kids." Both of them had enjoyed the healthy change of scenery and newly found freedoms enjoyed by their over the boarder neighbors to the north.

Rudy and Maria had to be in Winnipeg in two days to drop and pick up another load of hemp materials. It was going to be a long trip from Alberta to Regina The hemp industry was newly reformed and exploding into the Canadian economy. The Canadians Industrialists and farmers were jubilant. Rudy and Maria figured their next lay over in Regina would break the trip up a bit.. They had a one night lay over which would be welcomed by Rudy and Maria.

When they entered Regina, they drove past the Silver Sage Casino. Their hotel was just down the street and in with walking distance. Rudy and Maria decided to go to the Casino for a quick late night dinner accompanied by a little gambling. While on the black jack table later that night, Rudy was up and winning by thirty five hundred dollars. The dealer Hector, just dealt Rudy another winning hand and was replaced by another dealer. The roulette wheel spun in the framework next to the grand staircase.

Maria came over and talked Rudy into retiring for the night. Maria was getting a bit tired. She was up by six hundred dollars from the slot machines alone and found it as hard to quit as Rudy did. Rudy had never won so much, and was glad Maria coached him into quitting for the night. They both went back to the hotel happy winners! "This will help with our attorney bills from Nevada." Rudy told Maria before they retired for the night.

Maria contended. "Thank goodness for that. We'll need it."

Upon arriving in Winnipeg the next day they drove by another huge crowd. There was another big event unfolding before them. They drove the loaded down semi to the delivery terminal address, which turned out to be another huge hemp multi complex. As Rudy backed the semi's trailer into the bay the dock workers were smoking a joint on the side of the building. Rudy got out of the cab and they passed the joint to Rudy. Rudy quickly excepted the joint and greetings were than exchanged.

The dock workers were Chance and Cyrus. They both were young and had long hair. Rudy asked them "What the big doing's down the road". Chance proceeded to tell Rudy, as Maria was walking up. "That's the Winnipeg folk festival. It's an internationally acclaimed musical event sponsored here every year."

Maria asked to Rudy. "Can we go?"

Rudy explained. "I don't know if we'll have time."

Chance insisted. "You should make some time. I'll take you for a quick tour. I have free passes because we have a merchant's booth there."

Cyrus raved. "The festival has a wide range of music from blues to blue grass. Jazz and alternative to dance and percussion."

Maria excited persuaded. "Wow, we gotta go!" Rudy just looked on knowing they had a schedule to meet.

Rudy commented to Cyrus while trying to change the subject. "Is this the Hemp Processing Plant and adjoining Cannabis Complex."

Cyrus informed. "Yes it is we represent a big part of the hemp industry here in Canada. The hemp processing plant produces fiber for paper, wood products and insulation. We'll have the ability to make potential plastics, clothing, fiber board, hemp oil for burning or fueling automobiles. We employ over fifty people at this plant per-shift and another seventy-five people in the Cannabis Complex which displays our sales area."

Chance defined. "Manitoba was a major grower of hemp before being banned in 1938 here in Canada with the urging of the US."

Cyrus induced. "Manitoba will soon be a major grower of hemp for the world with this state of the art hemp processing plant."

Chance illustrated. "The farmers are happy with an income of five hundred dollars per-acre for hemp. They are tripling the size of there hemp crops acreage next year now that they know were serious about processing hemp, and they have a hardy legal alternative crop."

Manny asked. "Have you been busy?

Chance responded. "We've been getting busier everyday. We just had a representative from "Hemp-Argo International" call earlier today about farm acreage availability. They had a great crop this year and want to farm an additional ten thousand acres. They want to come here because we have the most modern hemp processing complex in Canada. "

Rudy enounced. That's fantastic! I like hearing success stories!"

Looking around the hemp complex Rudy noticed there was hemp literature available for general knowledge and promotional reasons. Chance explained him of the Canadian hemp network. The network supplied urban job creation in rural by shifting from raw hemp agricultural to the industrial use opportunities. Other reports by farmers, who were now growing hemp, spoke of the hardiness of the crop. Reports by those involved in the hemp industry were all positive. Commercial growers of hemp spread to all Canadian provinces. The scary hemp phobia is over from the government's earlier criminalisation propaganda hype. Canada is now growing the first modern hemp crop in North America hemisphere nationwide. Hemp cultivating and hemp industrial processing is becoming a renewed way of Canadian life on a startling pace.

Hemp Associations are forming internationally based alliances from this region in Canada alone. This region is looking for economic inducement and found it in industrial hemp production. Consulting firms for the hemp industry were busy with the new hemp business inquiries. Distributors were trying to keep pace with the new hemp business orders and the hemp mail order catalogues were trying to keep up with new hemp product orders. Hemp textile industry was exploding in the farmlands of the surrounding the Canadian Rockies. Hemp machinery was introducing the latest high tech hemp processing equipment. Wet spinning as well as dry spinning equipment allowed for state of the art processing of hemp fibers in commercial qualities.

Different hemp outfitters advertised their hemp wares here as well. One manufacture of different hemp products was on display, and also exported them around the world proudly displaying a "Made in Canada label." and one hundred percent hemp made stamp on the hemp products, and brochures was advertised there hemp sub-outlets. Hemp merchandise loaded on Rudy's semi for delivery to the United States.

Chance said. "Hemp fields are a common sight in Canadian farm fields now. The Liberal party of Canada has rescinded the six-decade-old ban on hemp cultivation. National growth of hemp is now permitted. Health agencies are now responsible for hemp instead of the police agencies. Hemp cultivation is to stay as big part of Canadian agriculture. Directories of Canadian hemp companies listed are immense, stretching all the way across the country and the world."

Cyrus continued for Chance and said that. "Commercial and Industrial hemp symposium reports are steady and readily available. The hemp symposiums have various speakers, talking about all aspects and avenues of hemp cultivation and hemp industrialization."

Rudy took a copy of each hemp brochure to take back to Houston to show Clint and his wife Chantel. Rudy had just called Clint to tell him about the trip. Clint told him to bring back information on hemp production and Rudy thought maybe Clint could set up some type of factory for hemp production or the making of raw materials into hemp paper. Clint knew already that hemp paper was the best in the world. Rudy told Clint on the phone from the hemp industrial complex he had all the fresh hemp information secured already in the Semi-truck cab.

Rudy and Maria decided to park the semi at the hemp terminal, while Chance and Cyrus took them to the Winnipeg Folk Festival for a quick look in the company car. Rudy and Maria were to leave Canada the next day and both wanted one more good memory of Canada to take with them.

The Winnipeg Folk Festival the cultural attractions were diverse. All the people and the music was moving to the soul. Rudy and Maria felt in the groove for the occasion as they danced at one of the pavilions. As usual the crowd noticed Rudy and Maria's dance routine and a large crowd had gathered around to watch. Chance and Cyrus took them around to all the fairways until, the festivities ended for the night, Chance and Cyrus took their new American friends Maria and Rudy back to the hemp terminal where they would retire to the semi sleeper for the night. Their semi truck was loaded and ready for the next day's run. Maria was exchanging addresses with their newfound friends and further inviting them to Houston. They again thanked both Chance and Cyrus both for showing them a great time.

Two semi trucks full of hemp seeds were to follow them to Shreveport, La for a drop off. The second semi driver's name was Ian. The third semi truck was not going as far as Shreveport, La. The third semi driver was to deliver his semi of sterilized hemp seeds to Minneapolis, Minnesota for tree free paper production.

The next day on their way out of Manitoba south to the United States of America, they viewed a large hemp field. A Canadian hemp farmer was pulling a wagon around the field with a John Deere tractor as they drove past in their semi's loaded full of hemp seeds. Rudy told Maria. "Isn't this remarkable." Maria said. "This is incredible to see history in the making," as they rolled toward the sun.

Rudy and Maria's caravan of Semi trucks sighted the Canadian and U S border. The two other semi trucks full of hemp seeds and their hippie looking drivers followed closely behind Rudy and Maria's semi with the cannabis manifested list. Commercial loads of hemp seeds and hemp products. Rudy and Maria already sensed they were going to be hassled by the custom agents.

Upon entering the U S Customs toll booth, Rudy and Maria were ordered for examination by customs agents. They pulled over their semi truck for the customs officer. The customs officer must have not of liked the cannabis advertising which encompassed the whole side of their sixty foot long semi trailers. The customs officer was unaware of new regulations which allowed hemp products and sterilized hemp seeds to be brought into the U S. After a tuff and thorough inspection of inside of the semi cabs and a fresh recap of the new hemp laws they were again on their way. Rudy and Maria and the other two semi trucks full of sterilized hemp seeds and hemp supplies, were then allowed to proceed on there way south into the U S.

As they drove though the Bad Lands of the Dakotas, Maria slept most of the way. They were on their way to Minneapolis to drop part off this load before they then departed to Milwaukee and then further south. The third semi was dropping his entire load there and departing north back towards Canada.

Ian's driving counted upon Rudy and Maria to follow south to Shreveport, La. Once in Shreveport, La they would make a drop off of all the hemp seeds and supplies at a newly established hemp paper and textile factory. Morris, the Hemp terminal manager in Alberta, promised Rudy and Maria that Henry the manager in Shreveport, La would give them a tour of the new American hemp processing plant in action.

As they went though the loop of downtown Chicago, Maria commented that she had never seen any buildings so high in her life. Rudy pointed out the towering Sears building, before they headed south through Joliet. They continued to roll their hemp smaller caravan down the southern highway. Rudy and Maria were now moving steadily though Illinois with the other semi driver Ian still following, before they all decided to pull over for breakfast in the next truck stop.

Maria as is now her habit walks over to the newspaper stand and sees the headline which reads. "Chicago Cop Charged in Drug Ring."

Maria sums up the article over breakfast to Rudy and Ian. "Police corruption is everywhere Rudy listen to this. A Chicago officer started out by robbing known drug dealers during the drug raid shake downs. The officer with the help of other officers than started protecting hard drug shipments of cocaine and heroin in a the drug ring ran by the gangs. The drug main drug cop operative then worked his way up the ladder to running the drug operations on a daily basis. The drug cop and his gang controlled the daily sales of heroin and cocaine in Chicago. The drug cop's large scale drug operation ranged from transferring the kilos of heroin and cocaine from Miami to Chicago like clock work to selling of the hard drugs on the streets. The crooked cop threw his unknowing fellow drug officers off the trail of his gangs drug distribution operation. How did this veteran cop of over twenty years would escort his gang members carrying large caches of heroin and cocaine through airport security, by flashing his badge and a smile."

Rudy divulged as he barreled ahead. "That's unbelievable! There is to much of this crooked cop cocaine transporter crap going on."

Maria pleaded. "This crooked cop crap is very involved and broad based."

Ian changing the subject ribbed. "Is there anything we can do around here for excitement."

Rudy looked at them both while they were having breakfast in a Springfield Ill. Rudy and said. "Do you know where were at."

Ian snapped. "No!"

Rudy's contended. "Were on Route 66. One of the most historic highways in the U S. was taking the historic route from Chicago all the way to St Louis, before we switch off to Memphis. This route traveled from Chicago all the way to L A, covering eight states."

Maria accented. "American History was Rudy's favorite class in school."

Rudy was now looking at the cassette rack in the restaurant for some new tunes when he turned and said to Ian. "You know the one tune by Jan and Dean."

Ian answered. "That was before my time."

Rudy continued to look at the tunes he kidded. "Well so is the Star Spangle Banner, but you know that one! Don't you?"

Ian disclosed. "I like alternative music and some old Rock and Roll!" Rudy being a part time D J and Musician said to Ian. "I have no negatives on Music. Good Music is good Music, where ever you hear it, whoever it's made by, or how ever it's made."

Rudy always sang "Rock, Rhythm, and Roll." It was an original he wrote and jammed from time to time with musical friends. Rudy had even made a CD, which he played occasionally while D-Jaying. Rudy said to Ian. "Listen Abraham Lincoln was before your time as well, and that's what I'm leading up to. Old Abe's house is right down the road from here. Were actually going to pass by the cemetery where Lincoln's Tomb is, when we make the turn to get back on the expressway."

Ian enthused. "I'd like to see his house." So they decided to detour to the downtown area of Springfield, where the house was in order to see it. They had to park their big rigs in a designated parking area. They were then all bused into the historic part of Lincoln's town. It was an intriguing thought to walk where Abraham Lincoln once walked and guided tours for Lincoln's haunts were free.

Rudy told his other travelling tourists. "This is great we can see some of our American history, the way it really was." Once at the house, they proceeded to take the tour of the two-story house. It was the only house that Lincoln would own.

Maria reading the tourist pamphlet and explained. "The houses and streets in the area are impeccably restored to authenticity and maintained as they were in Lincoln's day under supervision of the National Park Service."

Rudy informed. "The bank and courthouse contain many documents and ledgers in Lincoln's own elegant handwriting."

When they all drove away from the area, they went past an area where the train depot was. Maria told Rudy. "That is where Lincoln gave his farewell address before leaving for Washington D C to become our sixteenth president."

Rudy expounded to Maria. "I feel invigorated after being that close to such a rich part of our history."

Maria attested. "It would have been hard for any president to make decisions, during that period of American history." Rudy, Maria and Ian all connected that they learned allot about the country that day.

Maria continued to talk to Ian on the CB, while they were all trucking down the highway. Other travelers began talking about the civil war over the CB after they heard Maria and Ian talking about Lincoln's old neighborhood. It was as if they had opened up can of worms, talking about the civil war and President Lincoln.

Rudy and Maria rolled steady down the highway, and enjoyed all the new terrain. They chit chatted to all walks of life on the CB. It was an enjoyment to both of them and Ian. All of a sudden they were pulled over by one of Illinois finest an unfit in their opinion. Ian kept driving and CB'd back to Rudy "Ill meet up with you all at the next truck stop.

Rudy answered "OK" to Ian, before entering onto the shoulder with the cop's lights flashing on their semi's tail. Rudy had complied and pull over immediately when it was safe.

Maria asked. "Rudy what this was all about?"

Rudy explained to her. "It's smoky bear playing ticket master." Rudy continued to say trying to calm his wife's nerves. "I know why they'd pulled us over." The officer with a Smoky the bear hat on quickly walked up to the semi truck. The Illinois trooper ordered Maria out of the truck immediately. "Out of the truck" he said. Maria complied with the request.

The officer demanded to Rudy "Drivers license and registration." Rudy complied and the Illinois state trooper stared into Rudy's eye's with an intimidating hateful stare. Rudy admitted later to Ian. "I could feel the cold stare of that officer chilling my spine." Rudy was especially afraid for Maria. She was already petrified because of what they had to endure on the out skirts of Las Vegas.

Rudy looked at the police officer and nervously mentioned. "I gave you my drivers license and registration." The officer with his smoky the bear hat and badge beached on top, stuck his head into the front driver's seat of the semi truck said. "Boy you fuck with me and you will loose." Rudy at that time knew he was in for a rough interrogation. The officer ordered Maria who was standing on the shoulder of the expressway to get into the front seat of his squad car. All of a sudden two other Illinois police squad cars immediately arrived.

While Rudy was interrogated by one of the other officers, Maria was in the front seat of the first officer's squad car. That officer was calling her "wet back trash," trying to incite Maria into an argument. Maria knew not to let Rudy know of these actions by the officer until they were back in Houston. Maria didn't want to upset Rudy or get him into a fez with these officers. Rudy was placed into the same squad car with Maria after his interrogation. Their personal belonging's were out of the semi truck now scattered all over the high way. Traffic was blasting by in the middle of this sunny after noon creating a rapid rotation of windy vortices.

The first officer was just handed a pack of rolling papers, from one of the officers wearing rubber gloves who was searching Rudy and Maria's semi truck. The first officer now called Gabe by one of the other officers handed Gabe the rolling papers through the squad car window. The second officer just walked back from the semi with a pair of hemostats and handed them to Gabe. Gabe says to the officer. "Thanks Burt!"

Gabe now turned around in the squad car and says to Rudy in front of Maria. "Boy shit's rolling down hill for you fast Boy! I find one seed, one stick, or one stem of marijuana your both are going downtown to county jail. I'll have this entire rig confiscated and sold at the next drug forfeiture auction."

Rudy and Maria were now shaking in their boots so to speak and it wasn't from dancing all night. After the officers were satisfied there was no major contraband the officer known as Gabe, got Rudy and Maria out of the car. Gabe handed Rudy the homeostasis and Zig Zag rolling papers back. Rudy was afraid to take them, but reluctantly did.

Gabe commanded. "Rudy! Get out of here and don't ever let me catch you in this county again. Do you understand?"

Rudy still shaking in his boots reeled. "Yes sir! Were out of here!" After an hour of interrogation and the officers searching the semi from front to back, the cops had finally realized there weren't any drugs in their possession. Rudy and Maria were released. Rudy called Ian over the CB after entering back onto the highway heading south. Rudy told Ian they would meet him at a different pre-designated truck stop

Rudy pulled the semi rig into the mammoth truck stop to meet up with Ian. Concerned Ian asked. "Are you all right?"

Rudy embellished. "Yea! Just thoroughly shook up. This Hemp advertising on the side of the semi truck trailer will get you in all kinds of trouble."

Ian proclaimed loudly on the CB. "You're the luckiest son of gun!" Rudy laughed and both semis quickly re-entered the highway and headed south. Rudy continued to tell Ian, about the stop by the cops on the CB. Other truckers, and people on the highway with CB's were talking it up when they heard over Rudy and Ian's continuing conversation.

The highway travelers were all generally sympathetic with Rudy, while talking up a storm on their own CB's. The cop and pot topic of their CB conversation's was interesting and quickly drew opinions from all.

Rudy exclaimed to one lady traveler who's handle was "Lady Weasel." "Ya that officer Gabe even handed the Zig Zag rolling papers and hemostats back."

Lady Weasel asked. "What did you think when Gabe handed your the papers back?"

Rudy responded. "I was puzzled and felt reluctant to take them back."

Lady Weasel acknowledged. "I would be too. That's scary what these cops and courts are doing now to get promotions and raises."

Ian talking it up on the radio clamored. "I can't wait to get home and burn one in spite off in cops dishonor."

Rudy answered back on the CB. "What do you mean dishonor. It was down right dirt mongering!"

Ian cracked back. "It was honorable that he let you go without out planting any drugs."

Rudy confided. "I never thought of it that way! You're right! I'll help you burn that in Gabe's honor!" The highway travelers were incited by the cannabis conversation. Some truckers were now saying "I smoke wacky tabackie all the time." "To hell them porgy pigs!" One independent trucker who's handle was "Honey Bear" arrogantly said over the CB. "Yea I've got no use for them either." another trucker calling himself "Black Eye" would respond. Rudy and Maria started laughing.

One trucker who's handle was "Reefer Man" discussed. "The cops can't make their money catching real crooks doing real crimes so they invent horse shit nuisance laws or worse pull you over for absolutely nothing to meet their quota."

Black eye fumed. "I hear that! Like I said. I've got no use for them either." Semi truckers talked about scamp cop tactics like that on the CB into oblivion.

Rudy advised to Maria. "Let's quit talking and listen about all the gripes about cops the other truckers have."

Maria enthused. "That sounds neat!" New truckers always came back on the CB and had other new gripes about the cops for travelers to hear. Everyone had a story or two about bad cop encounters they endured and then some had true terror tales comparable to Rudy and Maria torture on the trail.

Rudy crowed. "That was a laugh!" They stopped for diesel fuel and separated from the other talkative truckers."

Maria divulged. "Were not the only one's out there suffering the injustice of being overly pulled over by the cops."

By daylight they were coming into St Louis, Mo. The caravan of hemp seeds, supplies, and hemp-farming implements was now approaching St Louis downtown area. Driving by St Louis the Arch over six hundred feet in height, the view of it prevailed over the old courthouse. Arching head over like a rainbow. The Arch now a national monument sits on the banks of the Mississippi River. Even the Pope on his visit to St Louis was impressed.

They were in full view of the Mississippi River at the moment. The design of the arch "The gateway to the West" is a prevalent object in the downtown area of St Louis. Maria told Rudy. "I'd like to visit Elvis Presley's mansion," during dinner the night before.

Rudy sweet talked. "Great we can do that baby. Anything for you baby." They proceeded to take the switch off route 66 to route I-55 south, toward Memphis. The excitement was now building, because Maria was a big Elvis fan. How many women weren't or aren't? The cannabis caravan drove all night to arrive the following morning in Memphis for a one day lay over. It would be a good break before the rest of the trip.

Arriving in the most southwest part of the great state of Tennessee, The tired truckers booked into a motel truck stop. Other semi drivers at the motel complex noticed the hemp advertising on their semi truck. The truckers became curious and walked over to the duo semi trucks to inquire about the hemp cargo. One trucker named Rex said. "What's all that hemp stuff about on that truck trailer."

Rudy gladly explained. "Rex! All I can say now is I'm a firm believer in the potential of hemp products and related hemp industry services."

One driver named Elliott asked. "Is there any opportunities brokering some hemp supplies from Canada to the states."

Rudy explained. "Yes! We started hauling supplies for the huge new hemp industry in Canada. Were making decent money at it."

Ian now in the conversation said. "The hemp industry has opened up in a big way. They need more drivers to transport loads of hemp supplies and products south."

Maria said. "We only have time for a catnap Rudy, if we intend to tour the Presley mansion this afternoon."

Rudy said. "OK see you boys later."

Maria said. "We have the motel room rented for the rest of the day and night. We can come and go as we pleased with this computerized entry key. "The motel is set up to transport touring patrons."

The motel clerk said. "The motel's van makes regular runs to all the Elvis attractions and the airport."

Rudy said. "Thanks!" Maria was an architect for arrangements. She already made for alternative transportation.

Maria said. "You just can't drive everywhere with a semi."

After a catnap and a shower all of the trucking tourists were in the motel van that was now taking them down Elvis Presley Boulevard. They couldn't believe the enormous build up of souvenir shops, museums, CD, record shops,

The motel clerk proposed. "The motel is set up to transport tourist's The motel's van makes regular runs to all the Elvis attractions and the airport."

Rudy marveled. "Thanks!" Maria was an architect for arrangements. She already made for alternative transportation.

Maria recounted. "You just can't drive everywhere with a semi."

After a catnap and a shower all of the trucking tourists were in the motel van that was now taking them down Elvis Presley Boulevard. They couldn't believe the enormous build up of souvenir shops, museums, CD, record shops, and tour buses ready to take patrons to Elvis's old haunt's. Including Elvis's Hume's high school, his birth place in Tupelo, Miss, Sun studio on Beale St, where they just dedicated a statue of Elvis, his karate school, and Elvis's dad's home the next street over from the mansion. The motel tourist transportation van was now arriving at the gate of Elvis Presley's mansion after souvenir shopping at a couple of close by stores. Rudy, Maria, and Ian couldn't wait to see Elvis's house.

The brick wall along the sidewalk bordering the estate of the mansion's elegant gated entrance was neat and articulating. Over the brick fence you could see through the trees on rolling hills of groomed lawns the pillars in front of the mansion. The pillars were prominent by itself and partially seen through the trees from Elvis Presley Boulevard.

The tour, which Maria had arranged ahead of time, was about to begin. Rudy and Maria were the first to walk in past the wrought iron gates with musical notes and Elvis playing guitar in elegant designs on both gates, which swung inward to the mansion from the center of the gate. Ian was following with the tour guide named Preston as Rudy and Maria continued to lead the way up the driveway path to the mansion. Preston welcomed all the tourists to Elvis's home. The light texture of the house was a good contrast for evergreen out doors of the Tennessee surroundings.

White wrought iron benches stood directly in front of the house and they were filled with visitors having their pictures taken by friends. In front of the house Rudy stared at stained glass peacocks among other seemingly priceless items. A large white couch rested in the forefront of the music room. You could see the grand piano Elvis used to play in the music room.

Rudy surprised. "Seems like every where we go in this mansion there is a chandelier hanging from the ceiling."

Ian maintained. "I like the dinning room with it's high back wooded chairs around the dinning table, one room had three TV's in a row."

The guide explained to Ian. "Elvis watched all three TV's at the same time. This room has seen a lot of action."

Ian rambled. "From what I hear this whole mansion has seen allot of action."

Rudy persisted to Maria. "This mansion is loaded with furniture."

Maria noticed. "Elvis had good taste didn't he?"

Rudy agreed. "Oh Yea! He sure did!"

The mansion tour guide Preston lectured. "Elvis back in the mid seventies had a two story structure added to the estate of his house. The bi-level had a hard wood floor for the racquetball court on the main level. Upstairs Elvis had his own dressing room, Jacuzzi spa, as well as other amenities in that new addition. Elvis was singing "Unchained melody" the day just before his death in this building. Elvis's trophy building is an eighty foot long room dedicated for his gold and platinum record albums and singles. Elvis has over a billion dollars in sales and sales are still climbing. Elvis has more sales for the recorded voice then any other recording artist. Elvis memorabilia here is from every era of his career. All memorabilia seen here is from his private collection in this trophy building. There is the famous gold suit from the fifty's, his two piece leather suit from his come back tour in 68' as well as his karate suit. Look at his colorful studded suit from the Aloha from Hawaii, broadcast via satellite special. There is his famous American Eagle cap which is also quit decorative."

Rudy, Maria and Ian were in the mansion automobile museum where Elvis's pink fifty's Cadillac was roped off. Ian professed. "I never seen any thing like it before."

Rudy raved. "I liked the Stutz Blackhawk with red leather interior and gold plated trim everywhere on the car." The truckers turned tourists walked past the swimming pool on the way to meditation garden. Maria led the way and knelt down by the grave of Elvis Presley bowing her head to say a prayer. To the left of Elvis's grave was his grand mother Minnie Mae Presley and to the right of Elvis's grave was his father Vernon with his mother Glady's grave and to the right of Vernon's.

Maria reflected. "It is an enlightening just walking through Elvis's home. It is then you realize the comfortable elegance he lived in. It's amazing!"

Rudy shared his feelings. "When you walk around his mansion grounds the fragrance from the floral gardens is evident."

Maria psyched. "You can feel his presence!" she persisted to Rudy and Ian as they peeked through the Graceland mansion grounds.

Ian sensed. "I know what you mean."

Rudy attested. "Elvis was a well documented man." The trio of tourists were now leaving the entrance of Elvis's mansion when Maria turned and take another look and picture of the mansion before they left.

The next morning they were up early and the caravan of semi-truck hemp seeds and supplies was back on the road. The semis were now moving fast toward Shreveport, La to drop off the hemp load at the processing plant for paper production.

Upon entering Shreveport, La., on Kings Highway, they could see the river boat casino on the banks of the Mississippi. They went past the casino straight to the hemp processing plant. Rudy then walked into the hemp production area. The hemp workers in this part of the plant were processing raw hemp fibers into hemp paper. With their own eyes Rudy and Maria were now witness to the pulping of non-wood materials into wood hemp particle board products, and all tree free!

Ian accented to Maria. "That's astonishing!" as they toured the hemp production plant.

Rudy was busy looking for his contact who Morris the hemp complex manager in Canada who had arranged a tour at this hemp processing plant in Shreveport, La. His contacts name was Henry Hendricks. Everyone called him Henry the Hempster, or just "Hempster." Morris said he was a tall and energetic sort and always was dressed completely in hemp clothing. The Hempster's apparel was all made in their hemp processing complex.

The "Hempster" was ready to give Rudy, Maria, and Ian and give them all an informative cannabis guided tour. The Hempster planned to explain the uses, processing, history, and potential use of hemp farming and hemp production. Rudy found an assistant to the Hempster named Ethan before he found the Hempster.

Ethan instructed Rudy. "Back your semi trailer into dock thirteen and we'll get you unloaded first. Then have Ian's trailer back in after your loaded with your hemp particle board."

Rudy asked Ethan. "How many semi trailers of hemp seed is your plant unloading here a day?"

Ethan informed. "Twelve to fifteen semi's per day are unloaded. The longer we are in business the more semi's we can process through the hemp processing plant, We keep on up grading with the development of new hemp processing technology."

Rudy asked. "Has your hemp plant been keeping busy?"

Ethan explained. "The Company set up profit sharing for the employees." Rudy responded. "Really"

Ethan further explained. "We put a lot of care into our work efforts here since this hemp processing plant is set up with the profit sharing plan."

Rudy asked. "Can we light up?"

Ethan enounced. "Yes! We allow our workers a smoke break no matter what their choice of leaves are. We have an electric fan vented smoking lounge. Our workers like it."

Rudy exhorted. "I'll be ready to check the smoker's lounge out after the hemp tour!"

As Ethan was walking explained the organization process of the plant. We have a paper recycling department in the other part of the building. The wood pulp paper can be recycled three times, but the hemp can be recycled up to nine times. Hemp has much stronger fibers in texture and a shelf life up to fifteen hundred years. The hemp paper is a high quality and long lasting product."

Ethan continued to tell them about all the hemp products they were making and were going to make in the future. Now the Hempster himself was approaching the inquisitive trio.

Henry after introducing himself with the hemp top hat on said. "How the hemp are Ya." The tall and flamboyant Henry dressed in hemp fringe garments was reflecting a uniquely new line of apparel. Henry further said. "Welcome to Shreveport." they all exchanged greetings.

Rudy told Henry. "Ethan has been filling us in about hemp seed processing."

Henry responded. "Good, We are trying to be a full service hemp processing plant."

Rudy emphasized. "Looks like your quite busy!"

Henry specified. "Yes! We are very busy and getting busier everyday."

As Henry went on to explain to Rudy, Maria, and Ian. "We make hemp products such as cigarette papers, stationary, card board, particle boards, insulation, automotive parts, etc. All made with hemp fibers manufactured here at this hemp processing and production plant. We even manufacture imitation wood looking two by four's developed from hemp fibers right here."

Ian confided. "I've never seen so many different products made from hemp in one place."

Henry told Rudy that. "This whole building and all the materials here are made from hemp."

Rudy raged. "This is one hell of a show case for hemp products!"

Henry claimed. "The building inspector was in for quite an education when they went through this specially built hemp building."

Rudy surprised. "I never imagined that raw hemp materials could be made into so many different safe and durable products."

The Hempster explained. "Yea, Our customers keep coming up with new hemp product demands. We keep trying to keep up with all the demands. The high quality of hemp fibers ends up being made into books, magazines, news print, packaging materials, and tissue paper."

Rudy asked. "Even toilet paper?"

Henry answered. "Oh Ya, The hemp tissue feels good on your ass." They all laughed as he gossiped. "My wife uses the new hemp Femi-pads."

Maria implied. "Hemp Femi-pads?"

Henry informed. "Hemp has been made into paper for over ten thousand years. In early civilizations hemp was the most widely grown crop. Everything from bible's, prayer books, artists canvas, artists paints, even the drafts of the U S Constitution, Declaration of Independence, and up until the late 1,800's ninety-five percent of all paper was made out of hemp fibers for paper. Hemp was advocated and grown by all the early state governments of this nation, as it has been and is still in many other nations. The processing of hemp raw materials requires no bleach, because hemp plant fibers are naturally white, which is not the case with tree paper."

Rudy was amazed at all the hemp product knowledge that was unknown to the general public. Henry went on to explain hemp production as they all looked at the hemp processing in action.

Henry lectured. "Popular Mechanics Magazine, back in the 1930's predicted that hemp was the next billion dollar crop. That was when they had inferior hemp farm harvesting implements, and hemp industrial processing facilities compared to today's modern standards of technology. Hemp being a standard raw fiber in the world economy, could produce a great many jobs in the American economy."

Rudy hyped. "I can see that."

Henry explained. "Hemp's tensile fiber strength and durability to make rope, chords, or twine all the way down to fine laces is incomparable when it comes to any other fiber competition against hemp fiber."

Maria avowed. "I like the high quality of the blouse I just purchased up front."

Henry now pointed to pictures on the wall of modern farming methods and explained. "From a farmer's point of view hemp is a hardy and easy plant to grow. It has a short growing season requires few or no chemical fertilizers for growing methods. This process is as environmentally friendly, as our water supply and does not contaminate like many other agricultural crops. Many of those other existing crops require a major amount of chemical herbicides and pesticides like cotton does. These chemical herbicides and pesticides from other crops enter our streams, rivers and lakes, with damaging affect on the water supply we all drink, and further damages the soil by stripping it of it's nutrients. Soil is not stripped of vital nutrients after a hardy hemp crop is grown. Industrial hemp farming combined with modern agricultural methods, leaves the soil for the following season in perfect condition for next season's crop. No till farming of the hemp cropland is recommended by the farm bureaus. This process lesson's the effects of soil erosion, because of the deep roots from the hemp stalks."

Rudy ranted. "This is a farmers dream, isn't it?"

Henry expounded. "It sure is Farmer's association's are also recommending hemp, when rotating agricultural crops. This process is favored for saving a farmer's time, and expense."

Rudy claimed. "I saw some fine healthy hemp crops in Manitoba."

Henry predicted. "Hemp will be a staple agricultural crop in the United States, because it is becoming one in the world community again. When the laws are lifted this country will be farming thirty million acres in three years time."

Rudy cheered. "I believe it!"

Henry proclaimed. "The present day supply and demand of hemp paper and card board products alone would support the hemp industry. The demand for hemp textiles will be hard to keep up with if American farmers don't get involved in hemp farming and production in a big way."

Ethan divulged. "We need the farmers to keep up with our hemp crop demands. The fiber's ratio per acre harvested is staggering in comparison. Hemp fiber's offer five times as great a yield, when compared to wood."

Henry explained. "That means a tract of one hundred thousand acres of agricultural hemp grown crops for hemp pulp, when compared to a harvested wood forest for wood pulp would take a half a million acres for the same amount of raw fiber material. Times this raw fiber figure by twenty years of hemp production and processing for hemp raw fibers, compared to the time it requires for growing another crop of trees that has to be reforested."

Rudy cracked to Henry. "My calculator would break!"

Henry hashed over as they continued the tour. "You know that's right! Various governors from different states, have created hemp and other crop alternatives such as kenaf. Kenaf is an East Indian hibiscus that yields a strong cordage fiber. However, kenaf is not as hardy as hemp with a weaker core fraction, kenaf is more difficult to ship, because of plant durability. Hemp is a hardy product all the way around even for shipping purposes. Farmer's want alternative crops and tobacco industries are looking into diversification as well."

Rudy asked. "Why doesn't the US grow it's own crop's now?"

Henry explained. "Current laws presently don't allow hemp farming. Specialty textiles and paper demands will soon dictate a different tune. In years to come when they cut our last trees down they'll have to grow hemp."

Rudy conveyed. "I don't think it's going to come to the last tree being cut down. I think hemp production will be legal again after people see the success the Canadians and other countries around the world are having in the hemp industry."

Henry enthused. "I hope your right Rudy! The US Government and DEA's office are still in opposition to industrial hemp production. They base this premise on not being able to distinguish hemp from its cousins plant marijuana."

Rudy attested. "That's not our problem."

Henry depicted. "That shouldn't be their problem. They think if they legalize hemp production, it would send a signal to legalization of marijuana. But the way the argument should break down is that the low THC pollen from the hemp crops would actually destroy the THC of the marijuana plants that people smoke."

Ian railed. "The government should plant forty million acres of hemp if that's the case!"

Rudy asked. "What's wrong with legalization of marijuana?"

Henry roused. "I don't see anything wrong with marijuana use. Marijuana should have never been outlawed in the first place. Marijuana has been used worldwide for thousands of years for thousands of uses. And after were all dead and gone marijuana will be used for thousands of years to come."

Rudy told Henry immediately. "Your right! I agree!"

Henry asked. "Why, do you wanna burn some Louisiana green bud?"

"Yea" Rudy's crowd ranted.

Henry paraded. "Let's go into the workers smoking lounge."

As they walked into the unique smoker's lunge area, you could see all the brightly colored walls. Fluorescent murals covered the walls.

Henry romped. "All of us that work here as a pretty tight nit crew. Around here most of us are related to each other or our best friends work here with us to accomplish the same goals. We have the same hemp profit sharing plan, and we also take a small amount of capital gains to invest in hemp commodity cannabis stock options which are available in other countries.

Rudy interested remarked. "Really stock options on hemp commodities!"

Henry presented. "Sure we all have industrial hemp stock options."

Henry took a joint out of his pocket and lit it up and put it. "Were liberal around here. We all work together, and we all smoke marijuana and go about our business every day. As you can see. We do good work!"

Rudy agreed. "Everything looks highly professional throughout the plant. Thanks for the whole tour."

Henry further stated. "World production and recognition is going up, and up every year. With the world wide shortage of productive fibers, the hemp industry will sky rocket." Henry now passed the joint around the horn, before continuing. "Hemp Manufactures and processors in the hemp industry exclaim, it will be for the environmental and economic well being of not only American citizens, but the world community as well."

Ian and Rudy noticed the "Think Green" signs that were all over the walls of the smokers lounge.

Ethan a farmers son prophesied. "Some strains of hemp grows eight to twenty feet tall in seventy to one hundred and ten days of growth."

Henry stated with conviction. "Hemp grows like Jack's bean stock with little tending."

"Wow" Rudy said in disbelief.

Ian asked. "That fast?"

Henry reiterated. "Oh gosh! Yes!"

Ethan asserted. "Oh Yea! Farmers like the idea of a such hardy hemp crop. Hemp products such as the shirt I'm wearing, will take us into the next century."

Henry portrayed. "We all have life time jobs."

Maria appraised. "That's a sharp looking shirt you have on Henry."

Ian agreed. "Yea I like the shirt also!"

Henry chuckled. "Thanks for the compliment." and further explained. "Hemp is an environmentally safe, and needed product. You can literally makes million's of household and industrial products, from upholstery, carpets, an endless variety of building products, the list just doesn't end with new innovative products. Were engrossed in a gigantic merchandise evolution worldwide involving strictly hemp fibers."

Rudy exulted. "I really am amazed! This hemp paper making craftsmanship is something else. The whole method of hemp paper making production is interesting."

Henry informed his new friends. "We get more and more business inquiries about hemp products everyday. The hemp industry is legal for hemp crop cultivation in Canada, France, Germany, Holland, Australia, Thailand, Jamaica, Africa, Austria, China, Hungry, Russia, Poland, Chile, Finland, India, Romania, Slovenia, Spain, Switzerland, Egypt, Portugal, Thailand, Ukraine, and in the United Kingdom, and the list goes on". Henry said, and "The hemp industry is thriving. The hemp industry worldwide is growing by leaps and bounds. Year after year. Even the Emperor of Japan wears hemp garments following in his countries established religious traditions."

Ian surprised. "I didn't know that!"

Henry further divulged. "China! Grows more hemp and produces the largest commercial crop of hemp, than any other nation on the planet. China has grown hemp for over ten thousand years straight and still does bigger and better hemp crops, production methods, and hemp products than ever. I'm telling you."

Henry's wife Heather, who also worked at the hemp processing plant was now walking up to the other's. She was quickly introduced to the inquisitive traveler's.

Heartwarming Heather and Modish Maria hit it off immediately. They both pranced off to the powder room together. Maria was probably glad to meet a person of the opposite gender. After being stuck with Rudy and Ian on such a long trip. Maria was probably, anxious to get home to see their kids. They all knew it wouldn't be long once they got on the road again. They had decided they would pick up their new semi loads in the morning and head out. Ian was to end his part of the caravan south. He planned to get his load of hemp paper and deliver the loaded semi to New York City while heading north. They decided they would spend one more night together having fun.

They picked out a local Casino in Shreveport for the evening. Henry and Heather wanted to go with them as well. Rudy and Maria stayed at the Casino Hotel for the evening, while Ian retired to the sleeper part of his semi. Before the evening was over Maria and Heather had exchanged addresses and Maria had invited Henry and Heather back to Houston the following summer. Henry the Hempster and his wife Heather the Hempstress graciously excepted. Before they knew it, Rudy and Maria were on their was south toward Houston again, with no other scheduled stops. They both, started to sing "On the road again" by Willie Nelson along with one of Rudy's CD's.

Chapter 3.... Presently; at the Houston Police Headquarters, the opposing forces of marijuana use ferment. Dick Dirkskin the Chief of Police whom and is the main nemesis of the pro-marijuana opposition. His force of loosly knit men were preparing to under go an intensive and all-inclusive training at a must be at police seminar.

This weekend the Houston Police headquarters hosted outside in their parking lot and inside their gymnasium is where the police seminar covering tactics and weapons. Girt was the head of the Metro drug squad, Officer Girt's job was to explain all counter drug operations. The seminar was being held to improve the image of the Houston Police Department.

Every one in the community was well aware of the six renegade police officers who were fired from the police department. They participated in a drug raid that ended in the death of an unarmed Mexican National. The Mexican man was killed after the police officers stormed into the mans apartment without a search warrant. The shooting started when one police officer was shot in the back by another officer by accident during the unauthorized drug raid. One officer fired twelve rounds off from his weapon and loaded another magazine in the weapon and fired off twelve more rounds at the unarmed Mexican national.

The weaponless Mexican National is fired on because of the rebel police officers unwarranted actions. The defenseless man was hit fatally by a dozen bullets in the small apartment. Over thirty bullets were fired in all, and yet no weapon was found on the helpless dead victim. The renegade police stated the raid was in search of drugs. Yet no drugs were found.

Ramone's mentor and friend Leon, a former deputy sheriff and Metro squad leader was sentenced to just ten years in prison for protecting two hundred pound shipments of cocaine for the drug cartels on a regular basis. Leon pocketed ten thousand dollars per load for protecting, transporting and distribution of these illegal hard drug shipments. Four different police agency's and over a dozen police were implicated by that one police internal investigation. Ramone narrowly escaped being implicated himself.

Ramone, Girt along with many other police officers fresh from the donut shop would speak on identification, detection techniques and symptoms people suspected of alcohol, or drug use exhibit. Ramone had a pocket size substance abuse influence guide, which showed papillary reactions to different drugs.

Sergeant's Godfrey, and Luke among others were managers, training officers of the Houston metro drug squad.

Capt. Reynold Renard head of special force operations was to represent the tactical vehicle squadron. He was also, the chairman of the police tactical vehicle seminar circuit, specializing in interception, inspection, and methods of interrogation. He embodied the one stop cop shop. Enrolment forms were being passed to all officers for the tactical driver's instructors coarse. The vehicle-driving courses included response team training, like pursuit driving. Other driving techniques include ditch jumping and preparing for a controlled immanent collision. These officers demonstrating for the Houston Police Dept were driving like nuts during their course preview in the dept.'s parking lot, and in the adjacent large field next to the tracks. Precision Immobilization Techniques was the best show. The presenters drove their patrol car into a moving car, and knocked the car out of commission like it was a real car chase. Courses like these cost thousands of dollars, and are essential for promotional jobs of magnitude in the police dept. His assistant. Sgt. Terry Thomas demonstrated a course protocol and course concepts of report writing. New traffic templates with multi functions were also being distributed on a trial basis. Sgt. Terry also mentions taking a field notes course for criminal law and evidence. "Court room testimony and convictions are denied or upheld because of an officers documentation" Sgt. Terry explained.

Corporal Conners demonstrated, Stun Batons with two hundred thousand volt's of arc, pepper spray's, and new personal tear gas canisters. At random all the police participants would either get stunned by the stun guns or pepper sprayed, as a matter of protocol. Effects and Safety were demonstrated, while the police officers were zapping each other officer with the stun guns, while some were still wiping pepper spray from their eyes.

Officer Larry demonstrated the new lead plated gloves available by hitting each officer for effect. The officer's were ordered to wear mandatory black combat boots for their militarized martial arts training that day.

Officer Maynard demonstrated hand to hand combat, and nunchaku techniques. The entire officer's force had to participate, either by hitting or be hit.

The canine trainers Denton Dukes, who was a one time trainer in the military K-9 unit. Professional K-9 training and Obedience skills were Denton's specialty. Denton went to other K-9 units to upgrade their dog training and attack techniques. Training must be intense and continuous for the K-9 unit to be effective in the war on drugs, or to track human prey. Dog searches were also done on a request by the school board. In one such incident Denton was in charge of a one hour search, while all students were locked down in there class rooms during a surprise drug search. A student was bit and scared by one of the police drug dogs. The student left the school building for the day to receive medical attention, she was given thirteen stitches to close the wound caused by the drug search dog.

Denton decreed. "That the girl moved to fast for the dog and the dog over re-acted. No drugs turned up in that High school. The dogs had sniffed all the locker rooms, and parked cars in the student parking lot after that. The school superintendent Shawn Staten ordered the surprise drug searches on the students un-announced. The school had a zero tolerance smoking, drug, and alcohol policy. I have an obligation to uphold to the community."

Parents were upset that the police reacted like it's citizens were living in a military state comparable to a third world country. The canines were on the far side of the police demonstration building parking lot, across from the Tactical Vehicle training on the other side of the building so the noise from the cars wouldn't bother them. Police attending the seminar, were carefully scheduled so they would have an opportunity, to see all the particular law enforcement demonstrations.

Denton had his dogs ferociously bite and hold participants in various dog attack drills. Witnesses were astonished and stared in horror, during the canine attack demonstrations. Denton went on to demonstrate canines, finding drugs in various places. The drugs were strategically placed for demonstration before hand. Some canine's found drugs placed in certain parcels of equipment that had been passed out to the unsuspecting cops. The cops were unexpected participants in the cop canine drug demonstrations. The dogs quickly rooted out all the cocaine and marijuana. The alliance between, beast and man, ran wild, at the same time as the military and police applications introduced.

Denton explained. "Their smell and hearing is far superior for a dog, than a man."

Tactical support officers were training other officers in counter drug training sessions and the corporal suppression of marijuana users, these officers were eagerly enthused with their counter drug training session. Overtime pay along with coffee, doughnuts were served for all the attendees of the day's events. The police chief decided to sponsor the day's events though the drug forfeiture fund.

New techniques in flashlight defenses was demonstrated with heavy lithium powered combat flashlights. Officer Larry explained that. "These flash lights can be used efficiently in close confrontations with disorderly civilians. Defense with out bruises or show-able damage to the victim is stressed. Tactical defense training for police was demonstrated by SWAT teams as well. Most of the SWAT team representatives had on body armor and fragmentation vests. Battering rams for knocking down household doors quickly for drug raids was also demonstrated, and new military issued holsters were given to all attendees, these tactical products were the latest in the counter drug arsenal. Police response teams for gang related crimes were also covered, through out this special tactics phase of the seminar. Talks went on about crack cocaine gangs. Crack gang members were ordered to kill innocent victims to gain full entry of the inner circle of the gang net work. They would then indoctrinate the new gang member with a gang tattoo, which identified him for the killing deed that was rendered. Everyone agrees these gangs and dealers of crack cocaine need to be taken off our streets and dealt with.

These were the guys the cops needed to concentrate on and eliminate the crooked law enforcement ambient factors, who work with the gangs. Because of the Cops blue code of honor they do not always rat out other cops even when they are suspected or known to have dealing's in the drug trade. These officers were known as the gang tactical unit were used for larger scale counter drug operations. They had a fancy way of demonstrating their shot guns quickly. They claimed it was a versatile and effective weapon, and a standard weapon in the police arsenal. Handling and short-range shooting techniques of the shotguns were demonstrated. You couldn't really blame the cops desire to be strong armed when they break into crack cocaine houses. Crack dealers are also well armed.

Pete in charge of the hard drug surveillance said. "The crack dealers and users are quite different from the normal marijuana user. The majority marijuana users don't want anything to do with crack or crack people. They don't have a crackers recreational high values. The marijuana smoker knows crack is a losing game. Crack Cocaine kills the soul. Ninety-eight percent of marijuana smokers are just like the Ninety-eight percent mainstream straight America, they want nothing to do with crack cocaine. They want crack cocaine off the streets."

One officer named Greg Greathead who was of Comanche and Mexican heritage asked. "Then why do we bust marijuana smokers?"

Peter grumbled. "Because that's the law, and our job, you're paid to uphold by all means."

Greg relayed. "I know citizens, who smoke marijuana and they lead OK lives."

Peter lashed. "Bust them all! How do you think we get promoted around here?"

Greg explained. "Don't you think enforcing out dated and outmoded governmental laws against marijuana user's is the real crime?"

Stunned Peter asked. "What did you say?"

Greg responded. "Smoking pot is another thing all together different then hard drugs, Marijuana is being constitutionally challenged. Nobody's constitutionally challenging hard drugs."

Peter stressed. "Greg, I want to talk to you after class about your intestinal fortitude to be a police officer. You sit right there until after class!"

Greg agreed. "Yes sir!"

This day at the police dept was one hell of a day of demonstrations, all crammed into a cluster of class training session. The day's police demonstrations were exciting. Chief Dick Dirkskin mingled with the heads of the other police departments from surrounding counties police dept. The chief was seeing many of his old and trusted friends some of whom were involved with county to county escorting of major shipments of hard drugs for the drug cartels.

When the cops who are supposed to be trained to "Protect and Serve", track themselves for personal gain all abuse's known to man seem to flourish under a system of repression of rights. This all accumulates from the lack of responsible government. Billions on top of billions of dollars from an open ended American taxpayer's wallet. Our dollars are being blown away endlessly on a continuous basis. All the money being spent by drug enforcement is really never explained.

Clint always thought, if the governmental accountants, can't explain what all the tax money is being spent on and where it's going, they should be locked up. All the high ranking public officials, who are in charge of spending our tax money accountable. Across the board every branch of government has to be reined in to provide a degree of accountability.

In the county building, the chief had support from an old staunch relic of a politician, Frank Forrester the county commissioner. He was supported by the so-called political moral majority. The unknowledgeable, and self-interested decision-makers.

Frank Forrester, the Commissioner, spent over two and a half million dollars on drug enforcement including marijuana drug busts and only four hundred thousand on homicide investigations. Marijuana drug busts where they zero in on easier prey, and statistically it looked like crime was being was being dealt with by busting marijuana users. There were over seven hundred thousand marijuana busts last year in this country and ninety percent of them was for simple possession of marijuana. What is wrong with this unbalanced picture? Besides that! There is no lucrative drug forfeiture money involved in solving murders cases. Cops only go after the cash crimes, no matter what.

There essentially is no police monetary incentive to get deeply involved in murder cases. Drug arrests is what put bread and butter on the cop's table. Frank and Dick were in total agreement with current marijuana drug arrest procedures, as long as they got their fair cut from drug seizures and forfeitures. It really didn't matter how the busts went down as long as the money kept coming in the till. It didn't really matter if the citizen was guilty or not, the judicial money machine must roll on. They were raking in millions splitting profits amongst the drug team and rolling on to the next charade of a raid. These legal crooks were no different than Quantrells raiders rampaging through Kansas. The drug forfeiture money should go to another party not to the police who use it as an incentive to bust marijuana users and line their police forces purse strings.

Police Chief Dirkskin on his drive home noticed his son Norman hanging out with some of his friends was shooting bow and arrows into targets. Norman's school friends were among the kids firing the arrows into a new hemp deer target. Norman's best friend Frank Jr from the military cadet school, they both attended.

Norman was leading the bow and arrow competition the kid's set up. Dirkskin was unnoticed from his position of approach behind the bushy tree line. He had parked his car walked and sneaked through the trees to watch the kids. Lowering the volume on his Motorola radio, he scanned the group of teens from behind a granddad hickory tree.

He watched his kid Norman lead in the bow and arrow competition. Then in shock Dirkskin noticed one of the kid's pass a joint to his kid, who was seventeen years of age. Norman hit the joint and passed it to one of the other kids, who passed it on around the horn. Norman was showing his friends his new hemp archery strings on his bow. Norman had earned the money for the hemp strings from his paper route.

Norman was telling his friend Frank. "I think the hemp strings make me a better shot." as he took his next shot, and hit a bulls eye.

Frank blinked and cheered. "Great shot Norm!"

Dirkskin sent his kid to an acclaimed military school with a reputation and stature for excellence. He was physically inflamed and astounded to see his boy burn a big fat green one, you could boil an egg on his head.

Dirkskin immediately called Girt on his radio. "Girt get over here to Gates Lane by the Gump bridge. I'll meet you there in ten minutes and bring reinforcements to surround the entire area. I want to teach some kids a lesson and arrest these pot smoking teens."

Girt after he answered the police dispatchers page responded from the local doughnut shop. "I'll be there in five minutes chief." Girt made sure he grabbed his bag of doughnuts on the way out the door, over re-action Jackson was enforce.

Ramone also heard Dirkskin's call over the radio, and headed to the area. Six police squad cars were now approaching the archery kids, who were all still shooting targets with their bows. Norman fires the last shot into the target and wins the archery competition. His friend Rance, whose parents owned the house and were at work said. "Great shooting Norm!"

"Thanks!" Norman voiced. As all the other kids came over to congratulate Norman and give each other high five's. The pugnacious chief of police Dirkskin suddenly ran up to the kids from behind the trees with the other police officers. The police commandos violently threw the kids to the ground. They hog-tied and cuffed them all tightly. Four joints of marijuana were found on one of the kids.

Dirkskin immediately and relentlessly beat his kid Norman in front of the other kids. "Wanna smoke a marijuana cigarette do Yea!" As he stomped Norm. He was in agony from being punched and humiliated. His social circle gaped in horror.

Dirkskin recommended charges against the boy Bruce Baxter, Norman's schoolmate, who first passed the joint originally. Dirkskin wanted the prosecutor to bring charges against the parents of Rance, who owned the house for contributing to drug abuse, even though the parents were not there.

Dirkskin wanted the kid's parents charged for maintaining and operating a drug house. Pete and Mittie Bacon's son Rance had a bunch of his friends over for the bow and arrow target meet in their backyard. Rance told his parents there wasn't a problem in the world until the cops showed up. Everyone was behaving and having a good time. "I hate those cops." Rance told his parents as he went into his room. "Look what they did to Norman." Rance cried as he left the room.

The parents of Rance ended up writing a stinging article in the newspaper's editorial section the following week stating: "The police tactics was brutal and unfair on these young men. Rance's parents article was well received in the community.

The next day after the bust Norman's military schoolmates were making fun of him. They humiliated Norman on a relentless pace. When Norman came home from school his father Dirk the jerk, would grind at him about smoking that marijuana joint, while Norman and the kids were shooting bow and arrows. Chief Dirkskin gave Norman a relentless amount of menial work to do around the house. Norman was also told by Dirk that he was grounded for the rest of the school year and the following summer."

After a week of abuse and being called names like "Narc" amongst his schoolmate friends Norman was depressed and blamed for the marijuana bust. Norman told his friend Frank Jr. "I'm gonna get even with my dad."

Frank JR asked. "What do you mean?"

Norman murmured. "Wait till tomorrow and watch and listen." Frank Jr was puzzled and he always stuck by Norman through it all. Frank was Norman's best friend.

That afternoon, before his mother Beverly got home, Norman loaded his fathers twelve gauge in his bedroom. Norman who may have smoked ten joints in his whole young life pulled the trigger, firing the slug into his head, ripping his face off. There wasn't any drugs or alcohol in Norman's bodying at the time. He died because of a humiliated and broken spirit. His mother arrived and found the body, crying on mercifully she called the station and told Chief Dirkskin. "Oh no." he said then immediately broke down and cried. Dirkskin knew he was too hard on the kid, but would never admit it.

Friends at school held a vigil in front of Norman's home. Norman's parents were mourning deeply. The funeral director Percy Perkins said. "This funeral is by far the largest funeral he could remember." Police Chief Dirkskin and his wife went into seclusion for a week to mourn.

The next week Girt was at the doughnut shop. A patron named Rex, who son was at the archery competition the week before and had been rousted along with the other kids, went on to tell Girt. "They should have left those kids alone that day. Norman would still be alive."

Girt riveted "Yea gotta put your foot down somewhere with these kids now days."

Rex. "Not like that! That was all Dirkskin's fault the man." Girt now embarrassed left the doughnut shop without speaking further. When he approached his car, he noticed a note stuck under the windshield wiper. Girt grabbed the note which read "PIGS". Girt now steaming mad got into his car and sped off burning rubber all the way down the shoulder of the road. Girt finally entered the roadway a half a block down from the shop.

When Girt finally arrived at his destination, he slammed on his breaks squealing to a stop as he pulled to picked up Patrolman Tim Harmons. Officer Tim was to assist Girt in the ensuing arrest of a political rival of Dirkskin's regime Bill Barker.

When Girt arrived at the large brick residence he immediately noticed Bill Barker's county car in the drive and instructed, Tim to follow him into the house. Tim was hot on Girt heels. Bill Barker (the City Planner) and his wife, Beth, were at home. The police officer and Lieutenant Girt barged on into the house and into the bedroom going right past Bill and his wife.

"What's going on? Wait a minute!" Bill scowled to Girt.

Girt answered. "Stand right where you are." Right there is where they stood.

Girt was relying on a tip from Jimmy Barker the grade school sixth grader who was Bill's son. Girt had interrogated Jimmy Barker at grade school, during the schools DARE program. Girt was informed by Jimmy that his parents occasionally used marijuana and kept the marijuana in a cabinet in the bedroom.

After knocking on his own bed room door, Bill still asked Girt in a civil manner. "What are you doing Girt?"

Girt responded. "None of your business yet, Bill but it's not a social call. I'm gonna look in this cabinet in the bedroom, your son Jimmy described it to a tee."

Girt immediately opened the cabinet door and looked in and retrieves the tray of marijuana holding a small bag consisting of a few joints. Girt looks at Bill and his wife and rattled. "Ha, ha, ha, what do we have here?"

Bill stated. "That is none of your business!"

Girt proclaimed. "It is now! We have illegal drugs here." Girt immediately reaches for his microphone from his portable radio and calls in back up Officer Logan Lamarz, who is on patrol near by came immediately and walked straight into Bills home with handcuffs in hand.

Girt, Tim and Logan promptly arrest both Bill and Beth. These hero cops bring Bill and Beth to police station for further investigation, interrogation, intimidation, and incarceration. Officer Logan was left at the house to further search for drugs and wait for the arrival of Social Services so Jimmy could be taken to the shelter. Beth was screaming at the cops. "Let me stay with my son." Logan says. "We can't do that." The kid was terrified, but all the crying was to no avail. The cops were going to get their vengeful way that day.

Once at the shelter the other kids taunted and made fun of him for helping in the DARE program and for squealing on his own parents. The kids at the shelter wouldn't let little Jimmy even hang out in their section of the youth home without torment.

Bill was now about to lose his position of over twenty years as City Planner. He and his wife smoked marijuana for over twenty-three years. They never had any problems whatsoever with conducting their everyday lives. They even smoked the pot away from their kids on a general basis and kept it from the family members who didn't smoke. Bill and Beth smoked with a tight group of friends, who enjoyed smoking marijuana amongst themselves. They were definitely not criminal types.

Frank Forester wanted to make a name for himself before the upcoming election. Two of Forester's councilman friends were just busted for taking bribes and the ranks of his political friends in his conspiracies was getting thin. Frank had one of his investigators, sneaking around Bill's house. The investigator was looking into the windows for marijuana use, prior to the pressuring of Bill's kid at grade school by Girt. Franks investigators could never catch Bill or Betty smoking a joint. Frank knew the only way to get to Bill was through his kid.

Bill was going to run for commissioner, that's why Frank wanted him busted. Bill was a public hero in the community after saving a young boy's life. Bill had jumped into the river ten years prior to save two boys who had fallen in.

The city gave him their highest civilian award for bravery. Bill saved both boys after diving in the rough and stiff currents of the river. One of the boys was Ramone Ramirez Jr. The same Ramone that was on Dirkskin's drug squad. Bill stated to one of the jail guards in conversation, while sitting in jail. "Doesn't anybody have a right to privacy any more?"

The guard maintained. "Not if we have our way about it."

Bill asked. "When is the government going to take the camera out of my living room and out of my bedroom, and not only my house but also every house in the nation? You people have gone too far! The constitution was not set up this way by our forefathers."

The guard looks at Bill and reeled off. "Yea, you are probably right boy, but we are making money and we do not mind stepping on anybody's toes in the process."

Bill stated. "No self-centered bigot bastard's orchestrating and implicating tyrannical laws will ever be respected or adhered to by the people." The jail guard laughed at Bill and walked away from Bill's jail cell, while another guard named Jarri walked up to carry on the conversation.

Bill professed. "Girt couldn't catch us smoking on his own, so he put pressure on my kid whose involved in the DARE program in elementary school."

The guard persisted. "That was a good move!"

Bill told the jail guard. "Drug training by police in our grade school's is similar to the other degrading youth league intimidating tactics."

The turn key Jarri asked sarcastically. "What do you mean?"

Bill answered. "The police ask the children to "tell on your mother and father" "tell on your brother and sister" and "tell on your friends and neighbors" that was exactly what the Hitler youth league was all about."

Jarri declared. "Ya right!"

Bill further said while sitting in his jail cell brewing. "These same tactics that are implemented in the youth DARE programs."

Bill in jail could only look at the guard and asked. "How DARE you? Just leave my kids alone! You temporarily turned our kid against us by egging him on to turn his parents in for marijuana use. Wait till my kid realizes what the government did to our family. There's something wrong when the government takes prayer out of public schools and replaces teachers with police."

The next day Beth realized the indifference at the jail, after she picked her terrified son Jimmy up at the youth home. Jimmy told his mother. "They lied to me Mom. They said they wouldn't do anything bad to you. The police officers said they just wanted to know so they could talk to you. They never said they would arrest you mom."

Beth's reassured. "It's OK son," as she tried repeatedly to calm the poor boy's emotion's down.

The next day at Clint's farm and the among friends, the conversation was heavy. Some of Clint's friends had gathered to play pool. It rained hard with heavy wind gusts for most of the day. The weather vane was getting a work on top of the wrought iron fenced and gated farm house. They all wanted to make the best of the bad weather situation.

Miles was ready to make a break by shooting the cue ball at the pool balls Igor had racked.

Miles announced. "The cops busted a friend of my wife's Beth and her husband Bill Barker."

Igor questioned. "For what?"

Miles disclosed. "Less than a once of pot. His political enemies set him up. The cops pressured their kid through the DARE program at the elementary school."

Clint asked. "That isn't right?"

Miles confided. "I know but what are you gonna do with unfair prohibition laws. On one hand we have non-violent users of marijuana and on the other hand we have the abolitionists, the moral majority and corporate leaders with self interests infested with greed and desiring to eliminate all competition to their own products."

Igor accented. "Tobacco companies wanted people to smoke tobacco leaves instead of marijuana leaves so they endorsed the idea of a prohibition. Alcohol companies wanted to sell their own spirits. The prohibitionists who were out of a job after losing the alcohol fight lobbied for a new prohibition so they could obtain their government positions."

Chris depicted. "Law enforcement agencies are now making money more with an abundance of the easy criminal prey in marijuana users now branded as criminals. The new marijuana laws create a brand new line of criminals."

Manny imputed. "Judges as well as prosecutors are setting quotas and dividing the marijuana forfeiture seizures for their own personal pork belly expense accounts."

Clint ranted, as he took another shot at the eight ball. "The DuPont's corporate lobbyists had help design, promote, the plan to contain industrial hemp their only viable competition. The Harrison Narcotics Act was to control hard drugs like cocoa and opium in 1914. In 1937 a federal law was passed making marijuana illegal. Hemp was included to eliminate all their competition. Other industrial and political giants stepped in collusion. The laws were passed because of their lobbying efforts."

Igor ripped. "The government did not want to see funding diminish in their judicial economy. All the partners were incorporated together by opposition forces concerning marijuana. The partners were working in unison to graft from the American public's resources and freedom."

Chris obsessed. "Targeting the easy prey of marijuana users so police can be heroes in the eyes of the public and pin a badge on their chests for heroic deeds in busting a new line of non-violent criminals is wrong. The crimes the civil servants and cops created after over one hundred and sixty years of free marijuana use and trade in the United States of America is without merit."

Clint emphasized. "The moral bigots shouldn't make laws against people because other people are not like them."

Clint viewed this resentful group of law makers as sleaze. "The new deal was no deal. Suppression and repression of the people's God given rights which were promised to be upheld by the constitution has eroded because of self interested politicians." Clint got wound up every time the subject was brought up. The injustice in the laws was appalling to him. "People should be able to govern their own destiny." Clint was adamant in his beliefs, as were most Americans he talked to.

Miles gossiped. "The President wants mandatory drug testing as a prerequisite before obtaining a driver's license. A governor of another prominent state, Governor Rickers, says "If you get caught smoking a joint, or any other drug offence, you will lose your driver's license, you will lose you professional licenses, and you will ultimately lose your children to Social Services."

Chris states while shooting at the three ball bank shot. "Another state representative proposes a law to sue drug dealers, who are caught no matter, who sells, what drugs to who."

Igor informed. "Some idiotic legislatures proposed a law to penalize firms which hire marijuana users."

Miles enounced. "Some states have already decriminalized marijuana use or possession. Marijuana possession or use is probational, requiring no jail time punishment what so ever."

Chris added. "The police and court records are automatically expunged from your record in two years. That law is a good start in some states but still far off base for full freedom of choice."

Clint exclaimed. "If they drug tested everyone running the government they'd have just as high of a per capita as the public for the tests being positive."

Miles stated. "Legislatures fail to realize that some employers are marijuana users and condone their employees use of marijuana. Some employers say marijuana use on the job or during smoke breaks is good labor relations."

Igor further told everyone while shooting pool that. "Pedro Penerez owns a tomato farm in North Beaumont, and freely smokes marijuana with the tomato pickers before they start picking tomatoes in the morning. They smoke a joint and go to work."

Igor specified Pedro told him that. "He had no problems with his amigos, working all day and into the night and smoking a bit of grass in between. It keeps my employees and me content all day. There are no problems with my employees whether they smoke or do not smoke. There is no problem among, them because of the marijuana. The government should not be so intrusive into our personal affairs."

Igor continued. "Myself and my construction crew smoke marijuana. My employer knows the crews smoking marijuana, however, the employer looks the other way because all the work is done on a timely schedule and projects are efficiently carried out."

Clint opined. "Ya just because you smoke pot doesn't mean you can't function or make good decisions."

Igor proffered. "If you smoke a joint and jump on a hundred pound jack hammer for twelve hours, You aren't in any kind of high state after starting to do any kind of exerting work. Marijuana is made for relaxation not physical devastation. Your marijuana high evaporates with the slightest adverse tension from your present experience."

Clint confessed. "I agree!"

Chris conceded. "Legislatures want to penalize firms which violate marijuana drug laws. Those who do not conform to testing their employees at any time or anywhere for use."

Clint offered. "If marijuana is only a small fine and no jail time for small amounts, and totally decriminalized in some states, you should be allowed to freely have marijuana in your system."

Miles stated while shooting at the twelve ball down the rail. "Marijuana testing is ineffective. There is no way to test whether some one is high on marijuana. You could have been at a party a week ago smoking a couple of joints, and test positive the night in question with out having any marijuana for over a weeks time."

Igor pressed. "The current marijuana testing procedures have unfair guidelines as they exist."

Miles affirmed. "The marijuana laws are unfair, they are morally invalid."

"That's true" Clint told Miles, as he took the next shot.

Chris disclosed. "Legislatures believe legalization of marijuana at the federal level will put a seal of approval on marijuana use nation wide. The federal legislatures encourage states legislatures to penalize marijuana users as well."

Igor regretted. "Pro-marijuana advocates are outraged that more and more discriminating laws being passed which stymie individual rights and freedoms."

Miles moaned. "Prohibitionist Politicians will be the last big hurdle before the legalization of marijuana becomes a reality. Pro-advocates of marijuana legalization are pushing legislature of their own for decriminalization use and possession of marijuana in small amounts."

Igor reassured. "We will fight this at all costs and no expense will be spared in the fight for freedom, no matter how much blood is spilt. It is agreed blood was being spilt everyday anyway with all police raids gone away and flagrant police corruption."

Chris griped. "The abolitionists are forming an alliance to destroy pro-legalization efforts. Pro-marijuana advocates on the other hand have a theory of separating responsible citizens from crooks."

Clint spelled out. "Drug seizures of six or seven hundred plants in different military operations were found by the National Guard. They were using weapon mounted lasers finding marijuana enterpriser's cash crops. Law Enforcement Agencies seized an enormous amount of marijuana on an eradication mission. Destruction of these large marijuana crops in corn fields and forests throughout the United States are condoned by the advocates of prohibition."

Miles explained. "They are known as enterprisers, which clearly separates the greedy aspirations of these people from small amounts of a normal user gratification's." while shooing the six ball with a little English on it.

Chris expressed. "Other marijuana growing operations by enterprisers are being conducted from inside their homes or other dwellings in order to conceal their marijuana growing activities."

Miles continued. "One grower was a real estate broker, named Ross Grimes. He owned thirteen different houses throughout the Houston metropolitan area. Ross had marijuana-growing operations in each home. Ross walked into his homes, while greeting unsuspecting neighbors outside of his various homes. Ross brought in greenhouse assistants into the homes of his real estate and green house operations. They were known as the caretakers of the homes to their unsuspecting neighbors.

Ross's business enterprise had profitable commerce role. Separate marijuana users from marijuana grow operators for large profit." As Miles told everyone.

Chris continued the conversation. "Most marijuana pro-activists do not have any problem with enterprisers getting busted. However, though major marijuana grow operations should be legalized, regulated and taxed. The marijuana could then be sold from the same enterprisers in this free society without repercussion."

Clint told Chris. "That's true! We live in a capitalistic society, which is based on a free enterprise system and free enterprise is what should freely prevail in my book." Clint shot in the eight ball for the game.

Igor reasoned. "Even with alcohol and tobacco, you can only make so much or grow so much legally for personal use, without being prosecuted. Citizen's should be allowed to grow marijuana for their own personal use, without any repercussion's."

Clint remarked. "That's right!"

Chris rehashed. "The government shouldn't be making such a big deal out of marijuana."

In the afternoon's eve the pool shooting party broke up for the day. The beaming sunshine had finally came out through the dark cloudy overcast after the turbulent lightning rain showers vanished. It created a mystic painted rainbow over Clint's farm.

Clint had previously dinner engagement. His friend's father Antonio SR came to America, and continued to make wine once a year in Italian tradition.

Making sparkling rose wine with California grapes, and another Zinfandel grape which made another nectar of white wine. Sr. passed the tradition onto Antonio.

Antonio Sr. proudly proclaimed during Sunday's Italian spaghetti dinner, that his wife Rosalita prepared in a hearty fashion for everyone. "The president wishes he had Zinfandel wine of such taste as rich and smooth." Antonio raised the full wineglass for a toast, while everyone said. "Salute!" as everyone said. Salute! as they then sipped their glasses of wine.

Every time Clint had dinner there, he waddle and roll out the front door because Rosalita cooks dinner like Italians are known to do. Especially after topping the dinner off with homemade canolis.

Antonio JR and Clint had burned one before their arrival for dinner. They both had a pretty good marijuana appetite. Antonio JR, Clint, and the Rattlesnake Round up crew were departing the following morning for the desert.

Antonio JR, Clint, and a group of friends often went into the desert north of San Antonio every year for the Rattlesnake Round up. After leaving the following morning for the Rattlesnake Round up, they were going to pick up the camp supplies, tepees, and tents on the way.

Clint explained to Antonio. "The Diamondback Rattlesnake's eat lizards, rabbits, and other small animals. The rattlesnakes are the same color as the desert sand, they hide by burying themselves in the sand to keep cool, so they escape the direct heat of the sun. They like to rattle the rattles on their tail to scare off their enemies."

Antonio appealed. "That's more notice than the cartel will give you."

Clint pressed. "There is always a snake pit to keep live snakes at the camp after they have been captured. We want to keep some of the snakes alive for handling. We'll all take turns milking the snakes of their poison and everyone handles the rattlers."

Antonio deemed. "The poison can kill you in short order."

Clint replied. "That's for sure!"

Next to the snake pit reptile collector's kept Gila Monster's that they ended up finding by accident.

Mangas decreed. "Everybody gets a kick out of catching these brightly colored creatures. I like how some are black and orange and some are yellow or pink."

Clint summarized. "I like those radiant bright colors!"

An Indian friend of theirs named Mangas was on the trip. Mangas recounted to them about Indian native traditions, and desert life. Mangus told them about the "water cactus" at night around the camp fire, then showed them to everyone the following day out in the desert.

Their camp had plenty of Creosote Bush, with its ever-present scent. Some of the high arms of the Saguaro Cactus around camp were over fifty foot high.

Mangas with his rattlesnake boots and belt buckle on said. "One tall large Sanguro Cactus can weigh over ten tons by itself. Cactus wrens build their nests into some of the Saguaro Cactus arms, they have plenty of flowers and fruits to eat among the Saguaro Cactus. The Saguaro cactus in the desert are also known as bird hotels."

Clint reassured. "Those wild birds don't have any heat or water problems living out here among the foliage and cactus's in the desert."

Mangus further explained. "The wood peckers usually make all of the carved out nest holes in the Saguaro cactus."

Roadrunners with lizards hanging from their mouth were buzzing about the desert foliage. Mesquite trees with their thick desert vegetation were also mixed in and about the desert camp.

Mangas defined "Some of those Mesquite trees have roots which go down in the desert sand over a hundred feet high."

Clint told Antonio. "Mangas knows everything in and about the desert. Everyone loved hearing him tell his stories about the desert."

Antonio excited. "I can't wait until tomorrow morning for our cowboy breakfast made with hot flour tortilla's for bread, scrambled eggs, refried beans, and fresh rattlesnake meat on the side."

Clint had Antonio JR get various seasonings from his mother's cupboard so they could cook rattlesnake deluxe out in the desert for three or four days in style. Nighttime's dinner was the best, Rib eye steak and honey basted chicken cooked over the coals of mesquite wood. Texas moonlight along with apple pie dessert was the topper, before the entertainment would start. They had the most desolate site in the state of Texas. Antonio brought some home made red wine.

Mangas drove his 4x4 Chevy was followed by his horse trailer. The trailer contained two fine horse for the desert round up.

Mangus noted. "I need my horse to scrutinize the desert's fossilized formations." Everyone in camp appreciated Mangas giving his insight on Indian cultures. They were sitting on the tailgate of Clint's 4x4 just grooving. Coyotes were singing their remote howls. The outline of the howling coyotes high on the ridge was in the forefront of the bright mooned background.

That night as usual, Antonio JR got his acoustic guitar out of his 4x4, and everyone, it seems, took turns singing different tunes. The round-up rattlesnake rustlers sat around the fire under the moonlight.

Chico as usual brought his horse drawn cannabis covered wagon. They all felt the night fall in pioneer style. They had camped out around the authentic cannabis covered wooden wheeled wagon and Chico played improvised tunes during the course of the evening. Marijuana joints were freely changing from hand to hand. Everyone was having a harmonic night.

Clint said confidently. "No lawmen equals No hassles, No trouble."

Antonio asked to Chico. "You got one rolled yet?"

Chico simpered. "Si Antonio, uno momento! por favor" Clint with a side thought wondered, while watching everyone have a harmonious time, Why even under the governments own admissions, that over forty percent of the American public is marijuana users. They don't make fairer laws. In the last thirty days, once on an occasion, or everyday marijuana users have smoked at least one joint. More people per capita smoke marijuana than they do tobacco cigarettes. Another twenty or twenty-five percent Clint figured know that marijuana is not the harmful evil that cocaine, heroin, whisky, tobacco and hard drugs are.

Clint still sitting and thinking while everybody was in a good mood, turns and says to Chico "How could this so-called drug marijuana have been scheduled a number one narcotic by our law makers, which classify marijuana with the likes of Heroin."

Chico aired. "It's all about money, power, greed and oppression. It keeps the law makers with a job and the economy moving, so they think."

Concerned Clint clarified. "Yeah! It is not moving our society in the right direction. Not when the government is hunting, hurting, jailing, killing and cheating it's good citizens!"

Chico expounded to Clint, "I agree Clint, it is not the dangerous drug it is made to be. Now pass that joint!"

Clint hashed over. "The government made marijuana out, when I was in high school, to look like it was like heroin or acid to us kids. I believed them. Until later I found out the truth about marijuana for myself." Clint said sincerely!

Chico responded. "I don't look at my friends and acquaintances as terrible or criminals just because they smoke marijuana."

Clint scoffed. "Yeah Chico! Last week the vice-president got on the television and reaching out with his hands and arms in his speech called his fellow citizens, brothers and sisters."

Chico pressed. "Ain't he got nerve!"

Clint induced. "That's what I thought. How could he call us brothers and sisters on one hand, and won't stick up for us Americans on the other. A friend of mine Nick, I know has smoked marijuana for over thirty years and leads a responsible life. Nick is a family man, yet; if he gets pulled over on the way home from work tonight and the cops bring the drug squad and the dogs in on him and they find one joint of marijuana, they are going to do everything they can to ruin his life."

Chico answered to Clint. "Just like more than of a few of our other friends who have had their lives ruined by these unjust laws already."

Clint responded. "Right!"

Chico replied. "Yeah Clint! I can't understand how the Vice President can call us a brother and sister, but if Nick gets pulled over tonight like you said, he is no longer a brother or a sister, he is a crook in the eyes of the law. Nick and his family is the one that will have to suffer the consequences because of these bigoted laws."

Clint discussed. "It does not seem right for a citizen to lead a responsible life in every other way and suffer repercussions because somebody in the government does not like your way of expression for individuality, or your choice of recreational leisure. When are we going to be judged in the judicial system on the content of real criminality? Our choice of recreational pleasures is harmless to other people."

Chico asked. "Hey Clint! Did you hear about the raid last week?"

Clint blustered. "No!"

Chico said excitedly. "Oh yeah! This seventy three year old man I read about in the paper and his sixty-three year old wife were busted for growing a marijuana plant or two."

Clint joshed. "No kidding! A man and his wife that old smoking marijuana?"

Chico continued. "Yeah. The pesticide man came over to spray the house and seen the marijuana plant in the closet and called the cops who came and raided the house."

Clint railed. "See! Even old people like pot!"

Chico hyped. "Yeah! The old man said he smoked pot all his life. They were only growing a plant or two for their personal own use. The old harmless couple told the cops that they used marijuana to ease their ailments of arthritis and old age."

Clint voiced affectionately. "They must be a cool couple of people. I wish the government and cops would just leave these good citizens alone."

Now the conversation turned light hearted. The camp side group was involved with the entertainment of the evening.

Antonio JR strummed the guitar in the background, and Igor on the harmonica, Manny played his small set of drums. They all drank beers, smoked hoots, and played there're tunes, while talking their tall tales. The congregation of so-called judicial cannabis criminals were engaged in another cordial and friendly night filled with light-hearted fun.

Clint sang on. "That was Many Moons Ago! We got Many More Moons to go!" an old favorite to the Rattlesnake Round up Desert Group. Over to the left of the camper was a homemade skin perch. It had twenty-four hanging. The meat from all the snakes was in a large black kettle above the fire.

The large campfire lit up our small cannabis congregation in the middle of the desert. This carousing cannabis crowd always had a sense of adventure. Rattle snake stories were circulating about, who caught which snake, who had the biggest snake, which one was the hardest one to catch. Everyone had the appropriate gear to safely apprehend the rattle snakes in their desert confines. Snake medicines of the an anti-venomous type was also with them. Everyone was grateful that they never had to use the anti-venom medicines.

Tonight was the last night of the Rattlesnake Round-up Competition. Free food for the contestants and their whole families was also included at the final judging of the rattlesnakes. Vendor's presented a full array of snake crafts as boots, belts, hats.

Everyone had to be back in Houston Friday night, by six o'clock at the civic club, which sponsored this rattlesnake hunt round up. Clint would stopped off at the Silver Dollar Saloon, close to San Antonio, with Antonio JR. the usual at the end of the rattlesnake round up. Patrons of the Silver Dollar Saloon stop showing off different Polaroid photos of the rattlesnakes they got on their trip. They had plenty of big rattler snakes in cages in the back of their pick up trucks and tales galore.

Everyone had a few drinks and talked to the other patrons of the bar about their luck at the round up. The round up was designed to eliminate rattlesnakes in vicinities of communities and livestock.

Different participants loved to tell their tall tales and round up stories about capturing the venomous rattlesnakes. Family, Friends, and Patrons loved to hear the adventurous stories as well. The deadline for the contest, in which the person caught the largest snake and the most snakes was to be the following day.

Saturday was the rattlesnake cook-off, and the best delicacies of rattlesnake dishes from the cookout were judged. Rattle snake chili, Barbecue rattlesnake, assorted rattle snake recipes were entered in the cook off as well. Judging was also done on the longest snake, for first, second, and third place, Weigh ins for the larger snakes was to be judged by 12:00 PM. The glamour part of the contest for the best looking snake was to be judged by 3:00 PM. The first place prize was a Remington carbine, Bowie knives, hemp camping gear, and supplies were to be awarded for the final judging. The judging was announced at the Cactus club late Saturday by video telecast. Miles arranged that with his media friends.

Everyone started to arrive at the Houston Civic Center and the attendance for the Rattlesnake judging was a sell out. Close competition was also expected. The numerous display's of the rattlesnakes that were handled by their snake charmers enhanced the ceremony for the patrons.

The Rattlesnake Queen did her rattle famous snake dance that began the judging event. Snake handling by the snake queen while doing the famed snake dance was an attraction in itself. Rattles and feathers were hanging all over the snake queen. Some of the spectators were aghast at the ease with which the Rattlesnake Queen handled the poisonous snakes.

Mangas had the biggest snake and won the five hundred dollars for the first place prize. His family stood behind him as he received the award. His oldest girl ten year old Lita was standing next to him. Clint had been there to help Mangas with his catch. When Mangas captured this huge rattlesnake amongst a group of many in a rocky cove among of the thickest cactus and brush line cover.

Mangas knew this particular desert cove and went back to the same rocky desert cove every year for his prized rattle snakes catches.

Clint reassured. "You can't beat an Indian in the desert." Clint was equally happy for him. The rattle snake events always ended with a rattlesnake eating contest. Who ever could eat the most rattlesnakes in thirty minute's won the famed rattlesnake belt with the gold plated belt buckle. The Rattlesnake party was always a rush in itself.

Ricardo who was at the rattlesnake round up the night before and didn't catch a serpent was having a tough time with Rita his wife. Ricardo stopped for some Tequila with his friends Hugo and Juan. Their actions were liken to drunken sailors from drinking alcohol at the Cactus Club all afternoon. They been drinking bottles of tequila at for several hours.

Ricardo's wife upon arrival was upset their at home because Ricardo was so intoxicated. She immediately started screaming "I told you I wanted you home earlier. I had a hair appointment."

Ricardo answered Rita, "Yeah, yeah, yeah" and nonchalantly walks by her.

Rita, with Ricardo's back turned slams him in the head with a heavy hot frying pan from right off the burner. Rita was steaming and screaming while as Ricardo falls to the ground.

Rita slashed. "I had a hair appointment! I was going to go shopping today with Tina." and she proceeded to kick him in the head. Ricardo gets up staggering saying. "Whoa, whoa, whoa, whoa! Wait a minute!" But Rita after dropping the pan continues to punch Ricardo who said. "If you would have gave me some last night, I would have not hung out, but if you are not going to give me none, I'm gonna go hang out."

Rita lashed. "You don't care about what I want!"

Ricardo railed. "Well you don't care what I want." As he and his friends walk through the door, Ricardo turned to Rita and moaned. "What the hell do you think I married you for? Just to feed you?"

Now staggering drunk with a couple of heavy lumps on his head Ricardo, Hugo and Juan arrive at the Amberillo Saloon for some more tequila drinking. At the door was a massive bouncer with a bald odd shaped head wearing multiple earrings in his ears and juju rings in his nose. Full body tattoos with a bulldog collar around his neck and a heavy black ring tattooed around his eye.

Ricardo was still intoxicated from tequila. He looked at the bouncer at the rear of the door as he walked past. He said to Hugo and Juan. "Look at that cutie!" sarcastically to the bouncer. The bouncer Brutes pissed. "I'll give you cutie!" Ricardo grinned and tracked his drunken friends through the lounge area of the Amarillo.

They all walked to the bar and sat next to Shorty, who is talking to the barmaid Ginger and she told Shorty. "I'm on birth control now Shorty."

Shorty looked at Ginger and said. "What did you do, get your tonsils out?" Ricardo and crew laughed outrageously.

The bouncer Brutes was eyeballing these fun seekers with a belligerent glare. These guys aroused Brute's attention when they entered the saloon. The bouncer decided to approach and instigate the removal of these guys from the bar after they ordered their drinks, which would surely tick them off. Brutes had another bouncer, Leroy, take their drinks after they were ordered and paid for since Leroy was the bouncer who let them in the club.

An argument soon ensued between Leroy and Hugo. Hugo said to Leroy. "You aren't taking my drink punk." Leroy immediately pushed Hugo. Hugo punched Leroy dead in the jaw sending him into the next world. All hell broke out! The bar was engulfed in a bar room brawl. Everyone started punching and kicking everyone.

Ricardo with his sledgehammer hands met all bar room brawler challengers. Ricardo knocked everyone down within reach. They were nailed with one punch.

As Ricardo left unconscious bodies laying about the bar floor, he proceeded to fight his way out of the saloon. Ricardo's friends were no match for the other bouncers. Ricardo assisted his friends by taking all comers from bar on. Ricardo left everyone in his dust face down. Ricardo, when pissed off was a one-man demolition crew. Ricardo was still totally intoxicated, and definitely feeling no pain.

Brutes after getting hit over the head by a chair, staggers up and walks out into the parking lot where Ricardo now is. Brutes is now mad and nodding and bouncing his head up and down looking directly into Ricardo's eyes.

Brutes hurriedly walks toward Ricardo demonstrating his bad attitude. Ricardo acknowledged the glare and nods his head up and down with direct eye contact to Brutes. Both men looked at each other from across the lot of the Amberillo Saloon.

Ricardo motioned. "Yeah you! Come on!" An enraged Brutes aggressively approaches Ricardo.

The two brutes charged each other with clenched fists. Ricardo with lightning fast reflexes pounds Brutes with a right jab, and floors Brutes to the ground knocking him out cold.

Hugo and Juan staggered out of the saloon and said. "Ricardo, Ricardo! Come on, the police are coming!" They all quickly leave through the back alley. Three or four police cruisers promptly arrive and the officers walk up to the owner of the bar. Seeing all the unconscious bodies and lying around on the ground.

The attending police officer Tom Turner conferred to the bar owner Pete Printers. "How many were there?"

Pete regretted to answer. "Only one."

Officer Turner echoed loudly. "Come on! Only one man did this?"

Pete proclaimed. "Yeah! He must have had one hell of an alcoholic adrenaline."

Ricardo had one hell of a reputation after that incident. Ricardo and his friends went to another tavern to continue, where they drank into the night.

Clint after hearing about what happened the preceding night said to Miles. "They all would have been better off in my opinion smoking pot for the day instead of drinking tequila into inebriation. Then they go out looking for trouble!"

Miles heralded. "I agree!" Clint and Chantel made arrangements for a party of their friends at their farm for the following Saturday. Chantel made the announcement at the Cactus club after the Rattlesnake winners were telecast to the club on that fact.

Chapter 4.... North of Houston's outskirts, just past Beaumont, Clint and Chantel Cole's family had a small farm of twenty acres. They built a greenhouse during the course of the year and grew tomatoes, peppers, and exotic plants in the indoor greenhouse operation. To keep the imported foliage and fresh produce part of the business going, Clint went to pick up semi loads of materials and plants from the Port of Corpus Christi. Little did he know about the events that were going to unfold, before his arrival back home? Law enforcement under the guise of marijuana drug irradiation mission "Operation Hemp" had been combing the county with aerial surveillance military helicopters. They would hover over various citizen's farms, barns, live stock, houses, soy bean, wheat, and cornfields at very low altitudes. Farmers would actually come out of their houses, which were shaking violently from the powerful down draft of the rotor blades of the military aircraft.

The farmer or house owner could see first-hand the military spotter protruding from the side of the helicopter. The military man with his special glasses or goggles attached to his head was looking between the cracks of the farmer's buildings for any marijuana growth. These Citizens clearly not in any marijuana drug operation or suspected of drug use were having their rights to privacy violated.

The farmers actually didn't know what was going on. As the military aircraft flew over the countryside looking for marijuana growing, wild or cultivated possibly by locals or enterprisers. The helicopter pilot said. "I see what's looks like a newly constructed greenhouse." The pilot couldn't miss the greenhouse because Girt had told him the coordinates before hand. The squadron of government officials then all observed the green house surroundings. The military officers and the DEA agent Greco who was in command seeing the top of the new greenhouse through the trees. Girt told the DEA agent in charge of the helicopter to tell the helicopter pilot him to descend lower for a closer look.

The DEA agent in charge ordered. "Bring us down for a lower look."

Girt detected. "There is a vent opening on the top of the green house. Let's look in."

Greco looked in the greenhouse from above said to Girt and the pilot. "Yeah, they have green plants down there, and lots of them. Looks like marijuana to me."

Officer Girt of the drug squad yelled at the pilot. "Pull her down closer" as they hovered with in ten to fifteen feet above the greenhouse. The plastic covering it lifted off the structure of the greenhouse immediately destroying the continuity of the greenhouse's rainforest effect. Officer Girt had done what he wanted to do. He'd brought the military helicopter close enough to destroy the green house. The small vegetable seedling plants, approximately a few inches in height were quickly destroyed by the dry heat coming in on the west desert wind. Dirkskin and company should be elated.

Chantel, Maria, and other greenhouse workers in the greenhouse trimming tropical plant cuttings went into hysterics. Chantel shouted. "They're destroying the green house!" The helicopter hovered just above the green house workers. The military helicopter quickly destroyed the green house plastic topping with a powerful down force winds created from the rotor blades like a hurricane. Workers were scrambling from the local warfare to secure the water lines, the plastic and the hanging plants, which were falling everywhere.

Children in the daycare set up in the corner of the greenhouse kids were screaming and crying form the military gun ships massive tourbillion force. Chantel and Maria tried to protect and calm the kids down. The shaking rafters and soaring plastic flats of plants swirled in mid-air striking some greenhouse workers. Some were knocked to the ground as the plastic covering tore off in shreds.

Maria screamed through the rotors thunderous noise to Chantel "Help me with the kids!" The military and police officers order of the pinched battle continued to take pictures of greenhouse contents. The plastic from the overkill was completely ripped off the top of the greenhouse.

Then DEA agent Greco leaned on the fifty caliber machine gun of the military gun ship and visibly laughed. The officers with guns on their hips finally finished their drug air search of the farm. The search and destroy drug raid was a police and military saber rattling operation was sponsored and directed by the federal government was now complete.

The military aircraft taking off to the north after completing "Operation Snoop and Goof" or called by the government "Operation Hemp." This was unwarranted open-wallet tax payer's mission. No drugs were found in the pictures of this governmental sponsored Ariel search and destroy mission.

These types of Constitutional infringements highlighted many busts that were merely marijuana hunting expeditions at best. The so-called law enforcement's planned drug raids ended up mostly being confirmed failures.

Clint, while in transit from Corpus Christi, heard over the radio that a greenhouse was destroyed. Clint had fresh produce and various hand cared plant cuttings from Beleize, Central America in tow.

When Clint arrived he would put all the imported plant cuttings inside the greenhouse. The workers planted the cuttings in trays, where the rain forest effect of the greenhouse keeps the young seedlings and cutting's healthy. The same rainforest greenhouse, no longer existed. The cuttings and young seedlings perished soon after Clint's arrival. All his tomatoes and pepper seedlings had dropped over from the lack of the water and soon died in the Texas sun in a manner few hours. The young seedlings and freshly planted cuttings died because of fragile and underdeveloped root system.

The politicians military posture law enforcement and repression isn't marijuana prohibition destroyed seedlings and plants.

The next day all the police and administers built up the drug searches in the press as heroes after a million-dollar investigation that yielded no trace of marijuana. Headlines and large pictures covered the front pages of the major newspapers relaying the story as the police portrayed the events. Police tactics with drug searches were often exposed and nevertheless the newspapers and media always seem to back the police actions with unchecked distorted facts. Printing what the government administrators and cops portray instead of the real truth.

When Clint arrived, Chris, Thai, Mike, Manny and Miles were investigating at the farm.

Miles jarred with skepticism invoked. "Unbelievable! This is really unbelievable! Wait until I talk to my editor for an exclusive story on this disaster. Were going to get the truth out about what happened here."

Manny stood in disbelief. "What's became of our country? Are we in Grenada, Lebanon, Ethiopia or Panama?"

Clint prompted. "Well, if the government is foolish enough to think I would grow five hundred thousand marijuana plants in my greenhouse, they are doubly foolish to think that I won't come after them for this uncalled for malicious destruction of my property."

Little did Clint know that Girt and Godfrey, the main lieutenants of the drug squad had set up the military fly by purposely to destroy Clint's greenhouse operation.

They told the DEA and the pilot to get closer to the greenhouse, than what they should have. They wanted destruction of the greenhouse, even though both of them knew perfectly well there were no drugs or marijuana plants in the greenhouse. Girt had the premises checked out in the middle of the preceding night by Ramone.

Girt told co-conspirator Ramone. "Leave a pack of zig zag rolling papers placed on the ground, so we can see me from the helicopter. Then we'll have reason to get closer." That was rational enough for Girt imply. "There's rolling papers down there! Let's do a drug search!"

Chantel called the police station to report the destruction. The police station dispatcher May belle said. "We'll send the next available squad car out to take a report."

Dick Dirkskin heard over the radio the dispatcher's conversation and intervened. Dirkskin told the dispatcher to send Lt. Girt and Sgt. Godfrey to Clint's. Dirkskin's wanted to control the investigation. While Clint and his family reported the losses to Girt and Godfrey, the officers lurked around and took notes.

Girt stated that the reason they got close. "There's rolling papers on the ground down over there." Girt instructed Godfrey to go over in front of the greenhouse and retrieve them.

Clint immediately grudged. "That's not good enough! Is that all you got for proof is a pack of rolling papers? And you come in and destroy our family's greenhouse and livelihood? Zig zag-rolling papers that they sell at any convenience store? And now I'm a criminal, so you cowboys have the right to bust my farm up? Because you seen zig zag rolling papers on the ground?"

Girt feuded. "Well Clint, it doesn't make you a criminal with zig zag rolling papers on the ground, it just gives us probable cause to search for drugs a little closer.

Clint shoots back. "You can use inferred and could clearly tell that there was no marijuana in this greenhouse."

Girt divulged. "Well we did not have an inferred technician on board today."

Clint emphasized. "Girt! You have it every other day. You could have walked up my driveway like anybody else and asked to buy a couple of tomatoes out of my greenhouse. You could have been shown around and seen for yourself like anybody else."

Girt pledged. "We don't make up a new set of rules for everyone. We have protocol. Godfrey stood in the back ground smirking now.

Clint heatedly said. "You didn't need a million dollar federal government sponsored military and police operation."

Girt nonchalantly decreed. "That's the way it goes sometimes in today's drug war."

Clint angrily demand. "I want damages Girt."

Girt shouted back. "I can't pay you any damages. I can't do much about this but take a report."

Clint poured out. "You're telling me you can't do anything about this Girt?"

Girt recoiled. "That's right boy, sorry about your luck."

Clint angrily aimed his extremity. "Let me tell you something Girt! If I was flying an airplane and I caused damage to a government facility, I would be rounded up and tossed in a jail, and locked up in Leavenworth with a very long sentence. And you're telling me I can't do nothing Girt? There isn't going to be no double standard on this one Girt! Get done with this report and get out of here, I have to call the governor as soon as your stinking ass is gone."

Girt and Godfrey finished their report, while Clint continued to scream at Girt "I'll have everybody in federal court over this one. Don't think this is all the justice this citizen is going to get around here Girt. I'm coming after you, your people and your marijuana propaganda laws."

Girt conveyed sarcastically. "We'll see Clint!"

Clint could hardly able to contain himself wanting so badly to grab Girt by the scruff of the collar and settle this man to man! Girt and Godfrey decided it was time to depart heeding Clint's anger. Clint sent them to the doughnut shop in a big way. Godfrey told Girt as they drove away. "I feel like I walked into a hornets nest!"

Girt responded. "Yea! Them boys were hot. It was definitely time to leave."

Clint his friends and associates were consulting about the events from the destructive drug raid.

Miles conveyed. "Clint I'm glad I'm here to personally gather information on this travesty."

Clint sincerely contended. "I've glad you were here to see first hand what's going on. Your one of the few consolations I have concerning all this."

Miles clarified. "Since I had heard what Lt. Girt reported. I've seen this destruction first hand. I'll ready to print truth!"

Clint and Chantel's plans for an upcoming party on Saturday were abruptly cancelled due to the destruction of the greenhouse. The farm grounds were a total mess with trash and green house debris hunkered everywhere.

The fenced in pen now the front of the property, and the buffalo still grazed peacefully. "Buffy" the Buffalo the main food entrée at the party was granted a reprieve by these events from law and order.

Igor joshed to Chris as he browsed through the penned fence. "Buffy the buffalo is the only lucky one of the day. She escaped the charcoal grill."

Miles reassured to Clint. "Plans for appropriate legal action are going take place. I promise!" An arch newspaper of Miles decided to boost the ratings of his newspaper by exposing only the police view of "Operation Hemp." The police never mentioned anything about destruction of any other property or of other farmer's complaints. Readers of the news never realize the official mis-representations. The innocent citizen's facts of the real truth aren't investigated or heard in the cop's version of events.

Clint and his Attorney Morgan ended up calling Miles to help follow up on Miles reporting. Miles already convinced the editor of his newspaper to do a full police investigative report. Miles was a journalist in the metro section. The editor let Miles do an exclusive on failed and flawed drug bust's. Miles felt that there were just too many of these bust's going bad and going the same way in too many cities across the nation to ignore them any more.

The editor Ed Edmond's decided to go along with Miles. After a thorough three weeks of exhaustive and intensive study, the story finally broke on the Sunday news in grand style. The follow-up Monday through Friday in a daily series will finish up in the following Sunday's paper.

Enormous amounts of documented police abuses were exposed with currant facts from incriminating intelligence. This newspaper exposed cases of injustice on the citizens by the long arm of the judicial system through a series of dynamic articles. The uncovering media hype continued in a frenzy. Exposing graphs and charts highlighting police operations, corruption's, political legislation and the common citizen's lack of knowledge about reprehensible police tactics. How much money the police department wastes was at the top of the agenda.

Miles editorial wanted to know where the unaccounted forfeiture drug money from drug seizures was going and told Clint. "Nobody accounts for how the drug forfeiture is allocated."

Clint was the target of their police and military investigative drug destruction mission, he called the governor's office of Alvin Amos to make a formal complaint about the military police actions which had had occurred on his farm.

Clint called the governors secretary. "Hello miss! then asked a multitude of questions rapidly. "Is the governor hearing about all the citizens complaints about the countless drug raids conducted by the police, that have gone wrong for some reason or another?"

The governor's secretary skillfully responded. "Well! That's a good question. I'll see if you can discuss this directly with the governor." as she put Clint through to the governor. Clint asked the governor. "Governor are you aware of all the carnage caused by the police tactics?"

The governor replied. "A farmer made a complaint to the police that his dairy cows north of Beaumont lost milk production because of the noise of the helicopter rotor blades for the second year in a row."

Clint divulged, "The Farm Bureau told me that a chicken farmer claimed a loss because his chickens quit laying eggs after the large military helicopter hovered over his commercial chicken operation, another farmer's barn wall collapsed from the downward force of the wind from the blades, killing their horse!"

The governor attested. "I'm glad you called to inform me because I really didn't realize these types of police exploits took place. I must confess your the second call I've had today. Another farmer Mr. Hooky called me today and asked. "Who makes the final decision about all these military aircraft running around the countryside on drug search and destroy missions. Hovering and hot dogging aircraft ten feet over my crops."

The governor admittedly disclosed. "Quite frankly, I'm dumb founded. I don't know where the buck stops as far as these types of drug search decisions are measured." before ending the conversation with Clint granted. "I will have my office look into this matter to get us hopefully some satisfying answers."

Clint stressed. "Thank you sir for your time! I hope to hear from your office soon."

The first cop corruption stories Miles were well received, with a massive collection of correspondence to the editor. One article about Clint's farm was well received. Most beseeched in favor of Clint's stand. The public opinion polls conducted by the newspaper supported Clint in an overwhelming volley.

Miles relayed. "I'll will talk to Ed the paper's editor. I want to do follow-up series, if this readers response keeps up."

Clint exulted. "That's great Miles."

The next day Miles told Ed. "Clint is not the only one being persecuted by overzealous law enforcement, other complaints are too numerous not to do a follow-up with more in depth media coverage."

Ed responded to Miles. "Clint's police miss-fortune is just an example of all the complaints against law enforcement tactics were getting."

Miles scorned. "The complaints about drug failed searches are happening at an accelerated stride."

Ed informed. "Police busts and surveillance of citizens are being conducted on a quota based system. The more you bust, the more money you get for your departments expenditure account."

Miles defined. "It's our obligation to expose the truth. Whether or not Clint is my friend is of no consequence in my decision to seek and expose the truth, where ever it goes."

Ed counseled. "I've got no problem with that."

Miles appraised. "My personal belief is that the way the police department is presently operating the marijuana drug war they are doing the public a much bigger injustice. Ed go out to Clint's farm with me to see for yourself the kind of people were dealing with."

Ed responded. "I'll drive out to Clint's farm with you this afternoon." Ed was going to get personally involved in trying to help Clint.

Miles said to Ed. "Thanks Ed, I'm glad your involved now."

The editor Ed replied. "I'm on the side of the truth, and that's my job to find and expose it."

Upon the arrival of Miles, Ed, and an editorial assistant Melody at Clint's farm inspected the greenhouse. The mayhem caused at the farm by the police military helicopters was self-evident. The picture of destruction was striking. Ed looked in disbelief and disgust at what had happened. Immediately he turned to Miles and said. "Wow now that I see this ruble first hand, I'll help any way I can."

Miles had told Ed about the round table meetings that were being established to counter prevailing police tactics. Ed among others was invited to attend the first of many round table meetings to come. All those in attendance decided, that they would establish round table parties on a regular basis on Saturday nights.

They congregated their thoughts on directing their fight in regaining lost freedoms. A master plan was being drawn up based upon the determinations of these round table meetings. Drawing a line of distinction and defining their goals, each of the round table participants would research their assigned topics and relate research results at the various round table meetings. Everyone agreed to no greed and to adhering to the indisputable information.

Clint convincingly said. "It is agreed that their is a distinct and definite difference between hard drugs and marijuana. And is it all agreed that enterprisers of marijuana are enterprisers and users of marijuana are users." All Yea's and no Nay's responded to Clint's reading of the meeting's formal opinion. The resolutions based on his findings from meeting's with participant's earlier that week.

Miles continued the round table meeting stating that. "Enterprisers need to suffer certain legal repercussions for growing large amounts of marijuana, without paying taxes. Paying fair taxes or lenient fines is the goal concerning marijuana decriminalization. Legalization in the privacy of a citizen's home of a soft drug like marijuana is the sanctioned goal of the round table meetings. Legalization for marijuana use in the privacy of ones home was an argument based on personal choice by the occupants of a home.!" People could than again govern their own households." Miles concluded his opening statement.

Ed explained. "All of us know marijuana use statistics show that well over forty percent of the American people have smoked a joint over the last several months. We all know that statistics also showed less than two per cent of our population does hard drugs. We all know you can not operate and maintain a useful life using hard drugs. And none of us are here to promote hard drugs or their use. We all want to be on the same page with our government infighting hard drugs. We all want the government to turn over a new page, and to respect the rights of responsible citizens, in making the decisions they make in their daily life. Let the citizens live in the privacy of our homes the way they choose. Ninety eight per cent of the people we all know do not use hard drugs. These are the same citizens who would be the first ones that wanted to get hard drugs off the streets of their neighborhood." Ed concluded.

Chico now sitting adjacent to Miles contended. "Heroin is more available, purer, and cheaper, than in the past. Cocaine is increasing in availability. These are evil and very dangerous hard drugs that needed to be off the streets. The president says drug use has decreased since 1979. He's full of shit. Marijuana has always been easily available in any city I've ever been in."

Clint continued. "Hard drugs are coming over the borders ten fold compared with past years, and the hard drug trafficking is only increasing. Last year there were over one hundred thousand cases of heroin abusers admitted to hospitals. Heroin is especially dangerous when mixed with other drugs as in cocaine, barbiturates, methamphetamine, ECT. There has never been a marijuana overdose documented in the last five thousand years.

Igor specified. "Last twelve thousand years."

Clint conceded. "Right the last twelve thousand years. We need to get the government and police force off the private marijuana users back. The government officials need to concentrate on real crime and major social problems in this country."

Igor relayed. "Chris and his friend Sam have finally arrived. They're have been viewing the destruction to the greenhouse."

When Chris walked into the room avouched. "What's wrong with these guys? Are they nuts? Look at the destruction they did to this place! Who did it and who gave them the right to do it?"

Sam's Uncle Leslie Lambkins was a member of the Congressional Black Caucus. Sam was introduced to the aggravated round table participants, and started his prepared assessment. "The guidelines in the law that make punishment for possession of five grams of crack is the same judicial punishment as five hundred grams of powder cocaine. Fifty percent of the black men being arrested for hard drug use is for small amounts of crack cocaine. These prison sentences are in dis-proportionate prison time to the same large amounts of powdered cocaine."

Sam knew what he was talking about and definitely had everyone's attention. "My Uncle Leslie wants healthy alternatives or fairer sentences for these men. He wants more education and treatment programs, instead of hard time to make more hardened criminals. There is something wrong when we have second hand educational facilities and first class prisons. We all want a safer community to live in. My Uncle Leslie will speak before Congress next week on this crack cocaine sentencing agenda."

Clint was clearly upset himself, he had truly worked hard, and also did his family and friends who had also put in a tremendous amount of effort and input into the greenhouse effort. All this erased because of some prejudicial cops.

Clint interjected. "I believe this was deliberate and malicious destruction to my green house."

Igor depicted. "No doubt about that!"

Mike a law student friend of Clint's pulled into the driveway. Mike didn't like what he was seeing on his walk into Clint and Chantel's home. Mike is making a legal thesis at law school on lawsuits filed by the victims of civil rights abuses.

Mike Moran was intending to explain to the group about a supreme court up held recent decision to award a lady from Oklahoma eight hundred thousand dollars for inappropriate police brutality. The core of the case, Mike Moran acknowledged after arriving. "The police department did inadequate qualifying investigation of one of their police officers, who had several physical abuse charges his wife documented."

Clint smirched. "The police personal department didn't do a proper background check!"

Mike answered. "They didn't do a good one that's apparent. The commissioner of New York alone had told the justices that during a three year span the city settled over twenty two million dollars in civil damages out of court over the conduct of police officers and prison guards. New Supreme Court ruling's, ever how; are making it even harder to sue the city for improper police employment practices."

Ed decreed. "They're going to make it harder to sue, when there's an injustice involved in hiring the police?"

Mike answered. "Yes! Now it's the police department's choice to hire cops of their choice and at their desecration, even if their proven to be bad cops."

Mike was worried with the new ruling's, but he was definitely going to do his best to bring his legal associates to help Clint and his family fight in this uphill governmental battle. Mike was going to contact other legal associates and colleagues for assistance in the fight.

Chico explained. "They raided my uncle's house in the barrio with no physical proof whatsoever. My Uncle Salvador from Equator says. "The drug cops raided his convenience store in broad daylight under the suspicion of a sale of an illegal drug." He told me "They come in, they throw you to the ground, they don't explain anything, they don't respect you, they treat us like dirt, then they find no drugs. The masked man barged in." He said. "I thought it was a robbery and here it was the drug squad from the Metro task force. He still maintained. "They broke the counter with their battering ram after they broke down the door with it. The door slammed down, busting the counter. The glass, shattered all over the floor, while it flew back and cut his wife Juanita's leg. The bleeding gash required twenty-eight stitches."

Clint asked. "They cut her during the drug raid?"

Chico answered. "Yes! She ended up cut pretty bad on her leg." My uncle said. Liquor and cigarettes were being pushed off the shelves and onto the floor by the so called drug investigators. They were actually destroyers." My uncle Salvador further said. "I was pushed to the floor by a police officer from the drug squad. The officer held an AR 15 automatic weapon pointed to the temple at my head." My uncle Salvador was shaking so badly after another officer smashed him in the face with a gun butt. Uncle Salvador was then hog tied, belly down, tying his ankles and yanking them up to his neck. My uncle then went into convolutions."

Ed said amazingly. "I've never even heard of these types of revolting abuses on our citizens. It's hard to believe we live in America. Believe me the staff and I will be following up at the newspaper."

Chico continued. "At the same time my aunt receives the same treatment while she is profusely bleeding from her leg wound. All in all the drug bust hinged on an unreliable informant who gave them the wrong business address for the drug raid the hopes of a more lenient jail sentence for himself.

My uncle had nothing to do with drugs but was dragged into the drug war by incompetent cops. The case was eventually settled out of court for four hundred and fifty thousand dollars. When this abuse going to stop?" as everyone nods in acknowledgement.

Mike affirmed. "I'll be ready for the next round table meeting on Saturday as well." Mike further pleaded. "Spread the word! Research facts for Miles and Ed. We want help them keep the heat up in the media. All newly obtain information will be helpful."

It was getting late and a few of the participants left for the evening, but most lingered on to present or listen to the new stories of injustice unfolding.

Chris offered something he remembered from reading an earlier article in the newspaper as well and said to the group still sitting around the table. "In the newspaper yesterday there was an piece about another four million dollar lawsuit claim being sought because of a drug raid gone bad at a liquor establishment."

Clint asked. "Another one?"

Chris reasoned. "Yes! The tavern owner claimed excessive force. The article stated that more than ten people have filed claims for over four million dollars who were at the establishment. The owner at a tavern was claimed to have been selling drugs by the drug squad."

Ed questioned. "Were there any drugs found?"

Chris continued. ""No, The tavern owner stated that the police humiliated the patrons physically and mentally after hog tying them. Then the cops stripped searched the lady patrons. The ladies were made fun of by male police officers as they were led out of the bar on their way to jail. The Groping of the women was, by far, more than just being patted down. The sexual abusive by the officers continued on the way to the police station. Again No drugs were found. Everybody got arrested on a whim."

Chris could not help but bring up an article that he now read to the round table meeting believing it was an opportune time.

Miles inquisitively asked. "I want a copy of that article, Please?"

Chris attentively confided. "No problem Miles. We need to elect politicians, who are really for people's rights. A government that does not abuse their power by feasting on citizens liberties."

Miles fidgeted, while sitting there wondering. "Where does it all end? The marijuana wars arrests keep going up and up. All they are doing is searching and busting someone for a joint here and a joint there and millions are spent in expenditures on these which herb hunts by taxpayers."

Ed criticized. "They are running a tax bloated burden on the citizens far over the limits of reason."

Mike concurred. "Over the limit, that's for sure!"

Chico reiterated. "Can't the cops get some quality busts? If you can't get a good quality crime bust don't bring me none."

Clint vouched. "I agree! Give me a quality bust, I don't want to hear about someone smoking a joint in their backyard getting busted by the cops. That's no crime against society."

Igor recounted. "Most of us here smoke, and we are none the worse for it, all of us conduct our daily lives in a responsible manner. A little recreational time taken at our desecration should not be a concern for the government."

Chico animadverted. "With all the real problems they have out there. Why should we be harassed?"

Mike reiterated to Chantel who now joined in the conversation. "You were here during the helicopter miss-hap. Give me complete and acerate description of the case? Minute by minute, second by second Chantel, I've got to have it that way."

Chantel looked and confessed. "That's not going to be a problem." Mike vindicated. "I want to hear the way things were before the drug raid, the way things were during the destruction of the green house by the armed helicopter, and the way things were after the ignorant drug raiders left."

Still anguished from the greenhouse destruction Chantel said. "I can give you an accurate description after the meeting concludes."

Mike emphasized "We also need to know how this greenhouse loss is effecting your family, and it's the aftermath."

Chantel responded. "OK Mike!"

Clint in the mean time, studied all the avenues of recourse available to him. Clint disliked the controlling philosophy of the government. He sarcastically felt that if you couldn't be free to choose your values the government might as well clone people for their perfect society.

Clint said. "I'm tired of hearing the government telling its citizen's what they can't do! I want to start hearing from the government, what we can do." He truly felt hampered by not having a right to choose his own destiny. Clint felt his friends were hampered by not having the right to choose their own destiny as well in this country.

Clint exclaimed to the other round table participants. "I'm happy! I'm a happy go lucky man! Most of all my friends seem to be the same as well. But what burns my ass is we don't need anybody telling us how to live in the privacy of our bedroom! Can't the government find some other action besides invading our living room or our backyard?" Clint seen the connection between a government dictatorship and it's citizen's because of all the new and impeding restrictions in a free society that were increasingly accumulating.

Clint's recent experiences caused by our government infringement had his nerves on end. The governments bad decisions, bottom line, had destroyed his livelihood, endangered his family, his workers, and his friends while on his property. Clint felt and said in his final statement that. "I have no choice but to get up, dig in, and fight all these allegations to the fullest degree of my ability."

Miles revealed. "Police chief Dick Dirkskin on the other hand, enjoys destroying the harmonious union of people".

Chico stressed. "Yea! They all seem to get off on cruelty to citizens downtown."

Igor sat there and looked at everybody's disgust, and seeing the disgust, says. "Don't drag your feet, do everything you can. Gather information for the truth, do all you can to get rid of these self defeating nuisance narcotics laws concerning marijuana." Igor still looking at Clint, Chantel, and friends states. "When it comes to helping our brother, I'll be there!" Everybody looks and extends their hand in the middle of the table, one hand on top of the other's. They all agreed to take a stand for the cause of freedom, and to further expose all the untruths along the way.

Manny concluded. "I'm going back to the Cactus Club. I'm deejaying later tonight." Manny stated before leaving "I'll seek help from my friends and contacts in the radio, TV sector of commerce. I'll tell other event planners. I'll tell all the patrons, friends, and the owner of the Cactus Club. I'll help round up the troops for the freedom of expression."

Clint averred. "I like that! Fight for the freedom of expression!"

They finally broke up the round table meeting at Clint's for the night on sound resolve to proceed forward. Some of the participant's at the meeting were headed to the Cactus club. The Cactus Club had a major dart tournament going on later in the evening.

Everybody involved at the roundtable meeting knew they had a tough task ahead of them. All were partners in the newfound freedom movement. They were gearing up for the long haul. Everyone was willing to help. They were going to feed off each other to keep the momentum going strong.

In the course of the evening at the Cactus Club Manny while deejaying burst out. "How are you guys doing tonight?" to Brothers Rick and Jimmy James.

Rick bemoaned. "I'm peeved after hearing about the governments police tactics regarding it's citizen's."

Jimmy exclaimed. "The laws are unjust! Everybody I know smokes pot!"

Rick fumed. "Me to! Everybody I know smokes pot. Why do they keep harassing us? What is their problem?

Manny groused. "That's what everybody is saying!"

Rick sneered. "They don't smoke pot but they know everything concerning everybody else who does smoke pot."

Jimmy grilled. "Who do they think they are? Yet! They still back laws condoning more harmful substance abuse with alcohol and tobacco. Those are the real leaders of substance abuse."

Rick observed. " I agree!"

Jimmy looked sideways at Rick. "Hey, you got one to burn?"

Rick set foot out as the others followed. "Yep! I got one."

Manny rebounded. "This song is almost over, wait a minute! I'll go with you! I haven't burned one all day." They all proceeded to the parking lot after the tunes were set. They burned a green number over some light hearted conversation about the upcoming Motto races. Manny was going to deejay the special Motto bike event. Jimmy and Rick were in the styling competition at the same time as the break between Motto races. All their friends were "Hot Dog" bike riders. The dare devils bike riders hated helmets as well, when they were running hard down the highway. After they all burn one, and finished their motto bike talks. They proceeded to walk back into the Cactus Club.

Jimmy and Rick caught up with their barmaid old ladies. They all continued to enjoy themselves with their ladies until well after the girls got off for the night. Rick challenged Sherry his girl to a pool game earlier, while she was on her break. Sherry already had the table won, three games later Rick had three more quick lessons by her. Sherry was on the Cactus Club's pool league and kept her pool game sharp. Sherry won the last pool game by laying in the eight ball on the break!

The next day Clint rummaged through what was left of the greenhouse. Clint noticed a paper that was on the ground. It was an advertising flier that fell out of the military helicopter. The flyer was for an air show involving drug tactical air support the following weekend. The event was to specifically featured the airman from local National Guard contingent. They were operating the fleet of military gunship helicopters in their counties. Clint figured these were the same pilots who flew this "Operation Hemp" mission and destroyed his greenhouse would be there. Clint a casualty of the Calvary's shock troops decided to take his family to the fly-in air show. Chantel was receptive to the idea. She gave Clint a cassette tape player to record any incriminating conversations that may occur.

Once at the air show, civic minded Clint, Chantel and their family enjoyed watching the Blue Angels, who were featured at the show. Many different military aircraft and historic aircraft antique aircraft, Tri-planes, BI-planes, were show cased at the air show. During and after the air show you were allowed to walk around all the aircraft.

The National Guard helicopters had their own roped off area. The crowd was allowed to mingle with the crews of the military guard's drug interdiction helicopters. None of the crewmembers knew who Clint was, but Clint knew who all the crewmembers were. Clint knew which helicopters were involved by the descriptions from the workers who were there.

Clint talked a warrant officer who was seating next to him. Both were reviewing the spectacular air show's squadron from the grandstands. The Military Warrant Officer Monty told Clint a lot about the drug operations on a general basis. He told Clint about the pilots of the craft, who conduct raids in the northern counties. The Monty freely talked about the government's marijuana drug eradication missions.

This Warrant Officer admitted to a certain extent that they caused destruction at different times in their searches for hemp.

Clint got extensive amount of information from a very qualified source. Clint later told Chantel. "I got the facts on tape mind you. I'm not done yet."

Clint made track's into the aircraft staging area. While Clint was in the aircraft display area, Clint's wife and kids began touring the Blue Angels aircraft. Clint went by himself to the pilots who were walking around the drug eradication helicopters. The Officers walked around in their fancy military uniforms.

As the pilots completed their briefing on air show aerobics performed Clint and the audience stood around and listen to the Officers in charge. Chantel decided to take the kids to the carnival part of the event. The kids ran straight for the Carousal, Ferris wheel and other various rides.

Clint continued to ask every conceivable question of the pilots about the raids conducted in the proceeding weeks without raising the suspicions of the helicopter pilots. The olive drab pilot Warrant Officer Jeremy Germs chewed the fat extensively. He foamed at the mouth as he continually bragged, and disclosed the drug raid operation the whole time.

This unrepentant military warrant officer explained his version about how they blew that greenhouse apart with the down force of the blades on their military helicopter.

Jeremy stated to Clint. "That drug cop told us to go closer to the green house so we did. The captain of the helicopter questioned the drug cop, and told him it would probably destroy the greenhouse. Never the less the drug cop in charge of the mission told the Captain of the military helicopter to proceed closer." He was boasting about how the kids were crying, screaming, and running while their mothers ran after them.

Clint could hardly contain himself. He was surly glad the tape on the recorder was going full blast. The officer told about how the cops really wanted this guy, and that's why we got as close as the cops in charge told them to. The warrant officer Jeremy admittedly said to Clint that " I would have not gotten that close through. It is against Federal Aviation Regulations for safety reasons."

The bad feeling's that Clint was getting after finding hardly any remorse from these mis-guided military nuts representing law in his American home land was enough. Clint found out enough through his own little internal investigation. Clint was so distraught he abruptly disengaged in the conversation with the Warrant Officer and walked away toward the carnival area.

The clowns were passing out helium air balloons free to all the kid's in this kiddy area. Clint walked over to his wife Chantel and asked. " Are you and the kids having a good time?"

She answered "Yes we are."

Clint asked Corey his son, to take his little brother Morey and sister Lori ahead of them. The family then walked to their pick up truck. The kids were going to spending a long weekend with their Uncle Tom, while Clint and Chantel were to going vacation to Colorado in a few weeks.

On the drive a home Clint told his wife Chantel about what he had learned from the arrogant warrant officer. "I want you to listen to the tape when the kids were not around. I don't want the kids to know all the information surrounding these bad events." Clint stopped on the way home at a fast food outlet with a kiddy land. The kids were in view playing in the slide maze part of the restaurant after everyone eats.

Clint and Chantel sat in the pick up with the kids in full view, close by. Chantel was literally fighting mad upon hearing of the warrant officer's arrogance. Chantel adamantly. "I want to contribute to the cause of the legalization of marijuana. I want to stand up for individual freedom. I want to invite some of my father's tobacco business associates from North Carolina to the round table meetings. Let's try to involve these tobacco company executives in lobbying the government on behalf of hemp in North Carolina. Both Tobacco and hemp produce smokeable leaves, both, also produce agricultural crops around the world presently."

Clint gushed exuberantly. "That sounds like a winner!"

Chantel's reasoning was that tobacco needed an ally to strengthen smoker's rights over tobacco itself she said. "1) To keep tobacco legalized, and 2) to get marijuana legalized."

Clint contended. "I don't know how their are going to be a decreased demand when thirty five percent of the American people smoke tobacco, and forty to forty five percent of the people smoke marijuana to some degree in the last year. Thirty five percent of the people are regular users of marijuana. Surveys have shown that more people prefer smoking marijuana leafs to tobacco by a huge margin.

The tobacco companies have been lacing their tobacco products for years with foreign agents to boost nicotine's addicting effects. These foreign additives known as nicotine enhances increase the tobacco smoker's demand."

Chantel elucidated. "Tobacco is a soft drug just the same as marijuana is in some respects."

Agreeably Clint professed. " If I smoked a tobacco cigarette, and me being a none smoker inhaling tobacco smoke into my lungs would knock me on my ass. I'd be dizzier than if I smoked any marijuana cigarette".

Clint conferred. "Since I'm a chronic marijuana smoker I don't get as high on marijuana. You build immunities to smoking pot, like the tobacco smokers do for tobacco. The marijuana highs evaporate as well from steady use."

Chantel reassured. "I can understand that."

Clint explained. "There is still a certain mild psychological effect from tobacco smoke. Tobacco smoking sooths smokers just like marijuana does. To a certain degree your equilibrium is off balance from the norm of tobacco smoking."

Chantel emphatically bellowed. "That's right!"

Clint contended. "If your don't believe this and you are a none smoker just inhale a good puff of tobacco into your lungs. Tell me that after you cough it all out if you're not buzzed. Your head will be spinning. Jump into a car immediately and start driving. Then tell me if it's the same as being a none smoking driver. Your buzzed harder than if you smoke a marijuana cigarette."

Chantel accented. "The big difference is marijuana smokers do not wake up in the morning chronic tobacco smoker's and spit flem out of their throats from the ill effects of tobacco smoke. There is also no alcoholic hang over. Marijuana is similar in a sense to tobacco, but marijuana smoke is so much less harsh."

Clint depicted. "You do not suffer the same harsh effect's in your throat from marijuana smoke opposite tobacco."

Chantel disclosed. "Most people that I know agree!"

Clint amazed. "Gee, What's that tells you is that pro-marijuana people are right."

Chantel equivocated. "After you start smoking tobacco awhile you get used to the smoke high. You don't get blown away such as in the beginning of your smoking tobacco experience. A tobacco smoker still inhales tobacco smoke for the mild underlining high you receive. Some similarities is the same desire of smokers share to smoke and relax after a dinner meal".

Clint clamored. "What element as a whole concerning tobacco smoking is the addicting part?"

Chantel responded. "What do you mean?"

Clint appraised. "Well, some of the tobacco's additive nicotine enhances and increases a smoker's chance of catching cancer ten fold. Different petro chemical combinations and portions which alter tobacco cigarette smoke increased the nicotine doses. My only concern is that the tobacco should not be altered but sold in a natural form, not with out nicotine enhances."

Chantel expounded. "That cigarette smoke is absorbed at a greater rate into ones lungs because of this altered petro chemical effect created by the tobacco companies. Tobacco companies she said, "Would argue that changes in the tobacco sold to consumers was for product taste and improvement."

Clint persuaded. "Tobacco smoking in it self is an addicting social habit. The petro chemicals induced into cigarettes by the manufacture's are harder to break down once absorbed into the lungs. Tobacco is a government approved and taxed commodity. This tobacco drug as it is now inhaled in smokeable form for human consumption into the lungs is a real killer." Both Clint and Chantel agreed that tobacco cigarette smoking was bad for your health, however the ultimate choice should be for the user not the government.

Clint further said changing coarse of the conversation stated. "A new viable crop of cannabis should be developed development for fabrics, textiles and medicines, that could serve as an alternative farm crop for the tobacco companies."

Chantel seriously said to Clint. "Marijuana should be grown for human consumption and taxed as such."

Clint predicted. "The hemp industry as a whole world wide would be a trillion dollar industry in the next fifty years."

Chantel agreed and laughed. "Write your congressman." After their long conversation the kids were finally done playing in the fast food restaurant play ground. The kids finally came back to the pick up truck.

The family was now on their way home. Clint and Chantel were glad they found new information about the National Guard. The tape would help prove collusion by law enforcement and the National Guard.

Clint and Chantel felt better after their big talk. They felt better about the current state of events they were both fighting on their return home.

Back at the farm. Clint talked to Maria who was at the farm cleaning the place up from the prior helicopter raid.

Clint told Maria. "I'm going to pass petitions out to stop these unwarranted helicopter raids on innocent citizens."

Maria remarked. "That doesn't seem to always work."

Chantel maintained. "Were going to try. Were not going to sit idle."

Maria suggested to Clint. "Why don't you run for Congress so you can make some real noise."

Clint vehemently said. "Don't temp me. Maria, Their already getting me worked up. I might run for a political position just to make a statement win loose or draw."

Clint and Chantel had arrived back home just in time.

Their friends and colleagues were arriving at the farm for the Saturday night round table meeting scheduled that night Igor, Chris, Mike and Manny were already there with briefcases, folders, various documents, news briefs, victims statements, videos, and magazines.

Manny at the radio station recorded interviews from drug victim's raids that had gone wrong. Manny also had interviews from a government response team to the media for the various complaints about police drug raids that went bad.

The participants at the round table gathering were all anxious to get the meetings started and moving. In a business like manner, they all moved to the conference attached to the back of Clint's house.

The conference room was draped with southwestern paintings and decor. The large stained glass chandelier hanging over a large solid red oak table set the tone for the conference room like atmosphere.

Manny was taking notes on the other side of the table, while; Igor was calling Chico to see if his Uncle Salvador could come to tonight's round table meeting. Uncle Salvador told Chico he was going to ride to the farm with

Aaron. Aaron reached Chico on the mobile phone. "I'll pick Salvador up on my way to the farm."

Chico thought and then conferred. "It is crucial for my Uncle Salvador to express his real ordeal during this terrifying drug raid. This is another example of government justice that was immoral."

Aaron Adams brought air brushed protest T-shirts to the round table meeting. Aaron pitched. "Clint! I just air brushed these shirts for you and Chantel last night. How do you like them."

Clint excited burst out. "I love it! It looks fantastic!" Clint warmly thanked and excepted the custom air brushed hemp shirts. "Thank You Aaron Thank you for all you've done."

Aaron reassured. "That's the least I could do for the cause. Custom air brushed hemp shirts are going to be made for all of the freedom fighters, who attend the round table meetings."

Clint decreed. "Great! That's a great idea." Aaron's wife Janice hand made hemp braided jewelry in American Indian tradition.

Janice was of Indian Heritage. Janice informed the round table participants. "I'm making for everyone who attends the round table meeting's a freedom crest. The crest will be made with a turquoise stone, and ornate hemp braiding like this one."

Chantel detected. "That's a beautiful and very unique freedom crest." to Janice. Everyone else quickly agreed.

Dinner was served buffet style during a break from the meeting. An assortment of chickens, Texas steer, and fruits and vegetables from the produce Clint had purchased at the port of Corpus Christi.

Clint and his wife Chantel always cooked more food than they could eat. The meeting lasted well into the morning, after Igor left at four-thirty-ish in the morning was finally done with the newly formed hemp strategies developed. The strategies were well orchestrated for an effective pro cannabis legalization campaign. The freedom fighters for marijuana were going to take on the prohibitionist oppressive political element of the government.

When they were done with the pro-marijuana protests, they wanted a responsible change in the way the government does business with its citizens. The freedom fighters intended on beating them fair and square by their own rules.

Mike had all the police documents, that were to be viewed in the round table meetings. Mike processed the information in an impressive manner and answered all the legalities for his associates the following day. "I'll take all this meeting documents back to our office and assign Martin my legal assistant to file everything onto disk for everyone to down load."

The legal summaries on Clint's behalf were to be filed the following week against the DEA, police agency, military guard, and the federal government.

Mike pressed his personal mentor in law, Morgan Motley, who's known for winning the most sensational human rights case in the state of Texas to aid him. Mike wanted to have Morgan himself represent Clint for the federal suit he was filing against agencies of the government who were involved in the charade that was called police drug raid.

Morgan's staff fully reviewed all the facts, which were to be presented for the complaint. The group craved to establish another legal front to change the current hemp and marijuana laws. After heavy debating of strategies the round table meeting dispersed for the night.

The leftover food from the round table meeting was dropped off at the shelter by Igor on his way back home to Houston in the middle of the morning.

It would only be a few hours before Igor had to start the asphalt conditioning crew up. Igor had an afternoon job assignment. A cracked and battered parking complex was ready for an overlay of new asphalt.

Igor walked into the old folks home at 8:00 AM. As Igor walked in he said "Hello is Skinner here?" to the receptionist. Igor also said "Hi" to everybody who was up watching TV in main gathering area. The old man they called Skinner always knew when Igor was coming and looked out for Igor's arrival. Skinner smiled at Igor's upon his entrance

Skinner questioned. "How Yea doing there young un?"

Igor added in a polite way. "Fine and you?"

Igor gamed. "Do you want chicken, steak or fish?" in a polite reassuring way.

Skinner jabbed. "Igor, you know I always take steak!" Igor then spent an hour's time passing the food out. The lunch plates were prepared by Maria, Illylia, and Chantel.

Igor started talking to the different elders about their life. The resident's enjoyed Igor's short stay. Igor enjoyed sharing part of his day, with the elders and always asked them if they needed anything that he could help them with. Igor's Uncle Pete had been in this old folk's home. Some of the residents like Skinner remembered Pete. Uncle Pete had since passed on. Skinner and the resident's thanked Igor for the food and his visit as Igor walked out the door to go to work.

Morgan, Clint's high profile lawyer, Clint and Mike all proceeded to the federal courthouse. They discussed the different parts of the legal procedures that would occur on the drive. Morgan told Clint. "You must understand the legal protocols, the total legal ramifications that are involved for the federal court fight."

Clint roused. "That's what I'm trusting you for!"

Morgan explained legal procedures they will have to go through, how many depositions they will have to take, and always how much money cost will it before the case is heard, and what to expect.

While walking up the steps, Morgan spots Senetor Stan Stalinski walking towards them and mentions to Clint. "He is the staunchest and most outspoken marijuana prohibition legislator in the country. He's admitted that he's never even tried marijuana in his life the newspapers."

Clint clamored. "And this guy wants to pass judgement on what we do in our own households?"

Morgan continued to tell Clint as Stalinski approached that. "The Senator is the most powerful influence in the government concerning the prohibition against marijuana for personal use in Texas."

Clint pointed his finger at Stalinski blurted. "Who that guy!" Morgan answered "Yes that guy!" Continued to tell Clint that. "Senator Stalinski drafted the harshest legislation for criminalization of marijuana possession and use laws in the country. He helped establish current harsh standards for criminalization of marijuana possession and use in the state of Texas."

Clint needled. "Really!"

Morgan continued. "All those marijuana laws now on the books are nothing but a nuisance to the people and the judicial system entrenched in our government."

Clint noted. "The governments arm is always dictating how you should live your life, what you should do with your life, and how you should act and think in the privacy of your home. Why doesn't the government make a law against human breeding and order strict human cloning."

Morgan sarcastically interjected "Then the government could have the exact society they anticipate."

Clint expounded. "It seems like the politicians are hell bent on promoting these anti constitutional laws."

Morgan told Clint. "Senator Stalinski stated that the raid on Chico's Uncle Salvador was a justified one!"

Clint remarked. "Really!"

Morgan divulged. "Stalinski said in the paper that the government never should have caved in for a financial settlement."

At that time Stalinski was closely approaching Morgan and Clint, and heard the word cave in from Morgan, Clint looked at Stalinski a few feet away, and Clint loudly said. "How would you like me to cave you in?"

Stalinski, stunned, looked up and arrogantly said. "What's your name boy?"

Clint defiantly said. "You see a boy you better get on your knees."

Morgan immediately grabbed Clint's arm and Stalinski approaching Clint is grabbed by an aide Meanie Mussini restrained Stalinski for political considerations. As both men cursed each other up and down the steps, both proceeded in their rightful directions. Clint said as they went up the steps and into the courthouse to file the case against the Federal government. "Stalinski You've got it coming, I'm not done with you."

Morgan groused. "Calm down he'll get his, when were done with him." Morgan continued to tell Clint "The Senator is backing Ted Slinky for the second term as prosecutor."

Clint speculated. "Who's that?"

Morgan revealed. "Slinky's own brother was busted for over a kilo of cocaine. Slinky went and begged for mercy from the court, twisted the judge's arm in the back room chambers. He asked the judge Zack Zenner in charge of the case. "Please let my brother off on the kilo of cocaine charge, please." The judge being a friend of Slinky gave Slinky's brother a much-reduced sentence. The first Judge Jeff Jenckle in charge of the case wouldn't budge. He turned the case over to the prosecutor's office for reassignment.

Jeff Jenckle called the two prosecutors, and the police in charge of the case a nest of perjurers, liars and thieves for not cooperating with the Federal and State investigation concerning other hard drug case where cops were found to be the crooks. Judge Jenckle always called them like he saw them "I call a spade a spade" he told the media. Newspapers loved Judge Jenckles candid assessments for the real fairness of facts.

Judge Zack let Prosecutor Slinky's brother off the hook, instead of strict affinity to a law similar like Michigan's mandatory life sentence for possession of such a large amount of cocaine."

Clint griped. "Essentially letting Slinky's brother off?"

Morgan recapitulated. "Ted Slinky was the only one that would get his brother off. Being well connected and having "The Power of Money" is still justice in this white mans court."

Clint exulted. "Ahh The power of money!"

Morgan appealed. "Most Attorney's won't defend you unless you offer them a golden calf. Their only ethics is money."

Clint responded. "One hand washes the other's."

Morgan adamantly assessed. "Right!"

Clint realized the harassment he had received and said. "The degrading my fellow citizens are receiving for simple possession of small amounts of marijuana isn't fair. More people smoke marijuana than tobacco. When the government finally makes marijuana legal, people will be surprised at the citizens that will come out of the closet."

Clint was fuming, while thinking of the governments double standards and said. "Slinky was in charge of the execution of a warrant on my farm."

Mike rebutted. "That charade of a drug raid!"

Clint explained. "Other people are rotting in prison for the rest of their lives serving life terms for the same amount of cocaine possession as Prosecutor Slinky's brother. Now, that same prosecutor runs these fictitious and flaky drug raids that are no more than fishing expeditions into somebody's private life. Drumming up dirt. The way we see it, the government does not have these rights under the Constitution or God."

Clint relayed what was on his mind at the moment. The determined group walked down the large hallways of the Federal Building. They proceeded up to the court clerk. Morgan had the legal papers for the case filed and the papers were stamped. Morgan said. "The judge for the cases is assigned by the luck of the draw".

Judge Perry Prisons, a long time federal judge was assigned to this current Texas federal judgeship. Morgan told Clint and Mike that. "Judge Perry has eaten at the federal pig trough for almost all of his adult life I've always been told, You don't bite the hand that feeds you, and this man has been fed by the federal government most of his life."

Mike relayed. "I've heard Judge Prisons is staunchly against marijuana users."

Morgan expressed. "Judge Perry's own son Chad was busted for selling a small amount of marijuana to under cover drug squad officer."

So be it says the clerk stamping the court filing. "Prisons is the judge." as the clerk time dated the document. Morgan continued to fill Clint in with Perry about the judge's staunch views against marijuana.

Clint assured. 'Don't worry Morgan, I know were in an uphill fight". Morgan moaned. "Now this case just went from a molehill to a mountain."

Clint professed. "I realize that!"

Morgan reiterated. "That don't mean we won't get over it."

Clint, Mike, and Morgan, were prepared to make a statement win loose or draw. They wanted to make a major statement.. Clint told Morgan. "I'm not here in the federal court to argue for a woman from Minnesota who was caught with four hundred pounds of marijuana while crossing the border in Nogalas. She got a fight of her own. She is an enterpriser. But she should be able to pay fair taxes on the four hundred pounds of marijuana and proceed to her sales outlet."

Clint felt the government should change the laws to reflect the times. "We have to cure social situations with liberalization and education."

Mike stressed. "Right!" as Clint continued. "No criminalization, or major discrimination, where small amounts of marijuana are concerned."

Clint, Mike and Morgan all settled in at the Cyber Coffee Shop after the federal court filing. Noticeable was a bunch of college students sitting amongst them. In this quaint little college café, you could do your own cyber surfing on the Internet. The variety of brands of coffee was astounding.

Morgan reassured. "You can have coffee any way you want, from anywhere in the world while your surfing the net in this Cyber Coffee Café." Mike says. "This place is cool. I've never been here!"

Clint rhapsodized. "Listen to that Morgan! That college student is complaining loudly to his friends at the next table." Clint told Morgan overhearing the kid loudly say. "I was pulled over by the police for my license plate light being out. The police quickly rousted me out of the car. The next thing I know suddenly there were two more squad cars there or maybe three altogether. Seven police officers wearing gloves on they're hands and a drug dog rifling through my car. Searching and searching and searching they finally found a half of joint underneath my seat. Seven cops, three squad cars, plus a canine unit from the police station."

Clint supplicated. "When did that happen?"

"Yesterday afternoon as I was on my way to college."

Mike queried. "That can't be legal?"

The student named Meryll, says "Oh yeah the cop told me the high court okayed the drug searches for any traffic stop's."

Mike asked. "That's just another way for the cops to invade your privacy. How much more privacy can they invade?"

Morgan counseled. "That joint could have been left in the car from a weekend headbanger or from an auto mechanic who worked on your car."

Meryll distressed. "And now, I'm driving along minding my own business and I have to answer to all this while I'm going to college. Why can't they leave me alone and everybody else as well? Who do they think they are just because they bust somebody for half a joint? Do you know how many people smoke a joint everyday?"

By now, Clint, Morgan and Mike had a feeling for exactly what Meryll was portraying in the past days event. Needless to say, they did not want to get into all the reasons why they were in the College Cyber Coffee Shop that day. Chris finally met them at the café. Chris had been looking up some new civil violation information in the library computer room attached to his house.

Mike and Morgan wanted Chris to help them get information on the different civil violation cases concerning small amounts of marijuana. They knew they were not alone in their civil pleas.

Morgan relayed to one if the students. "Yeah, now they have a no knock rule. That means in these drug searches, even if they have a warrant to search your home whether your guilty or not, drugs or not, drug law enforcement does not have to knock. The drug police can just take their battering ram and knock the home owner's door down."

Meryll demanded. "What kind of law is that? Violating some innocent citizens in their homes in hopes of catching a drug dealer!"

Morgan further said. "What about the people they violate during the drug raids who just happen to be living their everyday life in the wrong place unknowing of anything about the drug world."

Clint explained. "Tax dollars chasing tax dollars! Americans classified as criminals because they smoke weed."

Chris pleaded. "That doesn't make any sense!"

Another kid sitting at the table with Meryll a student named Seth, says "Yeah! The no knock rule! Our class at college did a back ground study on what cases we could find." In the course of our class search, we found one victim, a Reverend named Dexter Denning from Wisconsin. Whose house was invaded in style with the No Knock ruling by a metro drug squad. The cops now seem to think that they can do anything they want."

Meryll obsessed. "This was a traumatizing experience the Reverends wife who stated, "That she still cannot sleep at night, her stomach is nervous, she can't eat either or feel comfortable or safe in her home any more." The reverends wife felt they were going to be shot by these masked men after they stormed the house, breaking the door down and entering with an AR-15 being pointed to the temple of their heads. She said, "They were handcuffed hog-tied, belly down. The police ordered them not to speak, while the seventy one year-old preacher was gasping for his life." The storm troopers barged through every room demonstrating precision commando tactics. They all had an arrogant, and ignorant attitude. There's no respect here for the citizens." The wife said, in the aftermath to the media. "They don't listen." The victim's wife said the search warrant stated that. "Someone had bought an ounce of marijuana out of this home." She said, I told them, there is no way. That's how a seventy one year-old preacher was killed." Seth concluded.

Clint ripped. "What?"

Seth canted. "Yeah! That seventy one year-old preacher died of a heart attack." "The cops knocked down the old people to the floor, then they cuffed and hog tied them. While the one cop had an AR 15 automatic weapon pointed at the preacher's temple, the elderly preacher, who was so traumatized, he went into cardiac arrest. The cops bullied these old retirees. The preacher was trying to tell these police drug officers he was having a heart attack, but they all stood around and laughed. Then the drug police find out they busted into the wrong home. The preacher died in the ambulance on the way to the hospital."

Clint professed. "The heart attack was induced by the drug police force from the trauma of the ill advised drug bust? How come they never suffer any repercussions?"

Seth confided. "Yeah" The article was in last weeks Wisconsin newspaper. I read it while I was on holiday in the Wisconsin's Dells and brought it to school here in Houston. It was a clear cut case where these citizens were better off to be left alone to delegate their own life instead tormented from an intrusion by our government's trained robo cops of the drug force, who are callous beyond reason."

Clint disclosed. "These cops are trained to be a tactical mechanism blasting into anyone's home. Guilty or not."

Morgan enounced. "That's our government today!"

Clint protested. "Talked about being raped in the middle of the highway." "How about on your own living room floor."

Then Morgan the senior attorney accented. "Yep! That's the way the cops are doing it and it's only getting worse."

Clint decreed. "We have to take a stand men.!" They all joyously agreed

Morgan had Chris give all the students the address to Clint's farm for the next round table meeting. Seth, after saying he would attend the next round table meeting said. "There is too much of this cop intrusion into our rights going on not to take a stand." These college law students offered to bring in fellow law students to the next round table meetings. They wanted to help after every one aired their views on governmental injustices.

The very next day after court case was filed in federal court, one of Houston's biggest radio stations called Clint. The radio commentator, Woodrow Wallace asked. "Clint did you file these papers down here at the federal building for a million dollar lawsuit?"

Clint responded. "I sure did!"

Woody affirmed. "Clint we would like to put you on the radio and we would like to put you on the radio right now."

Clint espoused. "Well, I'd like to get on the air with you Woody right now but my attorney Morgan Motley says you have to call him first. If Morgan says its okay with him, then its fine with me."

Woody responded "OK Clint I'll get right back to you don't go any where."

Woody called to talk with Morgan Motley. Morgan okayed the radio interview. Woody called back Clint thirty minutes later.

Wallace concured. "Clint, Morgan said you can do the live radio interview, but just don't get wild."

Clint reassured. "Okay!"

Woody filled Clint. "You can begin now after this question."

Clint perceived. "Alright! I'm ready when you are."

Woody inquired. "Where were you when you first heard about the green house destruction."

Clint unveiled. "I was on my way home from the produce market at the port of Corpus Christi at the time our government's military air craft destroyed my families greenhouse at the direction of the police.

Witnesses stated. "The helicopters hovered ten feet over my house ripping siding off, then in the air ten feet over my seventy by seventy pole building, and then they hovered like ten feet over my fifty by one hundred greenhouse. The down force winds of helicopters rotor blades blew the whole plastic top off the top of the green house. These drug cops could have walked in and looked around like anyone else."

Woody summed up the interview with his radio audience. "So what was in the greenhouse? Exotic flower cuttings, five hundred thousand tomato and pepper plants which were all destroyed! Explained Clint.

Woody Wallace, Houston News Radio. Clint had no idea they would call. Clint, Chantel and green house crew were jumping up and down for joy. They felt their point of view had finally received notice about their injustice on the radio. Clint said to Chantel. "I can't believe how good the truth sounds over the air. I know Woody loved hearing the truth too." The majority of the callers into the radio station responded in favor of Clint and his family taking on the government in federal court. The radio pollsters said. "The public would want justice if a similar circumstance happened to them and their family."

At the same time unbeknownst to Clint chief Dirkskin was in the middle of a meeting when Clint's radio interview came over the air. The interview with Woody played over the air every half hour for the next twenty-four hours. The hog with the big nuts, Dirkskin could not believe the green house destruction was being exposed. Dirkskin went into a frenzy at that point and took personal charge to discredit Clint. The chief went to great lengths to protect his position in life. Dirkskin couldn't stand to loose his power or monetary position. Dirkskin states the following day to his men, Girt, Godfrey, and Ramone. "Look guys we have to get this guy no matter what, he is starting to bring some heat on us from the commissioner. Larry, take him out."

Larry pressed. "How do you mean Dick?"

Dick proposed. "Well you know those guys they always have a little bit of grass. Now if a little bit of marijuana showed up around that farm. We could turn up the burners on Clint and force him to drop that law suit."

Girt implored. "Ramone have some marijuana planted around and on that one kid who stays in that trailer shack out their on Clint's farm named Toby Turner.

Once the weed's in place in Turner's trailer we'll automatically be able to search Clint's farm knowing we can back up the drug bust in court."

Dirkskin desperately said. "Girt! When your at the farm during the raid try and throw a few pounds of weed in Clint's bedroom dresser drawer." Ramone said. "We can do that".

Dirkskin's philosophized. "Can you imagine the news headlines after we bust that loud mouth punk."

Girt directed. "Ramone line up some gutter rats from the barrio for the drug bust. Parolees who want lighter sentences who will Co-operate with the drug bust." Ramone had plenty of paroles who looking for lenient sentences to choose from because of all the marijuana busts alone.

Ramone affirmed. "I know that Turner's little girlfriends, Ashley, Sheila and Lisa, are constantly going over to Turner's trailer."

Dirkskin explained. "Have one of our guys go over there with one of the girls, like Lisa She's the one that got more twenty dollar tips from informing on her fellow class mates in the DARE program at the school than anyone else. She will be easy to pressure to our side when the shit hit's."

Girt commended. "I like your way of thinking Dick!"

Ramone assented. "Yeah! We can do this one. Gar will go for it." Dirkskin concurred. "Turn your man Gar on to her Ramone. Then get a couple pounds out of the evidence room and give it to Girt before the drug bust at Clint's farm." Godfrey says. "That is a good idea!"

Girt thinking to himself. "I'll just leave one of those pounds for the bust of Clint's farm at my house on the way to the drummed up drug bust so I can enjoy some recreational highs on the weekends myself." Girt, when ever the opportunity presented itself would skim weed from the evidence room and sell it to his friends or keep it for himself.

Dirkskin rebutted. "So he thinks he is suing us? We'll see who gets caught holding the bag here." As the meeting concluded Dirkskin went to the nursing home by himself to see an old mentor.

A former police chief, Garret Giles, who was Dirkskin's boss when Dirkskin was a rookie on a Colorado police force. Dirkskin was with Garret when he went up to a young long hair hippie, who was in a bar. Garret went into the bar grabbed the long haired young man up because he knew that smoked pot. The police chief Garret then took the young man out on the back roads and deep into the woods and blew the young mans head off with a twelve gauge shotgun. Dirkskin was a rookie at the time and never told anybody.

Garret avouched Dirkskin's. "Just take a couple of them young trouble makers out and shoot them. Then the others hippies will get the message and get out of this town." Dirkskin always admired Garret's boldness and visited Garret when he needed advice and extra gumption.

Ramone finally made contact with his drug informants in the barrio. A few days later the plan was in motion, Ramone had his criminal contacts introduced to the girls, Sheila, Ashley, and Lisa.

In Tiny Toby Turner's little trailer, everyone was smoking down on some grass. The kid from the barrio, named Gar for Garcia, planted a quarter ounce of weed behind Toby's dresser during the course of the evening. Toby rarely had any weed himself, because he spent time and his spare change on building model hot rod cars. As the party continued, they listened to some rock music. The kids talked about the various rock shows coming up. They were all hoping to go to the multi-concerts in two weeks. It was about nine PM. on a school night, and the school kids. After about two or three hours of music videos the party broke up. Dirkskin was happy to hear the marijuana drug evidence was planted.

Meanwhile, Mike and Clint had decided to go to Morgan's law offices to talk things over with Mike's law associates. They are gathering in the Legal Library of Morgan's law office. The library, disregarding the books, looks more like a mini-auditorium. In attendance was Miles, Mike, Ed, Morgan, some law students, a some victims of the drug wars, a police officer who was a friend to the cause and, of course, Clint.

One of the law students Roberto started out saying. "My Uncle Pedro Mendez and his wife were violently raided by the drug police back in Tucson. In a series of drug raids by the SWAT teams their house was mistakenly identified and raided. The drug raid was intended for the house next door."

Morgan interjected and said. "This is another typical case of the blind leading the blind."

Roberto further said. "My uncle was treated for back pain after being physically thrown to the ground by the police officers and cuffed. My aunt was hospitalized from trauma endured in the drug raid by an overzealous drug squad. The Police Department's spokesman states it was a regrettable mistake caused by human error."

Morgan supplicated the student. "Was Mr. Mendez taken away in an ambulance?"

Roberto answered. "Yes!"

Mike inquired. "On all these busts, whether they are innocent or not, the police have to break up bones in the victim's kingdom to make their statement in the drug war. They interrupt life as people know it. All this at tax payers expense. Tax spending fighting other tax spending because of a mistake."

Roberto proffered. "I don't know if my aunt and uncle will even sue the department."

The round table group now had twenty five to thirty people around the table listening to three or four of the researchers of civil rights abuses. The wrong raids being done on the wrong homes, and victims who were traumatized by the police officers. Other assorted abuses by police departments such as officers selling drugs on the streets, escorting drug shipments from New Orleans to

Detroit, right down to the Detroit police chief caught with millions of dollars from unaccountable drug forfeiture money were over whelming."

Morgan propagated. "Remember the million dollars in drug money ended up in the police chiefs attic in Detroit."

Clint imputed. "Oh Ya! I remember reading that article."

Morgan professed. "The police chief only got fifteen years."

Clint fumed. "Is that all he got!"

Ed divulged. " Drug investigative cops regularly keep money, drugs, guns, and jewelry from the raids. In some cases the only reason some of these raids are conducted is so that crooked police officers can steal the dealers or defendant's money knowing full well that these dealers had surplus cash, drugs, jewelry, guns, etc., lying about in excess. Marijuana users are easy prey and easy pickings for these under the guise of a badge in drug busts."

Miles imputed. "Most victims had day jobs and only sold marijuana as part of their smoking habit, or because some of their friends wanted some stash of their own. The unfeeling police and prosecutors would take everything these victims for worked for legally. After confiscating everything in their home for a couple ounces of marijuana with a value of one hundred and fifty dollars total. Leaving victims indigent."

Morgan appraised. "Ya! The police seized everything in a drug victim's apartment or home under the guise that it was all bought with drug money." The meeting broke up with everyone wanting to right this "Wrong" in our judicial system."

Chapter 5... Clint had just received a phone call from his friend Will a student in Colorado choosing fall semester classes at college in Leadville. Will had called Clint's house and Chantel to him and reach him at Morgan's office.

Clint's good friend Will was skiing in Colorado at A-Basin. He was on a break in the Alpine Hut area of the A-Basin ski lodge. Will had called Clint to rub it in about the great skiing. Will had known that Clint and Chantel always came here and talked about how A-Basin skiing was the best. This was Will's first time at A-Basin and he was impressed with the moguls on the mountains runs.

Will conversing with Clint over the phone "Did you here that?"

Clint chaffed. "I heard it. That's the avalanche mountain cannon. You must of gotten quit a bit of snow."

Will pledged. "There's a phenomenal amount of snow has just been felled by the avalanche canon."

Will informed. "I'm staying in the Idaho Springs area tonight. While attending college in Leadville. I've decided I'm going to try as many ski areas in this state as I can. I want you and Chantel to come out to Colorado and see me."

Clint answered. "I'd like to! Then Chantel and I can see my sister."

Will raved. "Good! I'll see you as soon as you can get here." Betty Clint's sister lived in Evergreen, Colorado.

Clint told Will. "I'll talk it over with Chantel tonight when I get home and see what we can do."

Will excited. "Great!"

Clint told Will. "If Chantel decides we can go we'll leave tomorrow. I know we need a break from the family business and current events."

Will prescribed. "Really Clint. That's why I'm calling. come on out here for some light hearted fun."

Clint disclosed. "I want to go out there and go skiing that's for sure. It will help take my mind off it all."

Will restated. "Theirs a heavy snow fall now and Arapaho basin ski lodge is open."

Clint relayed. "Arapaho Basin is known for the most adventuresome skiing Mountain in the Rockies and it's the first ski lodge to open the ski season, and the last one to close. The nice thing about A-basin is that it's known for it's natural snow with a wide variety of ski and snow board slopes."

Clint and Chantel had been there many times before. Clint's brother in law Bob worked at A- Basin as an instructor. Clint ended the conversation with Will by. "We'll try and be on tomorrows flight out of here for Colorado." Needless to say Clint and Chantel couldn't resist the ski trip and they both flew out of

Houston's airport the next day thanks to some quick dealing by their travel agent Kathy.

Will was at the Denver's airport when the plane landed the next day at noon. Will picked up Clint and Chantel he took them directly to "The Hemperor's" on Larimer street in downtown Denver. The Hemperors is the biggest hemp retail outlet store in the state of Colorado. The hemp store imported hemp products from all parts of the world. Chantel, while eating her hemp lollypop, bought hemp shoes for her entire family. Clint immediately bought khaki carpenter's pants by Hempy's after seeing the display. Chantel was collecting some current hemp literature from "Agricultural Hemp Association" (AHA) which was based in Denver, Colorado. Another bulletin advertised the "Great American Beer Festival" that was held recently, and featured a large variety of Hemp Beer's sold nationally.

They were soon on their way west, when Will told Clint and Chantel how great the skiing was before he explained to them the bad news. "Law enforcement set up a drug sting roadblock."

Clint surprised. "What?"

Will informatively said. "Not long after our conversation yesterday I left and end up in a long line of traffic."

Clint wearing his new natural "Hempton Green Cannabis Cowboy Hat" deplored. "That would just blow my whole vacation to go through that kind of harassment."

Will further said. "They targeted patrons as they left the ski lodges and headed down the mountains winding road. The roadblock was backed up fifty to sixty cars at any given moment. Each car was going through a gauntlet of investigators who were vigorously searching for drugs. Close to four hundred cars were stopped in one day leaving the different ski lodges. This led to thirty five arrests and no one had more than quarter of an ounce marijuana on them. The other victims in most of the cars searched were innocent and broke no laws. Their rights to privacy on a leisurely day were interrupted by a law enforcement rug sting perpetrated on the them. Sanctioned terrorism paid for through American tax dollars."

Clint and Chantel couldn't believe what they heard. Clint's said. "I've never heard of such a thing. That's never happened to us before."

Chantel affirmed. "Never."

Clint told Will. "I can't believe it."

Will explained. "All that were apprehended in the drug sting were marijuana users not dealers. They came to contribute to Colorado's tourist industries and were subjected to an intense marijuana drug search."

Cool headed Chantel said. "Now the cops are chasing off the tourists."

Will entreated. "These arrogant sheriff's are getting out of hand."

Clint responded. "There out of control big time! You go to a ski lodge, and bring a couple of joints to burn while on the high speed chair lifts and run the slopes. You come out here for some world class skiing to thoroughly enjoy yourself. You run up and down the mountains snow boarding and skiing all day and you have to go through a gauntlet of Gestapo tactics."

Will voiced. "Some mini vacation for the tourists. This is ridiculous. Is this all these cops have to do?"

Clint's summarized. "Hey Will! They must not have any doughnut shop up here?"

Wide eyed Will said. "Ya, they sure love doughnut shops! It's incident's like this that make cops a detriment to society."

Composed Clint said. "We don't need this type of expensive instigative aggravation by the police department."

Will reported. "I saw several police officers with plastic gloves were searching suit cases, under the seats, in the trunks, in the glove box, in my own pockets, in the cracks of my arm pits and even in my baseball cap stitching."

One snow boarder stated in the middle of a radio interview. "They just ordered me out of the car without any reason and acted like I had a weapon. I was really freaking!"

Another snow boarder named Clyde offered. "How can we really put the innocent citizens in jeopardy out there who have nothing to do with marijuana or drugs? Why victimize them in a holy anti-cannabis crusade, that's directed to morally correct anyone they perceive as morally unfit? In this case the government's wrong when they disregard an innocent victim's individual rights! The police tactic's are no different than third world Nazi type repression.

Another skier went on to question the reporters. "What would happen if one of these kids just freaked out and ran because he had a minor warrant out for him or a small bag of weed and the cops just opened up and shot him dead? Is that what has to happen before these road blocks stop? It can and will happen. The cops have made bigger blunders. Why can't we stop this madness before it happens?"

Wholesome Will reproved. "The attorneys for the road blocked skiers are filing a civil suit for unlawful search. Skiers were signing a class action law suit against the police roadblock for the uncalled for interruption of their holidays.

The lawyer for the skiers said. "Just say No!" to the police officers when your pulled over and asked by the officer if he can search your automobile. Do not give the police permission to search your car ever, because they then have permission to trample all over your civil rights. Don't put your head in a noose."

Another lawyer conceded in a the newspaper interview. "Probable cause has to be established by the police officers, before a motorist can be hindered by such drug searches. A probable cause for a search was never established here."

Will complained. "I felt discriminated against. I unequivocally disliked the powerful police search procedures. I was subjected to a traumatic ordeal according to my standards. A Denver morning's newspaper featured avouched. "The District Attorney's office will release a statement next week. A The skier vindicated. "The County commissioner assured the people. "Similar incident will not happen again. We will cease to have these roadblocks."

Will scorned. "Still, nobody gets reprimanded!"

Clint quizzically nagged. "Who ordered these insulting and assaulting road blocks to vacationers anyway?"

Will remonstrated. "Governmental officials can do whatever they want. They never have to answer for it. When they make a mistake, they just say they're sorry regardless of the injustice. Motorists coming from the ski lodge that day were held up in the police gauntlet, missed flights, in Denver returns from their vacations.

Signs were placed along the side of the road "Drug dogs one mile ahead", and "Narcotics Officers ahead". Americans in this country don't need this type of aggravation. Some vacationers were told by law enforcement at the road blocks that police were hiding in bushes with binoculars trying to catch the motorists as they threw drugs out their window as they approached the drug gauntlet. The police had everyone get out of there cars. The police body frisked all vacationers and further searched their cars. This is state sponsored police terrorism tactics at their best."

Chantel portrayed. "Your right we might as well be in a third world country."

Will stated. "Some of the vacationers asked. What do drug sniffing dogs prove by running in and out of my car? Some vacationer's were upset with the unscheduled interruptions. Some rental cars were turned in late forcing vacationers to pay for an extra days rental on the vehicle as well as missing their fight home, and maybe a days work."

Candid Clint questioned. "That isn't right?"

Will informed. "Fred Hall the manager of the ski resort was enraged that his patrons were targeted. These police actions defeat the purpose of all our advertising to bring vacationers here from all over the country and world to enjoy themselves here on the mountain skiing. How come my customers have to leave and go through the police gauntlet?"

Clint said. "That's Big Government's approach to treat US citizen's as cattle!"

Will rehashed Fred's news statement. "How do they expect us to bring vacationers here and stay in business with these police tactics? Who'd even come out here to go skiing any more?"

Chantel protested. "Nobody wants to go through a personal frisking on the way in and out of here."

Clint inquired. "Will is that only happening in Colorado?"

Will divulged. "No! This morning's paper said it's happening in other states as well. It's happening in Reno, it's happening in Wyoming too, and it's also happening in Ohio, it's happening across our country."

Clint and Chantel upon their at arrival were disappointed about the dirty police tactics. They were now driving on I-70 west toward Evergreen and Golden Colorado. They would take the cut off going up Lookout Mountain. Look out mountain was where the famous Buffalo Bill was laid to rest with his wife Nettie. The picturesque view of Denver at the base of Buffalo Bill's grave on the mountain was breathtaking.

Clint, Chantel and Will overlooked the valley to the east several thousand below them the inner peace was tremendous, while standing by Buffalo Bill's grave. This was a real tribute to Buffalo Bill a trailblazer and pillar in the memory of the American western frontier. They walked to the other side of the mountain top's historical retreat, where the Buffalo Bill Museum is found. The tourist museum is always fascinating, and full of souvenirs. Pictures of Bill as an Indian Scout and a Pony Express Rider graced the walls.

Chantel was already watching one of Thomas Edison's first movies. It featured "Buffalo Bill's Wild West Show." There was the colorful Buffalo Bill. He had on his best Western Indian garb. Bill was on his big white stallion, as he gallantly rode into the show under the "Big Top Tent."

Clint attested to Will. "Buffalo Bill had toured all over Europe in front of Kings and Queens standing to thunderous applause. Buffalo Bill brought the true flavor of the American West throughout Europe. A big part of the show was featured American Indians. Look here! There's a picture of Buffalo Bill and one of the Indian Chief's smoking a peace pipe."

Will proclaimed. "I love it!"

Clint reminisced to Will. "I think I come here just to see that picture." Clint talked so much about Colorado Rocky's to Will, that Will coerced him to show all the sights, he had heard mentioned about earlier.

They were now back on I-70 west for another exit or two. Clint pointed out a herd of hundred or so of the heavy fur coated buffalo grazing at the base of the mountain in the open meadows of the trees. Will excited. "I didn't noticed them on the way to the airport?"

Clint suddenly said. "Look at the horns on that big ram on the side of the cliff of that forested mountain! I'd like to mount that rack in my den." as Will turns his head sharply.

Chantel defensively said. "He's to pretty to kill!"

Clint calmly said. "That's why I'd mount him. He's a trophy for most to behold."

Will surprised. "I didn't see those mountain goats either."

Clint explained. That's because they stay high up in the Aspen Forests during the morning."

Will insisted. "I seen those large Elk though! I'd like to have one of those Elk over there hanging as a trophy in my den," as they drove and eyed a herd of over two hundred Elk in Elk meadow in Evergreen, Colorado.

Chantel remarked. "I'm glad there protected."

Clint scrutinized. "Ya, for most of the wildlife is protected year around. Except during hunting season or in hunting preserves." Will nodded in agreement as he passed a newly lit green bud joint to Clint.

Clint immediately said. "That you sir! I'll enjoy a hit of that green bud now thank you."

Clint depicted the story about how Chico, Igor, Rudy went hunting in the Northern parts of Montana. Clint said. "Igor fell asleep by this huge tree. The is the biggest deer I've ever saw. The huge racked deer stood in the field in front of him. I'm wandering down from the ridge where I was positioned. I'm wondered why Igor wasn't firing at the body under that gigantic deer rack directly in front of him."

Will appealed. "Igor still didn't shoot?"

Clint conceded. "No; and I'm to far away too get a good shot off myself."

Will curiously asked. "What happened then?"

Clint replied. "This colossal buck then lowers his rack and shoves Igor who was dead asleep. Igor had spread plenty of buck lure around the base of the tree he was sitting under."

Will bright eyed further inquired. "What did Igor do?"

Clint explained. "Igor suddenly woke up startled with his loaded pump shotgun laying across his lap. He try's to jump up but the shotgun gets caught in the buck's huge rack. The buck charged away with the shotgun involuntarily discharging shotgun shell's from his rack. The Buck was galloping as fast as he could up the mountain. The shots were in stride with the bucks pace."

Will recapped. "The deer's racked shotgun discharged as he ran?"

Clint raved. "Ya! We laughed so hard at that time. I just hoped the Buck ran out of bullets before he got up to the ridge."

Chantel asked. "Did you ever find Igor's shot gun?"

Clint answered. "No! We never did find Igor's Grand dads 1871, 12 gauge pump shotgun."

Bewildered Will burst out. "That's unreal!"

Clint amazed accented. "If you hadn't seen it you wouldn't believe it."

The vacationers were now on their way to Betty's house high up in the mountains. Betty was widely known at the Arapaho Basin ski lodge. She was the nurse working in the medical station at the ski lodge, and was accustom to a steady diet of injured skiers coming off the mountain. Betty told Clint all the time when he was at the lodge. "Those skiers who push their envelope of skiing ability beyond their limitations on the Black ski runs cause the worst accidents and injuries."

Bob and Betty sat in their hot tub on the balcony of there huge rustic cedar structure house built in the side of the mountain as the visitors pulled up. Betty noticed Clint and screamed. "Hi everyone! Welcome to Colorado!" Betty ran up to her guests after wrapping herself into her Cannabis Kamona and then hugged Clint and Chantel. The main high ceiling interior ballroom was loaded with live plants and Indian Art surrounding a "Canyon Stoned Mahogany Mantled Fireplace." One bedroom's the wall was actually the black rock of the mountain. Will confessed to Clint and Chantel. "What a way to live."

Chantel agreed. "You know that's right!" After greeting's were exchanged, dinner was served. It consisted of homemade lasagna, without meat, because Betty being a vegetarian registered nurse did not eat meat. She still made everything taste good without it and even Will and Clint avid meat eaters enjoyed the food.

Betty voiced to all that the kid's were in Denver. Her son Dale fourteen years old and daughter Diane twelve years old were there at the Paradise Rock

103

gym. Betty said. "The kids are attending a sport climbing improvement program. The instructors held diversified rock climbing courses for expeditions and mountaineering. The Paradise Rock gym always has safe and reliable instruction."

Bob added. "An avid rock climbing family needs to be in shape year round."

This family was also building an elaborate hemp card board space shuttle replica. Bob wanted his guests the hemp card shuttle which was being constructed in the garage of their home. "Clint I can't wait to show you what's in the garage. This week end is the Card Board Derby. Elaborate multi-color creations of cars, trucks, airplanes, Noah's ark were entered. Every part of the elaborate "Cannabis Cardboard Space Shuttle" here is made with hemp cardboard, paper, tape, and string."

As "Kudos" their cat ran around Betty chattered. "All the card board derby entries will carry a load of ski bums down the mountain as many as the builders desire. All the participants will to roll down the mountain to the Arapaho basin ski lodge. Ski patrollers made a huge ramp at the bottom of the hill so the craft would not plow into the lodge. This popular event is sponsored by a local Denver radio station."

Clint mustered. "The kids are helping too?"

Betty answered. "Yes! They wouldn't miss it for anything!". "The kids will be home shortly. Our neighbor Calvin and his kids are at the rock gym. Calvin said he'd bring them home after their climb."

Clint reeled off. "I can't wait to see that cannabis shuttle."

Bob rattled. "Let's go down stairs now and take a look at it now." Bob led the way towards the mountain home's steps. Everyone followed until they seen the Cannabis Shuttle.

Clint amazed. "Wow! This is an elaborate looking craft."

Chantel embellished. "I'm as amazed as everyone else."

Bob begged. "Guess what?"

Will inquired. "What?"

Bob conceded. "This whole shuttle is made from hemp, from the string, to the tape, and the card board, the paper, and even the non toxic paint."

Clint questioned. "Where did you get all the hemp material."

Bob answered. "From a industrial hemp processor and manufacturer in Canada who sponsored our hemp shuttle. He only asked that his name Pierre Berline and Hemp Industries and Materials made in Canada be printed on the side!"

Clint beseeched. "How did you find Pierre?"

Bob disclosed. "Betty found Pierre on the Internet by accident. Pierre was looking for somebody in this area to build the hemp craft. He was here at last year's card board derby. He'll be here tomorrow for this one."

Clint expounded. "His cannabis craft is large enough for a dozen people."

Bob relayed. "Thirteen people. We'll all be in it tomorrow."

Chantel chuckled. "I'm excited!"

Clint chortled. "Everyone's excited now!"

The door suddenly opened up! Bob and Betty's kids rushed into the room. "Hi Uncle Clint and Aunt Chantel" Clint's nephew Dale and his niece Diane said. They all promptly exchanged hugs, kisses and greeting with their Aunt Chantel and best liked Uncle Clint.

Will's friend arrived shortly after as planned. Bart and his girl Brook were college students from Colorado Mountain College in Leadville, it was also Will's college. Bart was entertaining for the night. Bart formed a group at college played local taverns and events in the area.

Tonight Bart and his guitar and played John Denver songs long into the night. Clint said. "This is really a Rocky mountain high." as he stood up with Bart.

They played an original tune of Clint's called. "I am, Who I Am, for What I Am." The song continues for the duel. "I'm right here right now to take a stand" the back ground chorus sang. "Isn't that grand to take a stand."

Will exulted. "That is a neat tune."

Brook vouched. "Ya! It's catchy but not to complicated."

The night went fast as everyone merrily sung along. They all had a great time before they retired for the night. Bart and Brooke's mountainside room was just below the hogback. Their bedroom was built into the declivity of the mountain below the cliff. The west interior wall of their room is solid black rock.

After an early rise, and a Colorado vegetarian breakfast prepared by Betty, the trio of vehicles left with everyone. Bob and Betty's drove their 4x4 GMC one ton pick up with the Cannabis Space Shuttle in tow. On I-70 west they pasted the "Buffalo Bar" in "Idaho Springs." In view was "Oh My God Road" which went straight up the mountain the back way to the other side to old wild west mining town of "Central City" nestled in Virginia Canyon. Central City's "Glory Hole Mine is thought to be of the same vein of gold as Idaho Springs "Argo Mine" on the opposite side of the granite walled mountain. They were excited to pass through highway's long and modern "Eisenhower Tunnel" at fifty miles per hour en route to A-Basin ski lodge for the Card board derby.

The trip from Evergreen to A-Basin was approximately seventy five miles. Along the route they traveled on I-70 west and continued through the Eisenhower tunnel. The Cannabis Space Shuttle took in it's share of gawkers along the highway. The colorful advertising on the Cannabis Space Shuttle and matching trailer underneath is red, white, and blue color coordinated.

Will snickered. "Look! Some of these gawkers are actually following us and our Cannabis Card Board Shuttle all the way to A-Basin." as they now past "Keystone Village" on their way up the mountain.

Clint spurred. "I bet they stay for the main event!"

Chantel touted. "I'll bet they do to!"

Once at A-Basin, Bob told everyone in the 4x4 king cab truck that. "A-Basin is one of the oldest ski runs and has by far the longest ski season of all the ski runs in Colorado."

Betty blinked. "Look! The card board derby contestants are over there. Look at the contestants very different card board crafts that are being inspected."

Bob discerned. "I'll drive into the ski parking area. The ski patrol has a derby line established over there." Betty said. "All the card board crafts are being brought up to the summit by the ski patrol for launching." Before the event started everyone geared their freshly waxed skis. They began skiing as soon as they finished suiting.

Young Dale sidestepped on a glance. "Lets go straight to the top of the summit from the ski lifts Uncle Clint."

Will examined the area once at the top. "The view is awesome and A-basin is the most adventurous skiing in Colorado I've ever experienced!"

Clint descried. "I can see that! It has the most exciting ski run moguls." as he aimed his skies down the slope not far from the peak.

Chantel squealed to Brook once at the top of the summit. "Did you see the ava-launcher canon going off?"

While riding past the Midway Steak house from the above ski lift Brook implored. "Yes! That must be a neat sight going off while riding to the top of the summit." of sum thirteen thousand feet on top of the solid snow coated mountain tops.

Clint and Chantel were the first skiers from the group to fan snow down though the alpine lined ski trails. Chantel smoothly sliding over the groomed snow trails down "Sundance Trail" turned back to Clint and spelled out. "I'll see you at the bottom of the hill." And headed straight down the black run around Pallavicini. Bart and Brook brought their own custom designed hemp snow boards. They were both going to try the snow boards on the more remote runs down hill. Bart and Brook were next finish the winding down hill run.

Bob and Betty were still at the bottom of the basin waiting to meet Pierre in the A-Basin Day lodge, Pierre was en route from Denver, with his wife Patsy. Pierre's very knowledgeable design and manufacturing manager Nolan was also attending this year's event as well. Everyone anticipated meeting at noon in the Alpine hut for a barbecue lunch .

The weather was sunny and clear, and heavy powder conditions made it great for the days event. The radio station had set up their broadcasting station to simulcast the card board derby live. The ski costumes and gaiety of the event presented a colorful collage, against the snow white back drop. The radio station was the first sponsor to have their card board craft go crashing down the slope. Most of the card board derby's entries disassembled long before the bottom of the hill, bearing in mind they were made from nothing more than what they were made of. How ever some did manage to make it to the bottom of the hill before crashing into the snow barrier below.   It was time for the Cannabis Space Shuttle to go down the hill. Diane says. "I'm excited"

Dale agreed with his sister. "I am too!" Everyone loaded into the craft. All of the party of thirteen were intact and soaring down the hill amidst the roars and cheers of an enthusiastic crowd in attendance. Everyone in the cannabis craft was hanging and waving out the opening's of the Card Board Shuttle. The hemp shuttle was one of the few craft to make it all the way down A-basin, crashed into the snow ramp and disintegrated into smithereens. Everyone on the shuttle went spilling into the pile of rubble laughing beyond control.

Clint yelled out as he got up from the snow. "That was great!" "The cannabis card board is a stronger fabric than that regular card board derived from lumber."

Pierre claimed. "I got what I wanted. A public sponsored event with a cannabis craft representing my company. This is a big promotion for the commercial hemp industry being established in Canada." Pierre said to Clint and Bob standing there after the event. "I'm going to use this video footage of the card board race in TV commercials and sales brochures for my company." Pierre even had the local radio station DJ's pose in the demolished cannabis craft for maximal advertising effect.

The hemp card board craft Pierre sponsored, and Bob's family put together was history. Clint said. "Bob you and your family were voted for the most unique and best entry of the card board derby event. That's great!"

Bob summarized to Pierre. "Thanks for giving us the opportunity."

Pierre summed up. "Let's do it again next year!"

Bob recited. "Agreed!" As everyone else headed for their skis or snow boards.

Clint set out. "I'm going up to the summit and down hill to the bottom of the basin on every ski run here."

Bart followed Clint and yelled. "I'm right behind you!" skiing into a snow race.

Clint gloated on the way up the highest ski lift chairs in North America with Bart. "The ski lifts is where everyone who smoked pot lit up for the relaxing ride up to the summit. The lift really gives you a birds eye view of the skiers. Look at those skiers in the cartoon costumes."

Bart descried. "Listen those skiers are playing the musical instruments on their way down to the bottom of the hill."

Brook fixed her eyes on the entertainment. "There is the clown who played a trumpet all the way to the bottom of the hill. He never missed a note as he skied to the bottom on my last run."

Clint proclaimed. "Previously, that clown was seen smoking a bong on the lift to the summit."

Bart quipped. "Did you see the three skiers going down hill in revolutionary attire from the era of the revolutionary war. They played their drums, flute and fiddle down the hill. The revolutionary costumed men had a large paper mache marijuana joint strapped to their back."

Clint conferred with his Pompeii Red ski goggles on. "Ya! That was wild. I like that." Everyone laughed hysterically on the ski lift up to the summit.

Bart scoured holding his puff. "Here Clint!" as he passed a big green one, he had just lit up. Clint and Bart smoked down on the way up.

Clint remarked. "Everyone is apparently protesting the roadblocks were set up by the police."

Bart responded to Clint. "The cops practiced their investigative drug methods. It was probably no more than a seminar for rookie cops to demonstrate their drug tactics on skiers vacationing on holiday." as they departed the ski lift at North America's highest Ski Station. During the down hill run the wind was blowing and howling loud close to the summit. In the sight was the endless peaks of the "Ten Mile Range" of the Continental Divide.

Clint on his skis embarked. "I wouldn't doubt it!" Responding to Bart.

Bart made tracks. "Only in America!"

Clint detected his wife among all the colorful skiers. "There's Chantel. She just came off her lift.

Clint said as he skied up from behind Chantel. "Hi!" as she caught up with Clint.

Chantel pointed out where Dale and Diane, Bob and Betty's kids were going down hill.

Clint amazed. "I see them in those bright ski costumes."

Chantel told Clint. "Did you see the radio station crew? They interviewed everyone including those costumed revolutionaries. Some other ski patrons concerned for individual freedom rights protested the police road blocks live to the local radio audience."

Bart chimed. "The radio station largely had a warm response from the radio audience, while telecasting live from A-basin. I was standing there with Brook."

Clint insisted. "Most people are getting tired of the governmental sham of complete mind and body control of it's citizens. After all were supposed to live in a free society with a right to choose our own destiny." What had always worried Clint was that other modern and industrialized countries were becoming freer than the supposed leaders of the free world the good old USA. Evidence was clear across the country people wanted a change. They wanted big brother out of their daily decisions with out any repercussions. Freedom of choice was the only fair way to delegate this change.

Everyone was to meet at the Dillon Inn after leaving A-Basin ski lodge. Pierre bought every one of the hemp shuttle participants dinner. He invited the radio station DJ's who gladly excepted. Pierre's video and photo crew continued to take advantage of the situation for maximal advertising footage with Pierre posing with the radio personalities at the famous Dillon Inn. Clint told Will who stood next to him drinking his rum and coke said. "The Dillon Inn was actually at the bottom of the valley in the old town of Dillon. It was one of the few building's brought to the top before the valley was flooded to make the Dillon mountain water reservoir."

Will appraised. "No kidding!"

Bart contrasted. "This is quite a scenic view with Buffalo mountain in the backdrop."

Bob divulged. "The city of Dillon is now modernly built up along the reservoir lake. All the new shopping centers, condominiums, and amenities are sprouting everywhere imaginable along the seven mile route between A- basin and Dillon."

Clint avowed. "The exquisite dinning in this most unique antique structure is such a treat."

Pierre standing next to Clint after dinner exclaimed. "Clint! I'm glad I had the opportunity to met you and your wife. I hope we can be of assistance to you for any cannabis information you may need in your pursuits."

Clint expounded. "Thanks Pierre! I'll be in touch with you believe me." Everyone exchanged parting greetings and hand shakes and most were now on their perspective ways home.

Clint, Chantel, Dale, Diana, Will, Bob, Betty, Bart and Brooke, were going to spend the night at Bart and Brooke's rented house. They had all made prior plans to head for Leadville for the evening. While on the way to Colorado's Mountain College campus they passed herds of white tail deer with gorgeous racks along the mountains sharp sloping evergreen forested trails.

Bart told everyone that. "Leadville is an old wild west mining town with views of the rugged weather augmented terrain of Mt Massive and Mt Albert two of Colorado's highest peaks along the Continental Divide." Brook said. "Nature trails were established along some Billy goat paths."

This gang of colleagues planned to take a hike the next day on a three hour trail trip. Signs for trail designations were arranged to guide everyone in and out. Signs posted all the do's and don't along the hiking trail. They were reminder's for a clean natural environment.

Bart talked about the trail hike to Clint. "If you pack anything up the trail make sure you pack it out."

Brook described "The spectacular view of the Colorado Rockies will make an excellent field experience."

Young Dale excited. "I can't wait!"

Bart and Brooke attended a Wilderness Studies Program at the Leadville campus. Brook admitted. "I love the natural settings of the mountains." The goals and curriculum were tailor fit for both of them. The study atmosphere was different than any traditional city campuses.

Mountain and Canyon Orientation, Snow shoeing, Rock climbing, White water Rafting, Outdoor skills, environmental studies. This was a smart and different choice for today's kids. Bart said. "Awareness of the environment is needed to balance the high tech society taking us into the 21st century."

Will exclaimed. "The state of Colorado has the right idea, when they made the all inclusive Timberline campus at the Colorado Mountain college."

Brook filled in. "The new resident halls and classrooms are in a spectacular location. Seminar and conferences are held year around."

Bart continued. "The state of Colorado has a lot of unique choices for learning at this campus."

Bob contended. "Mountain biking has flourished everywhere."

As a golden eagle was soaring overhead Clint decreed. "It sure has! Since I've been coming out here to see Betty and you."

Bob and Betty where avid mountain bikers and often took trips of several hundred miles over a few day period camping out with several hundred fellow bikers on prearranged trips. At times a van followed the mountain bikers fixing and assisting the bikers if they had flats or needed other repairs.

Bart while standing on a peaked rock depicted. "Around here we usually head north out of Leadville toward Tennessee pass to the biking and hiking trails. We'll sit out at night around the camp fire after we hike up to the crest."

Clint while standing on a peak leaped from one peak to another. They all gathered at the summit in a walled open rock shelter with a commanding view. You could see thunder clouds thousands of feet below rolling through the atmosphere.

Will after trailblazing another three thousand feet in altitude divulged. "We'll only be able to smoke very small amounts of marijuana, because of high altitude conditions and physical activities."

Clint with the vast view of the valley's gorges of the mountains disclosed. "Really I'm just glad to find some air at these altitudes." The high elevations and excruciating exercise of long distance mountain bike riding, won't permit heavy smoking for any leaves of tobacco or marijuana. Very little is consumed on this Saturday night evening for this mountain crowd.

Bart cleared the air. "The high elevations are tough enough for breathing the air alone, if you are not accustomed to the high elevations." as they hiked passed the tall trees along the snow covered ground of the mountain trail. They passed signs posted along the wilderness trails that say. "Pack it in! Pack it out!" meaning everything including refuge.

Clint professed. "Fun's fun, but mountain bike riding is an endurance test for most."

After hiking, biking, camping out close to the campfire on the Colorado Continental Divide, the rush ski trip from Houston for Clint and Chantel was ending the next day.

Clint and Chantel drove by herded "Elk Meadow" on their way up to spend their last "Rocky Mountain High" night in Evergreen at Bob and Betty's, before flying out of Denver the following morning. They had the special "Keystone Canyon Bedroom" with it's hemp sheeted king size antique brass bed. Clint told Chantel on the trip back to Houston. "What an action packed four day excursion."

Clint and Chantel were now invigorated to face Houston's finest's dirty tactic's. Clint had only one plan, fight fire with fire and may the best man win.

Clint never had a doubt about the outcome. His inner faith kept him motivated for a political fight, where he knew he was right. Clint expounded. "My philosophy is they won't be hard to beat, not their downright dirty discriminatory laws!"

When they landed in Houston. Miles picked Clint and Chantel up at the airport. Clint crowed. "Mile's!"

Miles responded. "Hi! Morgan's staff is having a meeting, and asked if you would attend?"

Clint asked. "Sure but when?"

Miles conferred. "Now!"

Chantel agreed to go back to the farm by herself in the family truck, which was still in the airport parking lot. Miles drove Clint straight to the meeting at Morgan's office.

Upon entering the office, Morgan's secretarial staff headed by Melanie was doing research of civil rights abuses. Clint said. "Hi Melanie."

Melanie greeted. "Hi, Clint how was your trip to Colorado?"

Clint responded. "Fantastic" and further said. "What's going on here today?"

Melanie divulged. "The staff is doing investigative searches, on how many wrong homes were raided in this country. We have found out about twelve wrong homes raided. The some victims of these wrong raids were hospitalized. Their lives were traumatized by the masked men in the last few weeks."

Clint implied. "That's a lot accidents. It's evident that there are major flaws in police conduct."

Melanie induced. "Needless to say the norm for all these wrong raids is another civil settlement out of court." Morgan walked into the conference room and said. "Hi Clint" Morgan would then went on immediately to explain to Clint. "These cowboy cops were at the wrong house, victimizing responsible citizens in the wrong way and act like it's O.K! It's part of doing business, just a common mistake."

With that in mind Clint responded. "The police department pays monitory compensation quick when they make a mistake like this."

Morgan scorned. "Because of the bad publicity they don't want these cases dragged through the media, they want to sweep it under the rug, again at tax payers expense."

Clint filled in. "Yep! They want to hush it up." Another law student, named Bill, stopped by for the meeting and said. "Police broke down the door of a forty year old lady, sprayed her dogs with Mace, and after they searched the place they found no drugs. The police department attributed the warrant a water meter reader man, who admitted calling the police after he smelled marijuana.

The repairman later noted. "The police overreacted! I only called them because I smelled marijuana and I thought I seen one growing in her basement." As it turned out the plant was nothing more than an imported fern from Australia. Needless to say with this flimsy evidence like that they can knock your door down."

Morgan explained. "That lady ought to get a good lawyer and hold the water reader man and his company accountable."

Bill reassured. "Oh, she is."

Lorrie another secretary on Morgan's staff said. "A week prior one family in Detroit alleged the police broke down their door in another wrong raid. The cops were horrified the family dog's barking, that was trying to protect the

111

family's home. The police officer shot the dog twice. The house pet ended up dying in front of the lady of the house, Mrs. Brown. The family pet was a Black Labrador Retriever trying to protect Mrs. Brown."

Clint reasoned. "The family dog had more of a right to be there in the that house than the cops."

Lorrie continued. "Mrs. Brown was handcuffed and hog tied, belly down, as was her husband Bertrum and her two teenage children Leia, and Linda. The police would not let the victims of this wrong raid talk until after they find out they had goofed again which seems to be normal police practice for these drug raids. And after a thorough and intense search by the police officers, no drugs were found, the house was indeed the wrong house."

Morgan persisted. "Your right Clint. That dog had more right to be there than the cops."

Lorrie continued. "The dog was doing his job of protecting the home for his owners. The veteran police officer Barret, who shot the dog with two twelve gauge slugs to the head is on administrative leave. Another law suit for a wrong house drug raid was to be settled out of court."

Morgan proclaimed. "The house next door was the one planned to be raided. All this because somebody said they smoked marijuana on the porch."

Various researchers at Morgan's round table discussions for freedom were giving different true scenarios and a synopsis of police mistreating citizens in conducted raids gone wrong. Explanations by the police. "We didn't know, we made a mistake."

Melanie asked. "I thought ignorance was no excuse?" Each constitutional and civil rights researcher exclusively confined their research to a specific subject area.

One of staff would talk about the crooked cops doing and selling drugs and they then would conducted raids with the idea of corruption and self interest. All subject matter and infringements on the civil rights of the innocent victims in the drug war were thoroughly hashed over at this round table meeting.

Clint promised. "We are not going to let these police abuses be continually swept under the carpet." After his staff prepared a synopsis of these improper police raids including Clint's green house, Morgan as promised approached the Attorney General the next day personally.

Morgan specifically wanted police chief, Dick Dirkskin, Ramone and Girt, the leader of the drug squad investigated. Morgan wanted their drug forfeiture fund to be accountable to the Attorney General's office. Morgan said. "I'm writing a letter to the Attorney General and recommending he look into how the drug forfeiture money is being spent."

Clint mentioned. "It doesn't hurt to ask."

Morgan was hoping that after the review the Attorney General would have enough evidence to lead to indictments against these crooked cops. A Grant Jury hearing was the goal and Morgan was now promised an investigation into Girt and company by the Attorney General.

Morgan told Clint later. "The Attorney General, Clifford Clements was not only the man of the hour but was also a man of his word. Girt, the drug squad commander, it was decided would be the easiest to target to look into for the corruption because Girt ran all the drug raid operations in the area. All the dirt stopped with Dirkskin the police chief."

Clint disclosed. "I'm ready to expose these idiots, some victims of drug wars are charged with possession of one ounce of marijuana on a drug raid when, in fact, there were over five pounds confiscated and personally pocketed by Girt."

Morgan professed. "Yea! Another man's home was also ransacked in the process. Jewelry, guns and money were missing after a raid from the guys house. The police promptly said they never saw anything but an ounce of marijuana. That's all the cops charged the victim with. The fine was payable by a quick fine of one hundred dollars and a "See Yea" by the cops later."

Clint counseled. "Internal Affairs investigations always seem to stall with the blue rogue dishonored badge of cop alliance." but the pressure was on from the Attorney generals office for answers to all the corruption allegations.

Morgan noted. "Clifford Clements assigned Rufus Remington to lead an independent investigation into the alleged police corruption. Rufus has an impeccable reputation for digging up the truth the matters on crooked cops. Rufus hates crooked cops. Rufus will do everything in his power to throw them in jail."

Clint ranted. "I like that!"

Morgan's staff in a meeting with his colleges explains the actions by the Attorney General Clement's office, that are now to be taken.

Melanie questioned. "Our concern is how can these cops keep targeting citizens on a consistent basis, ransacking there house, after busting the door down. Then the cops bust the rest of the place up, bust the citizens up, and say it was a mistake. We get the same thing over and over and over across the county. We want to know when is this marijuana drug policy going to be reviewed by somebody with a humanitarian conscience and authority?"

Clint was upset by the slow process, he wanted to bring these crooked cops to jail. "Nothing's ever going to change until the marijuana laws are totally decriminalized. That's why we are taking a stand here today! and asked, "We're all here for a change in the marijuana laws aren't we?" Everybody nodded in unison.

Morgan interjected. "Yes that is the one reason."

Clint pledged. "The government will have to convince me and a whole lot of other citizens differently. We know one thing. All the jails in the world will never stop or contain marijuana smokers. The government keeps filling the jails with marijuana smokers, then the guards sell them marijuana in the jail. They'll have to convince me through education if they want change. Nobody's perfect without flaws, but threaten me or throwing me in jail won't work with me or a whole lot of other people in this society. People in this country will always rebel for freedom and civil rights."

These constitutional meetings were kept on a professional level. You smoked pot before the meetings or after. The rule was no drinking booze, smoking of tobacco or marijuana products during the meetings.

Morgan looked to his secretary and said. "We're all here for a final push for sanity in these marijuana drug laws. Small amounts of marijuana whether possession or sales or use, should be legalized. Unlicensed larger amounts would still unlawful with our plan because these people are known as enterprisers. Enterprisers of larger amounts of marijuana should be regulated and taxed."

Clint appraised. "They are not just marijuana users, now, they are marijuana enterpriser's."

Morgan depicted. "They'll have to pay a tax or suffer the consequences of jail. None of us are here for the legalization of hard drugs. Although we need to look at the way the hard drug war is going. My staff is looking at the **"Manual of Marijuana Fair Laws"** an agenda for marijuana reform. One of the collage students brought the draft in. All of us are in the fight to rid our streets of hard drugs. None of us want our friends or our kids on hard drugs."

Clint explained. "None of us want to be violated for small amounts of marijuana. None of us want harsher penalties for such small amounts of marijuana on our citizens. Having the cops and their informants running around on a witch hunt, peering behind bushes and looking into someone's house to see if they are smoking a joint of marijuana is wrong and a total waste of tax payers money. Citizens being labeled criminal for nothing more than a type of smokeable preference."

Don a reporter at the meeting informed. "If they locked everybody up who smoked pot, they would have to take the equivalent of twenty states in our country out of fifty and lock everyone up. At that point it'll take another ten states of people to keep the other twenty two states caged and incarcerated and another ten states of people will be on welfare leaving the other ten states to work to pay for the whole show of putting all marijuana smokers in jail."

Clint asked. "What is this all coming down to? Is that they want it to comes down to devastation of personal liberty? We can't let this government's foolish marijuana propaganda frenzy continue."

Committed reporter Don explained about another raid. "The police officers fired weapons at each other because unknown to them. There were two separate drug investigations in this raided drug house being conducted at the same time. One by the DEA, one by the police department. Cops on both sides of the spectrum of law enforcement had no knowledge of the others. Both groups were in the drug house and in the midst of the raid ended up shooting and killing two of their fellow officers executing a warrant. Automatic weapons fired by the officers show little discretion for any innocent victims of the drug wars. One team went ahead of the other team during the search of the premises and had no idea the DEA undercover police informants were in the drug house as well."

Clint lashed out. "That's the real world!" and asked, "Can't we deal with it better? Let's get real!"

The informative reporter Don conveyed. " A Vietnam vet was living out in the middle of the woods for over twenty years and was going through some hard times. He was confronted by drug police officers. The decorated vet had saved the lives of his fellow soldiers in many of his battlefield firefights. The vet was suspected of marijuana possession. The vet freaked out opened up on the approaching masked drug officers. After the ensuing gun battle, the ex-Vietnam veteran laid dead."

His mother stated. "All he wanted to do was to be left alone. Cops didn't have to go up there in the middle of the woods and incite him by knocking the door down to his cabin." Our government should never abandon the men and women who served without question. I despise all the politicians and police officials who trade fair resolve for infested glory. What the cops did to that man was down right cowardly."

Clint a Vietnam Vet himself belabored. "This guy was trained by the government to go kill North Vietnamese people half way around the world when he was nineteen years old. Part of his training was singing in the morning "I want to go to Vietnam I wanna kill some Vietcong," during his morning five mile run before breakfast. Left! Right! Left! The sergeant counted off. The troops counted off in cadence afterwards. Left Right Left The government trained this man to kill along with a multitude of others. This guy lived with all the war gory glory memories, and still try and carry out a normal life."

Don depicted. "This man was given medals for gone deeds done for his country, now the country he fought for has turned it's back on him attacked him like they trained him to do to the North Vietcong. The police aggressors of the afternoon showed no remorse the following day in the media. They claimed the Vietnam Vet was an illegal drug user who resisted arrest."

Clint appraised the government's position. "So death by the government is the final solution for marijuana smokers."

Morgan stressed. "It seems to me a guy smoking pot in the middle of the woods ought to be left alone."

Clint asked. "Why the government has to go root him out of the woods? It's is beyond me. This guy had a wife and three kids. Those kids will never have a father again. Whether he was a pot smoking father or not, he was their father."

Don continued. "The cops involvement was again forceful". Don being a Vietnam Vet himself said. "The government sent us as teen agers to Vietnam so their buddies could get rich, while our buddies died. You wanna talk about what the government does to kids. It feeds them all the cigarettes and booze until they want and more. Then they send them to a war, where they give you more alcohol and cigarettes. Then when you return to the United States the government laws dictate your not old enough to drink alcohol after your year tour of Vietnam. A hypocritical government isn't much of a government." Don in a very opinionated manner stated. "They can just leave my kids alone!"

Clint groused. "Yes! They can definitely leave my me kids alone after hearing about the Bill Barker family!"

Morgan said. "Really!"

Don lectured. "In another media fiasco a football player's cousin that was killed by the police in a so-called drug stop? The police stated the man's appearance indicated he was high on drugs and for whatever reasons, this victim ended up handcuffed and beat to death." As everyone listened intently Don continued. "He then died suddenly in police custody and the autopsy proved the man was drug free. His cousin, an NFL football player, is following up with an investigation and a law suit."

Morgan protested. "These police targeted this man for a pull-over because of his profile. Him being black and in a luxury car!"

Karen walked onto the conference room and over hearing the conversation says. "These police do not know if a pull over victim has a chronic medical condition or not. The pulled over victim could be on prescription drugs as well. Prescription drugs is the sixth leading killer in the United States. People on prescription drugs, who get pulled over may be impaired with the slightest struggle. It doesn't take much of a struggle to kill them with any type of physical infraction. The sixth leading killer in the United States is prescription drugs. They are on record to killing more people a year than car accidents and all illegal drugs combined."

Clint fumed. "I don't see any political fronts fighting those outrageous statistics."

Morgan confessed. "And, a lot of these cop infractions with citizens aren't minor mistakes. These cops enjoy putting their hands, flashlights and clubs on citizens with the intent of causing pain and injury to their victims. They want to see if all the police fighting techniques they've been taught in class really work the same way as they were trained. Hit him hard in the knee and watch him buckle."

Clint induced. "It seems that when some of these cops pull you over their intent is to search and hurt citizens. Some of these cops are in relentless pursuit of creating new criminals for promotions and enriching the court system. They have no remorse for innocent victims. They know the citizen victim is innocent, but they still want a hard run at them."

Don firmly contended. "Blacks seem to get pulled over eighty percent more than white people. They are then searched by the drug squads more often. The cops deny using racial profiles but the proof of the matter is they do. Profiles include fancy hair do's, fancy cars, outlandish apparel, people carrying pagers, cell phones, or lot of expensive jewelry seen on minority men."

Morgan informed. "The cops say the large number of searches on minorities are just a coincidence. These profile check points violate the fourth Amendment with illegal search and seizure tactics. Different looking citizens going down the street are not a criminal and should not be treated as such."

Clint explained. "There are a lot of other people not willing to give up their individual freedom of rights because of the governments fanatical marijuana drug wars."

Morgan disclosed. "I know, I don't want my tax money spent on law enforcement chasing marijuana users. I don't want it spent on illegal drug raids or these unconstitutional herb stings against citizens for small amounts of marijuana. Hard alcohol which is legal is proven to be a much worse as a recreational substance."

Karen is one of the medical bio-tech students at the University. Karen is a volunteer for the ACLU on weekends. Karen has taken up the civil liberties issues and studies police privacy invasions statistics. Along with police promoted procedures having been implemented such as drug testing in the work place said. "Being forced to pee in a bottle is a gross invasion of personal privacy, and self incrimination. Hair samples, finger nails, blood samples, mouth swabs, and many more tests being demanded and sold for someone's profit at some one else's expense is ludicrous."

Clint asked. "What kind of mentality does it take for an all out war on marijuana users? All drugs are not the same. We shouldn't test anyone for marijuana. Marijuana is not heroin. I could see testing for hard drugs. I can't see testing for marijuana, unless your working in a highly sensitive area. But then even tobacco or alcohol would not be allowed, compensation should be required by the employers for employees."

Morgan questioned. "How much further are we going to go to lower our standards on freedom and dilute the constitution?"

Mike attested. "All major corporations are testing for drugs now."

Clint expounded. "You mean marijuana personal use fishing expeditions that are conducted automatically by employers and probation departments."

Karen reiterated. "What these companies are doing isn't right. What a person does in the privacy of his home on the weekend should have no bearing about the work he does during the work week."

Clint claimed. "Work performance will not suffer. Needless to say it's for nobody else to judge, including corporations or government on how somebody spends their leisure."

Morgan lashed out. "I agree!"

Dedicated Don enounced. "On ninety-nine percent of the jobs out there, there shouldn't be any problem if someone smokes pot. The other one percent of the jobs the employer can compensate their workers who they want to give up their rights not to smoke marijuana."

Morgan illustrated. "These workers who work in sensitive areas of our industrial complex in government would be the people who work in nuclear plants, have high security clearances in our government, are police officials in highly sensitive areas or medical staff doing operations."

Don conveyed. "It will be up to the worker to maintain the stringent guidelines he has agreed too!"

Clint advised. "They should be compensated for giving up their rights."

Igor walked into the meeting and over heard the conversation and interjected. "I know me and my boys burn an eye opener every morning before we start our job. It seems to make the day go by better and our workers are happier and work harder. I'd rather see them burn one than drinking a beer or whisky or doing any hard drugs which we don't allow on our jobs anyway. Anything more than a marijuana cigarette we don't like drinking alcohol until after work. It can be to much of a detriment."

Clint divulged to Igor. "I agree! Your right!" Everybody agreed that they would organize all the facts and figures for graphs and charts later. Melanie was to have them ready in forty-eight hours.

Morgan, Mike and his colleagues wanted to present the facts to the office of Alvin Amos, The Governor along with pleas of leniency in the law for marijuana users. They wanted the corrupt police and government officials to be targeted and eliminated. After all the of facts were analyzed, and they were all exhausted with hearing the endless amount of cop abuses, and all the corrupt cop convincing facts which stacked the round table. They knew there was enough of conspiracy against the citizens' and their rights. The evening was finally adjourned.

Over at the police station Chief Dirkskin standing in his office with Girt demanded. "I want to get something on everybody that is an associated with Clint, on any kind of charge, preferably drug charges.

Dirkskin wanted all those friends of Clint's. He knew that they all smoked. He targeted those marijuana users for his the drug squad for ensuing their arrests. Marijuana drug investigations were being done by who knows who, and tries to implicate anyone of them by searching their cars for anything, a joint, a seed, a stick, a stem. Dirk fumed. "I want to turn the pressure up on all his inner circle."

Officer Larry standing their with Lt. Girt in Chief Dirkskin's notified. "Hey Dick, Clint's brother Tommy is coming home this weekend from college. He usually comes home every other weekend. We'll stop them on I-10 and have Ramone come down to plant a couple of joints in his car if we have too, we'll get a little something on him one way or another." Dick says. "Yeah, that sounds good Larry, that is what I want to do, put the pressure on these guys."

Officer Larry ranted. "I'll get them Dick!"

The next day Tommy is pulling into the Cactus Club with enough weed in the corner of a plastic bag for a joint. As Tommy walked away from his car, he went directly into the Cactus Club. Tommy never locks his door to his car being the trusting soul he his. Larry opened Tommy's car door and looked in his car. Larry saw a half-burned joint in Tommy's ashtray.

Larry went into the bar with the other officers and walked up to Tommy in front of all the other patrons. Larry said. "Tom Cole" Tommy answered. "Yes, sir. I'm Tom."

Larry advised. "We are arresting you for marijuana possession." Tom had enough for a joint of marijuana in a plastic bag in his front shirt pocket as the Officer told Tommy to turn around so he can put cuffs on him. Tommy quickly grabbed the plastic baggy in his shirt pocket and began to swallow the bag. Ramone standing behind Tommy smashes his Billy club over his head.

Larry suddenly grabbed Tommy's head and smashes his forehead into his own knee. Tommy fell to the floor unconscious, where Ramone continually kicked and beat Tommy along with the other officers until the patrons of the bar were screaming. "That's enough! Stop! Your killing him!"

The bartender Bill Becker pulled a shotgun out from under the bar counter. Bill pointed the shotgun at Ramone's head and said. "You hit him one more time, I'm going to blow your head off." Ramone brings back his hand to hit Tommy one more time when he hears the hammer pulled back on Bill's shotgun.

Larry surprised blurted. "Easy Bill, you can go to jail for that."

Bill sized up the situation snarled. "I've got two rounds in this double barrel shotgun. One bullet for you and Ramone, if that boy is hit one more time."

Ramone snapped. "Wait a minute Bill!"

Bill still pointing the shotgun at Ramone proposed. "You hit that boy one more time and I won't mind going to jail, after I blow your head off."

Officer Greg Greathead responded to the radio call and walked into the Cactus Club. Greg seen Ramone holding Tommy's lifeless body by the scruff of his jacket with his other fist clinched and aimed at Tommy's head and roused to Ramone. "Hold it Ramone!"

Ramone looked up surprisingly at officer Greg, hesitates and induced. "OK!" and let go of Tommy dropping him headfirst to the cement floor.

The other cops ceased to hit Tommy. One of the women patrons tried to give first aid medical help to Tommy.

Bill told to the barmaid. "Ginger call an ambulance now." Ginger instantly grabbed the phone and dialed.

Officer Greg explained. "Don't expect me to back you up Ramone. Your all on your own." as he also calls for an ambulance from his radio.

Tommy's whole crime was a misdemeanor for simple marijuana possession payable with a small fine. Tommy was now in the hospital fighting for his life in a comatose state. Police officers stated they did not know Tommy was choking on the bag of marijuana.

The one cop who hit Tommy, and assisted in the arrest stated to Greg. "I came in here after the fact to help in the arrest. I didn't know he was in that condition."

In Clint's opinion that wasn't good enough, the Police were never charged in the incident. Prosecutor's refuse to file charges against the cops.

The newspapers ended up giving the bartender a bravery citation for standing up to the cops and saving what was left of Tommy's remaining life. Dirkskin tried to have the whole incident buried from the media. But even after the internal investigations were done none of the officers were disciplined. The police department refused to release any of the investigative reports.

Mike Moran convinced. "If that isn't killing the life of innocent victims in the marijuana drug wars, I don't know what is." while he was setting in the cyber coffee café the next day near Morgan's downtown office.

Clint had been there to discuss the options of legal reprisals with Mike. Several of his fellow law students are sitting with Mike discussing yesterday's events in the newspaper regarding Tommy. Eventually Mike's legal associate Morgan Motley and Miles, stopped by the cyber coffee cafe to discuss the events of Tommy's civil rights being abused. Clint had E-mailed Morgan's office for an appointment. Mike called and informed Miles on the cell phone.

Mike asked. "What do you think about the story this morning?"

Miles confided. "I can't believe it. Tommy didn't deserve that. He was a good kid."

Mike agreed. "It's pretty sickening."

Miles said. "We can't keep letting the police beat our citizens until they're comatose."

Morgan contended. "Then get away with it! Please talk to Ed?"

Miles agreed. "I'll talk to Ed and we'll do a bigger story in the Chronicle."

Mike asked. "Miles I want you to do me a favor? I want you to go to the hospital and interview everybody on the medical staff. Get statements for the truth of what happened last night. Find out the condition Tommy was when the paramedics arrived. Then stop by the Cactus Club and talk to the patrons, talk to the owners and get the skinny on what really went down there last night. Ask the doctor about the lacerations? See if he will release a medical report to the media on your behalf? Your a reporter! You should have access to a certain amount of information."

Miles cracked. " O.K. Mike, sure. Anything for you guys and Tommy I'll stop by later on this afternoon. He's still at St. Frances' Hospital, isn't He?" Mike replied. "Yep!"

Miles promised. No problem after the interviews, Mike, I'll call you.

Clint still at the cyber coffee cafe disclosed to Morgan. "I can't wait to see what Miles finds out at the hospital. It ought to be interesting."

Morgan reassured. "That's for sure!"

Clint proposed getting full background checks and surveillance on Girt, Ramone, Larry, and even Dirkskin. Clint was asking everyone to volunteer and bring in relative, or friends, someone they could trust to help with the counter surveillance on these police drug squad cronies. They were going to start following these cops every move. Clint was going to find out what makes these guys tick with a little help from his friends. This was now an all out fight to the finish. Clint's brother was dying in the hospital, because of these inhuman guys they call police officers.

Miles interviewed everyone from ambulance drivers, hospital doctors, and nursing staff, to the owners and patrons of the cactus club. Miles headed back to the Morgan's Law office after going to the hospital and the Cactus Club. Miles picked up Clint at the cyber coffee cafe instead. Miles asked Clint. "Go back with me to the Cactus Club? I want you to talk to the patrons themselves."

Clint decided to go back with Miles to the Cactus club to interview Bill the bartender and some of the patrons who may be there. Miles wanted Clint to hear first hand the disturbing news about the prior days beating of his brother

Tommy. Clint couldn't believe the cold blooded and callous beating his brother received by these so-called police officers.

Miles stated. "These guys, police officers are hired in the community to be peace officers not to be gangsters."

Bill told Clint and Miles about Tommy. "They flat out weren't going to stop until I made them stop."

Chico who was in the bar having a beer at the time confided to Clint. "I hate all cops, I don't trust any of them and I never will! I hope they all get exposed for what they really are and they all lose there jobs."

Miles explained. They're some good ones." as Officer Greg now walked into the club to do a follow up report.

Chico seeing Greg fumed. "What are you here for to beat up on some tax paying citizens?

Greg deplored. "No and I'm sorry for what happened to Tommy."

Chico confronted. "I'll bet you are," as he stepped closer eye to eye with Greg.

Bill conceded. "Chico give him a break! Greg helped stop them rogue cops."

Clint interjected. "What's on your mind Greg."

Officer Greg conferred to Miles and Clint. "Can I talk to you guys privately at the rear tables of the club?

Clint and Miles look at each other and then Clint turned to Greg and agreed. "Sure" as they all waked back and sat down.

Officer Greg explained. "Look Miles this is off the record but I'm telling you both on the QT that I don't like a lot of what I see on the drug squad. Most of the narc's I work with smoke pot. The rest drink alcohol. I've seen more of my police colleagues destroyed by alcohol. I have never seen one destroyed by marijuana. I wish they'd legalize marijuana because there is no way people are ever going to stop using it. When I make arrests I never have to fight a marijuana stoner. After twelve years on the squad I've only had to fight harden criminals, drunks or a hard drug user's adrenaline. We could fight hard drugs that much more aggressively once marijuana is made legal."

Miles jabbed. "That's the most sense any cop ever made to me in my entire life."

Clint conceded. "Until now I was thinking like Chico was ten minutes ago. I'm glad to know there a little heart left in the police department for the cannabis citizens."

Greg contended. "There's other's but we can't say anything because of our positions."

Miles professed. "I realize that!"

Greg defined. "I'll tell you one more thing. Watch Ramone I hear he's trying to set you up. I don't know the full details but I will keep you guys informed of any conspiracy. I'd let internal affairs handle it, but I'm afraid whatever there into, they're in it altogether."

Clint reassured. "Thanks Greg for all your help."

Greg again maintained. "I'm sorry about your brother. I hope he recovers."

Clint rehashed. "Thanks" again to Greg as Miles and Clint head back to the front of the club.

Clint stated to Bill. "Thanks for stopping them cops Bill. I can't thank you enough for taking a stand in saving my brothers life."

Bill clarified. "If you needed me to testify I'll be glad to."

Clint again said. "Thank you very much again!" as they walked out the door.

With that Miles and Clint headed back to Clint's farm, wondering if they would ever see justice or if Tommy was ever going to regain consciousness. Tommy had a serious closed head injury in addition to broken ribs and a punctured lung.

Rudy was in the kitchen with Chantel talking about Tommy. Chantel had just hung up the phone from the hospital to see if there was a change in his condition.

When Clint walked in Chantel gave him an update on Tommy's medical condition. Rudy told Clint. "I'm sorry to hear about Tommy, I hope he fully recovers."

Chantel aired. "Thanks Rudy."

Rudy explained. "Maria and I are having a bond fire party this week end. We've had it planned for awhile. We already have relatives, and friends coming in from out of town."

Clint shocked with everything happening disclosed. "Chantel and I will talk it over. Thanks for inviting us. We want to see how Tommy is first before we decide."

Rudy sympathized. "I understand"

The free spirited friends were itching to get together at Rudy and Maria's large house set back on a couple of hundred acres. An ideal spot for the party they were about to throw. Rudy and Maria's place was way out of the away. Nobody had a right to complain if people got loud and loaded. Everybody was looking for a cheer up from the stress letting out some wholesome harmless anxieties.

The cannabis caravan of pot partiers was on their way to the party stoned. They were rolling down a desolate part of the highway on the fringe of the desert in high gear. Rudy's Brother Jerry never made it past the city limits before he was pulled over by the cops.

Jerry wasn't drunk or drinking but the cop on a drug search of Jerry's car found a marijuana roach in his ash tray. The cops threw him in jail. While he was being booked the cops roughed him up dislocating Jerry's shoulder.

Brother Big (no relation just a nickname) rode shotgun in Brother Jerry's car, when they were pulled over by the police. Big had asked Jerry for a ride out to Rudy's party. Jerry obliged.

Brother Big ended up driving Jerry's pick up into a farmer's field earlier in the day. Big told Jerry he was going on a beer run. Big went into a farmers field and picked a pick up load of field corn from some farmer unbeknown to him. Big then took all the field corn to a busy intersection in Houston and sold all the corn as sweet corn. One customer a black man from Alabama, Questioned Big. The man said in his slow southern draw. "Are you sure that's sweet corn? That's some awful big ears for sweet corn."

Big immediately reeled off. "Oh Ya! I just bought all that sweet corn fresh today from the sweet corn farmer." Big would always have a follow up to his customers as he counted his money hand over fist from the corn sales.

Big would put his money in his pockets on the front of his farmers bibs, then grab an ear of corn peel back the husk and gobble up a few bits for the customer to see. Big would then said. "MMM mmmm That's dam good sweet corn" and continue to sell and eat the field corn.

The Alabama man then bought three farmers dozen of corn from Big. Big wanted to buy some cheap whisky, beer, and a bag of marijuana. Big always knew how to get somebody else's money.

Big was now driving Brother Jerry's pick up truck. Big took a set of Jerry's car keys out of Jerry's dresser earlier in the day. Since Jerry's pick up got towed, Big decided to hitch a ride with the tow truck driver after the cop cuffed and hauled Jerry off to jail.

Big loitered at the tow yard. When the tow truck attendant was busy Big quickly drove off with Jerry's truck and preceded to go to the party. Lighting up a big green joint up on to the party.

Rudy saw Big pull in Jerry's pick up said to Maria. "Big is so Big he can stash a forty once beer, a quarter pound weed, water bong pipe and a stack of rolling papers in the front of his farmers bibs, and you'd never know it".

Maria griped. "In his back pocket he carries his fifth of whisky, he's a wild and deranged kind of guy."

Rudy informed. "Make sure we keep an eye on him tonight. Brother Big is a sponging, scamming con man. Big is somebody you absolutely can't trust even if you were watching him straight on. He is over four hundred and fifty pounds on hoof, and he can eat a ton food in one sitting."

Big found out about Rudy's Party from the Bar. Big was never one to miss a party. Big knew how to invite himself anywhere. Big was just one of those kind of guys. Some one you'd like to lock up with Dirk, Girt, Ramone, Larry and company.

A semi truck driver Tracy and his girl friend Lucy were hauling the musical and stage equipment for the band to Rudy's party. Tracy was looking out his semi-tractor window and into the window of the Motor home going down the road in the next lane and said. "Wow Lucy Look! Look at all the partygoers in the back of the motor home. They have an orgy going on. Body paints and all." Tracy was freaking out on them. Lucy said. "Come on with it!" pointing at the partygoers while Tracy kept rolling down the road.

Lucy was riding to the party with him in the big truck. They were playing Tracy's new CD. "Ride along." as Lucy was rocking the semi's seat.

Lucy being young and liberated raved. "Lets party with them when we get to the party."

The caravan of vehicles continued to roll toward the party grounds. Lead by a pack of Harley Davidson's, and some with lady filled side cars. They were followed by another groups of on the road or off and road bikers. When ever the hot dog road riders could they would run their motor bikes down the highway one the rear wheel. Just to see who could go down the road the fastest and furthest on their rear wheel. When you see a dozen riders hot dogging down the road for miles up on end, it's a thrill.

Tracy railed to Lucy. "This is quite a treat!"

Lucy razzed. "I love it. Look there's Frankie." Frankie Free Style at one point was way ahead of the group when an on coming car passed an on coming semi-truck. Frankie Free Style had no choice with two on coming vehicles coming straight at him but to drive right in between them. All while going down the highway on one wheel at eighty mph.

Tracy admired. "Look at Margo she's right on his tail!

"Margo Motto" as she's known in the Motto circuit was close behind Frankie, while they passed the semi-truck and car. Margo was Frankie's only serious competition at the Motto track. Margo also rode on her rear wheel only, while flying done the highway on her motor bike.

Rudy was glad nobody was hurt to badly on all these motor bike stunts. Manny rode with Chico in his old 70's era Cadillac El Dorado. Richard their friend tried to follow road riders down the highway in 68 Mustang, while his wife Mary smoked a joint and tried to video tape the bike stunts. Richard paid more attention to his wife video taping and ran through a construction barrier, and nearly ran over a construction worker.

Mary screamed. "Watch out Richard!" as the construction barriers demolished and mangled the front of their Mustang.

Manny glanced. "Look over there Chico. The construction worker had to dive out of the way for his life."

Chico eyeballed. "That worker is laying on his back in a pile of rubble."

Manny gawked. "He looks unhurt though. Thank God."

Chico blinked. "I can't believe that! Richard doesn't smoke or drink."

Manny focused. "He's just a naturally nuts!"

Clint, Aaron, and Igor joined in the race with their 60's vintage corvettes. Red, White, and Blue were the colors of the 63' 66' 67'corvettes dressed in their chrome wheels. They typically stopped their corvettes on the Highway and burned rubber on take off then run hard from that point on. Every few miles the corvettes would stop. They did this over and over when there was no on coming traffic on the way to Rudy's house.

Teens were also racing their cars or whatever daddy gave them down the highway. Their custom painted "Low Rider Trucks and Cars" raced to the finish. Everyone was in a mad dash down this desolate part of the highway as fast as they could. Most of Rudy's crowd were all race car people and associates.

All on the way to Rudy and Maria's house. The drive was an ultimate rip roaring build up to the racing event that Rudy and his friends had arranged. Clint was the first to reach Rudy's yard party in his 63' corvette. "I won the race" Clint yelled to Rudy who was standing in the driveway by his own fancy car.

Rudy's Bahama Blue Bomber was parked out side at the front of his long driveway. Caribbean Cruiser was air brushed in bright lettering on the sides. The lettering "Make It Happen" was airbrushed on the rear of the Blue Bomber Hot Rod. You couldn't miss the only driveway with that type of land mark on the road.

Rudy and Maria wanted to throw a bash for some light hearted fun. They wanted to enlighten everyone's mood from all the troubling events that were unfolding.

Rudy's son Marty had set up a skate board platform. Marty had a ton of friends from school who came over on a regular basis and used the skate board platform. Marty wanted to get into the ski board competition in the next Olympics.

Marty was thrilled when his father Rudy had his Canadian connections invite the current ski board champion from Canada and a few others from that crowd who compete in ski boarding competition. Come for the week end. Marty had to try his new hemp skate board, and get skate board training on a professional level. Skate boarding is similar to ski boarding in respect to balance. Skate boarding in the summer was a good tune up for winter ski boarding.

There was an area out back where Igor and Rudy had put together motto runs a week earlier. Igor had all the bull dozing equipment brought in. Igor ran his excavating equipment while smoking a hoot on and off. The grader ended up perfecting a terrain of hills, and motto run valleys and carved in the terrain into a competition track for the Motto runs. Motto Riders were invited from everywhere. Groups of four wheelers drove the motto track down for the competition.

Chris's pastime was Motto Running with groups of friends. Hundreds were usually at his competitions. Chris invited forty or fifty Motto-runners to spiff up this extensive party's attractions.

Chris exhorted Rudy. "Wait until you see my friend "Frankie Free Style. He can really wear some shock absorbers out!" Free styling Frankie loved riding eighty mph on the rear wheel of his on the road off the road bike while accelerating lighting fast down the highway.

Chris boasted to Rudy while they both sat in Chris's Ford Expedition sporting an overhead lit bar and a rounded chrome front end grill. "I guarantee Free Style will win the Free styling event of the competition."

Rudy exclaimed. "Yea! I've seen him ride. Frankie is at the top of his game."

They intended on having a motto bike Free Styling Event. The motto bikes would do stunts of various types while jumping thirty foot off the ground. After a run straight up the projection ramp his motto bike flew in mid air over a fifty foot length of fire ten feet high.

The motto riders position and stunt movements such as lifting one leg over the gas tank and back in mid air over the blazing fire in front of the audience in the bleachers, who cheered when the bike touched down.

Frankie Free Style usually screamed like a wild man, while lifting his leg over the gas tank in mid air in front of the gasping crowd. Three jumps apiece by twelve motto free style riders of the motto event was to be based on the creative criteria.

The finale came down to two riders for the last free style jump. Mikie Motto and Frankie. Chris watched the Motto races on the sideline with Clint and Chantel and said. "Frankie's gonna win!"

Chantel dazed. "He's phenomenal!"

Clint surprised. "I believe it, that guy's remarkable!"

Chris responded sharply. "He's dam good!" The crowd roared with excitement and amazement with every jump Frankie Free Style made. On Frankie Free Style's winning jump the bike lifted off the ground into mid-air over the flaming cars below. The bike while Frankie negotiated the landing on the platform flipped head over end with Free Style slamming him into the ground in between the tumbling motto bike.

The crowd went to a silent gasp while Frankie lay on the ground next to the running bike. Frankie suddenly jumped up and the crowd roared now that they knew Frankie wasn't hurt.

The winner of the event was Free Style Frankie. Free Style usually always won. Other competitors jumping couldn't match this motto riding dare devils ability. The Motto Bike Dare Devil had a good attitude to boot.

Frankie always cracked. "I'd rather be a Dare Devil than belong to the DARE Program." Frankie always burned a few, and didn't mind who knew it. Clint said to Chantel. "I like that cocky kid."

Chantel chuckled. "Yes! He sure is exciting and spunky."

The TV commentators who followed Frankie's every sure shot jump said. "Frankie certainly is exciting and fascinating to watch, "Free Style" has jumped canyons in the outback, forty limousines, and has met most riding challenges."

Chris popped. "You never know what his next stunt will be."

A cement drag strip was also set up on the old small abandon air strip near the back of Rudy and Maria's property. Weird Willy as he is known to his friends was the first to take a vehicle down the track for the partying audience. Manny said. "Look at that messy mad man! He's driving that snowmobile down the cement track as fast as he can, while eating live sardines and outfitted in a red, white, and blue spandex suit on."

Rudy gasped. "Sparks are flying from the bottom of the snowmobile everywhere," as Weird Willy's snowmobile raced down the track. The audience laughed profusely at Weird Willy.

Marty who helped his dad organize the party of road racers told Igor. "Race Cars participating in the event have numbers on the sides of their race cars for identification."

Igor scanned the track. "Looks like there already for nine hours of straight drag runs." Marty said. "Ya, the race car participants are camped over night in a wooded area of the property."

Clint stressed. "Everyone is talking about the twilight featured race between the Gear Heads VS the Motor Heads."

Igor responded. "Those two groups of race cars are sponsored by two different groups of automotive businessmen. These two groups of businessmen usually compete six times against each other in a race season."

Manny talked with Clint and the boys on the side lines said. "That's one brave man, everyone calls Fender, he stands in front of the race cars at the beginning of the race track."

Somebody from the audience yelled out "Hey Fender bender bumper jumper."

Manny continued. "Fender does a jumping jack on the race track in front of and in between both Race cars. The race cars then barrel down the track. Burning rubber and fish tailing out of the hole right past Fender."

Rudy implied. "Fender will have to do the best he can to get out of the way, if one of those cars fish tail."

Manny later stated. "They call him Fender because he was hit by so many fender's as the cars came out of the hole."

Clint conferred. "Look at the wine bottle on the pavement in front of him and ten foot in front of the race car." Fender then came down off his jumping Jack cadence, both race cars would burn out past Fender down the track.

The Two Race Cars that were opening the event proceeded down the track at high speeds. Hemp parachutes popped out the race car tails near the end of the track slowing the cars down.

Manny noticed. "There's a lot of lady drivers in this racing event".

Rudy portrayed to Clint. "Some of the race car drivers wife's finally get to live out their life long dream. They get to drive the family race car in their first semi pro competition down a real drag strip."

Manny persisted "That's cool Rudy!"

Clint explained. "In a couple of heats one race driver let his seventeen year old daughter race another sixteen year old girl down the track."

Chico walked up and said. "Hey, Clint Rudy even had bleachers brought in and set up on the sidelines for all the people that were attending."

Manny proclaimed. "Rudy thought of every thing."

Clint rattled. "I wish Tommy could be here."

Rudy admitted. "We all do to Clint"

Marty remarked to Clint. "A Hemp Sponsor from Canada brought a Hemp Jet Car. The Hemp Jet Car burns Hemp Rocket Fuel, which burns much cleaner and stronger."

Clint asked. "How do you know all that Marty?"

Marty answered. "My dad told me."

Rudy mustered. "Once the Hemp Jet Rocket Car ignites in the darkness of the night. The ground will shake no matter were you stand, the flames thrusting backwards from the Hemp Rocket Car."

Marty asserted. "The sound of that rocket car is powerfully loud."

Rudy holding his ears screamed. "Once off of the starting line the Hemp Rocket Car can make it down the track in three seconds. The parachutes pop out half way down the track to stop the Hemp Jet Rocket Car while it goes down the straight away."

Maria informed. "The majority of the Hemp Jet Rocket Car was built with Hemp products. The Hemp fiber formed panels are similar in appearance to fiber glass stock, and made with a non toxic industrial process."

Rudy explained. "The car is bright red in appearance with fancy flame air brushing painted with non toxic hemp paints on it's side of the Hemp Jet Rocket Race Car."

Maria rehashed. "Rudy set up this event through meeting people while he was DJ-ing a Race car event in Dallas."

Clint looked at the rocket race car and told Rudy. "I like the Hemp Rocket car the best."

Maria observed. "Everybody is talking about the rally tonight, it's growing from a party to a small rally of protesters."

Clint reeled off to Maria. "Great!"

Rudy admitted. "What the growing consensus is from almost all of us, is that the drug task force busts, are often busts in themselves."

Clint maintained. "There's nothing quality about the marijuana drug busts. Making criminals out of hard working citizens because they choose to smoke weed. Get real it's time to stand up." All agreed that the governments way was the wrong way to fight the marijuana war.

Rudy predicted. "Education not criminalisation and respect for other's ways. Period. This is the opinion of the marijuana culture from the people who live in the marijuana culture."

A local rancher donated a large steer to be roasted Texas style before the night's end. Tex Rider was from the Horse Shoe Ranch. His son Wade was in a country band with Tommy. Tex wanted his son Wade and his friends to play in their band known as the Ombres at the parties night cap.

The party turned into a rallying point for Tommy because of the large number of participants that showing up. Chantel tried to console Clint and said. "Sympathizers are gathering in larger numbers to show their support for Tommy".

Clint recognized. "I appreciate that from of our friends and supporters."

Rudy predicted. "More citizen's are gathering and demanding less restrictive laws concerning marijuana."

Manny prophesized. "No restrictive laws or penalties for use and possession of small amounts of marijuana is the feeling among all the people attending the party."

Clint reasoned. "Enough stupidity and repression by the federal government's action's! Enough is enough! The federal law the cops feed off of is what may kill my brother."

Tex knew all them Young Ombres would bring in their crowd. Tex knew they would be burning them hoots and guitar notes. Wade was going to sing "Steer Horns" a song Wade and Tommy wrote. Tommy was the bass player for the group. Tommy's friend Nigel was going to stand in, while Tommy was fighting for his life in the hospital.

Clint told Chantel. "Nigel is a friend of Tommy's from college. Nigel and Tommy were in Musical and Arts class at the college."

Chantel told Clint. "That's nice of Nigel to stand in for Tommy."

Clint admitted to Chantel. "Tex burned some local weed himself in his younger days. And Tex was always one for freedom of expression and freedom of personal choice. Tex respects others for their personal decisions."

Rudy agreeably disclosed. "Tex is a Texas Cowboy from way back. Tex would always say a little local weed never hurt anybody."

Tex responded. "It's also saved many a people's day."

Clint conveyed. "I absolutely agree!"

This day was a perfect union for everyone involved today right down to a perfect closure on this harmonious night. All Clint and Tommy's friends were there to show their support.

Rudy divulged. "Again good times no cops no trouble."

Clint assessed. "Seems like the government don't like anyone to have fun, as soon as you have fun you're branded a criminal."

Rudy agreed. "It's gonna seem that way, until we get the marijuana law changed."

Clint expounded. "They don't want to legalize marijuana because they have to lay off fifty percent of the police departments and change the judicial system for fairness concerning all Americans."

Rudy professed. "I'll bust my tail to get it legal! It's something I believe in."

Clint obsessed. "I'll burn one for the cause."

Rudy laughed. "Do the deed!" as the night was ending.

Chapter 6........ Back at police headquarters, Police Chief Dirkskin was catching wind of the round table meetings, parties and rallies. Dirkskin exceptionally wanted to turn up the heat on Clint and Company.

Dirkskin knew Toby Turner was set up with a little weed stash. Dirkskin knew his drug search warrant would stand, when his drug police force proceeded to execute the warrant.

Dirkskin's told Ramone. "Were going to claim that Turner sold a forty dollar bag of marijuana to the kid from the barrio, Francisco "Gar" Garcia, Right."

Ramone disclosed. "Right, I had Gar place a bag of pot in Mr. Turner's household for evidence, when Gar went over there with the girls."

Dirkskin knew Sheila, Ashley and Lisa went to Turner's trailer with the narc stooge Gar. Ramone says to Dirkskin. "Gar is going to testify he bought weed from Toby on several occasions. Gar needs a reduced sentence for a felony house invasion and rape."

Dirkskin counseled to Ramone. "If Gar testifies that Toby bought the weed, and you or Girt plant that pound of weed in Clint's dresser drawer. Clint will go down, that won't be a problem. I'll arrange Gar's probation with the prosecutor myself."

Ramone divulged. "Gar's the man. He'll do it!"

Dirkskin boasted. "Then, We can legally search Clint's house, his pole barn, his green house, the fields. Then Girt will plant more marijuana in Clint's house to criminalize Clint, while he's cuffed outside".

Ramone explained. "I'll have Larry back Girt up, when the other police agency cops are there."

Dirkskin excited. "Sounds good Ramone." Dirkskin could now put a microscope on anything present at the farm to drum up additional charges against Clint, but this wasn't enough. Dirkskin wanted a last ditch effort to get Clint himself into a Catch 22.

One of the dispatcher's wives was a female police officer, named Marian. She was on the drug squad and Girt was already trying to talk Marian into informing on Clint. Girt told Dirkskin. "Marian will be introduced to Clint through Clint's green house operations as a green house worker in hopes of seducing Clint. We'll try to embarrass him at all levels, at the same time by having a mole in on the round table meeting's."

Dirkskin enthused. "Great Girt!"

However, When Marian approached Clint with the big come on. Marian was getting a little too close at opportune moments, like women do. Marian would discreetly brush her big boobs on Clint as she was carefully carting flats of herbs. Clint finally confided in Manny. "I wouldn't have anything to do with adultery on my wife Chantel. Do something with this dizzy broad. She's getting nosey. Find out what her bag is."

Manny quipped. "Clint I'll get to the bottom of this."

Clint told Manny. "I want to stay clear of her assertive sexual advances."

Manny said. "Yea, well I'm single I'll give that flussie a whirl."

Girt and Marian had decided to go for one of Clint's friends, Manny. And, hopefully Marian could force Manny into an informational encounter about Clint's green house operation, and round table meeting's. Marian told Girt. "Manny helps in the promotional part of the greenhouse business."

All this was arranged to get to at Clint, who was considered a threat. He was political leverage at election time in Dirkskin's eyes. Girt choose Manny for Marian's next target. He was chosen because of his free spirited lifestyle. Over the period of a few weeks Marian and Manny were hitting it off rather well. Their friendship became a little more than a marijuana drug investigation.

Clint had already discussed his suspicions about Marian to Manny. Manny told Clint. "I'm going along with Marian and her inquiring advances. I'm stringing her on."

Manny and Marian were alone after one of the round table meeting's at Manny's apartment. Unbeknown to Marian, Manny had a video camera set up in a bookcase. The video outlook observed the whole area of the living room, including the couch and floor of the living room. The video camera targeted Marian's anticipated arrival. Marian proceeded to get small bits of information about Clint. Manny lead her on. Marian inquired extensively about the greenhouse operations while sexually seducing Manny.

Manny snickered. "Marion! Let's get down on the bear rug."

Marian teased. "I've never did it on a bear rug. Come on Manny" After Manny and Marian were through with their sex capade. They watched another sex video or two. Marion said to Manny. "Do you have any reefer?"

Manny gushed. "I sure do baby!" Marian smoked a few joints in front of the video camera with Manny.

Marian seemed to love smoking the joint's, she continually said to Manny. "Roll another joint."

Manny pledged to Marion. "Sure baby!" In between joints Manny would caressed Marian's big tits, while Marian would bob the knob. When they were done, Marian left the apartment. She met Girt at 2:30 AM and discussed all the information shed discovered.

Meanwhile Police Chief Dirkskin's police thugs in criminal enticement with other county of law enforcement agencies across the country, from New Orleans to New York and beyond. These upholders of the law were traitors to the country. They were also involved in a conspiracy with other government and law enforcement officials to import and transport drugs from the ports of Houston and New Orleans north to Detroit, New York and Chicago. The bandit cops were making heavy hard drug runs. Most of the drugs that were run by these police officials were hard drugs like cocaine and heroin. There was a lot more money involved.

Dirkskin told his associates in the criminal conspiracy. "The cartels money can buy any branch of the any government."

Dirkskin told the new police chief Red Colburn coming into the cocaine courier club. "These hard drugs are coming from the ship Bogatel, straight from Columbia to New Orleans. The captain to the ship hands money to the Customs officers to look the other way when the cocaine is unloaded. All the cops here are involved in running the drugs with us."

Red inquired to Dirkskin. "The Cartel pays for a police escorts to follow the drug mules through their counties and safeguard the drug shipments."

Dirkskin conveyed. "Right, all our drug escorting officers are paid well for escorting the drugs to all points of the country with the help of other officers across the country police escorted county by county."

Ramone told Red. "Other counties in the drug route are in cooperation with the drug escorted shipments. New arrivals of drugs reach the gangs in the major cities on schedule of destination. The cooperating police departments escort the drug shipments the rest of the way for dispersal of shipments by local drug kingpins."

Red discussed. "These drug kingpins have houses which rarely get busted."

Dirkskin explained. "Our police will bust all the rival drug operations. We look the other way for our own sponsored drug houses."

Girt told Red. "Sometimes Ramone and Larry have young girls rounded up on the streets like those locked up in that cellar. After all us guys have fun sexually molesting them. Ramone heavily drugs the girls with heroin and gives them to the ships captain in trade for a couple of kilo's of cocaine for each."

Dirkskin admitted. "Those young girls are molested and raped all the way back to Columbia."

Ramone laughed and disclosed. "Then the captain sells the girls to the drug cartel to be enslaved in the sex camps in the jungle. The only way out is to be carried out." They all laugh and Red said. "What girl can I have?"

Dirkskin roused. "All of them," as they all laugh and grabbed the tormented girls.

Meanwhile Clint and his freedom fighting friends take a stand in the media. Clint vehemently denounced the government's tactics in the marijuana war during an interview with a radio commentator named Macy Rollins.

Clint preached. "Let it be known, that the law for arresting citizens for small amounts of marijuana must be changed," as Clint read his statement over a predominate radio station live.

Macy asked. "Clint what are some of the abuses you see?"

Clint continued. "Men and women are on chain gangs after being arrested, incarcerated, they suffer loss of property for small amounts of marijuana. This is ridiculous and we feel very unconstitutional as well."

Clint proceeded. "I challenge the federal government to respect the Constitution of the United States concerning individual freedoms. The lawmakers will be ousted when all the facts come out concerning their marijuana war.

Other young victims of law enforcement are subjected to cruel abusive behavior in state prisons further being violated by their unconstitutional incarceration. The prison gang rapes and abuse by the guards is never ending. Victims have to fight everyday for survival in prison after being criminalized for possession of three or four joints of marijuana."

Macy remarked. "Jails are filling up with low level marijuana offenders, while high level violent offenders such as murderers and rapists and bank robbers who are being released early because of prison overcrowding."

Clint agreed. "Right, and the heavy hard drug traffickers, and the drug king pens are never caught or apprehended. These are the people who need to be caught."

Macy rehashed. "I can see the government needs to change the way it does drug business. Let these marijuana traffickers bring their marijuana into this country with taxation. Put an end to the violent war".

Clint argued. "In this current drug war, all the money being spent on the drugs leaves the country. Truck loads of money have been leaving this country steadily for years."

Macy predicted. "Through legalization of marijuana by taxation, like it or not, the money from these transactions would steadfastly remain in this country."

Clint professed. "We are sticking up for the responsible people of America. We need responsible laws made by the lawmakers for our lawful and useful citizens. If there is no humanity in the lawmakers they will be no humane laws concerning a citizen's freedom of choice. Laws going against the norms of our culture must cease. We have to restore lost freedoms of choice back to the populace."

Macy a radical radio host favoring the pro marijuana freedom movement continued. "The corruption that belies the incarceration systems with guards delivering not only pot, but cocaine, heroin, antphetimines, barbiturates, women, alcohol, equipment for alcohol stills and more to the prisoners that are incarcerated must stop. Prison guards letting other guards or prisoners abuse prisoners also must stop."

Clint informed. " A Twenty year old female prisoners incarcerated for uttering and publishing was sexually abused by the prison guards. Some women end up pregnant while incarcerated, just like in the prison camps."

Macy explained. "One prison guard, in particular, ignored a prisoner who was dying of an overdose from crack cocaine another guard brought into the prison. The previous guard already beat the hell out of the prisoner. That prisoner begged to the hospital. He stated he was dying from an overdose. The guards laughed and when the paramedics were finally called in, the prisoner had died."

Clint portrayed. "These police abuses are common place and need to be stopped. Some prison guards are now pitting prisoners against prisoners, while guards and other prisoners take bets on the gladiator arranged fights to the death."

Macy professed. "The financial incentive for law enforcement with the current system feeds disaster and descent".

Clint observed. "When government and law enforcement work against everyday responsible citizens. It's time to stand up." Clint expressed to his radio audience.

Macy pattered. "Seems like the goal of law enforcement and government officials is to pull over someone who has drugs. No matter how small the amount. Then law enforcement seizes their cash assets and car for forfeiture under the citizen degrading drug laws."

Clint beckoned. "And money from such a bust is divided between the judge, probation department and law enforcement. The more marijuana busts the cops make with the more the built-in monetary incentive is to expand the drive for the marijuana busts."

Macy persisted. "Clint this is a classic conflict of interest."

Clint noted. "These same government officials store the confiscated drug money in their own attics until they decide how to spend the drug seized money on themselves." Clint continued to make these political accusations with out being interrupted by any adversarial conflict internally from the radio station.

Clint recounted. "These public officials who rule with scorn instead of fairness are not serving the public. They are serving their own power base, which is money. Letting people make their own personal choices in life is the truth. The truth is always healthy."

Macy concerned. "The racketeers of law enforcement are breaking more laws than the citizens they're watching over!"

Clint interjected. "It's time to address the current judicial system, when the Law enforcement, who pulls you over while your on your way home from work instigates and incarcerates you for it's own personal gratification."

Macy agreed. "Personal gratification?"

Clint stressed. "A system which preys on the public and cops acting much worse than the people they're pulling over must be eliminated. When deputy sheriff's are being sent to prison for major drug theft's from the police property room, and then found guilty of fraud, conspiracy, drug distribution. These cops operated on grand scales, not the scales of justice. We have no choice but to correct the system back to the basics of the constitution."

Clint concluded. "How much power do the cops have?" Clint answered his own question and said. "Too much power!" With that speech Clint concluded and left the radio stage platform.

Clint then invited Macy, the media and audience to Rudy and Maria's farm for the Freedom Rally the next week. This was a surprise announcement even unknown to Rudy and Maria. Rudy and Maria's farm would never have such a crowd in attendance.

Rudy commented. "I guess I'm elected. I have a few hundred acres to throw a political bash or a good event."

Clint mustered. "The farm is still warmed up from last party we had for Tommy's injustice."

Once the freedom rally started at Rudy and Maria's, Manny had arranged pro hemp bands proceeded to play. The freedom rally continued long into was a night. Party was enjoyed by everybody but nobody wanted to forget why they were there. Everyone was showing his or her support for individual freedom.

In the meantime there were cannabis conscious citizens passing out fliers about police corruption from counties all over the country.

The defendants were accused by deputies of being in possession of drugs, after the police found fifty five thousand dollars in their car.

The police chief who was in charge of the drug arrest and reported the drug seizure to the press was caught on video tape from a squad car directly behind the defendants car. The police chief was clearly seen opening the trunk of the defendant and planting drugs in the defendant's trunk.

The man reading a flier which stated in large headline prints. "The squad car video tape since has came up missing." The police chief and under sheriffs of the county police force who were involved with the phony arrest were implicated and convicted.

Clint explained to Rudy. "I remember that story about some fishermen who had fifty five thousand dollars cash and were non drug users. They were family orientated oriental men who were taking their life savings to the Port of New Orleans to buy a fishing boat."

Rudy moralized. "These innocent men were caught up with the corrupt judicial system we are now in. Search and seizure charges were drummed up so the bust incentive forfeiture system could flourish through corruption and criminality."

Clint deemed. "The marijuana law itself is wrong. It makes good cops bad. That's why, the marijuana cops lie in court. They are trained to persuade the jury, even by tainting and lying about evidence."

Rudy implored. "The cops don't think it is wrong to lie under oath, because the politicians are fighting evil in a anti-herb holy war."

Clint consulted. "That's their political excuse. They're all making a ton of money getting their cut."

The true menace is not somebody smoking a joint of marijuana in the privacy of their home. It's the marijuana laws themselves which infringe on our constitutional freedoms."

All the fliers distributed had similar incidences of well documented abuses. Friends of Igor's construction crew were circulating the fliers to the audience at the rally. Schedules for further rallies that were being held were also being circulated.

A couple of Dirkskin's drug squad officers were in attendance. One was hanging around Manny and Marian all night next to the DJ booth. Manny Deejays in between the sets played by the hemp bands. Manny made special announcements about up coming hemp events. The Freedom Rally ended on a constructive upper and again ending in a peaceful protest.

The next day Dirkskin got the inside information on the rally at Rudy and Maria's. Marian and his other informants had filled Dirkskin in. Dirkskin decided to make the designated marijuana bust on Clint immediately.

The masked raiders of Metro Drug Police stormed the farm and greenhouse of Clint and Chantel's. Their were a dozen people working around the farm on this Thursday mid-afternoon, a regular sunny green house work day.

Chantel was in the greenhouse working with exotic angel plants along with other co-workers of the green house operation.

"Police! Everyone down! Now!" The cops screamed.

Several other workers were weed whacking, mowing the lawn, and one of the seventeen year old boys named Raines, Everyone called him Rainy. The biggest cop knocked Rainy down as he was weed whipping the tall grass around the green house.

Dave, his friend, on the riding lawn mower was pulled off by the drug cops and cuffed belly down. The riding lawn mower Dave was on kept running riderless into the dusty field.

Rainy's girlfriend Irene was sixteen years old. She was also eight months pregnant. Everyone called Irene, Reenie. Rainy and Reenie as they were known. Irene was upstairs with her girlfriends, Ethyl and Cindy They were all helping out by vacuuming the floors and dusting the furniture for Chantel.

Clint and Brother Big were in the pole barn sweeping the floors, and helping other workers, who were preparing for the up coming party.

Over two dozen marijuana enforcement police cars stormed up the driveway. Clint erupted out of the pole building screaming. "What the hell is going on here!" Four cops quickly pushed Clint to the ground and hog tied him belly down.

Ramone with his black ski mask on kept an AR-15 automatic weapon trained on Clint's temple mustered. "Don't move Clint, or I'll hit a home run!" Most of the workers were still cleaning up the greenhouse mess from the military helicopter destruction from the preceding police drug raid.

Toby Turner the kid who was supposed to have made the drug transaction had just left for the store to get a case of Pepsi for everyone, when the metro drug squad cars came roaring up the drive.

The unmarked metro drug squad cars were the first to arrive on the scene to everybody's astonishment. This fiasco of drug officers looked like crazed killers with automatic weapons jumping out of their cars screaming "Get down it's the Police!" The Metro drug cops were running and knocking the workers down to secure the area.

Everyone was covered with an AR-15 on their head as they were hand-cuffed and hog tied belly down. Six officers ran up the steps of the house and using the no knock rule broke the door down.

The girls, frightened and screamed for their lives, thinking they were about to be robbed and raped. They were trying to hide from the Metro Drug Squad Officers, who were masked and dressed like the village people with automatic weapons.

These screaming herb cops grabbed, groped and threw the young girls to the ground and once again, hog tied and cuffed these innocent young victims. Reenie was screaming for Rainy to come and help. "Rainy help me!" Because of the overpowering police assault during the home invasion, Reenie was terrifyingly crying.

The masked commando's of the Metro Drug Squad resembled the village people and were armed with AR-15 automatic weapons. The government trained terrorists pointed their assault weapons at the temples of these peaceful working victim's innocent heads.

Even Irene, who was eight months pregnant, was treated in such an uncivil and brutalizing manner. Verbal abuse, intimidation and threats by the Metro Drug Squad Police officers never ceased through out everyone's incarceration. Within five minutes the police had secured the area in a brutalizing and traumatic manner. All these young people were innocent victims in this marijuana war.

Girt told Ramone. "We've got the area secure, Ramone. Get up to Clint's bed room and plant that pound of weed."

Ramone rebutted. "I can't, The Metro police are up there right now."

Girt deplored. ""Damn! Dick ain't gonna like that."

The Metro Drug Squad Police continued to ransack the home, the pole barn, the green house, searching for papers, files, pictures, then scanning and retrieving the hard drive of the greenhouse business computer.

Clint still lying belly down said to Big. "These power hungry corrupt cops would do anything to build a case against honest taxpaying citizens."

Big laughed and said to Clint. "Looks like all the law enforcement officials involved are on the gun ho wagon together from the judge, prosecutor, police chief to the robo cops on this drug bust."

Clint reasoned. "There not going to find anything, I don't understand what this is all about yet."

Big stressed. "That's easy they want to bust your ass no matter what and at all costs."

Clint "Ya, know Big I think your right." The big bimbo cop walks over to Clint and kicks him in his side hard and screams. "Shut up! Dirtball!"

The barking dogs of the police canine unit continued sniffing the victims crouches while they lay cuffed. One dog licked their private parts as the police laughed at the squirming victims.

Chantel was cuffed and thrown belly down into a mud puddle on purpose, just because she was Clint's wife. "Chantel looked at the drug cop and badgered. "You call yourself a cop!"

The masked drug cop screamed. "Shut up bitch!" while kicking her in the ribs.

Other canine units of police and dogs were running through the fields looking for marijuana plants.

Another police helicopter was hovering close overhead. All the Government Agencies involved were the DEA , the State Police, the county sheriffs and city police. School kids who were involved in the school DARE drug program also were helping to comb the fields. Big told Clint. "The police force is pulling this drug raid off because it's an election year."

Clint admitted. "This is the biggest charade of a drug raid I could ever imagine."

Big, while still cuffed belly down next to Clint pressed. "All this excessive governmental force just because some cop don't like you, he can sick the dogs on you hard." After four hours of snooping and going through the closets turning pockets of clothing inside out, the innocent victims of this charade were still belly down and cuffed after four hours.

Clint's face looked like a waffle from all the bug bites. Clint told Big. "Insects are crawling up my pants and chewing on my nuts."

Big moaned. "It's a bitch! I can't even scratch these bugs off my body, while being cuffed from behind in the tall grass for hours on end."

Clint griped. "There are a lot of bugs and insects in the grass this time of year."

Big fumed. "I never knew free people were supposed to bow to cops, who misrepresent the law."

Victims of the raid were being interrogated on a continuous basis and everyone was segregated from everyone else. Friends and workers, who unsuspectingly came up Clint's long driveway, were asked by the different police officers what they were doing at Clint's that day. Everyone said the same thing which was the truth. "Were working!" The girls were vacuuming the carpet The boys who were doing the landscape work. Clint, and Brother Big were cleaning farm implements.

All the victims of the ill fated drummed up police bust were innocently working on this Thursday afternoon for Saturday night's party. The police told everyone they could. "Your not having your party now!" and the cops laughed sarcastically.

The Metro Drug Squad regardless of the current laws had handcuffed fifteen and sixteen year old teenagers.

Clint confided. "The only marijuana found in the entire search was the quarter ounce of marijuana which was planted by Francisco Garcia in Toby Turner's trailer. Toby Turner's trailer was immediately emptied by the drug task force of all his personal possessions. Clint was hauled off to jail and charged with maintaining and operating a drug house.

The next day the newspapers displayed a headline which says, "It's a Raid" and all had gathered at Clint's farm in the aftermath of the Police raid. Eveyone looked at each other in amazement.

Clint scorned. "It wasn't a raid, it was a nightmare charade."

Igor raged. "A citizen can't even maintain freedom and privacy in his own domain. Can't choose his own herbal smoke." Igor who had just walked into Clint's sunroom, made his statement upon entrance.

Clint told Igor. "The local newspapers promoted the cops' interpretations, and made it sound like guns were confiscated, young girls were being victimized, major amounts of drugs were found, in order to justify their excessive expenditures. This was a pure intrusion of massive force into the privacy of our home."

Chico chuckled and asked while looking at the paper. "Hey, you know why they wear masks, don't you?"

Chris asked. "No! Why?"

Chico explained. "So they won't be identified when marijuana is legalized." Everyone laughed. After a week of the police parading themselves in the papers, radio and television, the drug squad henchmen made themselves out to be heroes by abusing citizens with tax payers money.

Miles disclosed. "The media is backing the governments push to eliminate pot smokers. The main stream media discourage marijuana use, and backs the so called pure, high and mighty. The media rarely give objective views!"

Mike conveyed. "They also discredit Marijuana user's and new laws of leniency being proposed or passed. The media will not transmit the truths with the same velocity in their news coverage."

Clint contended. "They in essence helped shut you up on the way to shutting you down."

Igor alleged. "The righteous governmental elitists control media hype, which has an unfair and intimidating effect from all the mis-information. Their war on drugs has not led to a drug free society in America."

Miles implied. "The tax loss and profit margins from the underground marijuana sales is to great to ignore."

Clint needled. "Police, prisons, armies, executions, righteous politicians do not have any effect in the slowing down of drug use. The fact is use of all drugs are on an increase. The war on drugs has been an expensive and dangerous failure. The police now seem to get away with any abuse they want and nobody seems to be able to stop them."

Forty-eight hours later Clint was released from jail, he were being charged for maintaining and operating a drug house. There was no drugs found in Clint's home. No excessive amounts of money or drugs were found to substantiate the police investigation, or drug bust. Not so much as a stick, a seed, a stem, a roach, rolling paper or any other drug paraphernalia was found in Clint and Chantel's home as well. Clint who fought for individual freedom for himself and others was now a victim of political and police repression.

Girt couldn't plant the pound as Dirkskin wanted because there were too many other DEA and officers from other police agencies around, whom Girt did not know. Girt later told Dirkskin's. "The bust was being monitored too closely by all the other officers and agencies involvement of the drug bust."

Dirkskin told Girt. "Wait till I destroy Clint's credit rating. I'll have the jailer charge Clint with two months of jail time, instead of two days. Clint won't know until well after the fact, I'll have the judge slip in the civil judgement on him. The jailer will say it's a billing mistake when Clint complains down the road."

Girt giggled. "I like that one boss."

Morgan Motley meanwhile made an appointment for Clint with the Attorney General. Morgan disclosed to Clint in his office. "Clint I want you to present the facts and figures of police abuse by the drug task force."

Clint reassured. "Morgan! That won't be a problem!"

Morgan asked. "OK, how so?" Clint continues and further implicates the police. "I'll burn Dirkskin and his drug squad with hard core video evidence. Manny has officer Marian in a self-incriminating video. The tape will show conclusively the police sponsored dastard tactics to discredit me."

Morgan questioned. "Where's the tape?"

Clint responded. "Manny has the tape, and he's making several copies of the tape right now. I should have a copy for you this afternoon."

Morgan enounced. "Great. I can't wait until we drop that bomb on these guys."

Morgan and Clint arrived at the Attorney general's office. Serious talks commenced after the greetings were exchanged.

Clint told Attorney General Clifford Clements. "The current marijuana busts are mere harassment on citizens with trivial amounts of marijuana involved. The drug task force spent over a million dollars on their investigation of me."

Morgan grilled. "What kind of a police state are we living in?

Clint conceded. "Two separate helicopter raids and an eighteen month investigation produced absolutely nothing."

Morgan avouched to the Attorney General. "The media helps to build and hype minor marijuana busts into major bust episodes. The climax of the media's coverage yielded a large police propaganda drug bust story, but no amount of marijuana was in Clint's household."

The Attorney General sat back and took it all in.

Clint is clearly upset about the false marijuana charges being drummed up. Clint continued to tell the Attorney General. "It's not just this city, it's cities across the board in this nation with our current unjust marijuana laws. When is this third world operation going to end."

Morgan reasoned. "The current marijuana laws and police tactics, encourage and breed corruption, it's time to clean it up our current marijuana laws."

The Attorney General sat and listened intently. "But Clint," he said, "The cops are only doing their job and it's the law. My hands are tied."

Clint continually told the Attorney General, "It's not the law to hound and frame virtuous citizen's".

The Attorney General refuted. "They wouldn't frame anyone."

Clint argued to the Attorney General. "Bull they framed me! I want you to look into this matter."

Morgan implored. "My clients constitutional rights are being violated by an overriding public nuisance law of the land, where responsible citizens are condemned because they enjoy smoking pot. Our forefathers set up the government for all its citizen's to have freedom of choice. Especially in the privacy of their home."

And Clint continued to tell the Attorney General about Hernando's nephew who at seventeen was gang raped at the youth home after being arrested for pot as he was leaving a concert with his girlfriend.

Clint conceded Attorney General. "The police frisked down the kid in front of his girlfriend and found a few joints on him. These kids are not criminals our government has no right to reach that far into a person's free life."

Morgan petitioned. "These young kids are being exposed to violent people in jail. The hardened criminals will only harden these young people like the wars hardened the people that go to them."

Clint pleaded with the Attorney General. "Help stop the Warmongering in the name of marijuana by the government."

The Attorney General revealed Clint straight. "Look Clint, the police can't prove this trumped up drug charge."

Clint told the Attorney General. "Can they restore my work stoppage and my reputation? That's what their destroying!"

The Attorney General stressed Morgan and Clint. "There is nothing I can do about the drug charge Clint."

Clint pleaded. "You can look into the mis-justice."

The Attorney General said. "I'll monitor the court and observe that all proper legalities will be preserved to assure fairness. There were no drugs found in your home. I can't make it look like I intervened in your case."

Clint posed. "You have an obligation to seek fairness for the citizens of this state."

The Attorney General affirmed. "After the court proceedings, I want a transcript. It will be in my power at that time to take a look and see if any laws were violated and see how the legal proceedings were conducted."

Clint and Morgan thanked the Attorney General for his time, and the meeting was concluded.

After the meeting with the Attorney General Morgan told Clint. "I think the meeting went well, you provided undeniably incriminating pertinent information and evidence about Dirkskin and his drug squad henchmen. We to find out the ins and outs of their marijuana drug busts. Who they're busting, and how they're busting. Why they're busting, and who the police are not busting."

Clint acknowledged. "I hope the Attorney General sets up a sting to go even further into Dirkskin's web of illegal and corrupt connections. I know he's dirty. I want the truth to come out."

On the drive back to Clint's farm Clint and his group discussed the plans for the approaching trial. They figured the best way to defend the trial was to put the police on trial pending the course of Clint's own trial. Make the police though court proceeding answer questions, which entrap the truth from the police.

They all met at Morgan Motley's office the following Wednesday and the trial was to begin on Friday. Martin said over the cell phone. "They're having the trial on Friday. That is an odd time, since it usually is the Judge's day off."

Morgan answered. "They don't want anybody there to see this trial. That's why the trail was scheduled on an off day, and no other court proceedings are on the schedule."

Clint was already offered a plea bargain deal by the prosecutor. Clint told his Attorney. "Tell the prosecutor I won't take J-walking to settle this."

As they walked into the trial room set up on one side are the members of the drug squad. While seated Clint looked around and saw members of Dirkskin's drug squad. Clint glared fiercely at his archenemies, staring and glaring them down with every glance.

The bailiff said as the judge enters the courtroom from his chambers, "Now rise" and after the judge enters the everyone is seated.

After a few formal court procedures, the prosecution called its first witness an undercover sheriff. Clint was fuming that the police represented the criminal side of the law. Clint knew this was the undercover cop who wore the mask on the day of the drummed up marijuana bust.

The cop presented himself by his physical build and his knowledge about the day of the bust. When he described what was found in the pole barn, Clint knew that this was the undercover sheriff was. The one who stole sensitive and private pictures of Clint and his wife Chantel in an intimate moment. The crooked drug cop proceeded to tell the jury and the court. "I found marijuana in the pole barn."

Clint, sitting there with his attorney, and now vehemently pounding his fingers on the desk, protesting to his attorney Morgan.

Clint blustered to his attorney Morgan. "The drug lab report in front of us clearly showed the marijuana found in the barn had nil value! It is my understanding that nil means none!"

However, the drug cop proceeded to tell the jury about marijuana being found in the pole barn on a continual basis just to drum up convincing twisted facts in these court proceedings up to get Clint bound over.

Morgan told Clint. "These cops are trained to convince the jury."

Clint raved. "Then educate the jury with the truth."

After testifying the prosecution dismissed the under cover marijuana cop, he briskly walked to the back of the courtroom.

The bailiff called the next witness against Clint. The bald-headed, seedy, withdrawn looking marijuana narc named "Guck," who also participated in the charade of a raid. This marijuana cop was now a witness against Clint, Guck continued lie. "Clint told me that he knew there was marijuana drugs in Toby's possession. Clint told me he knew Toby was selling marijuana drugs."

Clint came out of his skin from hearing the hooligan cop. Clint pounded his fingers even harder on the desk and told his attorney Morgan at his right side. "I didn't say that! He said that! And now he's saying I said that!"

Chantel sat in the courtroom with Maria and watched the court proceedings and said quietly to Maria. "That is the marijuana drug officer who interrogated Clint, After four hours of being hog tied, belly down on the ground with bugs feasting all over his face. That marijuana cop put Clint's face in an ant hill, while Clint was cuffed."

Maria relayed back to Chantel. "Then the marijuana cop intruders interrogated Clint with double edged questions. Questions that had no correct answer for Clint's innocence."

Chantel moaned. "All the questions during the marijuana interrogation without his lawyer were double edged questions. If you said yes you were committed and you said no you were committed."

Maria emphasized. "They clearly had their investigation tactics developed in a controlling method which proclaim guilt at the expense of a defendant's answer's."

After a little more interrogation on the stand of the marijuana drug cop witness, who was still being questioned by Clint's attorney. The judge sat with his chin leaning into his hand and his elbow stretched out on the podium and stared at the marijuana drug cop in amazement.

Clint later said. "That was giving me a signal or maybe the people in the court a signal that he wasn't going to be led on by improper police procedures. He recognized that this marijuana drug case was flawed, and the police corrupted case."

The Judge abruptly dismissed the case. "Case dismissed"

With objections from prosecutor Slinky himself who belabored. "But your honor, Jones VS: Smith!"

The judge interjected. "Dismissed!" again slamming the gavel down and avowed. "I'm quite aware of Jones VS: Smith!"

Now Clint hearing dismissed for the second time jumps out of his chair feeling like a free man who was reborn again.

The prosecutor Slinky seeing Clint is jubilantly on feet protested louder and harder to the judge. "But judge!" and the judge slammed the gavel down angrily for the third time and screamed to the prosecutor. "I don't wanna hear it! Dismissed! The defendant was hog-tied in cuffs! The man was in duress! The man didn't have an attorney present during marijuana drug interrogations, and you never read the man his Miranda rights! "Dismissed!" as the gavel slams down for the fourth time.

The Judge further scolded the herb cops and prosecutor. "You're a nest of perjurers, who will be lucky to escape your own up coming criminal convictions."

The Judge also put the prosecutor and under cover DEA Agent in charge of this case on notice. "Do not bring to this court these types of drummed up marijuana cases to me again!"

Clint turned to walked out of courtroom feeling a major sigh of relief. He thought hopefully that his good name would be exonerated. Clint briskly walked to the rear of the courtroom, when at the last minute he looked and noticed to his right where the three major conspiring culprits of the marijuana drug raid sat.

Lt. Harry Bines, Lt. Bob Boner, and as Clint called him Sgt.0 "Lying Guck Little" These were the main conspirators of Dirkskin's drug squad, Dirkskin, unknown to Clint, even had a five thousand dollar jail court judgement put on Clint's credit report to adversely affected his personal credit rating. The marijuana drug police had entered a judgement in collusion with another judge for further hindrance and harassment.

Clint had beat their drug frame up. Clint couldn't resist his urges. He stopped and bent over abruptly. He lunged forward with his fist clinched toward Lt. Bines as he was stepping out the court's door. After bending downward in an abrupt and fast manner. Clint's clenched fist and stopped within an inch of Lt. Bines's stiff face.

Clint with his clinched fist said. "Yeah!" in an exuberant forceful manner.

Clint slowly erected his posture back upward and walked out the court room's door. After Clint gave one last final and fierce glare to Lt. Bine's in an egging mannerism. Clint wanted Bines to get up and settle it now man to man.

Clint's attorney Morgan slightly pushed Clint from behind out the door of the court room. Morgan wanted to make sure no further infractions would happen.

As Clint walked down the hall into a private chamber with his attorney Morgan, their office door was open.   The two-drug cop Lieutenants, the drug cop Sgt., and the prosecutor Slinky, who lost this case walked by the office.

Clint discerned. "Look Morgan! The herb cops look like little kids whose candy has just been taken away." and Clint laughed.

The drug cops winced and whined down the hall after looking into the court house office chamber Clint and his attorney Morgan stood in.

The prosecutor stated to the drug lieutenants so Clint could hear. "Bonnie's never lost an appeal" and looked into the court room chamber at Clint. Clint in front of his attorney, laughed outwardly and inside thought of what a pathetic joke these drug cops really are.

Clint spieled later to his attorney. "I know the judge wasn't fooled by the lying cops. I was just glad that he stood by the truth."

Miles had his editorial associates from the newspapers, plus radio and TV commentators watched for Clint's courtroom decision. Miles told his associates. "The media needs to expose the excessive abuses of the police force. We need to take a stand for the truth. Home invasion is home invasion. No matter who does it. We have to hold these guys responsible."

Clint was prepared if found guilty in court to let the cat out of the bag about police officer Marian of the drug squad. Clint had decided to break the news the following day to maximize media attention.

Clint bared down in front of the media microphones outside the court house. "I'm happy with the court's decision. I'm discouraged that events like this take place in modern day America. I will have a major announcement in a news release for tomorrow night's news. I personally assure everybody that nobody will want to miss this news presentation."

One radio interviewer asked Clint. "What type of announcement?"

Clint further announced. "A video tape will be released to the news media to show direct corruption of Police Chief Dick Dirkskin, and involves corruption in his police drug force."

The same commentator asked. "What's on the tape?"

Clint stated. "I wish I could show you the whole tape but you'll have to go to an X-rated theatre to view the whole tape as it is taped with no blacked out areas."

Everyone laughed, and everyone was going to curiously wait until the next day. Clint then took this moment to seize the opportunity to announce. "There will be a freedom rally held at the end of the month. Look for a further announcement through the news papers."

The next day everybody anxiously awaited for the 5:00 o'clock news for the surprise story to break. Igor said. "The commentators are talking about the news release for tonight's news. They talked all day and this is what people have been waiting for the anticipated news bomb."

The TV commentator Riley Reece came on nightly news and said. "Good evening everybody. We have video of a female police officer on the drug squad who seduced a citizen in hopes of luring him into a drug implicating crime during a staged drug raid. The female police officer was video taped seducing a friend of the intended target of the investigation. The female officer is in explicitly clear the whole time our viewing of the video tape in a one hour sex seducing romp."

Now the TV commentator Riley Reece showed pictures of Dirkskin, Ramone, Marian, Girt, Larry, and some of the other drug cops on TV.

Igor said. "Check that out there's Dirkskin's walking straight past the TV crews cameras coming out of his office."

The TV commentator Riley Reece continued. "The female police officer is married to another police officer named Delbert Dane of the police force. The female police officer Marian admitted her part in the drug sting. She further acknowledged all the cops involved went over the boundaries of the legal guidelines. Officer Marion resigned her position from the police force immediately."

Manny was with the female police officer on the video. Marian told him during the sex-capade. "I love you Manny. Let's do sex in six different positions." Manny later joshed. "Marion loves her job!"

Igor yelped. "Ya! Blow job!"

Everyone laughed. Marion stated on the video tape. "I'm single, let's move in together Manny."

Manny stated at the news conference that. "She was free and naked as a J-Bird. "

Clint chuckled. "I loved your video Manny. We'll have to show that XXX one at the next bachelor party."

Manny excitedly pledged "She does know what to do in bed, as you can see on the video tape." The news media standing around all laughed at this disgraced police officer. Manny said to one commentator. "I knew something was fishy with her mannerisms. That was why I set the video camera up."

Commentators and the audiences were astonished at these staged events by the police drug force. Ratings on the follow-up news cast were sky rocketed. Headlines in the following days newspaper exposed the police drug tactics and the criminal elements with in our judicial system.

Dirkskin's drug squad was shivering and shrinking in their body with embarrassment. The police commissioner was personally reaming Dirkskin up one side and down the other, demanding that Dirkskin resign. Dirkskin tried to play dumb, but Marian would not lay down and take the fall for him. First they lose the bust, then the trial, and now publicly humiliated with the truth of corrupted entrapment police procedures.

Now, the heat was turned up on Dirkskin. Citizens watch groups watched his lieutenants the drug squad. The truth came about Ramone and another officer who kidnapped, raped, sodomized, and tortured the young Indian girl. They then buried her in a shallow grave in the desert on the remote part of the Indian reservation. Buzzards picked the corpse almost clean. Maggots had infested the rest of it.

On the Indian reservation the tribal police were notified by the locals where a grave was found. It was swarmed by black long billed vultures. Indian horseback riders had found the body after seeing the buzzards flying above the desert sand. The badly decomposed corpse of the little girl was sent to the forensic center for autopsy and DNA for identification.

Little pieces of evidence the killers left were found. The evidence incriminated some of the other cops at a later date.

The conventional media intensified the investigative scope of local law enforcement criminality in the communities. Jason Thatch spoke about Police Criminality per capita.

Various investigative articles came out on a daily basis from various news commentators. Whistle blowers from other police departments were speaking up. Amnesty was offered to police who spoke up against their crooked co-workers on the police force. The news commentators at the convention headlined the content of the drug related articles.

The various commentators could then check each other thoroughly about the articles they wrote or represented. The commentaries started and proceeded until all commentator's submitted their different derogatory information to be aired. How widespread these police department abuses are, and what can be done.

"Let the forum begin." the leader said as he circulated articles from the "The Boston Globe" was written by George. F. Will "Who Is Responsible When the Laws are not Fair "The decision to use drugs should be yours." Letters to the editor in many papers came out on a daily basis to decriminalize marijuana.

Marijuana legalization beats other strategies, marijuana laws infringe on civil liberties. Wide spread abuses are being exposed concerning police involvement with drug running. We can't keep storing inter-city youths in lock downs. "Prohibition of drugs is the problem" is an another article by Anthony Lewis.

"The drug war has failed miserably" writes Jerry Ebstein, who wrote articles concerning the border shooting of an American Latino by a United States Marine patrolling the US and Mexican boarder.

The young American Latino was herding his goats and was shot by the United States drug warriors during an anti-drug surveillance patrol being conducted by a four man marine patrol with M-16 automatic weapons. The young Latino man with no criminal record was an innocent victim. He is now dead from what seems like constant mistakes of the government in it's drug war.

The United States Justice dept acknowledged that the death was wrong. The family of the young Latino man settled the wrongful death suit for close to two million dollars with the United States Government. Civil rights activists made sure the U S Military did not cover up this deadly mishap by it's armed misinformed misfits.

Another commentator explained. "If we need bigger and bigger jails, then this is a police state."

Another conveyed. "Government sponsor's hard drugs! Doctors can prescribe hard drugs all they want but can not prescribe soft drugs like marijuana. The government sponsor's only soft drugs of their choice."

Miles induced. "In ounce by ounce illicit marijuana moves rapidly into the mainstream. Marijuana is widely accepted in most social levels around the globe."

Clint always decreed. "Marijuana has always been widely excepted socially for years and years all over the world."

Miles expounded. "The public is finally wising up to the hypocrisy of the drug war. The government is hooked on booze and cigarettes, because of all the tax base and graft that was already established."

The news commentator maintained. "The government is a partner in alcohol and nicotine distribution. The government should pay as well for past alcohol and nicotine medical abuses on its citizens. They shared in the profits with big business throughout the promotion and taxation of these government preferred legal substances."

Another article being expounded on by TV commentators outlined the anti-drug co-operation program between Washington and Mexico City. A program where United States tax dollars go to Mexico to fight drugs. The Mexican Czar in charge of fighting the drug war keeps Washington's money, and is in full cooperation with the drug cartels aiding drug shipments to the United States in the tons of hard drugs like heroin and cocaine at a time. The Cartels typically buy off Mexican police, the border patrols, and the local police on the fringes of the border and deep into the northern United States. The drug cartels are well organized. These drug shipments continually operate at a brisk pace. Sometimes in a drug conspiracy of government officials and police officers even elements of the CIA and Military join in and cooperate in drug running. Everybody gets there cut for their cooperation with the Drug Cartels. Drug king pins freely walk the streets of their home towns below the border."

"Another article presented and circulated states, "The enemy has overrun us!" Another article in the headlines stated. "Marijuana, prohibition and taxing gimmicks are failing. United States campaign against drug use has failed!" "To Big of A Battle is Being Waged Against Marijuana." The government's crack down against marijuana is heavy handed and wrong. The president's war on drugs is cruel, wrong, and un-winnable. The media commentators at this convention were all in sync with the truth.

"Drug costs now at twenty billion dollars a year to fight a war with no end" Another article stated. "Drugs Wars Are a Lost Cause." "Reefer Madness Strikes Again." "Alcohol, not Marijuana is the Big Problem." "The War on Drugs is Lost." "Kill It!. Go for Legalization, Freeing Up the Police Force and the Courts will Reduce Crime."

Another article in the Washington Host fully displays the attitudes of parents who are marijuana smokers themselves at present or in the past. One parent said. "The kids of the nation are not stupid. You can not tell them not to smoke and they see their parents, friends, neighbors and acquaintances on the street, who smoke marijuana on a regular basis conduct their lives responsibly. Kids know marijuana is not the impairing drug the government makes it out to be."

One parent at the forum revealed. "The government's strict marijuana policies will not be implemented through all the parents or to all the kids. The government should stay out of peoples daily lives. People can mostly police their own daily activities.

Clint declared. "A man is a king in his own castle. You can get a more useful citizen through tolerance of their preferred freedom in personal choices. A strict policy of moral adherence of repressive governmental actions of a socially acceptable way of life isn't realistic. You can't govern a free society by passing strict aggravation laws which enforce citizens to relinquish their personal freedom of choice."

The forum was developed especially as the pulse for the media, to see where the media commentators, new organizations, and its citizens stood. Clint at the forum podium instead of the sidelines cleared the air. "Nobody is here for legalization of hard drugs but a lot of us are pro-marijuana advocates." The idea of this forum is to regain certain constitutional rights which are a casualty of the right wing moral majority. Clint said. "Now responsible citizens are the real casualties of the continuing marijuana war."

The forum also addressed human rights abuses by drug police raids, where no crime was committed by the citizens but citizens were treated as criminals. The public audience sat attentively in the convention center listening to all the different news commentators related by pro-marijuana activists outlining strategies and addressing further abuse of the citizens by the cops.

At the end of the forum, the news commentators had an open question and answer town meeting with the audience.

The local television station broadcast the whole event, not only in the Houston Metropolitan area, but nationally and internationally through the APS. Inter-net polls were heavily in favor of legalization of marijuana and personal freedom changes. The forum ended in a positive and peaceful way.

The following evening, television news commentators invited police chiefs, legislators and medical personnel who favored legalization of marijuana to follow up rally. They gave them the forum agenda, which was printed in detail. This marijuana forum was planning to be given the following week as a fund raiser for the marijuana legalization drive.

The marijuana forum was now in process, after a week of preparation. The constructive get together turned into a hemp rally and other assorted pro-marijuana speakers. Hemp food and assorted displayed hemp crafts that were featured that night by hemp industrialists.

The police chief from St. Louis attended the forum, and lectured. "I've been on the force for thirty five years fighting the marijuana war. And in my own heart I believe the war against marijuana can not be won and I further urge legislators to aggressively endorse decriminalization of marijuana and pass legalization agendas for the safety and well being of the community. This marijuana war must end!"

The police chief continued. "You can only police the citizens to the extent that they want to be policed. You are not going to stop it, so lets stop the citizen abuse. Tear down this wall of our nations internal war which pits citizen against citizen." Everyone in attendance felt good that law enforcement was represented in the marijuana legalization fight. Various pro marijuana legislators were beginning to speak out as the weekly polls shifted toward full legalization.

Brant a representative for the labor community, who owns a large llama and ostrich farm clarified to Manny. "The keynote speakers labored all day in the hot sun of the afternoon. Cold hemp drink refreshments were served. Funds came from donors and pro-marijuana legalization sponsors for the event. Media arrangements and coverage were engaged globally.

Manny disclosed. "The final cut for the colorful hemp bands competing to play for this large hemp rally was an extremely hard decision to make."

Brant informed. "This forum hemp rally was intensely organized due to the media coverage in the weeks past. The speakers spoke passionately and pleaded for a change in the marijuana laws in their speeches."

One of the keynote speakers was a federal judge who concluded. "Drug legalization is the way to go after being involved in the prosecution of drug laws over the past thirty years."

The judge felt obligated to carry out the law to the best of his ability but stated. "I became convinced that drug enforcement is a failure, and can not and will not succeed as far as the war on marijuana users goes. The marijuana war should be ended immediately as far as this federal judge is concerned."

The crowd was overwhelmed hearing a federal judge who was appointed by the president to fight the drug war, and was now making an about face. The federal judge expounded. "Cease the Al Capone type gang wars between police, the drug cartels and marijuana users."

Another prominent jurist who spoke at the rally was from the Chief of Federal Appeals Court lectured. "Marijuana legalization is an easy way of reducing crime. Marijuana criminalisation of our citizens is a total waste of law enforcement efforts, time, and taxpayers money. Court dockets and prison space can be re-used for longer prison sentences for violent and dangerous criminals who will take their place."

The judge continued. "Decriminalization of marijuana is a sure route for reducing crime The real loser's are the taxpayer's, especially when real violent criminals are released, because of prison overcrowding. Let's go after real criminals by legalizing marijuana and give our responsible citizens back their constitutional rights. Freedom of personal choice period! Thank You!" The judge told the applauding crowd as he left the stage.

After the keynote speakers were finished. The hemp bands protest music entertained at no cost. "Bring the hemp bands on" was the banner line. Marijuana growers and smokers were coming out of the closet and to the freedom events. The hemp freedom events were sponsored by various donors and donations for cannabis freedom charities were accepted at all the hemp rallies. Fund raisers for marijuana legalization were announced as the next hemp rallies were scheduled. With the hemp bands and the crowed were roaring each other on.

George Barras is an International Billionaire, who is a pro-medical marijuana advocate. He is sponsoring some of the up coming hemp-festivals. He brought in the open stadium an elaborate laser light show for those in attendance. The huge lights lit the skies up to the full moon.

George's lady friend Dolores was an actress from Hollywood. She escorted him to this rally. Dolores enjoyed a remarkable movie career during the 1960's and she was now in her late fifties. Dolores grilled the host of a late night TV show when she was a interviewed. "Do you smoke marijuana?" The flabbergasted host did not answer the question and tried to change the subject.

Dolores came back again. "Do you smoke marijuana?" The host still didn't respond. Dolores steadfastly admitted. "I've smoked marijuana for years and I still do."

The host admitted. "What a week. Last night another lady guest asked me the same thing after she admittedly said. "I've been a user of reefer for years and I still love smoking reefer." The host wouldn't own up if he ever smoked pot or not.

Media camped out for the hemp forum event. Mainstream news anchors were now covering the hemp and marijuana issues on a more fair and consistent basis. Everyone was getting the feeling that the hemp movement for marijuana legalization was gaining momentum and rally after rally after rally rendered facts revealing the truth in rampant fashion.

Clint organized and attended many of these hemp rallies. Popular Clint was becoming known as the foremost pro-marijuana and hemp keynote speaker.

Clint walked up to the podium, and started by expounding correct marijuana facts and the wide range of police abuses in the present judicial system to the crowd. Clint pitched the audience. "Other countries including our Nato allies have legalized marijuana and/or are in process of decriminalizing marijuana."

Clint made it clear. "Germany's high court just rewrote their cannabis laws, and raised the legal hashish possession limit from two to four grams of hash, which can be sold or possessed by their citizens legally. The government of Germany recognizes and respects the right of its citizens in this regard and to freely choose, use and posses small amounts of hash or marijuana."

The crowd reacts with a loud favoring roar. Clint goes on. "Marijuana laws are being rewritten everyday favoring legalization. These other industrialized countries are realizing that the police have more than enough serious crime that needs to be researched. The governments must come to the realization that giving the people their constitutional rights back to make their own personal decisions on marijuana use is right. We feel the government is not right chasing pot people and make criminals of people who just use marijuana or hashish."

Clint who received three or four different pro-marijuana speaking engagements everyday. On the radio, on television, at colleges and for pro-marijuana and hemp events. Clint's lecture postings were detailed on the Internet, and updated everyday for the up coming hemp rallies. The crowds were stirred up and ready for change. The media scrutinized and promoted many of these pro-hemp rally events.

Keynote speakers who were speaking were actually victims of the drug war. Miles told his editor. "These victims can finally vent their frustrations by speaking about the police abuse. Attending the hemp rallies helps them cope. Giving first hand actual facts about the "no knock" entry in various drug raids by the victims is eyeing opening."

Ed conferred. "I agree! I've reported on many drug raids where families and friends have been victimized unfairly and deprived of their civil rights."

Miles discoarsed. "The victims are demonstrating the need for an investigative police panel to review the departments current drug raid policies. They want independent panels to oversee police operations with a scrutinizing eye to catch colluding police officers and criminal government officials."

Also speaking at this cannabis rally was, Bonita, who's father was victimized on a drug raid that had gone wrong. Bonita's father was shot in the leg in the course of the drug raid. The raid on her fathers house was conducted when police raided the wrong house by accident. The city promptly settled a lawsuit for over one hundred thousand dollars out of court. Bonita says. "The settlement proves the fact of irresponsible acts escalated by uncontrollable police conduct. It is our responsibility as citizen's of this country to ensure monitoring of the police department drug policies and procedures."

Bonita continued speaking to the audience. "Constitutional and Civil rights complaints are followed up on a just newly established hot line. All civil and constitutional complaints are being followed up by a special people's commission investigating police department's alleged misconduct. People! You and your neighbors rights are being abused everyday. Discriminating marijuana laws are not essential for a healthy free nation. Stand up and be counted. Help take our country back. Get the political marijuana prohibition bigots identified and vote them out of office. Free our proven responsible citizens who pay taxes deserve to govern their own live!" The crowd roared with affection as Bonita left the stage.

The next keynote speaker was Clarence Olson, who was an exemplary teacher for twenty-one years, fifteen at the same high school. He had earned national awards for teaching excellence. The school board at the school did an intensive and very intrusive background check." Clarence nervously said. "The school board found a marijuana possession charge for a joint of weed during my youth, twenty one years prior. I was promptly discharged. This same school board that permanently expelled a student for minor marijuana possession on school property."

Clint discussed to Miles. "The school board disqualified this teacher from teaching in their high school over a misdemeanor marijuana charge he received in his youth. This is an unreasonable way to treat a proven and responsible person of the community." Clarence told how his family and he have suffered immensely over the firing.

Grimly Miles expounded. "Ya! That's really digging deep for dirt."

Furious Clint deemed. "Drummed up dirt!"

The next speaker Benton Barrit a disabled factory worker claimed police brutality during his marijuana arrest. Benton said. "I use marijuana for medical reasons. I have been diagnosed with diabetes. I hated the reaction and paying for doctor prescribed insulin shots everyday. I quit after two weeks of taking the irritating insulin shots. I then began to smoke marijuana with my friends, who I knew smoked marijuana."

Benton further alleged. "My new weed habit seemed to lower my blood sugar level. My appetite picked up from my weed habit. In addition to that I felt much healthier. I grew some marijuana for my own personal medicinal use. The next thing you know I'm busted! I can attest to the incredible amount of police man power, tax money, and police abuse that goes virtually unchecked. The cops busted the doors off the hinges of my house with a battering ram in the middle of the night. The police drug squad commander then slammed my face into the floor, while cocking the hammer of an automatic weapon to the rear my skull."

Clint told Miles on the sidelines. "I know the feeling."

Benton emphatically wailed. "I feel like, I've been raped inside my house! All my possessions were destroyed or taken from me by a police moving van."

Benton continued. "One cop during the marijuana raid said Your lucky we busted you boy. Were going break you from your drug addiction, while the same cop was taking pictures of my disrobed wife for drug evidence in front of my kids."

Benton tearfully scorned. "I felt betrayed by my government and the cops. I will be bitter for the rest of his life over this ordeal. I am now on probation with terms that allow the police to walk into my house, with a no knock entry twenty four hours per day three hundred and sixty-five days a year. My family and myself now live in constant fear of the police. A badge and an automatic weapon doesn't guarantee consciences or compassion for citizens." Benton concluded his appeal to an arousing applause.

One former state legislator who spoke scoffed. "I was found with a marijuana cigarette during traffic stop. The officer searched me after I was ordered out of the car. Marijuana was found in my blood after a police instigated drug test." The state legislator was removed from public office for minor marijuana possession.

Mrs. McDonald a parent of a fifteen year old student in the DARE program, she proudly encouraged him to follow the DARE programs procedures. She said. "Unknown to me the school had a system developed among the students for informing on the other students their parents and their friends to inform on drug and marijuana users. My son Brett was given payments of twenty dollars per snitch lead, which caused another student drug user to be arrested. When the student got out of jail, he got together with a few of his friends, and they went looking for Brett. They beat and kicked him to death. The student Brett fingered was dealing hard drugs in the barrio. The busted students older brother was shot by drug king pins. He could not account for the drug money the cops recovered from busting his kid brother."

Mrs. McDonald continued her speech, crying most of the way through her story stated. "These students were trained to snitch on fellow students. I wish I never encouraged my son to get involved with the DARE program. The teaching and training tactics are similar to the tactics of a third world youth league. Snitching and informing in the drug war can be and is dangerous. I not want our kids fighting other kids and getting killed for twenty dollar rewards. The principal of the school promised to stop the informant reward system, but it's way to late for my son Brett."

Mrs. McDonald advised. "Keeping drugs and alcohol and tobacco out of schools is the right thing to do. Teachers should be educating our kids at school about drugs. Drug searches with the use of dogs should be after school hours not at the same time as class room hours."

Clint agreeably told Miles while watching Mrs. McDonald. "I always said. "Educating our children would be better than criminalizing them."

Miles answered Clint. "As real and scary as the facts are, the truth of the matter is drugs, alcohol, and marijuana is freely available in schools, in many homes, and in the kids everyday social life. It is up to us as parents to develop a responsible message for our children and the way we want them to be, while their brought up."

Mrs. McDonald disclosed. "The anti-drug lobbyist's are losing us and our kids. We need to win the war through education." she reiterates, "Not criminalization!"

Mr. Sam Smith another speaker had passed out drug testing literature earlier. He started his speech by stating. "Employees are being fired from their company after hair samples are being taken at their physicals. Where is the opportunity to plead the fifth amendment. The medical data from the hair sampling informed employers and insurance companies that the medical history of the worker also indicated possibilities of other health problems. Blood testing and your rights are finally being limited by the high courts. We need to all recognize the right and value to individual privacy."

Mr. Smith questioned. "What about the citizens who go to other countries where marijuana is legal?"

Mr. Smith answering his own question. "A citizen who smokes marijuana and then comes back to their place of employment after a vacation which involved smoking hash in Amsterdam. His employer has him randomly drug tested and than promptly terminated after testing positive for marijuana. Is this reasonable action for all concerned?"

Mr. Smith continued. "In some states possession or sale of less than one hundred grams of marijuana is a one hundred dollar fine and no possibility of jail time at all. People around the world have been smoking for thousands of years. No government is above the peoples choice of leafy herb for pleasure. Drug testing is an infringement on our rights by these companies, sanctioned by our government. Pro-marijuana groups are exploring abuses in drug testing alone."

Clint cracked to Miles. "Come on Mr. Smith."

Mr. Smith exclaimed. "What protects a man against unreasonable and unwarranted search? Do we control our own our body, and soul or does the government? Does the government have the right to destroy free thinkers. Because if we don't control our body, and soul then they might as well clone everybody and the federal government can have it's citizens exactly the way the government perceives it's citizens should be. Governmental prejudices against marijuana users rank up there with any racial, or religious persecutions in the history of mankind. A government which forces it's own interpretation of morality on it's citizens is an unjust government. Defining the crucial word is a reasonable question to be asked by any citizen. It is not reasonable to drug test so many people for so many indiscretions. Where discretion is biased and a mere fishing expedition with so little positive results. The governmental officials making the laws are by passed in the drug testing process. Some of these same government officials are the biggest drug offenders in the world. Testing for marijuana is unwarranted and unreasonable." Mr. Smith concluded to a standing ovation.

The rally ended with all the speakers feeling some relief that they could express their anxieties and trauma's related to negative governmental hype. The audience continued to listen to commentator's assessment of Mr. Smith's speech.

"What a comforting feeling." one speaker told Clint. "This Hemp Freedom Rally is concluding on another positive note for pro-marijuana activists." After the rally for marijuana rights was concluded, Clint was chosen to be a part of an advance team in charge for upcoming hemp rallies that were being established.

The following week after the rally a major decision was announced in the newspapers. Everybody is waiting for the federal judge in charge of investigating the use of excessive force by police and orders the sweeping raids by the drug task force. The investigation was coming to a head because of the excessive complaints. We all hoped the judge would hopefully rule in favor of the pro-marijuana activists and closet cannabis citizens.

It was Wednesday night at the Cactus Club, Clint was shooting pool and relaxing his nerves, while sipping on a beer.

Chris the computer hack was sitting at the bar hitting on a Blond headed girl full of make up. Manny was D-Jing that night at the Cactus Club. Igor was trying to persuade Manny to play the top forty instead of the Rhythm and Blues. Miles had just arrived with "Legal Beagle" Morgan Motley, who was primed with his black top hat on.

Everyone was surprised to see the conservative Morgan Motley at the Cactus Club. But Morgan wanted to be with Clint, when the news was announced on the six o-clock edition. While watching the television above the bar, and taking a shot at an eight ball at the same time. Clint waited to hear the expected announcement. It came by the federal judge. Everybody was hesitantly silent. At that point, you could hear a pin drop as the United States High Court stated there are limits to how police conducted searches.

The TV news commentator stated. "They have decided that the sweeping drug raids okayed by the no knock rule is ruled illegal especially for small amounts of marijuana."

The crowd jumped in the air and screamed and roared and danced that even a small victory was finally coming to the pro-marijuana activists.

Igor exhorted. "We as a voice are heard, not only in the media, but also by our government."

Morgan raved. "The government ruling states the police must have reason to believe the citizens are racketeering and enterprising in marijuana, before police can conduct drug raids."

Judge Zegler of the courts attested. **"Marijuana users have the right to privacy in their own homes, and that their constitutional rights to privacy should not be violated for menial amounts of marijuana."**

Morgan snickered. "The court went further to rule people are not cattle. The government does not own a citizen's body. Marijuana drug testing will cease. Marijuana discrimination must end against responsible citizens, who choose marijuana as a recreational high."

Clint professed. "Citizens can now grow three plants at a time for personal use."

Morgan further explained. "Exceptions to the marijuana legalization rules are some jobs citizens have in sensitive areas of governmental employment, the industrial complex, and law enforcement. Citizens in these positions must give up their rights to marijuana voluntarily, but are to be monetarily compensated for the drug testing. Only sensitive positions that require an utmost behavior would be required to give up alcohol, tobacco, marijuana rights."

Miles divulged. "The court also said. "Marijuana discrimination will transpire only through compensation in these sensitive job areas, not the general work force or the general public."

The crowd over hearing the judge's statements were ecstatic. Clint immediately bought a round for everybody. "The round for the house is on me". Clint yelled! Beers, cocktails, and Pepsi were flying everywhere! You would have thought they had won the Word Series!

Shorty sitting at the bar sneered. "They knew the drug raids on small time marijuana possessors was illegal all the time. The cops kept doing those searches on private citizens homes, and they keep getting around the constitutional law with all their finagling."

Clint reiterated. "Remember, this is only a partial victory. We are not done yet." Everybody had a cheer for more liberal renditions of our constitutional and god given rights.

Miles ventured. "Everybody knows what's best for themselves, They should have the right to make those personal decisions in life."

Dirkskin in the meantime is nervous with the on going investigations of his drug command. The sting of the truth is coming to a head. The hammer is about to be lowered down hard on him by the Attorney general Clifford Clements.

All the sweeping raids conducted by his drug squad unraveled and fell apart as the Attorney General's internal investigation by Rufus Remington uncovered damaging evidence from thirty nine separate marijuana drug arrests.

Rufus uncovered how tons of hard drugs were smuggled into the country with the cooperation of Chief Dirkskin's drug network of state and county cops.

The police chief and lieutenant Girt's informant Gar refused to cooperate any further after being interviewed by Rufus. Many of the drug busts were collaborated through insufficient evidence. Some like Clint's were flat out frame-ups. The witness "Gar" refused to back up Police Chief Dirkskin's key indictments after being investigated and interviewed by police internal affairs. Dirkskin was under pressure from the Attorney General Clifford Clements to resign.

The informant Gar admitted to false statements when he testified for the drug search warrants in front of the judge Dirkskin asked for a warrant. All of the drug arrests including Toby Turners drug cases came crumbling apart and case after case was exposed and then dismissed.

Dirkskin knew he was not only politically finished in the upcoming election, but he would now likely see prison time himself. Dirkskin's grandstanding in all the newspapers and in all the drug raids for the upcoming election was now proven to be a farce.

After the marijuana court cases were dismissed, the Attorney General had Dick and all his thug cops rounded up and thrown in jail.

Clint conferred to Morgan. "Evidence is now coming out that corruption was rampant throughout Dirkskin's administration. Investigations exposed various drug dealings, drugs frame ups, robberies of citizens and drug dealer pay off's."

Morgan attested. "All are now charged with criminal drug conspiracy and federal drug charges that have been brought up against all of Dirkskin's men."

Clint discussed with Morgan. "Dirkskin's will also have to explain where a million and a half dollars went from the drug forfeiture fund two hundred and forty- six pounds of marijuana and one hundred and twenty kilos of cocaine missing from the police evidence room."

Morgan recanted. "The drugs were stolen in the last five year period."

The implicated cop conspirators were contacting their attorneys, pointing their fingers at each other and pleading for mercy.

Larry quickly turned states evidence on Ramone for the kidnapping, raping and killing of the little Indian girl.

Clint was astonished! Dirkskin had even surprised Clint. "I never thought Dirkskin could go that far." After the revealing damaging criminal evidence came out on television, Clint told the bartender and everyone else in the bar. "I'm buying drinks for everybody and anybody for the rest of the night." Clint finally felt vindicated.

Clint asked. "I need a designated driver?" Morgan Motley, a non-smoker and non-drinker is designated for the duty. Smiling and drinking Pepsi, Morgan answered. "Obliged."

Chapter 7.... At the moment with little victories and realities of justice being realized, Chico's friends

Mile's editor at the newspaper Ed told Miles. "I to do a story on the drug cartels. I want to expose how Mexican drug industry and it's influences penetrate the United States from south of the border. I send someone down south to document the narcotic traffic from the inside of Mexico."

Miles reassured. "I'll see what I can do. I'll talk to Jose a friend of mine from college baseball. Miles knew he had relatives deep in Mexico. Miles told Ed. "I'll have Chico ask his friend Alfonso."

Alfonso was on his term break from college. He Chico's friend Jose from San Antonio also. Alfonso and Jose were going to go see Jose's cousin Poncho in Mexico City first. "Poncho is a cliff diver at an Acapulco resort on the Pacific Ocean."

Jose told Alfonso, where they both attended college together. "I realized in that call from Miles it was business. After all he worked for the large Houston newspaper."

Alfonso asked Jose. "Guess what?"

Jose questioned. "What?"

Alfonso anxiously acknowledged. "My friend Chico called. He work's in newspaper distribution in Houston." Jose fidgeted for explanation and muttered. "The newspaper want's us to go to Mexico on an investigative drug venture?"

Jose asked. "Why not? The newspaper is going to pay for everything." Alfonso answered. "I don't have the greatest amount of money any way, while I'm going to college. Were already going to do college reports while were in Mexico. What's one more report."

Alfonso razzed. "Let's go! I'm in!" Between them, they figured they had enough relatives to uncover drug related corruption. They'd heard about corruption of the Mexican government, military, and police officials.

Jose told Alfonso. "Miles established a money draw network with the banks. We can travel at ease with out a great amount of money on ourselves at one time."

Alfonso told Jose. "The newspaper wants us to come back with an unbias story of the facts in Mexico as we see it."

Jose's said. "I heard my cousin Poncho is well connected. His family is one of the principal economic families in Mexico City and the Acapulco area. Poncho I hear is well liked by the women in the Acapulco area, because of his fancy clothes and exciting adventuresome day and night life."

Jose's Aunt Leona arranged a big family reunion, by virtue of Jose had never been to Mexico City, before. His Aunt Leona visited Jose's mother Rita in San Antonio, and Jose, barely aquatinted with her from those visits, vigorously darted for this adventurous opportunity.

Alfonso and Jose's mission from the newspaper was to get involved in the Mexican community. Their cover would be the guise of studying the De forestation of the Rainforest and Archaeology of the Mayan Indian ruins.

Jose told avid Alfonso. "We'll try to get involved with the people, who direct the labor in the drug dominion. Even the people who mule for the main families."

Alfonso answered back. "That part's scary!" Despite that said. "But we'll chronicle the moods of the people and drug deals during our tour of the Mexican country."

Jose told directly Alfonso. "Ed is going to pay for this trip with an expense account established for new story development by his newspaper."

Alfonso calmly said. "Cool!" They were both literate in speaking and reading Spanish.

Alfonso's relatives lived in San Christobal de Las Cases. Alfonso told Jose. "My father Sonto crossed the border as a teenager and never left Texas. My dad became a citizen under the amnesty program, which allowed immigrants who could prove they lived in the United States for more than two years to claim citizenship. He has worked as a mason and cement worker, and sent both my brother and me to college so we could have a better life than he had!"

Alfonso conceded. "I'm excited about going to the Chiapas State."

Jose enthused pledged to Alfonso. "I can't wait to visit your relatives in the Chiapas State."

Alfonso told Jose. "My grandparent's still live in San Cristobal. I've never met either of my grandparents. Now one their grand kid form north of the border is coming to visit them."

Jose wheeled. "That's great!"

Alfonso decreed. "My five cousins from my dad's side are waiting to meet their new cousin in a couple of weeks time."

Alfonso and Jose cut for Mexico to see relatives in Mexico City, and Chiapas area. They converged down the coast by motor couch, till Brownsville, then trekked across the boarder to Motomoros, Mexico. In Motomoros they purchased their tickets and boarded the bus to Mexico City.

Jose professed. "Were finally on our way down the highway in Mexico." Both were well aware of the dangerous drug cartel turf wars, which had just claimed nineteen lives from three separate families, eight of which were children. They were all dragged out of bed in the middle of the night, some were tortured, and all were shot execution style near a Baja tourist resort area. These family members were now eliminated from competing with the major drug traffickers. "Massacre" was the daily headlines.

Alfonso divulged. "The bus will be stopping every so often for the Military roadblocks."

Jose asked. "What?"

Alfonso shrieked. "Yip! I've talked to one of the locals. The bus stops at the all roadblocks, then the Mexican soldiers board the bus and search everyone's belongings. Some of the patrons are usually ordered off the bus. The bus then proceeds on down the highway without them."

Jose told Alfonso. "I don't know if I want to experience Mexican hospitality first hand."

Alfonso imputed. "The Mexican drug Czar was busted for aiding and accepting payments from the drug cartel the last year."

Jose defined. "The Mexican Drug Czar was supposed to be somebody who is impeccable as described by our U S Drug Czar."

Alfonso conveyed. "The United States drug Czar says he's needs more help below the border."

Jose quipped. "He needs more help than he could ever imagine! Mexican involvement in the drug business include the majority of all politicians, military and police. I'd really like to know where is the United States drug Czar going to get help below the border?" He asked sarcastically!

Alfonso answered. "The International Bankers and drug barons are friendly together in laundering drug proceeds."

Jose told Alfonso. "A United States official stated in today's news article, that more high tech equipment is needed to combat the flow of cocaine into the country."

Alfonso disclosed. "Those cocaine barons are the ones who control all the drug routes. They even have a hoard of underground tunnels crossing into the United States where hard drugs flow like water."

Jose implied Alfonso. "Drug trafficking problems have no borders. The drug barons run the drug gangs. Certain Senators in the United States say that Mexico is not doing enough to bust drug barons."

Alfonso induced. "The United States wants the drug kingpins extradited from Mexico to the United States. The Senators do not want to rectify Mexico, because of the lack of progress in the drug war."

Jose said. "The former mayor of Mexico City ran for President and form another Political Party. He says there's to much corruption in the Present administration. He's trying to rally all the oppositional political forces to unite and topple this political regime in the 2,000 election year."

Alfonso told Jose. "It won't change a thing here in Mexico, until we change are ways in America. Everyone knows that the only people who get off for being busted for drugs are the ones who belong to the long arm of protection of the drug cartels here in Mexico. Corruption has reached the highest levels of the Mexican government. The Mexican drug Czar protected these drug families run their drug business, while eliminating their competition. That's the way it works here. Like it or not. It's reality."

Jose said. "It didn't help that over four hundred Mexican officials were found to have illegal drugs in their system after drug tests. Most had worked as agents of the Federal Judicial Police. Over half tested for cocaine followed by followed by sedatives and amphetamines. Ironically, only seventeen of the Mexican officials tested positive for marijuana. Most of the government officials were paid with drugs as was much of the cartel mules or aid the cartel."

Alfonso needled. "The Mexican drug lords have established a multi million dollar drug trade which has led to corruption at all levels of the government. Threats, Bribery, intimidation and acts of violence by governmental officials assure their criminal way of life. Seventy percent of all cocaine that comes into the United States crossed the boarder of Mexico and the United States."

Alfonso and Jose never navigated pasted the boarder towns. They were already experienced infringements on their movements and actions, they were uncomfortable in comparison to the U S A. The power shift to the drug lords consumed an economic twist, as well as a political indifference to democratic rule. Jose told Alfonso. "Indeed! I've never experienced military rule in such great a proportion like this before!"

Alfonso was reading one of Mexican newspapers on the bus about The Mexican Defense Ministry and in detail said. "Top officials have admitted wide spread corruption involving drug related crimes by military drug intelligent officers. Ties between the Drug lords and the military are noticeably evident to everyday Mexican nationals. Almost eight hundred drug fighting agents were fired after such rampant collusion and trafficking were exposed drug barons."

Jose read his newspaper. "The Mexican Attorney General admitted the drug force is in a state of anarchy. He further admitted that ninety percent of the drug task force is on the payroll of the murderous drug cartels payroll books. They maintain a free terror reign to do any feat at any ones expense for power, profit and pleasure."

Jose continued to read the daily newspaper about intelligence chief involved in kidnapping and killing a major competitor of a rival cartel. The TV in the bus station had a report on the news as well. Some people stood around and looked on with interest. "The alleged police and military conspirators transferred all the drugs along to the California and Mexican border," the announcer relayed.

Jose and Alfonso were barely into Mexico and their investigative trip, when signs of the drug trade seemed evident every where. Alfonso acknowledged. "Drug lords used the Mexican mules to hump their drugs into the United States across the boarder. You either do it, or you suffer the consequences of saying No."

Jose termed. "As the drug lords take a firmer hold on government positions, the job to stop the spread of hard drugs is harder as it goes. Presently seventy-five percent of the cocaine and eighty percent of foreign grown marijuana that enters the country from across the US- Mexican border."

Alfonso divulged. "Here's one well publicized case of Mexican federal police helped unload ten tons of cocaine from an air plane, then the Mexican federal agents help destroy the aircraft after it was unloaded."

Jose stated. "Links between the Mexican political system and wickedly corrupt influence of narcotic organizations is common place. The United States government is unwilling to confront their neighbors to the south in fear of straining relations."

Alfonso said. "Down here drugs are bigger just big business. It's a way of life for many in Mexico."

Jose said while looking at a newspaper story. "Violence and corruption are spreading across the border onto United States soil. In one case a United States Customs inspector was convicted for accepting one million dollar for allowing one ton of cocaine across the US border. Wow !"

Alfonso contended. "That's big news back in the states."

Jose professed. "I knew about these facts before we came down to Mexico. Mexican Drug lords have the financial strength to make things happen. Everyone from the President of Mexico to the generals, colonels, captains, down to the soldiers at the road blocks we have to go though."

Alfonso repined. "Well I didn't know it was that big. All the newspapers have strong content stories about the drug cartels." Bribing the military on a regular basis was their way of life."

Alfonso gamed. "Everyone loves the profits of money from drugs."

Jose discussed to Alfonso. "In the United States the Mexican Cartel hired Ex-green berets and former United States counter intelligence officers. The ex-military specialists are now on the payroll to help the cartel smuggle the drugs undetected across the border into the United States. The U S soldiers are highly trained in escape and evasion techniques. They secretly scout in camouflage the illegal areas to cross with hard drugs into the United States along the two thousand mile border."

Alfonso emphasized. "The newspapers are full of articles about drug induced corruption." On the buses they talked their intelligence mission strategy out and sorted out their information collected on the Mexican state of affairs.

Alfonso gossiped. "The country side they were going though and all the small towns and farm lands were enriching to the soul, being back in the country of your heritage."

Jose lucidly expressed. "This trip is an enlightening tour for both of us."

In Mexico City the bus dropped the young men off at the central plaza or "Zocalo" as it's commonly called. Jose and Alfonso were to meet Jose's Aunt Leona at the "Mercado." " Aunt Leona works there selling flowers, not too far from the "Zocalo."

Jose disclosed to Alfonso. "Mexico City is known for being the oldest and longest inhabited city in the world. Once was the Aztec capital city, known as Tenochtitlan."

Jose's Aunt Leona's friend Trelita from "Resorante Larcos," had a business on the next block. She delivered prepared food from the house specialty for the guests. When Jose and Alfonso walked in Aunt Leona and her daughter Rosala immediately swarmed them.

Aunt Leona kissed and hugged Jose, while Jose was trying to introduce his friend Alfonso. Aunt Leona called Trelita and had her bring the diner's for everyone. Aunt Leona, Rosala, and Pancho lived upstairs from the mercado.

Leona said. "Your Uncle Emmanuel is gone a lot, he has a job out of town." Leona affirmed to Jose. "Your Uncle Emmanuel always pays the rent on the flat on time."

She told Jose. "Pancho will be home tonight for three days. He typically leaves for three days on and three days off at his job in Acapulco as a cliff diver."

While in town this time Pancho wanted to show his cousin Jose and his friend Alfonso around Mexico City. Jose knew Poncho had many friends in Mexico asked him. "Hey cuz can you get me some Acapulco gold?"

Pancho laughed and called Jose "Loco" then said "Si. No problemo!"

Jose proffered. "While were going around to visit the tourist sights we want to smoke a few joints, we want a buzz on. Smoking Acapulco gold is the best buzz we can both think of." Neither cared much for alcohol other than a few beers on an occasion.

Jose conceded to Alfonso. "Were gonna to do this Mexican drug study but on our own terms and at our own pace."

Alfonso consulted to Jose. "I agree!"

Jose cleared the air. "Pancho don't smoke much marijuana at all."

Alfonso admitted. "I already seen Poncho with a bit of cocaine."

Jose contested. "I don't like hearing Poncho is into hard drugs." Both Alfonso and Jose turned down free offers of cocaine from Poncho.

Jose reacted to Poncho. "No thanks! I just smoke weed!"

Jose wasn't there to rock the boat with his cousin Poncho. Jose got to know Poncho and his friends fairly well over the next days to come. Alfonso said to Poncho. "The tourist and historical sights here are incredible." Poncho drove his own car and Jose bought all the gas. They were constantly on the go joyriding, and gathering Poncho's friends in their homes. Alfonso and Jose got a good feel from the Mexican natives on their sightseeing trip.

Jose admitted. "Smoking marijuana is socially accepted in Mexico, even in the city. Jose rolled his Acapulco gold marijuana cigarettes, and the natives liked the sweet flavor.

Alfonso hyped to Jose. "Walking around the sights a bit stoned is all that more intriguing because of all the interesting historical foreign sights."

Jose agreed. "Yea! I enjoy seeing the sights better scampering stoned."

Alfonso noted. "I like the impressive murals by Diego Rivera detailing key periods in Mexican History in the stairways of federal buildings."

Jose illustrated. "The National palace was built on the exact sight of Montezuma's palace. It conceals more breath taking murals by Diego Rivera."

Poncho described. "The historic Aztec market place in the plaza of three cultures depict Mexico city's evolution. The city of temples, palaces, and market places exhibit the National Heritage and indigenous cultures. At one time from AD 200 to AD 500 there were over two hundred thousand residents in Teotihuacan-Puebla just south of here. Cortez conquered and destroyed the city but the place remained and flourished."

Poncho on our last day of their grand tour, he took Jose and Alfonso to the Chapultepec Castle which served as a military encampment, controlled by the Spanish and Mexican dignitaries, and is a National Museum.

Jose listed. "This place is full of rich artifacts from eras of the past." Alfonso told Jose. "These Cathedrals are larger than I've ever seen." Jose also marveled at the Aztec massive stone altars.

Poncho pointed. "Ceremonials offerings were sacrificed there. Look at the religious paintings on the surrounding walls."

Alfonso radiated to Jose. "Again and again this city reflects it's religious spiritual presence."

Jose descried. "Mexico City is impressive and marijuana is no problem to get here, just as it is no problem to get in the United States."

Alfonso admired. "Yea. With Mexico City the Capital of Mexico and the commercial center of the country, everything should be here."

Jose and Alfonso did research in Mexico City libraries on Government facts concerning the de forestation of the forests, Indian Mayan ruins, and the collected drug report's from the Mexican newspaper's. They already knew what Mayan ruins, and rain forest they were going to visit after leaving Acapulco for the Chiapas State backcountry.

Poncho drove all the way to Acapulco via a one night lay over in Taxco. When they leave Taxco, they were going to stay in the poncho's villa he shared with another cliff diver Romano in Acapulco.

On the way to Taxco, the group went though numerous hills and valleys of the southern Sierra Madres Mountains. In Taxco, Jose said. "Light up a gold one."

Alfonso asked. "You want to smoke another gold one?"

Jose responded. "Yep!"

Poncho asked. "Can you see the brightly colored white and red stucco houses?"

Jose gazed and commented. "The back drop of this Mexican country side is gorgeous." They all went to the café Resorante and dined on Taco's and buritto's.

Jose offered. "I'll buy the cervazas with our lunch." As they all toured this colonial era town. Every building seemed to be making fine jewelry.

Poncho explained. "The tradition of silver smithing in this town has been carried on throughout the centuries. They are mining silver in the deep gorges as we drive into Taxco. There is a variety of Zapotec, Mixtec, Aztec, European and pre Columbian designed adornments that are made from Taxco Silver. The hand made jewelry is found in abundance in the surrounding shops. This is why I brought you Tourists here." Jose said. "The library in Mexico City said this was Spain's biggest source for precious metals after Cortez took control. Cortez sent tons of precious metals back to Spain."

Alfonso detected. "Walking down the cobble stone streets gives you the historical sense of value about what a National Treasure this place is."

Jose and Alfonso would never forget this elegant town of Taxco, where all the balconies of the villas are filled with ornate brightly colored flowers.

Alfonso was a busy taking pictures to chronicle the tour of events. They both kept mental notes and photos, while stalking the drug influence in the Mexican cultures and economy.

They were both careful, not to let on about their mission in Mexico. Not even Poncho was privy to the secret interrogative drug mission of Jose and Alfonso. Their entire intelligence gathering was done in subtle ways as to not arouse the suspicions of the locals.

The Mexican natives they met conversationally opened up once they were comfortable with their company. Alfonso told Jose. "Poncho is the perfect cover when mingling with the natives."

Most of the Mexican people welcomed Jose and Alfonso. They were welcomed as touristas. Which was the implication at all times, they tried to give off.

Jose and Alfonso sent all their Mexican drug information gathered of personal notes, photos and newspapers with pertaining to the drug industry corruption and economic articles assembled while in Acapulco, as planned back to Houston once they were ready to leave for the Chiapas.

Jose and Alfonso blended in with out many suspicions, after all they really hadn't pushed any buttons yet. After a festive night at a local tavern with live Mariachi Bands and all, and up next morning Poncho, Jose and Alfonso were on their way from Taxco to Acapulco.

Jose reeled off. "Thanks Poncho for your hospitable side track tour of Taxco."

Poncho answered. "Just remember to take me to an Astro's game in Houston next summer."

"Right on!" Jose said.

"Right on!" Alfonso said.

Poncho, Jose and Alfonso drove all morning from Taxco, they arrived at Poncho's waterfront villa. Poncho testified. "The best cliff divers get the best villas."

Surprisingly Alfonso said. "The best?"

Jose quickly stipulated. "Poncho is ranked among the best cliff divers in the world."

Alfonso announced. "I'm impressed with stature of Poncho's Villa."

Jose agreed. "Yea, I like the way the Villa is positioned on the beach front. Acapulco is everything I ever thought it was proclaimed to be."

Alfonso enthused. "I can't wait to hit the beach."

"I think I'll start cliff diving." Jose said kidding his cousin Poncho.

Poncho regaled. "We'll see how you feel after I bring you to the "La Quebrada" tonight."

"What's that?" Jose asked.

"You'll see!" Poncho predicted.

"La Quebrada" is world famous for cliff diving." Alfonso marveled.

The stay in Acapulco was only for two fun filled days full of thrills, before Jose and Alfonso were scheduled to depart toward Oaxaca on the Mexican continental divide. Poncho had arranged for Jose and Alfonso to attend a festival the following night. Poncho had plenty of girl friends for Jose and Alfonso's stay.

Poncho overlooking the Rivera mentioned. "Those girls over there on the beach are my friends. I told them you were coming. They will accompany us to the festival near the cliffs tonight."

Ballina one of the girls was into snorkeling stood near Jose. Jose knew she was part of the group that Poncho had picked out askd. "Do you know Poncho"?

Ballina answered. "Yes!"

Jose asked. "Are you going to the "La Quebrada" tonight?"

Ballina answered back. "Yes"

Jose asked. "By the way, what's your name?"

"Ballina" she confessed.

Jose quickly asked. "Meet me up there? Alright!"

Ballina enthused. "Si! I'll see you up there later." Then she asked. "Have you been to the cove?"

"No!" Jose reacted.

"Snorkel with me over to the cove." Ballina ended up taking Jose and Alfonso to a private cove, where they explored the reefs, corals, and sea life in the afternoon sun.

At night they met up with Poncho along with Jose's new friend Ballina at the La Quebrada. They all watched Poncho and his Cliff diving friends gracefully diving from the cliffs one hundred and thirty feet down to the surf.

Jose disclosed. "The suspense of seeing Poncho in mid air was a thrill to behold and it was worth the whole trip in itself. I never knew Poncho was so cut up in a muscular sense."

Alfonso averred. "I agree his muscles are really defined."

Alfonso said to Jose. "I never knew Mexico had so much to offer."

Jose said. "You do now, Al."

Al further stated. "I'll be back some day."

Twilight's evening set in and the sun was rapidly falling into the Pacific ocean, as the cliff divers enjoyed diving off the cliffs into the night. Jose, Alfonso, Ballina, and the rest of the girls were on the teak deck of the La Perla club a local out door cafe, watching the cliff divers with amazement.

The next day Jose and Alfonso went to their first bull fight. Jose told Alfonso. "Poncho has arranged for everyone to go to the bull fights. I will escort Ballina."

Alfonso implored Poncho. "They've taking a liking to each other."

Poncho conceded. "I can see that. There hanging all over each other."

Alfonso divulged. "They haven't quit kissing."

Poncho read. "Man against Beast" as they walked past the advertised poster, as they whizzed into the bull-fighting arena."

Alfonso said. "Some people think bull fighting is cruel and uncivilized treatment of animals. They are protesting outside of the arena." Everyone was in the arena stands, they observed the matador using his brightly colored cape to entice the bull to charge. With every charge the crowd roars with spectacular enthusiasm. Yip-ity Yoop-ity yells, roaring screams, ooze, ugh, zzzz the crowd staggered on.

Poncho jabbered. "Just the crowd gets excited with every charge of the bull. It's enough for anadrenaline rush."

Alfonso gasped. "The bull just got hammered! Did you see that matador's move. He stuck him good."

Jose bought some bull souvenirs to send back to Miles the next day. It was to be their last contact with Miles before leaving for the military overrun interior of the rainforest areas of southern part of the Chiapas State.

When they left the bull-fighting arena for Poncho's villa. Poncho wanted them to hurry to one more festival "You can meet some more natives on your last night. I want to take you to one more festival."

Jose pumped. "OK, we can't wait!"

Alfonso ripped. "Come on with it!" Poncho enjoyed his cousin and his friend Alfonso. Poncho said to both of them. "I want one more memorable moment, before the both of you depart for Oaxaca on the bus the tomorrow morning." Poncho had bought a rather large bag of Acapulco gold. "Here, Jose this is for you and Alfonso during your rubbernecking."

"Thanks very much. I'll smoke it in kind." Poncho knew Jose and his friend would enjoy the treat of Acapulco gold flavored marijuana. Jose and Alfonso could hardly thank Powerhouse Poncho and Blue ribbon Ballina enough for their hospitality. When they finally boarded the bus for Oaxaca, everyone was waving good bye to each other as the bus pulled off. Adios! Poncho yelled. "Catch Ya later!" Jose Spurted.

Jose squealed. "Wow what a trip!"

Al granted. "I have to agree," as the bus roared down the highway towards Oaxaca.

Once again the bus didn't go very far down the highway where upon it stopped because of roadblocks by the Mexican military. Jose said to Alfonso. "They sure keep a tight grip on things down Mexico way."

Jose said to Alfonso. "It seems like the further we push into the interior the thicker the Mexican Military presence."

They started a new phase of their Mexican investigations. The trip proved to get more interesting, as they both scanned the interior of the Mexican countryside. The main thing going was that Alfonso's relatives reside in San Chritobal. Alfonso never met his relatives was the only catch.

Sonto, Alfonso's father was proud to have his son meet his family.

After an all night drive, the bus pulled into Oaxaca. Jose said. "I hope you don't mind altitudes. Oaxaca's altitude is comparable to mile High City of

Denver in the USA. Both cities are on the fringe of the continental divide in their own countries."

A rider getting off the bus pointed. "See the historic district with it's Spanish colonial traditions."

Alfonso observed. "Look at the Colorful Indian markets peddling bracelets, earrings, chains, wood pieces, costume dresses, and wicker works."

The bus rider decreed. "This is the best preserved city from colonial times. Make sure you both go to the El Parian. It's a Mexican-style an excellent flea market, where Indian unique crafts and arts are sold."

Jose admired. "Look at that astonishing ancient Indian ruins." The Indian ruins were immediately noticed upon arrival in Oaxaca. It was at 7:00 a m in the morning just past sunrise. Jose and Al went straight to their hotel to book in. After dropping off their travel belongings, they tried to get a feel for the climate of affairs. They were on their own again, tried to listen to some of Poncho's advice. Steer clear of trouble especially in the Mexican interior.

Jose told Alfonso. "This time were not going to get involved with all the sight seeing. We want to see how easy it will be to get drugs in the Mexican interior. We want to see about the availability of drugs, mix in with a few locals and partake in a few smoke downs."

Alfonso gloated to Jose. "That's a good way to get the locals opinions on Mexican drug experiences. We want to see how far the majority of the locals are involved with drugs and the drug trade."

Jose professed to Alfonso. "The only way is to mingle with the Mexicans and observe." On one taxi tour driver Peron got them cocaine and marijuana in a matter of minutes.

Peron portrayed. "Drugs are readily available through out Mexico. It is a way to make money. It is a way of life under very difficult and different social circumstances."

Jose asked. "Doesn't the United States help stop the drug trafficking down here with your government?"

Peron answered. "The United States has no influence here what so ever on the Mexican people. We have to feed our families. We will never stop the flow of cocaine and marijuana. It's part of the way we do business in Mexico". Jose replied. "That's an awfully entrenched attitude if I ever seen one, " as they dandered back to there hotel for the night. Alfonso cautiously whisked over a nearby creek emptied the cocaine into the creek.

Jose relieved. "Thanks Al. I don't want those hard drugs." They both did what they wanted to do throw the drugs away in water.

Al conveyed. "I don't want to get caught with the stuff either."

Jose breathing easier said. "I'm glad to see that gone." Neither of them did hard drugs like cocaine. Smoking marijuana and an occasional beer or two was their personal limits. Jose said. "Well it's no problem. We found out buying any kind of drugs, including various downs and uppers are available anytime, anywhere, even this far into Mexico."

Alfonso assessed. "If you want any kind drugs it sure is not a problem. Drugs are big business in the United States and in Mexico. What's needed is better laws, better governing, and honest law enforcement to correct the hard drug problem."

Jose noted. "Honest cops are not in the largest part of the general mix of law enforcement down here in Mexico. Their all on the take that's the way it is."

Alfonso said. "If you're not on the take, and you're a drug busting cop you won't live long." That's the way Jose and Al both took it.

The next morning Jose and Alfonso were on their way farther down the highway into the interior of the mountain towns toward Tuxtla Guttierrez. They Kriss crossed the continental divide several times before reaching the city of Tuxtla Gutierrez.

Following the signs on federal highway 190, until late afternoon, when they finally reached the Plaza Civica in the main square. Jose and Alfonso went to a restaurant that had been newly renovated.

The restaurant had a horse arena inside it. While they had breakfast, these elegant horsemen pranced their fine horses around the ring. The horses were elaborately decorated with unparalleled silversmith bridle.

The windy waiter told Jose. "Horsemen are practicing for the big show tonight. The fancy horsemen are a new venue at the restaurant. The horsemen shows become an attraction for the city." When the waiter walked away Jose said to Alfonso. "That horse shit laying all over the dance floor kills my appetite." Alfonso laughed.

The following day they ride in an open-air jeep to the zoo called the "Miguel Alvarez del Toro. Al said. "I want to see the varieties of animals, so we can get aquatinted to the wild life of rain forest. You know Carmen's game plan is to take us on a mule trip into the Mexican interior of the rain forest once we arrive in San Cristobal."

Jose asked. "Are there any jaguars still in the jungle?"

Alfonso answered. "I'm sure there is. It's not like southern Florida where human habitation has driven the jaguars to near extinction."

Alfonso explained. "One of the main reasons we came is to research the de forestation of the forest first hand to help stop eliminating plant and animal life."

Jose answered. "We have to do our part to stop the de forestation and animal extinction."

Jose and Alfonso were doing serious research on their topics from the tropics. Over a dish of tamales de jacuanae Jose explained to Al. "The reports for the college we attend in San Antonio, is an independent study that I'm going to be graded "A" on for De forestation. Mr. Stoker is my Prof."

Al concurred. "I want to do an independent study on the Chiapas Indian uprising's. I want to get the story first hand since my kin folk and my heritage are rooted in the Chiapas part of the country. I'll do a back ground study on the Indian Mayan ruins for cover, but I really want to expose the abuses I've been hearing about my people."

During the independent studies they both would do, they would also do a report together on the drug environment in Mexico for Miles and Miles's Editor Ed. Speaking of drugs Jose lit a joint up on the plaza after lunch. Jose said. "Here Al! Light this gold one up."

Al responded "Don't mind if I do!" They went to a hidden part of the garden area of the restorante, they take their gold break.

As they stepped down the side walks of Tuxtla. Jose testified. "The newspapers are a big help in catching the trends of Mexican moods. Bad cops and politicians are busted for being involved in the cartel drug trade and replaced even more crooked cops. Drug money is what runs a large part of the economy."

Alfonso belabored. "Bad cops don't stay in jail long. The judges are bought off too."

Jose countered. "The drug kingpins are agents of antagonizing corruption. These drug entrepreneurs are involved in every phase of commerce in the Mexican economy. The drug kingpins ruthlessly pursue their drug monopolies. Sacrificing lives for profit is the way they do business."

Alfonso responded. "The narcotic cartels are the most successful businessmen in Latin America. They feed the mainstream economy."

Jose disclosed to Alfonso while they were alone talking and walking in the Zoo. "Without the influx of narco dollars into the Latin American their countries economy would collapse. That is why these politicians see things differently in Mexico than in Washington, D C."

Alfonso specified. "They have reasons concerning their state interests. The United States is hooked on drugs and the Latin American countries are hooked on narco dollars."

Jose admitted. "Mexican Economies bring in a minimum of two hundred million dollars per year in narco dollars. Were talking about the infrastructure of the Mexican economy."

Alfonso appealed. "The drug cartels will continue to line the pockets of politicians and police, and they all keep taking their cut. Your not taking their point of view are you Jose?"

Jose responded. "No! I'm down here doing an independent study on the drug situation for the new paper. These are the facts as I see them. I'm just calling it as I see it for now. What do you think Alfonso?"

Alfonso confessed. "The evidence seems over whelming so far. Let's leave it at that for now and we'll keep digging up some more drug information on current affairs, before we make our final assessment."

Jose relayed. "I can do that!"

The next day they finished their short run into San Cristobal de Las Cases in the state of Chiapas. Alfonso's cousin Carmen picked them both up at the bus station near the San Christobal market. Carmen brought them to Alfonso's kin folk huts on the village edge. This was to begin their extensive research work in the Chiapas State and the National Liberation Army.

Jose looks at Alfonso and depicted. "This is the same city that was taken by the Zapatista guerrillas in a past revolt against the Mexican government. The rebels as they're known took control of this Colonial City and five surrounding towns in the Chiapas highlands."

Alfonso emphasized. "The rebel revolt was caused by injustice in spreading economic wealth and health care to the Chiapas area. This is especially disturbing when a third of the crude oil produced in Mexico is from the Chiapas State."

Jose affirmed. "Their world is divided by rich, poor and racism. The majority of these Mayan Indians live in mud houses mixed with some wood slats. There is a dozen on average living together inside. Children die of malnutrition, dehydration, diarrhea of tuberculosis or a number of other curable and preventable diseases."

Carmen admitted. "Our leaders believe they have nothing to loose living this slow death. The revolt was the only way to draw attention to our state of affairs. Look around you! You can see many in poor health and with no decent homes for our families. We are descendants of the people, who built this nation first off and we have the least. We have no voice in the assembly of government. We have been largely ignored, we are left to starve to death in the modern world."

Carmen took Alfonso and Jose out among his peoples. Alfonso upon meeting his relatives and seeing them living in such appalling conditions immediately took the shirt off his back and gave it to one of his cousins Lino. Alfonso said. "Carmen! We are buying all the food and clothing for you and my relatives while were here until were broke. We will buy the provisions!"

Jose responded. "We'll send you some more money when we get back to States as well." Jose and Alfonso both wanted to help anyway they could. They called back home for more money form Miles.

Alfonso raged. "These poor people live in appalling conditions compared to the United States! Kids play on the shallows of the riverbanks for recreation. Most have no clothes on or real toys to play with!"

Jose expounded to Alfonso. "The living conditions are primitive, and crude. There is no relief here of any kind from their government. There is no real medical care here either. There is no food provided by the government to help these people. There is no clean water for everyday living, and no electricity. These conditions all lead to a negative social situation. These people are fighting for their very existence."

Alfonso griped. "The Mexican governments para-military attacks on these indigenous people is intolerable to the moral elements of the Mexico's Community, and the International community. International Monitors as well as these Indians are being forced from the homeland areas by the para-military. No free independent monitoring is allowed."

Carmen heard his cousin tell all. "The Mexican Government will have to show us by deeds, not words any longer, that they will have improve living conditions of the Indians in this area. A government proves it's a democracy when they take care of their own. A government that destroys its people is not a government of the people."

171

Jose recounted to Carmen. "Subcomandante Marcos the leader of the Zapatista's says he wants a peaceful Solution for his people but the government has reneged on all it's past promises repeatedly. Marcos says the government won't deal fairly with the indigenous people. Foreign aid organizations distribution of medical supplies and food have stopped. The are no longer allowed to go to the rebel villages. Even the missionary's have been expelled from Chiapas. The Mexican government has imposed strict travel restrictions on all foreigners."

Alfonso conveyed. "The Mexican government should make Marcos governor of the Chiapas State and give him large cash subsidies to govern since he is the one who really cares about the people."

Jose explained. "The Mexican government says on one hand it has new strategies of political over military containment, but cracks down on rebel villages. Detaining residents at random by the military police is routine. Top Mexican cops still fire on unarmed and innocent victims killing them at random."

Carmen described. "The Indian self governments created by the residents and represent the community are being ignored by the Mexican government. Indian protesters rights are squashed of their. The Indians of Chiapas are continually being pushed around and off their land as deforestation and Mexican urban building continues at a rapid pace. Poverty is rampant among our people. Our human rights are ignored."

Alfonso and Jose told Carmen. "We'll help you and your people anyway we can Carmen. Let us know what we can do."

The next day they left early for an expedition into the dense forest located high up into the rugged mountains. Carmen's friend an Indian guide named Lota will ensure safe passage into the rain forest by the mule train.

Carmen told Alfonso. "We'll be taking our journey higher and higher, winding up and around into the elevations of mountain country."

Jose conferred to Alfonso. "This is the thickest part of the jungle" as they were ion the trail of the mountain country side their guide Lota led them on their odyssey.

Alfonso identified to Jose. "Look at the poppy's that grow wild every where on the mountain sides." Through the hills across the rivers, lagoons, and through some almost impenetrable jungles they plodded there way. Cobwebs hung like fishing nets in lengthily cobbled webs. Giant spiders and large snakes beyond belief were in abundance and surrounded the explorers, they continued on with their guide. Lota illustrated. "The rain forest extended far beyond the ridges to the North, when I was young. The vast amounts of the rainforest are gone from the construction bulldozers. Gone are the animals and plants, that keep the rain forest alive."

As Jose and Alfonso pushed through the rain forest with their cousin Carmen said. "The sounds of the Macaws, toucans, motmot from the foliage above are more intriguing in the wild then at the zoo."

Jose agreed. "It's a majestic feeling."

Carmen groused. "The loggers have robbed the precious woods like Mahogany and Rosewood. We take to parts of the rain forest that is still left."

Alfonso scanned the rainforest. "The exceptional fauna and flora here is impressive."

Jose told Alfonso. "Our Indian guide has his own bud and doesn't mind sharing it, especially since we have our own Acapulco gold."

Lota harped Jose. "I like the flavor of your gold bud, we don't get much gold bud down here. We have plenty of Panama Red though."

Jose remarked. "That Panama Red smokes just fine."

Carmen told Alfonso. "The Mayan's hope to preserve this area of the rain forest and along with their heritage. Some Mayan's still practice religious ceremonies with marijuana as did their forefathers."

Alfonso prophesied. "I don't mind if I get spiritual like my fore fathers did right now. Light up a joint Jose!"

Jose and Alfonso would be taken to remote Indian villages. Carmen tells Jose. "People from the outside world rarely see remote rain forest villages." Foreign to Jose and Alfonso was the language and customs of these Indians. Dogs, chickens, ran free around village. Kids had small rain forest animals as pets. Small monkey's and birds were their item's of choice.

Jose and Alfonso knew Sub-commander Marcos was close at hand.

Jose portrayed to Alfonso. "The Federal Military groups intensifyingly thick tried to flush Marcos out the mountains of "La Realidad," where we are presently touring. Marcos said through the La Jornada newspaper: "What the Zapatistas demand is their right to live with justice, democracy, liberty, and dignity."

Alfonso claimed. "Marcos is a hero to these Indians in these parts, and demands better conditions for his people. Marcos is one of the only ones with balls enough to stand up for the Indian causes against the PIR who have controlled the Mexican government with their own self interest."

Our Mayan Indian guide Lota knew what time it was, and he knew how to avoid all the Federals. Carmen tells Alfonso and Jose. "Twenty-nine paramilitaries were just thrown in jail and only one has been convicted so far for shooting forty-five Indians, nine men, fifteen children, and twenty-one women to death. They were praying in a church in the mountain side village of Acteal. All the Indian peasants were unarmed. The National Human Rights Commission doesn't believe justice was fully rendered, nor has economic aid been provided in the area. There has been no reduction in the friction between the military and the peasants to control the violence."

Jose persisted. "What dogs these government military cops are."

Alfonso cried out. "Their gutless!"

Carmen continued. "The police commander of a nearby village is charged with collecting weapons after the slaughter. The Indians were thought to be sympathetic to Zapatista's cause."

Alfonso alarmed riveted. "Why isn't anybody speaking up for these people in today's modern day society?"

Carmen echoed. "Topping maters off three thousand Indians protested the massacre by the military cops peacefully. The protestors were shot at by government military commandos. They killed a young mother, shot her daughter and another boy."

Jose declared. "Those Mexican police who fired on and killed the innocent Indians were arrested and some admitted guilt."

Carmen deemed. "That doesn't matter the Mexican Military will let them all go free to kill Indians again."

Jose persisted. "Political opposition leaders say the Mexican government rule of force is waging a dirty war against the Indians in the Chiapas State. Although the governor stated publicly that the police are not there to fire on citizens for any reason."

Carmen gripped. "It's a little late for that! The citizen's want all para-military out of their villages. The police and Federals are not trusted in their towns. The Military Police enter the villages and incite trouble by provoking the citizens. The Indians are not going to be intimidated. We will continue to march and form human chains on the highway to stop traffic and protest the magnitude of this tragedy. We want the President of Mexico to resign! We wanted the paramilitary dogs of the PRI held accountable!" Uncontrollably Carmen fumed. Who could blame him.

Jose and Alfonso were in the middle of a war. "This abstract social environment was a long way from Houston."

Jose told Alfonso. "Light up a joint Jose. I've got to do something to help ease my mind of this senseless abuse. The Indians are mad and who can blame them. These people are abused by a system that is supposed to help them, not be a major problem to them. A government holding weapons over their heads to rule their land and resources."

Jose answered. "Poverty and injustice breeds depression."

Carmen recanted. "More than dialogue is needed now. Actions of great magnitude are needed to gain the confidence of these indigenous people. Good proposals need to be implemented to kick-start the peace talks that are still stalled over Indian rights. The Mexican Government is debating Indian Rights Bills in the Legislatures. But even now how will agreements hold up when peasant rights, and political officials keep getting killed at a sure and steady pace."

Lota explained. "The influential leader Rubicel Ruiz Gamboa of the Democratic State Assembly of the people of the Chiapas was gunned down the day before you entered the state capital of Tuxtla. The Mexican Media reported the killing, Ruby had endured death threats on a consistent basis. Ruby was one of the direct links to the Zapatista Rebels, holding out in the mountains. You can see by the pace of the events unraveling, that everything was being orchestrated by higher authorities."

Carmen disclosed. "Seven Tojolabal Indians were found dead in a deep mountainous ravine in the Chiapas. They were tortured then killed and covered with jungle brush. The Federal Police killed pro-rebel supporters, who were political opponents. The Federal police operational mode is no different than the drug cartels. These Tojolabal Indians were slaughtered for their oppositional political beliefs. The Tojolabal Indians should be dealt with fairly by the government. Instead were being eliminated. Our Indians by rights of the grandfather laws have more right to be here in the Chiapas than any Mexican Federals. We are being forced off our land by the well armed Federals."

Alfonso reviewed to Jose. "These Indian natives have to fight off poverty and racism in their home land. They have no way to express individual Idealism with out threat of death. Foreign church missionaries in the Chiapas are threaten, and driven off by military factions. The missionaries are no longer there to help shield the natives from the Federals."

Jose screened. "Understanding the Revolt by the "Zapatista's" can be realized with one look at the mud houses with dirt floors in which they live hard and die after a short life. These people have nothing. no food, clothes, education, housing, work, political leaders, or health care for themselves of family. They are constantly being driven off their land. Governmental powers are eroding the indigenous people off the face off the map. The Indians feel they have little or nothing to loose with no social resources available for them."

Jose and Alfonso spoke with Lota and Carmen in the Indian village hut had entered the area of conflict at a Heighten state of affairs in southern Mexico. They could sense and see the Indians of the Chiapas fighting for their rights and their very survival. International Human rights activists are outraged. Foreign observers and journalists are not allowed into the Chiapas State area.

Carmen mentioned to his cousin Alfonso. "These human rights violations in Chiapas must be addressed. Unchecked paramilitary groups rushing in with more and more extensive weaponry for total control of the Chiapas is terrifying."

Alfonso responded. "The Federals destroy, kill, or maim anything or anyone in their way. The Zapatista freedom fighters demand that the Federalises cut the number of troops in the area of the Chiapas as a condition for peace negations. Indian rights fighters are outnumbered three hundred to one by the federals."

Carmen was madly incited when he thought about the injustice presented repeatedly regarding his people. Carmen burned inside as the Indian village campfire flamed. "When Columbus first sighted the Americas, there were hundreds of different groups of Mayan and Aztecs Indians groups. The ancestors of these great Mayan and Aztecs cultures have been reduced to less than fifty groups. What's left of the existing Indian groups are almost near extinction. The lost Mayan and Aztec Indian Empire of past have few remaining ancestors to practice the ways of the past Indian cultures."

The next day it was hard for Jose and Alfonso to concentrate on the deforestation part of the project. They were determined to achieve all their scholastic goals. Alfonso's cousin Carmen kept them out of harm's way while in the jungle rain forest.

Jose told Alfonso. "It's time for a comprehensive study of the Lacandon Mayan way of life in connection to the rain forest dense jungle."

Alfonso rattled off. "Really!"

Jose continued. "It is estimated that there are no more than three hundred to five hundred Mayan's living in primitive stone aged conditions similar their ancestors. The "Hach Winik" as they are known live secluded in the rainforest. They have been pushed into an area of less than ten percent of what was originally the dense Lacandon rain forest."

The Mayan Indian habitat of thatched huts set along the mountainside abundant with wild life. Jose pointed out. "Look! That village boy is holding a young ocelot affectionately in his arms as a pet."

Alfonso counseled. "It's not like cartoons? Is it."

Lota disclosed to Jose and Alfonso. "Ten percent of the rain forest that's left, and ninety-five of the forest have been destroyed by the lumbering industry in the rain forest, traditions are continually getting harder to practice. The more gas and oil that is found, the more deforestation continues as well. Protection for the last of the rain forest in Mexico must come fast."

Carmen decreed. "The rituals and principles are purely Mayan in this village. We still face unprecedented changes from the massive settlement of the frontier. When you destroy the jungle, you destroy our world. Many indigenous cultures do not exist today because of the massive de-forestation."

Alfonso lamented. "The onslaught of immigrant homesteaders, continually come and destroy the rain forest. Cattle ranchers then exhaust the lands resources beyond repair. Farmers only yield two to three years worth of crops before the rainforest soil is depleted of its minerals. The soil than turns into red dust where the rich rainforest once was."

Carmen explained. "Lota is the son of the Mayan Indian village Shaman. He was educated in medical school, as a young man by Christian missionaries. He realizes that plant diversity is threaten by commercial logging. All the derivatives of medicine are destroyed before the plants can be analyzed for a productive use. The specialized flora and fauna of the rain forest tangled with tropical vines, have been undisturbed for hundreds of years, are systematically eliminated. Continuing illegal logging operations are never questioned."

As we cleared our way through the jungle trail to the Bonampak Mayan ancient ruins ceremonial center. Lota said to Alfonso. "Look, You can see the magnificent color murals which date back to 790 AD in the small temple."

Jose noted. "The reproductions in Mexico City and Tuxtla are no comparison to the artistic genius of these lost generations of primitive Mayan culture."

Lota depicted. "The monumental architecture of the ruins are a great spectacle in the middle of the jungle floor."

Alfonso told Jose. "I can feel my ancestors presence as we walk though the temples of the ruins." The silence was surrounded by stillness. Alfonso, Carmen, Lota and Jose lit up another gold one as they walked through the Mayan ruins. Each passing the burning joint from one another to the next.

Carmen spooked mewled. "Your right cuzz! It feels like their right here with us. We'll camp at the basin. Lota has a spot picked out for the night."

Alfonso chattered. "I'll sleep good and sound tonight." as the murky skies of temperate weather set in.

For nine days they had no idea, when and or where they would depart the jungle. They didn't care at this point.

Alfonso admitted. "I like camping out in the different villages and investigating the customs of the Indian people."

Jose responded. "I thought it was neat seeing the head chief men of the last village and listening to his stories."

Alfonso thrilled railed. "I like the story about the mountain lion that killed one of there dogs the night before we arrived!"

Jose depicted. "What's cool about this place is that you can hear the parrots and monkey's most always."

Carmen disclosed to Lota. "The other animal calls are strange for Jose and Alfonso."

The headman of the tribe in the village they were in asked Lota. "Does Jose and Alfonso want to visit the village Shaman?"

Jose asked. "For what?"

Lota responded. "The Shaman is the traditional healer in the village. The spiritual insight of the Shaman holy man bring good omens."

Jose and Alfonso quickly agreed. "Yes we will."

With an array of colorful Toucan's behind him Lota explained. "We entered the village at the right time. The em-powered Shaman is conducting a spiritual seance now," as they toed slowly into the hut.

Lota further explained. "The Shaman is treating a village women for stomach cramp. The seance includes chanting and singing various tribal-healing songs. Jungle herbs, plants, animal parts, peyote, mushrooms, marijuana are some of the different jungle foliage included in some remedies of the healing process." Alfonso attentively said. "I'm amazed"

Lota continues to explain. "These are precious sacraments which help them visualize their spiritual outlook. This helps give them a vision and strength to heal. This is a special spiritual process the Indians have done for centuries."

Jose looked at Alfonso and said. "I feel privileged to attend this sacred Mayan ritual." Alfonso looked at Jose and said. "I'm impressed. We'll never have an opportunity to see this again."

After another nights rest they headed back to San Cristobal the next morning, and expect to reach there in three days time.

Their trip though the jungle had been in part by mule train, bus rides and with the Indian rain forest natives by canoe up and down the river.

Now, that they were back in San Cristobal they thought they would visit Alfonso's relative's for a few days, before departing to Palenque to see the Palace another Mayan archaeological site. Alfonso's Aunt Delanta had a letter for Alfonso.

The letter instructed Alfonso and Jose to change plans and go to Nicaragua to observe a hundred acre plot of commercial hemp grown by Canadian Company "Hemp-Argo International. Pierre a Canadian hemp product manufacture wanted to invest large amounts of cash into the commercial hemp agricultural operation. He first wanted a independent hemp report, Pierre asked Clint and Miles if they could help. Miles told Pierre he would have the duo investigative hemp team on location in central America check thoroughly out. Plans were changed quickly and Jose and Alfonso were on a bus south bound to the Guatemalan border.

On the bus in Guatemala another traveler Carlos struck up a conversation with Jose. Carlos asked. "Where are you going?" to the travelers.

Jose told Carlos. "We're going to research a large hemp plantation in Nicaragua. we want to see how healthy the crops grow down here compares to other crops."

Carlos in their long ride into the interior of Guatemala told Jose about the recent truth commission was established to expose human rights abuses during Guatemala's long civil war. Carlos recounted to Jose. "Evidence was reported in mainstream news of the United States direct involvement in our civil war. They backed the government's ruling party that completely exterminated some Mayan Indian villages. They destroyed their homes, livestock, and food gardens. The Guatemalan's Paramilitary raped the women during the kidnappings, and tortured most before summary executions during the massacre's. They're is plenty of documented evidence presented at the Truth Commission of US involvement."

Jose fumed. "I hope our government brings all those in our country involved with these massacres to justice."

Alfonso quickly agreed. "They have been getting away with atrocities unchecked for years. We need to hold them accountable."

While still riding on the bus Carlos informed. "One German citizen on the panel stated. "It was clearly genocide and a planned strategy against the civilian population." the report said the United States was in support of these state sponsored criminal operations of killing innocent civilians during the civil war."

Jose asked. "Hey, Carlos the war is over isn't it."

Carlos replied. "Yes! For now it is." as the bus rolled on.

Alfonso said. "I've never seen so many coffee, banana, sugar cane fields or different kinds of birds in my life. Where the heck are we?"

Jose emphasized. "What else do you expect in the tropics?"

Carlos going all the way to Managua conferred. "Where approaching the Nicaraguan border."

Jose confessed. "This is a long ride.

Alfonso professed. "Especially non-stop!"

Carlos asked. "Where is the hemp plantation?"

Jose responded. "The hemp plantation is in Managua two miles from the International Airport."

Carlos specified. "I'll be going to Managua, that's where I live."

Jose proclaimed. "Great! We'll finish our journey to Managua together."

Uncomfortable cat napping they finally arrived in Managua in their early morning. After Carlos bid them good luck and good bye, Jose and Alfonso caught a taxi and went straight for the "Hemp Hacienda" at the hemp plantation.

Upon arrival Jose noted. "There's the sign! "Hemp-Argo International" big and plain as day.

Alfonso affirmed. "We're supposed to find the supervisor of the project Canadian horticulturist Dr Paul Wylie." They noticed straight off all the plantation workers in the large hemp field.

By now a worker named Julio came up to Jose and asked. "Are you here to look the hemp crop over."

Jose responded. "Yes! My name is Jose and this is Alfonso."

Julio remarked. "We've been expecting you. How was your trip?

Jose responded. "Cramped, uncomfortable, but I guess it beat walking."

Julio enthused. "Come this way and I'll show you to your accommodations." as Julio walked he explained the extensive hemp plantation's operation.

After they secured they're luggage in their rooms for the night at the Hemp Hacienda. Julio, Jose and Alfonso walked the hemp fields as the airliners were taking off and landing above their heads to Managua's International Airport.

Jose raved. "That is the biggest hemp filed I've ever seen. It's tasseled up beautiful."

Alfonso confided. "They must be harvesting. The have hemp stalk piles stack high over there in separate bunches."

Julio reassured. "Yes were harvesting now."

Jose noticed. They're stacking bagged hemp seeds over there."

Jose explained. "They ordered all the hemp seeds from China. It was the only place that they could get hemp seeds conducive to the tropical climate."

Alfonso appraised. "Hemp-Argo International" must have at least fifty Nicaraguans working here working this hemp field. These Canadian investors who sponsored this low THC industrialized hemp crop we'll be extremely happy with these crop results. The low THC level of the hemp falls within acceptable European and Canadian Standards."

Jose informed. "They want to plant ten thousand acres of Industrialized Hemp here next year. They are importing new European harvesting implements to handle the larger acreage for hemp project."

Alfonso contended. "I'm sure the financial investors will be real happy about this hemp project. Everyone is busy working this healthy hemp crop.

Julio conveyed. "That's where were making construction grade particle-board from hemp-stalk's. This is the larger mill over their as you can see is under construction. Then needed plenty of construction materials after hurricane Mitch blew through here. We sold all the hemp press board we made."

Jose asked. "Where did you get your seeds?"

Julio replied. China! Fifteen tons of hemp seeds were imported from China. They were inspected by US Customs in Long Beech, California. The customs officials emptied all the shipping containers of imported hemp seeds on the ground for the inspection."

Jose reacted. "On the ground?"

Julio conceded. "Yes, on the ground. Every part of the Hemp industry costs three times as much because of all the US government restrictions they pass along with foreign aid. They just won't let us develop a crop of hemp without paying more than it should cost."

Alfonso watched workers beating the hemp seeds from the stalks. Others eager workers were bagging the harvested hemp seeds.

Julio boasted. "When Hurricane Mitch came through it damaged a great amount of crops, but this hemp crop as you can see withstood the hurricane. We used no fertilizers or pesticides. What more can you ask for from a plant. Were pressing seeds over there for oil. Hemp seed's contain many essential amino acids. One pound contains over a hundred grams of natural protein. Would you like to see?"

Yes Please! They both said at the same time. Once in the press building other workers were using the newly installed automated hemp oil extractors.

Julio pledged. "Hemp seeds make the finest facial oils in the world. Ladies love the results on their face and hands. Many other products are made from hemp seeds too.

Jose told Al. "All we can do is go back to Houston and tell them we seen a large healthy hemp crop being harvested."

Alfonso professed. "That's the way I see it!" Both realized they have done their job to reassure investors. This was a viable hemp crop project with great commercial potential bursting at the seems. The investors are looking into several ten thousand acre plots, between Costa Rica, Panama, or any other country that would guarantee security for large tracts of tropical paradise to grow hemp. The investors want to process volume commercial hemp.

Alfonso disclosed. "Miles correspondence says they had to get permits the Nicaraguan government before they could even start planting."

Julio emphasized. "Yes! We have all the proper permits. The government officials were here last week praising the project."

Jose and Alfonso were tired from the trip. They had a long one back to San Cristobal. After late dinner they retired for the night in the Hemp Hacienda.

After a good nights rest and thanking Julio for showing them around some scenic volcano formed islands, they were both on their long trip back to San Cristobal.

Once in San Cristobal Aunt Delanta made a meal for everyone to behold. Over dinner Carmen discussed the trip to Palenque ruins Jose and Alfonso were going to explore.

Carmen accompanied Alfonso and Jose for that part of the journey before he would heading back to San Cristobal.

Carmen popped off. "I want to see the temple for myself!"

Jose disclosed. "I'll pay for your bus ticket to and from the ruins." Alfonso enthused. "Yea! That's a great idea!"

When they left San Cristobal Alfonso's Aunt Delanta gushed. "Here take some food with you! Al give this gold cross to your father!" Alfonso's father. is Delanta's younger brother Sonto.

After arriving in Palenque, Jose waved down a taxi. "Taxi" Jose, yelled as the driver finally stopped. "If your for hire, can you take us to the Tumba?"

The taxi driver gamed. "Si" The taxi driver then took them to the Tumba real. He explained. "That means the real tomb."

Jose railed. "I'm awe struck by the shear size of this monument!"

Alfonso compared. "The massive stone monument is well kept compared to Bonampak."

The taxi driver Frico conveyed. "Your more on the tourist trail here if you can call it that. Don't get me wrong though by saying tourist town, this still isn't Cancun."

Jose pledged. "I hear that!"

Frico confided to Jose. "There are guardians of the tombs who will show you around and explain the past history for a fee of five bucks American." The taxi driver Frico who also got Jose a bag of grass on the way to the tombs said. "Do you want me to get you some cocaine."

"No!" Jose quickly professed.

"Weeds it for us!" Alfonso said. They declined any hard drug offers at this point. The newspaper experiments are over so they all thought.

Harping Frico disclosed. "Cocaine is more available then marijuana." The taxi driver still asked them. "I can get you a kilo of coke cheap."

"No way! I don't care how cheap it is! I don't care if it's free!" Jose scolded him.

Alfonso attested. "We don't want any part of cocaine or a Mexican jail."

They knew they didn't have the power of the Mexican Cartel to back them up if they got busted, and they both didn't want any coke anyway. Marijuana was their high.

Carmen enounced. "Si, I like weed better to! You can still think and reason, when you're high on marijuana. Coke would definitely scramble your brains beyond reason like hard whisky."

Jose disclosed. "I'm glad we all think alike in that respect."

Alfonso and Jose were both having the time of their life. Jose, Alfonso, and Carmen didn't want anything to ruin it. They all stayed together for one more night at the main hotel in Palenque after they observed the ruins.

Carmen with a change in heart said to Alfonso and Jose at the last minute, before they departed north. "I'm going back with both of you to the United States."

Alfonso was dumb founded. "What!" Alfonso screams.

In a cold sweat Jose responded immediately. "I don't know Carmen!"

Carmen is Alfonso's cousin and he would be welcome at his family's home in Houston. Alfonso says. "There are no visas to get you into the United States and visa's are not that easy to get."

Carmen looks at both of them and sternly stated. "I'm going!"

Jose declared. "We'd have to smuggle Carmen into the states when we cross the boarder."

Alfonso admitted. "Even if we didn't smuggle him in we could set him up in Matamoros and it would be better than in the Chiapas. My parents and relatives could visit Carmen there until we figure something out."

Carmen then revealed next. "The cartel wants me to mule ten kilo's of cocaine into the states." Jose and Alfonso looked at each other and they both thought. This was one of the reason's they came to the country of Mexico. They wanted to find out the inner dealings of the drug world without being involved. But neither wanted to get totally involved in any kind of drug trading.

Carmen assured Jose and Alfonso. "The Mexican cartel will protect my journey all the way to the boarder."

"Wow! What a story that would be!" Jose clarified his thoughts. "I still don't know what to think!" Carmen just dropped a bombshell on both of them.

Alfonso compassionately said Jose. "We both know first hand how of a great poverty level that exists in the Chiapas."

Alfonso wanted his cousin to come to the United States. Carmen could stay with his family. Alfonso then wondered out load to Jose. "How do we engineer Carmen amidst the military road blocks."

Jose asked. "What if we get caught tying to help Carmen across the border?"

Carmen adamantly promised. "That's my problem!"

Alfonso emphasized. "No! That we'll be our problem!" Alfonso said to Jose quietly. "I don't want to see Carmen go back and live in dilapidated Palapa huts back in the bush. They don't even have clean water to drink."

Jose admitted. "Those living conditions are intolerable."

Alfonso further claimed. "I know if we can get Carmen back home in Houston things can work out. Carmen is young enough to make an adjustment to the United States way of life."

Carmen elucidated. "The Federals will let us go because I'm a protected mule." Carmen explained. "I'm supposed to contact an arm of the cartel in Veracruz. The man Navarro handles illegal alien drug mules from that point to all points of the Mexican American border for a big cartel kingpin. A friend of mine went to the states as a mule. My friend started a new life, when he reached the States. He' still lives there in the States, and he has never came back to the Chiapas."

Jose and Alfonso wanted to chronicle the drug trade for the newspaper but they didn't want to get involved heavy into drug trafficking. Carmen could come with out drugs they both thought.

Carmen contended. "The cartels will get me across the boarder."

The discussion barreled all night between the three of them, about how they would deal with this escapade. The arguing continued until the bus left.

Carmen was on the bus going northbound. Jose said to Alfonso. "Carmen cashed in his ticket to go back home to San Cristobal, and bought a ticket to Veracruz.

Alfonso decreed to Jose. "We'll were in for it now!"

Jose disclosed. "I know!" as he harmonized. "Were strangers in a strange land. Were gonna be hauling contraband."

Alfonso griped. "Don't even kid like that!"

On this on particular bus ride, a band was travelling on board. The band played a variety of instruments including an Accordion, box guitar, Congo's, and a few others. Bottles of Tequila were freely being passed to everyone on board. Marijuana passed freely. This part of the ride turned out quite festive. Jose spoke to Carmen. "Everyone is merrily going down the road with a lot of laughs."

Jose disclosed to Alfonso. "Were going to get that drug story after all."

Alfonso insistently repined. "We still have to distance ourselves from all the drug action."

Jose confessed. "I agree!" They arrived in Veracruz the next day.

In Veracruz they observed large coffee plantations, and knew the pleasure trip was over with. Jose divulged to Alfonso and Carmen. "This is going to be a dangerous game to play with the Mexican drug cartel, via your cousin Carmen."

Alfonso bitched. "You don't have to stick Jose."

Jose moaned. "I'm going! But I don't have to like it!"

Carmen avowed. "Don't worry! I'm the one who's the drug mule and by my own choice."

Carmen met Navarro at the Puerto of Veracruz on the wharf. Carmen told his two companions. "Navarro employed the day laborors for the ships that are in the port. The cartel has their man Navarro in place for travel arrangements for all the cartels drug shipments into the United States, Europe and beyond. The big ships in the harbor have produce such as coffee, bananas, and flower cutting's on board."

Jose itemized scanning the open ocean waters. "All the ships have drug shipments on them bound for all parts of the world."

Alfonso discussed. "The fisherman on the smaller boats are selling their catch directly off their fishing boats and onto the big ships."

Carmen noted. "Navarro is well known on the wharf. That's him in the black sombrero."

Jose gaped. "Look at all the Federal Military soldiers, they are evident everywhere."

Carmen detected. "There all Navarro's friends. Good luck I'll see you."

Alfonso envisioned. "Carmen your the one that's needs the luck. Were not going your way on this one."

Confident Carmen predicted. "I'll see you both in San Antonio!" Carmen left as the soldiers walked by."

Courageous Carmen approached Navarro on his own. Jose and Alfonso watched from a distance, while eating breakfast in a café on the wharf. They were all to meet later near the port's entrance. Carmen approached the terminal where Navarro was expectant. Carmen's friend Don Pedro from Tuxtla was Navarro's mule connection.

Keen sensed Jose contemplated while eating across the street with Alfonso across the street from Navarro. "The poor peasants are abundant from back in Tuxtla all the way to here. People are willing to make money dealing with drugs, instead of working a lifetime in their village."

Eyes sharpened Alfonso noticed. "Carmen is talking with Navarro. I'll bet he dropped Don Pedro's name already."

After approached by Carmen, Navarro immediately had Carmen taken into hiding with other drug mules. They are in a house expecting to be bussed north to the boarder. Jose and Alfonso had no idea what had happened to Carmen so quickly. Jose asked. "What happened?"

Alfonso answered. "They just scooped Carmen up, and cut out."

Jose had a taxi driver follow the car that took Carmen to the drug mule waiting station. The taxi driver knew that the tourists tailed one of the cartel's men.

The cab driver dropped off Jose and Alfonso called a cartel contact man. The taxi driver told them of the suspicious action of these so-called tourista's. The cab driver told the cartel contact. "There still at the café Carlita, near the north end of the wharf."

The cartel contact hawked. "We'll take care of it!"

The federal military police abruptly picked up Jose and Alfonso at the café for questioning. Alfonso thought real fast about an excuse for tailing Carmen's car. The Military Captain asked. "Why did you follow that car?"

Alfonso invoked. "I followed my cousin Carmen!"

The Mexican Military Capt. doing the questioning asked. "Why?" Alfonso quickly answered. "We wanted to go with him on his job, but he said we couldn't get hired."

"OK" said the Capt. after a phone call. "You can work with your cousin." The Federal Military police took them directly to the mule house where they were reunited with Carmen. Alfonso and Jose were unwilling mules.

Carmen couldn't believe Alfonso and Jose were at the mule station. Every one just looked at each other without saying a word. Everything was said through their eyes.

Navarro walked in and looked at the peasant mules and asked jokingly. "Is every body happy."

"Si" everyone said. "Good" he said. "I see we got a couple of more helpers." Navarro laughed as he left the room. All the mules were bought to the dock for two days of work. Navarro paid them for it so they'd all have a little pocket money.

Navarro collected thirty-five peasant mules at a time. The buses left Veracruz two to three times per week. The mule peasants were finally all herded into a cramped bus and transported north.

Jose said to Alfonso now. "Navarro didn't even tell us the destination on the border we were to penetrate."

Alfonso answered. "Not even how were going to penetrate the border."

Jose and Alfonso were now wondering if they would ever see their family's again. The bus drove day and night, yet rarely stopped for the military checkpoints.

Jose unlashed. "Unreal! I was just thinking how we got hassled more as tourist's travelling on the bus south. Now that were headed north with a busload of the cartel drugs and other mules we encounter no problems. What a fix!"

Alfonso blustered. "Yea! The Federal military personal just keep waving us all on as we sail right past the all Military check points."

While they went down the road. They all could see the road signs for Tampico, Monterrey, They were going straight up through the middle of Mexico. The bus driver drove day and night, stopping only for fuel, and were fed prepared food which was always ready at the designated stops.

Jose contended. "Miles ought to be happy, if we make it out of here alive. The story were all experiencing here is the drug trade as it flourished presently."

Alfonso defined. "Everybody here knows what's was going on here. Everybody makes their cut. They all do their part to bring the American Narco-dollars to their home land."

Carmen informed. "They feel better when they are feeding their families."

Jose professed to Carmen. "Starving and feeling righteous is no longer an option, with Mexican cartel acting as an employment agency."

Carmen explained. "The American government influence is minimal or none existent in everyday living for your southern neighbors."

Jose cracked. "I see can that!"

Alfonso declared. "Like it or not! We're all deeply involved in the drug trade south of the boarder now."

Jose jittery told alarmed Alfonso. "How it got to this point was beyond me." Jose and Alfonso had their American I. D.'s hid in the soles of their shoes. They didn't want to let the cartel know they were Americans from north of the boarder. Their indoctrination into the southern part of Mexico helped the situation they were now in. They felt they blended in with their dress and mannerisms. Carmen calmed their nerves, under these circumstances.

Once in the city of Torreon the bus met up with others in a bus staging area holding twenty to twenty-five buses. Jose said. "Look you can see all the buses are full of drug mules."

Carmen asserted. "This will be a two hour lay over."

The driver and a man in charge of our group of mules said. "Relax outside the bus in the picnicking area next to the park."

Jose picked up the local Mexican newspaper and read about the Tijuana Drug problems. "Alfonso look what's plastered all over the front page." Alfonso says. "What!"

Jose read. "A Mexican prosecutor has just been shot in front of his family. Six men carried automatic AK 47's calmly, dragged Mr. Gutierrez out of his car, and shot him with over two hundred rounds. They then drove their limousine back and forth over his corpse until Mr. Gutierrez body was dismembered into shreds of meat no bigger than six inches round.

The newspaper said he's the twelfth Senior Mexican law enforcement agent killed in recent months. Seems the prosecutor was investigating the murder of the last police chief, who turned down a hundred thousand dollar offer in bribes from the cartel."

Alfonso plunged forward with a heave and chuffed. "Jose, I just lost my appetite," as Jose read on about these drug cartel atrocities. Alfonso catching his breath questioned. "How many more people have to die before we change the laws to dismantle the ability of hard drugs to flourish on the black market?"

Jose confided. "The laws have to change, before the violence can end."

Alfonso asserted. "Tijuana's Drug Cartel kingpins are responsible for this latest uprising in violence." This paper further stated that. "One of the biggest drug smuggling king pins recently died during a minor surgery."

Jose agreed. "Yep! The paper says this guy shipped ton's of cocaine into the United States twenty-four hours a day. There's the problem, that smaller drug cartels are fighting to gain drug turf, and there's many reprisals."

Jose mentioned. "The Mexican surgeons who did the minor operation on the drug king pin, are found gagged, bound, tortured and entombed in concrete drums. The surgeons fingernails had been torn out."

Alfonso remarked. "The lawlessness of this drug corruption include every element of society and culture. The transportation ministry, the governors, the prosecutors, judges, military, police, and the people."

Jose maintained. "That's what the DEA and current drug laws are up against."

Jose exclaimed to Alfonso. "The DEA is preparing indictments against these drug kingpins but it is still up to the Mexican government, military, and law enforcement to enforce them."

Carmen rehashed. "A commander in the police down here makes eight hundred dollars a month. A body guard for the cartel makes three thousand to four thousand dollars a week. That's a lot of jack, no matter how you look at it. These officials don't only look the other way but they assist a majority to see that the cartels drug operations succeed."

"Wow"! Alfonso read "One of Tijuana's disco night clubs is where one of the Tijuana drug cartels hang out, they play popular music that glamorizes the drug cartel's functions. Triumphant songs of how the outwit and buy off officials."

"Alfonso" Jose gabbed. "It was widely known that the bloodthirsty drug lords are presently in command of the area and regularly cross over the border without provocation. They control the violent street gangs of San Diego."

Alfonso squeamishly claimed. "Jose, I don't know if I can go through this."

Jose reeled off. "Hold tight Al! We got no choice now. If we back out we'll end up like one of these news scenarios and quick."

Alfonso relayed. "I'm scared."

Jose harped. "Don't feel bad, you're not alone. I'm with you man. We'll all make it home." Then Alfonso reassuringly laughed a slight smile.

Jose remarked. "The newspaper further stated that the drug turf wars on the border have never been worse. Drug domain's deal drugs and kill in a frenzy to establish turf, which are presently controlled by another drug lord kingpin."

Alfonso admitted. "Cocaine as an under ground black market commodity was the real problem. The present drug laws establish this black market standard."

The chow truck arrived and fed the peasant mules. Alfonso wrapped his food up and took it on the bus with him. "My appetite will around later I hope after we go down the road." There was a sink with running water next to a latrine. They all relived themselves and washed up before they headed north fast toward Chihuahua.

The trio of unwilling drug mules were in some smaller village town. The bus had pulled over so people could relieve themselves. Jose screamed. "Draw a bead on this! Look hundreds of people are mobbing the jail."

"Where?" Alfonso asked.

Jose pointed out. "Directly in front of us in the towns central square."

One of the mules that came on the bus said. "They dragging and beating two men from the jail. One man is already beaten to death while the other is being hung there in the Town Square right now."

Jose shuttered. "There's over a thousand people watching that man hang."

Alfonso noticed. "They're cheering for the death of these men."

The mule that just back came on the bus said. "I heard from one of the locals say that these men had tried to kidnap four school girls age nine to eleven years of age in front of the grade school."

Jose terrified mustered. "This is a scene from the old west" as far as Jose and Alfonso were concerned.

Alfonso anxiously rattled. "I can't wait for the bus to pull away!"

Jose observed. "Look! The spectators are cheering for the men to be beaten and hanged." Alfonso still couldn't regain his appetite as the bus pulled away from the bloodthirsty crowd. The man hung high in the air with a noose tightly around his neck.

Jose bellowed. "Alfonso the mans body is still kicking!" as the bus rolled past the tree which served as the gallows and onto the highway. The whole busload of mules were frightened.

Finally on the outskirts of Ciudad Juarez, the bus pulled off the highway into an abandoned field. Alfonso said. "Look over there. There's some mules in that field next to some shacks."

Jose witnessed. "There's more mules are over there waiting."

Carmen viewed and said. "The ones by the latrine are talking about the Cartel gangland-style killings across the boarder in the United State the day before yesterday in a popular border town eatery. One victim's eyes were gouged out before his throat was slit in the parking lot in broad daylight. The rest of the gunman burst into the eatery and killed six people with automatic weapons before fleeing in a black limousine."

Alfonso shaking his head piped. "More drug related executions."

Carmen portrayed. "The drug cartels are known for their vast use and caches of weapons."

One of the mules Pero recounted to Carmen. "The border is plagued by Drug trafficking. U S trained Mexican pilots fly the drugs entering the country. The U S pilots were found to be shipping tons of cocaine into the United States with the drug cartels. These pilots know how to use sophisticated radar to help import the drugs into the U S."

Jose joked. "Great! Here it is again the United States tax dollars and technology aiding the drug cartel."

Jose, Carmen, and Alfonso were already scared. The next thing they knew. Carmen "What the hell is that!"

Alfonso announced. "It's a cargo airplane landing on the dirt strip in front of us."

The drug mule next to them explained. "The cocaine barons are shipping huge loads of cocaine in to us. Come on let's get our load!"

Jose previewed to Alfonso. "This must be a 727 Boeing. Look! All the seats are ripped out."

Alfonso surveyed. "This Airplane was made to haul nothing but tons of cocaine."

"Jose!" Alfonso noted. "The Mexican Military and police are all helping unload the drugs from this aircraft as well helping us."

Jose agreed. "Everyone helped unload the drug cargo."

Alfonso answered back. "Everybody that pitches in gets their cut."

Carmen suddenly realized. "This must be a two billion dollar drug load."

Jose responded in astonishment. "The cocaine load and the amount of people here working this load stagger's the imagination!"

Carmen harped. "Other buses and vehicles were loaded at a fast pace."

One of the other mules blabbed. "The buses being loaded over there are going to different parts of the boarder."

Jose beckoned. "The Mexican cartel is very well organized."

Carmen answered. "They keep the drugs flowing northward." Jose said. "It's a shame all this heroin and the cocaine is going to hit the streets."

Alfonso blurted. "Let's go quickly our part of the drug shipment is loaded on the burro's." Within minutes the drugs were loaded. In darkness there mission headed into the desert.

Alfonso reiterated. "I'm scared sick." Everyone knew at this point they had to keep cool, or they would all be eliminated by the drug cartel.

Carmen calmly peeped to his cousin Alfonso. "Keep cool Al! Were almost through this."

Jose squealed. "Everything seems to go like clockwork with the cartel's operation."

Alfonso agreed. "Everything seems to be going too fast."

Carmen followed up and sang quietly. "Back in the USA" Everyone laughed quietly.

Jose, Alfonso, and Carmen all had heard that U S and Mexican boarder ranchers have been terrorized by the drug cartels. The drug barons guided illegal aliens into the country, and take control of certain ranches that were in their way.

Jose divulged. "One rancher while hunting, frequently sees men in camouflage come out in the open often in daylight. The heavily armed guard's are followed with loaded down burros. The gunmen escort this caravan in columns from Mexico into the United States. The ranchers claim that the Mexicans bring in tons of drugs into the country with impunity."

Alfonso vented. "The ranchers on our southern boarder must feel as frighten and helpless as I do!"

Jose repined. "The ranchers are selling their ranches because armed drug armies cross their homesteads on a regular basis."

Jose and Alfonso did not know what to expect. They kept their mouths closed around most of the mules and all the drug bosses of the cartels.

As they walked the pack team of drug laden burro's northward. The man leading the way named Taro vaunted. "I run the drugs for the cartel every night."

Jose asked. "Every night?"

Taro boasted. "Every night! It's my job to pay some of the customs agents on the U S side of the boarder off. Once they are bought off they look the other way when we run the drugs across the border."

Taro's drug running armed assistant repeated. "The majority of all the mules get though. You have directions about who to contact, and where to go once you reach your destination in the United States."

Taro explained to all his mules. "You are going to a designated warehouse that is right over the border."

Jose confided Alfonso. "We're going to rent a car and get the hell out of there as soon as we get loose over the border."

Alfonso gossiped. "I wish we could get out of this mess."

Jose expounded. "To bad we can't double cross the cartel. If it wasn't for both of your relatives still back in the Chiapas. I'd pull stakes when we get further down that desert trail. You both know that I don't want anything to happen to them."

Taro told all the mules while they were all still under the stars. "Were on the border. You can see the lights in El Paso."

Taro's assistant depicted. "You can see the boarder guards."

Taro looking through his night vision binoculars. "Si, Taro said then gave hand signals indicating. "Two mules at a time."

Jose told Alfonso. "The cartel has the same equipment as law enforcement."

Taro disclosed. "Each mule will have fifty pounds of cocaine in knapsacks strapped to their back." As everyone strapped the drugs on their back. Taro was still giving instructions. "Run across the fields to the desert land, across the Rio Grande straight into the city. When you cross the highway by the high building, run between the buildings that are designated to the right."

Taros assistant now running across the desert with us snapped. "Once there a contact named Deante, will hurry you into a warehouse building. You will be given the five-hundred that you were promised."

Jose darting across the open desert commanded. "Hurry Carmen! Hurry Alfonso!"

Carmen evading obstacles in the night crowed. "I'll be right there!" All the mules ran desperately through the night into the United States penetrating the southern boarder.

Sure enough once across the highway into El Paso, Deante rushed them into the vacant ware house, a mini-bus picked everyone up minus the drugs. They were all given a ride five miles away and dropped off into the fields of the desert. The other mules were scattered every few hundred yards down the highway.

Carmen scampered. "Were clear of the cartel!"

Alfonso yelled. "Were in the United States." Jose, Alfonso, and Carmen jumped up and down for joy.

"What a trip!" Jose reasoned, as they sprinted down the road just before dawn.

Alfonso fluttered. "One thing for sure were all on American soil. That's just "Jim Dandy" to me!"

Jose seen a motel open. "Come on I'll get a room for us."

Alfonso admitted. "I can't wait to get cleaned up."

Jose then went and got a rented car so they could drive themselves to Houston.

Carmen rattled off. "I'm excited to be in America. Electricity, Running water, food and family. I would do it all over again."

Jose mustered. "You made it Carmen!"

Alfonso squinted. "We all made it!"

They were all glad to distance themselves from the cartel's criminal enterprise. They were glad they left on good terms as none of them wanted any reprisals against Carmen's family.

Jose told Alfonso. "Well we got our newspaper drug report."

Alfonso conferred. "We got more than we bargained for. If they don't like this adventure we just been on, Miles can go down there himself." They all laughed.

Jose claimed. "What makes the drug cartels so successful, elusive and dangerous is there ability to fade into the Latin community of America."

Carmen explained. "Mexican drug traffickers deliver Marijuana, heroin, cocaine, methamphetamines, and prescription drugs all kinds that are easy to get over the counter in Mexico."

Alfonso noted. "The drug cartel's have a profound effect amidst the communities across the states. Poor immigrants without any skills are drawn into selling drugs without reservation. These people are vulnerable to danger."

Jose admitted. "Americans still have a drug consumption problem. The Mexican government pleaded with the United Nations Human rights group to shape different angles of strategy concerning drug law enforcement. The Mexicans want to focus on demand, not supply."

Alfonso presented. "The Mexicans complain about hand me downs from the United State government. After they received seventy-five aging bell UH-1Hs helicopters to add to the another fifty aging aircraft.

The Mexicans claim that the helicopter engines are to weak to bring a full complement of troops into the high ridges of the Sierra Madres mountains, where the drug cartels operate. These are the aircraft, that they have available to fight the drug cartel."

Jose stopped and called his parents. " Hello Dad were home."

Jose's dad asked. "Are you all right? We've been worried about you."

Jose answered. "Yes! I just wanted you to know we'll be back in Houston tomorrow. We've got to go, see Yea."

Alfonso divulged to Jose. "I don't want to tell anyone, we brought Carmen back. I want to surprise everyone at once."

Jose agreed. "That's a good idea Al" and then called Miles. "I'm going to tell Miles were back and we have a lot of Mexican drug news information."

Jose called Miles at home and howled. "Hello Miles!"

Miles after picking up the phone. "I'm glad to hear that voice!"

Jose decreed. "We're back in the United States."

Miles asked. "Are you all right?"

Jose declared. "Were all fine!"

Miles remarked. "I'm glad you and Alfonso are all right. I received the different packages with newspaper articles and photos."

"Miles" Jose quipped. "Wait until I get there with Alfonso. You won't believe what we've just been through."

Miles conveyed. "I can hardly wait to talk to both of you."

Jose kiddingly said to Miles. "We want immunity before we spill our guts."

Miles asked. "What!"

Jose contended. "I'll explain when I see you."

Exuberant Miles roused. "Thanks!"

Jose raged. "I'll see you when you hit Houston."

Chapter 8.... Miles at the newspaper was in the middle of researching a drug case. Miles said to Ed. "A five hundred acre ranch was just seized on the Mexican Texas border by United States Customs drug enforcement."

Ed asked. "What Happened?"

Miles explained. "Even in daylight hours anyone can walk across the boarder from Mexico onto American soil with all the marijuana they can haul without being detected. Large shipments of marijuana are stashed then for destinations farther into the United States interior."

Ed squawked. "Law enforcement has high hopes this will stem the control of marijuana entering the country."

Miles maintained. "Marijuana is in the mainstream of America. It's here to stay. That drug bust is less than a drop in the bucket."

The time approached for a monach round table conference with all the big guns, all the pro-rights activists of the cabel cannabis movement attended. They were going to beat the government with active and concerned cannabis citizen's dialogue utilizing computers. They will use their reefer research to shed light on the truth.

Miles picked up Clint and drove him to the conference. Miles told Clint about the subject matter to be covered at the meeting. "The conference will be held at George's mansion on the Gulf Coast water front mansion. "You've met George over Leslie's haven't you?"

Clint responded. "Yes, I met George at hemp forums he's sponsored. He's a legend for freedom causes. I'm quit impressed with his approach to expose the whole truth."

Miles asked. "You haven't been to his mansion have you?"

Clint responded. "No I haven't! I've heard George Barras is a billionaire and a Corpus Christi resident. I know he has sponsored many of the pro-marijuana rallies."

Miles fussed. "Right! You'll like the house, the decor is strictly south western and Indian art designs. The furs, tapestries, Indian basket and bonnets are hanging on rustic wood walls."

Clint sounded off. "Chantel's favorite!"

Miles explained. "The fire place is an island centered on the lower leveled floor of the mansion. The high walled interior perimeter with it's vaulted ceiling is lined with adobe brick and terrain tan canyon stone. Part of a Redwood tree was imported from Northern California and custom carved for the unique centrifugal fireplace mantle."

Clint walked through the mansion with Miles reviewed. "Look at all animal trophy decor in every room."

Miles continued back to Clint. "The exotic animal trophies are mounted on the walls throughout the mansion."

Clint amazed persisted. "He must have a trophy from every continent in the world. I like the Polar Bear rug."

Miles marveled to Clint. "Look at the exquisite Indian rugs displayed on several of the walls and the floors. I can't let Chantel see this delicious decor play ground, or I'll be redoing the interior and exterior of our house."

Miles looked though the large picture windows from inside the mansion to the outside relayed to Clint. "George hired Mexican workers to maintain the grounds. They take care of the mansion grounds in an articulate professional lawn and garden manner."

Clint agreed to Miles. "They sure do! Let's go into the botanical gardens. Chantel would love these tree house floras, tropical trees and fresh green plants. Most of these are re-planted throughout the estate. This looks like the botanical gardens with the foaming sea from the rain bowed sea mist water falls."

Miles harped. "I love the reflections from the mystic pool!"

Clint claimed. "George even has large gold fish in the pond." As they walked back into the main part of the extravagant mansion.

Miles addressed. "These busy mansion workers have a torrid fire going under the mantle in the main ballroom of the mansion. That's where the cannabis conference is held."

Clint mentioned to Miles. "I heard George has a couple of black champion black Labradors. When he heard about the lady from Detroit where the drug squad shot the lady's pet of twelve years, he sent her family an eight week-old puppy."

Miles responded surprisingly. "That's right Clint?" And Miles continued. "The drug cops got another wrong address in another city using the same across the board gun ho barge in commando tactics. Her black retriever was gunned down in front of the lady by the cops subsequent an unwarranted and imminent ill-fated drug raid."

Clint commented. "I heard her and her family were ruffed up by the drug cops."

Miles responded. "Yes! They were ruffed up boldly by the herb cops. Nobody in the house knew who these masked men that barged in were. She's taken what little recourse she can, she sued the city for dire damages."

Clint rumbled. "They'll pay up, that seems to be the cops program for constitutional injustice."

The cannabis conference was about to begin. Extra tables and chairs were brought in to the conference room with folders, briefs and laptops flooded the platform. Political figures from various denominations and ethnicity's represented the community. Prohibition candidates were continually posted on the Internet pro-freedom movements web sites. All the voters were going to be aware of who not to vote for.

Leslie Lampkins was in the corner of the table. He is a leader from the black political caucus. The chaperone of the round table meeting George Barras told Leslie. "Leslie the current marijuana drug laws are ill advised and carelessly conceived."

George told Leslie. "I have given over twenty five million dollars to all pro-marijuana causes including special efforts for Medical Marijuana organizations from states to nations."

Miles conveyed to Clint. "George is one of the major contributors for recent medical marijuana bills that passed in California, Arizona. Several other states like the State of Washington, Alaska, Oregon, Nevada, Colorado are following suit, as well as the District of Columbia's Washington DC. George made sure the people were able to vote on medical marijuana in those states."

George continually told Leslie. "In Kentucky, the citizens are screaming for full marijuana legalization. In Congress, Democrat, Republicans, Libertarians, Reformers, Independents, Constitutionalists and Lobbyists urge for change concerning federal guidelines of use and possession of small amounts marijuana."

Miles expressed to Clint. "George beamed, that the medical marijuana bills he sponsored were passed with overwhelming margins."

Clint agreed. "Can you blame him. He did the American people a great service. He stood up for responsible citizens, while the government turns it's back on good and decent people."

Clint citing the fourth Amendment spoke. "What about the peoples right to feel secure in their persons, homes, papers and effects. The fifth amendment guarantees citizens not to be deprived of life, liberty, or property, without due process of law. We welcome the opportunity for due process of law. We just want our American brand of freedom to be heard. We want the war against marijuana users to end. We realize you can abuse any thing. The federal government abused their power as far as we marijuana smokers are concerned. The federal government's job is not to set agenda's for moral judgement's of its citizens."

Igor stood in front of everyone else and raved. "Right on!"

Clint listening to George for a moment. "The government is out of touch with the people, with this big marijuana drug war, they are draining all the money from the taxpayer's that could go to social programs."

Leslie agreed with George and Clint and asked them. "I want you both to speak at the Cannabis Rally tonight. We want and need changes in the black community concerning the government's firefight in the drug wars."

Clint told Leslie, after George walked away. "Your pro-marijuana support will be greatly welcomed."

Leslie told Clint. "I'll be there." and further stated. "Did you hear about the seventy one year-old retired minister from Wisconsin?

Clint lamented. "No Les. I didn't."

Leslie disclosed. "The minister was killed in the raid earlier in this year. He was a personal friend of mine." The police drug task force conducted a raid on the wrong house. The minister died from a fatal heart attack after being slammed to the floor and hog-cuffed by the drug police. The retired minister was not allowed to speak and relate to the drug police officers despite his serious health conditions. Essentially the masked men scared him to death."

Clint divulged. "That's the sorry state of drug law enforcement today."

Flustered Leslie scoffed. "This kind of Bozo government mentality has to stop!"

Subdued Clint unveiled. "That is why were all here! I'm sorry about the minister. I was unaware of the story. I'm saddened deeply as well about the continued police injustice."

Leslie demanded. "We have to stop this state sponsored terrorism!"

Compassionate Clint adamantly agreed. "That's right!"

Leslie explained further. "The minister helped me greatly in my earlier days of the ministry."

Clint soberly appealed. "I'm sorry for the minister's family."

The meeting began on a highly organized level. George announcing his plans said. "We've planned a major Rosta rally in Washington. I will help with travel accommodations to represent all states.

An attendee goal of several million people is expected to converge on the capital in the coming summer."

Clint testified. "The fourth of July would be great!"

George responded. "That's what I thought. We'll get the permits."

Clint verified. "They have to give us the permit for the rally."

The cannabis attendees made the final preparations for the International Hemp Bizarre in three weeks in Houston's Astrodome they sponsored.

Igor validated to Clint. "Andre Aires is preparing a Hemp made "Hot Air Balloon." The high altitude winds will carry Andre around the world. The Hemp balloon flight will be the first balloon to travel around the world hopefully setting a world record. Cruising speed alone exceed one hundred and fifty miles per hour."

Clint questioned Igor. "Is that Andre over there?"

Igor answered. "Yes lets go over while he explains the flight methods."

Clint, Miles, and Igor and Andre's group listened to Andre tell his staff at the meeting. "Hemp made fuel, riggings, canvas, and hemp products are exclusively used on this hemp balloon.

The Hemp Balloon Mission control will be in the center of the hemp-festival. The chief meteorologist of the command team anticipates no problems at this point. This Hemp made balloon will be bigger and carry more fuel than any balloon attempts previously made for an around the world flight."

Clint conceded to Igor. "That's very interesting."

Igor admitted. "It really will be great PR for the hemp movement."

Miles confessed. "Andre owns one of the biggest construction company in Texas. Andre puts up large scale home sub-divisions all over." Andre met Igor on a job site and Igor invited Andre to the hemp festival.

Andre explained. "The hemp balloon will take off in the beginning of the International Hemp-festival from the parking lot of the Astrodome."

George walked over and granted. "That's fantastic!"

Miles recapped. "Attending are vendors and speakers represent different state sponsored hemp farm organizations, who've been keynoting our recent hemp rallies. These National and International hemp farming organizations want to be represented at the International Hemp-Festival and bazaar. They are also engaged for our mammoth "Rosta Rally" next summer."

Clint appealed to Miles. "We can arrange that?"

Igor agreed. "We sure can!"

Miles affirmed. "George being the jet setter that he is, has Abraham Arms an actor flown in from Hollywood for this cannabis conference. Abe Arms is fiercely promoting the hemp industry. Abe represents commercial hemp lines of products such as hemp paper products, hemp rope, hemp clothing, even hemp made wood strong and sturdy enough to build houses."

Igor pressed. "Abraham's hemp house at the hemp exposition is completely manufactured out of hemp, right down to the insulation of the electrical wiring."

Catalytic Clint conveyed. "That's constructive and innovative ingenuity. Abe while interviewed by news analyst Craig Corners, pulled out a bag of pot out. He rolled a hoot in front of the news commentator. The kicker is the interview made national news.

The newsman known for his interpretive reporting said Abe. "That smells like good skunk weed? Do you mind if I hit that joint?

Clint revealed. "They passed the joints back and forth and continued the interview. Abe even gave Craig a joint to take with him for later. Cool ha!"

Igor responded. "No doubt. It sure is. I can't wait to listen to Abe now."

Abraham stood with a crowd around him lectured. "We can quit cutting down the forests the day industrial hemp becomes legal. All the representatives of the farm groups are expressing interest for a new vital hemp crop."

Adamant Abraham continued. "The State of Wisconsin's paper industry alone equals ten million tons of trees a year. Does anybody realize how many trees are cut down? How long will it be before we cut the last tree down, and then say well I guess we have to grow industrial hemp now for paper and wood products.

One acre of hemp grown commercially produced five times as much paper than one acre of trees. Lets see, that's one acre of commercially grown hemp harvested per year times twenty years, compared with how long the next wood crop comes in to make paper as a plot of the same magnitude.

Industrialized hemp is ninety percent THC free and there is no reason for hemp to be illegal. Farm groups and agricultural officials will attend the International hemp-festival. they all want to re-legalese the hemp industry now."

Abraham Arms explained. "Drug arrests are up ten-fold. The drugs on the street haven't been curtailed in this insane drug war. Never! You can get drugs anytime and anywhere. All walks of human life participate. We need a serious change on how were handling the drug problem. I want to give a special thanks to everyone for their attendance and their attention." Abe concluded his address at the round table conference.

Clint appealed to Manny. "We've been talking, Chico, Igor, George and me. We'd like to have you go to Amsterdam and go to the Marijuana Museum. Would you mind going?"

Manny responded. "No, I wouldn't mind, I wouldn't mind at all. I'd like to take a few days off anyway. How long is the planned trip?"

Calculating quick Clint conceded. "Three weeks!"

Mobile Manny asked. "Wow, three weeks in Amsterdam?"

Clint responded. "Yeah, but that isn't the only place we're sending you. George wants you to go around the world to various countries where hemp and marijuana is legal. He wants certain cannabis statistics, which are crucial for the extensive debates and rallies. George feels we can only accomplish this by sending somebody to get a hands on view. It's outlined in this reefer report. Glady's from George's staff drew up.

Glady's has your itinerary complete for each days events. You are to fly from Houston to New York."

Manny excited. "Wow!"

Chico crowed. "You're a lucky dog Manny! How come you get all the good runs?"

Clint continued. "Like I was saying. You're going to fly into New York, then you are going to fly into London for a few days. Then you will continue on too Amsterdam where you will spend three more days. You will proceed to different coffeehouses and taverns talking to the natives. You will be taking extensive notes in your off time. We want you to go to the marijuana museum while you are there, George will supply you with a brand new video camera."

Manny excited said. "I can't wait."

Clint continued. "George wants you to video tape everywhere you go, inside the coffee shops, inside the marijuana museum in particular, and all the displays in the marijuana museum. Glady's said there is another list on the back page here for some publications At the University of Amsterdam's library check out the cannabis book's outlined for you."

Manny quipped. "No problem with that." he sung out.

Miles reported. George wanted you to go to the mansion office as soon as you can."

Manny boasted. "I'm on my way guys!"

After an hours time Manny came back to the conference area and said to Clint and Miles. "Glady's has an immaculate and impeccable office. Everything including the artwork is hemp made and hemp orientated. All the office paper, stationary, envelopes, scratch pads, to the cloth covered journals are made from hemp fibers.

Glady's prepared hemp invitational envelopes for all the upcoming hemp events as I walked into her office. Glady's said. "I typically order all my hemp office supplies while on line. I also posts all the upcoming hemp festival, events, hemp farming associations meetings, and hemp legislative achievements on our Internet home page."

Manny expressed to Miles. "I can't believe Glady's office was so completely hemp orientated."

Miles relayed. "George told me Glady's stay's cannabis sharp. She wants to nail our latest cannabis achievement's or next hemp hurdle to cross."

Miles decreed to Manny. "She's really intense!"

Clint agreed. "She really is talented and committed."

Miles conveyed. "George had every politician and political figure he could video taped, while TV and Radio commentators asked them if they belong to the smoker's wing. The politicians had to state whether they believe a citizen has the right to possess and smoke marijuana in the privacy of their own home. In essence they have to state whether a citizen has personal individual rights or not. The politician's response of "Yes" or "No" is posted on the Internet web page by Glady's. Pro-marijuana candidates and their views are also posted as well as the prohibitionists on George's Internet web page."

Clint immediately depicted. "I like that. A place where we can politically identify all politicians and their views."

Igor agreed. "Yes sir! I like that pro-marijuana movement tactic too."

Miles continued. "Politicians are nervous about getting identified with government's harsh marijuana drug tactics on one hand or on the other hand be identified as pro-marijuana. The anti-marijuana league had their share of politicians as well who said. "No smoke of any kind."

Clint enounced. "It is becoming a political tightrope."

Miles informed. "Some anti-smoke groups are promoting in their commercials, that no cigarettes of any kind should be allowed smoked in a citizens home."

The second's day's round table conference was about to begin after a breakfast break from the preceding days meeting's conclusion. Extra tables and chairs had to be brought into the ballroom with folders, briefs and lap tops. Some hemp executives left, and others were scheduled for today's meetings. Clint didn't leave until the conclusion of the day's cannabis conference.

Manny in his poppy flower smoking jacket said. "I'm getting more excited, the more I think about the trip. I'm going on, an all expenses paid pot excursion." as he pops out a green bud in George's sparkle green smoking parlor already rolled. The Manny by striking his right hand with his left hand, the marijuana joint jump's into mid air and fly's straight into Manny's lips. Manny triumphantly sparks it up quick."

Surprised Igor looked at him. "That's the way to go, Manny! It's about time you break down with some green shimmer." As they pranced out to the parlor gardens."

Clint continued. "Manny you will be getting a rail pass to take with you on your tour through Europe from Amsterdam. Then through countries where hash and marijuana are legal.

Miles explained. "In Malaga, Spain. Glady's has a travel agency established for further travel arrangements. The travel agency is called the "La Linia Travel Agency."

Manny you are to pick up further travel instructions and on your lap top hook into George's Internet domain. Glady's will update our instructional files to you, and you will forward back to Glady's cannabis files back to Glady's on your progress.

From Malaga you will continue by bus to La Linia where you will spend your last night in Spain before walking over the border into Gibraltar.

In Gibraltar you are to meet one of George's contacts will show you around and escort you by Hydra foil to Tangier Morocco.

Once in Morocco you will go to the Casaba and you will meet Akil, who will take you to the various teahouses where hash is tolerated in Morocco.

After being met in Morocco by Akil, you and your contact will Hydra foil back to Southern Spain, then onto Bombay India. Once in Bombay you will research certain religious sects, which use marijuana as part of their religious practices.

Go to various hash houses and seek out their Indian customs in Bombay. When you leave Bombay you will fly directly to Sidney Australia. You will spend three days in Sidney, because we're going to give you a break, Manny.

Once in Sidney you will leave for Canberra, the capital of Australia, and talk to various lawmakers. Australia's drug policy is the model of the free world International drug policy is possession and smoking marijuana is legal in most of Australia.

From Canberra you proceed to Cairns, Australia give you a day in the rainforest in the Aboriginal town of Kuranda. You will smoke cannabis with Aborigines and use their pipes for an afternoon, while further researching their customs.

Then we'll let you dive the barrier reef because George wants some pictures of the barrier reef. You're a diver and George is a diver. George arranged for you to have a go at it while you are there with his personal under water Nakomis camera." Miles continued explaining the whole travel itinerary.

"Once you have completed your mission in Australia, you will fly out of Cairns International Airport to Panama. Research their liberalized cannabis initiatives before flying back here to Houston."

Manny chuckled. "Tell George I said thanks. I can't believe it."

Clint cracked. "Yeah! Get back here in three weeks!"

Manny questioned. "Three weeks!"

Clint asked. "Can you get the time off? George already has the tickets waiting for you at the airport."

Manny deemed. "Hell yea I'll take the time off! It's off for work and on for holiday."

Miles continued. "Tomorrow evening announce a few cannabis promotions on your radio show tomorrow."

Manny pledged. "No problem for something this magnitude. I have to tell my boss in the morning about the trip. I can get Rudy to cover my show for three weeks. I don't see where there will be any problem. Damm Miles! You got me excited!"

Igor stood in the background heckled. "Some guys got all the luck!"

George divulged to Aaron. "Brant from my management team is the hemp event planner for us. Brant is going over instructions for the planning the transportation. How the media would be covered and handled at the Washington Rosta Rally. We hope the hemp rally will force a major pro-marijuana debate. Which we have been consistently turned down by the gutless moral majority trying to govern how we should think and live our lives."

Aaron swore. "You know my family and I will donate all are time and effort by air brushing part of the hemp promotion."

George exclaimed. "Thanks Aaron for all your support."

Aaron filled in. "The drug Czar himself would not allow an election for legalization of marijuana at a Federal level."

Clint over heard Aaron and complained. "Those guys making the marijuana laws aren't subjected to drug tests. They're not required to have any formal cannabis education to be involved and in charge in the holy herb war."

Aaron implored. "Yet, they make ignorant laws against the constitution and the people."

Clint announced. "That's why we need a new political party."

George agreed. "I'm voting on the Constitutional Freedom Candidates from the cannabis wing. We want the federal level of marijuana law abolished. Let each state set their own standard for marijuana in society after the full legalization of marijuana."

Clint disclosed. "Most big changes seem impossible at the outset."

George confided. "Exposing the truth to everyone will be the trick."

Brant joined George and glossed over. "You can't be the big dog without taking big bites."

George clamored. "Let's do it!"

Aaron agreed. "All right!"

George told Aaron. "I want to know what type of anti-marijuana statements will be brought up at the debate."

Clint disclosed in a cocky manner. "George don't worry they can't effectively debate us when they're wrong. I'll go in there without any notes and debate any one of them point for point with facts and the truth."

George blustered. "I like that mans attitude!"

Clint, Igor, Miles, Brant, Aaron, and everyone who stood around laughed whole heartedly.

George asked Miles. "Who's that?"

Miles responded. "That's Patrick a law student going running for political office. Patrick handled the political front for most of our pro-marijuana agendas. Patrick sways public opinion with the stone cold facts and exposes the moral majority's the dreaded facts about hemp and marijuana.

Clint described. "He's a bright guy!"

Miles told Clint that. "His is very bright and is college valedictorian, absolute straight A's in school. Patrick pushed to complete a pot packaged strategy by developing a **"Manual for Marijuana Laws"** the government and marijuana users could both live by. "A Manual of Marijuana Laws" that is fair to all the citizens of this government."

Clint alleged. "I've heard about that from Morgan. He must be the college student that he told me about. That is a very commendable idea."

Everyone listened to Patrick lecture. "I want to be part of the electorate that legalizes hemp and marijuana. Our pro-cannabis movement doesn't want dummies from behind a desk in Washington deciding our daily life choices. Put up to the voters!"

Willard stood with Political Pat and asked. "What about the politicians, who say softening drug laws would give relief to drug dealers?"

"Pat answered. "You know that's not true. Were going to destroy the marijuana black market. Were going to keep American money in America and in American hands."

Willard asked. "What about penalties against doctors who prescribe to medical marijuana patients?"

Pat counseled. "That will never get by the Supreme court on appeal. It's just a political ploy of those temporally in charge of our government."

Willard asked. "What do you mean temporarily?"

Pat disclosed. "The cannabis movement is at the forefront of individual rights. We have to win! When will we pass laws that forbid the government from entering a person's private life choices."

Willard asked. "Are you sure?"

Pat told Will. "Will find out"

Willard asked. "What do you mean?"

Pat explained. "I mean. I'm running for State Representative in this county for our newly formed **Constitutional Party.**"

Willard questioned. "How?"

Pat informed. "Were developing a cannabis and individual rights agenda in this country for our pro-pot political front. State by state, county by county, city by city, village by village, person to person."

Willard elated divulged. "Great aspirations sound good to me."

Miles amused. "Good Luck Pat! Let me know if I can I help. Call me at the newspapers."

Pat told Miles. "I'm already counting on your help Miles."

Chipper Clint decreed. "Were all for you, Pat!"

Persistent Pat continued. "The major drug kingpins and political leaders of the government are making money off of these drug wars. The price of marijuana on the street is high because of its established prohibition. You have to pay one hundred and fifty dollars for a one once bag of weed to smoke from international drug dealing organizations, but you can't grow any marijuana for home use to eliminate the foreign black market. Eliminate the black market!

Common ground should keep American money in America."

Influential Igor induced. "He's got my vote!"

Patriarchal Patrick continued. "The last thing the drug kingpins want to see is marijuana legalized. The value of marijuana will drop. The consumers will grow their own or sell small amounts of marijuana amongst their own friends. The government could import marijuana for sale and further tax all incoming pot to this country. The drug kingpins would be out of business because the money that U.S. marijuana users spend would stay in this country instead of being continually funneled out by the truck loads."

Clint excited. "Yes Sir! You have my vote."

Pat asked Willard. "Does that makes sense Will?"

Assured Will answered. "Damn right it does!"

Clear sighted Pat defined. "Will, all we're emphasizing here is small amounts of marijuana for personal use and small amounts of money changing hands among the users. And, the users are defined by sales of less than five thousand dollars in the course of a year. In those parameters of marijuana use you would be considered a user. If they make a couple of dollars on it, so what. The only liability here is that the government doesn't get their cut, but they are not getting it now with the cash flow of marijuana leaving the country. As far as the government is concerned it shouldn't matter if Peter has fifty dollars in their hand or Bill has fifty in his hand as long as Pedro doesn't have Peter's and Bill's fifty in Columbia. I never realized that our present political figure heads are that blind."

Will wisely expounded. "They're not that blind. They're filled with self-interest."

Courageous Clint confided. "I agree! Most of our political figures are very corrupt when it concerns our right's."

Punchy Pat persuaded. "We've got to turn the heat up on these politicians and make them feel the heat."

Will gossiped. "Believe me Pat, they're starting to feel the heat."

Pat deemed. "We're going to scorch them with the truth. When were done with them they will be run out of office with their co called moral tails between their legs." Everyone laughs.

Rambunctious Roland is a highly controversial political commentator, who's quoted regularly in weekly Corpus Christi newspapers. Roland said. "Hey Pat, Hey Will, how you guys doing today?"

Pat answered. "Fine, Roland, how you doing today?"

Roland answered. "Not bad thanks. You still want to set up your cannabis political booth at the hemp-festival thwarting these marijuana drug laws and forfeiture's? Callers into the station are tired of our citizens getting humiliated, raped, robbed or even killed in their own homes."

Pat responded. "Sure, You know that's why we're all here. This time we're going to cross all the T's and dot all the I's."

Roland agreed. "That's right!"

Pat disclosed. "We've done the research and now we have the cannabis facts to prove it."

Chico excited jested. "We got the jazz baby!"

Pat explained. "City officials are talking openly about changing marijuana laws."

Roland asked. "Where at?"

Pat informed. "There is more than one town where different city councils are making proposals for more lenient marijuana fines for personal use."

Roland's questioned. "Will citizens still be getting fined?

Political Pat emphasized. "I can see getting fined if you're in hospitals, schools and such. Smoking a joint in public in most places should be tolerated. It happens a billion times per day anyway. So why punish these people. I can't see any fines for smoking marijuana in your back yard or carrying a small amount of marijuana anywhere."

Roland admitted. "The recent polls favor total decriminalization."

Pat continued. "I'll tell you what Roland. I'm going to be a **Constitutional Party Candidate** for the next election. The present leadership of this country promote family values out front, but pork's interns in the oval office behind his wife's back. Is that a moral leader or a moral pantomime?"

Clint grumbled to Roland. "Why should the innocent citizenry suffer and be victims of marijuana busts, especially when government officials smoke marijuana as much as the citizenry."

Roland protested. "Well a recent push to legalize medical marijuana in one state was denied by the states supreme court to even became an issue on an the ballot. The referendum to legalize marijuana was denied even with enough valid signatures were collected."

Patrick prefaced. "The medical marijuana issue must be put before every ballot box state by state not only for medical marijuana, but full legalization standards for Americans to make their own personal choices Roland. They can't stop an issue just because they want to. That is not how freedom works in America."

Roland continued. "I'm waiting for some kind of major legal break through."

Will revealed. "It's coming, it's coming."

Patrick specified. "Will is always the optimistic one. There are marijuana reform laws being proposed and presented to the voters in the next round of elections. More and more statesmen are jumping on the bandwagon."

Roland always the pessimistic one conceded. "City and state governments can't do nothing until we knock the federal governments marijuana laws not as they presently are. It's still on the books a person that a person can get five years in prison, and ten thousand dollar fine for possession of a joint of marijuana."

Pat grilled. "That tyrannical medieval law that butchers lives of citizens has got to come down to "Zero" discrimination for minor league cannabis possession." Looking at Roland, while they both nodded in agreement.

Pat stressed. "At least politicians are having open discussions now about changing the marijuana laws."

Roland implored. "We must get past discussions and we can't just keep getting stalled by the federal government. We have to get this pro-marijuana agenda for personal freedom over the hump."

Will pleaded. "It's coming Rollins, it's coming faster than people think. It's coming Roland."

Pat further stated. "Look Roland there are already DA's from various cities stating that they should start decriminalizing small amounts of marijuana for first offense possessions."

Roland asked. "Yeah, but aren't politicians and governmental officials taking a lot of heat from the just say no crowd?"

"Well" Roland, Pat reasoned. "We're going to do just that to the just no crowd, were gonna just say no to them in the November's elections. The just no crowd at voting time we'll get just no from the pro-marijuana movement. The opposition to marijuana reform candidates will be identified and targeted for the retirement home."

Will reproached. "They're going to have to change."

Roland agreed. "They're going to change, or be voted into retirement." Political Pat said. "I like that idea. They're going to belong to the smokers wing or be ousted. Fair marijuana reform will see to that. People have certain rights that will have to be adhered to and guaranteed under the Constitution of the United States."

Clint conceded to Miles. "Pat's firm back bone political position and adamant convictions for full legalization of marijuana have been long awaited. I like him, he is a bright guy."

On the other side of the pristine mahogany round table to represent the marijuana reform movement on the medical forum was Karen Kurtz, a U of M nurse who reviewed the medical uses to relieve pain. Karen said. "What we can prove is that marijuana has never killed anyone. We can also prove that the government marijuana laws and police have killed many more marijuana users and non users who were in the way of marijuana investigations. Bad politicians, make bad laws, which in turn have made many bad police officers. This has been proven to be very damaging to our society."

Karen is an adamant believer in Dr Lester Grinspoon, M.D. Ph.D. a leading authority who has proven marijuana's medical benefits. Lester is an associate professor at Harvard Medical school and was the first recipient of the NORML Foundation's "Lester Grinspoon Award for Outstanding Achievement in the field of Marijuana Law Reform." In over thirty years of scientific cannabis research Lester has penned numerous books and articles about marijuana medical findings.

Karen affirmed. "I just read what I believe explains the truth about the medical benefits of marijuana in "Marijuana, The Forbidden Medicine" in a book Lester and James B. Bakalar also a Harvard Professor wrote. They explained many remarkably safe medical benefits of marijuana. Safer medical benefits better then some legal prescription drugs currently being used on patients, in some cases with much better results. Book reviews by the medical community have been very responsive to his findings. Robert M Swift, M.D.,Ph.D., New England Journal of Medicine stated. "Cogent and convincing arguments for the legalization of marijuana and it's pharmaceutical active components.....this book provides an excellent overview of the subject from a medical perceptive."

Karen continued. "Uncle Sam's Pot farm at the University of Mississippi is a seven acre patch guarded by prison towers and twelve foot high fencing, and has been active since 1968, ironically the same year stiffer penalties came out against marijuana. All visitors are searched upon leaving the Huge Marijuana garden with large budding plants over twelve foot high."

Calmly Karen explained. "The Federally funded and American grown NIDA Marijuana project sows marijuana for research reasons. Various types of marijuana are grown in large amounts. Jamaican, Colombian, Thai are just a few of the many varieties and strengths. The joints are professionally rolled in cigarette production equipment. Approximately three hundred joints are done at a time. They are packed in tin cans and sent to prescribed destinations.

The Federal Government had supplied one patient with a medical marijuana prescription program of ten joints per day for the last twenty-one years straight. At that location the Government has grown millions of dollars of marijuana over the years.

One grandmother in her sixties has been receiving NIDA marijuana for glaucoma since 1989. Her seven grown children said if this relieves your pain, while it saves and improves your eyesight. Her family was for what helped grandma. Grandma excused herself to the bedroom and puff her five joints per day. Certain Science Evidence is mounting in great proportions that support medical marijuana use.

Research Scientists and Scientists at Harvard Medical School state that Medical Marijuana may be beneficial for multiple sclerosis, epilepsy, glaucoma, AIDS treatments, help relieve Chemotherapy treatment's nausea effect, migraine headaches, arthritis, menstrual cramps, pain from muscle spasms, old age and other ailment's."

Karen told the round table participants about her roommate. "At Medical College my room mate writes letters to AIDS and Cancer patients. Just to cheer these terminal patients up. She says many of these terminal patients choose to smoke marijuana. She has come to believe that if marijuana will relieve their pain then it's their choice. It's simply idiotic to ignore it's medical benefits."

Karen further explained at the round table meeting that. "Marijuana is also an appetite enhancer. fifty percent or better of those patients who use marijuana as a medication eat better. Some of it's proven medical helpfulness for patients is a better alternative than unproven prescribed chemical hard drugs presently available. Some prescribed drugs have adverse medical effects on patients in order to accomplish similar medical goals. Let everyone remember legal prescription drugs is the nations sixth leading killer. Not marijuana!"

Pot supplied by Uncle Sam should be prescribed on a much wider basis to citizens in need. We can end this unfair prohibition against marijuana possession in small amounts. Give citizens medical and recreational use in the privacy of ones home. These responsible citizens deserve to get their rights back." Karen concluded.

Clint commended to Miles. "That girl is powerful stuff!"

Miles verified. "She knows her forte very well."

This advanced pro-marijuana research round table forum was inclusive to all aspects related to marijuana. They truthfully intensified each marijuana subject matter.

Pat told Clint. "The legalization strategy session is progressing on a sound foundation."

Clint agreed. "I think so!"

The pro-cannabis movers want to submit strictly marijuana and hemp facts. They don't want to get into the gutter with the government and with the rest of the people who hate.

Each of the round table participants represented their own diversified outlook on cannabis subjects. They summed up concerns and hemp facts for their associates. They all believed that smoking is better than shooting and killing people, which the governments sponsored herb cops do.

Calvin Creater educates the public about the small legal victories marijuana users have gained yet not realized.

Calvin conveyed to the cannabis conference. "One lady told her story to the audience from a past rally about a judge who dismissed her case of marijuana use. She claimed her marijuana use was for medical reasons to ease her pain.

The judge agreed with her and the case was dismissed. The Judge also scolded the prosecutor. The Judge told him not to bring him any more cases similar to this any more. Bring real criminals to my court the judge said.

Calvin explained. "Another marijuana user brought before the court wasn't so fortunate. The judge, prosecutor, and cop slammed the book on this marijuana user after a roach from a marijuana cigarette was found in his ashtray. The police officer after interrogating the man and conducted an intensive search of this vehicle promptly arrested him and had his vehicle towed.

The man was on his way home from working at his five dollar an hour job. The judge ended up charging this man over five-thousand dollars in fines. The man spent over eighty days in jail, while missing work the whole time.

The man was then presented with a jail internment bill of forty dollars per night for eighty night's equaling thirty-two hundred dollars. This miscarriage of the law or should I say, miss-justice of the law for less than a half gram of marijuana. This harmless and honest man of simple values was fined in total costs of over ten thousand dollars. The only criminal activity here is state sponsored terrorism carry out by the government on it's good citizens."

Calvin with a sigh continued. "This man couldn't even afford an attorney making only five dollars an hour at his job. The man was earning a meager living at five dollars an hour. He should be commended instead of being slammed by the long arm of the law. This is an unfair and outrageous example of American justice while we are preaching human rights around the world. These drug cops are a gang of thugs and thieves who operate our judicial system by glossing over public scrutiny."

Clint whispered to Miles. "I like that, you can tell Calvin is getting mad even describing these governmental abuses."

Miles admitted. Yes! Compassionate Calvin not only has brains, he has heart for all the people too. He constantly promotes the resurrection of constitutional rights."

Chris told Clint. "Rudy is going to stand in for Manny at the International Hemp Rally and Festival. "Rock'n Rudy Roadhouse" will be featuring assorted hemp bands, which are backing the hemp cause at the festival. Their new CD with hit the song "Prohibition Puppet" will released at the Hemp Bizarre. Hemp bearing bands will alternate with Rudy D-Jaying in between sets played by the bands."

Standing erect Brant announced. "Pro-marijuana activists are free to mingle amongst their smoking friends without incrimination from the long arm of the law. George assured me that Hemp Political fronts have confirmed from the opposition that there would be no outside interference from law enforcement. The opposition said our permit to rally was assured, our call for freedom of rights at the hemp fare will be respected."

Miles divulged. "The Attorney General himself issued a statement for a hands-off policy by the police unless criminal activity transpires, which is different from marijuana use. This is indeed a viable political movement, and had to be respected as such."

Brant stipulated. "Volunteers will be passing out fliers to patrons for the upcoming hemp festival as they would walk in from the parking lot into the fair grounds."

Political Pat added. "Cannabis facts, figures and statistics will be presented on the fliers with info about citizen's tax dollars being spent on a futile marijuana war. The fliers feature volumes of documented police abuses. Our government has assembled and supplemented their marijuana drug war on fabrication and friction."

Clint walked over while Manny and Igor were standing by George.

George asked Manny. "What do you think about the round the world trip, Manny?"

Manny jumping inside for joy replied. "Thanks again. George, I don't know what to say, but thanks. I will do my best on this hemp, marijuana and hash assignment."

Everyone laughed. And George predicted. "I know you will, Manny." "And Manny" George asked. "Did you see the notes, I have circled where about you pick out a custom made pipe while you are in Amsterdam? The hemp made pipe will be raffled off at the International Hemp Festival and Hemp Bazaar in ruffly three weeks?"

Manny questioned. "What kind of pipe? George"

George answered. "A hemp made pipe to smoke marijuana in. You know an intricate one, something special. Please, send me the hemp pipe back as soon as you can so we can have it on time for the and upcoming hemp fairs."

Manny affirmed. "OK George! All right, no problem. I'll pick out a special pipe."

Raffle tickets were circulated for diversified hemp charities. The money was donated to medical marijuana clubs, which supplied marijuana to AIDS patients as well as to other patients with severe ailments.

All views and plans for upcoming hemp events were presented at this crucial round table meeting. A Democratic meeting in America is a tradition. Participatory philosophies with questions and answers are welcomed by everyone.

Most of the participants and their friends were anxious to attend the International Hemp Festival and Hemp Bazaar in a few more weeks.

Miles riddled. "Everyone looked for a good hemp informing time."

Chapter 9.. Once at the hemp festival started in the Houston's Astrodome hemp vendors organized and prepared their agendas.

Clint, Chantel, along with their kids Corey, Morey, and Lori were now at the Houston Astrodome for the International Hemp Festival and Bazaar. Chantel standing next to Clint was told. "This is the largest hot air balloon built in the world."

High minded Clint relayed. "Andre's team made a giant hemp balloon to go non-stop around the world, and hopefully will set the world record. Look Chantel, The twenty-five story hemp balloon with a pressurized hemp-fibered craft is presently going through final systems check is in the parking lot of the Astrodome now." Everyone wore a special cannabis wristband for solidarity.

Chantel enthused said. "The hemp balloon is already set float off and begin the Hemp Festival."

Miles caught up with Clint and Chantel and said. "Andre's flight will take off shortly. The hemp hot air balloon mission will be tracked around the world during the hemp festival."

Amazed Chantel said. "Look!"

Clint screamed. "There she goes!"

As the Hemp balloon lifted off the ground the crowd roared and waved at Andre.

Andre waved vigorously until the Hemp balloon was out of site.

Miles filled in. "Hemp fair goers can track the soaring hemp balloon into the stratosphere at the mission cannabis control. It's in the center of hemp festival."

Chantel railed to Clint. "I like the Hemp Banners streaming above the hemp product booths."

Miles continued his conversation with Clint. "Everyone is on the same page as far as nothing less then an all out full legalization for small amounts of marijuana."

The right to posses small amounts of marijuana without harassment or hindrance in the privacy of our homes. They want the right to choose there're own personal lifestyle."

Clint responded. "With no governmental red tape."

Chantel followed up. "That would be nice."

Miles agreed. "Yes the people here want a renewed hemp industry just like Canada did across the border. This three day hemp festival starting today at the Houston's Astrodome has a interesting array of informational hemp events."

Clint stated. "People want the show to go on with out a hitch."

Miles decreed. "Right! The invited world community is represented as well."

Chantel asked Miles. "How many hemp displays are there?"

Miles responded. "There are over one thousand different hemp exhibit's from around the world displayed at this hemp festival alone. The world cannabis smart governments are participating. America is one of the last countries on earth with these repression laws albeit personal choice are denied. Repression type laws are still on the books concerning the hemp industry in America."

Clint attested. "The hemp participants from around should tear down the evil marijuana war. Citizen's are concerned for human rights in their own country. I want to tear down this wall built by the marijuana war in our own country's society."

Miles agreed. "We've got to tear down this wall of governmental repression in our society."

Igor, Illyia, and their son Vladdie all were smiling and strolling in Clint's company. Igor said to Clint. "How do you like the Hemp-a-thon?"

Clint responded. "I really like this Hemp festival. I think it's about time Americans are allowed to show off their ingenuity."

Igor explained to his wife Illyia. "The "International Hemp Festival" started Friday varied vegetable and meat combinations before noon with "Chili Cook Off." The schedule says it starts on, and will be judged Sunday at 7:00 o'clock in the evening. Scheduled for Saturday is red meat/steak cook off, and followed Sunday with sweet meat entries mixed with hemp seasoning are featured to cap off the "Cannabis Con Carne Cook off.""

Rudy now present with his wife Maria, and their son Marty coupling in with Clint's Company said. "Pro-hemp bands such as the Bong Smokers, House of Smoke, Hemp Harvesters, Higher Reality, Comedy with Cannabis Carl are participating in the Musical and Comedy Entertainment scheduled. There are so many cannabis band entries they couldn't all be booked."

Chantel didn't beat around the bush. "No kidding Rudy!"

Rudy popped off. "Really but Music of all sorts will be featured at this three day hemp festival, from Reggae, Rap, Rock, Country, and Blue Grass. Theatre, and artist's cannabis creative work shops are another featured at this hemp fair."

Igor pledged. "Smokers of marijuana are from all backgrounds of life young, and old, rich and poor. They are encountered in immense ratio's here in America."

Vladdie ripped. "The Bong Smokers are going to release their new song "Just leave me alone with my home grown.""

Rudy yapped. "Cool!"

Vladdie and Marty told their parents. "Were taking off to inquire about all the hemp activities at the hemp shed. We've trying to catch up with Corey," who is already at the activities hemp shed.

Rudy clamored. "OK!" Then turned and raged to Maria. "They have some great hemp projects over there for the kids to participate in!"

Chantel told Maria and Illyia. "Men and women alike are walking around with very attractive and durably hemp made foot wear."

Maria noted. "They are uniquely different."

Illyia wearing her "Hemp Jumpsuit" accented. "Ladies are trying the stylish hemp perfumes and natural hemp scented oils. After one whiff of the sweet hemp fragrance, and the women swarmed to try samples."

Maria surprised. "I don't believe it! There are the new Hemp Femi-Pads. I've been looking all over for them."

Chantel disclosed. "World famous Tree Free Hemp Femi-Pads are also given in free samples to the ladies."

Illyia explained. "The hemp products sales lady had some specially lined Femi-pads for all the felines."

Maria's admitted. ""I'm trying some new "Hair Affair" hemp products. I like this "Hemp Hair Affair Booth." Free hemp hair conditioners, shampoo demonstrations, and free hemp samples were given out on request."

Chantel railed to her friends. "Hemp wear is every where" as she tried on some hemp made earring's.

Clint with Igor and Rudy expressed. "I wish I had a Cannabis Coffee House like that set up next to our camp grounds."

Igor excited. "That elaborate "Cannabis Coliseum" exhibit was really eye popping as you entered the fairground hemp exhibit area."

Miles, who just arrived stated. "In the center of the fairgrounds is one of the largest display and variety of hemp products ever assembled."

Clint snapped. "That's terrific news. I'll buy a round of drinks on that one."

Igor professed. "There is a huge hemp tent and teepees in the middle of the hemp festival.

Miles quipped. "That sign over there says everything in these tents and tepees is made from hemp including the canvas, poles, stakes, rope, the tents and the tepees."

Clint gawked. "Look over there! Those hippies are weaving baskets out of hemp like civilizations did ten thousand years ago."

Igor gazed. "Certain tent signs went further and say! Everything in this hemp tent was made while we were stoned on marijuana." Everyone got a kick out of that sign in particular.

Clint reeled. "When you look at all the hemp hand crafts, you suddenly realize how much work and artistic handicraft are involved to make all these hemp products. You have to commend all the ingenuity and effort of the hemp merchants and their promoters."

Miles canvassed. "These Cannabis Promoters are damn proud of their hemp products and the strong public showing."

"Right on!" Igor continued. "All the hemp products the top of the line products in product to product comparison studies. No wonder chemical and textile businessmen want hemp for competition. The hemp products are far superior, to existing similar product lines currently used and made without hemp."

Miles defined. "No smoking of any kind area's and nursery's were designated. This is to ensure hemp festival parents, who brought kids, a health safety net of their choice. The majority of people treat their kids or elder relatives with the same respect as if they were smoking tobacco. They respected others."

Igor ate hemp seed candy one of the vendors was handing out as samples. Miles tried the oatmeal cookies made out of hemp-seeds. "This tastes great! They're really delicious."

Igor painted in detail. "Hemp seeds is a staple food of the world for centuries."

Clint asked. "Isn't this where were supposed to catch up with non-smoking and drinking goodie two shoes Morgan Motley."

Miles quickly answered. "Yes! He's wearing his new dark blue "Three Piece Hemp Suit. He tells his clients it's the finest apparel available. It's quite a conversation piece."

Igor in his "Cannabis Cap" hashed over. "The majority of pot smokers do not smoke as much in capacity as tobacco smokers do cigarettes per day. And as far as being stoned on marijuana it's nothing like trying to cope with alcoholic drunks, When you're drunk on alcohol! Let's face it your drunk!"

Clint professed. "If your so called stoned on marijuana you can snap out of it in any instant given time. It is not a mind-controlling drug in anyway like beer, whisky, cocaine, or heroin. It's not much more than a strong cup of coffee."

Igor agreed. "Right, and you can't smoke coffee beans." everyone else laughed it off.

Rudy in his "Reefer Jacket" claimed. "A lot of marijuana smokers are happy with a joint or two in a month, or a week or a joint or two a day. Some people like Clint and the boys smoke a half a dozen a day."

Igor disclosed. "It' still much less use smoke wise than a usual cigarette smokers intake."

Miles admitted. "The inquisitive crowd is relatively hemp perceptive."

Clint in his "Cannabis Vest" curiously razzed. "The "Cannabis Crowd" wanted to see colorfully innovative and informative cannabis displays."

Miles conferred. "I've collected all the latest hemp updates, and brochures that were in this area. I like how all the non-smokers can order anything at the hemp festival from this non-smoking designated area."

Clint noticed. "The hemp product workers have cleaned up on the tips from all the trips."

Miles expounded to Clint. "This proves how gigantic the hemp industry is and how it is going expand for the next few years. Pro-hemp activists from all over the world sold their hemp wares right here in the good old USA."

Igor in his "Marijuana Muscle Shirt" and "Cannabis Jogging Pants" exulted. "Look over there on that stage there's "Cannabis Carl" himself doing his crazy cannabis comedy routine."

Clint laughed. "He's dressed up like a "Smoking Marijuana Leaf."

Igor roused. "Yea! That's' a rush!"

Miles raved. "It's not about who has the "Best Green Bud." It's about who has the "Best Time.""

Clint agreed. "That's right!"

Chantel wearing her new-sprung "Cannabis Shoulderette" and the girls are back from the ladies hemp fashion section of the fairgrounds. They freshened up with their hemp make up and showed off their new hemp clothing. Chantel told Clint. "There are seventy-four different hemp clothing lines from all over the world featured here today. Everything from diapers on babies bottoms, to "Hemp Trench Coat's" are displayed and sold here."

Maria wearing her "Hemp Grass Hula Skirt" preached. "I can't believe the amount of hemp made diapers the vendors gave out. The hemp diapers that are given out as samples constantly to mothers with babies."

Illyia explained. "They have one brilliant idea. The manufacture will sell millions."

Chantel disclosed. "One couple of back packers are dressed in full hemp apparel. Their hemp manufactured apparel included their hats and shirts, cool cannabis canvas jeans, hot fashioned hemp hiking boots, marijuana matching field bag, pot passport portfolio wallet, and even her jewelry and purse were all made of hemp."

Maria asked. "Did you feel how soft those cannabis towels were at the hemp home furnishing's display?"

Chantel answered. "Yes! You can tell they are superior to cotton. The couple stayed in their own hemp made tent in the middle of the hemp fair. This was a uniquely dressed couple with their own environmentally safe and strong hemp product lines completely covering their bodies."

Chantel depicted. "All the hemp products are soft and comfortable to wear, and much more durable than other clothing fabrics like cotton, wool, or polyester. One hemp display featured novelties and jewelry all made of hemp from all over the world. Many sales persons was handing out hemp product catalogues and hemp jewelry samples to the public."

Illyia relayed. "One huge hemp teepee full of women cannabis customers had different vibrant colors of hemp yarn, and twine, while crouching hemp blankets for their family."

Chantel stressed. "Don't tell Clint but I bought him a "Cannabis Chippendale Chair" with a matching cannabis coffee table at the "Completely Hemp Furniture Store," in the midway.

Maria snitched. "Heather bought the Hempster a "Hemingway High Chair.""

Chantel ribbed. "It sounds like he'll really get off on that."

Illyia laughed and giggled. "They all need a "Pot Parlor Chair." God knows they got the pot!"

Clint paraded in. "Hey! We've got to hear Abraham Arm's give his speech."

Miles flinched. "We all better hurry then!"

Chantel asked. "Who's Abraham Arms?"

Clint answered Chantel as they scrammed to his speakers stage for a house seat. "He's one hell of a famous Hollywood actor, who's stagecraft is unmatched."

Miles followed. "He's one great upcoming keynote speaker for the Hemp Industrial Complex. He's very knowledgeable and inspirational in his monologue"

Igor surged. "George had Aaron create and Brant build the hemp agricultural background scenery for Abraham."

Chris adjusted the angle on key house-lights accordingly, because expert Abe is precision after preparation."

Clint edged. "Academy Award Abraham" has a straightforward personality. He has recently had been arrested staging a protest for the hemp industry by planting "Industrial Hemp Seeds" in Kentucky."

Igor blared. "The nice thing about him is there's never a blackout."

Miles stumbled. "The Star had the media there in full force during the hemp seed planting, when an over jealous police officer arrested the peaceful hemp protester. Maximizing media coverage of the hemp seed planting was well received by the public, and pushed public awareness to new heights for industrial hemp. Teachers in public schools are fired for advocating some Abraham's view of the hemp industry.

Abraham hawked his audience of pro-hemp advocates and began. "The hemp farmers of Kentucky after being stripped of their hemp heritage. We have to give them their hemp agricultural rights back. The hemp industry will fuel the American farmer and American Agricultural sector of commerce. All the hemp board packaging is made out of industrial hemp at today's show. Hemp paper industrialists from other countries have displayed their hemp paper and hemp cardboard wares. Exhibits from sign posters employ hemp paint right down to hemp facial paints on children and grown-ups alike. Everything made in the world with other fibers are made out of hemp at this International Hemp Festival and Bazaars."

Clint told Chantel. "That's cool!"

Abe continued to speak. "Hemp wrapping paper and hemp eats are demonstrated for all fair goers. The perforated Styrofoam looking burger containers that have a cheeseburger in them are made from hemp. When you are done with the burger you can eat the hemp-burger container if you want to. Hemp food containers are available in different flavors. The hemp seed chef makes thousands of different hemp recipes." Abe concluded his speech to a heavy round of applause.

Max Miller is the owner of a hemp paper factory, and had on display hundreds of various types of hemp paper varying in contrasted colors and texture.

Max told his customers. "All paper products displayed are made with hemp fiber's, samples and products a like."

Max further told his inquiring audience. "Hemp paper makes the finest paper in the world."

Max invited the audience. "You are all invited for a free tour of my hemp factory in Detroit. You can see our semi-truck driver bring and unload sterilized hemp seeds from across the border in Windsor Canada. We process the raw hemp seeds and stalks at my Detroit factory."

Miles scoped a fancy hemp display and told Clint. "Check that hemp environmental sales guy out."

The hemp salesmen named Craig demonstrated. "All hemp products are biodegradable and safe for the environment. Further contributing to our Biomass conversion in an environmentally safe manner.

Craig explained. "Hemp Environmentalists say pollution from fossil fuels are causing eighty percent of the worlds air pollution. These toxic petro-chemical fossil fuels and toxic products can be reduced with Eco-friendly hemp production and products. The hemp vendors further explained the benefits of hemp grown for fuel. They will explained how much cleaner fuel made from hemp burns, which contribute to global warming. Large tracts of Industrial Hemp Production will help balance the CO2 cycle, which in essence would help solve acid rain problems. Reducing carbon dioxides from out cars combustion is what has to happen. Make sure you look around at all these Eco-friendly products booths here on display today." Craig concluded.

Igor emphasized. "Hemp ethanol fuel burns much cleaner through the entire car motor, when compared with gas. Out of all the vegetable fuels Industrial Hemp is the best!"

Clint stressed. "It so much cleaner throughout the earth's atmosphere too."

Miles conveyed. "Marijuana and hemp activists armed with literature are setting up with displays as well. Hemp petition drives of diversified classification's that concern hemp production are on display at that political booth as well."

Clint told Miles. "One hemp display the booth had an original experimental "Hemp Panel" from Ford Motor Company. The original Henry Ford engineers descendants produced these tough hemp plastic like panels. These hemp panels took heavy blows without denting like steel of similar thickness."

Igor accented. "Henry Ford grew his own hemp and tried many documented hemp innovations."

Miles exemplified. "Hemp products have been proven to be very durable. The "Industrial Hemp Farmer's Associations" that represent the hemp industry have set up booths and are dispersing literature on hemp growing techniques. They're explaining the difference between types of hemp to grow for industrial cultivation. You can review the John Deer tractors with a full line new of hemp agricultural implements were on display. The cannabis rights of the farmers were recognized. The hemp farming and manufacturing equipment on display is used throughout the real free world."

Igor praised. "That is impressive how the hemp field was made for the show here in part of the Astrodome."

Miles promoted. "Henry the Hempster will demonstrate the John Deere equipment for the harvesting show's audience."

Igor boasted. "Bring it on!"

Clint told Miles. "An old man over there stated the last time he had hemp seeds in his hand was 1937. He told me how his father lost their Kentucky farm when hemp was made illegal.

The old man thought it was a great idea to re-establish the hemp industry again. The old man also said he didn't get out of the house much but wanted to attend this hemp event. Is that all we can spend our money on is military, police, and prisons the old man said Turn society and the economy around Legalize cannabis across the board.

Give the people what they want. Give the people what they are comfortable with. The marketing opportunities for hemp is incredible Just look around." The old man said. "I always knew hemp was a good fiber. They should have never eliminated the hemp industry in the first place. I'd still be on my Daddy's farm in Kentucky."

Miles continued. "Hemp production and different fiber processes are being demonstrated at the hemp production center in the middle of the Astrodome. Hemp stalks freshly harvested from the middle of the Astrodome are reduced to hemp pulp and fibers. The different hemp processes break the hemp down."

Clint defined. "Canada, Australia, China, the Netherlands are among many countries involved in hemp agriculture industry. They are displaying their hemp farm hardware here today. They explained the different hemp growing and harvest seasons in the different regions. They told other hemp farmers where they can sell their hemp after being grown and for what price."

Miles explained. "Business techniques were presented at the hemp-festival in a small business recommendation display. The advantages of hemp production has to many qualities to continually be ignored by our country."

Igor induced. "Hemp for textiles is over there at another merchants cannabis tent. Making products with raw hemp material so spectators can see many different uses and products."

Clint exulted. "I'm impressed with the processed hemp wood like building materials. They're just as attractive, but much stronger than processed wood". Everyone finally ended up at Aaron's and his wife Janice's booth.

Aaron quickly conferred to Clint. "Were busy beyond our wildest dreams. Were airbrushing custom T-shirts made with hemp fabrics and hemp tie dye paint."

Aaron's wife Janice enthused stated. "I'm custom airbrushing everything with paints that are made from cannabis."

Chantel asked. "I want one on my cheek?"

"OK!" Their teenage daughter Alicia in her "Hemp Hooped Hip Hangers" as she welcomed Chantel. Alicia was painting funny faces on kids with non-toxic hemp paints, but Alicia couldn't wait to paint Chantel up.

Chantel asked to Alicia. "Did you see the "Pot Puppets" with the hemp made costumes, that are featured in one of the shows put on for kids."

"Yes" Alicia answered. "I took my lunch over there earlier, watching the puppet show. I liked the display booth next to the Marijuana Messiah's booth. The booth has hemp-crafted candles with colors of all sorts and hemp incense. I just love those "Cannabis Candles.""

Chantel teased. "I'm going to check the cannabis candle booth out just because you like the cannabis candle booth, Alicia."

Brant caught up with Clint and raved. "Key note hemp speakers are featured all afternoon. Rudy as usual readied the pro-activists hemp bands that begin at 8:00 O'clock."

"OK Brant, Thanks!" Rudy minced.

Karen at the Hemp Festival now gabbed to Chantel. "Hemp medical activists have a tent exhibit set up. They displayed hemp medical prescription drugs that are available through out the world. They are currently used medically for many different ailments. A sign over there says. "Healing Herbs Advice Here," which is the head line of the Medical Marijuana Clinic."

Chantel confessed. "I'm glad to have found you Karen. I'll come by the medical booth as soon as we are done at the political booth."

Karen attested. "All right I'll be looking for you!"

Igor and Clint walked through The Marijuana Messiah's Head Shop booth which displayed marijuana paraphernalia galore.

The Messiah summoned to Clint upon entrance. "This is the place where Zig Zag rolling papers have cannabis made rolling papers for sales competition."

The Messiah proudly showed his customers marijuana buds that were in the last cannabis cup contest in Amsterdam.

The Messiah puffed on his jag and wheezed. "I'm going to the next cannabis cup contest in Sunny Southern Spain. We also make custom home made pipes of all sorts, shapes and colors, to customer's specifications and requests, whether it be made out of stone, various woods, bamboo, hemp, deer antlers, amid unique curious oddities." The Marijuana Messiah boasted.

Igor raved to Clint. "The Marijuana Messiah has a video constantly showing a history of pipes, and a "History of Marijuana People" from around the world. Which pipes were smoked by who, and at what time in history. The intricacies of the pipes, and why people liked pipes. How it warms them up on a winters day a bit, and puts people in a better mood."

Clint discussed. "He's selling the marijuana informational museum video for fifty bucks right there." Clint said while pointing to the counter.

The Messiah rhapsodized. "When the Indians and the white man smoked the peace pipe it always worked out better than over the barrel of a gun. Peaceful parleys presided over a pipe, instead of looking over the barrel of a gun".

Clint contended. "The Marijuana Messiah is definitely right Igor."

Igor conveyed. "That's why were fighting friendly!"

Clint quickly responded back sharply. "You know it!"

Miles walked up to Clint and Company specified. "I want to see that hemp beer display in the Messiah's booth. The one that has the mini brewery."

Clint railed. "I want to see that to!"

Igor disclosed. "I didn't know that a hemp bier display was here."

Miles emphasized. "MMM Hemp brewed bier, that taste great."

Antonio walked up after tasting the hemp wines. "MMM I like the hemp wine."

Igor divulged. "The hemp wine is being sold for take out."

The Messiah walked up and popped off. "Gentlemen we have frozen mugs with ice cold hemp brewed bier samples today. The bier was made from imported hemp seeds."

Igor took a sip of the hemp bier illustrated. "I like the creamier head."

Clint summarized. "I like the herbal flavoring of the hemp bier."

The Messiah attested. "We substitute hemp seeds for barley and hops during the brewing process at our microbrewery. The Feds tried to stop us and another half dozen microbreweries from brewing the hemp bier, because of the image it presents to the younger populous."

Igor branded. "So the Feds would rather practice censorship on freedom, and encourage repression."

Clint stipulated. "When the Feds starts dictating their own policy instead of following policy and laws. When laws are hysteria based instead of fact based, and must be forcibly promoted based on their own perceived morality, it's time to eliminate the Feds promotion of values department in the government."

Igor agreed. "That is for sure!"

Clint pledged. "Thanks for the hospitality Messiah."

The Messiah further cheered hemp. "Try the hemp root tea samples they're good. The hemp root tea is offered for take out. Hemp coffee with hemp coffee filters are on display at the next counter."

Miles spelled out. "The hemp energy display has books on sale on how to make Hemp oil fuel, along with other how too hemp books. One "Stogie Master" burning one was reading a book on growing marijuana hydroponically".

Igor spurred to Clint. "Look outside the Messiah's booth. There's the "Marijuana Mobile" with vibrant colors of various marijuana plants and marijuana leaves encompassing the whole automobile. That's the Marijuana Messiah's personal auto." They all laughed.

Clint asked kiddingly. "Do a story on the Messiah! Miles?"

Miles answered. "How did you know that's what I was thinking!"

Clint and Company laughed with Miles and they all went on to explore the Hemp festival's next cannabis displays.

The hemp builders booth had quite an interested crowd around them.

Igor spouted. "Hey Clint! The hemp builders have special hemp festival price."

Clint confirmed. "These hemp builders will put an addition on your house. You can call a smokers parlor. Complete with marijuana stash and paraphernalia drawers. They even use hemp pressed wood."

Miles divulged. "Some hemp additions come with a hydroponics growing room including grow lights. The wood, shingles, and insulation for these show specials are all made from hemp fibers."

Clint disclosed. "That's wild how the hemp builders build complete houses out of ninety percent hemp materials."

Miles revealed. "That's amazing!"

Igor pointed out. "They're displaying the new hemp building materials of pressed particle boards which are much stronger than wood fibers. It is utilized as hemp made 2x4's, insulation, wall paper, ECT."

Clint proposed. "Let's take a look!"

Chantel and the other ladies in the mean time are at the Hemp Fashion shows that are being held from noon till 6:00 O'clock each day at an alternative stage.

Chantel pulled Maria to her side and glamored. "That is the Internationally renowned Cannabis Fashion Designer Emilio Avares. Emilio has assembled and brought in seventy-five models to display the new hemp clothing line sponsors for the International Hemp Festival and Hemp Bazaar show."

While the "Cannabis Queens" were busy, Clint, Igor and Miles found Political Pat. Clint suddenly lashed out. "Pat! You are the front running Pro-Marijuana political proponent in America."

Pat acknowledged. "That's right! Our political movement has formed the new Constitutional Party of America."

Clint answered back. "That's sounds political!"

Pat confided. "Thanks Clint! Come on in here and check out these other Hemp Political activists and candidates. This is the individual freedom and pro-marijuana candidates nationwide demo-graphic tracking station. All political agendas on marijuana reforms are logged here.

The computer screen here explains the different legislative procedures in the past, and the ones currently, being implemented now. We also have the marijuana legalization laws being developed for future implementation."

Mild Miles asked Pat. "Are you going to announce your Pro-Marijuana agenda and Hemp Candidacy platform for State Representative at this hemp festival venue?"

Perky Political Pat answered back. "As a political leader for the local cannabis freedom organization I sure am. Let's make it official right now! Miles your the first to know. I have just ending our exploratory activities. I've announced my candidacy for state representative."

Miles and Clint both answered. "Great!" at the same time.

Pat further explained to a cannabis inquirer and his audience that. "There has been over twelve million marijuana busts for possession since 1966 and a waste of money, and the aggravation on our society which could have been saved for the tax payers. Nothing has been gained by the hemp and marijuana drug war, and much more has been lost."

Miles taped the Politically Correct Pat so he could comprise a news story. Pat went on at length to explain to his political audience, "The views of the pro-marijuana political front I represent, want marijuana regulated in a fashion similar to government regulated tobacco and alcohol."

Impulsive Igor informed. "I'm voting for you Pat!"

Pat told the audience at his political booth. "An FBI background investigation found that the over twenty White House Staffers used drugs with in the prior year. The presidential candidate's staff also had members, and friends of the President, who admitted to drug use and said they had smoked marijuana on the White House roof regularly. The president even has admitted to marijuana use. State Senators as well as State Representatives, their friends and relatives were found to have used drugs much harder than marijuana as well."

Pat made it clear. "The pro-marijuana movement I represent wants to eliminate or curtail hard drug use. Our political agenda is to re-legalize the hemp industry and small amounts of marijuana for personal use in the privacy of our homes.

The Cannabis Wing of Constitutional Party will put forth legislation in congress for the legalization of cannabis as soon as the voters sweep us into office. Thank you very much!" Pat had a standing ovation in front of him."

Optimistic Clint convinced as they all walked to tour the rest of the hemp festival implied. "The Constitutional party candidate Politically Correct Pat is the next state representative for his district."

Igor agreed. "That's for sure!"

Carefree Chico clamored. "You know that's right!"

Aaron in another zone of the hemp bazaar took a break, and mingled the other air brush artists. Aaron noticed Clint and crooned. "Hi Clint!"

Clint asked. "Your a long way from your booth aren't you?"

Aaron explained. "I thought I'd get a quick look at all the other hemp art."

Clint cackled. "This Hemp festival is something else."

Aaron conferred to Clint. "The artists have great cannabis creations, and paintings made with hemp paints, canvas, even the easels are made from hemp like wood. I like the hemp art, sculptures and creative cannabis crafts. I'm here to pick up some hemp stalks, they make the finest art canvas and paper."

Clint asked. "Do you make your own art canvas?"

Aaron answered. "Yes! I also make my own hemp oil paints and stationary paper as well."

Clint described. "Everyone at the hemp show or representing the hemp show is wearing brightly colored hemp clothing outfits. They are all topped with vibrant hemp hats."

Aaron squealed. "That's cool! Everyone here gets to do what they want to do. If they didn't want to do it, they wouldn't be here. Nobody likes to be told or forced to do something they really don't want to do. If you had to do it you wouldn't enjoy it. Do you know what I mean Clint?"

Clint confided. "I sure do Aaron! That's why people like you are friends of mine."

Aaron retorted. "Thanks Clint."

Clint told Aaron. "Come one over here! I want you to meet some good people."

Henry the Hempster and his wife Heather are making projections at the "Hemp Financial Analysts" exhibit. Aaron recognized the Hempster and admitted. "I know the Hempster. I buy my hemp fibers from him."

After everyone caught up on old times Henry defined the hemp programs. "Businessmen are eager for a new cannabis financial market to develop in our country. They are making projections for the stock exchange if hemp farming and industries are legally free."

Heather relayed. "The hemp businessmen are showing potential hemp investors. How citizens of the world are already investing in other countries on a stock exchange currently for the hemp industry."

Henry represented hemp as a whole while on Hemp Financial platform and expounded in detail. "Business tycoons, investors, and entrepreneurs are very interested in the development of the marijuana and hemp industry in the United States. Hemp has two hundred percent better yield than cotton.

The hemp financial analysts predicted in the first year alone that ten million acres of hemp agriculture in the United States could be harvested. This is the most viable and durable crop in the world. The hearty hemp fiber is a very valuable commodity presently grown throughout most of the world. In three years American farmers can compete with the free world with thirty million acres of hemp production per year. Some demo-graphic seed strains still exist in Kentucky. "A Canadian firm Hemp-Argo International's hired Dr Wylie. He is a professional botanist who is developing tropical strains of hemp for this hemisphere in Central America. They even want to try the hemp strains in areas of the country where the soil may not be the best for growing. Hemp will grow healthy where other crops won't.

The hemp industry's modernized processing and manufacturing technology for a new full service hemp industrial complex. This complete hemp complex could be built in any poor rural economies, even if they have poor quality soil.

Hemp Financial Analysts predict a free trade hemp industry will generate over one trillion dollars over the next forty years in world wide revenues." As Henry continued Clint and Company went on to the Cannabis Teepee area of the International Hemp Festival and Bazaar.

Clint stressed to Chantel. "These are by far the best days for the pro-marijuana movement so far."

Chantel answered. "Yes, the people running the government will have to take notice of the large very successful pro cannabis turn out."

Brant ran into Clint at the festival and informed. "The Hemp festival will break up at midnight. The media commentators and the hemp vendors were tired from a hard day's work. The feedback from the public arena favor legalization of hemp and marijuana."

Clint resolved. "I could see at the conclusion of the hemp festival everyone is peaceful and has left in fine spirits, we were all invigorated with a sense of hope and direction for pro marijuana reforms."

Brant revealed. "Only hemp biers and wine were sold here today. Hemp sponsors wanted the great public showing. Pot festivities are peacefully more informative. Not like the alcohol infested rowdy soccer matches in Europe."

Clint agreed with Brant. "That's for sure!"

Brant contended. "The day was especially delightful because law enforcement wasn't looking over the publics shoulder here at the Hemp festival. The patrons of the hemp fair smoked freely as they walked in the open air."

Clint confided. "Isn't that incredible. People bustled around and enjoy themselves govern themselves, respected their neighbors and had day full of hemp activities."

Brant attested. "There were no problems what so ever with out the militarized robot cops in today's attendance."

Political Pat divulged to Clint. "The hemp fair agenda was held without police interference because of the enormous numbers in attendance. This International Hemp Festival and Bizarre the hemp and marijuana political front represented the best America has to offer!"

Clint looked at Pat said. "I agree! With this kind of pro-cannabis crowd were definitely making head way."

Chapter 10..... Manny has long been on his way to New York. On his arrival at Laguardia Airport New York City, Manny caught a cab to go through the congestion of the city to Kennedy Airport before departing for London.

On Manny's way to the Kennedy his cab driver a West African named Raphael, asked him. "Do you mind if I smoke a joint? It's been a rough day so far."

Manny asked. "You're going to light up a joint while you're driving a cab?" "Yeah! If you don't mind."

Manny smiled and protested. "If you don't mind sharing." As Raphael drives down the road he said. "I don't mind." and he passed the marijuana joint to Manny as they talk about world affairs.

Manny asked Raphael. "How do you like it here in America?"

Raphael replied. "I don't like it Man."

Manny felt that was odd that this guy wouldn't like America being that he was from West Africa. Manny thought anybody from the desolate area of West Africa would surely enjoy America. Manny said. "Why is that?"

Raphael answered. "Too much crime! Everywhere you go here it's crime, crime, crime. Crooks are robbing, stealing and shooting all the time here."

Manny asked. "Is that right?"

Raphael answered. "Yeah" As they went past the Statue of Liberty, Manny raised a toast with his Pepsi.

Manny puffed and railed. "The old girl is looking good today."

"Yeah, not too bad, Man." As Raphael drives on and dropped Manny off at Kennedy Airport. They exchange friendly good byes and parted ways.

Manny struck up conversation with a few other natives of New York by asking. "How do you like New York?"

Many residents responded. "There is too much crime!"

Manny questioned. "Is that right?." Manny was surprised to hear all these negatives from native New Yorkers. Manny was glad when he out got of Kennedy Airport to London.

On the flight Manny conversed to a Member of Parliament in the first class section of the Airliner. He was flying back from a United Nations conference to his native London.

George had set Manny up with classy accommodations throughout his three-week tour world reefer tour.

Manny listened to a member of the British Parliament Oliver Owens. He spoke about marijuana reforms in his country, and legislation being drawn up to decriminalize marijuana, and hash. Manny after overhearing the herb conversation asked Oliver. "Have the hemp industries been explored in England?"

Oliver answered Manny's question said. "Yes, there are hemp farmers in England are experimenting with hemp crops, which are being tried on a trial basis in the fields now

Manny avowed. "I'm glad to hear that!"

Oliver chucked. "Healthy cannabis crops too! The hemp farmers love the durability of hemp. Were bringing their own hemp heritage back."

Manny inquired. "What do you mean?"

Oliver expressed. "I mean. We've had a hemp tradition established in England for centuries. It died when the prohibition started. The politicians are wising up. They know that hemp is rope not dope. We are slowly reestablishing the hemp industry in jolly old England."

Manny responded. "I'm thrilled!"

As the airliner landed on the run way at Heathrow airport, London, Oliver asked Manny to met at the Hippodrome Saturday night in Piccadilly Square. Manny quickly excepted.

Oxford University graduate Oliver recanted to Manny. "I'll bring some friends."

Eagerly Manny retorted. "I can't wait for tonight!" as they departed ways for the time being. Manny traveled the train to London's central "Victoria Station."

Once off the train arrived at the Grand Old Victoria Station Manny maneuvered through the entangling passenger traffic in the vast open area surrounded by gift shops. He walked through the tile walled area that led from the platforms up the escalator to the open streets of London while the station announcer broadcast new departures and arrivals. After a money exchange he was off a stranger to opposite road drivers. Manny scurried past the oncoming black London taxi cabs. The city's busy double decked red transit buses were lined up for blocks.

Manny dined at a elegant sidewalk café while facing a many protruding arched-gabled layer-trough windows with a castle-coned steepled roof's topped on a gigantic structured building. He was reading the local newspaper. The papers headlines of the day and news articles were about the freshly knighted Paul McCartney, while a "British Bobbi" was pointed the way for a tourist.

Paul McCartney, still remembers the repression of being locked in a box for nine days for marijuana in Japan.

Roy, a British chap sat at the next table over, and saw Manny's travel bag with a small American flag. He asked Manny. "Where you from Yank?"

Manny responded. "I'm from Houston, Texas."

Roy excited. "Fantastic! Is your stay here going to be awhile?"

Manny hemmed. "No, not really!"

Roy noticed the article Manny was reading inquired. "You like the Beatles do you?"

Manny scrambled. "Yes I do!"

Manny liked the Beatles. Manny being a DJ further said to Roy. "Whatever the Beatles did musically is as good as gospel."

Roy quizzically asked. "Who's your favorite Beatle?"

Manny answered. "All of them! I'd like to see some of the Beatle haunts while I'm in London."

Roy replied. "You're in the right place, Paul McCartney owns a home right down the street."

Manny maintained. "Paul McCarntey is a friend of the people. I'm glad they made him a knight. I remember when our government investigated Paul's friend John Lennon."

Roy noted. "The American government leaned on John Lennon quite hard."

Manny claimed. "John endorsed peace, and the peace process. John was a staunch marijuana smoking anti-war activist. He must be a criminal the U S government officials concluded. Which in my opinion, I'm glad John spoke up for my brothers and sisters that had to go to that unfair lousy war."

Roy responded. "They wanted to silence his voice for peace with a whole bunch of other fighters for peace.

Manny agreed. "That's for sure! The Nixon Administration tried their hardest to deport him for strictly political reasons. John endured personal investigation's by the White House, FBI, CIA, and other assorted government officials of our free society."

Roy rousted. "John finally won that round with Nixon! He gained the immigration status he sought!"

Manny changing topics asked. "Is pot hard to get here?"

Rightfully Roy divulged. "We have no problem getting marijuana or hash anytime. It's all over the place. The government is leaning toward full decriminalization of marijuana and hash. Over half the people young and old want marijuana legalized."

Manny asked Roy. "Is that the opinion here?"

Roy responded. "Sure it is just like America. Right!"

Manny joked. "Right Roy!

Manny asked Roy. "Are there any hemp farms around here? I'd like to see hemp growing in the fields of England, while I'm here."

Roy who was an active member for "Legalize Cannabis Campaign" head quartered in London told Manny. "There are British companies licensed to grow and sell industrial hemp."

Manny asked. "Is hemp farming accepted in England by the locals."

Serious Roy stipulated. "People are starting to get the anti-prohibition message. That prohibition is wrong and has failed recklessly. While your here see if you can reach the people who represent the "Legalize Cannabis Campaign." or from "Legalize Britain." I sure think, they can be of help. Members of Parliament have taken notice. Some members admit to marijuana use, while others in Amsterdam cafes are caught on film smoking down marijuana and hash."

Manny professed. "People are smoking pot any way, why make criminals out of them? Why make our people go against their own wills if that's what they want?"

Roy explained. "London policy makers are discussing how to regulate, tax, and distribute marijuana. Public opinion polls around world support legalization of marijuana."

Manny stressed. "That's the way I see it! Marijuana is already the largest cash crop in America."

Roy further divulged. "Why fill the jails with marijuana users. They may end up being turned into real criminals? Prisons are breeding grounds for criminals. To place a pot smoker among harden criminals is criminal itself."

Manny decreed. "Everyone I talk to says the same thing. Yet, some of these governments can't get it through their ignorant heads."

Roy decided to show Manny around London town, who was shopping at the "Gift Flair" souvenir shop for post cards and a small souvenir "British Flag." Roy's girl friend Rhonda met them at Larco's restaurant just around from Victoria Station. She decided to tag along with Roy and his new Yank friend. They walked the streets of London past the spike topped high walled fence of Buckingham palace, and kept on until they were in front of Big Ben, House of Parliament, Westminster Abby. Manny said. "Roy Buckingham Palace is much longer to walk around the perimeter, then the White House in Washington, DC. I remember that from when I was a kid on holiday with my parents in DC."

Roy responded. "I didn't know that." as they walked over the "River Thames," while a barge with an aft wheel house cruised under with his horn sounding. They crossed back over until they reached the large well groomed green grass lining parkway along the river. A well dress lady walking Dash hounds passed when Roy decided to take Rhonda and Manny to Kings Cross on the tube. As the clock stuck 3 PM they walked past the ornate lamp posts and the tall structure of "Big Ben" to the "Westminster Station."

Manny on the way confided. "I need to go back to London for a month if I expect to even scratch the surface of these exciting tourist sights and attractions."

Roy responded. "You'll still never see them all!"

Manny told Roy. "There's a book store in Kings Cross, and my friend George wants me to retrieve some hemp reading materials."

After taking the illuminated event advertised arched-hall escalator down to the transit, Manny checked out the tube map on the wall before proceeding through the automatic entrance gates with a travel pass in hand. Travelers were walking against each other to get to their destinations, while a man played his guitar for money. Once on the tube Manny met more Londoners, who smoked marijuana.

On Manny's last stop of his sight seeing tour with his new found friends, they took him to the Abbey Road Studios.

Roy explained to Manny. "This is the place of some very famous Beatle recordings."

Manny exulted to Roy. "I'm really excited that you brought me here! I feel privileged! I get to take some Beatle souvenirs back for Clint and Chantel."

Roy laughed because it was no big deal for to him. Roy lived in London. He could go to the Abbey Road Studios anytime. Manny scouted the tourist attraction at length.

Rhonda laughed. "Watch Manny Roy! He is really excited to be here." As he excitingly toured.

Roy professed. "I know. I think that's great!"

Manny knew Clint was a big Beatles fan.

Manny asked to one of the patrons. "Did you hear that on the radio?"

"What?" the startled girl pleaded.

Manny explained. "Your Price of Wales just said he thought the government should do an inquiry about sweeping reforms concerning Marijuana use."

"We all want to legalize marijuana!" The young British girl alleged. "It's the Americans, that are stupid and stubborn. Our government is growing marijuana for medical research. The House of Lords scientific committee has approved the use of medical marijuana."

Manny looked at her and claimed. "You're right the U. S. governs marijuana in an ignorant mode."

The young girl known as Jenny stated. "Your politicians are more worried about getting re-elected, than doing what's right for the people."

Manny disclosed. "Unfortunately I have to agree with you young lady." as he strolled over to Roy and relayed. "Roy, I have to go to the hotel and get ready for tonight."

Roy turned to Rhonda. "Manny has to get ready for tonight. He's doing a guest appearance as a DJ at the Hippodrome tonight. Oliver Owens invited him."

Rhonda conveyed. "Maybe we'll see you up there."

Manny exhorted. "I hope you both do." as they said. Their good byes."

Manny, Roy and Rhonda departed their own ways.

Manny while having a beer at "Soho Tavern" decided to check out the fancy lighting in the sex souvenir shops.

In the early part of night Manny traveled the tube to Leisester Square. Then he moseyed on Cranbourn Street directly under the fluorescent tube facial sign of the Hippodrome's building. Impatient Oliver squinted at the door waiting for Manny.

Oliver told the managers of the Hippodrome about Manny. The American radio celebrity D-Jayed night club's in Texas on a regular basis. Oliver arranged the short stand in set for Manny. Manny was delighted to do it.

Oliver professed. "They'll love to hear your Texas accent, Mate."

Manny needled. "Now wait a minute Ollie. Let's get one thing straight. You guys have the accent, not us." Oliver laughed.

Oliver, and his guests, Trent, Trevor, Teresa, Tina and Tiffany made Exuberant Manny felt about the tour that George had sent him on.

227

After Manny DJ'd his set he left the Hippodrome for the night with Oliver, Trent and Trevor. Oliver decided to take Manny on a yacht tour of the river Thames in the middle of the moon lit night.

Trent's seventy-five foot yacht regularly entertained Parliament dignitaries. Trevor was a speechwriter for some of the most polished politicians in Parliament.

Merry Manny maintained. "Thanks to George flying me first class, I've met classy people, who are well connected."

Trent professed. "That's for sure were well connected."

Ollie quickly agreed. "Yes, we are all well connected."

Trent constantly told Manny. "There are some really hot places to enjoy while your tour in Amsterdam. There are many different coffee shops, and museums."

As Oliver handed Manny a business card he said. "Here's a contact named Heidi. She's a photographer in Amsterdam, and while you scour around to marvelous cannabis shop of Amsterdam, she'll personally take you too different coffee shops that participate in the Cannabis Cup. She'll observe the Hash, Marijuana, and Hemp Museum with you, and assist you during your gathering mission for marijuana legalization in America."

Manny psyched. "Heidi! He asked. "What does she look like?"

Trent jumps in. "You'll like her mate, she is really a neat person."

Manny exulted. "I can't wait!"

The following day after all his good byes, Manny took the short flight from London to Amsterdam.

On his arrival at the airport Heidi met Manny. Heidi recognized Manny immediately, because he wore a Houston Astro's baseball cap as planned for easy identification for Heidi.

As Manny approached Heidi at the airport she asked. "How you doing Yank?"

Manny greeted. "Hi! How are you Heidi?"

Hiedi answered. "Yes, I am. Trent said I'm to be your personal guide while you're here in Amsterdam."

Manny proposed. "Great! Where do we start?"

Hiedi asked. "Are you hungry, Manny?"

Manny answered. "Yeah! I could use a bite to eat."

Hiedi declared. "OK! We'll go to this nice coffee shop in the heart of the city."

Manny stressed. "Let's go! I'm geared!"

Heidi lead Manny from the airport to her car parked under the airport pavilion. They departed and drove to Amsterdam. Heidi pointed out different coffee shops located throughout Amsterdam. On the way past Central Station she turned on Rokin and went straight for the De Rokerij coffee shop.

Manny attested. "I can't wait to get the coffees house. This is cool. I've never been in a coffee shop before in my life," as he looked over the official coffee shop guide Hiedi handed him.

Heidi asked. "Do you want to eat or do you want to go to the coffee house?"

Manny responded. "Well, I guess we'd better eat second. I can hold back food. I'd like some green bud and black hash, and slam it down with a frosted mug of dark hemp beer."

Hiedi noted. "You sure know what you want. I think I can arrange that. Let's get to the De Rokerij!" as they drove by the Hemp Hotel. Hiedi explained to Manny about the grand variety of hemp beers, hemp wines, hemp teas, hemp snacks, and hemp sandwiches sold at the Hemp Hotel.

Manny expressed to Hiedi. "I've have to try some of those hemp treats." Hiedi assured Manny she would take him there before he left Amsterdam.

Hiedi recounted. "Last time I was in their "Hemple Temple NightBar" I overheard the owner's Mila's daughter Willy chuckled on phone to one of her cannabis customers. "You feel so well in the "Hemp Hotel!" Everything in the hotel's relaxing atmosphere from sheets, snacks, shampoos are fabricated from fine hemp products.

Heidi was the Cannabis Cup Fashion Queen from the prior year's Cannabis Fashions Show. Heidi knew all the right spots in Amsterdam. The coffeehouses all knew Heidi favorably.

Manny prowled into his first coffee shop with Heidi and noted. "I am astounded by all the people in line at the cannabis counter."

Hiedi admitted. "They're looking at the wide range of marijuana and hash on the menu."

Manny voiced. "I'll bet all their weed is good."

Heidi specified. "Yes, Were known for quality marijuana in Amsterdam. There is a menu for marijuana and hash on the table we'll be sitting at. Let's go and sit in our booth."

Manny confessed. "That sounds good to me."

Manny picked out an exquisite silver cannabis blend.

Heidi shadowed Manny. "After you make your choice, you can purchase five grams of any variety of hash or marijuana."

Manny answered. "I love it! I just can't believe it! Look around inside this coffee shop. It's very attractive."

Hiedi explained. "The "De Rokerij" has a very active decor some with Eastern themes."

They sat in the "Royal Seats" when Manny pronounced. "I like all colorful and innovative coffee shop theme's. They really run the imagination. Everyone takes ultimate pride in the cannabis trade. Look at that customer's hand crafted hemp pipe!"

Hiedi spouted. "That's unique. Look at it's black marble base and brass colored braided extension's. It's lovely."

Manny declared. "That is the kind of pipe I should get George."

After a few hours of smoking black hash and bubble gum green bud Manny asked. "Can we go to a coffee shop with an Internet?"

Hiedi answered. "Your lucky there's one right around the corner." as they soon left.

Manny conceded. "This is a vibrant Coffee house also. It's set up with computers for surfing the net. I want to e-mail Clint, George, and Rudy." Manny e-mailed current news about his trip. Then they were off to their next coffeehouse.

Manny conveyed. "All these coffee shops have plenty of patrons." while he smoked hash the in-house water pipe. They searched cyber space for some local hemp shops.

Hiedi revealed. "I'm chit chatting with a pro-marijuana activist from Canberra, Australia right now. I told them about you. They said for me to tell you good luck Yank."

Manny summarized. "Thanks tell them I'll need it. I can see other patrons are doing hemp textile research."

Hiedi stated. "Some Coffee shops only supply hydroponically grown marijuana. I like the hydro-weed when it's inhaled from a vaporizer. It's smooth!"

Manny pressed. "I'm trying the vaporizer," after a hit he said, "I think so too."

Hiedi looked on. "Good hit?"

Manny winced. "Really good hit. I prefer smoking weed. I can smoke only so much hash. The hash will let you know when you've had enough."

Heidi told Manny. "The coffee shops are well regulated. Patrons for the most part are well behaved. They are not like the alcoholic bars where the crowd can get much more than festive to downright rowdy."

Manny agreed. "That is for sure!"

Hiedi bird dogged. "That's Archie! He is the coffee shop keeper. Archie sells hash, marijuana and hemp apparel from behind the counter."

Manny noticed. "I like the way he's dressed."

Hiedi revealed to Manny. "Archie is clothed in hemp apparel. Look at the display behind him, all the apparel is made from hemp fibers."

Manny questioned. "All those shirts, hats, and garments are made from hemp?"

Heidi responded. "Yes, and they were all made here in Amsterdam."

Manny asked. "Was the hemp grown for the clothing fabrics in Holland?" as he inspected a hemp rope belt a customer had just purchased.

Hiedi attested. "Yes. The paper the menus are made from hemp fibers."

Manny astonished. "I can't believe the Dutch drug policy about cannabis and the availability and acceptability. It's really a good thing. I can't wait until the American government officials wake up."

"Archie!" Heidi called. "I'd like you to meet a Yank friend of mine. His name is Manny," as she introduced Manny to Archie. She patronizes Archie's coffee shop on a regular basis.

Archie in his "Weed Wind Breaker" greeted the American tourist. "Glad to meet you Manny. Are you on holiday?" He asked.

Manny answered. "Yeah, you can say that. I'm enjoying myself, so it might as well be a holiday."

Archie proudly proclaimed. "This coffee shop serves excellent food. Sushi is tonight's special, along with a menu full of other European favorites. You and Heidi enjoy tonight's special on the house as my guest."

Hiedi and Manny thanked Archie for all his help as they gracefully dashed to their table.

Hiedi told Manny. "The Coffee shops have a very diverse crowd. Professors, artists, judges, politicians, blue collar workers, young and old people alike. The shop managers always make their patrons feel welcome."

Archie walked over while they were dining and asked. "How long you staying for Manny?"

Manny responded. "Right now, it looks like three days Archie."

Archie chewed the fat. "Is Heidi's going to show you around?"

Manny predicted. "I hope so. I'd like her to take me to the Hash Marijuana Hemp museum tomorrow."

Heidi portrayed. "That's what we have planned."

Archie mentioned. "We have a brisk clientele of over six hundred patrons a day. And each patron on an average spend about six to ten dollars American. That's not a bad business Yank is it?"

Manny rattled. "No it's not. I wish I could have a business like this in the United States."

Manny and Hiedi enjoyed themselves for two to three hours smoking hash, cyber spacing, and sitting around chit chatting.

Hiedi told Manny. "Patrons have opportunities to sign new petitions for World Wildlife, Green peace, and a few other environmental causes the coffee shops sponsor. These coffee houses are politically involved. They have formed their own union, and are official accepted by the politicians. Their goal is to maintain a safe cannabis climate."

Manny dreamed. "I wish I lived in the free world."

Heidi suggested. "You can always move here."

Manny predicted. "Now that's a good idea."

Archie told Manny. "Over a billion and a half dollars of hash and marijuana are sold in Amsterdam throughout the year."

Manny asked. "That much?"

Archie answered. "Yes. This gives our people an alternative to alcohol, tobacco, cocaine, heroin, opium, barbiturates, amphetamines, and designer drugs and psychedelic's. Hard drugs are strictly forbidden in our coffee shops. Under Dutch policy they will close any coffee shop quickly if hard drugs are found to have been frequented in a coffee shop. Our policy in Holland separates hard drugs from soft drugs. We strictly go by those guidelines."

Hiedi explained. "That's one of the coffee shop advantages."

Archie relayed. "You know Manny, marijuana is less harmful than all the above."

Manny asserted. "You know that's right."

Archie recounted. "Well, enjoy yourself Yank. I'm going to get back to my work. Enjoy yourself while your here in Amsterdam."

Manny rehashed. "'I'm sure enjoying myself. Nice meeting you Archie."

Archie remarked. "Nice meeting yea."

Manny said. "Thanks Archie!" as he then went on to serve other patrons of the coffee shop.

Hiedi reiterated. "This café has different kinds of hemp products on display."

Manny and Heidi walked over to the other side of the coffee shop. Manny decided to take their black afghan hash he just purchased to the cyber station with them.

Hiedi said to Manny. "This café in part is set up for Internet access."

Manny decided to log on the Internet. He e-mail George's staff and size up how the tour was developing. He marveled at how Heidi had assisted him. Manny prompted after he was done. "As always I've got new instructions from George's office." When Manny and Hiedi were done smoking hash, they took their left over hash with them. Manny said. "I'll enjoy my hash as an evening nightcap."

When they left the coffee shop, Heidi said to Manny. "Manny I've decided to take you to a hemp harvest festival tonight. Featured at this hemp festival, where hemp products manufactured in Europe are featured."

After they both freshened up, they met up at the Hemp Festival. As soon as they walked into the Festival, Manny commanded of view of the hemp apparel display's and set forth. "Hiedi, Lets take a survey here?"

On further examination of the hemp clothing line Manny said to Hiedi. "Some of these hemp products, I've noticed, are imported from Germany."

Hiedi answered. "Yes, all are Euro-manufactured hemp products. All the hemp products are tagged and identified for what Euro country of origin of where they are made."

Manny asked Hiedi. "Would you help me pick some hemp products and clothing out. George gave me access to his business account to buy hemp clothing for his entire staff, and he wants it all sent back across the Trans-Atlantic's by air, before I leave for Germany."

Hiedi decreed. "That won't be a problem. I'll assistance you in selecting out your hemp apparel. The boutique will package and air mail everything back to the states for you. They'll be happy to sell you the clothes."

Manny evoked. "Good that's one less thing I'll have to worry about. The hemp sales lady claim's this was the best hemp line available in Europe."

Heidi agreed. "They are superior, when compared to their rivals."

Manny turned to Hiedi and conveyed. "I've decided to buy this robust ruby red shirt made from pure organic hemp."

Hiedi admired. "That's a beautiful Holland tile hemp shirt. I love the bordered intricate hemp rope braided seams on all the ultimate fringes of the shirt."

Manny admitted. "I'm glad you do, because I also bought you a matching blouse."

Hiedi schmoozed Manny a hug. "Thank you very much. I'll remember you, when I wear this special shirt. I must confess I would have picked this beautiful shirt out myself. It's superlative in comparison."

Manny proposed. "Let's put them on." referring to new hemp apparel they had just purchased."

Hiedi answered. "Yes, let's do! I want us to hurry to catch a sight of these hemp band's. Let's jet to the dance the night away."

Manny making tracks. "I'm hurrying!"

Hiedi jostled. "Come on with it Yank!"

Manny fled. "I'm right on Ya!" as they went straight onto the dance floor. Manny muddled through the crowd, and always a ham rushed headlong onto the dance floor. Moving grooving Manny fishtailed, and leapfrogged fluidly while romping wildly. Hiedi unrestrained wailed, wiggled, wagged, wattled, and waved

Hiedi rambled later. "Yank! Nobody here has ever seen such an elaborate dance routine."

Manny moon walked backwards. "Rudy taught me a few moves."

Hiedi smiling asked. "How do you like the festival?"

Manny answered. "This place is something else. Nobody second glances anyone. Nobody cares about anybody else smoking pot." as they side stepped everyone standing around.

Hiedi confided. "It's no big thing for the Dutch any more, it's common place. Hash and marijuana citizens are not stigmatized as criminals here. As a matter of fact the European Union is spiraled in the Dutch direction concerning their drug policies."

Manny excited. "I've got to admit. I love it." Manny and Heidi walked around the Festival in Amsterdam. Manny said. "Every time I talk to somebody they know I'm a Yank immediately."

Hiedi accented. "They express their greetings in an exuberant manner once they find out your an American."

Manny felt welcomed walking around and agreed. "They sure do. Just about everyone makes fuss over me just because I am an American."

Hiedi emphasized. "They are eager to talk to you."

Manny professed. "Especially the owners of the hemp businesses, they continue to ask me about how things are in the states."

Hiedi portrayed. "You always oblige, because of your popular personality."

Manny piped. "They treat me as a free spending American tourist."

Hiedi asserted. "That's right, because you are."

One patron at the hemp festival named Mole told Manny. "The coffee shops in Holland are so popular that they're spreading across the borders into Germany."

Manny relished. "The Germans have coffee houses?"

Mole proclaimed. "Yes! They have some. They've obliged their cannabis citizens." Mole realized Manny was on a fact finding marijuana mission said. "The Germans have concluded that from a study of our coffee shops."

Hiedi stressed. "I like the way the Germans have established some of their coffee shops. I've been to a few in Hamburg."

Mole dictated. "It's a way of life."

Manny pledged. "Smoking pot is a way of life in America. The government just doesn't want to admit it."

Mole stipulated to Manny. "I thought the Americans were the leaders of the free world."

Manny answered. "Not when it comes to marijuana or moral checks. We're the leaders of repression." Mole laughed.

Manny informed. "The marijuana reform organization I'm involved with is trying to overturn current federal marijuana laws in the United States. We want to reform marijuana laws and educate our governors to current way of life many Americans live. There shouldn't be double standards throughout the free world."

Mole expounded. "The European community is finding the Dutch way of life more acceptable as time goes on. They see there is by far fewer problems all the way around. Our Dutch harm reduction policy's has worked very well, because they take everyone in their country into account and make the best of it. Belgium Ministry of Justice has ordered prosecutors and cops to stop arresting people for cultivation or use of cannabis."

Heidi realized the night was getting late, and decided to call it an evening and asked Manny. "Would you mind if we left, so I can go home. We have to get up early tomorrow to go to the Marijuana museum."

Manny confided. "No problem, Heidi."

Heidi rehashed. "I'll drop you off at the Rokin Hotel."

Manny gratefully said. "Thanks." to Mole and waved goodbye they and left.

Hiedi instead hustled to the Green House Coffee Shop for a hash night cap. Manny could scuffle to the Rokin from there. When you approached you the "Green House Coffee Shop's" you first noticed the florescent tube crafted sign. Arjan the owner and his wife Brenda were working behind the counter, and assisting some customers. Manny and Hiedi went over and picked out "Great White Shark" green buds and the in house Nederhash "Shanti baba."

Manny disclosed to Hiedi. "I love that artistically chipped mirror, and the brilliantly designed and equally colorful wall. Let's sit at that special table in front of it for a photo." as they smoked away one customer said. "Would you like to try some Super Silver Haze?" As he looked at Manny the well dressed man without a word exchanged smoldering pipes.

Hiedi asked. "Arjan would you mind taking a photo with us Please?" as Arjan obliged his customers, his shop keep took a souvenir photo.

Manny and Heidi roamed along the canal's sea wall next to the waist high steel pillars lining the sidewalk. They causally strolled over the canal's bridges. The high steepled buildings along the canal were brightly light up. The street lamps reflection off the canal's picturesque waterway mooned sweet memories. They decided the next day they would tour the world famous Hash, Marijuana and Hemp Museum.

Gladys, George's secretary had gathered additional information on the Hash, Marijuana, and Hemp Museum for Manny.

Early in the day Hiedi said as they hiked past the Holland Casino. "Look at the marijuana moped near the door way to the museum."

Manny surprised razzed. "Wow! I like all those marijuana leaves painted on that motor bike in front of the museum." They embarked past the cannabis library to the American exhibit.

Hiedi enlightened. "This is a presentation of American slaves, diversified indentured servants and Indians in colonial times used hemp. George Washington and Thomas Jefferson both grew hemp. Thomas Jefferson re-designed, manufactured, and patented a hemp break.

This picture of the hemp break was first designed to manufactured raw materials of hemp. He made hemp fibers into industrial fabrics and paper. Did you know that?"

Manny admitted. "I didn't know that!"

Heidi looked at Manny and grilled. "Thomas Jefferson was one of your great leaders. Their is an exact replica of the original Declaration of Independence issued on hemp paper."

Manny agreed. "He is definitely one of the greatest presidents. He'd be the first one on our side fighting the marijuana prohibition."

Heidi gazed. "If Jefferson grew hemp and made the first patent hemp break, there shouldn't be any problem with legalization of the hemp industry. Jefferson attributed hemp. "The greatest service that can be rendered to any country is to add a useful plant to it's culture."

Manny belabored. "You know that's right!" As Manny looked through the myriad of hemp displays, he noticed that the early states of the US induced laws requiring farmers to grow hemp.

Hiedi inquired. "Are we having fun yet?"

Manny responded. "I'm having a great time. Look! There's a picture of the US Flagship the "Constitution" with all it's rigging and sails among many other items of the ship listed here constructed from hemp. Tons on top of tons of hemp, which virtually represents America's roots."

Hiedi investigated. "I see here. Hemp was grown in greater proportion to cotton for clothing, rope, canvas and paper. This was the way of life in America for centuries. This was an American tradition that was killed by special interest groups."

Mellow Manny moralized. "That's obvious."

Openly Heidi professed. "The Dutch government officials want to keep their youth and their citizens away from hard drugs. They decriminalized marijuana for that intention. Through their medical research regarding marijuana Officials have included from cannabis intensive studies that marijuana is less addictive than coffee. They've concluded that seventeen of the twenty-three different make's of coffee have developed cancer in laboratory rats, where cannabis has not procured any cancers."

Manny explained. "With spiraling discovery of the facts, I'm finding that the Dutch compared marijuana smokers to tobacco smokers. Marijuana came out ahead."

Hiedi recounted. "When marijuana's is grown naturally and used unaltered, even pulmonary researcher's concluded that marijuana smoke actually aids some asthma victims. While increasing the efficiency of your lungs marijuana protects the lungs' pores from some cancer agents, which may have been damaged arguably from prior tobacco smoke."

Manny vilified while reading the displayed brochures. "The Dutch conclude you must quit smoking tobacco for any improvements in your lungs to take place. In chronological order this exhibit shows how American's used marijuana. Marijuana use was developed throughout its history for various medicines. They explained the uses of bi-products extracted from the hemp plant for medical purposes. England's medical associations formerly made marijuana a medicine in the 1840's."

"Draw a bead over here Manny. They have an extravaganza of marijuana and hemp seeds, leaves, and hash on display."

Manny impassioned stated. "It's wild how they display live budding cannabis plants by the thousands in here and all the way out onto the side walk. Everyone in America should be at liberty to have one potted cannabis plant on their front porch."

Hiedi responded. "Look here at this budding marijuana plant in the storefront window of the Sinsi Seed Company. They sell high potency, high yield marijuana seeds by the millions on Internet mail sales around the world. They produce some of the best pot in the world with their team of growers."

Darren a cannabis judge who comes to the cup every year was from Baltimore. he stood beside Manny in the museum and divulged. "The people of Amsterdam don't care who smoke's pot. Their police here may light your marijuana joint if you ask them nicely. The Dutch cops are friendly and understand marijuana tolerance and tourists. The Dutch government knows there's over fifty thousand marijuana growers in Holland. By letting them grow pot here in Holland it stops the criminal elements of smuggling pot into this country."

Manny conferred. "That makes sense."

Darren addressed. "There are allot of things here in Holland that makes sense."

Hiedi agreed. "That's for sure!"

Manny attested. "Really! I'm going to see if a Dutch policeman will light my joint. I'll ask them nicely."

The cool headed cashier of the seed company avowed. "Ben Dronkers and his son Alan run the Sinsi Seed company, and the Hash, Marijuana and Hemp Museum. They subsidize hemp farmers who grow hemp here in Holland. They give them risk proof contracts even if they have poor soil quality. German auto makers are inquiring about hemp fibers for environmental reasons. The European auto industry is switching to environmentally safe hemp auto parts like pressed hemp fiber insulation. They can environmentally recycle hemp safely many times compared to other fibers."

Manny noticed. "That's interesting. I'm glad the hemp industry is taking a firm foot hold here."

The store keep acknowledged. "We are too! The owners recently bought an old flax factory to process the hemp."

Hiedi crowed. "My American friend is really impressed with all the personal freedom in Holland."

He gushed. "So are we," as he turned to wait on another seed customer. The museum and the seed company united each other in the rear of the store where all the budding marijuana plants are on display.

Manny summarized. "I've never seen such a sweet looking variety of buds. How do you know which one tastes the best?"

Darren answered. "There just like fine wine, if you try a dozen or so fine wines you'll like them all. These different high quality marijuana strains are the same. They have their own distinctive delicious taste."

As Manny and Heidi left the Hash, Marijuana, and Hemp Museum, they walked down a few doors to the Cannabis College. Manny looked into a peep hole from the side walk of Amsterdam. The peep hole was there with an arrow pointing to it so tourists could look in from the outside side walk and see marijuana plants growing. Their mission is to educate the public about the hemp plant known botanically as Cannabis sativa. The college creed was "Cannabis--- learn the truth before you decide."

Manny implored. "I recognize now more than ever as I walk the streets of Amsterdam how a genuine free society exists. I know now more than ever, something has to be executed in America."

Hiedi heralded. "I agree! And Manny your a judge at the Cannabis Cup highlighted most of this week. It starts tomorrow."

Manny responded. "That's right. I can't wait."

Manny and Hiedi dined at a side walk café. Hiedi explained to Manny. "The High Times Cannabis Cup competition this week will determine the best coffee shop, best strain of marijuana, best made hashish, among competing coffee shop entries. Many marijuana related categories will be judged."

The next day Manny dandered into the cannabis crowd for cannabis demonstration's, and to investigate hemp display's. Seed sales centered at the Pax Party House were enourmous. After a quick tour he went straight to the judge's room. Manny was ready to be one of the cannabis cup judge and cracked. "I'm going to enjoy myself for the whole week."

Hiedi reassured. "I'm happy for you. You will pick up a lot."

Manny expressed to Hiedi. "Thanks again for everything your doing for me."

Steve Bloom the music editor of High Times just introduced to the audience full of the cup's judges, Gilbert Sheldon. Gilbert Sheldon is the world renowned cartoonist of the famed "The Fabulous Freak Brothers" which is a collector's item comic book series. Gilbert an American flew in from his digs in Paris, France to be at the Cannabis Cup. Gilbert autographed a promotional poster for Manny. Manny said to Hiedi. "Look! He not only signed his name but he actually drew three cartoon characters on the bottom of my "FREEWHEELIN' FRANKLIN" poster. I'm going to frame this as soon as I hit Houston."

Hiedi popped off. "It's a great souvenir!"

Manny enthused. "I'll see if I can get another one for you Hiedi."

Hiedi obsessed. "Please do!" as Gilbert smiled slightly and quickly cartooned three more creative characters on the poster for her. He then signed his name.

Manny heralded. "Thank you very much Gilbert." as they both happily walked away.

Hiedi explained. "All the judge's are given samples of the best cannabis, and hash not only made in the Netherlands, but from around the world. Some cannabis cup competitions have in excess of sixty strains of marijuana."

Manny joshed. "I wonder who will win the smoker's championship?"

Salina continued. "Some judges use the large bongs standing four foot high. Judges are given access to a full array of smoking utensils, including magnifying glasses, pipes, papers, supplied by the competing coffee shops. All week judges smoke down before casting ballots for the best strain of marijuana the night before the cup awards are announced via satellite at the "High Times" awards ceremony."

Manny asked. "Aren't there other cannabis cups through out Europe over the course of the year?"

Hiedi answered back. "Yes, Spain has a cannabis cup coming up, and then there's the Dutch Cup." Many of the cannabis cup participants come back every year. Many new pro-pot participants are in attendance every year."

Manny smoked hash in the judge's room and beamed at his new "Addidas" hemp canvas shoes. Manny had just bought the shoes from the "Ohio Hempery." Right under the sign that read 1 800 BUY HEMP.

Heidi pointed out. "Look there's Author Lee Bridges. He's an Afro-American Poet who settled here in Amsterdam. He's been all over the world and tells quite a story through several his book's of poems. Come on Manny I'll introduce you." as she spoke loudly over the crowd. "Lee!"

Lee turned to Heidi and attested. "Hi, we meet again."

Heidi divulged. "This is an American friend of mine and I wanted him to meet you."

Lee conferred to Manny "I'm glad to meet you. I hope you enjoy your stay in Amsterdam."

Manny declared. "I sure am. It's my total pleasure."

Lee mustered to Manny. "Do you know why?"

Manny appealed. "Why?"

Lee professed before being whisked away for another autograph signing of his new book of poems. "Good Conduct makes Good Luck."

Manny predicted. "I like that that makes good common sense."

Hiedi harped. "Check that out Manny!" as she marveled at ongoing the vaporizer demonstration

Manny inspected. "They have vaporizers for inhaling marijuana over there in use at that seed sales counter."

Hiedi relayed. "There's free hit's of marijuana for anyone who wants to try the vaporizer. Eagle Bill is demonstrating to the patrons of the Pax Party House. The vaporizer is a no waste, non burning or smokeless way of injesting marijuana. This new revolutionary method also improves flavor and reduces harshness caused by flame combustion methods."

Eagle Bill invited the cup goers. "Step up and get your free demonstration." as patron's inched in line to try the vaporizer.

Hiedi portrayed. "Bill told me he was in a motorcycle accident and one leg is shorter than the other. For years he fought off the pain with heavy drugs like percodan and codeine. He started smoking pot to relive the pain instead of the prescription drugs. He can't understand how a plant that doesn't hurt anyone is illegal in the United States."

Manny revealed. "I wish the boys back home were here. They sure would want to dig in and make themselves at home just like Eagle Bill."

Hiedi conveyed. "I'm going to try some green buds from Sinsi Seeds. Organically grown Sinsi is my personal favorite in the water bongs."

Manny depicted. "I see all kinds of marijuana cultivation tips are learned at these cannabis cup competitions. I heard from one of the judges say that the Hemp Expo Cannabis Cups is coming soon. That one sounds like a rush. I wish I could go to that cannabis cup competition too."

Hiedi joked. "You can always fly back."

Manny followed up. "I just might be back with the boys."

While judging at the Cannabis Cup, Manny told Hiedi. "I am literally having the time of my life. These crystal green buds are gorgeous. I feel great to live in a free society. I like having fun without looking over my shoulder."

Hiedi responded. "I'm really glad you're enjoying yourself. Maybe one day Manny you can show me around a Texas town."

Manny divulged. "Hiedi, that's not going to be a problem for all the help you've been. It will be my personal pleasure to show you around. I'll personally ask George to fly you in to attend the big Rosta Rally were planning."

Hiedi confessed. "I appreciate that Manny. I'd love to see you in Texas." as she gave him another hug.

Manny helped promote and, along with thousands of other judges, decided the all around best entries for the different varieties of marijuana, hash, products, shops, and service related cannabis industries.

Manny declared to Hiedi. "I'm smoking different blends for the best taste and buzz."

Manny and Heidi mingled in the cannabis crowd. Marijuana exhibitor booth's were set up like a baseball card or computer show. Everything thing in this show centered around the cannabis products and culture. Hemp products, along with hemp clothing, marijuana seed companies, large variety of pot smoking apparatuses, cannabis candles, hemp and marijuana how to books and videos. Large marijuana plants in planters were displayed amongst the very heavy crowd. Many different pro-marijuana movement groups from all over the world attended this cannabis cup event. Heidi asked. "Isn't this great how everyone adheres to this friendly atmosphere?"

Manny phrased. "Everyone respects individual freedom."

Hiedi pledged. "Cannabis Coffee shop management and sponsors provide hemp natural juices, hemp biers, natural water to drink, and hemp food for the judges to eat."

Heidi advised Manny. "Look over there! That's Jack Herer world famous hemp author. He's also a celebrity judge."

Manny was excited to see such a knowledgeable hemp author. "He's autographing one copy of the "Emperor Wears No Clothes" right after another."

Hiedi elucidated. "It's the best selling book on hemp ever."

Manny explained. "I'm in line now to buy an autographed copy." After Manny purchased his book he told Heidi how personable Jack was and how he wrote a personal inscription for him."

Hiedi admitted. "Jack's been coming to this cup for years."

Manny decreed. "Jack's one of the greatest cannabis crusader's ever. I read recently where he's not stopping the cannabis crusade until all pot prisoners are free, and marijuana is as legal as toothpaste. Jack calls hemp the "Queen Mother of all Plants."

Heidi depicted. "He's authored the best book available on Hemp. I'm just glad to have a copy of my own to read."

Manny gamed. "Look at this Hemp TV Rockumentary video. It's called the "Cannabis Conspiracy."

Hiedi commented. "The film maker Kenya Winchell stated. "I just wanted people to hear the truth, without all of the anti-cannabis hysteria."

Manny ordered. "I want this video tape! It's advertised as "The Film Your Government Doesn't Want You To See!" and he made sure busy Kenya autographed his copy.

Hiedi raved. "I want one to Manny! I've seen the premier showing at the Greenhouse coffee shop. It's very good! It's an award winning film!"

Manny squealed. "Sure I'll get a few copies." as he was smoking the Greenhouse bio cup entry "El Nino". In the background of the Greenhouse was a song by Willie Nelson off "Hempilation" CD "Hempilation 2 is NORML's latest benefit twenty song CD with a wide variety of pro-hemp artists.

By showing the judges pass you were able to vote for the best weed, hash, or coffee shop categories at the Melkweg until 2:00 PM tonight.

Manny marveled. "I'm thrilled and touched at how this Cannabis Cup attracts so many Americans and other diversities here. It just goes to prove that pot people love hemp."

After the Cannabis Cup Awards were presented, Manny and Heidi left for another Coffee shop having a Jazz Hash Bash. Manny said to Hiedi. "This place parties all the time."

Hiedi remarked. "Were just a few blocks from Dam Square near the main canal in the town of Rembrandt."

Manny responded. "You can feel the breeze of freedom."

Hiedi expressed. "Yes. It certainly is a relaxing atmosphere in Amsterdam."

Manny exuberated. "I love Amsterdam!"

Hiedi sized up. "There's no place like Amsterdam, but Amsterdam!"

Manny stared down. "I believe it! It's a very articulately interesting society."

Hiedi noted. "We have a multitude of tourists. Some who have been here before and others, that are curiosity seekers."

Manny jabbering to an older man at the café. "This gives the young people a place to hang out away from the harder drugs and hard liquor that are readily available. These marijuana and hash coffeehouses are safe environments. I've smoked hash and marijuana all my life. I see no reason to quit now. I feel fine."

Manny listened to the old man. "Look around here everyone is getting along. Everyone is here because they want to be here. The fruits of god given life are present here."

Manny agreed. "You are one very wise old man."

The man now known as Herb continued. "Have you been to the red light district?"

Manny stressed. "No! I haven't."

Herb remarked. "Because of Dutch policy's, AIDS among our legal prostitutes is one percent compared with the rampant spreading of AIDS in your country, where thirty to forty percent are AIDS infected prostitutes in your country. No wonder innocent housewives get AIDS from their cheating husbands who patronize illegal prostitutes in your country."

Manny surprised. "I had no idea AIDS is spreading that fast in my country."

Herb expressed. "A lot of the people in your country have no idea, not until it hits close to home. Our prostitutes don't have to risk their lives here to make a living at the oldest profession on earth. Men can relieve their sexual stress here without reference or rape. In America should maintain at least one "Red Light District" in every state. They can also relieve their stress from everyday life by smoking a little pot, instead of American government's bottling of forced human time bombs. Then your government slaps their created time bombs in the face and wonders why tragic results continually escalate. Look at what happened in Detroit. Two men tried to buy prostitute, who was a police vice decoy. When

241

other vice cops swarmed one for the arrest the men grabbed a gun and shot two of the vice officers dead and wounded another. Your government doesn't understand the law of nature where the human sex drive is the strongest emotion known. Give all people a safe environment. Don't create dire problems."

Manny recognized. "Your so right Herb." as Herb continued. "While, I'm thinking, America should sanction at least one "Red Light District" and at least one "Coffee Shop District" in every state. This way people in America can slowly see that there are much safer alternatives. Your social problems in America can't be solved by making everything from drugs to sex taboo. Our young people here are now more inclined to believe our government about the dangers of hard drugs. Here they have safe alternatives instead of unsafe sex, hard drugs or alcohol. Your crime in America will not recede until you change your approach of governing."

Manny emphasized. "I like how hard drugs are way down!"

Herb pontificated. "Hard drug use is way down here, when compared to the US!"

Our teenager pregnancies are one seventh percentage wise, when compared with the United States, because of our birth control policies. The teenage abortion rate is fourteen times less than in the US. Dutch teenagers have the highest score in international mathematics and science tests in the world We treat all our people with tolerance and respect which in turn breeds respect for our government. Our "Collective Conscious Approach" does not demoralize people of different social habits. Our governments obligations is first for our communities and our society. The drug users utilize clean needles, the prostitutes use condoms, teen age marijuana smokers are no longer criticized but educated, suffering terminally ill patients are all treated fairly."

Manny concerned. "You'd think my country could get smart one day?

Herb deemed. "I doubt it! But after nearly thirty years of cannabis tolerance in Holland, scientific studies have concluded that if there's anything wrong with legalizing cannabis they haven't found it. One reefer researcher said After ten thousands years of use and studies there's nothing conclusively harmful with cannabis. It's proven safe!"

Manny interjected. "I agree!"

Herb pored over. "Your country pushing moral purity on it's citizens and bullying, badgering, beating, and locking the ones up who don't submit is unfit for humanity. We can't believe that a country like the United States is destroying itself by creating social anarchy."

Manny sighed soberly. "Herb our government leaders are very short on wisdom when solving social problems, that's for sure. Our government will never inspire trust of all it's citizens without giving them their due respect."

Herb scowled. "That's for sure! I hope they can turn it around for the people's sake, before it's to late."

Manny prophesied. "Really! The U.S. needs to take their hands off their citizens lives." as Manny and Herb concluded their concrete "Collective Conscious" conversation.

The following day, Heidi and Manny had their last lunch together at one of their favorite coffeehouses, but not before they toured the countryside setting of the "Cannabis Castle." Heidi said. "Manny at this museum you can touch any of the thousands of marijuana plants exhibited. Some of the marijuana plants are over twenty years old. The Cannabis Castle Seed Merchants travel all over the world to get marijuana and hemp seeds. They among others bombard the world with marijuana and seeds with their brisk Internet sales alone. You can take a ton of photos."

Manny scanned as they left. "This is a gorgeous green countryside drive from Amsterdam. How ling will it take?"

Helpful Heidi clarified. "Maybe an hour."

Once at the Cannabis Castle Manny posed. "Snap my photo with the "King of Cannabis" please?"

Manny exclaimed to the King. I'd like to have a crown of marijuana like yours."

The Cannabis King clamored. "You get the pot! We'll put it together."

Manny contended. "Cool!" as Heidi took a ton of photos. Manny posed in front of the sea of green cannabis.

Heidi after the tour asked. "Let's go to Haarlem?"

Manny envisioned. "Haarlem! That's in New York."

Heidi hyped. "No! There's a Haarlem, Holland."

Manny grilled. "What's in Haarlem?"

Hiedi responded. "The Global Hemp Museum. When I bought that hemp made shirt from Nol at the Pax, he invited us to his new hemp museum in a Haarlem's country setting. The city of Haarlem has a very clear soft drug policy. There are nearly twenty coffee shops that serve hash and marijuana but they do not serve alcohol and only three cannabis grow shops. A green house owner and manager Hank said he'll show us how to make hash at the museum with a fifteen ton hash press."

Manny pumped. "We ain't there yet? That sounds like an Amsterdam capper to me."

They entered into the Global Hemp Museum's front shop. Nol's newly released CD "Holland Holland Land of Sinsemilla" by "Cannabinol and the Inhalers" was playing loudly. There were hundreds of hemp based products. Products compassing hemp jeans to hemp paper were sold. The next area had live marijuana plants displayed with official permits. The exhibits after the grow area featured different hemp fibers, stems, hemp products, and related harvesting procedures.

Manny pitched to Hiedi. "I'd like to have a hemp-made snowboard like that one mounted on the wall."

Hiedi stipulated. "It looks just like fiberglass! Doesn't it?"

Manny spelled out. "It sure does! You could sell a million of those hemp made snow boards in the states."

Hiedi acknowledged. "I just read that one of the big ski companies are making hempmade skis as a product."

Manny espoused. "It would be another million seller in the states."

They proceeded past the marijuana medical display and through the marijuana art tunnel to the big Arabic water pipe taller than Manny. They were at an informational marijuana display area which shows the aspects of cannabis from around the world.

Manny pledged. "I have never been on a better trip in my life. I can't imagine anything topping this freedom trip." as they concluded the tour.

While Heidi while touring Manny to the train station whined. "This is my last bit of hash."

Hiedi shared. "Let's smoke the last bowl of hash together?"

Manny snickered. "That's what I want to do!"

Heidi avowed. "I wish you well Manny on the rest for your marijuana fact finding mission around the world."

Manny sweet talked. "I want to thank you all again for your help. I'm an American pot smoker who lived with respect without discrimination here in Amsterdam. It just goes to show a marijuana prophet is without honor in the United States."

Hiedi roused. "Your only without honor in big brother grasp."

Manny confessed. "I hope we finally get our self-respect back. It means everything." as he gave her a big hug and a kiss goodbye.

As Manny boarded the train, he looked back at Heidi one last time. Heidi waved and Manny waved back and yelled. "Bye, I'll see you in Washington at the Rosta Rally!" Manny immediately started writing and signing the hook line to a new tune called. "I got a friend in Amsterdam, No Threat of Who I am!"

The train moved rapidly toward Germany. George had Gladys book Manny on the expresso train. The trip to Germany was shorter than Manny had anticipated.

The first stop in Germany was Hamburg. Roderick was his new contact. Roderick showed Manny the newly developed coffee houses in Hamburg. Roderick explained to Manny German views on cannabis legalization as currently lived. "Did you enjoy your stay in Amsterdam?"

Manny announced. "Oh yeah! I'd sure like to go back some day."

Roderick promised. "Well if you enjoyed your stay in Amsterdam, you will enjoy your stay here in Hamburg." And, again Manny was on his way to a festival of swooshed people.

Manny called Roderick, "Rod" and asked "These German beer festivals are sponsored by the local taverns. Aren't they?"

Rod embellished. "They have micro breweries established in some of the German taverns here, they want to promote different brands and blends of their own beer."

Manny sized up. "I see the streets were barricaded off at each end of the block. People party right in the streets. Just like New Years Eve in Key West."

Rod prompted. "Yes! Lot's of alcohol is today's vice at this block party."

Groups of people revolved around with German steins of all types. Manny told Rod. "They must be drinking German beer with high alcohol content?"

"Rod responded. "Yes, you can clearly tell the difference between this crowd of alcohol consumers from a crowd of cyber cannabis stoners in the coffee houses of Amsterdam smoking hash."

Manny laughed. "That's for sure!"

The next day Rod and Manny scaled hash in a Hamburg Germany Coffee shop. Rod told Manny. "The German government just raised the legal limits from two grams to four grams of hash that are allowed on your person without being punished for any unlawful prosecutions. The Green Party lead's an active part in new government policy's. Actually German prosecutors have been told to stop arresting people for small amount possessions."

Manny conceded. "That's a good law respecting people. Letting choose to their own life styles. That's what we need back home."

Rod professed. "I agree! The next legislation on the docket is expected to legalize sales over the counter of marijuana, hashish. The governors want's to regulate THC and safe quality control of marijuana and hash. German government officials are exploring tax methods."

Manny disclosed. "The German government will collect a ton of taxes from hash and marijuana consumption."

Rod admitted. "Yes! The high court in Germany already ruled that marijuana and hash are safer than alcohol and tobacco. Marijuana and hash should be legalized. The government has acknowledged that General warnings about the dangers of marijuana are not taken seriously. The German government officials ruled that the government could tolerate small amounts of marijuana and hash for personal use. In fact to be considered criminal you must be in procession of more than two-hundred grams of THC. That can be usually found in two to four kilos of hashish."

Manny informed. "I like hearing this stuff."

Rod emphasized. "You'd be considered an enterpriser with larger amounts of cannabis."

Manny laughed. "Yea an enterpriser, equivalent to white collar crime. Someone other than that is just a user of hash or marijuana."

Rod stressed. "If you have a large supply marijuana or volumes of hash and you must pay taxes to the German government. That's the only way large sales of hash and marijuana will be condoned. The coffee shops have to buy hash and marijuana in large volumes because of the business demands. So you can't put the shop keepers in jail when our government condones possession and use of small amounts of hash or marijuana for its citizen's."

Manny preached. "That's what we need back home fair laws!"

Rod appraised. "So the coffee shop keepers pay the marijuana tax and roll on." Rods gestured with his hands expecting a marijuana cigarette to be rolled. Manny laughed and said. "No problem."

Rod told Manny. "The European Affairs Minister George Papandreou a world famous politician stated that Marijuana should be legal. He counseled hard drugs should be given to addicts, so all drug trafficking would come to a halt. We had an American trained sociologist, and a host of medical researchers from your country come here. They said. "Marijuana is no more dangerous than any other legal substance presently sponsored by governments."

They also stated that Zero tolerance policy didn't work, isn't working, and will never work."

Rod and Manny got into quite a conversation about current political attitudes, while they smoked hash in a newly established German coffee shop.

Rod instructed. "You have came to Germany in time for Europe's largest Cannabis trade show. I'll escort you around today to the cannabis show's numerous hemp displays. I will introduce you to hemp manufactures and distributors. There's always of heavy turn out at the hemp show. This is a very professional show which draws from of the industrial hemp industry."

Manny parleyed. "I've the compared different cannabis show hemp vendors. I watched them demonstrate their latest hemp growing techniques. They had some of the latest hemp products currently used in the modern world at the cup."

Rod proclaimed. "If you like what they had at the cup, wait until you see the cannabis trade show."

The next day Rod and Manny were on their way to the Hemp museum in Berlin. Rod was pulled over by the police for speeding. Rod told Manny. "Don't worry about the hash or even bother to conceal the hash. The police don't care about small amounts of hash or marijuana."

Manny astounded. "Sure enough! The police issued you a speed warning?"

Rod debauched. "The police never said a word about the hash, which in plain view on the dash of the car."

Manny affirmed. "Wow! I can't believe it. In the states we'd be in jail already."

Rod riddled. "No problems here! You like that don't you?"

Manny suggested. "You know I'd like that type of respect from the U.S. cops even if they gave me the speeding ticket."

Rod pried as they pulled up to the Hemp Museum for Manny's tour. "Did you look over all the brochures for the Berlin Marijuana Museum?"

Manny noticed photo's of an urn. "Yes, they have unearthed an urn from around the year 500 near Berlin. The urn contained cannabis."

Rod confirmed. "That proves we've been making cannabis clothing here for centuries."

The stay in Germany was only a quick two-day tour of Hamburg and Berlin. Rod took Manny to the airport to fly out the following morning.

Manny departed from the rail platform with a large hash bong and German Stein in hand.

Manny waved goodbye to Roderick after Manny had thanked Roderick for showing him a grand German time. "Come to the states for the big Rosta Rally in Washington."

Rod winked. "Das Vedanya!"

The next destination for Manny's tour was Malaga Spain. There he met a travel agent named Salina. Salina represented a local travel agency. Salina just arrived back into Malaga Spain herself from holiday in Greece. Glady's had told Manny that Salina was the best travel sales lady for her travel agency. Salina won the award for the most sales the preceding month. The prize was a free holiday to Greece.

Manny waltzed into the travel agency. Salina was talking with a client on the phone about a trip to Kathmandu, Nepal. Salina finished the sale. She had Manny's travel itinerary all planned. A blue folder sat on the table as Manny sauntered.

"Ola," Salina greeted Manny. "Ola, Salina, bonito, bonito, bonito." Manny always the ladies man, while Salina smiled.

Manny gazed at Salina and noticed friendly demeanor. Manny was intrigued at the elegance of this ornately dressed woman.

Manny diligently inquired. "Do you know when we will arrive in Gibraltar?"

But first Salina cleared up. "We'll tour Malaga before we hotfoot it down the southeastern Mediterranean coast of Spain together. We'll arrive in Gibraltar tomorrow evening."

Manny surprised. "I didn't know that Glady's arranged for you to escort me to Gibraltar and Morocco."

Salina lectured. "Glady's came here and met me on a trip to Malaga the year before last. Glady's told me! I'd be a good person to show you around in this part of the country."

Manny looked at Salina. "I can see that as well."

After a fantastic night in Maliga, they were on their mini-bus ride down the coastline for a commanding view of the bold blue water's of the Mediterranean. The final bus destination stop was La Linia. Salina's travel agency's headquarters was in La Linia, Spain.

Salina told Manny about a recent Marijuana grower's competition in the countries capital of Madrid. "Over fifty pot growers in white puffy clouds of smoke participated in Spain's first national marijuana plant competition. You are legally allowed to posses marijuana or hash in small amounts here in Spain. The large Cannabis Cup Competition in Cordoba Spain confirms the public's changing entrenched attitudes. The police don't bother anyone at the cannabis cup competition's just for pot. "

Manny disclosed. "I'm glad! I'm in another free country."

Slowly Salina enounced. "The Spanish Supreme Court deliberated granted permits for cultivation of marijuana for personal consumption. Advocacy groups pushed for the marijuana and hash drug law reforms. Growing for personal use will not be considered trafficking under these proposals."

Manny suggested. "Getting back to the cannabis competition I wanted to go. I wish I could have seen the winning plants at there Spanish Cannabis Grower's Competition."

Salina avouched. "There's always next year!"

Manny squawked. I'll come back! We'll go together."

Salina agreed. "Yes, we can." Salina knew Manny liked smoking hash. She took Manny to a local Spaniard's house, where she rapidly spoke Spanish and walked away with a few grams of hash the Spaniard gave her.

Salina, a non-smoker herself, took Manny to a local park. "Manny it's OK to smoke your hash in the park."

Manny posed. "I can?"

Salina nodded her head and answered. "Yes!"

Now in La Linia, Salina decided to walk down the crowded border towns streets and across the border from La linia to Gibraltar. She wanted to take Manny there before the evening got dark. She wanted Manny to see the view of Gibraltar and Spain from the Moorish castle high up on the rock."

Twilight light came as Manny and Salina walked past a play ground soccer field. A group of young Spanish kids kicked the soccer ball wildly against their opponents. In the backdrop of the playground is a magnificent view of the Rock of Gibraltar. Salina pointed to the impressive Moorish Castle for Manny to see. Salina explained. "The cliffs still have the remnants from craters and battle scare's from more then forty major battle sieges that were fiercely fought by the Moors, the Spanish and the British for control of military strategic Gibraltar."

Salina pointed vividly. "The cannon ball marks are still in full view from the war of 1701 by the British. Some are from in prior wars on the other side of the huge peak of the Rock of Gibraltar."

Manny beseeched. "I didn't realize it, but there is a lot of history here."

Salina explained that. "Admiral Nelson died right over there near "Parson's Lodge." The sailors of his ship put Admiral Nelson's dead body in a vat of rum and drank out of the rum which they called Nelson's blood." Manny who has a weak stomach was aghast. Salina and Manny capered along the new apparition's of Gibraltar, when Salina spilled the beans. "These new developments are literally being built and spread out right into the sea of the Mediterranean. The Spanish don't fancy the idea."

Manny ebbed. "You can see the Spanish coastline from this side of the Rock's peninsula without any problems," as they continued their jag along the old gold and black canon laced centuries old sidewalks of Gibraltar."

Salina and Manny met British citizens who were of Spanish descent smoking hashish in the open.

Manny blustered. "Did you see that? One of those men offered me a hit off his small bong." Manny lip's quickly took a hit off the small water bong. They stepped into the Trafalgar Tavern for some fish and chips.

Afterwards Salina and Manny continued on smiling and strolling all the way back across the Spanish boarder. They arrived at a quaint local Spanish tavern. Manny quickly ordered a Guinness stout while Salina ordered her usual, Pepsi.

Manny insinuated to Salina. "Even in Spain the police tolerate three to four grams of hash on your person, just like a ballpoint pen in your shirt pocket."

Salina appraised. "It's not on the Spanish policia agenda to question you about your marijuana use. Unless you possess large amounts of hashish or marijuana."

Manny roused. "Well that's cool!"

Salina disclosed. "The policia will not bother you"

Manny responded. "That's the way I love to hear it!"

The Spanish tavern barkeep who served the drinks overheard their conversation about the hash cheered. "Si, policia! No, problemo!"

Manny told Salina. "I am especially impressed by the young Spaniards standing in front of the tavern called The Jazz."

Salina confided. "What do you mean Manny?"

Manny hemmed. "These young Spaniards smoke their hash right out on the side walk. They saunter around as they brake their cigarettes in one hand and spill the tobacco in their other hand's cigarette paper."

Salina summoned. "Let's go outside and watch them?" as they scooted on. They watched the young Spaniards on the outside of the tavern. At one point they broke a bit of black hash up and mix it in with tobacco, while they all non-chalauntly stood around chit chatting. They talked to their friends as they then rolled this mix into a hash mixed tobacco cigarette.

Manny professed. "That's different!"

Salina broached. "This is a common practice in Spain. Everyone I know smokes their hash that way." As Manny and Salina stood outside the Jazz bar, the Spaniard, Benito, continued to role the mix in a cigarette paper, while another passed his mixed hash and tobacco cigarette. Manny was a non-smoker of tobacco. He knew couldn't smoke this cigarette mixed with tobacco and hash.

However, Manny tried to participate in this Spanish custom by smoking a small amount. During his first attempt to inhale Manny choked in their faces. With the slightest inhale of tobacco Manny immediately coughed profusely. Manny looked at the Spaniards and said, "I don't see how you can smoke tobacco. I never have, and I can't smoke tobacco."

The young Spaniards laughed. Manny red-faced picked up a Pepsi can. Manny said to the Spaniards. "Watch me." Manny depressed the side into on the opposite end of the can. Manny then proceeded to punch small little pinholes in the area of a dime in the indented part of the Pepsi can.

The Spaniards stood around quizzically looking at this American standing before them. When Manny was done with the Pepsi can, it was converted into a homemade hash or marijuana pipe.

Manny put a half a gram of black hash in the indented part of the can. Manny then lit the hash with a match and smoked the hash out of the can through the drinking outlet.

Then Benito rapped to his other friends. "Manny is smoking the hash out of the can as if it were in a pipe."

Maduro Benito's friend responded. "Manny doesn't cough now that he is only smoking hash. The Spaniards then tried Manny's homemade pop can pipe.

Benito exhorted. "Give me the Pepsi can?" I want to try the hash in the Pepsi can pipe!"

Salina informed. "The Pepsi can is going around the horn over and over with everyone chipping in a little hash."

Manny gawked. "I like how everyone just keeps the conversation and party going. Everyone is smoking hash without a care in the world."

Salina asserted. "The police don't care here. These social custom's of smoking tobacco, hash, and marijuana are realized at social levels in all the countries you've been to so far including America. People around the world enjoy smoking no matter what the risk long term health factor are."

Manny excited. "Really! That's the way it should be."

Salina explained. "Where marijuana and hash had been illegal in the European community for the most part it is now decriminalized." As Manny and Salina stood around in front of the Jazz bar, Policia drove by and the Spaniards would just waved at them and said. "Hi!" And in between smoking the tobacco and hash the Spanish walked inside and out of the Jazz Bar. The Spanish drink pop or beers in between their tobacco and hash cigarettes. Even Salina, who wasn't a everyday smoker, decided to hit the can of hash. "I just wanted to be friendly." she later told Manny.

A Spaniard named Benito told Manny. "Did you hear about the Gibraltar speedboat, that was loaded with five and half tons of hash, and traveled by launch from Morocco."

Manny professed. "No!"

Bernito shrieked. 'The police blew the boat right out of the water as it came into shore loaded with hash! They killed everyone on the boat! There are allot of speed boating smugglers here."

Manny emphasized. "They need to get over it! Legalize hash importation, and tax the hash! The Spanish mainline is a major entry for Moroccan hashish smuggled into Europe."

The Benito nodded in agreement and teased. "Growing marijuana for personal use has been accepted for years in Spain. We enjoy decriminalization and cultivation of marijuana."

After that final conversations Manny and Salina said. "Good bye," to their new Spanish friends, they embarked from the Jazz Bar.

The next day Manny and Salina lingered and discussed the prior evening in Spain at a sunny side walk café. A British Bobby quickstepped down the sidewalk and never second glanced at them or any other Gibraltar natives smoking hash on the beach.

They left the café and strolled the old Grand Casement Gates of Gibraltar, proceeded by a series of old British Infantry and Artillery Batteries manned with their relic cannons. In Gibraltar's downtown Manny mooched. "I have never seen anything like these cozy and quaint shops. These showcase storefront window's are plentiful with souvenirs from all over the world. I like how some stores have hemp apparel on hangers coving their storefront. These shops with there rich historical architecture are on the narrowest corridors of streets I've ever seen." as fashionably dressed shoppers and ladies with babies in their strollers passed by on the bustling streets.

Salina declared. "You haven't seen anything yet. Gibraltar is only three miles long and a mile wide. It is just a small peninsula on the bottom of Spain."

Manny depicted. "That must be why the old "Rock of Gibraltar" is rated in the Guinness Book of World Records as one of the worst places in the world to drive."

Salina quipped. "The only place you can maneuver your car is on this small peninsula of Gibraltar, through it's narrow streets and corridors. When you have to turn your car around in the Gibraltar shopping areas, you have to back up on the side walks to complete your turn around. People just move out of the way when small buses, cars or motor bikes come down the low stone walled lanes."

As the seagulls flew overhead Manny proclaimed. "You can always drive in sunny Spain."

Salina assessed. "Spain still wants Gibraltar back. Years ago Franco closed the border, the people couldn't drive to Spain. Franco shut off the electric to Gibraltar, which effectively killed the electricity at the hospital. A dozen or so British people died. It was extremely hard or impossible for the British citizens of Gibraltar to go into Spain at the time. Now on Gibraltar they make their own electricity at the modern incinerator plant."

Manny gauged. "I'm beginning to feel more and more like a political liaison for the marijuana reform organization. I love all its perks. Especially having you Salina as my guide."

Salina blushed as they strolled the centuries old corridors and reported. "You could see the overhead "Cable Car" take tourists up to the summit of the rock's station. Perched up there you can see across the straits of Gibraltar to North Africa and across the bay to Spain. Tourists can than visit the "Great Siege Tunnels" and some of the many other tunnels and caves of the rock."

Manny asked. "Are there any cool caverns?"

Salina smiled and expounded. "The crystallized interior of "St. Michael's Cave" from the glacial periods is a very natural unique beauty in itself. The lower chambers descend into a Cathedral Cave where they hold concerts, and ballets."

Manny proposed. "I'd like to ride to the top of the rock to check it out."

Salina responded. OK! Once at the top you'll see the interacting tourists feed the wild tailless monkeys peanuts at the Ape's den." After their monkey tour on top of the rock they went to Europa Point Light House" on the southern most part of Gibraltar by taxi. The wide banned red stripped white light house overlooking the straits is the southern most part of Europe. In solitude Manny sparked up another bowl of hash and revealed. "You can see clearly over the Mediterranean straits to the north shores of Morocco, Africa. The country of Morocco is in the northwest most section of the African continent."

Salina expressed to Manny. "I'm getting excited Manny! I've never been to Morocco. I'm really glad you are going with me Manny."

Manny asked. "Why?"

Salina told Manny. "I'm afraid to go by myself. I've heard a lot of stories about the Moroccan's poor haggling for money."

Manny appealed. "What do you mean? I thought you've been to the Kasbah?"

Salina responded. "No I haven't. I've only heard about the Kasbah from friends who've been there. From what I hear their standards of living are not what you are used to Manny. When you see the way they live on streets filled with beggars and hagglers and the accommodations of third world standards, you'll realize the very many other benefits you casually enjoy in the states."

Manny reassured. "Don't worry! I'll protect you Salina."

Salina elated. "I know you will, Manny." Manny began to feel a warm relationship develop between himself and Salina. Salina was equally admirable towards Manny.

Manny apprised. "I'm anxious to get on the hydra foil from Tarefica Spain tomorrow morning and depart for Tangiers, Morocco." Hiedi agreed.

Manny waived down a taxi driver. He asked the taxi driver, since it was getting late for service. "Can you take us to the King's hotel." He asked the driver, after the cab pulled over to the side of the street and who said. "Yes, I can take you there now."

They had separate rooms at the King's Hotel that was prearranged on the travel itinerary. However, Manny and Salina decided to stay up late and talk intimately in Manny's room late into the night.

The next morning after they both woke up together, they watched on TV the news of other countries like Austria, Switzerland, and Rwanda that have explored the legalization of cannabis.

A broadcast journalist Kendell Kox described the footage on TV. "The Rwandan capital of Kigali is a main staging ground for cannabis trafficker's in Africa. African's have smoked marijuana without hindrance by law enforcement forever." as they listened to the documentary.

Kendell explained. "Marijuana use is part of their social norm. They use marijuana for social, medicinal, and religious reasons. The Rawandans lock citizens up for genocide but not marijuana use."

Salina was as interested as Manny stressed. "One of the citizens stated that Marijuana use has helped him cope with the cold and hunger they suffer on the merciless streets."

The Kendell cross-examined the facts. "They are not concerned with hash and marijuana use in Rwanda. The streets are filled with orphaned children who cannot afford marijuana so they inhale gasoline or glue. Those types of intoxicants are extremely dangerous."

Manny and Salina proceeded to her room. She picked up her hair and make up bag. Manny picked up a Spanish newspaper Salina had requested from the hotel lobby.

Manny sweet-talked. "Let's go to the corner sidewalk café. I want to get a cappuccino. Would you like some orange juice Salina?"

Salina answered. "I'll just get a cappuccino." which is the custom for most the locals in the European community."

On their way to the wharf where the hydra foil was docked and ready to take tourists to Morocco Manny told Salina. "Let's walk along the shipping docks where the old fishermen are mending their fishing nets. We have time."

With her nostrils inflamed Salina said hesitantly. "Manny it smells like fish down here."

Manny lead the way and disclosed. "Salina were almost on the docks. Look at that one old man in particular, he is standing around rolling a tobacco and hash cigarette like those friends of ours at the Jazz bar."

Salina described. "The old man passed the jay on occasion to a few of the dock workers as they continually mended the nets." Manny wanted a photo of Spanish workers diligently doing their work, while burning a few.

Manny expounded. "Right, that's the kind of facts of life, I want to see during my marijuana mission."

A group of construction workers laid asphalt on the road, that lead to the dock of the moored Hydro foil as Manny and Salina soft-peddled.

One asphalt worker said to Manny as wheeled by. "Are you going to Morocco?"

Manny confessed over the production asphalt-paver's loud noise in a high voice. "Yes!"

The worker stressed. "You're both dressed too touristy for Morocco, watch your back."

Manny and Salina did feel trendy for Morocco, after they heard about the Moroccan living conditions.

Nevertheless, Manny and Salina boarded the hydra foil. The ship's deck hand explained Manny. "The trip by ship is forty-five minutes long, before we are in Tangier's Morocco."

Salina professed to Manny. "The crew of the hydro foil are all Moroccans."

Manny gossiped. "The patrons of the ship are mostly Spanish, Moroccan's and a few other European tourists."

The comfortable hydrofoil cruised swiftly for a powerful ocean ride, as they approached the windy port of Tangiers, Morocco. A Moroccan deckhand on the hydrofoil tossed the rope freely to the port hand on the dock, who snatched the rope's end in mid-air. The Moroccan dockhand's then tied the hydrofoil's rope to the dock's pillar, without hindrance from the rough waters of the Atlantic. The hydrofoil was firmly docked.

The boarding ramps were lowered from the dock to the boat. The Moroccan police then walked up the plank and onto the hydra foil. They gathered everyone's passport. Putting each of the passports in a box.

Manny disclosed to Salina. "The Police will hold the passports in their custody all the tourists, until the boat departs back to Spain. Then our passports would be returned."

Salina protested. "Are you sure we'll get them back?"

Manny alluded." No, but what choice do we have. This is a rather crude acting bunch of people. I can see that."

After they swerved through the Moroccan customs offices onto the mainland of Africa, a Moroccan approached them and asked. "American? Do you want to buy this Moroccan tapestry with an official government tag?

Manny answered "Not right now."

The Moroccan guide coaxed. "I will show you around. I will be your guide. My name is Amed"

Manny hashed over back to the Moroccan man. " Salina wants to go to the Solazur."

The Moroccan man stood among many other Moroccan's and blatantly demanded. "You must have an official guide!"

Salina still insisted. "I want to go to the Solazur International Hotel."

The Moroccan man refused. "No, no, I will take you to the Kasbah, you have to go to the Kasbah. I will show you the best of Morocco."

Manny and Salina finally agreed after much debate, and they reluctantly went to the Kasbah.

Manny immediately realized the Kasbah is the oldest part of the city, thousands of years old. "Salina, look where this Moroccan took us here, were walking down corridors not much wider than American side walks. Do you realize were lost in between this maze of the ancient buildings?"

Salina conveyed. "Were at the mercy of our Moroccan guide."

Manny popped off. "Well that's reassuring!"

Salina attested. "There are no signs we can read, all old building's and corridors look the same."

Manny informed. "All the corridor routes are built through this stone maze in the center of this ancient city."

All of a sudden they were swarmed by Moroccan's. They couldn't move anywhere. Salina recognized. "Were surrounded by Moroccan's who trying to sell us Moroccan hand crafts and trinkets."

Rushed by the crowd Manny unleashed to Amed. "Get these people away from us!" Amed finally shoos the mob away.

An old Moroccan man came out from behind the crowd. Then he placed a wicker basket in front of Salina, Manny, and Amed.

Salina and Manny looked at each with amazement. An old man opened the basket. Salina and Manny were shocked as they looked at all the snakes in the wicker basket.

Amed their guide knew what was coming next unbeknown to Salina and Manny. The old man and a few of the Moroccan Street Merchants who chased Amed's tourists were cousins of Amed's. Amed typically brought tourists here to give his cousins a shot at selling their Moroccan hand crafted wares. Sometimes Amed received kickbacks for the larger sales later.

They could freely talk Moroccan and make side deals. None of the tourists would ever knew the difference.

Manny shaking his head deemed. "Can you believe this old Moroccan man?" He continued to charm the snakes, pythons, vipers and cobra's." Salina and Manny were scared to say the least.

Salina expressed. "I think were OK as long as we don't get to close to the snakes."

Manny professed. "The old man handled the snakes with out a care." That put the travelers at ease, they were unquestionably strangers in a stranger world. They both realized now it was a show.

Amed reeled off. "The Moroccan Snake charmer wants you to pose with his snakes for a fee."

Manny feeling a little braver answered. "I'll hold a snake for some souvenir photos. Would you take the photos Salina?" Manny asked.

Salina proclaimed. "As long as I don't have to hold any of the snakes, I'll gladly take the photos from a distance." Salina took a roll of photos of Manny with many of the snake charmer's serpents encompassing his whole body.

Manny shimmering said. "I can't believe I'm doing this."

Salina excited. "This guy is a Moroccan Snake charmer at his best. Nobody is going to believe this unless we have the photo's of these snakes wrapped all around you Manny."

Manny was still in a maze of snakes. The old man kissed one of the cobra snakes on the head. He then put the head of the twenty foot Boa Constrictor down his throat, while it encompassed his entire body. You could see the Boa trying to squeeze his master. What an amazing feat Manny and Salina thought.

The charmer squinted and remarked. "All you need is a soft touch to hold one of the snakes." Salina still declined to hold any of the snakes, but continued to shoot daring photos.

At this point they left the Snake charmer, and Manny said to Salina. "I'm still completely turned around and confused to the demographics of where we are exactly in the Kasbah.

Salina interjected. "Don't feel bad! I'm a travel agent. I have no idea were we are!" Then Manny noticed a British chap walking around by himself with a camera dangling from his neck.

The man was being haggled by another aggressive Moroccan merchant. Manny interrupted. "How you doing, mate?"

The man responded. "Hi! American?"

Manny asked. "Yeah! What's your name?"

He responded. "Bradford,"

Manny quizzically said. "Bradford?"

He answered. "Yeah, Bradford."

Manny asked. "Well, where are you from?"

Bradford divulged. "Ireland."

Manny inquired. "You here by yourself?"

Bradford confessed. "Yes, I am. I've walked around here for three hours and I can't find my way out. The Moroccans continually follow and rattled my brain. They haggle me every step of the way."

Manny asked. "Have you been taking photo's?"

Bradford replied "Yes! I have. How long you are staying here?"

Manny told Bradford. "We just arrived today. Salina and I leave tomorrow to go back to Spain."

Bradford responded. "I'm taking the train tomorrow to Marrakech."

Manny stunned. "Marrakech?"

Bradford acknowledged. "That's right. If I can get out of Tangier in one piece."

Manny suggested. " You want to walk around with Salina and me for a few hours. We'll be tourists together?"

Bradford touted. "Yeah! I'd like that." Amed stood there and talked to one of his cousins before he said to Manny. "My cousin wants to take you to the tea house."

The Moroccan named Omar stood next to Manny. He pulled on Manny's arm wanting all of them to go to the tea house.

Manny mentioned. "We've never been to a tea house." Amed was still showing them all around the Kasbah pleaded to Manny. "It will be OK! You will all like the tea house."

Omar specified. "Come! We will go right now." They decided to make a go of it. Then they stepped up the narrow ancient stone walled steps to the upstairs of the teahouse.

Manny noted to Salina. "These steps must be over a thousand years old."

They entered through the darkness three flights up and into a large dimly lit room with a bar. Manny realized that they were the only tourists in this drab Moroccan setting.

Bradford expressed to Manny. "I noticed right off we are the only Anglo-Saxon males in the tea house."

Manny revealed. " On top of that were the only ones who are not dressed in rags and we have shoes on."

Bradford told Manny. "Don't worry Amed and Omar's are with us."

Manny groaned. "Are you kidding! They're the ones who brought us here."

In the smoke filled room they sat and watched the United States soccer team the Moroccan team on the television. They sipped on minted tea which was served. Hash from the Rif mountains was in the water pipe's bowl the teahouse's supplied.

Bradford and Manny hit the pipes, so did Omar. Bradford conveyed to Manny. "We've been here about fifteen minutes and the United States is trouncing the Moroccan team on the television. I think us it's time for us new comers to leave."

Manny clarified. "I like your way of thinking bud."

Bradford disclosed to Omar. "Were leaving!"

Amed and Omar quickly demanded "No! No!" Bradford and Manny quickly attested. "Yes! Yes!"

The ruffled tourists rose to their feet. Salina was already walking to the other side of the room towards the steps downward, Bradford and Manny followed.

Once into the streets, Omar announced. "I want to sell you some hash." The tourists quickly repeated. "No!"

Manny thought of the movie Midnight Express, they all began to feel that experience.

Manny clamored. "Let's go! I don't want any of us to see the inside of a Moroccan jail." Manny, Bradford, and Salina stoutly refused Omar.

"No way!" Manny groused to Omar again. They were walking to the out skirts of the Kasbah, when Manny hailed the next taxi in sight down. "Whoa!" Yelled out Manny. "Take us to the Solazur!"

"Yes." the driver said and they all piled into the taxi and felt relieved that their next stop was the Solazur International Hotel.

Manny told everyone. "I'm happy for all of us to get out of there."

Bradford contended. "Omar really tried to push that hash on us."

Salina professed. "They sell you their hash. Then they tell the Moroccan police, who arrest you. The police then tip the hash vendor after they arrest you."

Bradford alleged. "You then have to buy your way out of jail."

Everyone agreed. Omar who they tried to ditch followed in another vehicle trying to catch the tourists.

Manny suggested. "The taxi ride from the Kazbah went fast."

Bradford affirmed. "Right around all these stone corridors is the Hotel."

Salina stressed. "I'll feel safer now that we have arrived into a more open setting along the road here close to the sea's edge. I want to go to a modern part of Tangiers."

Manny agreed. "Everyone feels safer."

Once in the Solazur International Hotel, Manny took off his Moroccan cap. Manny tried to blend in the Moroccan word work, but they can tell a fish as soon as they see one. They all approached the richly carved wooden bar and sat down.

Manny immediately asked the bartender "Sir, how many star's is this International hotel?"

The bartender responded said. "Four Star."

Manny relieved said. "I feel everyone of them." As they all looked at each other, they enjoyed their cool refreshments. Manny and Salina talked about meeting up with their contact Akil.

George had arranged for Manny to meet Akil in the Solazur. When Akil walked in he immediately recognized Manny from the Internet photo Glady's had e-mailed him. Akil asked Manny. "How was your journey?"

Manny said. "Everything's going great so far. Are you Akil?"

Akil answered. "Yes I am. Welcome to Morocco!" Everyone really felt reassured once they met Akil. Akil came and sat down at their table. Akil then invited them to a Moroccan restaurant he owned. Akil further conveyed. "We have a twelve piece Moroccan band. They are a treat to watch." The tourists graciously accepted the invite.

Once Manny, Salina, and Bradford walked into the restaurant, they immediately noticed the many different musical instruments the Moroccans were joyfully playing on stage.

In between musical sets, some of the Moroccan band members came over and talked with the tourists about America.

Akil told Manny. "The band members all have hashish on their persons." They offered some hash to Manny, and Bradford, who then smoked their hash with them. "I like their water pipes." Bradford admitted.

Salina, not much of a smoker, sat and watched contently. "I'll stick to the mint tea drink. Thank you."

Manny confessed. "I like the cocktail, I have. It's called black hashish."

Akil explained. "The hashish comes from the Rif Mountains. Which is not so far away. This is the main production area of hashish in the world. Most of the hash is from the small province in "Ketma Valley."

Manny expressed. "This hashish smokes real nice Akil. I wish I could bring some back to America with me."

Akil deemed. "You can, if you want."

Manny told Akil. "I want, but I don't think customs would go for it." Akil laughed.

Manny asked. "Is it hard to get the hash?"

Akil answered. "No it's not. We get five kilos at a time. That's how they feed their families by making and selling hash. They earn their way "Thanks to God. If we had time I'd take you to the mountains, and show you the hash production center."

Salina asked. "Does some of this hash go to Europe?"

Akil responded. "Most of the hash goes directly to Europe. The Europeans came down here to show us how to step up production. The shunky hash smells great and it's very good medicine. Everyone in the family chips in to work the fields. Then they make hash from their harvest."

Manny queried. "Do you have any problems moving hash around the country?"

Akil dreadfully answered. "Yes! As a matter of fact we do. Our king wants foreign aid from the US. The US government wants the King to shut down the hash production area before giving aid. The problem is our Kings ancestors granted and blessed these mountains for hash production to our people. Now they have a military police check point on valley's road entry to the Ketma Market. The government made it tight. Before ninety-five percent of the hash went through the valley pass, now maybe one percent passes. The villagers take larger quantities of hash over the mountain ridges."

Manny pestered. "I sure would like to see that hash production area."

Akil reasoned. We'll see what we can arrange."

Manny divulged. "I see the American government is sticking their foreign policy nose over here."

Akil conceded. "Unfortunately yes they are."

Akil gave Manny a Moroccan candle to send back to George. Moroccan rugs were for sale and display in the adjoining room next to the entertainment restaurant.

Akil spelled out. "I'm going to have my assistant show you the Moroccan rugs you are to pick from."

Manny and Salina picked elegantly colored and designed hand made Moroccan rugs.

The assistant showed rug after rug after rug in front of them.

Astonished Manny stated. "I can't believe there are so many hand made rugs."

Amazed Bradford conceded. "They hope you buy all these rugs."

Manny admitted. "I am, because it's George's money; not mine."

Salina explained. "George had them ordered already. We just have to pick them out."

Manny consulted Akil. "Let Salina pick out of that pile of gorgeous rugs."

Akil informed. "Some of these hand made rugs take three to four years to make."

Manny grumbled slightly. "She's been looking at those throw rugs for a long time. I can see why they're so expensive."

Bradford buzzed on hash rumbled. "I like it here Manny. Were not being followed and haggled by all the street merchants trying to sell us their Moroccan trinkets."

Akil asked. "Let me take you to the market? Nobody will bother you with me there. I promise!"

Manny chirped. "That sounds great Akil, Let's do it." As they walked down the streets.

Manny told Akil. "Do you come to the market often?"

Akil told Manny. "Yes everyday. I'll take you to open air markets with fruits, vegetables, rugs and more trinkets."

Akil enounced. "Old men sit around smoking hashish from water pipes."

Manny told Akil. "What a drastic cult change!" Akil then took them to the motel he owned and located on the ocean front. He gave them rooms and said. "I'll see you all tomorrow morning. Get a good night's rest."

In the cafe morning at 8:00 AM, Akil met up with his foreign friends and took them to the open air market.

Steve, Salinas's cousin met up with the group at the open air market. Salina introduced Steve to Manny and Bradford and explained. "Steve lives in Gibraltar. He was on a dive holiday at the Red Sea. Steve just flew into Tangiers from Cairo, Egypt" Steve responded. "The plane tickets are cheaper that way."

Manny asked. "How are you doing Steve?" As hand shakes were exchanged between everyone.

Steve cheered. "Really good. How is it going with you?"

Manny answered. "It has been going smooth. We have some pretty nice accommodations."

Steve asked. "Where are you staying?"

Manny divulged. "We all stay upstairs in a condo. It has a view overlooking Tangiers and the ocean. Akil has made everyone comfortable in his or her own rooms on the upper floor of a building he owns.

"Look at what Salina bought me." Manny posed as he showed Steve the rug that Salina bought for Manny as a present. Manny revealed. "The rug merchants showed us these beautiful rugs earlier. We purchased some of those Moroccan rugs for our friend George back in Houston."

Bradford admitted. "The rugs Salina picked out for George are really beautiful."

Salina told Steve. "Manny thinks one bright red rug would fit in George's business room."

Manny stated. "Yes the room off to the side of the conference room where the round table meetings are held in his mansion. George's staff wanted George to remember our trip's goal."

Salina added. "The goal of marijuana decriminalization in America."

Manny told Salina. "The pro-pot plan is to force my country leaders in America into a full debate after the next major marijuana and hemp Rosta Rally in Washington."

Manny told Bradford. "George sent me to check out all of our NATO allies. I've lived in freedom this past week and a half. I realize now the legalities of cannabis in other free countries thoroughly."

Salina spouted. "Manny thinks they'll win the decriminalization of marijuana fight."

Manny emphasized. "That's right we will win! Real freedom has to win."

Steve decreed. "I hope so. I'll go on holiday there when you get the marijuana laws straightened out there in the U.S."

Bradford stayed with Manny. He decided to go back to Spain, instead of farther into the interior of the Moroccan countryside. Bradford told Manny. "Akil left a little hash for us here in the foyer."

Manny railed. "Light it up! Let's have a night to remember out on the balcony."

Manny while sitting on the balcony with the others relayed. "That Akil is one rich and well connected Moroccan businessman."

Salina divulged. "Akil has a friend who owns a taxi escort. His rug customers go back to the hydro foil dock without being hassled."

Manny noted. "We'll all be on the hydro foil back to Spain tomorrow morning."

Steve followed up. "And then Gibraltar!"

Once on the boat, they all felt relieved to leave the Moroccan shoreline.

Steve, Salina's cousin from Gibraltar, had an ounce of hash. He purchased the hashish in Morocco. Steve put a gram in a pipe and lit it up on the top deck of the boat and stated. "Heck with it! We are in international waters now. I'm not in Morocco now." Steve then passed the bowl of hash to Manny who quickly hit the bowl and passed the pipe to Bradford.

Manny acknowledged. "Bradford is flying to London out of Gibraltar's Airport tomorrow."

Steve joked. "Cool! Go to Soho and get a ho for me."

Manny told his group of friends. "This has been a breath taking adventure for me here in Morocco."

Bradford agreed. "Really!"

Steve sighted first the coastline of Spain as the hydrofoil approached the port of Tarifica, Spain at a good clip.

Once docked Manny walked down the plank of the Hydrofoil, and onto the Spanish mainland Manny said. "I feel like I just returned to the United States of America."

Steve bemoaned. "I wouldn't know, what that's like."

Manny invited. "Come to the Rosta Rally in Washington, we'll show you around." Manny then asked Steve. "How is the availability of marijuana and hash in the Middle East?"

Steve told Manny. "Hemp and marijuana go back thousands of years in these Middle Eastern cultures. Even in the pre-Christian times hemp marriage rings were made. They were replaced year after year in marriage customs of ancient Egypt."

Manny recounted. "From what I've heard marijuana is quite prevalent in Israel, and that hash is made in the close by Beka valley."

Steve admitted. "Most of the pot is grown by the Israelis for their own personal use. Israel's police get calls from residents about other residents growing marijuana on their balconies. The Israeli police do not want to fill their jails with Marijuana smokers, so they do very little about such complaints.

The Israeli archaeological digs have discovered remnants of hash in graves of women from before the time of Christ. The hash was found in the rib cage area indicating that the women used the hash medically for menstrual or birthing labor pains. This is scientific proof from ancient eras of the past that marijuana has been used throughout the centuries. Egyptians texts placed marijuana use medically centuries ago, even before this latest archaeological discovery."

Manny implied. "I'm amazed by all the cannabis information I'm continuing to uncover."

Steve told Manny as they all walked down the streets of Tarifica, Spain. "The Israeli government admits decriminalization of marijuana is being discussed in the Knesset drug committee. Government officials are drawing up a new agenda for their soft drug problem. Its called decriminalization."

Manny confided "Good. I love it."

Steve revealed. "Egypt's Mt Sinai has a large availability of marijuana and hashish. The cannabis trade flourishes out in the open-air markets without hindrance. It's a backpackers paradise."

Steve told Manny. "I was there on Holiday. I know." Manny's schedule was beginning to tighten up. Manny had to leave the following morning

Salina and Manny were having such a good time together and they had talked about finishing Manny's trip together. Salina, could fly stand-by because of her travel agent status. She decided to go to Sydney, Australia with Manny after he asked.

Salina gushed. "I've decided to finish the tour with you Manny."

Manny insisted. "I couldn't be happier."

From Gibraltar Manny and Salina's next stop together was Bombay, India. Bradford left Gibraltar Airport the same morning after they exchanged addresses. Bradford said. "I'll see you at the Rosta Rally." as they all departed ways. Manny and Salina were in route for their brief one-day holdover in Bombay.

Salina and Manny visited a hash den their upon arrival as arranged. Rashish was the keeper at this hash den. Rashish lived and worked on the main fare way in Bombay, India.

Manny relayed to Salina. "I can't believe were here. As poor as this country is, they are hash and pipe rich. Look on that wall."

Rashish explained. "The Indians have never made cannabis illegal throughout their history. The Indian Hemp Drug Commission instilled a minimal intervention policy concerning cannabis. Over one hundred years later the government of India still has these pro cannabis principles intact."

Rashish told Manny and Salina. "The abundant hashish and marijuana tea houses in Bombay are normal social activities. Hashish and marijuana has been prevalent through out India for centuries."

Manny asked. "You have no problems, because of it?"

Rashish told Manny and Salina. "No, and in some cities marijuana grows in the streets to no avail. No one so much as gives the marijuana plants a second look. India has never had a problem with marijuana."

Salina asked. "What about the religious customs I've heard about?"

Rashish with black hashish in his hand answered. "Certain sects of the Hindu Religion still use marijuana in their religious sacraments. Much like wine is used in the Catholic Religion. Smoking marijuana cigarettes during religious ceremonies happens in many parts of the world, and has through out man's time."

Manny told Salina. "Judging religious interpretation is not the government's job in the United States. There is supposed to be separation between the State and church in the U. S."

Rashish admitted. "The United States tried to force anti-hemp legislation through foreign aid influence and intervention."

Manny questioned. "And India resisted?"

Rashish answered. "But of coarse we resisted. This is our country."

Manny asked. "Can you get in trouble carrying hash in India?"

Rashish explained. "You'd have to possess more than one hundred grams of hash here in this country to be in trouble."

Manny exclaimed. "That's a good law!"

Rashish agreed. "You can grow all the marijuana you want to smoke. Come into my backyard."

Manny walked into a patch of marijuana growing randomly everywhere in Rashish's back yard. Manny noted. "I can't believe they're so high."

Rashish agreed. "Yes, you are allowed healthy marijuana plants. In Nepal they grow plenty of hemp. They make allot of different hemp products like those I showed you in the den."

Rashish took Manny and Salina on a fast sight seeing tour of Bombay. Manny and Salina were to only spend the day in Bombay, before they off.

On the flight the next day Manny E-mailed George's staff with all the new cannabis information he had gathered. On the next day's flight into Sydney, Australia you had a commanding view of the white capped waves and the spastic rowers in Darling Harbor. The Opera House and the traffic on the Harbor's Bridge were detected as the plane landed.

Manny disclosed to Salina once they arrived. "I want to go straight to King's Cross! George said it's known for it's night life. It's where we have to meet an Aussie named Mel. He's made arrangements us for our trip to Canberra and then to travel the eastern gold coast of Australia. We'll proceed through surfer's paradise, and on though Brisbane, Townsville, and finally to Cairns."

Salina asked. "Where do we have to meet Mel?"

Manny responded. "King Cross Tavern near the water fountain?" After they arrived at Tavern, Manny called Mel and he came to meet Manny and Salina.

Mel recommended. "Let's go over near the water fountain which centers Kings Cross to talk about your trip north of here." they walked towards the fountain's misty spray.

Manny described. "Look at the cloud of water mist from those spinning faucet heads. I have never seen a four separate tiered lit up pools around a fountain like this one."

Mel promised as they casually walked along. "You won't see one like this one anywhere."

Salina interrupted. "I believe it!"

Mel explained. "First though you both will go to Australia's National Capitol Canberra, then back here to Sydney before JD will take you both to the wild life sanctuary Billabong outside of Townsville. It's where kangaroos are like puppy dogs. They beg for peanuts from the tourists!"

Manny excited. "That sounds like a photo shoot for me."

Mel enthusiastically said. "It sure is. You'll both enjoy it."

Manny burst out. "Mel is that guy smoking a joint?"

Mel reassured. "They smoke out in the open in King's Cross. You can go into the Beer Tap next to "Joe's Poker Palace" and buy beer. The store keep will open it for you. It's no problem here mate."

Manny surprised. "That's unreal. No problem's right!"

Mel replied. "No worries mate. Not here!"

Salina with her stuffed toy koala in her arm asked. "Is that Sydney's revolving Tower Restaurant?

Mel answered. "Yes it is. You can see it from everywhere in Sydney. I'm going to take you for dinner on the water's edge. Dinner includes prawns, and barramundi fresh from the fish market. Is that OK?"

Manny trumpeted. "That sounds like a very tasty idea."

Famished Salina exulted. "I'm ready!" as they drove to and than dined in the open cafe under the bright blue cloudless sky. The heart of Sydney's city centre is the elegant enclave of sparkling Daring Harbour."

Salina told Manny. "That is one big glass topped pavilion storied shopping mall." she commented while dinning.

Mel divulged. "After the modern make over the Queen herself dedicated the harbour." as the boats cruised and graced the showcase harbour with the high risers of Downtown Sydney in the backdrop.

Salina attested. "I could go shopping here for a month. I love the open park area, the ponds and scenic artificial water flowing along the palm lined walkways and park areas." as they were finishing their meals.

Manny emphasized. "They defiantly had the right idea here. This harbour with it's wrap around tourists play ground is happening." while pigeons were eating crumbs on the sidewalk.

Salina accented. "The kids really like it. They haven't stopped playing in the and water overflowing receding inward spiraling staircase to the round cement ball in the center."

Manny cheerfully admitted. "I can get use to staying in Sydney real easy." as the small train trolley rolled by filled with tourists.

Mel posed. "Are we ready?"

Manny asked Mel. "We ain't to the grower's house yet?"

Mel now standing with his tasseled kangaroo coat on notified. "Yes! I have that arranged. Let's skedaddle!" as they drove out of the city's heart to Bondi Beach. Manny quipped. "I'm not used to being in a car going down the wrong side of the road."

Mel informed. "Manny your not on the wrong side of the road in Australia." as he goosed the car faster around the curve. The paddling surfers filled the endless waves along the sandy shoreline of Bondi Beach. The surrounding rock and foliage accommodated the rough billows. Mel's friend Derrick had a place close by.

Mel introduced Manny to his friend named Derrick. Derrick said to Manny and Salina. "Let me show you several of my marijuana plants in my grow room."

Manny obsessed upon seeing the little marijuana operation. "Nice set up! I like how you have thick crystal buds with red and purple hairs."

Derrick explained. "Most of our varieties came from marijuana seeds ordered from Amsterdam."

Derrick than lit a bowl of fresh marijuana bud up. "Here Manny try this!" Derrick then passed the pipe of marijuana to Manny.

Manny hashed over. "This is great taste! I like the set up, and all the marijuana plants your growing and smoking. It's perfectly legal in Australia?"

Mel induced. "Yes! In most of Australia marijuana is legal. We still have a few dry spots. You know like the dry counties for alcohol in the states."

Manny confessed. "I'm enjoying the connoisseurship of this marijuana mission to the max!" Everyone laughed.

Mel took Salina and Manny to several more marijuana grower's homes. They drove over the Harbour Bridge's arched tunnel toward Mandly. They sat around at each grower's house gloating in amazement. The fast paced tour was on schedule. Mel had Manny and Salina on their way to Canberra the following morning.

Mel gave Manny the next set of arrangements before he left Sydney. "George has radio interviews set up for you Manny. In Canberra, George has arranged for you to meet a member of the "Australian Parliamentary Group for Drug Law Reform." He wants you to talk about pro-marijuana issues in the states telecast live with radio host Katy Kangaroo."

Manny professed. "Katy Kangaroo. I've heard of her in the states."

Mel explained. "She will do a questioned and answer type interview about your world marijuana mission tour of legal inquiry."

Manny anxiously said. "I'm up for that. Let's have a go at it."

They were now at the radio station. Manny press on into the "Live on Air" booth as Katy began the interview. "Yes Mamm! My name is Manny. I'm a true American from the State of Texas." in his choused southern draw. He then begin to tell Katy's Australian radio audience about the evils of marijuana prohibition back in the States.

In the surroundings of the Black mountains of Canberra, George had Manny in front of the Australian legislature. Manny gave the legislature a synopsis of the pro-marijuana political movement back in the States. Manny had asked the legislators for advice for their pro-marijuana political movement in the States.

Manny told Salina. "Look they gave me copies of their current marijuana laws. The Australian drug program is the renowned as the world's unfolding model."

Salina pledged. "The Aussie's are also a staunch ally of the United States, but they view your marijuana laws as prohibition. They see how ineffective the prohibition s and decriminalized marijuana."

Legislature Sam Straight conveyed to Manny. "Decriminalizing marijuana has had no ill effects on our communities. We Aussies changed the marijuana laws for the better with legalization for cultivation and personal use. Citizens can grow marijuana for personal consumption. Marijuana possession for small amounts is legal without criminalisation. We sponsor educational programs on drug about abuse. Under the new reforms for marijuana users have been released from jail. We have implemented judicial fairness for our cannabis citizen's. Small or no fines, and no possibility of discrimination or jail whatsoever is realized in the majority of Australia."

Manny noted. "I see the government officials of Australia have taken legalization of marijuana a step at a time to reform the nation's marijuana drug laws."

Sam professed. "Yes! Growing a few marijuana plants for personal consumption is legal in most parts of Australia. Possession of Two grams of cannabis oil or up to thirty grams of cannabis leaves can attract small fines at worse. These are all steps toward total decriminalization of marijuana."

Sam told Manny. "Penalties will remain for cultivation, or possession of large amounts of marijuana. These are the citizens who import, grow, or are in possession of large amounts of marijuana. The governing officials don't want their kids thrown in jail with hard criminals. We don't want their kids to be threatened with jail. We'd rather speak of the health risks to our kids than scare them with prison sentences for smoking marijuana. Some Members in Parliament have been smoking marijuana for years and still do." Sam admitted to Manny as they walked through hall.

Manny acknowledged. "Some Members in London's Parliament came out and admitted marijuana use for years. They advocate decriminalization for small amounts of marijuana possession or use."

Sam admitted. "Yes they do, but it's still illegal in England."

Manny revealed. "It's been a rush Sam! Come to the Rosta Rally in Washington, DC. George will fly you and a few of your pro-marijuana colleges."

Sam excited. "I can't wait!" Manny and Salina were on there way back to Sydney by train.

Manny called on his cellular telephone to Clint back in the United States. He keep Clint tuned in with fresh updates about the marijuana current laws from around the world for hemp rally ammunition in the States. The only way to beat the bigot warriors was with accurate media exposed information.

The next day in Sydney, Mel introduced Manny and Salina to JD over a kangaroo sandwich's and crocodile for a side dish. JD was the trailblazer to take them all on their way to Cairns in his Land Rover.

After a nights rest at the local hostel, they were on their way to Cairns. Manny and Salina, and JD drove his Land Rover practically none stop Townsville. After another night's rest JD wheeled Manny and Salina to the Billabong in Townsville.

JD told Salina. "The Aboriginal word Billabong means "Waterhole" In Townsville the Billabong is a refuge for some of Australia's animals. The Billabong animal refuge is arranged for tourists to see Australia's unique animals. Crocodiles, four foot high birds known as Emu's, Koala Bears sleep twenty hours a day. Kangaroos run around the tourist areas so they can hand feed them."

Salina exulted. "That sounds really neat and interesting."

JD reported. "It is really neat to see all the different varieties of wildlife." JD lit up a joint bush weed as they all strolled through the rain forest paths of the Billabong.

Manny reacted. "I love all these beautiful and very different animals," while looking at a bush bird's exhibit of large bats hanging upside down.

The park's ranger cracked the whip to the ground, as the tourists stood around the water's edge and watched intently. The ranger tied a chicken onto the end of the whip and pitched it into the murky water foliage covered water. Suddenly the hidden crock snapped it's jaws as the chicken hit it's snout after being thrown by the park's ranger. The started tourists loved it!

Salina enthused. "Look at the monkeys scatter across the crocodiles back! as the crock opened his jaws cracking sharply at the monkey.

Manny snapping his fingers pointed. "That's wild! That crocodile must be over twenty feet long." in a natural water garden pond filled with Yellow Flag's, Water Lily's, Lizard Tails, Brown tasseled Cocktail's, and a White Faced Owl perched high above.

Salina admitted. "I love nature. It's alive and colorfully exciting"

Manny followed up. "I'm impressed. This is a great rainforest and animal orientation. We have to protect and preserve this valuable entity." while passing the joint back to JD a pair of peacocks walked on.

Salina appealed. "Look at the baby monkey hanging on it's mother just below the jungle canopy."

Manny said. "I really like the Billabong's natural habitat, and it's jungle atmosphere. The calls of the wild never cease here." As the flocks of wild birds, parrots, herds of monkeys, and kangaroos were being feed by the tourists. The Billabong's ranger was showing a seven foot python to those brave tourists who wanted to get close."

JD while feeding a small kangaroo proffered. "The tourists can hold one if they want to."

After the quick tour of all the animals, they left the Billabong and it's exotic creatures. JD yelled. "Come with me! I'll give you both a ride into the bush!"

While slapping a fly Manny asked. "How do you get away with that JD?"

JD cross-examined. "You know we drive on the wrong side of the road with the steering column on the wrong side of the car."

JD touted. "I use the Land Rover exclusively mainly in the outback."

JD took Manny and Salina to the Worlds largest indoors live coral reef aquarium located in Townsville at the "Great Barrier Reef Wonderland." Manny and Salina walked through and around the coral reef aquarium.

Manny clarified to Salina. "Gees-o-peets. The Aussie's have a glass tunnel through this live coral reef aquarium as large as a truck." While an octopus stuck to the glass, a Lionfish was devouring live shrimp among the cabbage coral.

Salina answered back. "When you walk through the glass arched overhead tunnel of the aquarium the large sharks and other fish swim over our heads."

Manny told Salina. "Look at the under sides of the sharks and their eerie looking teeth!" as the sharks swam directly over their heads.

Salina implied. "I like the live coral's best." as they swayed back in forth from the aquarium's current.

Manny conferred. "This might be the most interesting aquarium in the world." while a group of blue parrot fish swam by the front of the glass.

JD exclaimed. "Wait until I get you both to the bottom of the Great Barrier Reef." as a school of large angel fish swam over a few sand sharks.

Salina noticed. "The smaller aquariums have delicate ornamental fish like sea horses and lion fish. They are the most fascinating."

JD avouched. "The Lion fish are common and very poisonous. Watch yourself when your diving on the reef, they'll blend in with the spectacularly colored corals and the multitude of reef fish. That Lionfish is sure a fast eating shrimp machine."

JD drove them north to the rain forest city of Cairns before his 4x4 Land Rover took them into and through the lush foliage of the rainforest to an aboriginal village named Kuranda. Kuranda is the location of the "Australian Marijuana Party" JD said. "I have an Aboriginal friend named Cola, he'll smoke some good outback weed with us." JD with his guests drove his Land Rover ruggedly all the way up the dense highland's winding trail to the village.

They were now at "Tjapukai Aboriginal Cultural Park" in Kuranda. Once in Tjapukai's Boomerang restaurant JD had delicious spicy kangaroo and green peppers on fresh papaya, while Manny had Baked North Queensland Reef Shark with wild lime and ginger amenities. They both shared a side of crocodile. Salina had the Queen's variety platter of fish from the Great Barrier Reef. Afterwards they watched an aborigine cultural show by the Tjapukai dancer's in the outdoor covered Rainforest Marquee amphitheater.

Manny told JD as they left. "That was a very unique and thrilling experience. I'll never forget it."

As they walked into the thatch house of JD's aboriginal friend Cola. Cola was JDs friend. Cola was smoking his hand crafted pipe with a few of his friends from Kuranda.

"Wow!" Manny predicted. "I'm going to smoke a pipe of marijuana with the Aborigines in Australia."

JD explained. "Aboriginal cultures have smoked cannabis for years."

Manny in his blue bush hat replied. "This rain forest weed is smooth."

While close to Kuranda market JD remarked. "Boonga's Boomerangs are being demonstrated on the outside of the hut by Cola's kids and their friends."

Salina asked. "I want a boomerang souvenir?"

JD informed them. "There are many different brightly colored hand crafted aboriginal boomerangs, spears, and aboriginal art. They are on display for souvenirs right out side of Cola's house."

Manny and Salina bought aboriginal made Australian Bush hats for each other.

Cola suggested. "Make sure you visit the Nocturnal habitat just down the trail from here."

Manny agreed. "That sounds fantastic. We will" and then said. "Thanks Cola for all your hospitality. It's been our pleasure."

Once inside the Nocturnal creature exhibit you seen animals that only come out at night. The bats fly in their cage were in full view of the dimly lit display.

Manny raved. "Look at all the night creatures moving around the rocks and on the ground of the exhibit."

JD disclosed. "The only way you'll see these animals is at this exhibit or with a flash light in the middle of the night in the rain forest."

Salina defined. "There incredible." as they left for the short walk to the train station of Kuranda through the meticulously groomed flower gardens. Manny and Salina for their return journey from Kuranda boarded a historical train built in the 1890's at Platform one.

Manny admitted. "This train ride sounds exciting."

JD said. "I think it was to exciting at one time! When outbacker's cleared the way for the railway years ago, the aborigines ate foreigners who came into their rainforest surroundings for food."

Manny bemoaned. "That's crude!"

Manny confided before departing JD. "Salina and I appreciate all your Aussie hospitality. This has been another remarkable part of our tour." JD stayed in Kuranda and announced as the train revved up. "See you in Washington at the Rosta Rally."

Manny yelled back. "That's for sure!" As the train started it's roll forward from the old rail station. The old train chugged down the rail's through the thick foliage of the rainforest's scenic mountainside and many tunnel's along the river as Cairns was coming into view. All the way back down to Cairns was a real exasperating scenic experience. The train stopped at "Barron Falls" a scenic outlook of a deep drop off in barron's gorge. The water falls were out of season. From the high rock cliff's to the lower gorges and over the tall spanning bridge's of the route were breathtaking.

Salina expressed to Manny. "The train ride I'll bet is as exciting now as it was so many years ago."

The old train paced down the countryside of the mountain, until the rainforest meet the wetlands. Cairns was in full view in the lower lands. You seen from a distance where the rainforest meets the Great Barrier Reef.

After they stayed in a hostel for the night, they booked a dive trip out to the great barrier reef. The local dive shop operator Tim booked Salina and Manny for a three day stay on a one-hundred and ten foot dive ship, which renovated from an ex-American PT boat.

Tim told Manny and Salina. "The relic PT Boat was given to the Aussies by the American Government. The PT Boat had seen plenty of service against the

Japanese during World War II. The boat has since had been gutted of its original motors. The cabin berth is converted into a modern live aboard dive ship."

Salina, a diver herself asked Tim. "Can I do a deep dive to one-hundred feet with Manny on one of the dives."

Tim responded. "Yes! There is one dive, where you can do a deep dive. There is also one night dive on the schedule for the brave and bold."

Salina enounced. "Manny and me are brave and bold! We'll do it!"

Manny testified. "I can't wait!" as they left the dive shop. They went straight to the dock where the dive boat was moored.

Manny and Salina walked onto the dive ship. They had their first dive orientation as the boat left the shoreline. The next day after a night's run out to the big fish habitat we were moored in the deep waters over the wreck of the Angola.

Manny asked Salina as they got up from their cabin. "Are you ready?"

Salina responded. "I can't wait let's do it." After the dive meeting twenty-five divers from all over the world jumped over the side of the dive ship straight down to the bottom.

The party of divers passed through groups of barracudas on their way down to the tabletop coral reefs. There was an abundance of sea life in full spectacular surrounding the ill-fated "Yongala" wreck which went down in 1911 with the loss of one hundred and twenty-one lives. The crew and passengers all perished on that relentless stormy night in the turbulent seas.

The Kiwi ship hand Kevin promised to show some of the tourist divers, including Manny and Salina a set of binoculars that went down to the bottom with the unlucky ship. Kevin took Salina into the crust of the metal haul to show her the ship's old rusted and barnacled binoculars.

Before the divers came to the ocean's surface though all the air bubbles on there first dive, they had seen manta rays over twelve feet in diameter with their large limp like flapped wings moved out over the sand. The large reddish brown coloration of the giant loggerhead sea turtles, were very large in diameter. They were swimming along with the divers, who were going to the surface slowly.

Manny and Salina were back on the boat with the other divers. Exuberant Manny confessed. "This is absolutely an under water photo paradise."

Salina revealed. "This is an ultimate reef experience. The multituded finesse of colored of table top and finger corals surrounded sea green grass and fern plants. There was the Blue Star fish and cone shells right in the middle of that sandy cove."

Manny relayed. "Yes! Some fish were nibbling at the sea grass, while gropers swam by bigger than my car. I've never seen anything so intensely beautiful in my life as the oceans floor's Great Barrier Reef. There must have been two hundred feet of visibility."

While he filled the air tanks at the fill station Kevin explained. "There's good visibility when the seas lay down like this."

Salina raged. "It's just amazing exotic reef scenery, ecspecially when the balck tipped sharks cruise by."

Manny giggled. "You like the sharks?"

Salina affirmed. "Oh Ya! As long as they keep cruising."

Kevin lectured. "The passage liner Yongala remains as you can see. It is encrusted with white, red, yellow, blue corals, soft corals, barnacles, sea shells, algae, even living corals with all kinds of assorted vibrant colors. You two went down to a ship that went down to the bottom of the ocean some ninety years prior to its final resting place."

Manny granted. "I love the multitudes of fish and sea creatures of uncountable varieties that engulfed the remains of the ship."

Kevin asked. "Magnificent wasn't it?"

Manny admitted. "Yes! It was a very exciting dive. The schools of brightly colored fish are magnificent. It makes one great artificial reef."

Salina brought a broken piece of coral and a sea urchin back up from their dive. Manny told Salina. "Throw the broken coral back! Their are strict laws that prohibit taking anything from the Great Barrier Reef!"

Salina complied and threw the broken coral back into the blue water and offered. "I'm sorry I didn't know." Manny and Salina did three dives on that day.

Manny told Salina. "Salina let's go up onto the upper deck.

They climbed to the upper deck in the late afternoon after their morning and early afternoon dives. Startled Manny forgot he was in Australia, when he saw all the beautiful girls on the ship from all over the world. They laid on the promenade of the ship deck. All he women sunned themselves with the tops of their bikini's off. Manny looked at Salina and said. "The bosoms are sunny side up!"

Salina smiled and beseeched. "It's custom in Australia and most of Europe."

Salina had already taken her top off, while Manny checked all the other girls breasts out. Manny eyeballed as he rubbed cannabis sun tan lotion on Salinas back. He turned his head around for a minute and said. "America is really out of touch with the world and with the reality as far as I can see." as he smiled and looked on the other girls laughed along with Salina.

Manny chuckled. "I love Australian beach rules!" as the days crisp sun reflecting off the ocean warmed everyone up.

After a day's dives were complete the patrons and crew of the ship had a beer or two. At night they sat around the alcohol bar of the ship. Manny and Salina went out to the upper deck at night. The boat mates supplied the dive tokers with some Australian bush weed.

The Kiwi Kevin asked. "Do you want a hit or two of bush weed?"

Manny avowed. "Yes Sir!" while he reviewed the promenade deck. As the joints circulated the crowd got bigger, and bigger. The bar area of the ship shrunk. Nobody wanted the alcohol's heavy content of beer in their system. They just wanted a light hearted buzz smoking a joint or two. That was their hearts desire, before they went back down to the bar for a Pepsi. Most everyone returned to their beds shortly after for the night. They wanted to be good and ready for the next day's dive.

In their cabin berth preparing for their morning dive Manny told Salina. "That Kiwi from New Zealand is the best ship hand on the vessel. He looked out for the welfare and the safety of the passengers at all times. I like how the Kiwi came out with the dingy to get us when the current was taking us stranded divers further away from the boat."

Salina moaned. "The Captain is a broken up old sea relic from WWII. He told me some gruesome WWII Stories between dive spots."

Manny admitted. "Yes. He's a senile old bore." They were about to dive down to the World Famous Cod Hole on the barrier reef.

Kevin briefed the divers about cod hole terrain during their ongoing reef ecology program. "Everyone please be careful not to touch the sea life, corals gardens and plants on reef. Preservation of this precious and exotic reef is the golden rule here in Australia."

Manny confessed. "I'm glad they are so conscience minded. They constantly remind us of all the rules prior to every dive."

Salina defined. "That rule is mentioned at these dive informational and instructional meeting's prior to every dive we make."

Manny recanted. "They want to make sure that everyone has their pre-designated dive partner in sight at all times."

Twenty-five divers from around the world and a few of the ship hands with a bucket of apple bits dove down the ship's anchor line at once. As everyone descended to the bottom of the sea floor, the Codfish realized were bigger than the divers imagined. Manny took pictures constantly of Salina with the big Codfish.

 Salina now armed with George's under water camera took pictures of Manny. Manny spoke under water to Salina with the latest under water communication equipment.

Manny communicated while under water. "Look Salina one of the dive hands from the boat is video taping all the divers."

Salina talked back to Manny while underwater. "The dive boat staff sells copies of the videos to the divers who want a great souvenir."

Manny ranted. "I like how the Giant Cod are friendly with the all tourists."

Salina discussed to Manny. "The boat hands are feeding the Giant cod bits of apples. That's why these giant fish love to see us." The big Cod devoured the small apple bits while everyone took under water pictures of an underwater paradise. With everyone at their safe limit of air, they ascended slowly.

With the divers back on board safely Kevin informed. "As you know these magnificent fish are all protected. I'm glad to see that only pictures were taken. Thank you all very much!"

While taking his dive gear off Manny divulged. "They are so politely direct here at times."

Salina rallied. "Seeing the large family of Potato Cod in their own habitat is the biggest thrill I've ever had."

Manny professed. "You mean it beat the snakes in Morocco?"

Salina crowed. "Of coarse! I wasn't holding any of the snakes. I was only taking the pictures from a distance." as she grinned. The dive tourists were presently on the outer edges of the Great Barrier Reef.

Manny told Salina and Kevin. "The dive services in Australia are very professional over many other country's services, I've experienced." Manny

Kevin conferred. "We cater to clients from around the world. The dive boat operators do all the small things to make the dive safe and comfortable for the dive and snorkel tourists. Some Australian natives literally fly across the continent to get to dive the reef."

Manny conveyed. "I see some divers here are very experienced, while others are new divers. Some divers need to be catered to a little bit."

Kevin stated. "The boat's advanced dive classes are on going for divers who want to up grade their certifications."

Salina cheerfully noted. "The awesome Aussie's are fun to dive with."

Manny clarified. "Having the Great Barrier Reef below the vessel doesn't hurt either." They are finally on their dive excursion.

After an over night ship's voyage while everyone sleep in their cabins Lizard Island was their next stop.

Lye another diver on the boat relayed. "That old geyser of a Captain better navigate this vessel carefully into the cove!

The another diver lounging on the deck popped off. "I hear there's lizards that roam the island bigger than men."

Lye roared. "That's right!"

In the early morning's dawn while standing at the ship's rail Manny said. "The Kiwi is leading this large vessel with only a small motorized dingy and a tow from one hundred yards in front of us."

Shirtless Lye explained. "Were entering a very shallow harbor in the lagoon. The captain has to be absolutely careful." You could hear a pin drop over the low motor idle into the lagoon

Lye accented. "This is the blue lagoon where Captain Cook once sailed into for refuge. He damaged the Ship Endeavor's hull on the shallow parts of the Barrier reef. The Captain and crew stayed here for some time until the ships hull was repaired right here centuries ago on Lizard Island."

Manny asked "What happened?"

Lye disclosed. "He hit a few bumps out here, but was still the first one to map this entire eastern coastline of Australia."

Salina interjected in a low whisper. "The Kiwi ship mate is still negotiating the ship into the shallow inlet as the boat slowly inches forward."

Inspirit Manny told Lye. "That was an amazing feat back in those days, and this is an amazing feat right now." as he pivoted away.

After stepping their way through the deck's water bubbles and up the aqua foamed stairs, they climbed past an indentured wood carved Sea Nymph and Water Lily Seahorse. Manny and Salina then lounged on the coral gabled promenade deck by themselves in light of the morning's silent sun. The ship finally docked in the middle of calm waters in the early morn blue lagoon.

After the dive meeting some of the divers suited up for the morning snorkel or dive into the shallow water. Others went ashore for a brisk walk on the beach. After a few day's on the ship, dry land felt great to everyone.

Kevin offered. "After the dive. I'll take anyone else who want's to go ashore on Lizard Island in the small dingy."

Manny roused. "I'll go Kevin. Come on Salina."

Kevin quickly said. "Let's go!"

The dominant coastal colors of rugged cliffs and the sandy shoreline of Lizard Island were scenically intimidating sitting in the keen blue waters.

Lye also with them on the sandy shore depicted. "Some divers came ashore with their wives take pictures while they smoked a joint of herb on the huge earth toned rock formations." as they the hermit crabs scampered across the sandy beach.

While standing near large tropical plants with vines growing out of the ocean cove's edge Manny synopsized. "They're really posing up a storm on those rounded raisin rock boulders that shaped like mini-mountains near the beach shoreline."

Salina gushed before they head back in. "I wish we had one of those sailboats that dote the harbor to sail the world."

Manny joshed. "That would be exciting."

Lye appraised. "The divers are excited because there are three daylight dives and one night dive where we will see the shallow lagoon's scary night sea creatures."

Manny looked at Salina. "They only come out at night!"

In the evening Manny asked one of the mates, Rip, about the Australian government's push to legalize sales and taxation of marijuana.

Rip admitted. "The politicians here are really hip and in tune with the times." The earringed mate further relayed. "They want to be fair to all the people they represent."

Manny asked. "Like regulated availability of pot?"

"Yea," the mate acknowledged.

Manny sounded off. "That's good news to my ears."

Rip continued. "Regulated availability of marijuana is going to be a reality in Australia. Their idea of the Cannabis Decriminalization Act proposal for marijuana sales over the counter is to sell marijuana at medical pharmacies."

Manny cracked. "Cool!"

Rip explained. "Marijuana grown under Australian licensing, and regulation will be as strictly controlled as alcohol and tobacco." While Manny and Salina listened intently the mate said. "The government just paid hundreds of marijuana users twenty dollars. To relive there experiences with marijuana use for the government's scientific study."

Manny induced. "I'm glad! I have friends and mates like you around the world who advocate for full legalization of grass. I see you're country is on the top of the current progress with the new laws being proposed. Were all happy your government has explored and implemented fair avenues."

Rip disclosed. "Were ahead of you yanks that's for sure."

Manny conveyed. "I can see that, and so is Canada," and further asked What do you think were fighting for?"

Rip stressed. "We live with freer marijuana laws here in Australia. You can grow ten plants for personal use in parts of south Australia.

Manny appraised. "Yea man the hydroponics industry must be going wild down under."

Rip stated. "Once the people obtain hydroponics equipment, they grow good grass for themselves. Then they start experimenting with fruits and vegetables organically grown without pesticides. The people get back to nature. Most people who grow pot plants end up growing other plants."

Manny agreed. "That makes sense" Manny told Rip while Salina listened on, while sipping on a beer. "What a life!"

Rip explained some of the drug problems. "One thing the government is trying to stop is all the imports of heroin into the country mostly from Chinese immigrants. The big drug lords are from mainland China. They run the drug cartels here. They control production of heroin in the golden triangle region of Asia for export. That's why there's more of a problem with hard drugs, than marijuana ever could be legalized or not. The government figures they're only getting about ten percent of the heroin entering the country." Manny nodded in acknowledgment while gaining a new understanding.

Manny disclosed. "We'd like to stem the flow of hard drugs in our society. Hard drugs lead to no where. But on the marijuana issue that's were we draw a hard line with the government's law. I can see the Australian government put some sanity back in the world."

Rip asked. "You like that ayy?"

"Yes I do. It's amazing!" Manny contended before everyone retired back to their ships cabin.

The following morning the escalated eastern mountains of Australia were paraded along the seaboard from the ship's western view. Salina loved the sight at sea of the mountain chain from the distance. Salina and Manny really enjoyed their essential fact-finding furlough. Salina was helpful to Manny on the all-absorbing marijuana law mission. This was to be their last day in Australia. They were leaving the following morning from the International Airport in Cairns.

Once on shore in Cairns, Manny retrieved his laptop from his hostel room. Manny quickly e-mailed Glady's with an update on the trip. Glady's changed Salina and Manny's flight to land in Bogota, Columbia for a quick stay, before going to Jamaica.

Before returning to Houston Salina over heard the conversation with Glady's and after Manny hung up the telephone; Salina gave Manny a big hug. Manny said "Yea man!" After they dined on Emu liver, and with a side of wahoo they were on the flight to Bogota within a few hours time. Manny took some smoked marlin with him wrapped in Asian vegetables.

He told Salina that the stop in Bogota Columbia for a few hours. They had a six hour lay over that could be dangerous. Salina saw Manny's nervous behavior and said. "Don't worry I know Spanish, and I've always wanted to go to Columbia."

Manny told Salina on the flight east. "George has a half dozen Macaw parrots, another dozen assorted tropical birds, a few dozen tropical plants and two champion llamas he wants imported back to the Untied States."

After the airliner landed in Bogota, George arranged for a Columbian native named Rico to take Manny to the Colombian government's exportation department.

Rico explained. "I have the proper export certificates so the animals can be shipped directly to the port of Houston. They will be accepted for quarantine with these papers."

They drove through downtown Bogota's unruly and festive streets. Rico's cousin Juan drove the taxi. Juan knew Manny was a pro-marijuana activist, and he promptly lit up some Colombian gold.

Excited Manny stressed. "Rico! I haven't had Colombian gold in over twenty years. Rico. This is the best joint so far on the whole trip. I haven't had that rich gold taste in over twenty years! Wow."

Rico relayed. "George told me you'd like to try some Colombian gold."

Manny admitted. "I'd like you to be my importer once we get marijuana legal in the United States for import and export."

Rico answered "No problemo."

Juan cheered. "I liked the taste of this Colombian Gold."

Rico advised. "We have to go through the Colombian custom's office for the final pay off and signatures on the animal export papers." Then Rico took Manny and Salina straight to the airport.

Rico crowed. "Salina Thank you. You were very helpful in the Colombian customs office, since Manny can't speak Spanish."

Manny praised. "Thanks Salina!" On their way around Bogota, and back to airport Manny stated. "Rico, I couldn't help but notice all the Military Police."

Manny asked Rico. "I've heard allot about of the political dangers in Columbia. How serious is it?"

Rico answered. "This is the main cocaine producing country in the world. Hard drugs produce major crimes and violence. It comes from the lucrative trade and heavy hard drug abuser's craving."

Manny asked. "Have you been able to contain the hard drugs?"

Rico answered. "No, the drug addiction rate from cocaine, heroin, sniffing gasoline, or glue is high in Columbia, because of the abundant supply and easy availability."

Juan informed. "All type's of hard drugs are available here to get high on. It consumes these hard core addicts. Sub-stance abuse is extremely heavy on the streets. Our country's social infrastructure internally suffer from the extreme violence caused by hard drug turf wars. Hard drugs equal hard violence for the movers and shakers of the seedy underground hard drug world."

Disappointed Manny said to Salina. "Look at those kids on the street sniffing glue. All the street kids sniff glue as a daily ritual."

Rico intervened. "Sometimes they are sniffing gasoline, when they have no glue. That's common here on the streets."

Juan confessed. "The drug cartel's support the guerilla groups who control the Cartels different coca patches, cocaine production labs and packaging operations."

Manny asked. "There's allot of cocaine here?"

Juan admitted. "Cocaine is readily available here like water is in your country unfortunately. There's ton's on top of ton's of cocaine here."

Rico affirmed. "The cartel operatives then escort the drugs to shipping points around the world along with political, military, police protection."

Juan pressed. "For some of these peasants and people involved here, this is their only means for an economic living. The drug cartels take care of those who take care of them. These people don't get welfare or social security checks like in America."

Rico revealed. "We may need the right international intervention to stop or curb the production of these hard drugs."

Manny stated. "That's for sure!"

Rico stressed. "These hard drugs are rooted throughout the social infrastructure of this country."

Juan resolved. "A lot of people would like to see the hard drugs gone, but the drug cartels are much too powerful."

Rico specified. "The people of Columbia have to make some hard decisions and generate brave action to stop the corporate cowboy's of the cocaine cartel's. These drug operatives are the chairman's of the board in these Latin American communities."

Juan divulged. "They like your countries American dollars, that's for sure." Rico said. "They won't just go away. These cartels are entrenched and sophisticated criminal organizations. They are very influential and powerful in their business."

Juan appealed. "Everyone is scared to death of the drug cartel's business."

Rico told the story of the town. "Bogota has the highest murder rate per capita in the world, because of the hard drug operatives violence."

Juan pleaded. "Another problem is the leftist rebels. They control over half of Columbia."

Rico explained. "They set up roadblocks all over the countryside. They then confine and steal from travelers."

Juan conceded. "The well to do people can't even go to their large estates in the interior. Kidnapped people are sold to leftists guerillas. They hold them as hostage's for ransom."

Rico admitted. "Extortion from kidnapping is going on in great proportions."

After hearing that Manny and Salina asked Rico. "Are we close to the Airport yet?"

Rico laughed. "Almost!" While driving down the winding road toward the Bogota International Airport Terminal. Military Police were prevalent everywhere they went in Bogota. After some quick, good byes Manny and Salina were on their flight to Jamaica. Rico and Juan told Manny everything he wanted to know.

Manny and Salina kept track of their informative inquiry of the Columbian drug trade. They kept mental notes until they boarded the plane. Manny with his lap top hooked up on the airliner, e-mailed his findings to Glady's.

Manny told Salina on the plane to Jamaica. "I'm glad we left Columbia. Some how I didn't feel safe there. It sure can't be a safe vacation area."

Salina commented. "That's why we didn't stay long."

On arrival in Kingston, Jamaica, George had Manny and Salina shuttled from the International Airport straight to Ocho Rios resort. With increasing attacks on tourists, some robbed by gun point, Jamaican officials ordered foot soldiers on beach patrols. Undercover security officers were posted in the most troubled spots. Even with the abundance bicycled police, Ganja was in plentiful, everywhere in Jamaica.

Manny gamed. "I'm wasn't even out of the airport and two taxi drivers tried to sell me Ganja."

Salina reasoned. "That was quick, we haven't even been here fifteen minutes, and you already have a bag of weed Manny."

Manny laughed while looking at his bag of Ganja. "Yea! I beat my best time in country for possession of marijuana."

At mountainous Ocho Rios Mediterranean village on the Caribbean Sea. Manny talked with Clint on the cabana's walled phone from an inclusive luxury resort. It is an exclusive resort for couples only. Clint told Manny. "George is ecstatic you're getting such incriminating crucial facts concerning the cannabis culture. Manny your cannabis investigative material is self-explanatory. Your round the world marijuana mission is a total success. We all elated "Globetrotter."

Manny joshed. "Goldtoker" would be a better explanation."

Manny slowly reassured. "Well thanks! I'm glad our mission was accomplished. Salina and I will be very grateful to see you and Chantel when we hit Houston. See Yea!" At the exotic gourmet restaurant, the charming waiters and busboys treated Manny and Salina like royalty. Salina and Manny swam in the large Olympic style pool, and used the steam room and whirlpool to no avail. They both had there own masseuse rub them down before they left for the evening.

That night Manny and Salina were scheduled to attend a beach party on the white sandy beach waterfront. The tourists stopped at a Jamaican hand craft market first. Manny picked out a beautiful hand carved wooden pipe for a souvenir. Manny lit a bowl his own Ganja up.

Bob the Jamaican pipe salesman blustered. "Here Man! Try some of my weed," the manager supplied a sample of weed for every pipe bought from him."

Manny answered' "No problem" as he quickly put the pot in his newly bought pipe.

Bob conceded. "Were smoking our way into the next century. It is better than shooting our way though it."

Manny ranted. "I hear that! I wish our politicians back in the United States realized that."

Manny asked Bob who looked like a beach bum. "Would you accompany Salina and me to a beach party later tonight. You can supply us with some more of that good Jamaican weed."

Soon Manny and Bob struck up a conversation about the politics of marijuana in Jamaica. Bob told Manny. "Were pushing to formally legalize the "Ganja." That is the main campaign going on in our country."

Manny informed. "My country too." They all laughed.

Bob apprised. "Yea, but at least they don't bother marijuana users here so much. Jamaican weed is accepted here by our society."

Manny divulged. "Well I guess that's a break!"

Bob adamantly said. "The prominent heads of our state government are pushing for full legalization of marijuana. The movement is gaining public wide support in Jamaica."

Salina investigated. "Do the Jamaicans use marijuana for religious beliefs?"

Bob attested. "We had a lady doctor come here from a nursing college in Iowa. She was a reefer researcher from your country who claimed to have never smoked marijuana. She came first hand to understand and judge for herself. She lived in our villages to see Ganja used among our people's everyday life and for religion. She has seen how the men, pregnant women, old men, and children live in a Ganja society. Her reports were all positive despite all the political pressure she received from reporting her truthful findings."

Manny induced. "All the intelligently analyzed reports on cannabis are positive."

Bob continued. "Their are some Rastafarians, who use and smoke marijuana in religious rituals, and adhere to their strong African cultural beliefs. They firmly detest their interpretation of their religion by foreigners or governments. The Rastafarians claim the government has recognized that preventing Rastafarians from smoking Ganja is a breach of their religious liberties. Ganja helps to give us a vision to see. The Rastafarians say using marijuana in their rituals is inherent to their beliefs."

Salina enounced. "That's interesting, Manny and I have found other religions around the world who have said the same."

Bob explained to Manny and Salina. "Others simply enjoy marijuana better, than alcohol."

Manny asked. "Have there been any extensive studies concerning marijuana here?"

Bob answered. "The Ministry of Health has done marijuana legalization studies. These studies have concluded, again that the use of marijuana is no more of a threat than other legal substances."

Manny emphasized. "Actually marijuana is much less harmful than other legal substances. All major institutionalized studies of marijuana use showed no major ill effects from chronic use, and found no abnormalities of the brain physiology."

Bob admitted. "Jamaica's own police commissioner also said legalize all drugs instead of this mad and insane drug war. Prohibition plays into the hand of organized crime. The Jamaican police commissioner said the U S drug officials know Jamaica is a large staging point for trafficking of drugs into the United States. Stop this drug war!"

Manny exulted. "I'll second that!"

Bob further stated. "My government concluded that the reasons marijuana is illegal are economic. Drug barons make out the best because of the black market drug trade. They get richer and richer and more entrenched into the economy while the lucrative drug war continues."

Salina recanted. "That's the way it is all over."

Bob said to Manny. "My wife Bari will watch the bosses hand craft and pipe business. Let's go to the beach Manny. Let's have a good time."

Manny lashed out. "Yea man!"

Salina railed. "Yea, man!"

Manny professed Bob as they paced. "I'm really digging the fact that were in another country where the women are allowed to take off their tops on the beach."

Bob asked. "They don't take off there tops in the U.S.?"

Manny admitted. "No Bob, not in the greatest majority of the U.S." The new found friends were under a cabana on the beach. Pina coladas were carried to them on the beach by the waiters. They waited for the nighttime party, while the festive Bob Marley music played well into the early evening.

Manny pledged. "I enjoy being in countries with liberal views on marijuana.

Bob persisted. "In your opinion marijuana legalized would be the cat's ass."

Manny embellished. "Yea, if it were legal for personal choice, that would be politically correct." Manny thanked Bob for his hospitality, before going back to the motel room for the night.

Manny persisted. "I'll see you in Washington. here's an airline ticket for you and your wife. Compliments of George."

Bob promised. "I'll see you in Washington for a Rosta Rally. I'll bring all the Rastafarians I can round up!"

Salina marveled. "Cool!"

The following day was spent in complete leisure, jet skiing, scuba diving and snorkeling up and down the Jamaican barrier reef. Wind surfers skimmed over the waves of the sparkling seas. Under a sterling blue sky, the resort's glass bottom boat filled with reef tourists left the pier.

Manny remarked. "Look at the catch. I've retrieved twenty four bugs from the ocean floor."

Salina rattled. "Bugs!"

Manny quipped. "Yes, bugs that's how they are known to the scuba divers. There actually lobsters."

Salina admitted. "I love lobsters, with a little butter on them."

On the last night of Manny and Salina's trip, and before their flight in the morning to Houston, Salina and Manny cooked their cache of lobster. The lobster was basted with only butter and a light touch of sweet and sour sauce.

Manny prophesied. "Lobster is an ultimate cap on our very fruitful trip." Manny and Salina spent a peaceful last night together.

Chapter 11... As they arrived in Houston the next morning, George, Clint, Miles, Chris, Igor, Chico, Alfonso, Jose, and their girlfriends and friends them picked up in three limousines.

After greetings were exchanged, everyone was abuzz. They talked about the upcoming hemp rally strategies. Last minute strategies still had to be planned for Clint. The stream of limousines went straight to Clint's farm to work on the new pro-marijuana agendas.

Miles had various hemp reports and publications from newspapers and magazines, Internet web sites from the movement's current pro-marijuana agenda.

Miles than lamented. "Well! I hate to break the news but the hemp farming and manufacturing operation of "Hemp-Argo International" in Nicaragua that Jose and Alfonso just visited got raided!"

Everyone was asking questions like. "What do you mean?" "What!" all at once.

Miles expounded while everyone listened intently. "Dr Wylie went to the bank to get the payroll for the fifty workers. They were on there way back when some of the black hooded DEA trained National Police anti-narcotics brigade motorcycle drivers pulled up and sprayed their car with bullets. The attackers identified themselves as police and dragged Dr Wylie off to Somoza's old dungeon prison. A US employed DEA Agent in Nicaragua said it looked like marijuana under a microscope. Hemp-Argo's hemp field at Sabana Grande near the Capitol of Managua was confiscated. Government official's who gave the permits denied they gave the hemp permits."

Clint asked Miles. "What is the Canadian hemp company's position?"

Miles continued as he read the press release. "The President of Hemp-Argo International, Grant Sanders said they have spent thousands of dollars in research, development, and planting, and that this is a true injustice in a society that has it's own rules. We had all the official permission to grow "Hemp" in their country. We have been cheated and abused by the government of Nicaragua. It was our intention to help the people of Nicaragua and give them an agricultural alternative for the new millenium. The government is not only hurting us but destroying the hopes of their people."

Clint raged. "This is another prime example of our government "Hoodwinking" and meddling where they shouldn't have no concern of who's growing industrial hemp."

Miles noted. "On the brighter side our fight, the media is sizzling and finally starting to support the people who favor marijuana legalization. This political movement is going to get the debates for decriminalization of marijuana and with the media coverage that we've pushed for."

Chris informed. "Pro-marijuana activists across the country seized the moment. Their demands for fairness and truth are expressed in most media venues."

Igor relayed. "Opposition to legalization has sparked up Sen. Stan Stalinski's nasty disposition. The opposition wanted to pass legislation ending cannabis rallies. One prosecutor said. "He would seize the property that sponsors any hemp rally which openly celebrated an illegal substance."

Miles counseled. "That clearly violates the first amendment, and blocks the people's right to peaceably assemble."

Clint unloaded. "Bargaining in bad faith by the government to it's citizens is their norm. Argumentative "Meanie" backed up ill tempered Sen. Stan Stalinski in the media. The staunch prohibitionist attacked all opposing venues of the pro-marijuana movement with a vengeance."

Clint and the pro marijuana group kept a cooperative attitude throughout all proceedings. Clint said to everyone. "The truth calms my nerves."

Igor professed. "The truth make the government leaders nervous."

Miles vented. "Distinguished decriminalization campaigns expose the swarming hot beds of organized crime throughout the nation concerning police corruption, mismanagement, miscalculation, which is all directed at public enemy number one the marijuana smoker."

The meeting at Clint's went on for six hours before Clint, Igor, and Chris took their plane in waiting to Ann Arbor, Michigan for the Annual "Hash Bash." Some of the talk circulating the rally concerned medical marijuana patient. The wheel-chaired activist protest lit a joint of marijuana in Rep Bill McCollum's office. McCollum's co-authored bigoted pending legislation to end nationwide medical-marijuana initiatives against sick people.

Clint confirmed after hearing about the bigoted overbearing proposed anti-medical marijuana federal legislation. "She is a very brave women! Igor call Miles! See what we can do to help!"

Igor responded. "I'll get right on it! Who the hell does that McCollum guy think he is! Nobody elected him to shit on the Constitution. Let's make sure our voting fire power down there in Florida eats him up in the next election."

Clint reassured. "That's for sure!"

Clint, and Chris went straight for the University of Michigan's Diag, the site of the Hash Bash. Joe Astro is signing his latset pro-cannabis novel." Clint remembered visiting a war buddy and attending the 1973 Hash Bash. Michigan State Representative Perry Bullard smoked a hemostated joint of marijuana in front of newspaper and television cameras.

Clint told Chris. "I was impressed with the man. He was ahead of his time. He stood up for what he believed was right. Perry was strong and unbending in beliefs. No matter how unpopular the truth is or what political repercussions he could suffer. He unselfishly put it all on the line"

Chris asked. "Did he get in trouble?"

Clint answered. "Scurrilous ignorant legislatures attempted to censure Perry in the Michigan Legislature but failed. He was re-elected and never backed down. He also supported legal prostitution."

Chris surprisingly said. "He did?"

Clint responded. "Yes he did! Do you know, he was right! If they listened to him years ago, this AIDS epidemic would be diminutively contained. Serious crime would be way down and society would be adversely safer."

Chris reported. "A statement by University of Michigan director of Public safety Leo Heatley reported on a past Hash Bash Festival said. "This was a mellow crowd, no trouble at all."

Clint conceded. "This is the mid-west's foremost and fun cannabis show of continuity." after the featured speakers the cannabis bands played on to a joyous audience.

Nobody would question Energetic Body Building Igor in his chiseled physique. He enounced to patrons as they were steadily entering the line to sign the new "Michigan's Medical Marijuana Initiative." petition. "I'm trying to locate the medical marijuana patient that smoked that joint in Rep McCollum's office who was arrested for protesting the medical marijuana laws?

One Hash Bash speaker said. "The government wouldn't listen to her! So she lit the joint up. Now she's received National coverage."

Chris hashed over. "They really have some informative speakers here! They emphasize in their fight against the prohibition to "Fight Intellectually Smart" as everyone listen to Guest speaker Tommy Chong speak.

Now, at the hemp rally in Madison, Wisconsin, Clint read his "American Cannabis Society" literature out-loud to Chris. "This is incredible cannabis information. Everyone should read real news. I hope to meet some of their members."

Always in support Chris stated. "I agree! They also have Alaska and Florida Chapters. There is anther cannabis group based here called "American Marijuana Political Action Committee." but their calling for you now."

Clint acknowledged. "OK Chris!" Clint then walked up and opened his speech. "The news is still fresh in my mind about a Wisconsin youth, who was shot down by a police officer during a drug raid which netted three marijuana cigarettes. After a no knock entry the dubious police drug squad implemented it's search warrant. No firearms were found in the families trailer, yet the unsuspecting marijuana user was gunned down in the privacy of his home.

The Wisconsin youth, who was a father himself, was shot dead as his son slept in the next room. The innocent son after being awakened watched the paramedic's take his dead father out of the trailer on a stretcher. The father left a blood trail on the trailer floor all the way out the door. The marijuana-using father was pronounced DOA at the hospital.

The anguished boy is in custody with his grandparents, and with an everlasting indelible mark on his karma. The drug squad deputy who shot the father is under investigation by the Wisconsin government. At the grand jury hearing, the officer testified. "I do not remember pulling the trigger of the gun which killed the Wisconsin man."

Clint asked his audience. "How can we have cops who participate in drug raids on our cannabis citizens, and then can't remember what he's doing. These drug officers are inadequate misfits. They represent our government with nothing more than a con, a sham and a total rape of the tax payers money."

Clint conveyed. "We will spread the truth and expose the evils of the marijuana war going on across this country. Citizens groups support citizens who are unjustly branded as criminals just because they are using marijuana in the privacy of their homes. It's realized by a large majority that the marijuana drug war is wrong. Most citizens feel that smoking a marijuana cigarette is no crime at all." Convincingly Clint concluded his speech at the to an excited and applauding audience. One hemp protestor from the "Institute for Hemp" came down from St. Paul, Minnesota to show support cheered Clint on.

The pro-marijuana strategists at George's office are going over all the hemp rally's polices. Brant and Chris of the pro-marijuana political management and marketing team continued to plan the agenda of the hemp and marijuana rallies.

Brant professed. "Our preparation for the next Rally at the Boston Common's is going to be today's task."

Glady's affirmed. "The Hemp Parade Buses will follow Brant and Chris as they walk in the Float Filled Hemp Parade which proceeds the Rally."

Brant avowed. "I'm concerned about pace of the hemp friendship float at rally. I want to know where the media cameras and other recording equipment to document the upcoming event are placed for maximum exposure."

Glady's informed. "My staff is concerned with the timing and calculating of each hemp rally. We want to make sure we cover all the rallies with our best resources. These informational marijuana and hemp rallies are getting bigger and bigger every year."

Brant explained. "The National Organization for the Reform of Marijuana Laws (NORML) are usually in attendance at the marijuana rally's. The NORML Foundation was established in 1972 and has since stood up for marijuana reform. NORML people will educate people with literature with their views concerning marijuana re-form laws."

Chris reinterated. "Look at this NORML Leaflet quote from their Executive Director R. Keith Stroup who said. "NORML intends to give voice to the millions of Americans who smoke marijuana, and send an unequivocal message to our elected officials: Stop arresting marijuana smokers."

Brant roused. "I totally agree!" as did everyone else engaged.

Clint now at the Boston Commons told to the audience. "The political pro-marijuana groups have organized hemp rallies in numerous communities throughout the nation. Were active in every city and state. Depending on where the hemp rally is held, each pro-marijuana political force will have there own pro-marijuana and hemp speakers. They all have their own personal stories about police abuse and civil liberty violations within the marijuana wars."

Clint while on stage told the audience. "I'm sorry for the widow of a recent ill-fated raid that went wrong by the drug squad in Massachusetts. The widow's husband was a frail seventy-five year old minister.

The overtrained trained narcotics officers killed the minister in the middle of the raid. He died choking on his own vomit while handcuffed by narcotics agents, while their home was being ransacked by the other drug officers. The narcotics officers later admitted that they were at the wrong address and apologized."

Clint divulged that a friend of the minister told him. "There is to much of these ill fated drug raids going on in our communities."

Chris positioned next to Clint announced. "Political marijuana reform organizations and clubs are circulating petitions for marijuana legalization initiatives. Please sign the petitions at the entrance booth if you want marijuana legalized."

Clint professed. "This hemp rally is equal in stature to the staggering magnitude of the Boston Tea party. The Boston Freedom Rally is the biggest pro-marijuana legalization rally on the East Coast of the United States.

These are authentic American citizens of the homeland. No truer Americans exist. Admiralty of the pro-marijuana populace exists between those who attend these Freedom and Hemp Rallies. Instead of citizens objecting to the King's tax. The people object to their lost freedoms from a governmental dictatorship. The issue of personal choice concerning marijuana is what we want fairly addressed. These good citizens here are casualties of the American drug war." as they walked off the stage.

Igor disclosed to Brant behind stage. "Some forsaken citizens have had enough. We stand tall in our large numbers at these freedom rallies."

Brant stated. "United we the people are strong. Police will not wade into the mutiltude to make mass arrests. They arrested over forty participants who set up the pro-marijuana rally, before the large crowds had gathered for the day. The police did consider bringing water cannons to disperse the compelling pro-marijuana crowds."

Clint lectured. "Once the crowds are seventy-five thousand strong here at the Boston Common the youthful crowds will light up marijuana pipes and circulate marijuana cigarettes as is casual custom. You can pass your joints from one rally attendee to another. The support and camaraderie of the people who smoke marijuana is self-evident. The high volume of protestors lit marijuana joints and pipes as a strong protest for broader public support."

Brant explained. "The MBTA officials set record highs in commuter trains, and subway riders arriving into the city, they actually broke the attendance record at this rally. Bus's rolled in non-stop with adult citizens and teen-agers to the Freedom Rally. I like how the pro-marijuana speakers at the rally blasted lawmakers for jailing marijuana users. These speakers were here to protect free speech and the pro-marijuana associations they represented."

Police in uniforms were called PIGS by some of the uncompromising elements of the crowd. They heckled the police for not being able to catch real criminals who do real crimes. One protester yelled. "The cops are the ones who deserve jail time."

Another man yelled. "Nobody deserves to go to jail for smoking a joint of marijuana!" Everyone felt life wasn't supposed to be lived as a individual litmus test.

Later Clint, Brant, Chris, Pat, Igor and the other hemp rally participants had gathered at Clint's. The Constitutionalists pro-marijuana freedom fighters talked over the hemp conferences, hemp rallies, and other pro-marijuana political gathering's results and demanding accountability. Were against prohibitive extra costs charged to the tax payer. The Constitutionalists were tired of seeing the losing drug war machine feed itself at the expense of the freedom, which has made us the freest country in the world. The government tears into innocent citizens lives in monstrous and incriminating proportions by over taxing, and over bearing judicial policies which dominate and deprive us of our individual freedom.

Clint started out the meeting. "The Police had plenty of undercover vice squad members mixed in with the pro-marijuana crowds at all the rallies. The crowds are generally peaceful. The hemp goers are resentful of police who repress freedom in America. They are recreational users of pot at best. They are no different from any other citizen in their communities, who don't smoke marijuana. They lived similar lives in every other sense of reality. They are here to protest at the hemp rallies. The time has come to quit incarcerating marijuana users. We are here at the hemp rallies to test the American system."

Brant illustrated. "The federal law making marijuana illegal is what is scary, not pot, or pot the smokers. The Libertarian Party Candidates was in attendance. They talked about the rights and freedom being denied and how marijuana should be legalized for personal use without prosecution from anyone."

Igor while in attendance with the crowd noticed. "The cannabis users smoked joints, and pipes right out in the open in the park and listened to the free hemp music on stage. Everyone enjoyed themselves. Where there were no cops, there were no hassles."

Chris induced. "I liked hearing about the marijuana medical relief that the Florida resident enjoyed. She suffered from the pain of glaucoma and was one of only eight people in the United States federally allowed to smoke marijuana. She emphasized the positive about how smoking marijuana kept her glaucoma in perspective."

Political Pat stopped by and informed. "Different States are gaining momentum and continually approving forums for the legalization of hemp industries and some are endorsing all out marijuana legalization.

Certain governors have ended military operations in their states searching for marijuana and hemp fields, where the herb searches turned up menial amounts. The lawsuits that developed from failed drug busts have reached epidemic proportions. Justification for the governors to cease the marijuana searches is evident."

Brant equivocated. "Hemp rally after rally, more and more mayors, police chiefs, legislators and responsible citizens of the community are coming out of the closet with endorsements for marijuana and hemp legalization. Amnesty for all citizens convicted for small amounts of marijuana is now proposed by the Cannabis wing of Constitutional Party Candidates. Right Pat!"

Pat exuberated. "That's for sure! Jails from state to state should release prisoners convicted for small amount's of marijuana possession or use. Probation departments have been requested to drop small marijuana offences for off their books. The backlogs for probationers and minor warrants are impossible to keep up with.

Brant came back. "What about the drug warrior's continuing effort?"

Pat consoled. "With an anticipated Constitutional Party's victory into the White House, we will abolish the office of the Drug Czar. There will be no Czar of any kind over any American. We will abolish any agency that cannot distinguish the difference between marijuana and hard drugs like cocaine and heroin. We will abolish any agency or arm of the government that tramples on American citizens individual constitutional rights."

Clint pledged. "Sounds like the way to go Pat. Keep the freedom ingenuity up!"

Brant imputed. "I'll read the synopsis of the Colorado's pro-cannabis movement from an industrial hemp conference in Colorado. Hemp sandwiches were served, different farmers associations and many businessmen from around the country and world were in attendance. They were in attendance to discuss the latest results from last year's experimental crops of industrial hemp. This hemp program has the support of the farmers.

Container companies have bought hemp fibers to manufacture commercial packaging. The businesses constantly display their new designs at the hemp rallies, and all the packaging is made from hemp."

Pat expounded. "One farmers association representative promoted hemp agriculture. He wouldn't give any pro marijuana groups any interviews because they said their cause was for rope not dope."

Clint limned. "Let me tell you something. Even the prejudice straight lacers in the hemp farmers association should thank all the pro marijuana groups for exposing the truth about the espionage of the hemp industry. I'll guarantee you one thing! The hemp industry definitely wouldn't get it's foot back in the door if it wasn't for the pro-marijuana and other hemp movement associations who are strongly affiliated trying to keep American politicians honest.

Pat notified. "Established hemp farmers weren't even allowed to grandfather their livelihoods or family traditions, even though hemp had been such a valuable and proven commodity that is so extensively intertwined throughout American History."

Clint decreed. "That was just another slap in the face for the American farmer!"

Pat explained. When they destroyed the hemp industry in America they in essence destroyed the strains that were compatible with their own demographics. We have to get rid of those evil forces that oppose a free democracy!"

Clint agreed. "That's a must!"

Brant continued. "There are reports that America is losing over one-hundred million a year because of imported hemp seeds and products currently entering the country legally. Businessmen have expressed interest in entrepreneurship for hemp products at an escalating pace. Over two hundred and fifty thousand hemp products are currently being made around the world."

Chris expressed. "I think we've presented all sides of the issues today for the upcoming hemp rallies. Quality hemp paper made tree free for letter heads are available here by my laser printer." He suggested at meeting's close.

Clint consulted. "Brant were you able to make all the necessary accommodations?"

Brant exulted. "Yes! I've arranged all the travel accommodations."

Clint chortled. "Great Brant! This will officially close this cannabis strategy session. I'll see you all at the next Hemp Rally in Kentucky!"

All the pro-marijuana players were at this very large hemp rally in Kentucky. At a cannabis rally in Louisville Kentucky, was the governor of Kentucky stated. "I created a hemp fiber task force. I acted on information concerning all aspects of the hemp industry. I just recently visited the Hemp Museum in Charlottesville, Kentucky. Thanks to the Turner Foundation our national heritage is being acknowledged. Government subsidized deforestation has alternatives as you will see if you visit the Hemp Museum."

The controversial governor spoke in between rounds of applause from the audience. "I'm seriously listening to new law and business proposals from pro-marijuana and hemp activists. The pro-marijuana activists propose to build a city named Hemp Town.

Hemp town once is established on the Ohio River in the state of Kentucky, marijuana would be legal to smoke and grow for personal use as well as hemp agricultural purposes. It makes not only sense, but a lot of dollars as well. Hemptown will be a world port with import access and exportation egress for all concerns of the cannabis industry. The largest cash crop in the state of Kentucky was hemp at one time. It was abolished by industrial special interest's meddling with the federal government.

A recent lawsuit has been filed in Lexington Kentucky U S District Court suing the Federal government by hundreds of past and prospective hemp farmers. Hemp farming in Kentucky is going to be realized. It's just a matter of how soon.

The hemp farmer plaintiffs argued that hemp prohibition violates constitutional doctrine in separating governmental authority. The hemp farmers argued that there is a big difference in making rope and smoking dope.

The DEA countered that if hemp farming was legal real marijuana could be hidden easily in the crops of hemp, since both related plants are from the cannabis sativa plant. The hemp farmers argued that hemp seed is by far more nutritious than soybeans. Hemp seeds are high on B, C, E, vitamins and do not contain THC. Soy beans don't possess the same high quality potent content as hemp seeds. The hemp farmers argue that all other industrialized nations grow industrial hemp. They asked what country is the leader of the free world? When can this free nation compete in the world's hemp industry on an even playing ground in a free world market?

The governor strongly proclaimed. "The hemp industry will be re-established in the state of Kentucky." to an applauding crowd.

The governor said at the Louisville rally. "At one time. "Kentucky grew over ninety per cent of the nation's hemp, and with the grace of God we'll do ninety percent again. I want the State of Kentucky's legislators to sponsor a bill to change the name of one county in the state to Cannabis County. The county would then receive a state grant, and pro-marijuana, subsidies for the new establishment of Hemp town as the new county seat."

"The Governor's name for Cannabis County, Kentucky has a ring to it." Clint relayed to Igor while listening to the governors speech in Louisville, Kentucky."

The governor continued. "Cannabis County will receive subsidies from the state to establish a Hemp Industry Complex. The Cannabis Complex will be complete with Hemp Mercantile Stores. The complex will be a model for the nation. If the Federal government doesn't want to share the expense for the new hemp complex, then the federal government shouldn't expect to tax the hemp goods. If the federal government wants to take away our federal tax subsidy money, the state can more than make up for that chicken change through the profits from hemp after the state funding of the hemp industry. Kentucky is losing tobacco growing farms, because of a decline of tobacco sales. The farmers want and need an alternative cash crop. Profits are much higher and safer for hemp production than tobacco. Environmentally intoxicating properties involved in growing hemp are non existent. The farmers want lucrative alternative crops now."

The governor went further after an approving audience aggressively cheered. "Taxing marijuana use and keeping the peace with citizens is the way to go. We can then get on pace with the rest of the world's economy by getting involved in the hemp industry." The governor then concluded his speech.

Another Kentucky Gubernatorial Candidate had proposed a one thousand pound for personal use and possession tax on marijuana. Estimations for the hemp industry tax revenues are between twenty to fifty dollars per acre for growing hemp industrially. One Estimation for personal consumption of marijuana in the State of Kentucky alone was for over one-million pounds per year.

The political candidate joining the political race for governor in the State of Kentucky is known as the "Last Free Man in America." He said. "We can restore liberty by taking government out of our bedrooms, our bloodstream's, our bladders, our brains, our businesses and our back-pockets."

Clint told Miles before his speech. "Speaking of the Gatewoods's statement. I couldn't of said that better myself!"

Political Pat disclosed. "I'm not alone with my cannabis views in the political arena."

Clint contended. "That's for sure. Your not alone!"

Clint walked to the podium at the Kentucky rally and began his speech. "The states rights will prevail over the federal government's totalitarian standards. Similar standards from the norm are practiced in Las Vegas, Nevada for gambling and prostitution. You can go to any chicken ranch out there in Nevada and buy a prostitute. But Nevada has some of the stiffest marijuana laws and some of the most crooked cops in the country.

Of coarse all the cities, counties, and states across the country have police miss-management of police training that breeds confrontation and repetitive demographic corruption problems. It's like Cancer that needs drastic chemotherapy shocks.

Toxic free hemp textiles factories can be established in newly formed Hemp Town. Hemp manufacture and exported hemp products from Cannabis County. Hemp Fashions shows are presently being held in Knoxville on a weekly basis without Kentucky grown hemp. Show support and go and buy hemp products wherever available. We need Kentucky grown hemp!

This is a new Manual of Marijuana Laws created by the Cannabis Wing of Constitutional Party. Candidate Political Pat has presented the proposal to the Kentucky's State legislature. If implemented Kentucky would lead by example in our national marijuana drug policy. Fair and lenient laws that allow possession, sale, or bartering small amounts of marijuana amongst peers without persecution, prosecution, or prison should be established. Police could longer to use small marijuana as a guise to roust citizens. Police would no longer be allowed to kill, maim, rob, or intimidate marijuana users in their homes.

Rural areas of the mountains where the economy doesn't thrive like New York City grow marijuana and hemp crops to feed their families. Some people are plain tired of being poor. Under our proposals residents could grow and sell marijuana to support their family without prosecution in Kentucky, just like the farmers below the boarders of the Rio Grande River do. Other states will follow suite to be more in touch with their cannabis citizens. Less chance of government and police corruption in a new streamlined governing system of free choice and fair laws, that are being proposed by the Constitutional Party of America's Candidate Political Pat. A more Citizen friendly governmental management system will be established. If a citizen gets pulled over by the police and the cannabis citizens passes the marijuana Motor Skills endorsement test on your license. Then you are allowed to drive your car, just like using tobacco or using your cell phone. Simple fines at best when concerning the roadways. The joint best be out by the time the police officer gets to the car or a fine of up to five hundred dollars could be levied. You still have to show respect and stability under the marijuana code book for use, and personal possession guidelines. No fines in homes or for endorsed areas of cannabis use.

Citizens are responsible for their own mistakes. Under the cannabis code book guidelines marijuana could never be used as a defense for a citizens personal mistakes or ignorance of the law in court. Similar guidelines for Marijuana Laws are established in other parts of the free world. Fines and penalties remain stiff for school ground marijuana sales. The same as for tobacco and alcohol. Governmental regulations would now exist similarly for all three. Alcohol is a real problem on the roads and public highways. If people who drink alcohol on the highways smoked marijuana only, alcohol related accidents rates would be down. In essence this Manuel of newly formed marijuana proposals would give the public a much safer substance for recreation where everyone benefits.

The Marijuana Industry in the State of Kentucky is already thriving with an under ground black market. There's no social end one way or the other legally as far as marijuana use is concerned. The only difference is if it's a free and open market or not. Free enterprise should finally rule again concerning the hemp and marijuana. The truth is healthy for everyone. People should feel free to come out of the closet, without fear of prosecution. These are the same ideals upon which America was founded.

Creative Artists have been flocking to the proposed Cannabis County Kentucky Free Enterprise and Expression Zone. A safe haven for freedom, just like a church sanctuary. Cannabis Attitudes and their own moral beliefs will prevail in the proposed Crittenden County. Crittenden want's to take the huge financial package of incentives offered by the State of Kentucky to invest in the county. The County Residents will to be given priority for jobs in Hemptown. Hemptown will be established and built completely on barren land on banks of the Ohio River. River boat barges will go to up and down the river running hemp supplies, commodities, and textiles.

The first Hemp dedicated agricultural mill will be built in newly Historic Hemptown. The states first cannabis café's will also be established in Hemptown. The Kentucky Gubenatorial Candidate was adamant about change. The people of this state want to give hemp legalization a go. Pro-marijuana political activists have moved in-groups to the former Crittenden County to establish a voting power base. Political Candidates from that area are pro-marijuana and were put on the ballots for every electoral position. Pro-marijuana politicians of the Constitutional Party had gained control of a pro-marijuana county.

Hemptown City Hall will be built with Hemp Materials grown in Kentucky. The opposition marijuana politicians said. Smoking Marijuana is like opening up a commercial moonshine still. Yet, every one here agrees Marijuana smokers are much more coherent and level headed then any abusive alcohol user. You can talk to a marijuana user. You can't talk to an alcoholic drunk, unless your drunk.

The Pro-marijuana political goal is to have the first hemp auto-fuel full service gas station in Hemptown. All illumination from the gas station will use clean burning hemp fuel. Hemptown will join many other United States counties, cities, and township's with the same namesake.

Gone! Is the wide array of extensive bribes and payoffs by governmental officials. The value of black market of the marijuana drug war would be eliminated. The deception, lies, cover-ups will also be eliminated because of the new marijuana decriminalization proposals. These new laws take the teeth out of marijuana's taxable profits continually leaving our state. Days of marijuana as an untaxed illegal commodity for the most part will be gone."

Clint told the attendees who followed the hemp festivals. "The days of the war on marijuana smoking citizens are dwindling down fast. Repression in our country's history must be eliminated at all levels of society."

Clint said now quoted **John F Kennedy. "A nation is not free until all it's citizen's are free."** Clint continued speaking to the crowd which was in a frenzy of approval. "A government saying you can have apples and peaches, but you can't have pears is gone. The government shouldn't be able to make personal moral judgement calls for its citizens. The government needs to get out of the personal morality business, The government teaching tactics of war on citizens isn't the way of being neighborly. This state has eliminated criminal marijuana laws. This state now allows possession of small amounts of marijuana.

The pro-marijuana activists will take any county in the United States as a free marijuana rights domain, including the poorest county in the country. We'll move there just to escape federal persecution. Give us some space and see our beneficial and peaceful progression into a free society. This society will be built on diversity. Citizen creative diversity must prevail." Clint trotted off the stage with his speech being applauded.

The next hemp rally was in Miegs County Ohio. The students on the campus of Ohio State were aware of Miegs Bud. Miegs County along with a few others in the Ohio river valley are world renowned for their home grown pot. Miegs county was viewed for the Hemp town concept along with Lawrence County in Ohio. They both wanted hemp subsidies that went along with the distinction.

All players were at Clint's farmhouse office. They discussed details of the past and upcoming hemp festivals. Miles summarized a Tennessee hemp festival. "In Tennessee a prominent United States District Judge joined a list of over one-hundred federal judge's who favor legalization of marijuana. Some want all out marijuana legalization.

The judge cited that billion of dollars are spent annually on the drug war. A drug war the government always has lost on all avenues. Who commands this fruitless marijuana fight crush citizens individual rights? The government has fought this pot war for over sixty years. The government hasn't made any headway, they have lost ground every year since. Partnership for drug free America is a farce. One former federal judge stated. "The marijuana battle has been lost."

Miles continued. "At another rally in Chicago, A speaker told how the Supreme Court spoke out against sweeping marijuana raids by law enforcement. Committed pro-legalization Federal judges are just saying no to small time marijuana cases because they yield little benefits in a judicial system punishment is just not working. The judge will be at the next forum. He thinks congress should take a serious look at legalization of marijuana."

Chris told Clint and Company. "One speaker at the hemp told of a Police Chief in a Chicago suburb accused of racketeering, extortion, and bribery. A federal jury found him guilty of collaborating with organized drug gangs and protecting shipments of heroin, crack, and cocaine. The sneaky police chief fixed cases, warned the drug gangs about on going drug investigations, and always arrested rival drug dealers."

Another speaker lectured. "This kind of police action and corruption is going on across the board in our country. One of the chief's subordinates is charged with planting marijuana for evidence on a suspect, and lying about it to a grand jury. Then the police officer admitted to smoking marijuana on a regular basis."

At a marijuana rally in Pittsburgh a former Police Chief talked openly about the drug corruption arrests made internally in his department. The former chief said a Pennsylvania law officer was charged with growing marijuana in his attic. The officer admitted to smoking pot on the job just like cigarettes.

The former chief emphasized. "Police who smoke marijuana are just like everyone else." The crowd roared on that note. "That officer had been on the force for thirteen years."

Clint explained. "These documented offenses concern other officers who are guilty of planting marijuana on a prisoner at the jail. These same police officers went into a court of law and swore on their honor to tell the truth, while testifying against the defendant. This is a gross violation of the police code of ethics. Can you imagine what the accused person thought after this cop did this to him and he wasn't guilty? The lying cop's testimony had put an innocent man in jail for marijuana possession. Yet the cop smoked himself on a daily basis. If marijuana was legal nobody would be in trouble." The police chief said in his speech.

Miles informed. "In an Oklahoma Rosta rally a trustworthy paraplegic named Jimmy was set up on a special platform in his wheel chair. Jimmy and his wheel chair friends had attended the "Wheelchair Walk for Medical Marijuana" scheduled event from universities to city halls, from Boston to Washington D. C. during a month and a half period. This wheelchair bound medical marijuana users story was featured to open the rally. His peers honored the man that day. This man was another casualty of the drug war on American Citizens. His life sentence was finally reduced to ten years on a marijuana related drug charge.

Jimmy had carried two ounces of marijuana when busted. Not much weed at all for a medicinal marijuana smoker. The police officer who testified against him was later found guilty of embezzling drug property. He was caught red-handed stealing drug forfeiture money out of the drug property room. The officer said it was a typical practice of drug officers. This practice is known as skimming but rather it's stealing.

Jimmy smoked marijuana to help relieve the raw inflamed pain of his flesh and bone disorder. The crowd applauded this man with a standing ovation as Jimmy left the stage in his wheel chair. "Where is the humanity in our country?" someone yelled from the crowd.

Brant specified. "I liked the West Coast hemp rallies, let me explain gentlemen. In Seattle, the Hemp-festival is known as one of the West Coast's biggest legalization Hemp Rally's, I think it was as big as it's east coast counter part in Boston.

Igor explained. "The Seattle Hemp Rally exceeded over fifty-thousand participants. Over one-hundred hemp speakers, vendors, and pro-hemp bands participated on several stages. A student from the Washington State University had a hemp fiberboard in his visionary display. Hemp fiberboard is twice the strength of wood particleboard's the student claimed."

Miles conveyed. "I talked to a representative from (TIME) "Truth In Marijuana Education." I was impressed with their attitude. He was convinced were on the verge of breaking the legalization issue wide open."

The "Humboldt Hempfest" was endorsed by the cities Chamber of Commerce and sponsored by Humboldt Cannabis Acton network" in Arcata, California. The hemp rally is in Redwood Park proved to be a successful event. Hemp Industry Representatives of International Cannabusiness from Europe will promoted, displayed, and attended this Redwoods surrounded California Hemp festival." "Northern California Cannabis Growers Association" endorsed and attended along with many other organizations. A county official representative from Redwood City said they had applied to the US Food and Drug Administration, and the National Institute on Drug Abuse for permission to test marijuana on humans for a three year study.

The Hemp Rally organizers were trying to get Bob Denver of Gilligan Island fame to attend and speak at the rally with Mary Ann. Gilligan was recently busted for minor marijuana possession. The rally organizers wanted the pro marijuana people to come out of the closet be counted. Help contribute to tear down this wall of war in our society."

Chris informed the group. "One Rallier wanted Tommy Chong who still smoked pot to speak. The hemp organizers wanted to answer the call from the U S Drug Czar's office which said Medical Marijuana is like Cheech and Chong medicine. The cannabis organizers were upset that the drug Czar is an uninformatived, ignorant, imbecile in charge of the nation's police state. This appointed self Righteous Morality Minded Drug Czar Warrior constantly ignores the pleas for fair marijuana initiatives by responsible and honest citizens

Tommy Chong recently said. "Everybody thinks it should be legal. I think it should be mandatory especially for postal workers. Get those fuckers stoned." As reported in High Times by Steve Bloom.

Miles responded. "I liked the three day WHEE2 Festival last summer just north of Eugene, Oregon. The Rainbow girls decorated in cannabis leaves were killer!"

Brant smiled and pitched. "I'll bet they were!"

Miles disclosed. "I talked to a member from the "Cannabis Research Institute" he was very informative."

Chris explained another cannabis rally. "At a recent marijuana and hemp rally in Idaho. Representatives for human rights organizations attended. Much of the hemp rally's agenda exposed police abuses and other causalities of the drug war.

Questions to be answered as this rally were. Is this criminal prosecution or is it a cultural persecution? A twenty-four year old lady with four kids, after arrested, she received a jail sentence from fourteen months to two and a half years. All this for less than two ounces of marijuana. The lady then is charged and convicted of major conspiracy drug charges, and received a additional thirty-year sentence. She's served over thirteen years and is still in prison."

Clint informed. "Hemp Rallies in Missouri, Hawaii, Colorado, North Dakota, Kansas, Kentucky, Virginia, Vermont, Iowa, have hemp industry bills in commitment and legislative committee."

Chris added. "The Missouri Hemp Bill passed in the Senate Agricultural committee by an over whelming vote of eight to two. The extent of our legislative stage's are being presented at each of the cannabis rallies. The hemp educated State representatives spoke on current legislative updates. Why, and how the hemp industry will proceed at the different speaking engagements of the rallies is clarified."

Clint defined to his group of peers discussing tactics. "The time is coming and coming soon, when the legalization of the hemp industry and marijuana for personal use."

Igor contended. "The crowd always cheers the pro-hemp legislators at these rallies, especially when we make positive truthful statements."

Brant illustrated. "I agree! Get them going with the facts. They crowd love it. Agricultural hemp and industrial production is reality, another civic leader group representative said. There's one hemp participant right after another at all the hemp rallies we've attended."

Miles explained. "One women pleaded in court for the release of her husband from jail He was an Army Veteran who had smoked marijuana since he was thirteen-years old. He was a family man with teenage kids. He owned his own asphalt paving business to support his family. Two marijuana plants were found in his back yard by a drug cop. The man ended up sentenced to a five year mandatory sentence in prison.

The sentencing Judge came to the rally and spoke after the women left the stage. He was convinced, the judge said he was not dealing with a drug dealer when sentencing the man. He said he had to abide by the guidelines of mandatory sentencing minimum as it's written. The Judge noted that it was an over kill sentence, but he had his hand's tied behind his back. We are not serving justice by breaking up families."

Miles further explained. "Other citizens of the marijuana drug war protested their loss of hard-earned assets through the marijuana drug wars. Courts and cops feed off the public. The government punishes pot prisoners more than once for the same crime. Once with court fines, Twice with incarceration, and third if you own anything like your car, house, assets, self-esteem or something else you've worked for all your life. You loose your personal property under the guise of drug seizure for simple marijuana possession. Money earned from employment, that is legally yours through hard work. This is honest money to support your family. The government than takes that property away through civil forfeiture.

A couple who smoked marijuana was arrested for five pounds of marijuana. The couple claimed to use the marijuana for medical purposes on advice of their doctor. The couple both received five mandatory years apiece in prison for a relatively small amount of marijuana. The drug swat team came to their house in the middle of the night and literally destroyed their home. They broke their property and stole personal items from the house. The police were looking for the marijuana they had grown for their own personal use." Miles further explained. "That is why I'm standing here today."

Chris explained. "One politician from Missouri said. "The State of Missouri Senate looked into commercial production of hemp. Supporters of pro-hemp production educated the opposition about current hemp legislation. Hemp is a viable alternative crop for farmers in the State of Missouri. Hemp products offer huge profits for businessmen and enormous worker employment opportunities for Missouri. Politicians have proposed a county dedicated to a hemp and marijuana production center similar to Kentucky's. Hemp supporter's presented the framework for a well-regulated hemp industry structure from grain mills to hemp industrial production centers."

Amused Chris conveyed. "Missouri already had the advantage of a head start. Uncle Sam's Pot farm is at their State's University."

Miles depicted. "A Hemp Rally in Davenport Iowa turned violent when police moved in to arrest festival participants for marijuana. Some hemp festival participants threw rocks while resisting arrest. The crowd defended the hemp festival goers who were arrested. The of the hemp festival party stood up to the government and police tactics of repression. They stood up and demanded their constitutional rights back. "I'm proud of those pot patriots," the radio commentator told his live audience. "They have a moral right to their individuality! They have a right to choose freedom of their choice!"

Another commentator notified. "The police are wrong to interfere with peaceful political demonstrations!" The commentator would not withdraw his opinionated remarks.

Igor confided. "The producer was in the background nudging him to cease or ease his comments. "More mass rallies are needed to protest the loss of constitutional rights! Under the Constitution of the United States of America the government doesn't have the right to stop a peaceful assembly! These hooligans are at fault, when they instigate problems, just like Kent State, or Wounded Knee!"

Clint followed. "This commentator went wild with freedom expression and nobody pulled the plug. Ratings for the radio station the following day were astronomical. "Citizens called into the radio station and expressed their views for a change in the marijuana laws after they reviewed the results of militarized police hysteria."

The radio station manager stated. "The police instigated a riot by interfering with the peaceful festival." One caller said who was at the festival the day before. "There were no problems at the hemp festival, until the militarization of the police dept demonstrated a hard core approach towards the attending crowd."

Another one of the hemp goers, who was a stone thrower explained. "The Police were spraying pepper spray and mace into the face's of the hemp festival goers who were resisting arrest. The mace and teargas went into the direction and faces of the crowd further infuriating some in the crowd. Police chased hemp festival goers down and violently threw them to the ground before arresting them."

On further analysis Miles reported. "One hemp rally attendee told the radio commentator. "The police have too much time and money if that's all they have to do is bust marijuana users at a pro-marijuana political rally. These actions by the police with wrecking crew tactics make a good case for a healthy tax cut for the American citizens by cutting the witch hunting cannabis cop force out of existence."

Another protestor bemoaned "These sadistic cops are so stupid, ill trained and blood thirsty they kill there own during drug raids. Let alone look at what they do to peaceful demonstrators in this country. It's our right to have freedom of speech and expression in this country."

The media cited one police official who commented. "Were not going to look the other way!" So they start a riot to socially correct hemp festival supporters."

A student who attended all the hemp rally revealed. "The police stirred into the crowd. They intimidated and discouraged peaceful pot participants. They flat out interfered with a peaceful demonstration."

The commentator expounded. "Discrimination of expression and right a assembly were clearly violated here by police today. I can't believe the abuse I've witnessed today. A member from (NICE) "North Iowans for a Cannabis Education" stated "We'll have our day! They all have an education coming!"

A prominent Constitutional Rights Organization attested. "Hemp Festival participants feel they have the right to smoke marijuana and display hemp crafts. Everybody was there because of their own choice."

The commentator disclosed. "There is way to much of this police bulling and brutally going on toward the cannabis citizenry."

Another news TV commentator was sympathetic to the hemp festival attendees and stated. "All this happened when the Iowa's delegates voted to give hemp a try. The Iowa farm bureau protested police interference because they were to promote the event for the hemp industry." As he concluded the Iowa summary.

Brant professed. "Virginia farm bureau and legislatures have approved hemp for farmer alternatives with no opposition. I want to visit (ACRE) which stands for "American Cannabis Research Experiment" on our next cannabis campaign.

Chris conferred. "In Florida a Cannabis freedom festival permit was denied at the last minute. The organizers threw the bash anyway. They were arrested peacefully. The cool part about it is they sued the county officials in federal court for the violation of there first amendment rights which guarantees freedom of speech and assembly. The festival organizers won fifty thousand dollars from the county, because they were denied a permit. Now they have the "Cannabis Freedom Festival" every year in style. Thanks to the county officials."

Clint confided. "I love that story it has a happy ending," as everyone laughed. "But we need more comfort zones for marijuana smokers," and everyone seconded that.

Chris reported. "Were trying to contact (FORML) "Florida Organization for the Reform of Marijuana Laws or "Florida Legalization Organization to assist us for a cannabis show.

Brant suggested. "How about contacting (TEACH) Therapeutic & Ecological Applications of Cannabis Hemp. They would be an excellent cannabis illustrator."

Clint agreed. "That's a good one!"

Igor discoursed. "We just need the cops to respect our right to privacy, and give our freedom back in our own households!"

Manny and Salina arrived at Clint's Farm. They told Clint about Manny's findings on his around the world journey. Clint loved hearing about all the positive worldwide cannabis news.

Clint informed. "Look at today's headlines! The California law proposing, possess or smoke a joint you lose your drivers license. It was struck down overwhelmingly by the voters."

Manny expounded. "Power to the people!"

Igor agreed. "That's right Manny!"

Manny told Clint. "Hemp oil is sold in stores for cosmetic purposes like aloe is for sun screen. The stores can't keep enough cannabis products in stock." All the round table participants are reliable people. They are associated and politically involved with all avenues concerning the marijuana and hemp movement.

The participants today showed in force, and armed with new information to fuel the drive back to freedom. Clint wanted to restore the richness of the hemp history and culture. He wanted to expose the assassins of democracy, and get them voted out of office.

Ken strolled into the room at Clint's house with a radiant smile. Ken's sharp appearance attracted respect. Ken was always hemp dressed to the tack and was very well organized. Ken walked into the mini-meeting and gave a marijuana chronicle history of cannabis as a medicine.

Ken a friend of Karen's assisted his fellow collegian who was loaded with volume's of marijuana medical information they had accumulated. Karen clarified. "I think it will take four speakers to present this medical information at the forum. All with modern studies of medical marijuana is safe and effective. The medical benefits of marijuana use aids many ailments. Glaucoma, appetite stimulation, muscle spasiticity, muscular dystrophy, epilepsy, adverse affects from chemotherapy, spinal injuries, analgesia, irregular everyday pains, inflammatory disease, asthma, depression, mental illness, alcohol and drug dependence are some very beneficial uses."

Karen informed. "The myths about marijuana having no medical benefits is explained by the National Academy of Science concerning marijuana and health. They stated "In retrospect experimental studies in human beings have failed to yield evidence that marijuana use leads to increased aggression." Just as most of these studies suggest marijuana has a somewhat sedative or tranquil effect. Marijuana may reduce somewhat the intensity of angry feelings and the probability of a personal aggressive behavior."

Karen told the round table participants. "A driver affected with road rage would benefit from smoking a joint of marijuana before taking to the road. The driver would slow down a bit and enjoy the ride, because he wouldn't so uptight. Smoking enough to take the edge off. Hopefully, his angry feelings would be gone. Minimizing road rage enough to tolerate the drive home without an aggression level. In other words in personal mad moment the best advice from mother is to "Count to Ten" which in effect is what smoking a joint of marijuana equals."

The medical forum at the medical university will be a medical pre-forum warm up for the main marijuana medical debate. Karen went over other crucial facts. "The history of England showed that the established medical community realized medical marijuana's therapeutic values in the 1840's as a popular medicine. The Italians used medical marijuana much earlier. In early American history, medical patients used marijuana to ease their pains."

Brant interjected. "The medical marijuana forum time table for presentation in a weeks time. The forum is followed by questions and answers from the audience. Legislators have picked up momentum to fight current repressive marijuana laws."

Glady's George's secretary tracked marijuana and hemp promotion and institutionalized studies at the main office building of George Barras. Glady's said in their telephone conference. "The Million Marijuana March" in New York will have over two marijuana pro-marijuana supporters attending. This will be a strong show of public support!"

Clint enthused. "By George! That's great!"

Glady's explained an upcoming hemp rally to Clint and Company. "The marijuana rally in Wisconsin is expected to be especially explosive in nature compared to preceding hemp rallies in the weeks past. Another minister was just killed in a drug raid because of overzealous police drug task force over the week end past.

The media attention had failed to simmer the Wisconsin youth from the trailer court was gunned down by a police officer who couldn't remember pulling the trigger. Pro-marijuana activists converged on the Milwaukee fairgrounds after a pro-marijuana rally was permitted.

300

The minister's wife who's husband was recently killed by the cop marijuana raiders in Milwaukee was expected to speak. The speech is expected to be an emotional one at the marijuana rally for the people who have protested the drug squad police tactics."

Chris explained. "New marijuana ordinances passed in Milwaukee make marijuana possession of twenty-five grams or less a municipal ordinance violation instead of crime. Essentially decriminalizing smaller amounts of marijuana. Fines still in the range of two to five hundred dollars or imprisonment are the new measure of the law."

Brant expounded. "All they're doing is unloading case loads from one court to another. The discrimination, sanctions, and fines against citizens should be completely eliminated for those in possession of small amounts of marijuana. Pro-marijuana advocates argue that this is just another smoke screen for ultimate control of a person's soul."

Clint conveyed. "The marijuana rally participants want marijuana reform in Federal marijuana sentencing guidelines. I just had just spoke to a police officer who head's the police Academy in Gainesville, Florida who called me. He said he'd probably get in trouble with his superiors but said he wanted to speak in favor of marijuana legalization. The officer said. He'd seen many of his police colleagues destroyed by alcohol but he's never seen one destroyed from marijuana use."

Brant railed. "Fantastic! That's great news."

Chris professed. "The "Cannabis Action Network" in Gainesville is based nationwide. They might assist us if we throw a cannabis show."

Brant hyped. "Thanks Chris. I'll check that out."

Karen explained. "The marijuana rally participants want Medical reform now. Period! With no red tape! Reform of current marijuana laws, without being stigmatized, criminalized, or looked down by governmental officials. I've contacted "Texans for Medical Rights" in Houston to see if they will assist us."

Clint relayed to Karen. "I'll bet they will! Direct and intense pro-hemp and pro-marijuana lobbying efforts at congressional offices is going to intelligently proceed. Pro-marijuana activists examined and exposed federal laws and all it's flaws. Pro-marijuana brochures are distributed to the congressional leaders of our findings and pleas. They found that decriminalizing marijuana proposals for change is the best alternative from the existing federal laws."

Miles divulged. "The United State Sentencing Commission must answer to the media about fairness in their guidelines on imprisonment for marijuana users. The National Institute of Health was asked by the pro-marijuana activists to take a more active roll in decriminalization for all medical patients using marijuana. Different church organizations were asked to speak out in favor of the movement on humanitarian grounds alone. Freedom of personal choice is morally right in regards to marijuana. Isn't that what the first Amendment is all about?"

Brant equivocated. "The activist pro-marijuana organizations have expanded their membership at a rapid pace. Their combined effort will force a major show down with the federal government. Media interviews are being given on a daily basis to pro-marijuana activists across the country."

Clint acknowledged. "The rally at the Wisconsin's fairgrounds is a week ahead of the major Rosta Rally in Washington DC. This Rosta Rally in Washington will by far be the biggest cannabis rally ever. The momentum is building. Million's of participants are expected to converge on Washington for the upcoming Rosta Rally."

Brant affirmed. "An assortment of pro-cannabis entertainers, news organizations, paparazzi are converging on Washington for our Rosta Rally."

Chris proposed. "If you want to assure yourself of a view at the Rosta Rally you'll have to arrive there three to four days ahead of time."

Brant reported. "Transportation for the pro-marijuana education team is organized by George Barras staff. The buses in route to converge on Washington were organized in advance. George wants his part of the Rosta Rally to proceed without a hitch."

Chris stated. "All states who are represented will have transportation supplied by George's pro-marijuana political organization. Jetliner's with "LEGALIZE HEMP" in large letters on the side of the craft are flying in people from Hawaii to Alaska and back to Puerto Rico. We want to assure pro-marijuana Americans are represented from all the states."

Brant explained. "When the lead pro-marijuana buses George sponsors leave the capitals from their prospective states, there will be mini-rallies staged on their prospective state's Capital steps as a last gathering point before departure of the lead buses to Washington's Rosta Rally."

Chris unveiled. "The pro-marijuana buses were creatively designed by Aaron, He airbrushed the buses for cannabis freedom tour. Some of the buses are advertising the new Constitutional Political Party. Aaron has several Constitutional Party symbols and several different "Horse" designs similar to the mustang airbrushed on some of the city busses.

Brant explained. "Aaron airbrushed the Constitutionalists Party Banners. There ready for display during all the rallies and debates. Everyone worked with Aaron on the design for the special Cannabis Wing Banner."

The cannabis caravan of protesters is headed toward the nations capital as we speak. Monitored and tracked by satellite lead buses are coordinated and in communication with George Barras's staff. George wanted to assure that all the pro marijuana buses are to meet designated parking area so all our associated pro marijuana groups would be represented at the Rosta Rally."

Brant specified. "Other nationally known wealthy donors who advocate legalization have contributed, and their efforts are purely philanthropic. They have joined in an effort to liberalize marijuana laws. These generous contributor's gave hundreds of thousands of dollars to get pro-marijuana initiatives passed. Large money contributions to pro marijuana and hemp campaigns is an effective tool for getting the word out."

Chris resolved. "Pro-marijuana Grass root organization's gathered signatures on petitions for getting a legalization vote on all the state's ballots.

George wanted to get pro-marijuana legalization initiatives on the ballot in every state of the union. "Let the voters decide!" George always says."

Karen verified. "We want doctor's to make decision's for our medical marijuana use without hindrance from the federal government. Doctor's and doctor's alone without intimidation's and interference from political enforcement should be allowed to freely make recommendations to their patients concerning medical marijuana use."

"Let the doctors do the doctoring!" George said as he walked into Clint's farmhouse round table meeting.

Miles informed. "Our freedom fighters want immediate elimination of cannabis related criminal records. The marijuana criminal records should be totally expunged. We also want complete and unfettered amnesty for all non-violent offenders convicted of small amounts of marijuana. They can rejoin society and smoke a marijuana cigarette without fear. Police and cannabis citizens should socially exist in society without warring. This would create a nucleus of harmony with citizens to combat real crime."

Chris revealed. "Laws are proposed to require judges to give treatment not prison for hard drug users."

Clint who helped to form the newly instituted political party called the Constitutional party affirmed. "I belong to the Cannabis Wing of the Constitutional Party. The grass roots of the Constitutional party has gathered signatures in every state of the union. They want their own presidential, congressional, state and local government representatives to represent people fairly in all branches of government.

The people in this political struggle in America are sick and tired of the stalemated, stagnate and corrupt popular parties. All the bickering and backbiting is not taking care of the countries business. Backroom bureaucrats and watered down pork belly bills line the pockets of the rich in congress. Were tired of the same old type of politicians who run for office and are in control. They are always rich and overbearing. They fragrantly violate our constitutional rights. Ask any blue collar worker.

Americans have little say about how their tax dollars are spent. Is our tax dollars taking care of the business of the country? What we know for sure is these are the same politicians who for years have drained the social security fund, we have all paid into for a lifetime.

Miles concurred. "I can see right now! We all feel America need's a viable third political party."

Clint continued. "With George's money we can get the Constitutional party established in every state. The people want another choice on election day. A strong third political party will keep the other two existing major political parties honest. The Constitutional Party will break the headstrong deadlock of the Republican and Democratic parties. We want to carry out mandates in favor of individual freedom. We want the Constitutionalists Political Party of America!" Everyone in the room at the round table meeting applauded Clint's speech and Clint smiled, because of the group's gesture.

Miles mischievously reported. "The leaders of the Congressional Hall of Shame are nervous. The staunchest marijuana prohibitionists are in an uproar because the permits were granted for the Rosta Rally."

Igor infuriated. "The Hall of Shamer's tried for an injunction to stop the Rosta Rally. The public uproar created by pro-marijuana rights activists against the prohibitionist wing of the government put an end to their injunction through the supreme court."

Clint revealed. "The abolitionist establishment lost this round in the Supreme Court. The abolitionist's tried to ban pro-marijuana web-sites on the inter-net, and pro-cannabis radio stations, which sanction the pro-marijuana movement. They have been blocked steadfastly by the courts. Advertising sponsors on the Radio stations in turn increased their advertising venues after the court decision.

Senator Stan Stalinski publicly niggled in the Washington Host "I denounce the Rosta Rally for freedom." Stalinski still fumed from the last fourth of July "All American Smoke In" held at the White House and the Jefferson and Lincoln Memorials sponsored by the "Forth of July Hemp Coalition."

Clint told his peers "Our rally for freedom will not to be denied by any last minute back room finagling. Our day will to come."

Miles relayed. "Senator Stalinski personally had a hand in trying to block the pro-marijuana event. Senator Stan is associated strongly with anti-drug crusaders. They wanted to ban web-sites of marijuana advocates and advocate publications. The anti-drug crusaders are still leading the lobbying effort and campaign against marijuana."

Clint contended. "The last thing the anti-drug crusaders want is a fair playing field, or be forced into the showdown of debate. Were not going to go in there and genuflect in front of their domain. Were not anti-establishment! Were mainstream!"

Miles depicted. "The pro-marijuana groups stress their displeasure for unregulated illegitimate crops of marijuana. They want to grow safe crops. They also state the bureaucrats, military and police force are out of control while intimidating citizen's."

Chris explained. "One hemp business owner's business was confiscated and destroyed by the county prosecutor and police for displaying sterilized hemp seeds bought legally in the United States. The sterilized hemp seed displayed came with the certificate of authenticity in the storefront window. The hemp seed food store was located within a short distance of the courthouse. It became a focal point for political forces wanted this hemp business shut down. The hemp food business remained open from donations the local business chapter. They helped this hemp business with his hemp legal battle."

Brant remonstrated. "The pro-cannabis groups stressed that marijuana grow teams OK'd by the government should allowed for taxable sales. The government could pick and choose what big corporations could take on commercial cannabis sales. They can authorize and regulate smaller growers for sale of taxable weed.

Professional marijuana growers argue that the police should leave them alone. They tired of selling marijuana behind closed doors. Change the law! Keep the peace! Let's proceed on with safer communities! The government should concentrate on hard drugs. Marijuana is a soft drug, much softer that whisky, beer, and cigarettes. The constitution was of no value to these government prohibitionists who are repressors of freedom, the pro marijuana groups furthered argue."

Chris rebuked. "Drug users categorized under special legislation in Congress, give the government special legislation, which deviates from the constitution. In essence they passed laws which boycott merchants of the hemp industry and related marijuana paraphernalia. Congress took away powers of the judges who must adhere to tough mandatory drug sentencing guidelines. It calls for the removal of soft judges who show compassion in sentencing. Congress imposed laws which terminate employment or school of all drug users who test positive, and takes away their constitutional rights further. Drug related religious rituals and holy sacraments from all denominations practiced for centuries are now illegal. The government then made mandatory laborers out of their incarcerated drug prisoners. Censorship by the government is a strong reality in suppressing the truth. Yet, former head of the CIA and Iran Contra architect George Bush said we'd have a kinder gentler nation. These present laws in Congress and governmental attitude concerning cannabis and their handling of all drugs parallel NAZI Germany's laws of repression passed by the Third Reich from 1924-1939. These tyrannical and fanatical policy's concerning drugs is the reason our nations prison population exceeds every country on this planet.

Miles consoled. "Senator Stan Stalinski will try right up to the opening speeches of the Rosta Rally to get the rally cancelled. His actions will be to no avail. Some marijuana activists say if the government lets the KKK get a permit to rally and are allowed to spread hate and disorder, the pro-marijuana citizens should be allowed a permit to spread freedom and peace. Media pressure is persistent. Lucrative advertising contracts for major television and radio sponsors, who carried the hemp events live have exploded."

Clint railed. "The deal is sealed. Media news organizations are converging to the Washington Rosta Rally. The hemp rally event's are arranged and in place. Any cancellation of the Rosta Rally would create a public outcry at this point. Cancellation will outrage to the merits of the freedom fighters in the United States." Everyone involved in the cannabis freedom promotion is exuberant. Their efforts made a difference. They want an end the tyrannical twist of government. They want to kill the federal law of marijuana citizen criminalisation. This unjust federal law for menial amounts of marijuana, which presently exists in our nation.

Chapter 12... The Friday night before, the Rosta Rally approached, George secured and arranged cannabis events at a motel in Alexandria. George rented rooms for our immediate political group.

Clint and Chantel and kids, Miles, Chris, Igor, Chico, Morgan Motley, Manny and Salina, Rudy, Maria, and many more enjoyed their own private gala the night before the rally on the Potomac. Excitement was in the air. The enthusiasm for the hemp events brewing. Speakers and pro-marijuana activists groups for supporting all issues were flying in from all over the country and the world.

George served buffalo steaks flown in from Montana, especially for this celebrating group. George said "It would be a good omen to have buffalo as a dinner the night before." Clint agreed and so did Igor, and Manny.

Chief Cloud and his Indian Pow Wow Cannabis Congregation represented the Dakota Indians. George had a hemp teepee centered in the ballroom of the hotel. The congregation smoked marijuana out of a peace pipe brought by Cloud and his followers. Cannabis cigarette girls passed out pot pleasure. Cigarettes, Cigars, Chewing tobacco, and even Blunts were burned and passed around as protest. Hand rolling tricks of all types were demonstrated in many types of cigarette papers.

George smoked a three thousand dollar cigar for the occasion since he rented the whole hotel. He filled every room with pro-rights activists from all walks of life. The Cannabis Wing of the Constitutional Party is strong said Tex while talking with Clint sported a smoking corncob pipe from his adolescent days.

In the ballroom a couple of pro hemp bands who were playing at tomorrow nights Rosta Rally mingled with the pro-rights activists. The pro hemp bands and comedians entertained all night with marijuana punch lines, and creative jingles continually music with acoustical back ground music mingling from the sharp licked guitarists. As advertised the entrance area was the only smoke free zone for this majestic and jubilant smoke down.

Manny Deejays and read pro-activists statements in between original pro-hemp activist's songs. The pro-hemp band members wrote these songs especially for the Rosta Rally. George roused in his speech. "You have to force these old corrupt goats to change." As the night festivities ended, everybody went to their rooms and sensed victory from their motivations.

The hemp for victory parade the next morning began at 11 am for scheduled events. The hemp crowd was more congested then a hit Broadway Show. Cannabis celebrants rushed and jammed into every available space.

The hemp parade entered from Alexandria and crossed the Potomac River Bridge, past the Lincoln and Vietnam Memorials and down Congressional Avenue on its way around to the White House on Pennsylvania Avenue. It then proceeded all the way back around to Congressional Avenue. The hemp parade was cut short after two hours. The packed multitudes of pro-hemp spectators and vendors were non-ending.

"Hemp for Victory Parade!" ended on the steps of the Jefferson Memorial. The pro-cannabis activists pushed for full and open hemp and marijuana debates. They'll be held at a federal level if this Rosta Rally proves to be successful. The crowds stretch all the way to Rockford. One TV commentator said. "If you weren't at the rally early, the only way in was to parachute."

George had a ninety-four year-old doctor flown in to speak at the Rosta Rally. He favored marijuana. Federal judges, legislators, mayors, police chiefs, officers, prison officials, probation officers, and citizens spoke up at the Rosta Rally.

All were in favor in legalization of marijuana for small amounts, especially in the privacy of everyone's own home. One former judge said. "Were not a police state and shouldn't act like one with our citizenry."

Public officials were taking notice at the immense numbers of marijuana users in lock-downs, while prohibitionist politicians and violent criminals preyed on these victims in the political and prison system.

The world looked on Washington, while cannabis citizen's demonstrated the democratic process globally in a pot peaceful manner. The staunch prohibitionists like Senator Stan Stalinski were aghast that the handle of the totalitarian social nerve would fall from their grasp. Stalinski personally led the way to assassinate individual Constitutional rights of every American to choose the way they want to live. These bigot politicians made delicate decisions and mandate intimate individual choices in every American's daily life. Many lie on a consistent basis to the American public. They're confirmed to have no better morals than the populace.

Clint professed. "Senator Stan Stalinski is as mad as a staving baby. It's about time Senator Stan Stalinski feels a little bit of what a tired tax American payer is about. Let him come out here and sweat it out in the street doing Manuel work and scrimp by. These hoggish head's of state lavish in luxury at our expense."

Some guilty politicians are soul searching trying to decide which side of the political border they choose. Politicians broke ranks in favor for freedom of rights. Polls favored legalization of marijuana and more citizens' rights.

Headlines in Friday night's Washington Host read "Rosta Rally Ready!" "The Constitutional Party Lead's Rosta Rally Parade." Were the headlines from other city's newspapers.

The Cannabis Wing of Constitutional Party were readied for the Confrontation. Clint leading the Cannabis Wing of the Constitutional Party fully intended to use all the integrity and ingenuity of the hemp industrialists at America's disposal for economic growth.

Once the pro marijuana speakers started at the Rosta Rally the truth started to come out in a big way.

One speaker a pro-marijuana political candidate conveyed how she was busted for growing a few plants of marijuana in her apartment in order to relieve her chronic pain from chemotherapy treatments for cancer. She claimed it relieved a great amount of the nausea caused by the treatments. She went on to describe how the police had set her up with an informant who infiltrated her inner circle of friends. The drug police informant persisted in asking her for marijuana. She eventually gave her a few joints. Now she was arrested for selling a couple of joints to pressuring undercover officers who were sent to discredit her before the political election. The political opponents targeted and hounded this pro-marijuana candidate just over a couple of joints.

Another speaker is a quadriplegic is afraid of going to jail again after being caught with a marijuana plant growing in his backyard. The speaker named Dusty claimed marijuana relieved some of his pains, where prescription hard drug pain killers failed.

Dusty told the crowd "Try being restricted to a wheelchair. Your body racked with pain and tell yourself your not going to smoke marijuana because it is against the law. If it wasn't for the excruciating pain I may not have considered smoking marijuana." He also stated he was afraid to go to prison if he was convicted for growing a plant of marijuana in his small garden for his personal use.

Dusty's friend Lonnie another paraplegic and confined to a wheel chair sat on stage with Dusty. Lonnie told how he had a serious back operation the remove part of the disk from his spine. The delicate nerves were re-arranged with precision by medical surgeons. His younger brother had sold a small bag of weed to a police drug under cover informant.

Lonnie was still recuperating from the operation he stated. "In the middle of the night our front door was barged in with a battering ram! The drug police came into my room ripped me my out of the bed and kneed me in the back while they cuffed and hog tied me with my hands behind my back. I screamed in shear pain from my back. I had just had my back operation three days prior. I didn't even smoke weed then. These cops ignored my pleas for mercy."

Lonnie after a moment of composure said. "I do smoke weed now to help relieve some of the pain. It is approved by my doctor." Lonnie then lit a joint up with the roaring crowd's approval. Lonnie and Dusty's wheel chair attendants rolled them off stage while they passed the joints from one to another.

Large screens erected in many park areas throughout the city broadcast the speakers live from the Rosta Rally.

The Dutch cannabis organizations represented ethnic countries from all over the world. They explained how these countries moderated their drug laws.

The Dutch spokesman who represented multitudes of marijuana users in the Netherlands said. "We have over eight-hundred thousand cannabis users. Less than fourteen-hundred persons a year volunteer for programs to stop smoking marijuana and hash.

Pharmaceutical companies should manufacture Marijuanaette in similar fashion to Nicorette Gum for tobacco smokers. A gum for marijuana users who want to quit at some point in their life would be beneficial. We have the technology, as a people, we can do anything if we work together. We can do this! But we can not tear each other apart if we want a progressive society. Respect goes both ways between the citizens and the government. Progressesers of harmony must come to compromise."

The Dutch spokesman concluded. "Marijuana users have no higher a mortality rate than non-users. We sanction medical use of marijuana. Pro-marijuana medical associations supporter's are in attendance. They'll tell you very few marijuana users try hard drugs. The average are the same as straight people percent wise. Since cannabis has been legal in Holland, less people use marijuana, and hash than before we ended the marijuana soft drug war. Glue, petro-chemical, and solvent sniffing aren't ever heard of in Holland. The basis for the Dutch Drug policy is identifying the difference between hard drugs and soft drugs, and then dealing with it."

Banners for physician protests with the Federal Government said. "Leave it to the pot patients and the physicians."

Pat told Clint during the rally. "Were promoting no professional disciplinary action, sanctions, legal prosecution for doctor's recommending marijuana use to patients. The right to privacy between doctor and a patient shall prevail under the guidelines of the Constitutional Party."

Clint confirmed. "We'll see to that! For now on I want all our grass roots organizations to protest outside of courtrooms every time there's a pot prisoner on trail. We're going to start taking every single cannabis case personal. Do everything we can to maximize media exposure to the injustice!"

Owen from Karen's staff spoke to the audience and explained. "Patients suffer legal prosecution for growing marijuana in their dwelling. Cultivation and sale of marijuana is not a violation of law amongst these medical marijuana patients." It was not enough for the Freedom Fighters! They wanted it all! They wanted their freedom back. They wouldn't settle for anything less, than the riddance of the federal government's smoke screen and red tape. Another poster read "Drop The War Against Marijuana Consumers!"

George, Clint and their party at the Rosta Rally awaited their turn to speak at the Rally. Another pro-marijuana statistical analyst said. "I want the American people know the extent and percentage of busts the police make for drugs which ends with another foolishly fatally! Facts and figures of failed raids reflect costly turf battles between law enforcement and its marijuana citizens." The pro-marijuana analyst continued at the Rosta Rally.

Clint told George in the background. "I'm not going to wishy-washy around I'm going to lay the facts on the ground."

George agreed. "I like that. Let the chips fall were they fall."

And now George made his compassionate speech he worked on especially for the Rosta Rally. George talked about the credibility of the people in his pro marijuana political circle. They were from all elements of society who wanted a change for a better America.

George asked the audience. "What kind of free capitalistic society are we? The free market should dictate policy, where hemp is concerned! Are we a free and open society or a closed totalitarian society? Who killed the hemp industry in America and Why? Where's the federal government claim of ultimate individuality ideology? Only when our rights and rights of others are respected can these things be true. Legalization of cannabis is the only way to improve economic and social stability, while improving International relations on all levels

We are here to help the federal government determine the depths of reality. The want freedom to be a reality. We need our freedom back. The truth will feel good." George gave a stirring speech. The audience cheered George on with a standing ovation.

Washington, DC clearly had never witnessed such a strong peaceful pulse from the people in any prior events. People from all over just wanted to be part of the Rosta Rally. They showed support to regain and maintain freedoms that had eroded. Enough was enough!

The Rosta crowd had grown from protesting marijuana laws to protesting other different freedom fighter causes. Different cultures, political groups, and elements of society for various reasons responded to the political uproar against the government.

The array of diverse issues represented throughout the Rosta Rally in attendance spoke multitudes. Guest speakers on a continuos basis overjoyed to express their pro marijuana concerns and views. The media had a field day. They gathered around the pro marijuana speakers, and assured them they'd be heard.

Political supporters were anxious to speak out on pro-marijuana issues. Staunch opponents of the marijuana rally were given an opportunity to talk. The prohibition players represented the crude criminalisation process of mid-evil proportions concerning marijuana, they refused to attend or speak. They are afraid to show their colors, and then get booed off the stage. They refused to listen to the pulse of the nation or to our pro marijuana pleas. They refused to acknowledge, use or know anything about the facts of marijuana. They were adamant about "Just Say No!" not only for themselves, but for every one of the country's citizens.

The show of support for the cannabis cause was bigger than anybody anticipated. Media coverage was global. All nations covered the Rosta Rally and what the United States independence stood for. The Canadian newspaper. "The Lethbridge Herald" states. "It's time for proper debate on marijuana."

This Rosta Rally clearly showed change was eminent. You either got on the battle wagon or you lost your political chair. More than enough evidence of governmental cover ups and police corruption was presented to the public through the media.

One statesman stated. "Legislation proposed now will judge people not on their morals, but on real criminal actions. If passed marijuana use between consenting adults could enjoy their habit without prosecution." The crowds thrived on every speaker's plea at the Rosta Rally.

Different marijuana clubs held signs. They had flags custom made with a marijuana leaf with an inscription that said "IN MARIJUANA WE TRUST'.

Another poster had a pair of large glasses on and a marijuana clover, "Reduces Inoculator Pressure" was posted in the medical reserved section. Another poster had 'Bill of Rights" from a freedom union who filled an area with union activists for freedom's cause. They had the same governmental enemies and abhorred the defamation of the constitution. These freedom fighter's held a large replica of the constitution high in the air made out of hemp paper.

Mayor Bill Barnett had given a touching speech about legalizing pot to his city council the preceding year, and now Rosta Rally on lookers. "Legalize pot and legalize it now!" The city counsel had been outraged and demanded a recall of the mayor for suggesting the legalization of marijuana.

The mayor explained. "Look! We have spent two million dollars fighting marijuana abuse and only four-hundred thousand for homicides annually. What is wrong with that picture people? We are on a budget here, not an open wallet! It is not just our district, but all the districts across the board in this country. This drug war drains our tax base for progress. When and where does the hypocrisy end? Legalization is the way to go." The mayor stated. "Let's get marijuana prohibitionists off our back! Let's make them put their noses back on their face and out of our business. I commend the people here today that are part of this revolution." Many prominent police chiefs after the mayor spoke were in unisons with the mayor.

Police chiefs representing different countries gave their separate pleas for marijuana legalization. "Take the hypocrisy out of the drug laws!"

The chief looked at the police officials themselves and said. "Respect the citizens! You can only police the people to the extent that they want to be policed. Internal polls of the police department back decriminalization of marijuana. Opportunist's and hard drugs will adamantly be fought under new marijuana jurisdictional guidelines being proposed."

In the police chief's back ground his peers listened intently. Police officers representing police associations and police unions steadfastly wanted change.

Other signs not far behind the Rosta Rally were the tobacco activists. They feared new restrictive laws concerning tobacco use. Tobacco smokers wanted guarantees from the government that smoking tobacco would remain a freedom of choice.

Simon Smith represented a police association from Orange County California. He protested a decision by the county commissioners. The ruling by the county commissioners made it illegal for police to smoke tobacco cigarettes. This coupled with the fact that police have to abide with stringent residency rules. This freedom struggle has encompassed all avenues. Fighters with diverse interests and entities joined together in harmony to assert fairness.

The public spoke up on the real issues, that effect every day living in the community. The rally called for a positive but drastic change pertaining to cannabis laws. A real call for action was demonstrated. Assured priority seats and accommodations at the rally were cancer chemotherapy patients. These patients belonged to the San Francisco cannabis clubs. They can freely relieve their pain by smoking marijuana without prosecution. They voted for medical marijuana laws that are not being respected by the federal government. The enormity of the Rosta Rally crowd and the presentation jelled the powerful show of force for the pro-cannabis movement.

It was Clint's turn to take the podium. Clint thanked everybody from his own pro marijuana organization. Clint then thanked everyone else involved and all the other organizations that support the freedom Rosta Rally. Clint denounced the federal government tactics and declared **"We will never stop fighting for our freedom."** Clint challenged the president and his cabinet to participate in "Truth Presentation's" on the steps of the Jefferson Memorial.

Clint at the Rosta Rally stated. "Our group is here today to restore the laws as they were for 162 years in our country, when cannabis was once legal and black markets were not established."

Clint with that statement issued a thirty-day challenge for debate with the federal government concerning federal marijuana laws. "Effective immediately!" Clint further proclaimed "An all-inclusive debate on marijuana legalization. Right where we stand today at the Jefferson Memorial! A full debate with global media converge on the Potomac here in Washington, DC. to show the world our individual independence." The crowd roared with Ha Rah's of approval. The enthusiastic crowd drowned the largest amplifying speakers out. The crowd in roared unisons. Clint the speaker summed up. **"Our rights will not be denied!"**

Several people from the entertainment industry also spoke. The stage featured live bands shown on the monitors. Satellite projected the Rosta Rally entertainment throughout the world.

The cannabis bands conveyed freedom that night and sang jubilant songs and chants for cannabis freedom! Their music had meaning's similar to 60's protest songs from the Vietnam War era. The crowd dispersed, during all hours of the night many felt that they were about to be emancipated by the spirit of Lincoln from constitutionally and unlawful persecutions.

The conclusion of the Rosta Rally started when several hemp rocks bands played. "Freedom Speaks for Itself!" All the bands featured pro-hemp songs from CD's they had written. Some CD sales profits went for patients who belong to cannabis clubs in San Francisco. Spectacular Fireworks over the Potomac ended the day's events, topping off a magnificent day with a brilliant evening ending send off. Everyone on the plane planned for the upcoming full debate on marijuana. They wanted the debate on the Jefferson Memorial steps.

Stanley "Stash" Hopkins protested the government's marijuana laws. He was arrested in front of camera and radio telecasts. Stash smoked a joint on the steps of the Jefferson Memorial. As the police took Stash away other protesters lit their joints in protest. Stash quoted **Patrick Henry "Give me liberty or give me death"** as the camera crews kept filming.

Igor divulged to one of the camera crews interviewing. "I think the prohibitionists prefer death."

Later Stash was released on a small bond, but the publicity was profound. Stash disclosed. "I'm proud to stand up for what I believed in. I will never quit smoking pot as long as the government has it listed as illegal."

Our pro-marijuana forum at the Rosta Rally challenged the President, Congress and the drug Czar to a major satellite debate on the legalization of cannabis. Clint proclaimed. "I gave the government thirty days notice for debate." the headlines read, "Thirty Day Ultimatum" in some newspapers quoted Clint.

George's exuberant party was happy. Clint had made the challenge at the Washington Rosta Rally. They slowly left to go back to the hotel in Alexandria, the fireworks display dazzled the sky. the various pro-hemp and marijuana speakers concluded speaking for day. The crowd dispersed that night and in a friendly and peaceful manner.

The Rosta rally showed a convincing vote of emotion for legalization of cannabis. Cannabis users were looked on in a different light other than being criminal. Responsible people were going to be treated as responsible people. The government did not control every aspect of a citizen's life. The attendees from George's pro marijuana political organization were flying George's corporate 747 jetliner the next morning back to Houston. This political group felt more in touch with the citizens than the president himself. The "President's just a poll watcher," some one said. "He'll sway, or we'll have our day at the polls," said another.

The cannabis crowd, and business associates, George, Clint, Mike, Chris, Aaron, Leslie, Morgan, Miles, Manny, Igor, Chico, Chris, Armondo, Alfonso, Jose, Henry, Rudy, Pierre, Terry, Bob, Dale, Mel, Chantel, Maria, Illyia, Betty, Hiedi, Salina, Gladys, Alicia, Diane, the whole gambit of freedom seekers consumed the flight. Clint relayed to Chantel. "Just being with all the people, who worked so hard to get everyone heard, make this flight that much more enjoyable.".

Clint disclosed to George "They have to give us a full debate on the issue of cannabis. We all stood together to make a point! We showed them where the people's heart is."

Leslie made a great point at the debate. He appealed. "How come black neighborhoods are targeted for cocaine and crack cocaine sales? The flow and sales of cocaine is to well organized. It's too steady of a supply into our neighborhoods. Black men go to prison at alarming rates, because of these unjust drug laws. Other people are being intimidated and killed. One prosecutor told me. "Cops carry out a reign of abuse."

Leslie appealed. "We have to change the attack on drugs. Current drug laws hinder racial equality among Blacks, Hispanics, and low income whites. Unequal incomes equal unequal household wealth and opportunities. They face the barriers of racial indifference, that damage opportunities. Health and education should be paramount on the government's drug war agenda." Leslie told his group of listeners on the jetliner.

Leslie stressed. "We need more education, and rehabilitation. We need less criminalization for marijuana. We need the cocaine and heroin off our streets! We need a change in our government! We have a black man who was granted clemency by a governor for selling two grams of marijuana for ten dollars over twenty-five years ago. Then is extradited from his family and successful business to answer the charge across the country. For two grams of marijuana! For two grams of cannabis, he should never have been bothered by the long arm of the government at such a large expense of the taxpayer or our civil liberties."

Leslie an adviser to the Congressional Black Caucus was impressive and well armed with urban facts and figures he presented at the rally. Leslie implored. "I'll expound on all facts about this issue's in the our debate. The expense of incarcerating thousands of citizens for low level drug infractions is beyond reason. One marijuana smoker is arrested every forty-five seconds. At this rate in year 2010 it's estimated that more black men we'll be in jail, than on the streets. Is this what the government's trying to do? Is that the final solution? Stop Now! We need to put more money into education, drug treatment and prevention." Leslie concluded.

Armondo a leader of the Latin community talked about the power of belief and on what levels individual, community, country, and the impact of those beliefs attested. "The Oklahoma federal building bombing was horrific. The bombing Japan with a nuclear bomb was horrific. Decision's believed in and lived out. One country made the decision to wipe out the demographic area of another country's city. Another party bombed abortion clinics. Another party bombed the World Trade Center. Some parties don't have any beliefs, and don't care about the end results or tragedy to them or anyone around them. All these actions have serious and tragic consequences."

Armondo speculated. "My point is people who believe in the legalization of marijuana are like anyone else other than smoking marijuana. They believe in their right to smoke marijuana in the privacy of their home adamantly. Citizens should feel comfortable in protecting their rights in their home. Their home should be their sanctuary. I've never seen a crazed person just because they were high on marijuana. There is no documented cases of human malfunction just because they smoke marijuana."

Armondo pleaded. "If your a thief your a thief! If you were a thief before you smoked marijuana, your still a thief. Just because you smoke a joint of marijuana isn't going to make you an honest person. I absolutely don't foresee the legalization of marijuana as a great threat to our selves or society. People who smoke are going to smoke no matter what the law is. If your a health nut or just don't care to smoke your not going to smoke no matter what the law is. That's your own personal choice. In popularity of mild mind bending drugs, Cannabis is in forth place behind caffeine, nicotine, alcohol."

Armondo told the story of a ninety-six year old man in South Africa, who lived in the bush. "This bushman smoked marijuana all his life. The bushman called marijuana in his South African homeland "Dagga". The old man still used marijuana today to ease the pains of old age. The man has four generations under his belt. Maybe we could learn from this old man. He revealed about native women who uses marijuana while giving childbirth to relieve the pain.

The seeds from marijuana were ground up making assorted dishes of food. One food in particular was made for weaning the newborns. He told me The South African Coal mine owners encouraged smoking marijuana. The owners of the coal mine said it made the coal miners in South Africa work harder and showed less fatigue.

The old man explained. "The Suto people have always used "Dagga" for social or ritual habits. "No one is looked down on because of marijuana use. One government law to fit all is not realistic." There's people in all places and ages that smoke marijuana."

Armondo was doing the world report part of the meeting on culture traditions and relayed. "In the north part of South Africa, Congo tribes cultivate marijuana, then make food and clothing. The tribe smoke "Dagga" in everyday life and "Dagga" has been a tradition for centuries. In one ritual a pipe forty inches in diameter is administered to a person of the tribe has punished for small crimes. The tribesman smoke from the pipes until he passes out. The convicted tribal member just gets tired after hours of smoking and fall asleep." Armondo concluded.

Clint snickered. "Wouldn't that be a way to take a licking!"

Igor agreed. "It's not like a hang over, or hard drugs which takes control of your physical system the next day. There's no after effects the next day of impairment from smoking to much marijuana."

Arthur Carter is a pro-marijuana speaker and a champion debater assigned to the debate team. He served as a cannabis educational liaison and was a Harvard scholar. He wrote dozens of books concerning marijuana legalization and constitutional rights. Arthur scolded the government officials in a live radio newscasts interview called. "Thirty Days!"

Arthur told the radio audience that. "Our political group has every study in the world on marijuana available, and the facts are in! We agree with all other serious marijuana studies of the past. Concerning cannabis the politicians have escalated every adverse campaign, passed every damaging law, promoted every piece of misconceived information, and continually break important elements of our constitution." Arthur said in a steadfast manner voiced. "Politicians who refuse to reason or listen to the citizen's will be identified and voted out!" Arthur scolded puritan politicians who repress marijuana reform.

As they gathered at Clint's farm the next day, senators of the anti-marijuana opposition issued an icy statement. Senator Stan Stalinski said. "It is scandalous to make such political demands." Senator Stan Stalinski continued to talk about the evils of marijuana. Senator Stan Stalinski said.. "The chairman in charge of the committee won't sanction such a debate."

Clint countered the next day in the media. "It's not up to you Senator or the chairman of the committee. It's up to the people you work for. That's the

American people! We want and demand a full cannabis debate." Clint said. "This is in full accordance of what Thomas Jefferson, or Abraham Lincoln would call for if present."

Clint said in follow up radio interviews. "Let's settle this cannabis issue fair and square. Let's let the chip's fall where they fall. If we the American people can't get a debate, we'll call for an all out media revolution."

Clint suggested. "We should follow the principles of Thomas Jefferson who was a very fine patriot. Thomas Jefferson who was the most accomplished writer of the constitution of the United States. The first Constitutional drafts were written on cannabis paper. The hemp paper was grown and processed into writing paper by Jefferson at his plantation home "Monticello."

Clint said. "Zero Tolerance" will never be a reality! We as a people have to deal with this issue of cannabis fairly. A full debate on cannabis legalization is the only way to introduce a sound policy that's fair play to all. We will ride together on the Canvas Covered Constitutional Political Wagon Train into Washington DC. The Constitutional Party Horse's will serve as the Party's Mascot's. They will lead the parade into Washington, D. C. right down Constitutional Avenue."

The marijuana prohibitionists led by Senator Stalinski cringed with boiled hatred for vengeance. They want to maintain they're entrenched, act of war, anti-marijuana position that besiege harmless pot prisoners, and blockade their constitutional rights. This pitched battle is an all out war of nerves. The camouflaged reality of the social civil war had to be addressed. Counter intelligence by the prohibitionists conceded political damage to their ranks. They promoted an all out fire fight to avoid defeat of their doomed totalitarian entity. Gunboat diplomacy was the order of the day's battle for victory encouraged by ferrous Stalinski to route and sabotage the cannabis citizen's freedom activities at all costs.

Clint remarked. "Making Satanist's out of a marijuana user's in the privacy of their home is the prohibitionists passion. They are nothing but dirt mongers sticking their noses in and ruining someone else's private life and business."

Miles pitched. "Politicians from behind a desk in Washington pretend to know what's better in some one else's household. The government prohibition party's announced there wouldn't be any legislation to legalize marijuana."

Radio broadcasts carried the war of words between the prohibitionists, and the cannabis freedom fighters for days on end. The drug Czar in an interview called on parents, to bring there kids to the table and explains the evils of marijuana.

Igor concurred. "Problem is there's to many parent's and kids who smoke pot already. Parents or kids can get pot anytime that they want to. Laws don't change that."

Woody a live open forum TV commentator, the group was listening to on the radio avouched. "Hard alcohol and hard drugs are a parent's real fear. The scare factor about marijuana usage to parents and kids has worn off. The kids

316

know their parents have smoked marijuana. They know that they lead a respectful life. They know their parents aren't hooked on hard drugs. Most parents don't do hard drugs, and are happy if their kids don't. Concessions have to be made even to kids in order to gain their respect. Respect is worth more than any new law. There is an internal war in the government itself. According to the polls politicians are divided and fearful about how to deal with the issue of marijuana use. The only reason they're scared is because they're ignorant of the truth."

Chanters in the TV commentators audience chanted. "The drug Czar's War! Not our War!" Woody continued. "Marijuana research groups are supportive of pro-marijuana legalization. There is no longer public sentiment or confidence in standing with the anti-marijuana prohibitionists and activists. The teens here in my back ground today appear as whole approve of marijuana not as a crime, but a safer choice when compared with alcohol, or tobacco. Lighter alternatives for recreational highs usually are more acceptable for those who care to recreationally indulge. The government deceitfully over played the dangers of marijuana into overbearing laws. People flat out don't believe the government's assertions and propaganda about the marijuana drug war. Young people have grown up and seen their Baby boomer parents make it while defying the government's accretions that they would have grave mental and physical impairments from marijuana use.

Stern and threatening messages from the governmental propaganda machine to the kids about the ills of marijuana use fall on deaf ears. People aren't stupid. People want to choose how to live their own lives. In fact the kids parents are their idols. The same people who have demonstrated the most cognitive actions of thinking, learning, reasoning, and staying active to their kids.

Their parents give them the love they need. The government wouldn't know anything about personal family love and affection. Teens as a group advocated decriminalization of marijuana. They feel it would get rid of major drug traffickers. Marijuana use has increased among teens over the past ten years and has not gone down by any means. Any claim by the government forces that marijuana use has gone down is an out right lie.

Since the sixties marijuana use, availability and acceptance has been steadily growing. Marijuana has never been a problem to purchase in prior decades. The nice part about the trade off is a teen who normally would get drunk on alcohol, instead gets recreationally stoned on marijuana. Cannabis is one hundred and eighty degrees safer!

The number one drug problem at schools is alcohol. Period! Hard drug problem's need containment. The government brings in big guns to burn up the taxpayer's money by busting marijuana users which serve no purpose. A fatal dose of marijuana for a consumer is to smoke fifty pounds of marijuana in thirty minutes. This is impossible.

Teens exchange pot between themselves in every high school in America. Teens from every high school nation wide smoke marijuana. This is a fact of life! Teens hang out together drink and smoke after foot ball games. They go to friend's houses and motel parties. Parks are another big place for kids to hang out. Things are cool for fifteen to twenty kids with everyone just talking or laughing until the cops show up. Then cars are searched by the cops and kids are busted for weed pipes, rolling papers, and small bags of marijuana. Many kids prefer to smoke a little pot and don't use any alcohol. This make a much safer roadway, and keeps recreational substance use by kids safer. Many kids hide their smoking during high school social events. Everyone from football players, cheerleaders, nerds, and even the greasers have friends and acquaintances, who regularly smoke pot."

Pulling a fast one Stalinski's partner in crime Meanie scorned. "So what you suggest is we feed drugs to our kids?" while being interviewed.

Woody responded. "No I don't! Not all drugs are the same! Kids experiment! Give them safer alternatives! Some parents are cool and let their kids bring there friends over to hang out even while they are away. Some parents rather see their kids at home than all over the streets. Our attitudes are not lax on hard alcohol and hard drugs. Our attitudes are smart on drugs. Hard drugs have no place in constructive everyday functions of social living."

Woody continually rolled on with his own marijuana attitude. The Meanie had since left the radio station.

Woody explained to his audience. "Cannabis has been used for generations worldwide. Cannabis possesses qualities of merit and is here to stay."

The biggest part of the news coverage of worldwide was positive. The people were exuberant that they could express their pro-marijuana views by presentation. The ballot box promised to be the final executioner of marijuana and hemp law repression. It is where the pro-marijuana movement will be united in the next election.

Marijuana users are no longer being targeted, unless marijuana possession or use is in prohibited areas like federal buildings, downtown districts, school zones, hospitals, et cetera.

Morgan confided to Clint on the cell phone. "Major marijuana dealers are looked on as enterprisers. Th marijuana enterprisers will be treated similar to white collar crime. Stiff fines are assessed for large unregulated possessions and sales. Marijuana enterprisers will be penalized under the new tax code being introduced for the cannabis and hemp industry."

Henry the Hempster on a cell phone conference call with Clint relayed. "The marijuana and hemp industry is projecting a one trillion dollar growth in the next fifteen years. Hemp manufacturing and production are included in the future projections."

Political Pat on a follow up phone call filled in. "Historic modern drug measures are drawn up and have passed in several states. The presidential plan implemented by the drug Czar should be declared unconstitutional. They show prejudice for personal choice. Personal choice freedoms that are denied by the existing cannabis laws.

Pro-marijuana legislators are taking part in the movement. They are drawing up pro- marijuana legislation at a rapid pace. The marijuana reform laws will be voted on to change existing federal laws which compared marijuana to heroin in federal sentencing guidelines as a schedule one narcotic."

Clint asked. "Pat can you come over now?"

Pat replied. "I'll be right over."

Karen came over next and stated. "With a death sentence like AIDS, AIDS victims should receive marijuana at their own discretion. With marijuana AIDS victims will be able to face what little happiness they can tolerate. Marijuana is used by their patients to help them cope with the excruciating physical suffering and mental anguish they endure from wasting away."

Chris took his turn to explain. "With industrial hemp already being implemented in the free world, court studies show that the well over ninety-five per cent of the adult users of cannabis have never used any other hard drugs.

Upon legalization of marijuana the country's hard drug use will still be less than the two per cent of the country's citizen's. These people are shown to use hard drugs of heroin and cocaine presently.

The Swiss office of public Health conducted a heroin prescription program for hard core heroin addicts. The heroin addicts reported three times a day to get their heroin injections under this ambitious Swiss medical program.

Crime and unemployment sharply dropped by sixty-percent in the group of heroin addicted participants. They no longer had to steal for their fix. The general health of the hard core drug participants went up. The Swiss office of public health says their program was a success."

Terry in from Canada informed. "Vancouver Canada considered the same type of program for their heroin addicts, citing heroin overdoses, rapid pace of AIDS infected people and dirty needles due to the influx of the heroin availability.

Canada's federal health agency said. They'd try clinical tests where doctors could supply heroin injections to addicts. All these trail programs sponsored by different governments have an interest in reducing hard drug addiction diseases and crimes.

Police officials state these government Health actions make crime fighting and economic sense by deterring hard core drug addicts from human and property crimes. These actions by the government curtail the hard core intravenous drug users from chasing their drug habit with a fist full of dirty needles and further spreading AIDS in rampant proportions. Continued hard core drugs creates hard core crimes by the addicts.

Modern health programs sanctioned by different governments are the most effective way to handle the hard drug menace in our society. HIV infections run rampant from intravenous drug users in our cities. These governments agency want to curb the spread of AIDS through this government sponsored program." Terry concluded.

Clint reasoned. "Ideological barriers by the moral crusaders in the American Government must be broken, before any progress on this front of the drug wars can be realized in America."

Political Pat disclosed. "Ironically the US Conference of Mayors sponsored a resolution ending the federal funding ban for needle exchange programs for hard drug addicts."

Clint responded. "Find out Why! Even the drug Czar backs clean needle exchanges. See if it's a moral issue or monetary."

The same day, Manny had a marijuana question and answer marathon live at the radio station and fielded questions for twelve hours non-stop from his radio call in audience.

Manny conferred. "The public polling shows over whelming support for the pro-marijuana activists. In a recent poll eighty-five percent of the citizen's were in favor of legalization for small amounts, sales, use, and cultivation of marijuana. Marijuana should be taxed and regulated."

Manny interviewed many of the Rosta Rally participants and viewers from his broadcasting station in Houston.

Cannabis citizen's were committed to seeing pro-marijuana legislation's drawn up, voted on and carried out, without further delay.

Fielding questions for twelve hours non-stop from the audience and input exposed from the audience. In polls the following day represented overwhelming support for the pro-marijuana activists. Eighty-five per cent of the recent poll was in favor of legalization for small amounts, of sales or use, and cultivation of marijuana.

One caller into the radio station was a former governor, who joined other world class citizens, and has spoken on behalf of change in the global drug war approach. These well healed world class citizens said the drug war caused more harm than good concerning drug abuse. Some of these world class citizens sanctioned the Lindesmith Center in New York and included former United Nations Secretary-General Javier Perez de Cuellar, Nobel winner Oscar Arias, and former Secretary of State George Shultz.

Marijuana should be regulated and sold to the public after being taxed. The force of people demonstrating freely and peacefully. They urge our government to seek immediate resolutions of decisions at the marijuana policy forum."

The pro-rights group headed by Clint, and George formed overall policy directions to make fair cannabis proposals.

Chantel told Maria. "Clint is pursuing independent cannabis positions for the international marijuana infrastructure for demonstration on the steps of the Jefferson Memorial."

Maria depicted to Chantel. "George has the computer's working twenty-four hours a day. He wants to win this debate. He knows this is the super bowl of debates."

Chantel noted. "Intense media coverage will scrutinize the win or lose situation for the cannabis movement."

Maria professed. "The grass roots of a democratic movement are rising. Old established governmental concepts of values have to change concerning marijuana. The social stigma and the governments negative hype must be overcome."

Pat convincingly stated. "An attorney friend of mine Charley Sharp heads a league of pro-cannabis attorneys. They've prepared for the cannabis curriculum of the debate well. The networking of laws and by-laws fair to the people will be complex. For the legal work demanded in an exhaustive time frame. Discussions for the debate are diverse and intense concerning hemp and marijuana."

Brant recounted. "The established cannabis debate team is extremely knowledgeable. The convictions and facts are being presented in an intellectual and manner in favor of the pro-marijuana activists."

Pat contended. "Everyone in the community got involved in reviewing the cannabis facts. Anti-prohibition leagues from around the country are geared up to get their voice heard. The People want a less intrusive government concerning personal choice."

The last get together for all proponents of the pro-marijuana movement was at Clint and Chantel's farm.

Brant's event management team read off last minute debate preparations and Glady's gave itineraries to the participating pro-cannabis debaters and their perspective debate teams.

Glady's enounced. "Those pro-marijuana debaters sharpened their debate skills right to the last minute."

Brant explained. "A panel of correspondents will listen to discussions on our subject matter on the preliminary day of debate.

A Cannabis Chairperson from the sponsors of the debate visited each camp. He will gave strict debate instructions. Statements will last approximately thirty minutes in duration, an opposing statement of the same amount and follow up statements for the debate are ten minutes in length.

Comments and questions will follow for sixty minutes from the panel of correspondents and citizens via satellite. Each subject matter will take four hours including an hour in between each subject. Three subjects per day time six days of full and complete debates. Twenty-four different subjective analytical cannabis subject's will be covered."

Clint expounded to Igor. "This cannabis debate is needed to bring the issue directly to the forefront of the American people. The problem has to be dealt with fairly We can't skirt the issue, and pretend it does not exist. The problem won't go away until, we, the people deal with it!"

Chapter 13... The day of the marijuana legalization debate began on the steps of the Jefferson Memorial as the director Kevin Keller made opening statements.

Mr. Keller started. "This is the showdown, the volcano, the hurricane, the tornado, the twister, and tidal wave all rolled up into one. This is democracy at its best.

The American people want to clear the air once and for all. This battle is being waged on facts and figures, hashed out in a free democracy instead of the usual limited or no participation by the citizens. The citizens are tired of the drug wars affects on everyday life governed by decisions made in the back rooms of congress.

On this day abuses and excesses in law enforcement, judicial officials, prisons, and virtually all other aspects of government functions in regards to cannabis will be exposed. All pro and con views should be based and presented on sound facts.

Allen Ashtown, a Civil Liberties advocate stated. "The war on drugs has moved to a Civil Liberties War. The ACLU advocate continually stated and campaigned for drug decriminalization. ACLU researchers advocate decriminalization.

Allen continued. "This forum will present the marijuana facts to educate the unknowledgeable people. Presently lawmakers are throwing sand in the wind by waging a war on marijuana. Lawmakers have faced an up hill battle, that will not go away. We need to take some criminality out of drugs and drug enforcement. Stop wasting our federal tax dollars! Harm reduction strategies are needed. Let us bring an end to the smoke and mirror show of our government propaganda machine concerning hemp and marijuana. We are all tired of the re runs."

Allen laid it on the line. "There's a difference between hard drugs in society, large amounts of non taxed marijuana, to the small amounts of marijuana responsible users possess. There was a difference between using marijuana in the privacy of your own home and hard use. Hard drugs are very much like hard alcohol. Hard drugs can derange and control your sounder thought process. Marijuana is in a harmless league of its own. Marijuana rights for our conscious cannabis citizens must be restored without reservation."

The Supreme court recently ruled in favor for individual privacy rights. The police do not automatically have the right to search a motorist, who's pulled over and ticketed for speeding. The marijuana charge against an Iowa man for the marijuana pipe found under the front seat was dismissed. The court found no reason to search further for evidence of speeding."

Allen stated. "United States prisons, and county jails are jammed with an enormous amount of non-violent prisoners. These non-violent prisoners should not be shown the way of harden criminals. These non-violent prisoners should not be put in harms way of the violent criminal confines. The drug offenders consist of fifty percent of the prison populations. Locking citizens up for every taboo has not stopped the illegal flow of drugs across our borders. It has not stopped the laundering of our money from the United States to other countries. The drug cartels dictate to international financial institutions the direction of the money laundering. Legalize marijuana and stop the social internal war.

This would increase the amount of money on the side of citizens to fight hard drugs and their operatives. Getting hard drugs like crack cocaine off our streets is a practical goal. In a real sense these cannabis citizens would fight with the police who would no longer hunt and persecute them. These marijuana users could legally walk up to a police in a sanctioned area and say "Sir, they're selling crack cocaine on the corner, get that stuff out of the neighborhood." Drug Cartels could then be broken. The marijuana money has been leaving the country on a steady basis for years."

Allen after another applause stated. "No wonder the government has to keep printing new currency, the money keeps going to drug producing countries. Money from legal marijuana drug transactions in America would stay in America. Smoking and selling marijuana with other citizens in Americans keeps American money in the United States of America. Having the money stay in America instead of continually going to Mexico or with the Colombians, et cetera. Marijuana users are well documented as a whole do not commit violent crimes. The marijuana drug war should be called off throughout the Western Hemisphere."

Allen concluded. "Imports of marijuana could be allowed in and taxed under new guidelines in some states. Prices of marijuana would come down. There is no need for a totally unregulated black market. The pro marijuana alliance is sowing the seeds to restore our freedom movement back to new heights."

The main debate foreman Cory Shaft for the Cannabis Wing Constitutionalists trained the pro marijuana debaters to effectively debate their prohibitionist counterparts.

Cory's persuasive debate tactics was incorporated into the team of cannabis debaters. Cory attacked the federal marijuana drug laws themselves. "There are literary millions upon millions of marijuana smokers in America. The percentage of America that smokes marijuana exceeds tobacco smokers by far."

Cory clarified. "We can't lock up America! I've worked with world leaders who are disenchanted with the disaster of the current drug laws."

Cory's task countered all government claims during the debate. His vast hemp and marijuana knowledge truthfully disprove the federal government's marijuana and hemp propaganda campaign.

Cory stated that. "Every marijuana governmental, institutionalized, or major independent study has recommend decriminalization of marijuana. The marijuana drug warriors fill their pockets with good citizens cash from the marijuana drug war. The drug warriors do not want this marijuana drug war to end. All these marijuana decriminalization studies are available through the library or Internet. We commonly counter the government's propaganda with their own facts from hemp and marijuana studies. All avenues of serious marijuana studies conclude the government's holy war against marijuana smoker's is wrong." Cory concluded.

Smokers alliance groups wanted their say. Smoky Sanders spoke for this group. This national smoker's alliance group presented facts to the FDA for the right to smoke.

Smoky in his brief synopsis divulged. "We smoke, we enjoy it, we die that's are choice. Let those who understand it and enjoy it decide. Let those who ride decide!" Smoky represented a motorcycle club from Chicago.

Elder Rivers spoke for medical marijuana club from San Francisco and stated that. "The District Attorney must recognize the rights of American citizens to possess and use small amounts of marijuana for medical reasons. Courts at there own discretion could only give-educated advice for new modern studies for supposed marijuana use effects. All medical journals from modern world industrial countries agree that marijuana use even long term is not detrimental to your health. The same can't be said about tobacco.

The many available Medical Journals also state that marijuana is widely used worldwide for medical purposes and has been for centuries. Our psychological make up is part of our body. If the patient feels better and they're in a better mood, that's what a lot of legal hard core prescription drugs are all about. Some legal prescription drugs have much more damaging side effects on our human body. Marijuana use is reasonably safe. Marijuana decriminalization is not a major threat for the health of consumers.

Industrialized Nations are following the Netherlands approach for a much more citizen effective drug policy. Decriminalizing herbs, that are the healing of the nation, effectively means law enforcement is no longer required to chase and to convict cannabis citizens.

Users, sellers, and possessors of small amounts of marijuana and hash should no longer be stigmatized as a criminal element.

Criminal elements of the marijuana drug trade would dissipate. Prices would drop do to legalization and black market would no longer be needed. Hemp industries analysts project for hemp manufacturing of textiles alone would exceed economic rates on all avenues. Hemp clothier lines would give the cotton, wool, and polyester industry serious competition from a far superior product. Marijuana already serves as a medicine in pharmaceutical form. People could actually smile at each other, the police and it's citizens over marijuana use. Doctors wouldn't be caught in the middle. The citizens would live in a less sticky, red taped governmental relationship.

Law enforcement would be responsible for serious crimes and have more man-hours to spend on important tasks of finding deceptive and violent criminals. The Political football is in the government's hands. Marijuana decriminalization issue can not be ducked. No drugs will be allowed in the schools, as is the case right now.

The marijuana decriminalization laws would still be strict concerning children. Adults contributing to minors would be strictly dealt with. Crime innocent victims are losing their property through unfair drug forfeiture laws. Personal property earned honestly at their employment is stolen by the government, in the guise that small amounts of marijuana were found in their possession.

The police and prosecutors against simple marijuana users escalate charges of small amounts of marijuana to larger judicial guidelines. Some state governments require victims to loose their car their license and professional license for drummed up marijuana charges. Their car, cash also their positions stating that it was drug-related money. When the Police know clearly the money was from their payroll check." Elders said.

"Citizens are Incriminated, Intimidated and Prosecuted in a free society for minor marijuana drug dealing. Possession of small amounts of marijuana demand forfeiture and incarceration consequences. Clearly repression tactics of choice by police and prosecutors who equally split the wealth and fame at our citizenry's expense. Criminally tattooing cannabis citizens who are other wise productive citizens is dead wrong." Elders convincingly concluded.

The government repeatedly tried to gloss over the entire pro-marijuana political platform. Desecration's were clear. The facts were crucial and incrementing to the federal governments demise. Once the truth was exposed and understood by all, the governors of the country's cannabis fight was futile. On various pro marijuana and hemp topics, when push came to shove and the government officials were thrown overboard. Opening statements by each side began the debates.

Curriculum for debate is as follows.
Pro-marijuana Debaters Debating the Prohibitionists

Constitution and civil rights-Travis Truth	Wilton Whitewash
Religion and marijuana---John Javaz	Nily Nevers
Drug testing--------------Kent Jones	Blunt Baggit
History of marijuana---Ellis Edison	Gilbert Giles
Alcohol, tobacco, marijuana compare-Bobby Barret	Benedict Burns
Medical marijuana----- Karen Kurtz	Austin Annoytin
Hemp production--------Abraham Arms	Nortin Nonutin
Marijuana production, and sales—Mickey Matson	Ross Bossly
Government Mismanagement—Winston Wells	Bert Bares
Graft and corruption- Jerry Thompson	Dottie Dork
Cocaine production----Carry Carleton	Put Pan
Cartel Drug smuggling—Steve Grown	Pat Crabbinich
Cocaine street sales------Peter Penn	Kim Cantel
Violence Factor-------Burt Bennet	Lane Little
Police abuse--------------Roscoe Repares	Zane Slain

Money and money laundering-Kevon Parker	Mike Batner
Tax Commodity---------Penny Parker	Rupert Riddle
NHTSA-------------------Nolan Bates	Sarah Stalls
Prison Population-------Sherwin Smith	Otto Aso
Schools--------------------Ted Edgars	Weldon Wicks
Present laws --------------Vince Boyd	Bertha Ingels
New law proposals------Mason Voight	Ray Robert's
Cannabis users themselves-Brutes Baron	Dean Dobson
Final orientation---------Clint Cole	Stan Stalinsky

"Participants will have ample time to respond to all questions being posed in the cannabis debate." The director of debates Kevin Keller stated.

Travis Truth a clever civil rights attorney knowledgeable of marijuana laws stated. "Democracy is a system of compromise. Re-Legalizing marijuana will enable good but criminally coded cannabis users rejoin a constructive free society."

Travis pointed to himself. "Just as the emancipation proclamation did for the black folk of another era. This marijuana reform proclamation will set generations of Americans free. The values of truth and understanding will prevail. Possessing marijuana or hash is not a crime under the guidelines of the constitution, or a violation of International law. Small amounts of marijuana and marginal profits is tolerated under the guidelines of the constitution. Where is the America that expound on the fact that the free market should prevail. Jail terms and penalties for American citizens for cannabis is wrong!

Sanctions against a citizen's driver's license for marijuana convictions is wrong. Smoke a joint and lose your license. Over Thirty-two states have already opted out on those tyrannical choices of federal marijuana mandates that have been proposed. States need to govern their own states without interference or threats formed in Washington, D C. These are the hypocritical politicians, who protect themselves and their own from small amounts of marijuana convictions, but go with a vengeance after others. There have been different type of protests over the years."

Travis continued. "Jimi Hendrix funded Abbie Hoffman's Yippie's to mail three thousand joints to unknown people in the phone book. The marijuana joints were sent out on Valentine's day in the New York area. Publicity was prolific and positive note for marijuana users. It seemed to mark the beginning of the movement to end the long prohibition of marijuana in the United States.

The National Organization for the Reform of Marijuana laws was established not long after. In the mid-seventies the State of Alaskas Supreme Court declared the Citizens of their state had the Right to Privacy in the home. Declaring Citizens possession of one once of marijuana in the home was legal. The right to privacy took president over tyrannical federal laws, which were passed and enforced by business lobbyists and the federal government for self-interests. The marijuana law wasn't passed in the cause for freedom of choice.

Federal government doesn't have the right to dictate to each state's choice in Industry, Moral and social Practices. Each state should monitor their own demo-graphic area. Laws from state to state are completely different on a variety of issues. One state treats marijuana possession like a traffic ticket and the next state treats possession of marijuana as a heroin felony.

Travis now **Quoting Jim Morrison "When the truth is known the Judges will be proved the true criminals."** Travis Truth concluded.

Wilton Whitewash a rude governmental prohibitionist said. "Nobody's rights are being violated. The government has a right to maintain control of all aspects of drug policies." The crowd disgruntly looked at Wilton.

Travis interjected. "What gives you the right to repress individual freedoms guaranteed under the constitution?"

Wilton preached. "There is no constitutional guarantees as of such!"

Travis countered. "They're isn't! That's why we need to broom ignorant people like you from all aspects of government out! If you don't take a creed to uphold individual freedoms guaranteed in the Constitution for all citizens, the Constitutional Party of America we will not consider you for any public office. Not even "Dog Catcher!"

Wilton walked briskly off stage from the jeering crowd.

John Javez a heavenly priest from a Chicago Catholic Church said. "During my research I once asked a young college student if she thought Jesus smoked Pot. She immediately responded. "Yea! He sure looks like he did." You know she's right. He does. We know Jesus wouldn't want persecution in Gods church. This government was formed somewhat on Christian values. Some people of the Christian Church have used cannabis at all times throughout the centuries. Look in the Bibles that are over one hundred years old in the passages from book of psalms. Prophets smoke hashish in their religious sacraments. Who are the false prophets who censored the bible?" What else was censored from the bible? I thought there was separation between the church and the state. Historians of early Christianity claim, there are numerous religious documentations though out the centuries that has used marijuana among other drugs for religious purposes. Many religions of the world still practice religious sacraments with cannabis today.

The book of Genesis, God says"....I have given you every herb bearing seed, which is upon the face of the earth....to you it will be for meat" (29-30) designating seed as the primary food of mankind. The peaceful inner sanctuary of someone's beliefs of any individual should never be abridged by anyone or any government. Practicing your religion is the greatest human freedom.

United States Religious Restoration Act of 1993 guaranteed religious freedom. Thing is the same government that regulates how you practice your religion around this country. This government dictates how you freely worship. They change your individual belief system much like Stalin did in the Soviet Union to his citizens.

St. Mark established the Ethiopian Zion Coptic Church in the first century. He smoked marijuana in his sacramental rituals. "green herb of the

327

field." The Ethiopian Zion Coptic Church of Florida claim to be an offspring of a Jamaican sect of that Religion. The Coptic's claim marijuana, which they call by the Jamaican name "Ganja" is the herb mentioned in the Christians Bible's in numerous places. They have no doubt in their right to freely choose their cannabis essential sacraments to practice their believed religion. The Coptic's are heard chanting their sacred music during religious ceremonies in their commune. The Coptic's created quite a stir in their southern Florida digs with their interpretation of religion. However they continue to practice their faith. Hopefully, in the future with out government interference. All law enforcement agencies in Southern Florida argue that they have investigated the Coptic's and their relationship to large marijuana busts associated close to them. They are suspected of importing marijuana. I say let them, just tax their imports and sales of their marijuana. Life goes on peacefully.

However persecuted their religious views remain true and solid. They declare that Ganja is free and has always been free. The Coptics claim their sacramental rituals date back to a Jewish sect called the Essenes. The Essenes used marijuana medicinally. The same religious sect who are thought to be responsible for the Dead Sea Scrolls.

Your belief system should be yours to choose freely in a free country. Spiritual renewal with the safe enhancement of marijuana has been practiced for centuries in many different religions and cultures all over the world. Doctor's around the world pray with their patients if they are asked. Most patients feel better after their prayer session. This is part of the marijuana enhancement's medical healing practice.

These marijuana practice's have been grand fathered through the centuries. Cannabis will be here for centuries to come. It just a question if we live in a dictatorial prohibition or not. Catholics use the drug called alcohol as in wine to enhance their religious ceremony presentation.

Zororoaster an ancient Persian Prophet gave top billing to cannabis in the Zend-Avesta text. The Zoroastrians religion spanned over a dozen centuries until the 4th century AD. This ancient medical text listed over ten thousand medical healing plants, which marijuana came out in first place for healing powers from this ancient civilization. Widely used marijuana was their main religious sacrament and is believe to be called "Magi."

American Indians and non-Indian members of Native American church during unique and bona fide religious ceremonies are allowed marijuana, piote, and mushrooms use for religious purposes freely in this country. These guarantees for religious and other purposes are covered in "American Indian Religious Freedom Act Amendments of 1994."

Even a dozen Ethiopian monks were caught selling marijuana. They grew marijuana for over fourteen years before their marijuana grow operation was discovered. They grew marijuana at different monasteries. Some of the monks used marijuana in their religious ceremonies."

On the other side of the world an "Indian Hemp Drug Commission Report" states religious and social customs in India use hemp for social use and religious ceremonies. In one custom hemp leaves are made into a liquid mixture. It is then handed around in a cup with festive participants taking part. Hemp is mixed with sweet meats and is also passed in the custom.

The custom known in India is celebrated at the Durga Puja festival and has been practiced for centuries. Families and guests who participate in the Durga Puja festival embrace one another and exchange greeting in this joyous conclusion to the festival. Many Indians sanction hemp as part of their religious services in India. They possess the mystical knowledge to seek the ganja god.

Natives of Nepal use hemp for inspirational religious purposes also. Hinduism, Buddhism, both have reference to cannabis in there religions. The Bantus Religion of Africa use of"Dagga" is deeply rooted in their religious sacraments and medical customs. These religious rituals and customs are documented and still practiced today around the world.

These and other religious rituals around the world are sacred to those who believe and practice them. The Vatican disapproves of other religious rituals as less of less relevance or void of value. The Vatican has just revived and approved an exorcism ritual from four centuries ago. This catholic ritual is meant to drive the demons, devils, and Satan himself out of those who practice these sanctioned catholic religious traditions. Even the pope has preformed this exorcism ritual to drive the devil out on a withering women who was brought before him. Inspirational beliefs of other religions around the world have just as must relevance to those who practice their religious beliefs, established around the world. Their illusion of religious beliefs are just as viable to them as the catholic church exorcism rituals is to themselves.

Use of marijuana for religious spiritual enhancement is a viable reason for marijuana use. We're all only passing through this world. Everyone should be able to live their life like they want to. Where is the separation between church and state we were promised?" John concluded to an applause, while wearing a specially designed religious hemp robe made for him in Napal. The Red Hemp Carpet was rolled out for John to walk down.

Prohibitionist Nily Nevers------blind to individual beliefs, bitterly bias bent, and mentally inert was the best way to describe Nily after making a statement that "Marijuana smokers don't have brains enough to have firm religious beliefs." Nily was roundly booed off stage, and refused to walk down the red hemp carpet.

John looked on and shook his head in disbelief at Nily's irrational comments.

Kent Jones---Was an authentic authority polished with current drug testing facts for the pro-marijuana movement. Kent began. "Countries like our neighbor to the north Canada have declared drug testing illegal. Other countries are moving for individual freedoms. They have declared that drug testing is nothing more than fishing expeditions and as such is an infringement of their human and citizen's rights. By far too many laws are being past too fast without fair judgement or consideration of the United States Constitution, which bottom line guarantees freedom of individual choice for every citizen. This is the constitution that the blood of our nation was spilled for. All I know is the surest way to get people to smoke marijuana is to make marijuana illegal. Any problems our society has to be thought threw for all concerned. We have to think our way through it!

If you are like the segregates who are the prohibitionists, your day will come, and come soon it will. We will cut your bigotry out of the big government society, like you have cut us out legally from social society. We want to keep the peace where the government and police don't. Militarized trained cops who attack like pit bulls on marijuana users is not my idea of freedom constitutionally guaranteed rights. The government does not make good decisions for all its citizens. It hinders and sanctions free Americans, who choose their personal destiny.

Taking away citizens freedom is counter productive. Government's limiting a citizen's ability to express individuality is wrong. Where's the free government justice we were promised and guaranteed? Constitutional freedoms in a free society mean you have to put up with your neighbors beliefs even though you do not agree with him. Big Brother drug testing violates the protections from unreasonable searches and seizures guaranteed by the United States Constitution. No American has to open up for self incrimination, hindering his right to due process of law."

Kent continued. "Unconstitutional random drug testing for marijuana should halt. Somewhere along the line we lost guaranteed rights. Somehow, somewhere, at some time from governments past. The new deal was a raw deal. A raw deal should be no deal. A deal is only fair is when the deal is fair for all that's concerned."

Kent quoted another famous political candidate Gatewood Galbraith who said. "Did my father's generation hit the beaches of Normandy and Iwo Jima so their children would have to pee in a cup to hold a job in America?"

Kent said. "Truer words were never spoken. The government has ancient laws on the books, which they constitute, uphold and preserve. These ancient attitudes but current laws dictate and state what kind of sex your allowed in your bedroom, or herb you smoke in your household. These are laws against humanity's morals. These are laws against nature and social stability."

Kent who analyzed and inspected all the morality laws on the books against natural acts of comfort and compiled. "It's what many, many Americans do and enjoy. Smoke marijuana. Containing harm to our selves in the privacy of our homes is our right. Why is it Washington D C rated the fifty-first worst place to raise a kid, and this is where they dictate policy on how we live our lives in the privacy of our homes. Government control of your life and molding your children's attitude is bad policy. Kids learn about violence on TV and at school. Parents can now own their own drug tests to give their children. The drug tests are given to parents at reduced rates by some police departments. The parents can judge their child for governmental correctness. The child must pass a litany drug test to be included for full family status. They send their child's urine test into the laboratory for the drug test result's There is no bond of trust with these random drug testing tactics, further driving a wedge between parents and their children. These drug tests are not one hundred percent accurate, and do not gauge the extent of a marijuana smoker's intoxication, or if a person just ate hemp snacks. Other people who do not smoke marijuana have failed drug tests and have suffered the consequences of losing their positions in life. Some parent's know their kid smoke a little grass, but refuse to do anything about it. They decided to take a more progressive approach. Some parents who smoke pot have never hid the fact from their kid. They say hiding it from their kids only reinforces the fact that pot may be bad or wrong.

Some of these parents arouse the kid's interest in another direction if they could. Instead they would give their kids vitamins. They take him hiking, or white water rafting at every opportunity. They spend time and talk with their kids. This is your best defense. Most parents do not want to be vindictive to their kid. Some parents figure the kid will grow out of the cannabis habit just like they did. Some parents were glad that's all their kid did was smoke a little grass and that they kid carried on with a good life other wise. They know marijuana use is less harmful that alcohol.

Other testing done by the United States Custom's Agent's now check the inside the body of suspected drug smuggling tourists with x-rays when entering the country. Sobriety tests at police department require vials of blood, hair samples, urine, mouth swabs and a breathalyzer. Some employers require the same drug tests. One State just expanded the drug requirements of their state employees. Clean drug screens are a requirement for any employment position of the state. Reasonable suspicion of employees using drugs is cause for further random drug testing.

The state bargained with the workers unions about their complaints of privacy violations. However the new drug policy is to take effect soon. Some of the opposition to certain state's new drug testing policies. They complained only the rank and file personal is being drug tested. While the decision making employees of the state are not drug tested. The union stewards said. "It's not possible that the only drug users are in the rank and file. The ruling class against the sub-servants should be drug screened first. There is going to be a serious civil liberties court challenge." A union representative declared. We don't need big brother to make our moral and personal entrapment decisions in our lives." Ken said as he continued on.

"The government made moral decisions when they authorized the CIA to develop LSD, then conduct experiments on unknowing American citizen participants. They picked at random military personal from the armed forces. LSD was formally banned in 1968, after exposure of the drug was in the stream of the public. How many CIA agents made money from LSD, when they were the only ones authorized to have the drug. There's an example of governmental drug testing on human guinea pigs.

One experiment in our country was with artificial blood. The blood was given to unknowing or consenting patients. Science learns from human sacrifice because all of those injected with the experimental artificial blood are dead.

Local teachers in Oregon are opposed to a bill in their legislature that require mandatory drug testing. The teachers stated. "It is wrong and unconstitutional. Pay for the drug tests come directly out of the teacher's paycheck. One teacher said. "We should go out to drug test all the parents if they drug test all the teachers. These measures will not stop the nations youth from experimenting with drugs." The teacher said. "People should be glad if kids stick to marijuana than any other harder substances that are readily available to them include sniffing household products. Experts state one in five kids are experimenting by sniffing household products."

One teacher who had a drug conviction in 1974 was recently fired, after the conviction was found twenty-five years later on a performance review. The fired teacher has decided to run for State Representative. The American Civil Liberties Union has voiced strong resistance for drug testing.

The drug free work place is ludicrous, without stepping on the citizen's civil liberties." Kent said. "Our full time employers are now the governments lead dog in their drug fight on it's citizens. Drug testing is condoned and endorsed. Drug testing for employment positions should no longer test for marijuana, except sensitive positions of the government and industry, only if rights are voluntarily given up. The employee should also be compensated for giving up his constitutional rights.

Federal courts have ruled that an employee can sue after being fired by United Airlines for failing a drug screening. The employee was using legal prescription cannabis substitute Marinol filed the suit for disability discrimination. Some employee drug screening's don't distinguish the difference between marijuana and Marinol. "No employer has the right to discipline or dismiss an employee for using a legal drug prescribed by a physician," NORML Executive Director R. Keith Stroup, Esq. said. "This is another case of the 'War on Drugs' run amok."

The Canadian Civil Rights Association complaint filed with the Canadian Federal Court of Appeals which eventually ruled in a two-one decision that drug testing violates the Canadian Human Rights Act because it could discriminate against certain employees and because it isn't sufficiently related to job performance. Martin Doane, the commission's legal council stated. "The policy overshoots any reasonable mandate for drug testing and constitutes a significant infringement on the privacy of individuals who are required to submit to it." The Toronto Dominion Bank hiring procedures that include drug testing is discriminatory. One of the ruling judges Justice J A McDonald said. "A finding of a trace amount of drugs in one's system does not mean that the employee is unproductive or about to engage in a work-related crime." Drug testing should be a prohibited hiring practice.

Governments can drug test everybody on a continual basis. It will not curtail the nation's drug problem. Marijuana and hash are legal in more countries than not in the world. Recent surprise tests of a New Jersey police and fire dept found over twenty of the department's employees tested positive for marijuana, or cocaine. Mass drug urinalysis the cops and firemen claimed of the random drug testing violated their rights against unreasonable search and seizure. The cops said that imagine that."

Kent further said. "Upon further surprise inspections of the police and fireman's lockers, the search turned up hard drugs. Our law keepers are the lawbreakers. However it's not unreasonable for school children to be rounded up and have an internal inspection through mass drug urinalysis of all students. Responsible Citizens are not going to stop using recreational marijuana no matter what. Concerned cannabis parents of kids go into other parts of the house to respect their kids and others health aspects from smoking marijuana. Marijuana smokers do will adhere to unwritten rules already similar to tobacco cigarettes.

The Government can't lock everyone up, when forty to fifty percent of the people in this country have smoked at least part of a joint in the last month. Over seventy five percent of all Americans have smoked a marijuana joint in their lifetime. The Constitution guarantees everybodys the right for personal choice. Dehumanizing our marijuana-smoking citizens isn't what our constitution is about. The government and police can lighten up on it's marijuana smoking responsible citizens. It should be of no concern to the government who uses marijuana in the privacy of their home.

The government's understanding would be much more respected instead of their demands. Education and leading by example is the key for our kids. Marijuana smokers are not criminals or a danger to society. Everybody's right until they do wrong. No matter what there personal habits are. We must consider serious crime wrong.

The U. S. sponsored marijuana war by our government sprayed chemicals of parquet on Mexican, Central and South American marijuana crops in the 1970's. Public out cry through the media stopped the program after acute parquet poisoning deaths attributed to smoking the contaminated and poisoned weed. The parquet poisoned the weed, people of the world, Eco-system of the waterways, vegetables we eat, animals we treasure, soil we sow, and the air we breath.

Today our government still sponsors similar programs that poison hemp growing wild in ditch lines in rural areas of our country. None of these plants yield THC. Yet the irrational fumigation war continues unmitigated.

The DEA has been spraying chemicals and herbicides virtually unchecked for years. These drastic killing chemicals and herbicides used by the DEA in ditch weed eradication programs cause great illnesses among our people. Biological impairments to citizens in these areas are common. Environmentalists were astonished at the DEA's disclosure. The Drug Czar under the Reagan administration, Carlton Turner in 1983 went on National Television and explained the DEA's spraying of parquet in Georgia, Tennessee, and Kentucky stated. "It would teach a lesson to any or hundreds kids who died from smoking parquet poisoned pot." After Turner resigned in disgrace from media exposure, he then joined the drug testing industry. The urine test kits is a gigantic money making industry in itself. Their entity of rich man schemes is at the expense of every American's right to privacy and individual freedom. Even our self-incrimination rights under the fifth amendment are violated. Marijuana drug testing for probationers of minor offences, including marijuana possession, sometimes have men and women urinate in full view of a government or health official eyewitness. Urination is a very private part of your life which is now under a government microscope. Industrial and government employers drug tests use similar standards, further violating your right to privacy. It has been ruled in federal court of violating your right to privacy under the fourth amendment of the Constitution of the United States. Citizen lawsuits and Class action suits against the drug testing companies, and their agents are being filed in court on a steady basis. If we have to sue them until their bankrupt were going to get our Constitutional Rights Back. The lawsuits are demanding damages for emotional distress, and also punitive damages for illegal firings. This is a gross invasion of privacy.

I've seen a bunch of dirty tactics pulled on our citizenry by the government. Our Current Drug Czar Barry McCaffrey said. "It's silly and sad" about the overwhelming passage of medical marijuana initiatives by the voters. We'll I think it's a sad day in America when we have a retired military covert action authority in charge of everyone's social inner stability. I'd like to know how he knows how everyone in this country feels inside of their body. And I'd further like to know how and why he feels he has to try and change everyone's personal beliefs about themselves. Everyone knows the aches and pains of their own body better than any Czar. I'd like to see his educational credentials to make personal and intimate decisions in every American mind and body. I challenge the shallow and gutless drug Czar to a full debate concerning hemp and marijuana. I'd like to know how many of his friends get commissions on drug test kits? We are here today to put a stop to federal government's marijuana war. Now!" As Kent concluded his tough laborious debate issue stressing final his point to a very enthused audience.

Blate Baggit----Blate's dreadful reply was. "Drug testing is a necessary toll in the drug war."

Kent---Responded. "Drug testing is unreasonable in a country that's stresses personal freedom. Drug testing is to much to ask of non-violent honest tax paying citizens."

Bobby Barrit---"Tobacco had their prohibition through the centuries when the Czar of Russia, and the Ottoman sultan executed tobacco smokers on the spot in the seventeenth century. Others countries had similar prohibition laws like Bavaria, Saxony, Zurich. Alcohol had it's bout with prohibition wars. Marijuana Correct Comparison Studies have shown that marijuana is much less harmful to the lungs than tobacco cigarettes. Marijuana contains over six hundred less foreign agents than some altered tobacco nicotine enhanced brands. There is no acrylic tar and nicotine in marijuana. The tar in marijuana is water-soluble. Even chronic use of marijuana does not impair the lung ability to function, or does pose significant danger to lung function. Effects of marijuana use usually last a couple hours at best. You can snap out of these mild effects with any situation that arises. Depending on the importance of the shock situation that may arise. Like a large strange barking dog running at you in a furious manner. Your high on marijuana has just been blown away. Much like a police officer pulling you over with the flashing lights. The intoxicating effects of marijuana dissipate, where as alcohol, or cocaine still have adverse lingering effects.

Marijuana is not the mind altering narcotic or controlling drug as portrayed by the government. Non-users have no idea, what the mild high of marijuana is like. Being stoned on marijuana is one thing, being stoned cold drunk on alcohol is something drastically different. Motor functions are impaired immensely from alcohol than when compared with the mild effects from the high of marijuana. Motor functions are sometimes enhanced from marijuana use. Like getting in the grove to calmly go about your business. Alcohol is killing people on the roads where marijuana is not!"

Bobby further stated. "Fact is people who drink alcohol or smoke tobacco are worst off than people that just smoke marijuana. The hypocrisy centered around tobacco, and alcohol as well as legal drugs, where as marijuana is illegal and bad drugs is unacceptable as the facts of social level of acceptance and use prevail. Marijuana is less harmful than some foods we frequently ingest. Throwing users of marijuana in jail and making them criminals doesn't work. This tyrannical action by the government does not deter marijuana users. Marijuana re-education camps run by the government are also ineffective. Some citizens believe marijuana should be freely available and taxed at commercial outlets. Yet, unlicensed if grown for personal use."

Bobby continued. "The current drug policies are counter productive to society. The United States of America is not the leader of the free world. When leading democratic countries of the world like Australia, have much more liberal laws concerning marijuana. Australia concedes that there are no major or serious side effects from marijuana use. Tobacco is the leading killer worldwide, followed by alcohol, than hard drugs, prescription drugs, aspirin and coffee. Again marijuana has never killed anyone in the history of mankind, but the government keeps tobacco and alcohol legal. I often think just because it does kill methodically.

Tobacco companies which have targeted youths to gain a larger control in the substance abuse market. Philip Morris will begin a media campaign to dishearten smoking among kids.

The Marlboro man and Joe Camel rode into the nation youth's aspirations through intensive tobacco advertising. Adolescents are susceptible to appealing tobacco advertising. Some tobacco companies marketed to the public have their cigarettes artificially induced with higher levels of nicotine to keep smokers hooked. Genetically altered high nicotine content of some American cigarettes are sold in foreign countries. Nicotine rich altered tobacco plants are grown in some South American countries by big tobacco companies. Some of these high nicotine strains of tobacco plants have been grown in this country as well.

Big tobacco said they do this nicotine enhancement process to improve the taste of their product. Tobacco Studies and results they say are based on consumer tests. The U. S. Food and Drug Administration wants to regulate the tobacco industry like an addictive drug. Lawmakers are presently arguing over how little or how much authority to give the U S Food and Drug administration to regulate nicotine levels of cigarettes.

It is my belief that any organization that can't distinguish the difference between marijuana and heroin by having contributed to both being listed as schedule one narcotic should be totally re-vamped. Any organization that uses the public as guinea pigs should also be re-vamped. Any organization that is responsible for prescription drugs being the sixth leading killer in the United States should be re-vamped. It only shows there are much more serious problems to be solved then comparatively harmless marijuana use.

Lawmakers ought to be working eighteen hours per day trying to establish a national tobacco policy, and not a policy to throw big tobacco out of business either. Taxes as part of the tobacco settlement will make cigarettes prices go up substantially. Lawmakers can't be overly harsh on tobacco companies because we do not want to bankrupt these companies, that would create a huge black market. With big tobacco settling claims in the majority of states and territories for health cost reimbursements this is the new way tobacco business will be established. Tobacco products should be sold and used in the natural state as marijuana is with no altering additives.

Most people start smoking between the age of fifteen to seventeen years of age. The Surgeon General released a statement that if an adolescent doesn't start smoking cigarettes by the time he is eighteen years of age. That person is likely never to start smoking. Some law makers contend that kids smoke in the boys and girls room in schools as much now as during the decades of the 40's, 50's, 60's 70's 80's and 90's no matter what the laws have been."

Bobby suggested then. "Educators teaching kids about smoking with educational programs, including video's and smokers with blank lung. Showing the student's ex-rays of smokers and none smokers. The students see firsthand the inside of the black lungs of cigarette smokers.

Florida teens make anti-tobacco advertising for lawmakers now of their own design. The anti-smoking commercials for TV and Radio are being written for the "Florida's Governor's Teen Summit." They target their audience with gross-out topics for maximize impact among their peers. Teens making anti-cigarette ads is a good program, as long as they point out the ills of smoking.

Blue Cross and Blue Shield Medical Insurance want to recover losses from the tobacco companies from tobacco related illnesses that they claim are related to tobacco smoking. Law makers looking at over fifty-thousand freshly released tobacco company documents. The government and the medical industry knew the dangers of smoking tobacco. They advised and advertised health adversities to the public for decades about the ills of tobacco smoking. This didn't stop the government from collecting and spending the tax dollars of big tobacco. This didn't stop the medical insurance companies from selling health insurance policies.

Lawmakers are doing a state by state assessment of medical expenditures. Some states have over thirty percent of its citizens smoking tobacco cigarettes. Any proposed tobacco settlement will include the high costs of tobacco related illness.

Two large health groups the American Heart Association and the American Lung Association criticizes the tobacco settlement for being to lenient on tobacco companies. The Tobacco Industry liabilities would be limited in future lawsuits under current proposals.

Law makers said the tobacco settlement process is moving slow due to all the haggling from all parties involved. They also cited no shows by lawmakers unwilling to participate in the tobacco settlement process.

In any event the tobacco companies will pay a large settlement to stay in business. Medical compensation tax will be part of all sales. More educational programs will be established to make all citizens aware of the dangers of smoking. Questions still linger about limiting future tobacco liabilities under new proposals. Tobacco companies want to cap all future liabilities.

Over five-hundred billion tobacco tax dollars will be collected over the next twenty-five years under present proposals. That's a small amount compared to the seven-hundred billion some of these same law makers already robbed the social security administration fund of at present of our retirement. Now the law makers are short to pay social security to it's citizen's in the projected future.

The General Accounting Office Auditors upon reviewing financial statements from twenty-four government agencies found billions upon billions of American tax dollars unaccounted for. The United States Government officially admit they don't know what happened to the billions upon billions of the tax dollars. There is no end to the government's fraud, that is propounded on the America taxpayers.

The government has a blank check from American taxpayer dollars at the expense of all workers hard sweat. The government's accounting financial statement of the tax payers dollars stink. The tobacco farmers association want the tobacco farmers to get part of any big tobacco settlement. Tobacco crop share is already receding. The farmers feel money should be available for them to switch to alternative crops like hemp with any settlement with big tobacco. Most farmers cite that tobacco growing is part of their culture.

State lawmakers stated they want their cut of Big Tobacco's settlement to stay in their own perspective states. Federal Officials with their hand out are already objecting.

The Treasury Dept released statements that tobacco or marijuana smoking shortens work life. I will counter that by how many people put up with their job just because they consider or enjoy a smoke break as being part of their quality time. Many people lengthen their workday because they smoked some marijuana. Most smokers said they will not quite smoking tobacco no matter how high, the tax on cigarettes go to. People know that smoking cigarettes is harmful to their health but they still refuse to lay their cigarettes down, until when and if they are ready.

Some restaurant owners in California refuse to honor tobacco bans passed by the government. Some bar owners refused to tell their patrons to put their cigarettes out. They do not want to run their customers off. Some Celebrities of Hollywood have protested the cigarette ban in bars. Calling the latest cigarette ban on encroachment of smoker's right's. Smokers protested the restaurant ban. Magazine, book, TV, and radio personalities staged larger and larger protests.

There is no documented proof smoking marijuana has killed anyone after ten thousand years of use. Cannabis should not be considered a gateway drug to hard drugs, because all hard drug users started with government sponsored tobacco and alcohol mood altering substances, not cannabis, which is by far less harmful. Prohibition of marijuana serves no meaningful purpose. Alcohol and tobacco have their guidelines. They have certain known intoxicating and health risks. Marijuana is much less of a risk health wise. The marijuana prohibition has failed and should be eliminated. New fair marijuana use governmental guidelines should be reestablished.

Police rather deal with cannabis citizens and their so called high on marijuana involving contemporary relaxation, than hard liquor consuming citizens who are obnoxious and puking drunk from alcohol. Officer's have dealt with cocaine induced rowdies. Trying to arrest them is rarely a pleasure cruise. The adrenaline effect of hard drugs, and alcohol can have over whelming intoxicating effect. These stimulants from hard alcohol use and hard drug have strong adverse effects when compared with the mild effects of marijuana use.

Marijuana highs can compare to tobacco or coffee comparatively. The American public would be much safer when the customers leave from proposed cannabis coffee houses close at days business end, instead of our strictly alcohol taverns which multitudes empty customers on to our roadways nationwide.

In 1976 Robert Dupont, President Ford's chief adviser on drugs, declared that alcohol, and tobacco are more dangerous than marijuana and further recommend marijuana decriminalization. We need to get over the disaster phobia that has been created. We need to get people accustom to the facts, not fallacies promoted by the Federal government.

Marijuana smokers understand the difference between marijuana and all other drugs. The laws concerning marijuana have to be relaxed. A survey of drug users stated they had good experiences on marijuana, however they have bad experiences on barbiturates, heroin, cocaine, crack, and pharmaceutical tranquilizers. Citizens surveyed also admitted that they spend forty percent of their leisure money on cannabis, and thirty-eight percent of their money on government sponsored tobacco, and alcohol. Marijuana is the preferred herb of the people." Bobby concluded.

Benedict Burns lectured. "Cannabis Dependence causes a manipulative impairment as characteristic withdrawal. The narcotic marijuana causes curtailment of important activities such as occupational and social activities. Recreational activities are also reduced. Cannabis use results in failure concerning obligations as school, work, or activities around the home. Further neglecting household responsibility, or children. Cannabis use can be physically hazardous when operating machinery or an automobile. Cannabis dependence disorder further goes against social norms." Benedict concluded. "It takes weeks for marijuana's effects to ware off, if at all."

Bobby countered. "Even if half that garbage statement were true, marijuana is still not a detriment against humanity. Marijuana use is a matter of self choice, with out detrimental, lingering or long lasting effects. Clinical tests of marijuana users worldwide substantiate mild effects at best for marijuana's high. It is enough to take the edge off, but not enough to rob a person of mental and physical control. Marijuana use has helped me cope with a loss of my father from the Vietnam War. All I ever had of my father were pictures as I was to young to remember him. Now I have children of my own. I don't need the government interrupting our home life or own home values." Thank you all very much.

Karen Kurtz's started her opening statement soundly. "Set free a suffering humanity! Case studies of merit conclude there are no serious health risks associated with marijuana use. A multitude of medical marijuana institutionalized case studies of merit have been firmly established. Marijuana smokers presently have to hide smoking marijuana from their doctor, friends, colleagues and their employers. There are presently no government guidelines for safe medical marijuana use."

Karen went directly into her inspired medical presentation with her assistants close by stating. "The chief surgeon in Nero's Roman Empire praised cannabis for the stoutest medical chords. Cannabis is used intricately in many medical ways through out history to modern mans medical time.

Sir Russell Reynolds of England prescribed cannabis in treating menstrual cramps. As Queen Victoria's own physician claimed in magazine publication's in the 1890's that cannabis "When pure and administered carefully, is one of the most valuable medicines we posses."

Karen further stated. "Medical Marijuana's potential is endless, not only in smoking form, but in phamicutical adaptations as well."

Judge Francis Young of the DEA's administrators said "Marijuana is one of the safest therapeutically active substances known to man." after reviewing the enormous amount of creditable evidence. Included in medical marijuana issue's fight is U. S. Rep Barney Franks (D-Mass) legislation, which lets the states determine their own medical marijuana policies. Former U S Attorney General Ramsey Clark also endorsed a change in the government's drug war.

The indisputable credentials of medical societies, specialists, senior citizens groups, legislatures and knowledgeable influential citizens are firmly behind medical marijuana initiative's being proposed and passed in our nation. Tell me what walk of influential life you would except cannabis credentials from? I'll deliver!"

Karen named many relief's from marijuana use. "Medical marijuana users should immediately be able to start growing their own marijuana for personal use. Ironically, the citizens voted for medical marijuana use in California and Arizona. The Arizona repressionists senators nullified the voters choice on the medical marijuana initiative Prop 200.

Some of the same government leadership that is immune to drug tests, and their governor is convicted of serious felony counts and has to resign from the State of Arizona's highest office in disgrace.

Arizona Medical Marijuana pro-activists groups have collected more than twice the amount of signatures in time to place in medical marijuana referendum for the voters for a second vote in November, and again Medical Marijuana passed overwhelmingly in the State of Arizona

The cannabis conscious citizens of Arizona reaffirmed their first vote for medical marijuana. The pro-activists seek parole hearings of non-violent marijuana offenders as well in Arizona. The appeals court in California re-instated an injunction against a Cannabis Buyers club. That's like a slap in the voters face after California Prop 215 was passed overwhelmingly by the voters the cannabis club founder said of the judges decision. The cannabis club has been a constant on again off again entity.

California people want and need medical marijuana and have spoken at the polls. The leader of the Cannabis clubs in San Francisco quoted a Civil Rights activist "We will not go to the back of the bus." These un-American political repressionists all need to be voted out, he further said. Marijuana should be accessible to those who are severely in pain to ease their suffering. Marijuana Pharmaceutical's developed in other countries of the world are being used presently.

Dennis Peron from San Francisco headed the "Peron Cannabis Cultivators Club" has been a hero for medical marijuana patients in California. He has been persecuted by our government. He has sacrificed relentlessly for medical marijuana patients in need. The clubs motto. "This isn't about pot, it's about love." is true. Dennis's medical marijuana club had over ten thousand active clients, people who could call each other friends. These cannabis cultured people of all ethnicity's, sexual orientations, ages, peacefully co-exist without interference from cops. Dennis Peron indeed is a hero to some. Dennis has endured much hardship in the drug war of America. The pro-medical marijuana activist and provider's farm has been raided several times with the marijuana plants being confiscated by the herb cops. The herb cops then would hold legal medical marijuana patients at gun point, while stealing all the medicine of marijuana plants from the sick, and elderly patients. Dennis immediately replanted donated clone marijuana plants for medical patients as a defiant protest, holding a large protest party the following week end after the herb raid. These people won and are endorsed by the voters. The medical marijuana initiatives in the State of California won, yet they are still persecuted. That cannabis club will reopened.

The California Attorney General further said that the owners of the cannabis clubs face charges of sale and transportation of marijuana. How can they do this? People are sick and dying with aids and suffering with other serious ailments! The government won't give marijuana out, so the marijuana clubs are needed. We have a marijuana club sanctioned by the voters of the state of California being threaten and forcibly closed by the federal government. We have a right to be here without fear of prosecution, or jailed for sale, possession, or use of marijuana. Medical Marijuana had a major victory at the polls. The people have spoken but our government doesn't want to concede to the people's chosen mandate. AIDS Coalition's have demanded the White House allow medical marijuana to seriously ill patients.

Some doctor's don't always like to prescribe hard drugs like codeine and Prozac. Marijuana is a lot less harmful than some prescription drugs in the long run. Medical marijuana has been practiced for ten thousand years for a wide variety of very safe therapeutic uses. The majority of prescription drugs have only been tested for last ten to fifty years. It is estimated that safe therapeutic marijuana use could replace ten to twenty percent of prescription drugs currently being used for over a hundred different diseases.

When the patient and the physician agree on medical diagnosis, where does the government get their totalitarian authority to medically interfere with patients. Licensed Medical doctors, without threats of intimidation, should do the doctoring. The government officials don't have the authority or the education to override a licensed physician's counseling to a patient.

Doctors are legally allowed to prescribe marijuana without persecution or prosecution in California. Why do lawmakers threaten and arrest doctors for honoring prop 215. Pot club members have the right to obtain and use marijuana without persecution. Where's the compassion? What kind of message does this send, that the voters in the election of the State of California, in the United States of America, if the agenda for medical marijuana reform isn't respected after the ballets in ballot box are counted. Where's the credibility of our law keepers and makers.

This is a struggle in the mainstream of the American lifestyle and conviction. Vote these despicable politicians out, who don't honor the voters choices. We need a change! Clean sweep em out! This marijuana drug policy reform campaign is going to sweep the nation. The medicalization of marijuana will be back. We want non-profit growers Co op. We want safe gardens, with organically grown herbs. We want to furnish our patients with a high grade of safe marijuana. We want our patients to know what their buying.

The government's HMO Marijuana Traditional lock them up law enforcement are over. Were done with these political and police scare tactics".

Karen continued. "Other states like Alaska, Washington, Oregon, Nevada, and Colorado have followed California and Arizona's lead to reform marijuana drug laws. All these states passed reform medical marijuana bills overwhelmingly. Oregon's Democratic Party has endorsed medical marijuana. Alaska's medical marijuana initiative is currently in affect. The state of Maine and many more states will have a medical marijuana initiatives choices in their states ballot boxes next."

Karen elaborated. "The Washington State Medical Marijuana Initiative 685 was tailored after the Arizona Medical Marijuana Law already passed by the voters. The bigots of the Washington State Supreme courts decided that Medical Marijuana was of no importance. The voters of the state felt different and reality did speak in November. The Washington Lt. Governor opposed the state drug reform initiative 685. Lt. Governor Brad Owen was found to have spent thousands of tax payers dollars to sway the results, which is prohibited by federal law. The Lt. Governor was fined by state Executive Ethics Board seven thousand dollars for trying to influence the result's of Initiative 685, while utilizing public funds.

NORML Foundation Executive Director Allen St. Pierre said. "The fine against Owen should put all elected officials and anti-drug bureaucrats to local sheriffs or narcotics officers, on notice, Public funds may not be used to influence public opinion in advance of an election or initiative. It is hard to imagine a more repugnant and threatening specter than a government willing to spend taxpayers money to actively campaign against free elections." Was St. Pierre's response from a NORML News letter. The voters of the District of Columbia, Washington DC also have passed a Medical Marijuana Bill on the ballot last November.

The two-hundred and fifty thousand signatures for the ballot were collected in three months. Margins of two out of every three voters passed the medical marijuana initiative. Government officials now discuss distribution of the cannabis.

Possibilities being discussed was to establish a marijuana supply agency much like Oakland California has called the Oakland Cannabis Buyers' Cooperative. On regular member of Oakland's Cannabis Buyers Club is allowed to carry One and a half pounds of marijuana for his own personal medical relief stash. The marijuana stash is what the Oakland city council figures is a three-month supply for this medical marijuana user. The medical marijuana user said. "This is the how I deal with the pain of a motorcycle accident that has left me paralyzed for over twenty years." The City of Oakland's Council is the most liberal for medical marijuana since the voters passed Proposition 215 in the State of California.

Merciless federal prosecutors regardless of patient suffering sued to close the state sponsored medical marijuana clubs but failed. The same federal law that allowed undercover law enforcement agencies to sell cocaine, heroin, marijuana, and other drugs in drug stings, allows the city officers of Oakland Marijuana cooperative to distribute medical marijuana without prosecution while performing official duties of the city government sponsored by the voters of the state. These Oakland City Officers would distribute the marijuana to the medical needy in hopes of shielding the states medical marijuana patients from federal prosecution.

The state of Oregon medical patients light up now without fear of prosecution even though opponents still try to side step the new law. Some patients readily admit that they have smoked marijuana for over thirty years illegally. Marijuana medical patients claim relief for asthma, arthritis, glaucoma, severe nausea, muscle spasms, seizures, tumors, AIDS, chemotherapy treatments, depression, stress related headaches, and many more documented and safe therapeutic methods. Nightmares of the police breaking into your house on a home invasions is also relieved by passage of medical marijuana initiatives.

Marijuana medical patients will be issued a state registration card. Voters overwhelmingly are much more compassionate than our present governors.

The British Medical Association overwhelmingly back medical marijuana use for patients for the many different medical benefits use in their country.

A Canadian Health official stated. "Marijuana is no different than aspirin. We are prepared in emergency situations to prescribe marijuana as a legal medicine in a case by case deliberation."

One Canadian Judge Frances Howard said. "The occasional to moderate use of marijuana by a healthy adult is not ordinarily harmful, even if used over a long period of time. There have been no deaths from marijuana, assuming that current rates of consumption remain stable, the health related costs of marijuana use are very, very small in comparison with those health costs associated with tobacco and alcohol consumption. Others are free to consume society's drugs of choice, alcohol and tobacco, even though these drugs are known killers."

Medical patients who choose the soft herb over sedated prescription drugs lead a much more normal life. These people choose a soft herb for medical purposes over readily available legal prescription hard drugs. The pharmaceutical companies want to sell you dangerous synthetic drugs as Prozac instead of a natural herb to treat depression. Let there be no doubt drugs like Prozac have serious side effects. Pharmaceutical companies are profit driven, which over ride patients health.

Some of Canada's top doctors have evidence that marijuana use increases stamina and relieves pain from a rare neurological bone disease. Marijuana may boost the strength of our patients as the medical tests have indicated. They're is no reason for medical marijuana to be illegal. Still formal recognition of medical marijuana and legalities by the Canadian government hasn't been realized even though marijuana medical co-ops are springing up all over Canada. One patient who suffers from chronic pain said. "I've tried over fifteen different drugs and the only one that worked gave me extreme muscle tremors. That is why I tried marijuana. Since I started smoking pot, we've recorded remarkable improvements in my physical strength."

The recent medical marijuana class action law suit ruling by a Philadelphia Judge Marvin Katz questioned the Justice Departments policy. The medical marijuana supportive federal judge denied the federal governments request to dismiss the case. The judge empathized the equal protection issue with the federal government concerning medical marijuana patients. The judge asked the attorney for the federal government why they halted the IND program (Compassionate Investigational New Drug program). Why from did the program dwindle from thirty patients down to eight patients? Would it be fair to only give eight patients nationwide morphine?

This federal government claimed they had the right to regulate drugs as interstate commerce. The lawsuit was filed by one-hundred and sixty plaintiffs from forty-nine states. The plaintiffs (The Action Class for Freedom of Therapeutic Cannabis) declare the federal government's ban on medical marijuana is unconstitutional and further violates the first, fourth, sixth, eight, ninth, and tenth amendments, The plaintiffs claim their right to due process and equal protection under the law has been denied. The unjust prohibition of medical marijuana denies disease suffering patients from a remedy that does work for them. The scientific proof of the worthiness and value of medical marijuana is undeniable.

Over Thirty-five states have recognized the value of Medical Marijuana, Marijuana decriminalization, and need for re-instating hemp production. Many States have various bills concerning marijuana and hemp agriculture at different stages of government that are being debated and voted on in their state legislatures."

Karen armed with fresh facts from "International Cannabinoid Research Society" said. "Medical Prescription Cannabinoids derived from marijuana's THC treats "autoimmune" disorders. Researchers in laboratory tests injected animals with encephalomyelinitis a disease damaging the nerves like multiple sclerosis in humans. Of the animals that were injected with THC Cannabinoids first one-hundred percent lived. One-hundred percent of the animals died that were not given the THC Cannabinoids first. Israel physicians uses cannabinoids nerve preserving power called dexanabinol for prevention of brain damaged induced from strokes.

San Francisco General Hospital is currently conducting tests for Medical Marijuana. One patient with HIV smokes marijuana three times per day supplied and machine rolled by the hospital staff. A nurse regulates, calculates, and records the marijuana smoker. The hospital's experimental marijuana smoker was down to one-hundred and sixty lbs. from his HIV condition. So far thanks to this experimental marijuana program this patient is on a health rebound. His serious illnesses receded to undetectable levels. The governmental assertions that medical marijuana is ineffective has been consistently proven wrong. The opinion that research must go on is against already proven medical marijuana research. Marijuana medical methods have been thoroughly established for hundreds upon thousands of years by proven medical physicians through research and medical marijuana use of their patients. It's time for the government to get in step with all its people." Karen continued to explain.

Karen's bare bones medical facts stood up hands down and over political mis-information propaganda distortion. Karen's constant calculating of medical facts certainly were consumed by the concerned crowd.

Karen then personally thanked a federal judge who was in the audience with other colleagues of his legal stature. The federal judge in preliminary hearings sided in a class action law suit by medical marijuana patients. He asked the feds to explain the medical marijuana ban. The federal judge asked the United States government to contemplate providing medical marijuana to patients. "This is a needed program to aid sick people." He said to Karen.

"The British government has sanctioned a huge marijuana plantation for marijuana medical research. The overwhelming medical evidence and benefits from medical marijuana that exists can no longer being ignored. The European community is considering full marijuana legalization, where seventy-five percent of the countries have already decriminalized small amounts of cannabis."

Before Karen concluded her debate position, she turned the podium over to Dr Casey Casper.

Dr Casper illustrated his hands on experience with patients, who use marijuana medically. The Doctor explained his position of being against marijuana medically just a few years prior. However, as a medical general practitioner his family ran clinic had a medical clientele where fifty percent of their patients were infected with HIV. The Doctor said. "I've seen marijuana use by patients relieve pain without prescribing Marinol. Marinol makes patients drowsy. It then knocks the AIDS patients out for bedtime."

The Doctor lectured." The mild affects of smoking marijuana helps his AIDS, cancer, and severe problem patients overcome some of the pain and still carry on most normal functions. Most of these AIDS marijuana smoking patients get through their day, while staying coherent.

The Doctor continued. "I'm glad I knew the truth! My medical marijuana research has led me not to trust the government any more. I would rather find out for myself through our own medical research. I further would like to know why "The National Institute on Drug Abuse" took their time in releasing information on Ibogaine. This treatment is known to cure some people from coke, heroin, cigarettes, booze for months on end or a lifetime. "Instant De-tox!" Don't our decision making politicians read or under stand the articles on Ibogaine from "The New York Times." Are the politicians keeping good information from the public, so they can sell pills like Tylenol, prescription drugs like Prozac, whiskey with sky high alcohol content, and nicotine enhanced cigarettes? Did anyone see ABC News a few years back on what happens when you mix a couple of Tylenol's and a few beer's? Did you know you could die from liver failure? Where were the consumer warning's from the FDA? Did you know Tylenol and Budweiser are large finical sponsor's for a drug free America? The Doctor concluded by blatantly criticizing the drug Czar for his ignorant and reckless view on the benefits of medical marijuana.

Austin Annoytin—"Federal experts disagree with pro marijuana advocates." Austin started out. Boos immediately came from the audience.

The moderator Kevin Kellar quickly told the audience. "Quite down!"

Austin further stated. "The levels of THC are much higher today than in the 60's and 70's. Also stating that Marijuana is a health hazard, which causes respiratory disease. Therefore it should not be legal."

One spectator yelled. "Then put a health warning's on the pack of marijuana and sell them." Referring to selling marijuana with a consumer warning on the packaging similar to tobacco.

Spectators who heckled or hindered the debate were escorted away. Some couldn't refrain from expressing their view.

Austin explained some of the drug Czar's ignorant deeds. "The Czar condemns efforts of AIDS marijuana activists. Experts disagree on medical benefits of marijuana. Finding no marijuana benefits is the Czar's position."

In the backdrop AIDS activists and cancer patients were represented. They felt they knew what was best for their well being. They relieved pain of seriously ill AIDS patients with medical marijuana. The drug Czar, the Activists felt this was meddling with health policy issues. They feel the drug Czar had no jurisdiction here.

The protesters had signs with statements like. "Doctor-Patient relationship, without Federal Interference."

One AIDS Activist in the backdrop explained his point of view to a group of TV and radio commentators. "Some of these patients lose a lot of weight. Marijuana helps increase their appetite. For others it relieves their pain without heavy doses of prescription narcotics.

Eighty percent of the people polled in all types of surveys Newspaper, TV, Radio, or Cyber, favored Medical Marijuana patients.

Government ID cards at the very least could easily identify these people. Give them what they need and leave them alone. Marijuana is not the dangerous drug the government make it out to be."

One Aids patient said to a commentator who was interviewing him in the backdrop. "Why such a war over weed? Why worry whom smokes and who doesn't smoke? I smoke and so do many of my friends, that does not that make them criminal in my mind."

Another man yelled. "No! It does not!"

The commentator agreed. The marijuana medical users further said. "These people need to get judged by the content of their character, not on if they smoke marijuana or not. Most marijuana smokers are fun loving people at heart."

Karen Kurt rebutted. "Marijuana level of THC has not changed in the last thirty years. Levels of THC at street levels have remained the same. Smoking Marijuana is known not to destroy someone's health. Marijuana is not loaded with foreign agents in production similar to tobacco. There is a health advantage for users of marijuana that holds over the legal drugs of tobacco, and alcohol.

All studies have show that the killer weed claim by law enforcement has been proved erroneous. Research programs on marijuana use show time and time again that marijuana and a short death span have no link. Marijuana use does not curtail a persons mortality rate." Karen and company enchantingly concluded.

Idealistic Ellis Edison a perpetual and accomplished history buff spoke on history of marijuana. "The word marijuana first came from supporters of Poncho Villa in the Sonora Mexican region. Their enlightening Mexican songs sang of looking for and smoking marijuana. The word reefer was first used by African-Americans. Musicians commonly used marijuana Jazzman Louis Armstrong in 1930 was busted for criminal possession of small amount of marijuana.

Positive cannabis reports conflicted with the governmental propaganda campaign against marijuana use. The government's Panama Canal Zone report conducted by a civilian and military panel of experts in the 1920's concluded no long term ill effects and further that cannabis is not habit forming or dangerous. The government sponsored Panama Canal report recommended taking no action for sale and use of marijuana among its soldiers or the citizen's our nation.

California was the first state to outlaw marijuana and Texas followed shortly after. However in the course through times, California, and Arizona are the first to change marijuana medicinal use laws. Some countries have never had Marijuana or hashish illegal like India. Some people think smoking marijuana is hereditary. It's been a major part of history through out modern man's time. Hemp production is a leader in industrial circles. Earliest recorded uses of marijuana started in 10,000 BC by one of the Chinese fathers of medicine. Since than numerous records of various useful methods in use of marijuana have been recorded.

Marijuana use from the ancient Egyptians, Indian, and Chinese civilizations realized marijuana's many uses. The Greeks and Persians used marijuana for it's anti-depressant qualities. The French used marijuana for it in the nineteenth century. China today is the world's largest hemp exporter of hemp textiles and hemp paper. Look through 1840's medical journals of Britain and you'll realize the many different medical marijuana benefits."

Ellis explained the difference between hash and marijuana. "Hash or pot can be eaten or smoked have the same high properties. Hash is a condensed form of marijuana smoke properties. Hash is often smoked in a pipe. Marijuana is smoked usually is in a cigarette paper or a pipe. The THC content level for the high is the same, as the THC level is what it is and that's that. Long term or short term effects from marijuana or hash are equal. Even heavy smokers of marijuana over long periods of time do not show signs of lung malfunction. You don't see marijuana babies, but you do see hard drug and alcohol affected babies with malfunctioning bodies."

One spectator yelled from the audience. "Tell it Ellis!" Ellis then responded. "See what's so wrong with marijuana." The crowd roared with enthusiasm.

Ellis continued. "Marijuana is one-hundred percent non-toxic, the same cannot be said of the legal, taxed, and government endorsed substances of tobacco, alcohol and prescription drugs. The European community has relaxed cannabis across the board, Germany, Spain, Netherlands, Italy, Greece and on and on. In England in the 1,500's Elizabeth I ordered the larger farm owners to grow hemp or face fines. If only today's Queen Elizabeth in England had the same foresight of her hereditary namesake. The Spanish ordered hemp to be grown through out their empire in the part of the Americas they controlled. Cannabis cultivation has been here for centuries. Cannabis cultivation will be here for centuries to come. In the United States Police confiscate marijuana crops of seven-hundred plants at a time in helicopter drug raids. Seven-hundred fully mature marijuana plants times one-thousand dollars equals seven-hundred thousand plus dollars. Why do you think people risk all for these type of enterprising ventures?

A cannabis crop in Tennessee had over six-thousand plants were recently discovered and destroyed by the Sheriff's Dept. Value of the marijuana crop was estimated at fifteen-million. The history of the drug laws are similar to the history of alcohol concerning the prohibition. High crime goes with prohibition. When the eighteenth amendment was repealed which ended the prohibition on alcohol, high crime rates declined. When marijuana is decriminalized it will have the same effect. No more wrong raids on marijuana users homes where the police kill the residents during arrest procedures, before the drug police realize they are at the wrong resident. Cannabis has been and will be used by the people of the world long after were all gone." Ellis concluded to a standing ovation.

Gilbert Giles. "History has ended for hemp in America." Gil was booed and egged off the stage fast.

Abraham knew hemp is one of the oldest commodities and trades on earth. Abe started out by quoting Thomas Jefferson. **"Thomas Jefferson said. "Hemp is the first necessity to the wealth and protection of this country."** Who knew more about the nation's foundation, and future then Thomas Jefferson.

Lobbyists from companies like Dupont were hell bent on destroying all their competition, they helped destroy the hemp industry in America. Dupont wanted to use their petro-chemical's to process wood pulp into paper.

Dupont had a patent on their sulfuric acid used in the wood to paper manufacturing process. Dupont also wanted to prevail in making synthetic products without competition. Dupont had filed patents for their sulphur/sulphite process to make paper from wood pulp. Dupont filed another patient to derive plastic from fossil fuels from oil and coal. Hemp which is a bio-mass fuel producer was eliminated from the marketplace. The wide range of bio-mass hemp derivatives includes gas, liquid fuels, and fuel pellets. These environmentally safe hemp fuels would reduce petro-chemical fossil fuel and even nuclear power considerably.

Dupont lobbyists played a role in the governments elimination of the hemp industry in America. Manipulating public opinion, and back room federal directives. Industrial and political espionage corruption were as rampant than as they are now.

Hearst's headlines in publications of. "Marijuana Makes Fiends of boys in thirty days, Hashish Goads Users to Blood Lust." Going further with articles degrading Negroes, Mexicans and the youths who used marijuana. Hollywood's collaboration in movies as in Marijuana's – "Assassin of Youth," and the seedy satire of "Reefer Madness" hype of constitutional corruption. Dupont's Synthetic rope products would replace hemp products as rope, riggings, paints ECT. Literally thousands of products would be eliminated with hemp being outlawed. Another blatant bigot in the cannabis conspiracy former United States Drug Czar Harry Anslinger stated in 1937 that in front of congress that. "Marijuana is the most violence-causing drug in the history of man kind." Ansliger however can produce no sound facts just opinion based on hysteria. Marijuana was made illegal without any research on the assumption it was a narcotic, which then was subject to Prohibition. Anslinger hated blacks and jazz musicians. He kept surveillance and records on who smoked marijuana. Anslinger was part of a government that turned the police on it's own citizen's. Government policies which cause much more harm than marijuana use itself. The ignorance of reefer racism hasn't stopped! Conclusive and positive reefer research should not be stoned walled.

Mayor LaGuardia of New York City on the other hand, believe marijuana is did not cause violence in the city and emphasized the positive concerning marijuana use with their citizen's.

Dupont didn't mind stepping on people rights in this business process. Citizens ending up on a chain gang for smoking a joint of marijuana was a reality after the combination of effort by big business and big government. The industrial espionage which abolished the hemp industry intern filled railroad cars with petro chemicals. The petro-chemicals eventually through the industrial complex is spilled onto our soil and waterways. Much of the environmental damage is either by accident or direct spillage of these chemicals. Where do all the laws come from that destroy all the land, waterways down to the coral reefs down to the mercury infested fish of Lake Erie, forested timber land is now barren land, and toxin filled air barreling up into the upper stratosphere. All further destroying our eco-system, Perennial green plants, and eliminate homes for forest animals. Extincting most into history. US Fish and Wildlife Service claims excessive chemicals from agricultural crops, bleached pulp and paper products, plastics, disinfectants, solvents, and Organochlorines are all related to killing our wildlife. Rare birds like wood storks, white pelicans, great herons, ring billed gulls, egrets, and other fish eating feathered friends that inhabit the wetlands of Florida are in danger. They eat contaminated fish and become fatally infected. Deformity's of reptiles of the water lands are now more common than deformity's for those for live under high tension wires of the nuclear plants. Our environment is the air we breath, the food we eat, and the water we drink. Scientists belief humans and mammals are affected by the chemical mis-management. Toxic free hemp agriculture can help restore our natural environment in many ways.

The Dupont's, the Hearst's, the Cotton industry, alcohol breweries and the tobacco companies had no interest in saving the hemp industry. Hearst publications processed their paper from huge forests they owned. These businesses were among the big shooters in shooting down hemp as a competition. Their financial gain would be enormous with the elimination of the hemp industry. These decisions by our government to side with the competing hemp industries were horrible decisions. The government even destroyed hemp related studies and documents from public records.

These decisions effected private lives of countless marijuana users by hunting down and criminalizing citizens. Just because the government passed a law doesn't mean the government's decision was right, fair or just. Looking for patches of marijuana cultivation with police and military agencies nationwide and further are today's norm.

Hysteria created by the government beyond your wildest dreams about the disruptive natures of marijuana. Creating a massive black market involving a violent worldwide underworld.

Dupont knew modern machinery was developed to process industrial hemp. With the hype from Hearst publications they helped destroy their cannabis completion. This chemical company was free to pollute the planet. Poison the air and waterways of the world.

Dupont should be held responsible along with the government in the form of a class action lawsuit for violations of rights against our citizens, hemp farmers, and hemp manufactures. Their lobbyist's help eliminate the hemp industry, along with the right to privacy, and freedom of choice for people and industry alike.

The government turned to hemp during WW II. They promoted the hemp industry with "Hemp for Victory film. The film urges farmers to grow hemp. The farmers got deferments from the war as an end result. Again governing with two different policies.

The Billion-dollar Hemp Industry predicted by "Popular Mechanics and Mechanical Engineering" in an article in 1938 "New Billion Dollar Crop" was put to an abrupt end. Popular Mechanics said Hemp is. "The Most Profitable and Desirable Crop than can be Gown."

New farming and textile equipment developed for the hemp industry suddenly became useless. The bright outlook of the Hemp Industry was crushed along with American values.

Back in the mid 1930's farmers produced over sixty-thousand tons of hemp per year to make varnish and paints. These hemp paints were made without toxic petrochemicals.

The production of hemp did not discard poison BI-products into landfills, rivers, lakes, soil, air, and oceans. Hemp paper was popular in choice. All the textiles from heavy rope, nets ship's rigging, Book's, to finely tailed clothing was made from hemp grown in the United States, before being shut down by governmental self interest.

Today over one-hundred different products are made around the world from hemp pulp. These hemp products are made safely. It is predicted if hemp were made legal for cultivation in the United States. Over two-hundred and fifty-thousand hemp products would be developed on short term. Including panels made of hemp for automotive industry. Henry Ford grew hemp for automotive development. Researching hemp for fuels. Hemp per acre grew sixty times more fuel possibilities than corn. Of fuels made from vegetables, hemp was the best.

Some car manufactures of the automotive industry use hemp for matting of the car floors. Mercedes cars are already use hemp in their headrests. Many other auto hemp products are being produced or in the makes world wide presently. Children are exposed to or die from toxic chemicals in paints, if these products were processed with hemp pulp. Hemp would be a trillion-dollar business over the next fifty years. Competition is healthy and the hemp industry should be re-instated. Give Kentucky back their largest cash crop.

Hemp paper is the finest paper in man's creation, though out all times. Presently the paper industry itself consumes hundreds of thousands of tons of paper per year relying heavily on trees only. The Moslems started Europe's first hemp paper mill around the year 1150. Hemp accounted for the most of the paper making for nearly a thousand years. The benefits of this all-natural ingredient hemp paper are enormous. Saving the water supply contamination and there is no air pollution environmentally Large crops of hemp nation wide competing worldwide would help refurbish the world's atmosphere, essentially reversing the damaging greenhouse effect.

We could stop cutting down forests once hemp is made into a modern crop in the United States as it is now in most parts of the world.

Industrial Hemp was made into non-toxic paints before the prohibition started. Industrial Hemp would compete or replace cotton's market share. Industrial hemp unlike cotton requires little or no pesticides, fungicides, or herbicides for commercial growth. Cotton on the other hand accounts for a large amount of the nations soil and plant petro-chemical additives such as pesticides and fertilizers, which ultimately enter our waterways.

Hemp fibers are eight times stronger than cotton, and much softer. Hemp produces more fibers per acre, and their fibers demand higher prices than fibers presently on the market.

Wood chips for example sell for seventy-five per ton. High grade hemp pulp fiber's sell for five-hundred per ton. The highest grade of hemp organic fiber's sells for two-thousand per ton. A one-thousand acres of hemp could subsidize the taxpayers of some forgotten rural area. It has been estimated that thirty-million acres in United States farmland could be used for hemp production. All other free countries of the world are farming hemp, and some are regulating taxing revenues. To some of the cultures it's always been just a way of living. Growing hemp and making hemp products.

Hemp is made into a replacement wood in other countries like Canada. The hemp pressed particleboard is proven superior to woods. Hemp is much stronger. The Canadian Non-Wood Fiber Symposium attracted thousands of visitors who witnessed alternatives to supplement wood fibers. The Commercial & Industrial Hemp Symposium among other hemp informative events are growing in acceptance by leaps and bounds.

With many new harvesting techniques hemp production has grown by leaps and bounds every year. Hemp production is the leading industry in a China, India, Hungry, Turkey, Poland, Romania, and many countries produce high volumes of hemp production like Egypt, Thailand, Burma, Portugal, Brazil and Greece. Ninety percent of the European community produces industrial hemp. Hemp is an extremely viable and profitable crop with enormous emerging markets. Let the free market decide! Competition and the Truth is the ultimate heath cure!

Jamestown, colony in Virginia ordered into law that all farmers to grow hemp on their plantations or go to jail. Along with the early settlers of Vermont, Massachusetts, ECT. Our early pioneer's canvas covered wagons were made out of hemp. The word canvas comes from cannabis. Ben Franklin cannabis based paper mill was one of the first in this country, which vastly contributed to the Colonial free press.

The first few drafts of the Declaration of Independence are made on hemp paper. Bank notes in most countries are still printed on hemp paper. During WWII American farmers produced fifty-thousand tons of hemp fibers.

George Washington urged farmers to grow hemp for a domestic industry, instead of tobacco. Thomas Jefferson among other legislatures called cultivation of cannabis a necessity. Thomas Jefferson and George Washington both preferred hemp to tobacco.

George smoked hemp flowers, wooden teeth and all. They both also cited soil exhaustion from growing tobacco. There wasn't a problem for farmers with soil exhaustion concerning hemp. They noted how you couldn't feed your cattle from a tobacco crop. You could feed all your livestock however from hemp in the 1790's

George Washington cultivated "Indian Hemp," citing the superior quality of hemp over tobacco. In 1815 Jefferson's hemp breaking machine he invented was recorded at the U S patent office. This hemp break machine would do the work of a dozen men.

Shipping industry of the time depended on the superior quality of hemp in marine use. Both of these countries founding fathers promoted hemp. All the old Iron sides were made of hemp rigging in they're day.

Anyone going against these great men's beliefs is not in the country these great men had envisioned. Seventy-five percent of the fabrics and textiles were made of hemp during the 1820's. Hemp made the strongest long lasting garments.

The Agricultural benefits are enormous. Up until the 1840's hemp was the most traded commodity in the world. In 1841 the United States Congress ordered the U S navy to increase hemp expenditures. Increased production of domestic hemp followed. Hemp was used heartily in the commonwealths of the Americas.

In the 1870's United States Pharmacopoeia listed Cannabis as medicine in treatment's for many different ailment's, treating tetanus, epilepsy, rheumatism, rabies, fevers, mensal pains, ECT. Orally taking hemp roots or teas.

In the same decade the hashish and marijuana exposition was served at the very first American Centennial Fair. There was no mayhem at the fair. People smoke hashish in a public outing and nobody gave it a care.

In the ten thousands hectare hemp fields of France, some of the hemp stalks are innovativly used in a housing project. This housing project is made entirely out hemp. From the foundation on up including cement blocks insulation, particle, and wallboard. The insulation on the wire is made out of hemp. These hemp houses have a life expectancy of one-hundred years.

Canadian forests are currently being destroyed at a rate of one acre every ten seconds. That is a scary fact. Wake up people. Currently nearly one-hundred percent of the worlds phone books are made from eight-hundred and fifty year old trees off the Rocky Mountain slopes of British Columbia. Farmers who grow industrial hemp for paper would eliminate the devastation our precious forests. These forests takes decades and some centuries to replace.

Seventy five to ninety percent of books, newspapers, paper money, until the turn of the last century were printed on hemp paper. The bible, Alice in Wonderland, Mark Twain are among many famous books of publication magnitude that were printed on hemp.

They Ogalala Sioux tribe distinguished the difference between marijuana and hemp. They plan to cultivate and manufacture hemp products. They will enter the International marketplace where hemp is grown in over thirty different countries. In accordance with (GATT) the Ogalala Sioux tribe classify hemp as a commodity in difference to any narcotic. Their large scale industrial hemp cultivation of a commercial crop is expected to greatly benefit their demographically poor Pine Ridge South Dakota Indian reservation.

We could curtail or stop using fossil fuels with hemp's non-toxic seed oil. Making different fuels from hemp would eliminate depletion of our limited resources of fossil fuels as coal, petroleum, natural gas, and timber. Suitable top-grade diesel fuel made from hemp seed oil is already a reality. Hemp has been developed fuel for semi-trucks, cars, industrial machinery, planes, ECT. There are many fuels and auto parts made out of hemp. Hemp could be the next oil giant. Freezing the import of foreign fuels. Keeping our money in America to build America!

Eliminate our scorched earth policy! You can help save "Mother Earth!" Abraham concluded his speech to an applauding audience. Everyone involved with the cannabis now knew they couldn't choose sides of hemp or marijuana, they all had to step across the line together in their concerted fight with the government to regain lost rights.

Nortin Nonutin quoting a field of expert reports for hemp as an agricultural crop, Nortin began. "Consultants for non-wood fibers of all types, point out that hemp pulp has little value in the countries paper industry. If hemp was so good why didn't people grow it, when they could. The hemp crop was on a decline, when it was made illegal. Large crops of hemp if made legal would increase the drug trade activities.

Hemp will never compete with soybean, cotton, and canola crops. Hemp production is theoretically speculative. Hemp production would be a minor agricultural commodity at best. Large markets for hemp fiber would not become a reality. Farmers further fear that their many legal obstacles are to numerous to over come. The hemp industry infrastructure is non-existent. There are no investors to develop the hemp industry infrastructure. Farmers would never realize financial benefits of hemp production." Norton Notutin concluded.

Abraham countered all objections to the hemp industry in convincing fashion. Blasting back. "The opposition hasn't laid one good reason, on why the hemp industry should not reinstated. A coalition of farmers in the state of Kentucky are suing the federal government for exceeding their authority through the strong-arm of the DEA, which classifies hemp as a narcotic the same as marijuana. Industrialized Hemp does not have the THC content it's cousin plant marijuana has.

The Eastern District of Kentucky civil jury trail request against the Justice Dept and the DEA is to figure out and explain the rights of the hemp farmers. The suit by the hemp farmers is only to recover rights to grow hemp in their fields without being arrested for growing the hemp.

The DEA's argument is that marijuana growers will hide their plants in hemp crops, which will make them undetectable. They are wrong again. The low THC pollen from the industrial hemp crops will destroy their cousin plant marijuana's higher THC content. In effect helps the DEA get rid of smoke-able marijuana crops, which would be rendered as rag weed.

The Kentucky farmers want the DEA's ban on hemp to end. The Dept of Agriculture lists industrial hemp as an extremely viable fiber. Hemp production in the Group of Eight industrialized nations is banned only in the United States. Economic hemp realities are staggering. The hemp farmers should go ahead and raise hemp just as they have always done. Trouble is the hemp laws never get consideration for change by our inferior leadership of congress in this great country. International agricultural treaties have recognized the difference between marijuana and hemp and have changed their laws accordingly.

Canada grows industrial hemp in Canadian farm fields from shore to shore. The hemp laws were rescinded in their country after sixty years. Police, industry, agriculture, with environmental concerns put together a set of regulations for Canadian farmers to grow hemp. Hemp makes fibers. Fibers make textiles. This creates legal cash flow. This is an industry, which puts people to work. This gives farmers another crop to grow.

Canada hasn't decided if they will let farmers sell the hemp outright or set up a government runs industrial hemp board that compare to other grain boards of the agricultural industry. The grain board than would regulate and set the pricing on the commodity exchange. The hemp grown in Canada hemp has less than 0.3% THC content, same as the European standard.

Canadian businessman and farmers cultivating acres for hemp research project cultivation of thousands of acres of commercial hemp. The hemp industry is another avenue for farmers to make money.

Canadian farmers are reaping unreal profits from hemp cultivation, while American farmers are left on the sidelines. Drop the drastic regulations, which stop farmers from their work of choice in the United States. Canadian farmers just north of the American border reap the benefits. They are pleased enough to increase their hemp crop sizes next season. Over fifty growers have requested special permits to grow over two thousand acres of hemp for one Canadian company alone. The new specially designed hemp processing plant with state of the art hemp manufacturing equipment has just recently been completed. Similar new hemp processing plants springing up all over Canada. The hemp managers claim they have a high demand for hemp from the automotive industry alone. The hemp boom market blossomed like a bouquet.

Hemp crops deep roots rejuvenate are aerate farmland, while alternating with crops of vegetables, soy beans, wheat and corn. Hemp roots then replenish the farmland with fresh nutrients. Cycles of plant diseases are broken from other

354

crops by alternating with hemp crops. These practices produce healthier and larger yields as a result. The rotation crop properties of hemp is profitable in itself.

The Canadians built an all inclusive hemp infrastructure nation wide from the ground up.

Soy beans weren't grown a few decades ago at today's level. Now soybeans is the nations second largest crop. Hemp will be an American staple crop as well if given a chance to the American farmer.

Countries around the world, which grow hemp and have always grown hemp, claim their industry is vibrant. They claim to do a brisk business in the hemp trade. Hemp is on the stock exchange already in certain countries around the world."

Abraham claimed. "There already is and has been a hemp infrastructure established though out parts of the world. To say hemp industry will never happen or couldn't happen is ludicrous. It's already established in the world community. More and more countries have ended their bigotry of hemp as an industry. Other countries steadily pass decriminalization laws to grow hemp." Abraham was pumped. "Were gonna tear you apart with the truth of the facts."

Nortin Nonutin stated. "Greatly manipulated hemp facts deceitfully downgrading all the true hemp proof." The audience caught on quick. Some openly laughed while others painfully tried to be polite.

Mickey Matson shrewdly direct stated. "The desirable and valuable commodity of marijuana should be legal. It is hard to estimate the retail marijuana crop in America. With all the avenues around the world that marijuana enters the country. Colossal crops in the interior state of Idaho have been seized in amounts of seventy-plus thousand plants. Plants in excess of ten feet shocked residents of the community. Most of this marijuana grow operation was found on the land owned by the Bureau of Land Management. Similar busts were made in Ohio, Kentucky, Tennessee ECT. This is nothing compared to states that grow marijuana on a regular basis. The ones that are known to grow heavy crop every year.

Autumn in the American homeland is marijuana harvest season for many residents. National forests and farmlands are loaded with marijuana plants across the country. Seizures of marijuana crops are larger every year. The civil air patrol, Forest Service, National Guard, or local police agencies in coordination with the DEA organize most cannabis crop sweeps.

The National Guard in their Army Black hawk helicopter with their powerful down drafts hover lower than the FAA permits to find marijuana fields in full bloom. Dressed in camouflage with combat boots these officers of the law gather and burn large marijuana fields. Some of the cops keep some of the marijuana for personal use or sale.

Large cash crops found in Northern California, they usually dorf the Idaho crops found. Industrialized size pot garden raids are more intensive there as well. It's impossible to estimate the indoor marijuana crops in this country grown domestically. Millions in pounds of marijuana all together are grown domestically for American consumption. Busts by police of indoor operations range from greenhouses, house basements, all the way to mansion's full of marijuana plants.

A recent mansion in California was busted with over four-thousand marijuana plants growing. These marijuana plants were at different stages of growth. Estimated black market value is over twenty million dollars. Stakes are high for a quarter pound of marijuana seeds of growth. Modern equipment available to grow marijuana hypnotically indoors is readily used and available. The corn fields and wood lines out in countryside hid enormous amounts of marijuana grown domestically. It would be nice if the marijuana farmers could come out of the field, and not be criminalized.

The government taxman could then estimate the marijuana crop. Taxes would be paid on the sales of these marijuana crops. Life could go on peacefully for all citizens. Police would no longer be involved. Cannabis court cases could be completely eliminated. Streamlined America for social peace of mind. That is rally call from this crowd. Mickey concluded.

Boss Bossly explosively arrogant stated. "Morocco wanted European financial support to eradicate cannabis production in their country. They wanted to stop illegal migration as well. The King looked for social and economic reforms in the Rif Mountains of Northern Morocco. This is a major production area of hashish. Over two-hundred thousand acres of marijuana is grown in this region alone. Hashish factories are abundant in the Rif Mountain communities. The King wanted to promote other economic growth in their area with European businessmen. The King wanted the Euro-Moroccan free trade zone to become a reality. Spanish port of Cueta, Morocco is a major exportation point of hash from Northern Africa. The King wanted financial support to end the hashish trade." Boss concluded.

Mickey countered. "Morocco would throw their support either way depending on the key word Financial Assistance." The crowd got a chuckle out of that response. Under an agreement fair to all they could still make regulated amounts of hashish for use and export. The country could reap it's own financial benefits once legalized, taxed, and regulated." Mickey concluded.

"Rigid" Ross Bossly with his tough stance on marijuana said. "All dealers of drugs marijuana or other wise should be sentenced to death. The crowd booed and immediately disapproved. "Killing our citizens doesn't make sense!" One man in the audience blurted out.

Another yelled. "We'll vote you out bigot!"

Ross argued. "We have to protect the children.!"

One protester yelled out. "Killing their parent's doesn't protect the children!" Ross was booed off the stage.

Roscoe Repares overwhelmingly spoke about the militarization of the police force abuses. Roscoe holding a copy of "The New Yorker Magazine" high up in the air sporting the cover with a police officer shooting target cutouts of people in the carnival shooting gallery. The featured story covered four cops firing forty one bullets at an innocent unarmed man. There laid an innocent dead man, who believed in the system. Cutting into clear-cut civil rights abuses by the cops. Tell me why a Specially trained unit of the New York Police force killed an unarmed immigrant who was trying to make good in America. The man was shot and struck nineteen times at close range after forty one bullets were fired by the expertly trained four police officers. All this good unknowing man did was walk out of his apartment into a hail of government sponsored gunfire! It's your uncontrolled tax dollars at work. All the people here that didn't vote are in part responsible. Correcting the major flaws against humanity in our government system should be your top priority. Get back to the constitution while we still can.

"Citizens have lost faith in the ability of the government's judicial system to work in fairness. I can see why marijuana is dangerous. Police kill marijuana users for what they believe in. Police stop citizen's freedom of choice. Police criminalize and de-humanizing the nation's citizens. They invade other countries and destroying their marijuana crops. This government bribes and bullies other nations to repress marijuana and hemp.

A property seizure by the government in the guise of a drug enterprise for marijuana use against law-abiding citizens is unfair. Non profit think tanks have looked into hundreds of property seizures and have concluded that the prosecutors and police are allowed to violate laws they are supposed to uphold. The pro-rights group supports changes in our current drug laws.

The study recommends law enforcement is not to receive benefits from the drug seizures. Eliminating conflict of interest. Law enforcement must show specific relations between the crime and the property. The amount of forfeiture cannot exceed the crime."

Roscoe continued into the hot sun of the day. "The study from the non profit think tank recommend that the drug seizure laws be made to help citizens get their property back, and be compensated for the illegal drug arrests if they win in court. The abuse of civil liberties is outrageous.

You have to do something when violent criminals are released, and marijuana users take up the prison space. Violent predators are released from prison for good behavior. Numerous backlogs of warrants for violent cannot be followed up on and the warrants are shelved. Murderous police regimes, which promote false arrests, are a fraud to the American people.

There is an abundance of real facts and abuses of an enormous proportion. How can you in good conciseness sponsor serious abuses to our citizens. Sychonising militarisation of the police force with tricks, and tacky tactics and armed with a Stalonistic attitude to feast on good citizens is wrong.

Evidence fabricated and presented in a prejudicial manner in court by the police departments. Rampant misbehavior in court procedures, prosecutors encouraging police to lie for prosecution and election ramifications. Police and prosecutors send innocent victims to the chair as in electric.

When prosecutors twist the truth and cops hide the evidence they conspire in criminal corruption to railroad citizens. Our judicial system has failed! Crossing the line by any government officials should be punished more severely than any citizen. Punishment should be doubled, because of the breech of trust with the citizens.

One cop crusading for the anti-drug crowd with his Detroit cop formed music band called the "Blue Pigs" played for schools. The cop was involved in a drunk driving hit and run incident. He fled the accident scene. Internal affairs at the department's urging buried the incident. That is until a local TV Station got wind of it from the accident victim's and blasted the truth of the accident all over the five o'clock news. What kind of an example is that from the Blue Pigs! We need more whistle blowers! Those people should be rewarded!

The police aggressors of our civilization are supposed to uphold the motto "Protect and Serve " when they actually "Roust and Wreck." The real problem isn't marijuana use it's getting caught by the police, just because marijuana is illegal.

The forfeiture's by law enforcement of hard working American assets for recreational use of marijuana is unwarranted. It is a direct violation of their civil rights in every sense of justice. How can we give police unlimited authority and immunity with their actions?

Our citizens suffer under laws passed by an influence of Corporate greed in an era of world's past conflict. The decision of past times was clearly unconstitutional. The laws passed were without the voter's conscious.

You can only police people to the extent they want to be policed. Decision-makers should be fair and diversified to represent all the people. Public apology's by government for improper raids by law enforcement is not enough. Judges have slammed law enforcement agencies for unauthorized drug raids. Saying that there sorry for mistakes of busting in a law abiding citizens falls short of the freedoms they are promised and guaranteed in the constitution of the United States. There's way too much of this crap going on by law enforcement.

What do you say to the kids who watch drug dogs search their home as their parents are handcuffed belly down? It's a little late to say their in the wrong house. The kids are as terrified as their parents. These cowboys of drug law enforcement had no right to disturb these families watching jeopardy on TV in the privacy of there own home. Sometimes these same drug commandos use their high-tech snooping thermal imager to invade the privacy of homes without warrants.

There is documented proof of Federal Marshals on these raids shooting a kid, because they thought the candy bar in the kid's hand was a gun. They even left him bleeding on the ground handcuffed. The drug cops were all congratulating each other. This kid who was shot and bleeding on the ground was a high school soccer star. You can't even walk to the store and get a candy bar." Roscoe said.

"The kid said he turned around and was shot immediately. He didn't know what had happened. There is violence in the drug trade no matter how you're involved in it. I personally I'm on the side of citizen right's. Period!

Yet! Despite the government's harsh crackdown and arrests on these cannabis citizen's the "American Bar Association" concluded illicit drug use has dramatically increased. Offer's by the White House to curb illegal drug use in half is a very ridicules assessment considering such a large percentage of the population socially smoke pot. No matter how much money is spent, what propaganda is produced or what harsh law is passed by our government!" Roscoe impressively concluded.

Zane Slain countering any abuses by stating. "The police dept abuses are overblown, scarce, and scattered around the country."

A sign in the background held up in the audience with **Martin Luther King's quote of "Injustice to one is Injustice to all."** The crowd roundly booed unpopular Zane back to the plains.

Winston Wells narrative detailed report of Government Mismanagement. Winston said that. "The marijuana war the government sponsors is a waste and a tax grafting money cow that is a killing machine. Killing the very fiber and tradition that America is made of. The beginning of marijuana illegality began with actions by the Federal Bureau on Narcotics, and outside business interests.

William Randolph Hearst the newspaper magnate of the 1930's orchestrated and drummed hysteria anti-marijuana campaign, which intern included the hemp industry. Helping to sponsor and promote a prohibitive tax in the USA for hemp production.

The forum of collaboration including competing industrialists like Dupont whom would gain significantly by eliminating hemp as an industry. Elimination of a whole hemp competing industry created a monopoly for many of the company's products. Were tired of all the politicians talking out of both sides of their mouth. The pure, pompous, pathetic, politician who is drastically destructive and calculating options for containment of human rights.

Police department's after legalization of marijuana, would have time to concentrate on deadly hard drugs and crime. Wouldn't that be a shame if the police had to do real work of value." Winston said sarcastically.

Politicians demand more prisons, prosecutors, police, and paramilitary operations. This leads to a police state that has abandon any sense of reasoning. They are contributing to establishing a police-state society. Digging through someone's car or garbage for a couple of roaches to bind a cannabis citizen over in a court of law. Where's the citizens right to choose? It's non-existent in cannabis America!

We need a different politician, a different agenda of day, and a different way to delegate authority fair to all the people. Untaxed and unregulated money that leaves this country by the truck loads to Latin American drug cartels. These drug cartels rival oil, and steel industry economic profits in their demographic regions.

Legalizing marijuana for social consumption is a good start. State legislators could enact laws similar to Australia. Citizens could grow marijuana for personal use, and the government could realize revenues when the plant is sold or bartered. The Australians are not enforcing the American approach to marijuana use with its citizens. They are going to stop being the freedom oppressors. The Australian government was going to represent all the people in their country fairly.

Since the government tried to tax marijuana out of existence after the 1936-film reefer madness, and wrong facts concerning marijuana were aggressively promoted. Hyping hysteria through media moguls of their day William Randolph Hearst. Back room decisions to address the marijuana issue in governmental forum did not address the hemp farmers association, and medical Associations, until one or two days before the forum condemning marijuana, and Taxing marijuana into oblivion came about. Giving no time for any objective view to be heard.

They gave the American Medical Association only two days notice before the internally arranged governmental forum abolished marijuana. The AMA did not know this forum was about the elimination of marijuana and the hemp industry. A clean sweep with one marijuana and hemp prohibition law. Giving all hemp competing product companies no voice or choice but to close down all hemp farming and industry operations. Only back room Washington insiders with the chance to financially gain were allowed to participate in decisions to make hemp illegal. Corrupting political forces pulled a fast one on the American public. They passed their agenda for prohibition unnoticed in the seediest fashion.

Marijuana was sanctioned for medical use until than. The National Oil Seed Institute was not allowed to attend this hearing. The citizens were never invited to a town hall meeting to discuss the prohibition of marijuana. Again no chance of voice to respond. Stripping rights of our country's citizens across the board without notice.

Why is the government rejecting research from New York Mayor LaGuardia Marijuana Commission in the 1940's, which results concluded that, "Marijuana causes no uproar in the community. There is no recognizable violence in citizen's use of marijuana. The Commission further stated positive results from community marijuana usage." Tell me were the politicians lying then or are they lying now?" Winston soberly said.

Of over ten thousand scientific studies by Educational Institutes and others by different government that were sponsored, marijuana was evaluated favorably with definite benefits. No more than fifteen of the studies were less than favorable.

"They haven't been able to curtail marijuana use. Use of marijuana has grown by leaps and bounds. Marijuana seed banks flood the world with seeds. You cannot stop demand, use, or deny the safe medical benefits especially when compared with prescription tranquilizers. Importation of the illegal herb marijuana has increased every year without hindrance. There are a billion cannabis users on this planet today. Marijuana users see marijuana as political symbolism. Cannabis users like its social excitability and it's recreationally safe alternative.

National Research Council of the National Academy of Sciences did research on the Marijuana Legalization Issue. The report called the Analysis of Marijuana Policy, 1982 was when the report was concluded.

360

The report recommended from the results by NAS on Committee on 'Substance Abuse and Habitual Behavior' for states to set up methods for controlling marijuana. To decriminalize and regulate marijuana as it does alcohol. Federal penalties could than be removed. Why don't we follow research that was put forth? It seems fair to all. It's not so one sided in the government's favor is that the problem."

Winston continued. "In California a Research Advisory panel's findings concluded similar findings concerning decriminalization of marijuana and in 1989, as a way of ending the war on marijuana. They made other determinations on drug policy as well. They expressed educational programs. They recommended change in the prohibition of marijuana policy, as do all smart free thinkers.

Why didn't we listen to them ten years ago? Now these marijuana drug warriors tell us what they're going to do in the next ten years with our tax money. They haven't been able to slow any flow of marijuana to the streets for the last sixty years of their imposed marijuana prohibition. There is more marijuana available now than in any time of our prior history. The pot is available on a regular basis to all American consumers. The government is making a lot money on the back door. Even cops smoke pot because they can hide use on the job, were they can't hide alcohol's heavy give away.

Marijuana as medicine is greatly endorsed in the world community. Federal response to the voters of California and Arizona has been negative. The federal government is interfering with doctor and patient relationships. Patients can suffer according to the federal government. Compassion is not in the federal vocabulary. Freedom of choice does not exist in the federal government of America.

The White House and its surrounding politicians are only concerned about re-election day only. They take the same entrenched negative stand and avoid the real call for change." Winston gratefully ended his informing corruption session of the debate.

Bert Bares defiantly disagreed with Winston he said. "America wanted these laws and that's why the federal government made marijuana illegal. Marijuana threatened the infrastructure of society, and killing the youth of America." Roundly booed off stage.

Winston walked back up to the podium to a rounding applause. Winston said. "So the Federal government starts an internal war in society including prosecution and internment of marijuana smokers, and shuts down the hemp industry. What does that do to the freedom of choice infrastructure of our American society?" Winston then left the stage to a cheering crowd.

Jerry Thomson an above board honorable family man headed the debate on "Graft and Corporation" Jerry stated. "Corruption has no bounds. Corruption has no limits. Corruption is the killer of our country. Entrapment of our constitutional rights demeaned American Citizens. Drug entrapment, wire taps of citizens is at an all time high. Along with high bail bonds, forfeiture of property and illegal search and seizures are all too common. We are here to expose the common police corruption ways related to the drug trade. Continuing political and police corruption across the board supported by the present governmental drug policies. Bad cops are ruthless beyond conciseness. They operate like a pack of wolves. They are no different than bandit raiders conducting raids and preying on innocent citizens. If you think we like to talk against the police force, your wrong!"

Jerry stated in between applause's. "We just want good laws and good cops. Respect and fairness for all citizens, there comes a point when the government is into everyday citizen's private life is too much. We want the government to get out of the dark ages of repression. Eliminate hypocritical double standards. Get out of our living rooms!"

Jerry uncovered tantalizing facts, that he presented to the debate audience. "We could be here a month on this a part of the problem. We would never get to explain all the documented drug convictions of police in our country because of there is an enormity in volume. It has been hard to cut it down to the few cases of documented proof we present here today."

Jerry continued. "Vice drug squads in southern Florida were armed with information of the drug smugglers operations and habits. These drug cops were found guilty of robbing the cocaine smugglers of their drug bounty. The drug cops threw them live into an ocean of sharks to drown and no return. The Vice squad police than sold the stolen large shipment of cocaine and kept the profits. These cop drug operations breed corruption."

Jerry depicted. "Another sheriffs dept in Florida was found guilty in shaking down citizens in fake busts to steal their possessions through the forfeiture laws. The police armed with inside information plant drugs on the victims.

Over one-thousand pounds of marijuana was stolen out of a southern Florida police head quarter's evidence storage room with street value of over three and a half million dollars. This was the forth major heist from the evidence room in recent months. Police drug evidence rooms in Texas have drug officers on videotape stealing cocaine. The same police are caught selling the cocaine on the streets. Another narcotic officer jumped out of airplane over the state of Kentucky with over thirty kilos of cocaine strapped to his body. They always said it takes a good crook to be a good cop.

A DEA Agent was arrested with over twenty-five kilos of cocaine stuffed in his suitcase at Logan International Airport. Recently more and more DEA drug convictions of their agents are reality. Internal Police Investigations have reached an all time high, involving cocaine-dealing cops. They investigate the tight knit drug organizations of drug dealing cops. Cops hired to watch cops.

Police chiefs in major cities are convicted in America diverting millions of dollars from the drug fund, that's meant to make drug buys end up in their own bank account. The corrupt police chiefs are falling like dominos. The trouble is the new chief that replaces the old chief follows the same corrupt path. Another police officer fought a high steaks campaign against drug use in schools though the media was convicted in a court of law for selling heroin. He took the heroin out of the evidence room of the police head quarters.

Federal Grand Jury Indictments are at an alarming all time rate nation wide, against the large numbers of government officials and police involvement in the corrupt elements of the under ground drug trade. This issue of organized cop corruption had to be addressed, because of the scope of involvement nation wide. Greed has no bounds with these corrupt officers of the law.

What if we were like the North Vietnam Government is today. Take our police commissioners, captains, and corporals out and shoot them to death in the Town Square when found guilty in drug protection and drug conspiracies for large shipments of hard drugs. When police are found guilty of dealing, excepting bribes for the heroin and cocaine trade, take them out and kill them in a mass execution, upon conviction in a court of law. North Vietnamese sentences are always carried out immediately. What's good for the goose is good for the gander.

How long would it take to straighten our police force out? How long would it take the flow of cocaine and heroin to quit entering our neighbors hoods in such an organized and corrupt manor? How long would it take to clean our streets up with no major hard drug integrating our communities? The number of police and political leaders of syndicated hard drug operations would be eliminated from dealing these major amounts of hard drugs. Word would quickly get out, You're caught, and you're done, Said one government official in North Vietnam said from Downtown Hanoi. "We needed a new approach. Executing conspirators of large shipments of hard drugs in the town square showed we are serious. When Police and public officials breech the trust of the citizens, We should take harsh actions. Hundreds of kilos of cocaine and heroin transacted on a timely basis conducted by these political and police officials. That's what this country is doing." The North Vietnamese government official smiled and said. His telecast was simultaneously simulcast from half way around the world to the event. The informative view from large screens from different countries around the world was to include everyone who participated in the debate.

In Laos smoking opium is a part of their livelihood US Drug officials concede. Foreign tourists flock to the opium producing Golden Triangle to smoke down. Laos bordering Thailand, and Burma welcomes International tourists and ignores US pleas to prosecute foreign drug offenders."

The incredible number of documented prior convictions of police corruption startled viewers. Major poor hiring practices were also noted. Why not take the recent forty some police officers recently caught from Northern Ohio in one circle of major amounts of hard drug sales and criminal conspiracy corruption and shoot them in the town square. These so called police officers protected and distributed major amounts of cartels cocaine, and heroin. These officers of the law up are supposed to be our protectors. Not our community destroyers inspired by power and greed. These corrupt officers of the law profit of the hard drug trade at the expense of its citizens. We should take hard justice to these corrupt police officers because they breached their oath to the citizens and their integrity of the office. Sentences of crimes and corruption by police and government officials should be triple in sentence when compared to citizens.

Recently over five hundred officers of the law in over fifty cities have been convicted in connection with the hard drug trade in the United States. When United States law enforcement is caught and convicted in such a large scale drug operations, that says something about the nature of the beast in this government drug war. These police officers helped transport and distribute hundreds of kilo's heroin and cocaine to our communities. That many cops found guilty in a court of law in one regional sweep means there something is drastically wrong in our government. When all sorts of law enforcement and public officials are found involved in the circles of corruption across the board."

Jerry was endless in his accounts of documented cases and convictions. Documented by the government's own records of abuse in these Republics of the America's. Whole governments are bought by the influence of the drug cartels. They are more than an influence group, they have become policy makers. The drug cartels own hand picked officials are put into all areas of the governments, military, and police. These drug cartels have more influence in these political circles than the United States federal government.

Evidence exists that Aruba a popular tourist resort has laundered billions in cartel drug money. Aruba is a shipping point for drugs. Antigua has opened dozen or so off shore banks to help launder the cartels drug money. There are no boundaries in this drug war. Virtually no island or nation is off limits to the drug cartels. Restrictions by forum time limitations were unbearable. All the facts would never come out at the debate so a columnist ascertains were compiled for anyone to review.

Listed were the facts, figures, and events. CIA was implicated in drug running all the way down to the street cops, covered up by judicial and governmental officials. Millions of dollars were stashed in Swiss bank accounts of relatives of the drug operators, and their political cronies. The drug trade has encompassed the global economy.

Black activists, and progressive leaders, down to people on the street ask how come there is so much cocaine, and weapons in the streets, particularly in the black, Hispanic and low income areas. When an eight year old can buy cocaine and heroin in their neighborhoods street corners easier than candy at the party store?"

Newspapers have suggested in different articles of a CIA link between Latin America and the USA. The drug trade is too organized, deliveries are to regulated, just like Mc Donald's. One CIA officer was indited for importing over a ton of cocaine from Venezuela to the United States. Another is connected to over thirty tons that entered through the Port of Miami. The "San Jose Mercury News" Chronicles the CIA Cocaine pipeline to the United States. Smugglers with CIA ties were common place in circles of the cartels in the southern Americas. The "San Jose Mercury News" retracted their stories, but many don't think their stories were off base.

Russian Mafia has joined forces with the drug cartels of Latin America. They're exporting cocaine, and heroin in vast amounts to Europe. Marijuana is of small value for transport because you can buy marijuana legally throughout most of Europe. Organized crime flush with money expanded their domain of hard drug sales. Cartels buy Planes, Airliners, Helicopters, sub-marines, Ships, boats, semi-trucks, off shore banks, sophisticated electronic equipment, along with sophisticated weapons, like surface to air missiles.

These Cartels organizations compare to the United States government's best drug-fighting arsenal. Cartels have access to billions of dollars. The Cartel's move like clockwork, entrenched in the woodwork of world. These cartels control thousands of drug distribution gang's worldwide. They move large amounts of hard drugs right under the noses of drug enforcement, or with cooperating authorities. It is rough to catch the Russian part of the drug trade because of the language problem. Typically the drug cartels buy off whole governments from the president on down. Political officials, military and police everyone gets a cut. The rampant bribed corruption paralyzes the government's anti-drug fighting effort. Some high ranking government officials live the drug cartels in bunker like dwellings. The bunkers are heavily armed and fortified.

Some intelligence reports should be made public so the public is aware of this enormous problem caused by the corruption of cocaine and heroin traffic. When a dozen Latin American countries are solid cohorts with cocaine cartels. To pretend the drug corruption doesn't exist here is ludicrous.

U S boarder patrol and custom agents are busted all the time in drug related crimes. The customs agents help or look the other way when it comes to drugs crossing the boarder. They always get a cut of the action that way.

The Mexicans recently busted thirty-one police and army officers in connection of a ton of cocaine being stolen from the evidence room. The drugs were sold back to the Mexican Tijuana cartel. This was the same special Mexican drug-fighting unit that was busted is the same that is funded and trained by the United States Drug and Law enforcement agency. Ghost agents were found to be on the payroll, which the U S government paid for. The United States drug fighting plan has either fell apart or has never been intact. The American trained Mexican Special anti-drug forces and military equipment are not used as intended in the south of the border anti-drug campaign. Mis-trust remains between the both countries drug fighting forces. The drug agents on this side of the boarder do not want to share information. The first thing the Mexicans want to know is where the US got their information, The next thing you know the informant and his family turn up dead. People who investigate the cartel end up dead.

United States policy helped corrupt the law enforcement arm of Latin America. The link between the Mexican Economy, the government, drug traffickers and the support of the people are all impossible odds for the American government to contain.

The Mexican government give the DEA token busts to get drug certification money. Then it's business as usual with the drug cartels. The Mexican government officials said policeman are paid three-hundred per month. The Mexican cartel typically pay them one thousand a week to assist their drug running operation. The Mexican government can't compete. The recent arrest of the second most powerful member of the cartel was replaced immediately with underlings of the cartel. There's to much money involved for them to just walk away.

Jerry disclosed. "A US DEA Administrator Thomas Constantine informed the Senate Caucus on International Narcotics Control. "Mexico's effort's against narcotics trafficking are failing and corruption is hampering joint programs. Because there is little effective law enforcement activity leading to the arrest of major traffickers in Mexico, investigations have been compromised in some cases." Suggesting there's no serious effort to reign in the heavy drug traffickers.

He further stated. "Corruption in elite Mexican counternarcotics units trained and vetted by the United States, coupled with the "rapidly growing power and influence of the major organized criminal groups in Mexico, cause us great concern about the long term prospects for success." Even a dozen or so Airmobile Special Forces Group in charge of "Mexico City's Airport" were charged with drug related trafficking. Long term trusting relationships in drug fighting with Mexico is very doubtful in plain English. The drug traffickers operate with business as usual.

About the most recent five year narcotics investigations Tom further stated. "The power of the (Mexican) criminal organizations has grown virtually geometrically" and further "Unparalleled to anything I've seen in thirty-nine years of law enforcement."

He also informed. I know one drug Mafia in Mexico alone that makes two billion dollars every single year selling cocaine and methamphetamine in the United States, and has better technical equipment and counter surveillance equipment and armored cars than we do."

Yet even after all that "Slick Willie" says we have made solid gains in the illicit drug trade and says Mexico is fully cooperating. Cocaine cartels run rampant over our borders with semi's filled with cocaine. Then the return semi's have loads of Yankee dollars. Mexico continues to release jailed cocaine kingpins and refuses to arrest of extradite any of them back to the United States.

As Jerry continued. "Some of these cartel kingpin's have ties with the Mexican president's brother who's help orchestrate the drug trade in Mexico. Hundreds of millions in bribes were paid to protect drug shipments to America during his tenure. The former Mexican president has fled his country, while his brother is sentenced to fifty years in prison for ordering the murder of his brother's political opponent. He was also convicted of major drug activities. They want him to explain the hundred of million in Swiss bank accounts which prove rampant corruption south of the border.

Major investigations of high ranking Mexican officials like the Quintana Roo Governor is under investigation for cooperating with the drug cartels. This will test the dexterity of the United States and the Mexican forged anti-drug relationship. Several luxury hotels and many more luxurious homes were confiscated from the cocaine drug investigations. It's estimated that four to five tons of hard drugs like cocaine pass through the governors state. It's apparent when cocaine is readily available in the tourist resorts. The paradise tourist resorts of the Caribbean are plagued and surrounded by the drug smuggling trade. Elaborate and sophisticated drug smuggling schemes are mixed into the unsuspecting tourist crowd who are sometimes dangerously drawn in. Recently the whole the security force of Cancun's International Airport was terminated because of their drug cartel ties. They even filmed US Federal drug fighting agents for the cartel. They protec.ed drug traffickers and their drug shipments on a regular basis. Leading Cancun businessman have requested the governor step down because of his alleged linking to drug organizations. American drug fighting agents are usually tortured and killed when identified by the brazen cartel. When American Drug agents call their Mexican counter part in the anti-drug fight to arrest a drug king under surveillance the Mexican drug fighting official stated he is tied up and can't help.

The FBI in Houston said. "The INS agents are also involved in the drug smuggling. Some U S Customs officials joined in the Mexican Cartels smuggling. Customs agents were found to be involved rampant drug smuggling efforts.

Yet year after year for thirteen straight years our congress rectifies Mexico as a drug partner and give them a ton tax payers dollars all nearly catra blanche. Only a minority in Congress speak up for change even after the Mexican Government abuses of the people from the Chiapas state.

Cartel corrupted Mexican police were involved in the torture of an under cover US DEA Agent. Another dozen Mexican Police shot and killed an investigating state drug officer. Recently four sheriffs from Laredo were caught stealing more than a ton of cocaine. The Laredo cops then tried to sell the cocaine back to the drug cartel. These large quantities of drugs are moved across the boarder, with the help of the boarder agents who except the drug cartel bribes.

Eighteen wheelers also bring multitudes of hard drugs into the country with the other customs agents turning their back as the hard drug shipments cross the boarder. One semi-truck stopped by the Texas police had two tons of cocaine on board. Agents also seized four tons of cocaine in a New Jersey warehouse after following another eighteen-wheeler.

The eighteen wheeler in Texas was bound for assorted destinations across the country, dropping off cocaine along the way. These eighteen wheelers, fright trains, and cars are non-stop across the boarders hauling drugs. The traffickers are usually triumphant over law enforcement, especially when the local police help the drug cartels.

In Canada a whole town of law enforcement was arrested for drug trafficking. Residents testified against the towns police officers who delivered bricks of hash their dealers. These police were linked to well organized drug cartels. This type of corruption is across the board, through out all the countries with no bounds.

Police officers have been convicted for turning a blind eye to their own relatives selling drugs. The extent of the law enforcement drug corruption and the scope of their drug-related crimes is innovative and surprising to perceived realities of law enforcement.

Over sixty percent of drugs that enter the US penetrate the US and Mexican border. I'm dumb founded at the facts and the proof is staggering. We here to do something about it today. As far as were concerned. If the government can't run a clean ship, the government can't run." Jerry finally concluded.

Response by Dottie Dork—"Mexican Specials forces in helicopters of the DEA just busted a cartel operation in the mountains of the Sierra Madre and the cartel opened up with ferocious gunfire. These military tactics are similar to guerilla warfare. The drug dealers were overcome by the Police military firepower and four traffickers were killed. Twenty-four more were captured. A large amount of weapons were confiscated. Automatic AK 47's to grenade launchers.

The DEA with the help of these special drug units of the Mexican Federals have made five such busts in the last several months in this mountainous region. These troops are motivated and aggressive in their fight against illegal drug trafficking. The struggle with the drug cartels can be won."

She further stated. "The Colombian and Mexican elections are not being influenced by drug cartels. Opponents to the cartel's aren't afraid to run against the drug cartel sponsored candidate." The crowd now booed Dottie of stage because in disbelief.

Jerry countered. "Cartel's typically kidnap and torture candidates of the opposition. Observers of the Organization of American States, which monitor elections, were kidnapped in some recent elections. The tensions build on every character of miss-justice. Some peasant voters are killed for voting. Others are intimidated into not voting whatsoever." Kevin Kellar asked Jerry to cease to respond because of time restrictions.

Carry Carleton---With the debate heating up to inflamed proportions Carry commenced his oracle. "Drug cocaine processing laboratories are set up throughout South America. The Mexican cartel's process major amounts of cocaine now too. However, South American countries as Colombia, Peru, Brazil, Chile, ECT are still very much in the cocaine manufacturing mix.

These drug cartel bring to their counties Yankee dollars by the truck loads far south below the boarder. The cocaine cash flow buys more and bigger drug processing laboratories. The drug cash buys more influence in the southern Americas Politicians, military, police, and their people. How long can we keep sending our money by the semi-loads below the boarder?"

Carry explained. "Jungle covered cocaine processing laboratories that are prevalent through South America. Where all the people work together in that highly profitable business. If you were a peasant in South America and it came between feeding your family, and working in the cocaine industry. Or starving and watching your family dying from disease of malnutrition. How people would turn it down? We are a product of our environment. You have a right to survive. Put yourself in their shoes to understand what's going on in South America.

The people here on welfare have a wealth of living benefits, down to health care, clean running water, electricity, ECT. Counter-narcotics operations by South American Military and Police on these jungle cocaine laboratory raids make only tokens busts.

Peasant farmers are given the poppy seeds by the cartels to grow the raw material for heroin and opium. Other farmers are given coca seeds to plant. US eradication efforts are made with Blackhawk Army helicopters that spray weed killers on the crops.

In these countries the government officials want the United States to give them drug certification money to fight the drug war. They want their cake and eat it to. Brazil refused the United States money. The offer was far less than what the drug cartels pay. A Brazilian government official said. "A million dollars was too paltry." The cartels pay them and everyone else much more. Again all the American money is going south fast.

Haiti's government seems to be completely bought off by the drug cartels. One Colombian man was arrested at the International Airport with a few pieces of luggage full of cocaine headed for the United States. The luggage weighed over seventeen-hundred pounds. The drug trafficking suspect was allowed to leave Haiti several weeks later. Nobody when questioned at the police department knew what had happened to the drug suspect. The cocaine had also come up missing.

On traffic stop by police in Haiti the driver of the car was found to have over two-hundred pounds of cocaine in his trunk. A senior Haitian Law Enforcement Official ordered the car, driver, and cocaine released. Narco dollars go along way in Haiti. People are in need of everyday essentials. They have turned to the Narco-dollars. There have been no prosecutions for drugs in over two years in Haiti. Corruption is wide spread. The cartels buy the government of the people from top to bottom.

Drugs from Haiti, and the Dominican Republic travel though extensive drug routes including Cuba, Puerto Rico, to Miami ECT. Puerto Rico is a big funnel into the country. Mail in Puerto Rico is not regulated like overseas mail, since it is a United States entity.

There are no custom checks from Puerto Rico to the United States on over seventy flights per day to the mainland. A single container from a Cargo ship holds over eight thousand pounds of cocaine, while bound for all ports to the United States. The United States coast guard vessels have a hard time keeping up with the drug cartel operations.

Honduran Judicial government officials on the cartels payrolls have been caught tipping off drug cartels for drug raids pending by court employees. Judicial Courts orders must be obtained first by the police. When the police drug raids are not carried out fast enough the drug cartels take brisk measures to curtail the police drug raids.

The nut shell games conducted by the drug cartel's never end. Drug transshipment points from these Caribbean Island amounts to an estimated flow of thirty percent of all incoming drugs to the United States. Cocaine has corrupted these fragile Caribbean governments. Cocaine traffic has wreaked havoc on the social fabric on these islanders.

Cocaine is a viable commodity that has to be dealt with. Over half a million of the Dominican Republic's population of eight million do cocaine on a regular basis. The heroin and cocaine the cartel leave behind as payment for the shipments infiltrate and pollute the populace. Hard drugs give the people a hard way to live.

Police bust all the small drug dealers in the run down neighborhoods for crack, powdered cocaine, and heroin. Parts of these cities are completely over run by drug trafficking. The government sent in national guardsman and took over these drug encompassed low income areas.

Drugs are sold retail and wholesale without interruption. Crack pipes, syringes, bags of drugs were confiscated after house to house searches for the drugs. The drug crazed cocaine and heroin heads from the searches were arrested. Yet, no big drug kingpins who ship these large amounts of hard drugs to all points of the U S and the world get caught. The drug cartel kingpins go on and on with their political and social influence's." Carry concluded.

Put Pan rigidly obstinate started. "Brazil passed new laws which allow the Brazilian Air Force to shoot down airplanes they suspect are smuggling drug shipments. This law is a strong deterrent. "We will shot these unlawful flights into our country down," a government official stated. Brazil's dense Amazon jungle and vast demographic area will receive a modern radar surveillance system in the year 2002. The SIVAM, as it's known, is the most modern system available. This system will help the government of Brazil to monitor their boarders.

Laws to curb money laundering have recently been established in Brazil. Brazil stressed that these new laws and counter drug measures were passed with internal governmental decisions only. Brazil's official state that drug trafficker's will roam freely in Brazilian air space." Put ended his speech.

Carry countered. "Brazilian peasants sell beans for less than fifty cents per kilo. Marijuana grown and sold by the same peasant is thirty dollars per kilo. In five months of field work One Brazilian region produced more than two million tons of marijuana in one growing season. This is only one region in one country of South America. When you feed your family and yourself there is very little choice, what crop are you going to grow. Over fifty percent of the population in Brazil is unemployed. Marijuana has solved a lot social problems for many Brazilians in the growing regions of the Brazilian Interior. Food on the table for the family is a first essential.

Marijuana keeps the trade routes moving. Hard drugs is what needs to be reduced the Brazilians maintain. Why should we stop the money flow into Brazil? The Brazilian first lady also said. "We should decriminalize smoking marijuana."

Things are very much different around the world than the in U S A. You Americans are in for a drastic culture experience, when travelling from a free world to a third world country."

Carry continued. "To counter that may be a good law, shooting down drug cartel planes, but when the cartels money buy off government official's, who can stand in their way. The laws really don't make any difference. These cartels have a green light with all the enormous cocaine profits. The power of the cartels money will over ride any law passed. The Cartels influence and their drug operations will not be deterred. In fact the coca plant growers biggest problem is the bugs. The bugs devour thirty-five percent of their coca crops. Law enforcement only confiscate ten percent of their crops." Carry ended.

Steve Grown---Exposed major drug smuggling routes. "The Colombian Cartels from the Caribbean brought in drugs into the country from traditional routes such as Florida. The Mexican cartels bring the drugs into the country over our two thousand mile southern border. They account for eighty percent of drugs that come into the homeland. The Colombians move the cocaine overland, then send it on ships. It's then off loaded into smaller vessels, which speed inland to Florida. Small planes drop off bundles of cocaine into the ocean. Speedboats pick them up and bring them to shore. Isolated dirt airstrips are also used in the Everglades of Florida. Some planes are abandon on remote airstrips in southern Florida. Some abandon planes on our mainland had over three-hundred and fifty kilos of cocaine for cargo.

FBI and DEA during an International drug investigation busted sub-divisions of a major drug organization. A trucking business in Michigan transported and distributed upward of six-hundred and sixty pounds of cocaine in a three-month period, and more than six tons in less than a three-year period. The semi-truck owners and accomplices were arrested. This is only one sub-division in a demo-graphic area by one cartel. Let it be noted that in the same three year period, the narcotic semi-truck company transport and distribution only brought in twenty three pounds of marijuana. The marijuana is more bulky to transport, and not nearly as lucrative per pound as cocaine. This drug operation had been going on for years, from Tijuana, Mexico to the northern state of Michigan. A drug route of over four-thousand unimpeded miles one way on a continual basis. The trucking business had drug drop off points along the traveled route across the country. Over eleven-million in cash was seized from this truck operator and owner.

How much influence can that money buy when multiplied x times around the country by all these different arms of various cartel operations. There is never a slow down to the streets. I repeat never is a slow down of the drugs that enter and are available in the United States.

Protection is bought off in a big way when forty-some police officers were charged and convicted in a drug sting, which involved five different United States Law enforcement agencies in cocaine collusion.

These officers took cash bribes to safe guard large shipments of cocaine from the drug cartel organizations established in Cleveland and in Northern Ohio. Some of these twenty documented cop protected cocaine shipments were over fifty kilograms, and seven-hundred pounds of marijuana at a time. These officers guarded the shipments and sales of these hard drugs.

Police correction officers sold the drugs to the prisoners. These cocaine cops who are crooks are the people in our society who need life sentences. The enormous amount of officers involved in the drug conspiracies are proof of the penetration by the cartel into the law enforcement agencies of the United States.

These officers do the same thing as the Mexican officers that took bribes. Bust competing drug elements, protect shipments, buy and inflence judges, prosecutors, and politicians by the handful. This bought off element let's those they protect to sell all the cocaine they can, so they can get there cut of the action. These police drug networks are set up presently nationwide. For everyone organized police drug operation you know about theirs twenty-five or more you don't know about.

Another Detroit Michigan core of cops face federal charges for the same type of drug running operation. Standing guard while cocaine shipments in excess of six-hundred and sixty pounds of cocaine are distributed locally. Involving a twenty-seven year veteran police officer to the chief deputy chief on down to the road patrol on and on. Police escorted drug filled vehicles from point A to point B.

It's the same in Chicago, New York and on and on. There is a staggering and an endless amount of documented police drug convictions proving widespread involvement. We need a new approach!"

Steve continued. "The Colombians created their own competition. The Colombians no longer can afford the cost of paying off the Mexicans. For every one-thousand kilos of cocaine cost, it would cost one-thousand kilos of cocaine for protection from the Mexican Federals.

The Mexican gangs have their own distribution networks established through the states. A DEA official said. "The cartels across the boarder use fax machines, pagers, encrypted phones to distribution centers through out the heartland of the United States. Shipping marijuana in Semi-trucks, large motor homes, cars with trailers, ECT across the country, blending into the woodwork of our country."

"In a recent bust of cartel underlings documents were confiscated of INS agents who deported illegal aliens from Houston back to Brownsville. The INS agents dropped off the aliens in Mexico. Then the INS agents had their U S government bus loaded with a million dollars worth of cocaine and marijuana by the Mexican cartel in Mexico. The INS agents brought the shipment of drugs to its destination in Houston without any interference. The delivered load of drugs by law enforcement is norm for corrupt cops on both sides of the boarder.

Bribing public officials is not a problem. The Mexican Cartel's enforcers have no problem with government official cooperation. Mexico has serious drug problems. Violent criminals run these cartels with no remorse. Cartel gangs roam around with silencer equipped Uzi's, eliminating any one their way. Gang wars over trafficking turf cross the boarder more and more.

With documents mounting that the Politicians, U S Military and Police are involved in smuggling drugs proves the ineffectiveness of our present drug fighting strategies. If we are serious about fighting drug abuse, turn to social and medical scientists. Generals, soldiers and cops have proven ineffective ever since the drug war started. One California Narc was busted twice for stealing drugs.

He was indited last time in connection for six-hundred and fifty pounds of cocaine stolen from the evidence room.

A recent bust found in Columbia of nearly twenty tons of marijuana stashed in milk cans was ready for shipment to the United States. Cocaine and heroin is regularly found on cartel infiltrated Colombian Air Force cargo planes. Some Colombian military drug shipments are intercepted at Ft Lauderdale International Airport by US Customs agents. Recently a Colombian Air Force plane brought in a ton of cocaine and twenty pounds of pure heroin. Colombian security chiefs and their subordinates are arrested but replaced with other cartel operatives. It's a never ending cycle. It doesn't matter if the Colombian President is on the plane, there's a good chance there is a shipment of cocaine on board.

Another cocaine shipment on a Panamanian cargo ship exceeded over five-thousand pounds was intercepted by US Customs the prior month. Some anti-drug agents of Colombia make large cocaine busts in Colombia. They stop speed boats filled with cocaine as they leave the shoreline.

As usual in the drug war operators pit their skills against the anti-drug warrior's strategy. They continually beat up on each other at the expense and safety of the citizens.

These cartel cocaine cowboys are ruthlessly violent. The Port of Miami bust upwards of two tons of marijuana at a time off ships and planes. The cocaine is uniquely hidden in different import products coming into the country. There are not enough customs agents to do through searches of all shipments and entries into the country. Many drug-laden imports are never given a second look.

The drugs once identified by customs officials are allowed to proceed to their destinations. Numerous drug trafficking arrests are made at that point. The Mr Big's are never around.

The most wanted drug lords visit the United States on a regular basis to run their gangs drug operations or just relaxation. The Tijuana drug gangs are ruthless and blood thirsty, when it comes to protecting their drug operation enterprise. It is no problem for the drug kingpins to cross our boarder back and forth over and over again." Steve concluded.

Pat Crabbinitch deceitfully told the audience that. "The DEA had all the major drug routes identified and secure from large shipment penetration into the country."

Peter Penn began narcotics agents bust organized cocaine rings in all types of neighborhoods. A sixteen-year-old girl was arrested at an Amtrak train station in Detroit. She had a ticket to Minnesota and a kilo of cocaine in her luggage. Under Michigan mandatory lifer law for six-hundred and fifty grams of cocaine she could spend the rest of her life in prison. Another young boy was taken into custody at the same station the next day for possessing over two hundred grams of crack cocaine.

At recent suburban house was busted a kilo and a half of cocaine, after neighbors complained of traffic at all hours of the night. Sales of crack cocaine twenty-four hours a day just like seven eleven. Drug scales weapons and drug paraphernalia, ECT were found at the residence. The owner was charged with possession of more than six hundred grams of cocaine. The charge carried a life sentence in the State of Michigan. The cocaine was repackaged for sale and distribution. It is believed these people were involved in thousands of dollars in drug sales over a long period.

The crack cocaine sold like candy. People went to any lengths to get money once addicted to crack. To crack heads no low life underhanded deal is too low to keep going on crack twenty-four hours a day. Girls offer their body and their very soul for the glass cock. They all con and steal for their crack high. The best advice to crack heads is not to take the next hit. Whether it's offered for free or you dumb enough to buy it. It's a loser's game. These are facts of a crack heads and hard drug operations."

Peter informed. "Twenty billion plus to fight the drug war per year hasn't stopped the flow or availability of drugs on the streets. Drug use has gone up with all drugs including alcohol, and tobacco sales. Youths in gangs are typically busted in dope dens. They have fifty or so rocks of crack cocaine for sale at any given time. That is worth about twelve hundred dollars in street cash sales. Semi-automatic weapons, cell phones and beepers are part of these different gang's drug organizations. Crime runs rampant in the hard drug circles.

Gang members who are caught and proven to be in gangs are given jail time with no early out. You get a ten year sentence for prison time on federal drug related crimes, you do ten years of incarceration. They also run drug sales in some circles of schools. Those who supply hard drugs to elementary school kids need jail time.

They estimate hard drug users in recent surveys is higher than previous survey's suggest. The White House Office of National Drug Control Policy released the study. This study is a national estimate of habitual hard drug users. Hardcore drug attics described as crack cocaine, powder cocaine, and heroin use in the last eight months.

Availability is widespread nation wide. Cocaine dealers sell heroin, which is now more readily available. Cocaine still dominant's the hard drug under world." Peter concluded his difficult speech.

Kim Cantel quickly acknowledged. "There are substantial street sales, but all use is down." The audience booed Kim off stage. The audience was tired of hearing the same old bull from the governments wasteful and ineffective drug war position.

Burt Bennet a non smoker is a sympathetic man toward the non-violent marijuana smokers labeled criminal. Burt is a firm believer that violence is not caused by marijuana use. Burt argued. "Cannabis use does not alter your basic disposition. Marijuana use reduces aggressive behavior. The violence factor comes from the US Government's sponsored drug war. The drug operating capital's influence of the cartel's narco-money out rival by far the dollars the United States spends on drug deterrent programs in Latin American.

Cops kill cops to protect and maintain their cocaine trade profits. The cartels live and invest in Latin American Commerce everyday. One Latin American was found dead himself in a stolen car from San Diego. He was the chief of an elite assassination group, who assassinates rival drug dealers and police for the Tijuana cartel. These people brutally kidnap, torture, and murder anyone who gets in there way. Violent crime escalated to phenomenal proportions in Tijuana.

One kilo of powdered cocaine is made into four times as much in crack cocaine. Crack cocaine has a much more addictive factor. Both types of cocaine are addicting. The violence factor involved with crack cocaine is a dangerous element in our society. We have to deal with eliminating the streets of crack cocaine.

Cops share in unwarranted violence as well. It is the nature of their aggressive militarized training. Cops beat harmless victims to death, because they have drugs in their hand. How many more people have to be beaten to death or shot to death by the police on drug searches gone wrong? Why put our citizens and our police force at risk in a senseless and reckless frenzy? Just because there is a law against marijuana use, doesn't give the cops can kill cannabis users.

The politicians, judges, prosecutors, and cops, manipulate and hide behind the law. It still doesn't mean their right persecuting marijuana users. The government's social projections and promotions devour the real America. How come marijuana users are branded addicts, pushers, or criminals but never identified as common social recreational users. Like common tobacco users. Like common beer drinkers. Marijuana is nothing like serious common whisky drinkers.

In Colorado a woman was hospitalized after eight DEA agents broke into her house. While the drug cops cursed, slammed and kicked her to the ground. They beat her in the head as she screamed in terror. Then they realized they were in the wrong house.

Wheat Ridge Mayor wrote that "Drug manufacturers must be controlled but not by people who can not even get the address right for the drug raid correct."

In Akron, Ohio a black clad drug police officer terrorized a mother and her kids in the middle of the night on a wrong house raid.

Another California cop blotched raid ended up accused of shooting an innocent businessman. He's is now suing the DEA and Customs Department. The drug cops used an untruthful paid drug informant.

In another California raid drug agents of the local sheriff's department attacked a ranch foreman. His wife's bathrobe was ripped off so the police could look at her naked body. "The Police were the real crooks." The rancher later said. "These cops acted like crazed druggies." The residents of the home said. The Sheriff's Dept later admitted. "We were one-hundred and eighty degrees off."

Another in California drug raid ski masked terrorist cops broke down the door, then stripped searched male and female residents. He drug cops already maced them in the face, cuffed and hog tied them belly down, ransacked their house, and ordered the man of the house to shut up!

Cops screamed. "You bitches shut up!" Their little girls were dragged out of the house and thrown on the lawn by these so-called heroes, they call cops. They were again in another community in the wrong house raid. Miss-managed, miss-guided, miss-trained, militarized, miss-informed, make- misfits is the tax payers miss-fortune.

One raid in Guthrie, Oklahoma Police knocked down a front door with an axe. They pointed guns at the mans wife and daughters while wrestling the man to the ground. The police then realized they were at the wrong address.

In Oregon a couple just got a of one-hundred thousand for a blotched wrongful raid on their house.

In Venice MO the cops bust down the door of the Mayors house in another blotched raid with pistols drawn. The Police again claim the wrong address.

In Florida a couple busted for suspected Marijuana turned out to be Elder berry bushes. "They don't even know what there looking for." The couple later said.

"In Washington State Drug agents ransacked a home. They forced little girls out of their bed in the middle of the night at gunpoint. Dragged their parents out of the house. Placed the kids in diapers out on the front lawn in the middle of the night. Again no drugs were found.

The coast guard on the high seas during a routine inspection had a sail boat towed all the way to Key West, Fla. The sailboat was stripped looking for drugs causing over eight thousand in damages. The owners of the sailboat a man and his wife figured they were kidnapped and terrorized for four days for no reason. The coast guard never paid for the sailboat to be repaired.

In Jacksonville, Florida police were charged with planting crack cocaine on suspects. This illegal police action tainted over two-hundred pending drug cases.

In Indiana the police barged into the couple's house after their eleven-year-old daughter opened the door. The couple was rousted up in the night time out of bed. The women told the officer she wasn't dressed. The officer said. "I don't care get out of bed. The officer kept the flashlight focused on her breasts. Then taking pictures of her breasts." He later said it was for evidence.

"They are very arrogant and hateful in their actions. They treat you like dirt." The lady also stated. "She felt like she been raped in her own house in front of her family." There are so many complaints and lawsuits, and settlements which are a direct result of bungled police commando procedures during unjustified drug raids.

We don't have time to go over all the police miscarriages of justice here today. However these police miscarriages must be addressed. These police created miscarriages of justice and freedom are spread across this country, brutalizing and terrorizing innocent victims in random drug raids just because that cop or informant said so on a whim. Cops stopping motorists for minor traffic violations just to shake them down. The police academies in this country are uniformly filled with militarized robot cowboy commando types, exploiting citizens rights with intimidating fear. These citizens have constitutional rights that police are supposed to uphold not suppress. We need politicians who are man enough to admit their wrong and come out of their bigot ways like George Wallace did before you die!" Burt firmly ended his part of the debate. The applause was genuine.

Lane Little amending her prepared speech to contradict the pro-marijuana group said, "I Steadfastly agree that violence is the biggest factor in the drug war. Most of the violence is perpetrated on victims by the drug cult, not by the police department."

Burt quickly countered. "What about all the violence and deaths created by the police drug raids. Marijuana raids are on record to have killed more innocent civilians than any marijuana use has killed. "

Kevin Kellar stopped this part of the debate stating the debate time as run it's coarse for this time frame.

Sherwin started. "There has come a time when theirs to many nuisance laws. You can pass a law that J-walking is a felony. How fast will you fill the jails then? Now there's to many prisons built for those convicted of the nuisance crimes. There comes a point when to many laws created are injustice and rally repression. How about marijuana users being small timers getting hard time? The results are that hard timers get small time.

Millions in drugs have taken off the streets but at what cost. Federal Government Massive Money Miss Management of illegal drug police tactics and their ineffectiveness contradicts fairness in the judicial system. We keep filling the prisons, while there is no slow down in availability of drugs in the streets, what so ever. Law Enforcement can listen to your phone calls, scan the hard drive of your computers, examine your medical anatomy with a single strain of hair, freely search your car after they pull you over from what ever reason they dream up.

The U S Bureau of Prisons populace doubled in the last ten years, adding more than a million new incarceration's. Prison building and Prison incarceration is big business. Predatory profits by the police are prolific. Prosecutors and Prisons is one hell of a booming business.

More crime laws, equals more prisoners, equals more lawyers, equals more prosecutors, equals more judges, equals more jails, equals more paved parking lots. These profits are unequalled for the prison business at forty-thousand to fifty-thousand dollars per year to maintain each prisoner no matter how trivial the crime of conviction.

These non-violent drug prisoners are now in prison to be trained as professional criminals. Prisons are a breeding grounds for hate. The government winds these non-violent prisoners up for disaster. The government does not wind them down into a normal society. Young kids end up in hate mongering violent racist gangs.

It's a disgrace the cops have such a high anti-marijuana expenditure, and pin badges on each other for the minor weed busts, when their own cities have the highest murder per-capita's in the country.

The American Gulag make state and commercial products built with free labor. Homes, roads, furniture, license plate, ECT. They are no different than Soviet gulags. Repression is repression. When Freddy Fender is throw in prison for three years for less than six grams of marijuana that's repression.

Political opponents of the governments marijuana drug war were jailed like John Sinclair for possession of two joints. He was sent to prison after receiving a long sentence.

Amnesty International now lists the American prison system among others for human rights violations. They claim the prison abuses are widespread and very regular. "Cruel, degrading and sometimes life-threatening methods of restraint continue to be a feature of the US criminal justice system," according to the Amnesty International report.

We want to end this marijuana apartheid in America. Punish cold-blooded killers not marijuana smokers. We want a constitutional structural balance for marijuana consumption and possession.

Drugs are more prevalent than ever. Marijuana users forfeit their possessions in drug raids. Over eighty five percent of all marijuana users work for a living, contributing to a better society. Their money is earned honestly. These working citizens use marijuana in a responsible manner. Our government eliminated their individual Constitutional rights.

These government officials are the money suckers of society who deprive a citizen freedom of choice.

People know what's better for themselves than the government. People work together with or without a government. We need more government working with the people, instead of against the people.

There will be a time and place in this country when freedom and equality will mean something different than all those rich white farmers.

Those same rich white farmers that rigged elections in the south by making blacks and minorities take an impossible Literacy test. He's a copy of the literacy test in my hand from the State of Louisiana. This is another government sponsored program of we know what's best for the people from our governmental dictatorship.

Freedom means how deep is your pocket of cash? The Federal Bureau of Justice statistics continually add an enormous amount of new prisoners every year to our prison system. Some innocent victims can't afford to pay for lawyers who bribe judges.

Our prison system's meant for violent offenders not somebody for marijuana possession and use. There's over a two hundred percent increase in marijuana related crimes of use and possession in the last ten years.

The prison hospitals are always filled and over crowded. Do you realize how much costs for doctors to examine prisoners along with hospital and medical care alone? Do you realize the arrest, incarceration, Courts, probation, parole department's, the whole ball of wax combined cost the American taxpayer for one prisoner alone that is convicted of marijuana possession and use crimes?

The prisons are over crowded. Harsher sentences for marijuana users are not a deterrent. Unfortunately hard core drug addicts who are sent to prison or gulag still come out of prison drug addicts.

Availability of drugs is no problem the prison guards and inmate visitors see to that. Two-thirds of all prison inmates are drug addicts from hard drugs. They use hard drugs on a regular basis. Some guards know inmates from the street. They trust them to distribute the drugs in prison. Inmates walk around the running track in the morning and pass their joints to one another. One inmate told me pot and hard drugs are easier to get in prison than on the street. Guards are busted for bringing drugs into the prisons are common place. One guard was recently convicted for smuggling large quantities of heroin into the prison. The gangs in the prison control the sales of the drugs. Over a dozen Dade country Florida correction officers were incriminated in a drug dealing network of peddling cocaine to inmates. Drugs are readily available in prison.

Other who cops strung out on cocaine rob banks in broad day light in hopes to supply their crack cocaine drug habit. These cops usually succeed for a few bank robberies before brazenly being caught.

Some Drug treatment programs work compared with the alternative of prison. Methadone clinics for heroin abusers work to get hard drug abusers off the drug so than can enter the work force.

Statistics prove they reduce hard drug use of patients as much as seventy-five percent. The methadone clinics are proven to be an effective in treatment of cocaine, heroin and other hard drug abusers.

Doctors recommend treatment not jail. They want to turn former drug addict's into productive members of society. The New England Medical journals endorse medical use of marijuana. Voters approved medical use of marijuana in several states. Patients have a right to use medical marijuana without interference or harassment.

Some prison guards sanction gangs to have gladiator type fights to the death with prisoners for entertainment purposes. The guards and prisoners bet for the death of an inmate. Some prison guards sanction physical, and mental abuse. They make prisoners live and think on the level of pit bull mentality. Barbaric and medieval state sponsored incarceration and abuse.

Prison guards have also raped their women prisoners. Some of these women prisoners were in prison for simple marijuana possession. Guards allow privileges to female inmates exchange sex for favors. Sexual harassment and rape are everyday occurrences. How do you think over one hundred female inmates become pregnant every year?

The violent gangs that internally run the prison are a major nemesis. These violent gangs dictate who lives and who dies in the prison system.

Some out of state to privately run prisons have failed to clean up allegations or weaknesses. Indictments of jailers is reality. Some guards have been video taped kicking prisoners who were ordered spread eagle naked for a cavity check. The cuffed prisoners were ordered to craw on the floor while being probed by stinging shots from the electric stun gun. Guard dogs bite the gentiles of some of the prisoners who screamed for there lives. Some of these privately owed prisons also fail due to the high rate of escapees in Ohio. The state is considered taking over the prison.

Marijuana users do not belong in prisons with these people. Marijuana users do not belong in prison. Marijuana users constitutional rights are violated. Empty our prisons of marijuana offenders. Even former Attorney General Edwin Meese III leading an American Bar Association panel admitted curbs have to be made concerning federalizing so many crimes.

We need politicians who stand up for all American's or we don't need them!" Now Sherwin is infuriated by all the penal code injustices. On a limited time frame he is not able to describe all abuses of the penal code system in detail and concluded. "I'm only sticking up for the little guy, not any hard core criminals. Period!"

Nervous Otto Aso stated. "The prisons are not over crowded, that we just keep pace with the rest of the world's penal systems."

Sherwin interrupted. "The United States has the biggest penal system in the world, where overcrowding is the norm. The blinded drug war is what keeps building new jails, prisons, and incarceration camps in demand. One Correction Officer John Baird said. "We take all the responsibility away from them (prisoner), then kick them out and tell them, OK, get a job, pay your bills. We're not correcting a damn thing. The (Department of Corrections) should be renamed the Department of Confinement." Legislatures now question the high expenditure prison spending proposals." Sherwin concluded.

Chairman for the board of Educators Ted Edgers started off. "We must tell our kids the truth. Thomas Jefferson said. "We are not afraid to follow the truth wherever it may lead." The truth is always healthy. Ted told the audience. "The government's social stigma placed on youths that smoke marijuana is wrong. Criminal records mark these young people as criminals if caught in possession or use of marijuana.

Random police dogs conduct sweeps of schools are heavy-handed and unconstitutional. Those drug-sniffing dogs should be tolerated only when kids are not in attendance in order not to stigmatize the students.

Some kids readily admit they can get drugs before school, during school, and after school. It's up to the parents of kids to keep them involved with intellectual, physical, and social activities they approve.

Over fifty percent of school kids admit use of marijuana in the last thirty days in recent surveys. No one condones giving marijuana to kids, but not everyone thinks we should stigmatize these kids as criminal either.

In schools your kids are more susceptible to flues, friends, enemies, peer pressures, sex, cigarettes, alcohol parties, gangs, marijuana, other forms of much more harmful drugs, and some other habits parents do not condone.

One student was suspended for seven days brought marijuana into the school for a show and tell session. He said he was going to participate in the drug education class. The DARE program in our schools has failed. It is a program with internal conflict, which pits people against people. Citizens against citizens.

Parents in large numbers as well question the DARE Program. There are no answers for their questions. The students are told not to bring the DARE workbook home. The DARE program is in approximately seventy percent of all schools, and has no problem financial wise. More than half a billion per year of the tax payers and money sponsored contributions is spent on the feel good DARE program. Major city council members question the DARE Program's effectiveness. National studies show that DARE's feel good program, that does not work or possess any lasting power. Many students say they feel uncomfortable in the DARE classes.

The ineffective feel good DARE Program has been examined effectively by intellectuals nation wide. Their findings are all similar as to nil effectiveness of the DARE Program when compared statistically.

The DARE students when compared with students that did not participate in the DARE Program, do not show any significant statistical difference in the following years, when it pertains to alcohol, tobacco or drug use. Students grow out of the program. Kids can't remember much about the programs study book in the following years.

Narcs and drug sniffing dogs operate at the school like a military operation conflict with teaching programs. Learning the effects of sub-stance abuse can be done in a much different manner in schoolroom classes. Parents can question their own kids about all drugs. Some parents sanction marijuana use, other parents find pipes, papers, and weed among their kids possessions.

Most kids, who use marijuana, really don't experiment with other harder drugs. Staying on a stupor equal of government sponsored hard whisky is what a parent should worry about. They know the difference light hearted fun and totally drunk.

Socially mild experimentation with marijuana is no great danger what so ever. A person whose addiction is alcohol, which is approved by the establishment, is much harsher health wise than any marijuana. Marijuana is excepted cultures wide. We need more of a learning atmosphere than subversive and tyrannical DARE program teachings.

A program that pits Americans against other Americans create another Ka-oss of conflicts. Police in uniforms teach DARE students for seventeen weekly sessions.

Some parents question. Why untrustworthy militarization classes are taught to our kids in school classrooms?

The Canadian's reported that the DARE program did not curtail drug use in their country. The real world differs from schoolbook ways. Researchers and professors alike who report the true full facts in national studies of the DARE Program say they are branded druggie slang names.

The DARE Program backers have been accused of jamming radio and TV stations when adverse information is released about the DARE Program. The Reporters are intimidated not to report the true full findings on the DARE Program, and accused of journalistic fraud.

The DARE Program has not worked or is it effective to curb drug use. The DARE program actually promotes marijuana and drug use by instilling the drug topic's into the kids. They could be learning the arts, physical Ed, science ECT. DARE has done a lousy job curbing drug use, that's the bottom line.

The cops have made snitches into a big business, pitting friends and family against each other.

Police and school officials praised one kid publicly. While the kid got an award his father sat in jail for simple marijuana possession. Cops who initiate kids to their bust parents in their own household is the real crime. When full debate is required, the DARE Program backers refuse to participate until today, and only because they were forced them here today to show their hand.

One ten year old turned in his parents through the DARE program. The police officers promised they would not arrest his parents. However, they lied to the student in the video movie to the children the student said, "They promised they would never said they would arrest my parents." The cops eventually arrested the parents. The ten-year-old watched his father arrested after being handcuffed by the police. His mother lost her job as a result of the drug investigation and arrest. The father did four months in jail for two joints. The parents wound up getting a divorce, because of the ordeal. The hard drugs turned out not to be cocaine, but an anti-phedimine.

The former DARE program student graduate said his rights were violated. The parents have sued the town's government. There are dozens of documented similar stories.

One fact remains is that drugs are more readily available to teen-agers in school than on the streets. Drugs are common in the school system. The parties the tee-agers attend often have marijuana circulating among alcohol and cigarettes.

Many students who do drugs say they all started using alcohol and cigarettes first. Their parents or other adults use government sponsored alcohol or tobacco. Smoking illegal marijuana's light hearted high is much preferred by students.

Marijuana is as easy to get as tobacco cigarettes. Anyone can purchase pot in anywhere in the United States. Alcohol is the real gateway drug. We all knew that. Virtually drug free schools seem to be non-existent.

An undercover agent recently planted in a high school nabbed over twenty students in a drug sting. Most charges were marijuana related. The kids felt betrayed because this cop posed as a friend to them.

Kids rarely tell their parents about marijuana use among their crowd, unless the have marijuana smoking parents. Many kids have just that. They don't feel marijuana use makes them stupid. Most claim they have smoked and have friends that smoke marijuana.

Research has proved that over ninety-percent of school kids have tried alcohol, over fifty-percent of the kids have smoked a marijuana joint in the last few months. Social norms and peer pressure take precedent in their lives.

Marijuana is the number one herb of choice among students and the adult population as well.

Role model parents are not consistent with other kids. Where they say! Do as I say, Do not do or as I've done. Some parents actually promote marijuana use. They would rather have their recreational substance indulging kid involved with just marijuana on a peer party night than alcohol, tobacco, tranquilizers, valiums, cocaine, sniffing glue, inhalants, or any other much worse substance.

Four high school girls who made an anti-drug video were killed in a car accident shortly after. Toxicology reports concluded the girls had "Difluoroethene" in their blood streams. A spray can of Duster II which contains ingredient was found in the car. Doctor's treating teens nationwide from sniffing inhalants say there are over one thousand over the counter household products widely available. The kids prefer inhalants because they don't have to hid any pipes, cigarette rolling papers, etc. Most kids no not realize the dangers. Dangerous inhalants public awareness is close to non-existent. It's estimated that over a million school kids will try the inhalant euphoria high which affects the circulatory and nervous systems of the human body. Consciousness loss and cardiac arrest vary from the amount and dangerous strength of the many different glues, deodorants, cooking sprays, pesticides spays household inhalant's available. Reality check is kids experiment with their peers. In Holland kids using inhalants is unheard of. Their approach to teach kids the truth is way more effective when compared to our disastrous time after time stupid and deadly educational approach.

We don't need a DARE scare we need the FAIR stare to teach truth. Promoting jails with the DARE warmongering programs have no place among our young people trying to develop there own personal initiatives in life. Governors who sponsor drug tests for all students are counter productive. Some of the same governors line their pockets with political contributions from drug testing companies for the wide spread use of drug test kits that are now deemed mandatory. The spot light should be on the graft by government, educational, and police officials.

With academic freedom and reason in mind while we are standing here on the Jefferson Memorial, I'd like to honor and quote Thomas Jefferson again. ".....the Superiority will be greater from the free range of encouraged there, (rather than) the restraint imposed....by the shackles of a domineering hierarchy, and a bigoted adhesion to ancient habits."

Doctors urge teaching students about the safe use of herb marijuana. Strict abstinence calls from some parents and law enforcement fall on deaf ears, when it comes to today's youth. Effectiveness of DARE's feel good drug education programs is limited at best, and ineffective in reality.

Two seniors from college were just thrown off the College football team. They were in possession of a small amount of marijuana at a drug search roadblock set up by police. The small amount of marijuana was found in the back seat of the drug search.

One college cancelled its basketball season after seven player's recently admitted smoking marijuana. The players felt they had to make a stand for personal freedom. Other collegians claim to smoke marijuana and get straight A's. "Marijuana is purely is a light recreational drug at best," these college students said.

"Marijuana is the drug of choice in modern America society, so you figure it out. Our politicians ought to get with the program. Retire to the old folk's home would be a good step in the right direction for these relic politicians. One school chancellor recently resigned after he was arrested for a small amount of marijuana, because the adverse back lash.

Teachers found in possession and use of small amounts of marijuana in past years are dismissed or not hired for prior convictions from decade's prior. These are some of America's brightest. Smoking marijuana, tobacco or not. Some NBA Basketball players are speaking out in opposition to marijuana drug testing.

Tobacco rights groups support our cause, now fearing the tide would eventually criminalize tobacco smoking. Shifting gears they heavily back the pro-marijuana activists. Some tobacco smokers feel that maybe some day they might not be able to smoke a tobacco cigarette in the privacy of their own home.

Laws are passed to punish teen smokers. Police write thousands of teen smoking tickets. Problem is the court system can't hear all the cases. Most of these teen smoking cases end up dismissed when they are contested. The court ends up dismissing a great majority of these teen smoking cases. The court system is already bogged down beyond belief or relief, smoking tobacco tickets confuse the bog down court procedure's even more.

Draining the taxpayers courts resources have certain communities asking for a change in the teen smoking law. Police write tickets for teen smoking, but the court can't act on because of the increase in teen felonies. The teen felony cases take president in juvenile courts, over underage smoking. Smoking tickets don't do much. They light up with their friends no matter what the law is, if they so choose. Teens in some state are required to adhere too much tougher restrictions on their driver's licensees. Learners permits time requirements have been extended. No teen driving in certain parts of the day.

Smoking tobacco or marijuana encompasses school kids, college students, and teachers, to professors. Not bad if you look where all these schooling graduations bring you. These schooled marijuana users fair just fine, without police interference. They keep the pace with A's and peace in the community." As Ted concluded to a rousing audience applause.

Wheeling-dealing Weldon Wicks immediately began. "We need to drug test every school kid, every teacher, every policeman, every fireman, all military personal, all farming and factory personal." The audience booed Weldon right off the stage. Nobody wanted to hear about any more stiff-armed tactics to control morals of the country.

Penny Parker started to explain. "Marijuana is the modern day moonshine but much less harmful. Marijuana should be regulated and taxed, when grown in larger amounts. You can target legal marijuana sales, because they want to be targeted. Research show a trillion dollar industry projection between the hemp and marijuana industry. Marijuana is an established under ground black market thriving and growing steady. Trouble is we need to rein the tax money in, and release freedom of personal choice back to the people where freedom belongs. Right now this marijuana drug war concocted by the federal government is costing billions per year. All drug profits by the billions steadily leave this country on a regular basis. You tell me what's wrong with this picture? We don't need pot police. Fire them all! We need pot tax collectors." Penny concluded after accurately accessing the legal pro-marijuana industry sales projections.

Rupert Riddle said. "I'll tell you what's wrong with that picture! We are winning the drug war. We will win the drug war." The crowd started with chants of "No more lies!" The chants grew louder and louder until Rupert knew what time it was and sheepishly walked off the stage.

Admirably trustworthy Nolan a retiree from the National Transportation board talked about the real dangers on the road. Nolan had a report by the National Transportation Board in his hand. The report said. "This comprehensive study show the real dangers is alcohol, not marijuana on the roadways. It went further to say that. "Marijuana users have no more higher rate of accidents than none users."

The study was done out of blood samples from highway vehicle accident victims where over fifty percent were alcohol related. Less than eighteen percent showed drugs. Marijuana was less than seven percent, but two-third's of highway accident victims had alcohol in their system. Accident fatality victims involving marijuana by itself shows a very little difference in the accident rate victim verses of straight people.

Some argue smoking marijuana while going down the road eliminates their road rage. They slow down, awareness increases, and enjoy their ride better. To some they consider marijuana a friend that help's them down the road. I know in the last thirty years I've logged hundreds of thousands of miles while driving stoned on marijuana. I'll tell you what. It's the best feeling in the world to come out of the closet."

Nolan admitted marijuana uses this to the crowd. Nolan said. "We've all stayed in the closet for years. I've had to hid smoking pot from my family, and some of my fellow workers. Now, that I'm retired, I want to speak up and tell the truth. I've been driven around with friends, and acquaintances, hundreds of thousands of miles over the years, without a second thought while passing joints in a moving vehicle. Smoking marijuana kept everyone alert, comfortable and conversation lively while going down the road safely. It has not been a hindrance. Marijuana is not a controlling drug like cocaine, heroin, alcohol, barbituetis, ECT. Those drugs are mind and body altering and cause real driving impairments.

The adverse effects from marijuana's THC in driving performance are minute, to nil. Driving skills are not impaired or impeded. Some actually say their driving skills improve. Some drivers say their are more consciences, and various driving feasibility studies have concluded the same.

Paying attention to the roadway, instead of just blaring down the road in a straight road rage. If you ask me a few more people could afford to try marijuana. It would help the great majority of people who have a bad attitude on the roadway. Smoking marijuana lowers a person's highway speed to a degree. The driver after a bad day at work isn't so uptight on his way home. Theirs' different reasons why marijuana use is helpful."

Nolan explained. "The biggest reason is people seem content for that time. Being content is half the day's battle. For some people marijuana is their little helper. The congestion roadways are intolerable for schedules that some have to keep.

In the last twenty-five years the amount of cars on today's roads have over doubled. There has been a only six percent increase of roadways. Did the highways over built then or are they under built now? In some places driving seem worse than the rock of Gibraltar, because of the congestion.

Chronic marijuana smoker's admit marijuana is a safer easier form of tobacco's relief. They smoke just because they enjoy smoking in itself. These people continue to do their chores around the house or farm. Whether it's driving tractors all day long, cleaning or painting. They continue to do their jobs even if it's a construction worker who jack hammers concrete or policeman who patrol in their squad cars." The crowd roared with that note.

"Smoking marijuana has very little to do to detract one from their abilities. It's a proven fact people using cell phones while driving their cars down the road are involved in more accidents. Smoking marijuana makes some just feel content to go about their business with a better attitude. A calming of the nerves, and relieving some tension's from everyday living. Without being on edge, wanting hit somebody or taking prescription hard drugs. Marijuana use is much better even than counting to ten. Marijuana use keeps some on their best behavior. It helps others with self-initiatives. Why would you want to detract from these facts?"

Nolan further said. "The government's taxed and regulated cup of tea is tobacco cancer sticks. Some cigarette's were found to have six hundred plus foreign additives. The peoples popular choice of marijuana is a less harmful form of a recreational high pleasure, which presently this government doesn't tax or regulate."

Nolan looked at the audience and said. "These are some of the government conclusions. They are documented by the Government's own National Transportation Safety Board but not advertised. There is no indication that marijuana use by itself cause's fatal car accidents. These are conclusions from your fellow citizens. When marijuana by itself is used while driving there is no statistical difference in fatal accidents.

Of the eight industrialized nation's highway studies and investigated accident reports, all have concluded that marijuana is not the problem in the roadway. Alcohol remains the most serious problem. When the alcohol bars empty out onto the roadways there's drunks at the wheel. When the coffee shops of Amsterdam let out at night and the patrons hit the fresh air, they are soon straight.

The most comprehensive study on marijuana related accidents was conducted by Australian Transportation Department. The report stated. "The accident rate between marijuana smokers when compared with straight drivers was actually lower."

Dr Jason White researcher from the University of Adelaide said. "The findings hold world wide significance. Alcohol produces the greatest impairment to driving. Marijuana smokers he speculates. "compensate for impairing effects of the drug. They are more cautious, less likely to take risks, and they drive slower." Why don't we try a modern approach to help empty our nations highways of alcoholic drivers." Nolans exemplary explanation of transportation studies driving facts conclude.

Sarah Stalls stated. "It is reprehensible to suggest that driving skills are improved by smoking marijuana."

Nolan quickly reiterated. "This government document in my hand is from the National Transportation Safety Board, it clearly states their studies have concluded that there are no statistical significant difference in accidents between marijuana users and non substance users." Nolan holding the NTSB paper in the air and told the audience where they can get their own copy from the government.

Accountant Professor Kevon Parker divulged. "The drug money in our country is leaving by the zillions. It's about time we change the law for the money of the drug trade to stay here in this country. Let money change hands for small amounts of marijuana, between our citizens. At least our money stays here in this country in American hands. The majority of marijuana consumed in America is imported into this country by international drug cartels with cooperation of many of our government officials.

In turn money paid for all these drugs go to foreign countries at an alarming rate. Government controlled sales of cannabis would create millions in taxes at an escalating rate for our country. Our American money would stay here. Marijuana money making elements of the drug cartels would be eliminated. The legal sale, bartering, and regulation of marijuana would eliminate the foreign black market.

Give the people want they want! I don't know whose in charge of draining our national reserve and exporting our money overseas? It's because of the way our government handles the drug problem.

One cartel alone laundered over fifty million through one Mexican Bank source alone. One hit man for the cartel was arrested with over two million dollars in his possession. He was on his way to launder the money with this financial institution. These drug traffickers are very rich, powerful, and influential. If a connected men like him ends up in a Mexican jail his release is usually imminent.

Yet, Mexico has gained U S certification to fight drug smuggling year after year after year. The president certifies and the senate reject the certification. The Senate does not believe that Mexico is doing enough to counter the flow of drugs into this country. Some senators have changed they vote for certification of Mexico, because the certification plan to fight drugs has failed. Mexico's wide involvement of the police and military in the drug trade is the reason cited for the non-certification votes.

The Mexican government can give you a good show on the one side but business remains as usual for the drug cartels. The Mexican drug cartels have been proven to do volumes of business with Chase Manhattan bank, Bank of America, Citibank and many other financial institutions as well. Citibak officials asked very little of where Raul Salinas, the brother of the former Mexican President where he got his one-hundred million he deposited with them. The former Mexican President fled his country, while Raul got caught holding the bag.

The Congressional report from the General Accounting Office accused Citibank of operating "a money-managing system that disguised the origin, destination and beneficial owner of the funds."

All the money washers of these drug financial institutions should be terminated, and banking institutions strictly regulated."

Kevon ended his speech in an revealing a clear view of where the money goes now, and where it should go. Kevon convincingly demonstrated changes that need to be made.

Mike Batner started right in on discrediting Kevon studies. Mike stated. "We bust these financial drug laundering institutions dealing with the drug cartels. We project shutting all cartel money laundering financial institutions down with in three years".

Kevon countered. "How can you promise busting these drug money friendly banks in three years when you haven't been able to through the whole drug war?"

Vince Boyd eloquently speaking about the drug wars failure of politics and present marijuana laws. Vince said. "The Civic leaders are ineffective with outdated with judicial marijuana policies. We don't have adequate security at our embassies around the world, but we have billions to fight millions of citizens in a marijuana war, that the citizenry doesn't want.

The civic leaders and politicians with self-interest are persuaded by special interests. Where's the man or men who govern this government for all classes of people. These present government leaders are out step and touch with society. Anti-drug hysteria campaign promoted by the government has not reached the morals of the people, who live down on earth.

Morals as lived in by society differ drastically from the laws made by the governors for society. We need laws that do no buck the majority of the citizen's beliefs, and livelihood actions. Jailing marijuana users is counter productive in America. The reality is smashed American Liberties. If you count all the people who smoke, that would have be forty to fifty percent of the people in the United

States, and more than seventy-five percent of the people have tried marijuana. Yet, not one has died from marijuana use.

Our studies have shown us that at least one joint was smoked by that amount of citizens. That's an equivalent to the population of twenty-two to twenty-five states of our union. This division that cannot be ignored. This class of citizens of created criminals by the government must be terminated. The government presents mystical fears to the citizens of the world about marijuana use to non-users propaganda filled with mis-information, and mis-truths.

We need a government that focuses on real criminals if were talking about a law and order society. Where if man is not the king of the jungle? He certainly can be the king of his castle, without reference or strings.

We want to be free to choose in our society. Quite frankly were going to get it. If we talk about a faith or group as Jewish, Catholic, Baptist, Protestant Hindu, Hispanics, Blacks, or native Americans, we'd fight to preserve their rights. We would not work to take them away. Marijuana smokers are no different from any other American fighting for their rights. Marijuana is embedded into the mainstream of the world including America.

Some law enforcement officers in the drug war are forced during the drug buys to smoke crack from the drug dealers. Then that officer is given a new assignment. Some main stream law and order types who are hard core drug fighters advocate selling a shot of heroin, and cocaine just like a shot of whisky. This would cut down on crime by hard core addicts and eliminate the drug cartels. America would deal with its drug problem here. The drug war in this society would be over. Stemming drug substance abuse has to be done with education not criminalization.

Drug producing nations claim the U S drug consumption problem encourages coca crop farmers to produce. Colombian economy alone brings home over six billion dollars a year of American dollars from the cocaine trade.

Marijuana serves as an alternative for alcohol, and hard drug dependency. No matter how many marijuana users they arrest the marijuana trade continues to thrive and flourish. Trying to arrest every marijuana dealer and user is senseless. We put plenty of people in jail, but the government has not accomplished the goal of zero use by no means. Under the convictions of conspiracy laws the government fill prisons up without documentation or evidence.

Criminologists concede the criminal justice system advances social anxiety instead of being a protector of peace. The government should promote harm reduction policy's instead of inciting state sponsored violence. Drug violence will subside only after the government's wasteful drug war stops. Only then will the black market of drug world be eliminated.

We need to change our approach. Judges are not given the leeway to fashion sentences that fit the crime. Mandatory sentences give all the power to the prosecutors regardless of circumstances. The prosecutor does what the cop's request is period. There is no discretion for the judge. Why have a judge?

Non-violent drug defendants of the criminal justice system receive longer prison terms than rapists and murderers. How dumb can our government legislatures be, if they think getting peaceful marijuana smokers off the street is going to stop real crime?

Many police chiefs and federal judges openly admit that the drug war is a complete failure. They want a change. Some federal judges refuse drug cases which require mandatory sentencing for convictions. One judge felt depressed for his part in the war on drugs for the cruel sentencing standards which has done more harm in society than not.

Marijuana laws differ from state to state. In New York twenty grams of marijuana is a one-hundred dollar fine and no jail.

In Nevada possession of two grams of Marijuana can get prison time, but you can buy all the whores you want and gamble all your money away legally in the state of Nevada.

In the state of Wyoming you can cultivate any amount of marijuana, and cultivation is a probational offence. In Texas sale of large amounts of marijuana net ninety-nine years in prison. In New Hampshire State legislatures sponsored a bill to decriminalize small amounts of marijuana down to a traffic ticket. Industrial hemp production regulations is also in the states mix. Industrial hemp has nothing to do with drugs. It's rope not dope!

In New Mexico drivers licenses are not taken for marijuana offences, while the state of Georgia suspend your driver's license and your professional license. In Iowa the Supreme court ruled blanket drug searches of non-consensual, motorists without cause and search warrants by law enforcement is illegal. Reversing a motorists possession of marijuana conviction.

California all marijuana offences are probational, no what matter the circumstances. Some states have all misdemeanor marijuana convictions erased from their record and destroyed automatically after a period of two years. The overbearing Federal marijuana laws are the most stringent. All Federal marijuana laws should be revoked. Individual states should monitor their own marijuana policies.

The inroads of intellectuals, journalists, and legal thinkers, favor drug reform. This pro marijuana movement grows by leaps and bounds everyday. Everyone has second thoughts about current drug laws and the ills they bring. Prohibition of marijuana will be a thing of the past. Individual freedom will prevail.

Look at the message the Arizona and California voters overwhelmingly sent to the federal government. The Federal Government officials still don't want to honor the voter's decision. Prison orientated drug control policy's will fall like communism across this country. Drug prevention and treatment will prevail over current law. A safer America will be established.

We don't need broaden police state powers for marijuana's sake. We don't need broaden police search and seizure powers. Wouldn't it be a shame if cannabis crimes went down because of marijuana legalization and we had to lay off a few cops to save the taxpayers money?

The government should not decide the people's self-interest. That's not what the foundation of this government is about. We need to get back to the basics of the Constitution of the United States. Degrading laws concerning cannabis citizens has proved to be a total failure.

The United States war on drugs has few victories, and violent unfair turf battles remain on all sides. Our four hundred billion-tax dollar loss in an effort to fight the drug war in the last ten years has to be re-evaluated. The victors are the leaders of the drug cartels, because of the black market value of their cocaine. United States has created this black market and drug war. We can stop one part of this battle by legalizing marijuana. Then we can concentrate on getting the harder drugs from entering our neighborhoods." Vince concluded to applause.

Bertha Ingels countered. "We have fresh break ups of marijuana rings. These rings were well organized to distribute more than three hundred pounds of marijuana to the streets of one Pa community per week. We just recently cleaned up one marijuana drug ring, and a Drug infested LA neighborhood from selling crack on the streets."

Vince countered. "They may be off the streets but drug vendors are still selling drugs out of their many strings of houses on a continual basis."

Mason Vought expounded. "Stop the Assassination of our citizens. It's time for the government to ease up on its cannabis citizens. It's time for the heartless Federal government to open its heart to real citizens. This is the time to decriminalize cannabis for personal use without reservation from Washington D C. An in-trenched government cannot grow with one type mind set. One type mind set isn't a free society. The government campaigned for over sixty years in an all out war of miss-information, intimidation, incarceration, inhuman treatment of free citizens. The government tried to make people do something they don't want to do. The try to make them be something they don't want to be. People do not want to be a clone of the government's perception of citizens.

Where's the attitude? "I may not agree with what you do but I will defend your right to do it." We have to establish fair and just guidelines for all citizens. We want to get this marijuana war over with so all Americans can go on to bigger and better things.

Washington DC endorsing legalization of marijuana will not increase marijuana use. Washington sponsors Alcohol, perspiration hard drugs, and tobacco that don't mean they promote widespread use.

Kids realize drug abuse from childhood until death. Marijuana has it's time and place in society. The only plan our present government running Washington came up and implemented is inadequate, and totalitarian. The best plan was the one our forefathers set up with the Constitution. The plan where marijuana is completely legal, the plan, that does not impede on freedom of choice for individual citizen's. We won't consider voting for any politician for office that opposes that plan. The deep seated anger and hate of the right wing morality promoters must be eliminated from government. Freedom of individual choice must prevail. Get rid of the "Snitch for Profit Program" on who smokes pot. It's irrelevant!

Today's marijuana drug control plan is dictatorship mixed with facism. We terrorize cannabis citizens our forefathers did not consider criminals in any way. We want our old freedoms back. We standing today retaliating with the truth. Look around prohibitionists you're being abandoned everyday by your most staunch anti-drug supporters, because dictatorship is a loser.

Politicians, Police, Judges, Prosecutors, people from all walks of life are here today to protest present federal law. A big part of our populous want to see change in our drug war. My question is do the people in charge presently in charge here, see and hear them. The populace will not overlook the marijuana smokers rights abuses any longer. These important players in the drug reform initiative are supporters who realize we need a serious change in our approach to the drug war. They are here to help establish new drug reforms. There are here to support the legalization of marijuana. The truth and the people will win."

As the debate audience applauded Mason he continued. "Our retired general the drug Czar, needs to be retired again. We need responsible leaders in touch with the communities, not dictator's of social policy in our households from a Washington desk. Society does not always approve of what different parts of society do. These diversities make a free society competitive. Washington should endorse individual freedom. Not divide citizens up with a line in the sand. Freedom of our citizens is what will keep this country the best on earth.

We the voters, can vote every single one of these out of touch incapable righteous politicians right out of office in a clean sweep. The politicians who do not believe in smoker's right to choose marijuana or tobacco in the privacy of their own homes will be identified and voted out. More governmental red tape in society is not the solution to our problems."

Mason said. "Were dealing with real people here. There's polarization in all these points of view. One is the war on drugs and it's warriors and it's consequences. The second is the push for marijuana legalization and the legalizers. The third avenue is to deal with the drug problem itself. With the legalization of alcohol and cigarettes being legal, it doesn't make sense to fight the war on less harmful marijuana. Alcohol, Cocaine, Heroin, and other hard drugs are the real menace to society. They are the real corruption to society.

We need to concentrate on pragmatic approaches to circumvent the drug problem. We need to curb demand here for hard drugs in the United States. We are the biggest consumers of hard drugs in the world. We have the best available information for analyses.

New Regulation and drug laws are needed, but not to enforce a social norm. The laws shouldn't punish citizens with jail for marijuana use. What they government is doing is destroying peoples lives. A government protecting a person from themselves in a method that destroys a citizens life. Giving these citizens what's equivalent to half status in life to keep a cash bloated police drug expenditure cookie jar is wrong.

The governmental marijuana control process kills and maims citizens individuality further spending of our taxes out of control. Just open your wallet and give it all to the government, and law enforcement in the name of fighting marijuana. This outrageous tax payer bilking isn't right. Get out of marijuana criminality business like many other countries have!

Prison space should be used efficiently for hard criminals. Marijuana smokers are not hardened criminals, who need incarceration. They do not deserve to have their civil rights violated. Incremented changes are needed with concern of drug laws.

The government law can't have a worse effect on our citizens than letting the citizens choose their own destiny as far as marijuana is concerned. It's not the government's job to protect people from there own peaceful behavior, when it comes to marijuana use."

Mason explained. "Over sixty percent of these people surveyed concede that law enforcement is not successful in curtailing marijuana use. And ninety percent of police chiefs nationwide advocate a change in the drug laws. Only ten percent choose punishment as an option to reduce marijuana use. Only two percent of law enforcement say that current drug laws are effective. Is this a no brainier or what by their own."

Mason explained the new law proposals. "The effects to be realized though drug reform legalization would make our communities safer. Safety should be everyone's number one concern.

One problem is the Republicans and Democrats can't agree on anything let alone a controversial drug reform bill. We need more than two major political parties in this country, to break the tie and keep the Republicans and Democrats honest.

A former Republican Secretary of State George P. Shultz with influences all over the world said. "We're not really going to get anywhere until we can take the criminality out of the drug business and the incentives for criminality out of it."

Reduce the price and regulate the flow of drugs would destroy the value of cartel drugs. The organized business of smuggling and selling drugs across our country will be over. Destroy the cartel's valuable commodities is the only way to destroy their economic influence.

Experts agree some types of drug legalization is the only way to curb the profits of the Cartels. The drug cartel influence would dissipate. Taxpayer dollars and lives would be saved. Police can concentrate on crimes against the people. Prison over crowding would be eliminated. Court systems would be free to concentrate on quality crime cases. Police and governmental official corruption would be greatly reduced.

If you smoke marijuana, your labeled by the government an addict, pusher, dumb or criminal. You're never considered a responsible citizen, who works hard and pays taxes. A citizen who proves to be a good American deserve their individual constitutional rights.

Drug reform laws would automatically save taxpayers money that could be regulated tax dollars to more worthy venues.

Fighting terrorism, organized crime, finding serial killers, rapists, white crime and dishonest cops is real crime.

Marijuana Reform Legislation also bring consumer protection. Marijuana is now unregulated with present consumption. Marijuana has no warning labels on black market sales. From the enormous amounts in legal sales of marijuana, and incoming taxes dollars from the vast amount of marijuana sales would be realized in the millions for most states counties and cities.

If a consumer would like to quit smoking marijuana, counter products could be developed and purchased over the counter much like nicerette is for cigarettes. Drug legalization would reduce the spread of Hepatitis, AIDS because intravenous drug users would be supplied clean needles to prevent spread of infectious diseases. Hard drug users would also have a safe soft herb alternative.

Reform drug laws would prevent the erosion in regard to personal liberties of the citizens. Foreign countries would be safer to travel and live in, because guerrilla groups that protect the cartel poppy fields would not have a valuable drug commodity any more.

Major funding for these guerrilla groups would dissipate. Latin American Countries realize the need and recommend change in our drug war approach. The rest of the world has taken steps to stabilization of drug trade, without impairing safety of its citizens. Realization that the elimination of drugs would never be possible. Co-existence with drug users on our own terms is the only alternative.

These drug laws are falling all over the world, as we know them. Drug reform legislation would put U S Relations with other countries on equal understanding. Anti-American sentiment would be curtailed. The thousands of coca growers in Latin American countries who chant "Death to America" "Up with the coca production" Would have their poppy field economy regulated to reasonable prices. This act alone would eliminate tensions, between all countries concerned.

Everyone would be on the same page. Mutual respect would be established, between all the countries. The foolishness of the American Federal drug laws strikes fear into the vein of freedom. Special investigative divisions of police and military personal assigned to witch-hunts of finding out who smokes pot, so they can bust them, will end.

When Marijuana becomes legal our money would go from one Americans hand to another, when marijuana changes hands. Money exchanged in America for marijuana happens everyday on a grand scale. The real trouble is the bulk of the money keeps going down below the boarder. The cartel then keeps large amounts of cash coming home to buy more government influence.

We need to legalize sales of marijuana. The money will stay in our country, the United States of America. When are we going to think about all American Citizens. There is a high percentage of Americans who think marijuana should be legal other than the marijuana users. Some citizens, who have smoked marijuana in the past know full well it's not a hard drug.

We are not for legalization of Cocaine, and Heroin. People who get caught with a pound, or more of cocaine or heroin needs to be locked up. Politicians, who sponsored lifer laws for possession of six hundred and fifty grams of cocaine, now admit it was a mistake. The politicians are letting the lifer convicted cocaine criminals out of jail. The tough cocaine law did not get the big fish or curtail cocaine use on the street. We the people have a big enough battle trying to curtail the flow of cocaine, and heroin into this country. Small amounts of Marijuana should be regulated like an aspirin. Casual use of marijuana is much less harmful than legal alcohol, or tobacco." Mason concluded.

Ray Robert's countered Mason. "There are new strategies to fight drug trafficking by the government. The fight to win the drug war is multi- directional on all cartels of the drug trade. The attack is centered on the control and command elements of the cartel's operations." Ray Robert's further promised a major blow to the drug cartels. "The United State government is funding their present air interdiction and eradication of opium and coca poppies in the Latin American countries."

Brutes said. "Virtually everyone in society has talked to someone on marijuana and has never suspected use by the marijuana consumer. Look around out there. Look all around you and there's no mayhem in the streets, because of marijuana use, only the laws that presently govern use of marijuana cause mayhem." Brutes ended the pro-marijuana debater's forum.

Dean Dobson walked to the stage and simply said. "We must continue the drug war at all costs." Dean briskly walked off the stage at that point ending the debate part of the forum.

Now, the debate on the Jefferson Memorial steps featured two bitter opponents. With cameras projecting the events globally. Clint walked over to the podium to a cheering crowd and glared at marijuana prohibition leaders on the other side of the isle.

Once at the podium, Clint looked directly at Sen. Stan Stalinski and decreed. "Once again I've listened to your people try and gloss over the truth. You people who on that side of the isle are all ignorant punks! You have small minds from ancient times. The issue is your either for an American citizen's right to choose a life style, or you're agenda for making the cartels richer and richer and richer as it is presently happening on a consistent basis. The people on our side of the isle are here on shear guts with symbolic motives. Where we are clearly motivated and determined to take our freedom back. We want to know why you oppose freedom in a free society. We are all here to root out the truth." Clint pointed out. "Why don't you lay it on the line, Senator. You're doing nothing but lying. You lied about this country's early involvement in Vietnam and your still misleading the country's citizens today."

In between applause's Clint said. "I'm committed to human rights right here at home. You prohibitionists do not have the hart and soul of our forefathers. They were on the side of the American citizen's individual rights." Clint said. "I've got Abe Lincoln on my side. Who stated in 1840 that. **"Prohibition will work great injury to the cause of temperance. ... for it goes beyond the bounds of reason in it attempts to control a man's appetite by legislation and makes a crime out of things that are not a crimes. A prohibition law strikes a blow at the very principles upon which our government was founded." Abraham Lincoln, Dec 18, 1840.**

Who do you have on your side Senator Stalinski, Hitler and Stalin?" Clint intimidated Senator Stalinski at this time. "Thomas Jefferson and Abe

Lincoln is on our side. Anybody going against the principles and values of Abe Lincoln and Thomas Jefferson should find another government to govern, because the voting citizenry will run you out of here."

The crowd stood up for a standing ovation as Clint spoke on. "The prohibition on marijuana has failed miserably. Just like the alcohol prohibition during the roaring twenties failed. The government was forced to give the people back their god given rights, which they are Constitutionally guaranteed. Any restrictions on the constitution is treason. And those responsible should be held accountable. Trust is the most important factor in relationships, between the government and its people should be restored. A government of the people should be for all the people."

Clint laid it on now that he had his opportunity. "The facts that were presented this week are overwhelmingly in favor of pro marijuana rights activists. You would have to be null and void of reason not to give the people back their rights. Our movement has used common sense in our theories. The government hasn't demonstrated any fair workable theory at all."

Clint continued in between applause's. "Are you immune to reason? If your neighbor smokes pot, stays out of trouble and works hard. What's wrong with that? If your suspicions run wild, we are here to solve those suspicions. Were the leaders of the free world, yet other NATO allies and industrialized nations aren't busting people for smoking pot. Busting pot smokers doesn't have to be what makes the police departments of this country successful. Here in the USA our government should be able to distinguish the difference between human rights and human abuses."

Clint attested. "We cannot be the leaders of the free world until we lead in progressive liberties for the citizenry on all fronts, including a modern drug reform program. Other nations are way ahead of us with their drug policies. Stop dehumanizing our brothers and sisters. Stop the war on the people. Legalization of marijuana is coming very soon. Legalize marijuana all the way now!" as Clint rolled on among the applause's.

"America don't get mad. I am part of what you made me. I'm here today to stand up for my rights with conviction. I'm a crusader for our lost constitutional rights. Get rid of this stumbling block to our freedom. Stop the drug war on the herb marijuana. We have a vision and belief that the great politicians will have a change of heart. Were not going to wait thirteen to fourteen months for decisions. We want the right to choose now and that's what it's all about!"

Clint continued. "I challenge congressional members to make the right choice with constitution decisions. Your either ill-advised, uneducated or have alternative motives when your in the opposition decriminalizing marijuana. A free government can't impose its moral concept on a free people. People have their own morals they accept and live by. The government Legalizing freedom of choice in marijuana use, and further more promoting the hemp industry will be a good start on containing this drug war. We are not going to learn much of anything as a people if we don't try new ventures. If we don't change we'll stay in the same status quo. Bringing the truth out of people is always healthy."

Clint smiled to an applauding crowd and continued. The people don't want a government that keeps telling us what we can't do. We want a government that let's us make the decisions, we want to do. I'm going to stand up and be counted."

Clint already standing up at that point, and looking at the prohibitionists Clint lashed. "Marijuana smokers have counter parts here who want to throw us all in jail. No doubt some people consider smoking leafs a bad habit. Those people still have a right to choose their own destiny under the constitution. Their rights must be restored in the privacy of their homes. These people must be allowed to govern their own affairs."

Clint further asked. "Do the prohibitionist politicians acknowledge the rights of the smokers alliance? The smokers alliance believes they have the right to posses and use tobacco or marijuana in the privacy of their home."

Clint warned that. "All Politicians at all levels of government will be asked and will have to admit that they are for the smokers alliance or against the smokers alliance. You will have to admit one way or the other if you belong to the smokers wing of the Republican, Democratic, Liberation, Reform, Constitutional or any other independents before being considered for our votes. You will not be allowed to skirt the issue. The Cannabis wing of Constitutional Party of the United States of America will root you out. We are going to make sure the politicians we vote for possess the education and firm stand for strong individual rights first for all Americans before we allow them privilege of running our country."

Clint further said to the prohibitionists. "There will be no talking out of both sides of your mouth. Our smokers alliance movement will elect or reject your candidacy by your decision. Criminal Laws should be based on criminal acts, not personal morality choices guaranteed to all Americans. Were going to turn you around to the truth or were just going to turn you out to pasture. You don't have the heart and support of the people! Your gonna go with the people or your just gonna go!"

Clint rhapsodized. **"True Americans will take America Back!"** Clint left the podium and the people waved to him. Clint proudly waved back.

Sen. Stan had to follow crowd rousing speech by Clint and an over whelmed and applauding crowd.

Sen. Stan Stalinski still sheepishly walked to the podium in a slow manner. Sen. Stan Stalinski after a cold stare into the crowd proceeded to tear into the pro marijuana group. Boos came from everywhere instantly as Senator Stan steamed internally and from the podium.

Stan asked Clint. "What if the Marijuana that's being dealt turn your kid into an addict?"

Clint responded. "I've raised my kid to make good decisions if life. My kid knows the difference between hard drugs, alcohol, tobacco and soft drugs. That won't be a problem in my family. What I won't teach my kid is to hate or discriminate against his neighbor just because he smokes marijuana. Your war is not our war. Haven't you heard enough government and police abuse? When your raids that go bad end and up in lawsuits. What about citizen abuse and death to innocent drug war victims by cops. The users of small amounts of marijuana are thrown into prison while felons get released because of over crowding."

Sen. Stan deemed. "Marijuana is a narcotic!"

Clint challenged Sen. Stan. "Show me one report or institutionalized study that says marijuana is a narcotic!"

Sen. Stan preached. "The DEA has it listed as Schedule one narcotic."

Clint firmly repeated. "Show me the scientific verification that identifies the plant cannabis as equal to a manufactured hard drug such as heroin and cocaine in writing!"

Sen. Stan admitted. "I don't have the report available right now."

Clint proclaimed. "That's because there is no report to be found. If you don't know that facts, how can you make decisions in our lives? I'll tell you one more thing Stalinski. The Constitutionalists are going to get rid of all the self interested ignorant politicians. Government management wings who can't identify the distinct difference between marijuana and hard drugs are history in this country. Were going to make sure of that. Our present government managers are so self defeating with their stupid medieval attitudes. " Clint concluded.

Senator Stans prohibition associates Sen Bennet Horn told Senator Muggins that. "Every thing that Stan asked Clint. Clint came up with a good answer." Senator Muggins is swayed to the pro-marijuana views. "That's because it's they're personal right to choose. They have the power of the people on their side."

Senator Vanders is leading the way to pass a Bipartisan medical marijuana bill through conventional state legislative measures other then voter popular state marijuana initiatives. Senator Vanders stood up and admitted. "I went to Amsterdam. I saw firsthand the continuity of the people, who live under liberal marijuana laws. It is a much more practical way for a government to co-exist with it's people."

Clint continued. "How can they continue to fight of marijuana war by spending billions of the tax payers money at a time into a useless and endless self terminating hole. We've got people starving out there. Legalize hemp and marijuana and we can end that." Clint told the audience from the sidelines, while everyone watched Senator Stalinski squirm.

Igor quietly conferred to Clint. "It's ludicrous to think people won't help people. Legalize weed and we can feed the homeless."

Clint pledged. "I hear that!"

The audience chanted Marijuana. "Marijuana now!" As Sen. Stan Stalinski continued on to talk about the ills of marijuana. The audience noise grew loader and loader, showing disapproval for his speech.

Stalinski finally storms off the stage. He knew his speech had fallen for the majority on deaf ears.

Chapter 14.... As the debate came to an end, Clint and his group felt the week's cannabis facts were presented in a compelling and convincing way.

Clint felt that the Federal government had to own up to the reality of the times. The people wanted their own personal freedom to choose, over a Federal dictation of lifestyle which is not freedom. A government pro-active for individual citizen's right's instead of re-active. The president were nervous as a crap shooting dice roller to make the right decision. The president was nothing more than a poll watcher. This is the tenacity he based all his decisions on. The president was a flag was sailing in the wind. His cabinet members was split on decriminalization of marijuana. The presidents radio program last Saturday spoke of new proposals to end drugs in America. The President said. "Drugs have been reduced by fifty percent in the last ten years. I will reduce drugs by another fifty percent in the next ten years." The president told the American people to fight drugs at their kitchen table. Trouble was that not all citizens sit around the kitchen table like the tax sucking politicians and their lobbyists. A lot of citizens smoke pot. They believe there is nothing wrong with smoking pot. The morality of the president has been proven human, not a fairy tale as always presented. The people want a people's president.

Clint, immediately after his arrival back in Houston the next day, packed his bags for a cruise trip to Alaska. After breakfast with Chantel, he decided they should get away for a few days. Clint felt drained from the pro-longed decriminalization struggle.

When they arrived in Fairbanks, they shutted to the one of Alaska's five star ships. Clint and Chantel wanted to enjoy the scenically spectacular wildlife encounters. The incredible dazzling ice glaciers landscaped the rugged mountain terrain and enhanced the cruise ship's comfort.

They sat in the glittering domed restaurant and enjoyed king Crab legs, Alaskan Salmon, lemon baked cod fillet and desert of apple crunch cake topped with Alaskan berries. They dined with a commanding panoramic view of unprecedented landscape that is unmatched. While on the teaked promenade deck of the elegant cruise ship abundant wildlife was overflowing. The natural beauty of the soaring bald eagle's graced the sky.

Clint mustered. "Look at the sight of the Beluga whales! The beluga whales graced the waters as the tourists steadily took pictures.

Chantel responded. "The tourists have a great photo shoot! What an eye opening experience."

Clint professed. "I've never imagined Alaska's beauty was so breath taking full of intimidation.

Chantel persisted. "What an exciting adventure tour this glacier cruising is!" as they explored the rest of the ship.

Clint stressed. "We'll have to come back just to explore Alaska's interior for a complete wildlife tour. They have the right idea up here. They are securing nature's habit for the future. I'd like to see grizzlies, caribou, moose, and a larger variety of wildlife in their habitat."

Chantel proclaimed. "Anytime you want to come back here, I'm ready."

Clint told Chantel over breakfast the next morning. "Sen. Stan's outlook make a fine speech, but he only glossed over the real facts. Trouble with his position is that a good amount of citizens who sit around after dinner with friends and family don't believe him."

Holding her terrier on a new hemp leash Chantel winked. "Everyone we know, and then some."

Clint asserted. "They sit around and smoke marijuana as a social outlet. A great many American's condone, or use marijuana. Hiring, training, and outfitting police with more of the tax payers money to fight marijuana users is unrealistic."

In a following news conference, the speaker of the House blasted the President as ineffective in the drug war. The Speaker said. "In fact drug use of all sorts have increased. Teenager drug use has increased by over seventy-five percent. Get tough policies on marijuana smokers has not worked for the last sixty years. Current drug fighting policies and new drug proposals define failure. The tax paying American citizens is a loser again."

Miles explained to Brant at the local cyber cafe. "Congressional members know they are going be identified and targeted in the next election. They have to admit alliance to the smokers wing of their political parties or be smashed by the momentum of the people in favor of decriminalization of marijuana."

Brant relayed what one of the pot protestors said. "Our country indeed has more serious problems to conquer than creating new ones with bad laws. We need to eliminate the bad laws that exist, which hurt good people."

Marijuana investigative reporter Miles said. "Our newspaper polls at the end of the marijuana debate condone marijuana use by responsible citizens. The majority of all viewers accept the polls. Marijuana use is much less of a threat in the eyes of the American people, than the war on marijuana."

Brant expounded. "Stinging assertions by the prohibitionists of marijuana kept viewers of the media on needles and pins. This is the Armageddon debate concerning cannabis total decriminalization for use, possession, or bartering of small amounts."

As the other "Pot Patriots" stood around Miles conveyed to Brant. "A Congressional showdown will be held in fifteen days, I think after bitter battle in congressional the hearings we'll win this one."

Brant decreed. "The Constitutional Party representatives have joined Congress from previous elections. More and more Constitutional party politicians raise money and are part of the new clean imaged Constitutional political party. There are no scandals to look back on from the Constitutional party."

Miles disclosed. "Our present political parties are the equivalent to used car salesmen. They are nothing more than a third party with their hand in the pie full of flagrant double standards. It's very obvious we need a political cleansing.

I'd like to know where in the constitution it says that they government has the right to make moral decisions for the citizenry."

After pulling up in his spectacular new cannabis custom painted 2000 model year "Thunderbird" and hearing part of the conversation Clint claimed. "That's what I like is that even if a third party is established and only garners twenty five percent of the vote, that party wins because the Democrats and Republicans are always split on everything they do."

Brant suggested. "Maybe it will get them to consider to agree on something right together for a change."

Miles convinced divulged. "That's is what the people like about the Constitutional Party of America. The Constitutional Party can break the stagnant dead lock of congress. We force the government to work for the people. Any government that blocks individual rights is not a free democracy."

Clint informed. "Any government branch that blocks agriculture of industrial hemp, and marijuana cafe's is against free commerce."

Brant admired the thought. "I like how we already have Constitutional Ave in DC named for our political party."

Miles agreed. "Really! Right down there close to the White House."

Clint wisecracked. "They drew the line in the sand! Watch the citizen's of this country rush over it all at once and roar. "Were here!"

Chris rampaged into the Cyber cafe. "Did you hear? The Federal government decriminalization of marijuana. We finally won by a large margin in congress. States are to control their own demographic marijuana situation."

Cannabis Celebrations began nation wide. Headlines around the world applaud the Americans on stopping the war on marijuana users. "The Americans Stopped the Marijuana War!" "The Americans are now in step with the world community" were only some of the headlines.

The pro-marijuana movement's creed "You Stand up for what you believe in or you don't stand." Served them well. A marijuana party was established on August 13th for "Cannabis Celebration's" at Clint's farm. Every one, who participated in the decriminalization of cannabis struggle, gathered to celebrate the "Total Federal Marijuana Decriminalization Act."

Igor exulted loudly. "We the people stood up to the callous corrupt giants and took our country back!" as the celebration rolled on everyone felt proud that freedom prevailed! Personal freedom is the most important element of life. No government or person has the right to impede.

In the background the cannabis duel "Jay and Bongs" played their new cannabis celebration song. "Freedom Rings Again!" Everyone jammed to their hard cut rock. Clint said at the cannabis celebration party to Igor. "Citizens can't be tested for marijuana. Fishing expeditions on marijuana use against cannabis citizens have ceased. Freedom in America meant all Americans could decide their individual rights. All laws against morality choice's are now abolished."

Igor crowed. "Great! The marijuana law hasn't been fair with my truck drivers. They smoke pot at weekend parties and go to marijuana tolerant states or countries. If they're drug tested for pot during the week, while they're driving, they will not pass the marijuana drug test. Now at least they are protected by the new personal freedom laws."

Clint induced. "All politicians and police officials who make the marijuana laws should be tested for marijuana first. What was fair for the citizens is fair for the officials. If they wanted to know what is in our body, they have to let us know what's in their body."

Three different pro-hemp bands played at Clint's farm for the celebration. Their pro-cannabis CD sales were at the top of the charts. "Woodstock freedom spirit prevailed." The intensity gave the musicians a passion to feel their music.

Rudy accented. "The evening is perfect. The gathering is friendly. The buffalo is on the rotisserie. The Texas sunset is picture perfect."

Miles attested at the celebration. "The majority of people are happy to see that the democratic system in our country has worked. They are glad the marijuana war is over. The pro-cannabis activists now have an unofficial marijuana holiday declared by the cannabis wing of the Constitutional Party."

Igor defined. "Hemp town, Cannabis County Kentucky is an American example of cannabis industrial and social living where marijuana is condoned. The first cannabis café opened in Hemptown, Kentucky. Cannabis County is growing fast because people from all over wanted to go where marijuana was first legally sanctioned by the state legislature again. They wanted to be among people of their peers, morals, and social values."

Miles enounced. "Volunteer Marijuana Tolerance clinics have been set up as well, and marijuana tolerance pills handed out just like they do for tobacco cigarettes. The clinic has had less than a half percent per capita of total marijuana use for it's business. In other words they had no significant amount of volunteers to quit smoking marijuana after they started smoking. Never the less marijuanaette is available nationwide. The gum is designed to help stop smoking marijuana."

Clint yelled out. "The war against the people concerning marijuana is finally over."

Miles told Igor. "The political, governmental, industrial, religious, moral majority's shotgun re-education internment program against marijuana smokers was finished. Religious freedoms are allowed again. Marijuana for sacramental use in America is with out hindrance or persecution again. Other detrimental and crazy laws against people's nature will be scrutinized and eliminated."

Brant emphasized. "Cannabis crooked cops, conniving prosecutors, convincing cash heavy businessmen filled with greed, politicians filled with self-interest, and uneducated ignorant lawyers have finally lost this insane battle of marijuana against the citizens. The government graft manipulating money managers and their devious back room schemes of corruption are eliminated from the black market because of the decriminalization marijuana."

Clint informed. "Marijuana deals for small amounts is allowed above board now. The government collects taxes on imports of hash and marijuana. Twenty-five to thirty percent of the marijuana taxes go to the health funds as tobacco has settled for as well. A conference of American Cannabis business men was held to decide the how hemp industry would be implemented and established."

Igor raved. "Hemp beer and wine is now being served at liqueur establishments across the nation. I'm applying for a commercial micro-brewery cannabis beer license."

Chantel and Maria sat having a toast with delicious hemp white wine next to the brightly lit wall aquarium filled with Corey's exotic fish collected.

Brant conferred. "Hemp agricultural, industrial textile, and paper mills are now being built for the anticipated fall hemp crop. Thirty million acres of hemp will be realized by American farmers with in a few years."

Miles explained. "Hemp processing complexes similar to Hemptown are popping up all over the country. American Farmers have a viable alternative cash crop to grow as their counterparts already enjoyed in the free world."

Mangus stressed to Clint. "I've been importing hemp chordage for horse bedding at the race track. It's the finest quality horse boarding stables. I've bought so much horse related hemp supplies that the Canadian company I deal with made me a hemp products distributor. They even sent me those hemp made horse blankets."

Clint expressed. "Those are beautiful blankets."

Miles proclaimed. "Now we can deal with home grown hemp, and manufacture industrial hemp in America.

Chris explained. "The earth's Eco system will greatly benefit from large clean non-toxic hemp crops. Some tobacco companies have followed suit in growing commercial and industrial hemp."

Miles divulged. "Tobacco companies have settled their law suits around the country for it's incriminating medical miss-deeds, but the smokers alliance felt the government was partly at fault for sanctioning medically damaging substances. The government collected a lions shares of taxes over the years. They have to work out fair solutions for the changing tobacco industry. The tobacco industry want to offer their former farmers alternative crops without subsidizing idle farm land."

Clint discoursed. "Tobacco Companies had to stop practices such as advertising cigarettes to kids, and inducing stronger doses of nicotine into their cigarettes. Hopefully, many of these tobacco practices have changed in our country."

Igor contended. "Greenhouses are applying for tax permits for commercial growth of marijuana for future sales to citizens. Our pro marijuana political group want to limit commercial growth too small amounts of marijuana being grown. We want a greater amount of average people, not only large corporations growing marijuana. We to spread the financial growth of the pot industry."

Clint stressed. "I don't want large corporations to make all the money and leave the smaller pot growers out."

Miles explained. "Cannabis buyers clubs want to re-establish their own greenhouses to serve their medical community with organically grown marijuana who prefer this type of marijuana use for medical purposes. Commercial advertising for marijuana use will be non-existent. However industrial hemp will be allowed to advertise their hemp wares."

Igor eagerly conferred. "The hemp industry sponsored a race car for the Indianapolis 500 with the race car body made with hemp-fiber-glass. The turbo-engine will run on clean burning hemp fuel."

Abraham Arms was at an extravagant cannabis legalization freedom celebration, while smoking a big green one he said. "One Great Broadway Show called "Cannabis Kingdom" will be featured in New York next week. It has a creative cannabis theme with cannabis costumes and outlays on stage. The Broadway show has their own cannabis video and cannabis CD called "Cannabis Kingdom" as well."

Political Pat advised. "Stock investors have invested huge amounts of capitol in the billion dollar hemp industry of the new established industrial hemp commodities market. Industry financial analysts made projections of a trillion dollar for the hemp industry over the next forty years. The hemp industry is realized by the financial analysts as a safe investment with the "Red Taped Middle Man" out of the way. Marijuana is established a commodity on the worldwide stock market. Marijuana investors broke all records on the New York Stock exchange for large money investment for new commodities."

Manny reassured. "Every day living under the new decriminalization of marijuana is welcomed and respected by most. The bigotry has been publicly identified and not dealt with fairly"

Pat conceded. "Clint! I forgot to tell you. The Constitutional Party has drafted a resolution nominating you for Ambassador to Holland."

Clint excited. "I can handle that Pat. But nothing really is going to change around my household as far as marijuana use, except the fear of the police breaking down my door. However I've raised so much hell with the government. The senate gave me one those special government marijuana growing permits allowing me to grow one hundred plants in a greenhouse for commercial, recreational, or medicinal use. They said. This cannabis grow permit will be the first one and the government will use this greenhouse as an example. I going to import my first seeds from Holland."

Miles triumphed. "That's terrific news!"

Clint granted. "The marijuana grown in the greenhouse will be regulated and inspected by marijuana auditors, tagged, taxed, and then it can be sold for profit."

Pat lectured. "We're passing a resolution were legislators have to be qualified on subjects before they can draft up judicial concept laws. In other words before they can draw up hemp legislation, they must prove they are knowledgeable on the subject of cannabis. The politicians will have to attend classes at the Cannabis College in Holland or another institute of it's magnitude.

Miles reassured. "That will put them in check!"

Pat professed. "Checkmate!"

Manny implored to Clint. "Were glad your brother Tommy is coming out of his coma." An unspecified amount of money was paid to Tommy's mother, which was settled in an out of court settlement for her son's severe beating.

Clint offered. "The greenhouse as it turns out has been good therapy for Tommy."

Terry flew in from British Columbia to attend the celebration snickered. "Cannabis coffee houses are springing up on the Canadian side of the Canadian-American boarder. Toronto, Windsor, Vancouver, Thunder Bay, and even in Quebec, Americans are flocking to the coffee houses for holidays, faster than the Canadians are going to Atlantic's City."

Pat the pot party politician told Morgan and Mike. "The Constitutional Party of America is made up from true American philosophies and has been re-established in every Federal, State, County, and city government. The Constitutional Party's mascot horse represented our political campaigns and debate forums effectively. The Constitutional Party made serious challenges to the White House and the Constitutionalists are an active component in making government policy's."

Terry opinioned. "One Canadian City has legalized smoking marijuana at a newly established gambling casino. The Rolling Roulette Room at the Cannabis Casino features imported marijuana joints for gamblers instead of alcoholic drinks. The Casino's Cannabis Hotel has hemp bedding, towels, soaps, carpets, virtually every thing there is made from hemp. The slot machines pay off in gold coins or gold bud tokens. The Reefer Restaurant features a revolving floor, and serves delicious hemp drinks and foods.

Chantel unveiled. "The exotic hemp food was tasty."

Clint and Chantel had traveled by air for the grand opening Chantel explained. "I walked up to the casino and a girl was sitting in a police car rolling a joint of weed. The girl then got out of the car and walked into the casino smoking and dangling the joint from her mouth unhindered and without any further ado."

Clint revealed "I told Chantel. I wanted to smoke a joint before I sat at the black jack table."

Chantel proposed. "I wanted to smoke one before I played the slot machines." We smoked our joints, which were supplied by the casino. We were than primed for a night a gambling and everyone had a great time."

As he used his new very creative and colorful electric exhaust smokeless ashtray Clint specified. "American Business Entrepreneur's have lobbied to established their own set of cannabis rules for limited cannabis coffee houses which supplies marijuana to customers of age. It's the Domino affect to them! They ready to cross the line!"

Terry enthused. "Seattle is the first city to apply for a cannabis coffee house license in the United States. Entrepreneurs and Investment Franchiser's want to start a cannabis chain of coffeehouses. One café in Amsterdam already established was called "Clint's Cannabis Café" its motto being "The Worlds Finest Cannabis Served Here."

Miles pledged. "Billionaire George Barras was nominated for the Nobel Peace prize for championing marijuana legalization. Marijuana keeps pace in the endeavors of economics."

Clint decreed. "What is really great is we have a new socially stronger conscience developed. A new generation will be born into the "Collective Conscious" environment in America. These intensive, and proven, social studies prove the common sense value of right and wrong way of governing. Governments that have implemented techniques of the Collective Conscious have benefited safer society's. Where drug addicts have a choice to use clean needles or walk in on their own accord to quit and ask for the habit killing drug Ibogaine. Making the decision to dry themselves out and kick their habit. Where sick people and doctor's freely choose the medicine that's best for the patient. I like the serious effort made by the Constitutionalists for creating the "Citizen Friendly Harm Reduction Programs" that have been implemented."

Igor explained. "The new laws just passed by Constitutionalists will be implemented in every state in the Union for the "Coffee Shop Area's" are very welcome in the interest of commerce alone. Every state now has their own "Red Light District" where would be rapists have a choice. Prostitute's have a safe work environment. Constitutionalists mandate government laws to work with the citizenry instead of against them.

Clint spouted. "Medical Marijuana Freedom fighter "Mary Jane Hemp" is now recognized in as much of the freedom fighter of merit as Rosa Parks is for her cause by the Cannabis Wing of the Constitutional Party. She refused to give up her Constitutional Rights. She's one gutsy woman."

Pat responded. "We've finally reached the "Age of Reason. We've also passed a resolution to honor "The Hemp Plant" for it's special contribution for freedom and economic stability to our "National Heritage" The Hemp Plant is the "Plant of Distinction." After all the first American flag was hand sewn with hemp material by "Betsy Ross.""

Miles discoursed. "After an association of ideas and tremendous public outcry, and protests our national nightmare is over. The police and the people now enjoy a safer community. By eliminating the wide spread mistrust people and police are establishing respect toward each other and a real community peace."

One month after the decriminalization of marijuana laws were passed Clint finally looked at Chantel on the porch of his farm at puts out his marijuana cigarette. He looked at Chantel and hyped. "I quit!"

Chantel quizzically resolved. "What do you mean?"

Clint reacted. "I mean after thirty years of smoking pot I quit! One of the reasons I smoked all these years was because I despised the law against smoking marijuana. I would have felt that if I quit it would be in part, because the government made me quit. When I decided to quit smoking. I wanted to make sure that I quit! I want didn't quit because the government forced me to!"

This Novel written by Joe Astro is currently being converted into a Screenplay. The "2002" Screenplay will be accompanied with an Original Musical Soundtrack. This is a book based on Truths, Facts, and Real life scenes, and some scenes were fictionalized. This Novel is written and portrayed in a storybook manner. It examines the Truth concerning our Individual Constitutional Right's Concerning Current Cannabis Laws, Use, and the blatant injustice to the Hemp Industry.

I hope you enjoy Joe Astro's version of "fictional realism"!

"2002" Novel Published by
Joe Astro Productions
P O Box 130, Dundee, Michigan 48131
Printed in the United States of America

Date Published March 31, 1999

www.joeastro.com

Acknowledgements: Joe Astro Productions thanks
mainstream news, Internet resources, cannabis
contributors, and the televised and radio broadcasts
which helped articulate the facts.

Disclaimer: Work which involves strong opinions always
has opposing forces. For those who disagree with
conclusions or statements contained herein, the author
welcomes any comments or corrections. This novel singles
no person or party out for retribution.

Joe Astro sporting his Hemp Wear!